OTHER WORLDS THAN
THESE

Other Anthologies Edited by John Joseph Adams

Armored
Brave New Worlds
By Blood We Live
Federations
The Improbable Adventures of Sherlock Holmes
Lightspeed: Year One
The Living Dead
The Living Dead 2
Seeds of Change
Under the Moons of Mars: New Adventures on Barsoom
Wastelands
The Way of the Wizard

Forthcoming Anthologies Edited by John Joseph Adams

Dead Man's Hand
Epic
The Mad Scientist's Guide to World Domination
Robot Uprisings (co-edited with Daniel H. Wilson)

OTHER WORLDS THAN THESE

STORIES OF PARALLEL WORLDS

edited by

John Joseph Adams

NIGHT SHADE BOOKS
SAN FRANCISCO

First Edition

ISBN: 978-1-59780-433-2

Night Shade Books
http://www.nightshadebooks.com

"Go then, there are other worlds than these."

—Jake Chambers, to Roland Deschain of Gilead
(from *The Gunslinger* by Stephen King)

TABLE OF CONTENTS

FOREWORD

LEV GROSSMAN

When I read The Chronicles of Narnia as a child, it didn't so much introduce me to the idea that there was another world as confirm my already grave suspicions on the subject. Even at the tender age of eight I was—as I suspect you were, and are, if you're reading this book—one of reality's natural critics. Oh, I knew that the real world had its good points. One must be charitable after all. Candy, for example, and cats, and hot baths. But by and large the material was just a bit thin. The jokes weren't funny, the catering was uneven, and the less said about one's fellow players the better. I had a powerful urge to see what was on in the next theater over.

Until I read *The Lion, the Witch and the Wardrobe*—and *Alice's Adventures in Wonderland,* and *The Phantom Tollbooth,* and *The Wonderful Wizard of Oz,* and The Chronicles of Amber—I thought I was the only one who felt that way. Of course this can't be all there is: this ludicrous excuse for a universe can only be a rough draft, a temporary substitute, the amateur opening act before the main event, which will be more magical, more exciting, more meaningful, more ecologically sound and otherwise superior in every way.

This wasn't actually the point of any of those books, of course. That fact was lost on me then, but it isn't now. Now I understand that the children in the Narnia books went to another world in order to imbibe crucial life lessons at the paws of the lion-god Aslan. Then when they were deported back to England at the end of the book they could experience reality, such as it was, with a renewed appreciation, and they could spread the Word of Jesuslan to the unenlightened.

That would have been the "correct" lesson to draw from The Chronicles of Narnia, but if any child has ever read those books correctly I will eat my hat. When he wrote them Lewis unwittingly let loose a monster of an idea, one even more powerful than the idea he was actually trying to put across. The lesson you receive from The Chronicles of Narnia is that reality is not where it's at, my friend, so get out by any point of egress you can find and get into somewhere better.

Of course, Lewis didn't invent that idea. It's an old fantasy, far older than Narnia—far older, I suspect, than Christianity. The idea that you can enter another world, generally heaven or some heaven-analog, without having to die first exists in any number of religions; it is technically known as ascension, or assumption, or (my personal favorite) translation. The Virgin Mary managed it, as did Elijah, and for that matter Bilbo and Frodo Baggins. It was given new life in the twentieth century, and a new spin, pun intended, by the so-called many-worlds interpretation of quantum theory, which posits the idea that all possible universes are in fact real, and the multiple possible outcomes of every event spawn multiple universes in which each of those outcomes is realized. Schrödinger's cat is dead in one, and alive and purring in another. This theory is actually taken seriously by quite a few non-insane physicists.

Far more compelling would be a very-many-worlds hypothesis, in which all universes exist, both the possible and the impossible, but unfortunately no one sane believes that, not even an old traveler in the realms of gold like me. Fortunately there is a device, entirely real, which can take you into those other realities. Not permanently, but for short, ecstatic flights that are very much worth taking. You're lucky enough to be holding one such device in your hands right now. As Aslan would say: further up and further in.

INTRODUCTION

JOHN JOSEPH ADAMS

W hat if you could not only travel any location in the world, but to any *possible* world? That is the central conceit of this anthology. Or, to be more precise, it aims to collect the best stories that fall into one of two categories: parallel worlds stories or portal fantasies.

A portal fantasy is a story in which a person from one world (usually the "real" world) is transported to some Other World (via some magical or unexplained means), usually one full of impossibilities and generally much stranger than the one they come from.

A parallel worlds story is one in which a person from one world (usually the "real" world) is transported to some Other World (via some scientific/ technological means), usually a parallel universe/alternate reality either just slightly different than the one they left, or else vastly different, with different physical laws, but strictly scientifically plausible.

As you can see from the parallels in those two descriptions, the portal fantasy and the parallel worlds story are essentially two sides of the same coin; heads, you get fantasy, tails you get science fiction, but in each the characters' journey is essentially the same: to explore and wonder at these strange Other Worlds...or to do their damnedest to get back home.

When I first set out to assemble this anthology, I had been thinking primarily of parallel worlds fiction, until the above realization occurred to me. Once it did, I knew that if I were to consider one side of the coin I had to also consider the other, and at that point the entire anthology clicked into place.

(Accordingly, it felt to me like the two types of story should be in dialogue with each other in the context of the anthology, so I did not separate them in the table of contents; instead, both types of story are mixed together throughout the book. It should also be noted that I shied away from including any stories that are primarily based on time travel—as time travel stories are their own genre, though of course time travel does, in essence, create parallel worlds.)

The tropes of Other Worlds fiction have fired the imaginations of millions of readers over the years. The portal fantasy has the earliest roots, with prominent early examples including *The Wonderful Wizard of Oz, Alice's Adventures in Wonderland*, and The Chronicles of Narnia. The tradition has continued, with modern day writers picking up the torch, such as Stephen King (The Dark Tower), Philip Pullman (His Dark Materials), and Lev Grossman (*The Magicians*).

Although one might assume that parallel worlds stories are of a more recent vintage, the hypothetical idea of multiple universes has actually been around since the late nineteenth century, and, indeed, some early examples of parallel worlds fiction can be found in the works of science fiction's most prominent early practitioner, H. G. Wells. (However, it is fair to say that the majority of this type of story has been written after the many-worlds interpretation theory of quantum mechanics was first postulated and popularized in the late '50s.) For parallel worlds stories, there are fewer obvious classics to reference, but there are *The Gods Themselves* by Isaac Asimov, *The Female Man* by Joanna Russ, and *The Big Time* by Fritz Leiber, with recent examples including The Neanderthal Parallax trilogy by Robert J. Sawyer, *The Mirage* by Matt Ruff, and Alastair Reynolds's *Absolution Gap*.

(For more Other Worlds novel-length works, see the "For Further Reading" appendix located at the end of this anthology.)

So let's take a trip through the looking glass…or into the universe next door. Thirty different Other Worlds await you; to visit the first, simply turn the page…

MOON SIX

STEPHEN BAXTER

Stephen Baxter was born in Liverpool, England. With a background in math and engineering, he is the author of over fifty novels and over a hundred published short stories. He has collaborated with Sir Arthur C. Clarke and is working on a new collaboration with Sir Terry Pratchett. Among his awards are BSFA Awards, the Philip K. Dick Award, and Locus, Asimov, and Analog awards. His latest novel is *Stone Spring*, first of a new series.

B*ado was alone on the primeval beach of Cape Canaveral, in his white lunar-surface pressure suit, holding his box of Moon rocks and sampling tools in his gloved hand.*

He lifted up his gold sun-visor and looked around. The sand was hard and flat. A little way inland, there was a row of scrub pines, maybe ten feet tall.

There were no ICBM launch complexes here.

There was no Kennedy Space Center, in fact: no space programme, evidently, save for him. He was stranded on this empty, desolate beach.

As the light leaked out of the sky, an unfamiliar Moon was brightening.

Bado glared at it. "Moon Six," he said. "Oh, shit."

He took off his helmet and gloves. He picked up his box of tools and began to walk inland. His blue overshoes, still stained dark grey from lunar dust, left crisp Moonwalk footprints in the damp sand of the beach.

1

Bado drops down the last three feet of the ladder and lands on the foil-covered footpad. A little grey dust splashes up around his feet.

Slade is waiting with his camera. "Okay, turn around and give me a big smile. Atta boy. You look great. Welcome to the Moon." Bado can't see Slade's face, behind his reflective golden sun-visor.

Bado holds onto the ladder with his right hand and places his left boot on the Moon. Then he steps off with his right foot, and lets go of the LM. And there he is, standing on the Moon.

The suit around him is a warm, comforting bubble. He hears the hum of pumps and fans in the PLSS—his backpack, the Portable Life Support System—and feels the soft breeze of oxygen across his face.

He takes a halting step forward. The dust seems to crunch beneath his feet, like a covering of snow: there is a firm footing beneath a soft, resilient layer a few inches thick. His footprints are miraculously sharp, as if he's placed his ridged overshoes in fine, damp sand. He takes a photograph of one particularly well-defined print; it will persist here for millions of years, he realises, like the fossilised footprint of a dinosaur, to be eroded away only by the slow rain of micrometeorites, that echo of the titanic bombardments of the deep past.

He looks around.

The LM is standing in a broad, shallow crater. Low hills shoulder above the close horizon. There are craters everywhere, ranging from several yards to a thumbnail width, the low sunlight deepening their shadows.

They call the landing site Taylor Crater, after that district of El Lago—close to the Manned Spacecraft Center in Houston—where he and Fay have made their home. This pond of frozen lava is a relatively smooth, flat surface in a valley once flooded by molten rock. Their main objective for the flight is another crater a few hundred yards to the west that they've named after Slade's home district of Wildwood. Surveyor 7, an unmanned robot probe, set down in Wildwood a few years before; the astronauts are here to sample it.

This landing site is close to Tycho, the fresh, bright crater in the Moon's southern highlands. As a kid Bado had sharp vision. He was able to see Tycho with his naked eyes, a bright pinprick on that ash-white surface, with rays that spread right across the face of the full Moon.

Now he is here.

Bado turns and bounces back towards the LM.

After a few miles he got to a small town.

He hid his lunar pressure suit in a ditch, and, dressed in his tube-covered cooling garment, snuck into someone's back yard. He stole a pair of jeans and a shirt he found hanging on the line there.

He hated having to steal; he didn't plan on having to do it again.

He found a small bar. He walked straight in and asked after a job. He knew he couldn't afford to hesitate, to hang around figuring what kind of world he'd finished up in. He had no money at all, but right now he was clean-shaven and presentable. A few days of sleeping rough would leave him too dirty and stinking to be employable.

He got a job washing glasses and cleaning out the john. That first night he slept on a park bench, but bought himself breakfast and cleaned himself up in a gas station john.

After a week, he had a little money saved. He loaded his lunar gear into an old trunk, and hitched to Daytona Beach, a few miles up the coast.

They climb easily out of Taylor.

Their first Moonwalk is a misshapen circle which will take them around several craters. The craters are like drill holes, the geologists say, excavations into lunar history.

The first stop is the north rim of a hundred-yard-wide crater they call Huckleberry Finn. It is about three hundred yards west of the LM.

Bado puts down the tool carrier. This is a hand-held tray, with an assortment of gear: rock hammers, sample bags, core tubes. He leans over, and digs into the lunar surface with a shovel. When he scrapes away the grey upper soil he finds a lighter grey, just under the surface.

"Hey, Slade. Come look at this."

Slade comes floating over. "How about that. I think we found some ray material." Ray material here will be debris from the impact which formed Tycho.

Lunar geology has been shaped by the big meteorite impacts which pounded its surface in prehistory. A main purpose of sending this mission so far south is to keep them away from the massive impact which created the Mare Imbrium, in the northern hemisphere. Ray material unpolluted by Imbrium debris will let them date the more recent Tycho impact.

And here they have it, right at the start of their first Moonwalk.

Slade flips up his gold visor so Bado can see his face, and grins at him. "How about that. We is looking at a full-up mission here, boy."

They finish up quickly, and set off at a run to the next stop. Slade looks like a human-shaped beach ball, his suit brilliant white, bouncing over the beach-like surface of the Moon. He is whistling.

They are approaching the walls of Wildwood Crater. Bado is going slightly uphill, and he can feel it. The carrier, loaded up with rocks, is getting harder to carry too. He has to hold it up to his chest, to keep the rocks from bouncing out when he runs, and so he is constantly fighting the stiffness of his pressure suit.

"Hey, Bado," Slade says. He comes loping down the slope. He points. "Take a look."

Bado has, he realises, reached the rim of Wildwood Crater. He is standing on top of its dune-like, eroded wall. And there, planted in the crater's centre, is the Surveyor. It is less than a hundred yards from him. It is a squat, three-legged frame, like a broken-off piece of a LM.

Slade grins. "Does that look neat? We got it made, Bado." Bado claps his commander's shoulder. "Outstanding, man." He knows that for Slade, getting to the Surveyor, bringing home a few pieces of it, is the finish line for the mission.

Bado looks back east, the way they have come. He can see the big, shallow dip in the land that is Taylor, with the LM resting at its centre like a toy in the palm of some huge hand. It is a glistening, filmy construct of gold leaf and aluminium, bristling with antennae, docking targets, and reaction control thruster assemblies.

Two sets of footsteps come climbing up out of Taylor towards them, like footsteps on a beach after a tide.

Bado tips back on his heels and looks at the sky.

The sky is black, empty of stars; his pupils are closed up by the dazzle of the sun, and the reflection of the pale brown lunar surface. But he can see the Earth, a fat crescent, four times the size of a full moon. And there, crossing the zenith, is a single, brilliant, unwinking star: the orbiting Apollo CSM, with Al Pond, their Command Module pilot, waiting to take them home.

There is a kind of shimmer, like a heat haze. And the star goes out.

Just like that: it vanishes from the sky, directly over Bado's head. He blinks, and moves his head, stiffly, thinking he might have just lost the Apollo in the glare.

But it is gone.

What, then? Can it have moved into the shadow of the Moon? But a little thought knocks out that one: the geometry, of sun and Moon and spacecraft, is all wrong.

And anyhow, what was that heat haze shimmer? You don't get heat haze where there's no air.

He lowers his head. "Hey, Slade. You see that?"

But Slade isn't anywhere to be seen, either; the slope where he's been standing is smooth, empty.

Bado feels his heart hammer.

He lets go of the tool carrier—it drifts down to the dust, spilling rocks—and he lopes forward. "Come on, Slade. Where the hell are you?"

Slade is famous for gotchas; he is planning a few that Bado knows about, and probably some he doesn't, for later in the mission. But it is hard to see how he's pulled this one off. There is nowhere to hide, damn it.

He gets to where he thinks Slade was last standing. There is no sign of Slade. And there aren't even any footsteps, he realises now. The only marks under his feet are those made by his own boots, leading off a few yards away, to the north.

And they start out of nothing, it seems, like Man Friday steps in the crisp virgin Moon-snow. As if he's stepped out of nowhere onto the regolith.

When he looks back to the east, he can't see the LM either.

"Slade, this isn't funny, damn it." He starts to bound, hastily, back in the direction of the LM. His clumsy steps send up parabolic sprays of dust over unmarked regolith.

He feels his breath getting shallow. It isn't a good idea to panic. He tells himself that maybe the LM is hidden behind some low ridge. Distances are deceptive here, in this airless sharpness.

"Houston, Bado. I got some kind of situation here." There isn't a reply immediately; he imagines his radio signal crawling across the light-seconds' gulf to Earth. "I'm out of contact with Slade. Maybe he's fallen somewhere, out of sight. And I don't seem to be able to see the LM. And—"

And someone's wiped over our footsteps, while I wasn't looking.

Nobody is replying, he realises.

That stops him short. Dust falls over his feet. On the surface of the Moon, nothing is moving.

He looks up at the crescent Earth. "Ah, Houston, this is Bado. Houston. John, come in, capcom."

Just silence, static in his headset.

He starts moving to the east again, breathing hard, the sweat pooling at his neck.

He rented an apartment.

He got himself a better job in a radio store. In the Air Force, before joining NASA, he'd specialised in electronics. He'd been apprehensive that he might not be able to find his way around the gear here, but he found it simple—almost crude, compared to what he'd been used to. They had transistors here, but they still used big chunky valves and paper capacitors. It was like being back in the early '60s. Radios were popular, but there were few TVs: small black and white gadgets, the reception lousy.

He began watching the TV news and reading the newspapers, trying to figure out what kind of world he'd been dropped in.

The weather forecasts were lousy.

And foreign news reports, even on the TV, were sent by wire, like they'd been when he was a kid, and were often a day or two out of date.

The Vietnam War was unfolding. But there'd been none of the protests against the war, here, that he'd seen back at home. There were no live TV pictures, no colour satellite images of soldiers in the mud and the rain, napalming civilians. Nobody knew what was happening out there. The reaction to the war was more like what he remembered of World War Two.

There really was no space programme. Not just the manned stuff had gone: there were no weather satellites, communication satellites. Sputnik, Explorer and all the rest just hadn't happened. The Moon was just a light in the sky that nobody cared about, like when he was a kid. It was brighter, though, because of that big patch of highland where Imbrium should have been.

On the other hand, there were no ICBMS, as far as he could tell.

His mouth is bone-dry from the pure oxygen. He is breathing hard; he hears the hiss of water through the suit's cooling system, the pipes that curl around his limbs and chest.

There is a rational explanation for this. There has to be. Like, if he's got out of line of sight with the LM, somehow, he's invisible to the LM's radio relay, the Lunar Communications Relay Unit. He is linked to that by VHF, and then by S-band to the Earth.

Yeah, that has to be it. As soon as he gets back in line of sight of the LM, he can get in touch with home. And maybe with Slade.

But he can't figure how he could have gotten out of the LM's line of sight in the first place. And what about the vanished footsteps?

He tries not to think about it. He just concentrates on loping forward, back to the LM.

In a few minutes, he is back in Taylor Crater.

There is no LM. The regolith here is undisturbed.

Bado bounces across the virgin surface, scuffing it up.

Can he be in the wrong place? The lunar surface does have a tendency to look the same everywhere…Hell, no. He can see he is right in the middle of Taylor; he recognises the shapes of the hills. There can't be any doubt.

What, then? Can Slade have somehow gotten back to the LM, taken off without him?

But how can Bado not have seen him, seen the boxy LM ascent stage lift up into the sky? And besides, the regolith would be marked by the ascent stage's blast.

And, he realises dimly, there would, of course, be an abandoned descent platform here, and bits of kit. And their footsteps. His thoughts are sluggish, his realisation coming slowly. Symptoms of shock, maybe.

The fact is that save for his own footfalls, the regolith is as unmarked as if he's been dropped out of the sky.

And meanwhile, nobody in Houston is talking to him.

He is ashamed to find he is crying, mumbling, tears rolling down his face inside his helmet.

He starts to walk back west again. Following his own footsteps—the single line he made coming back to find the LM—he works his way out of Taylor, and back to the rim of Wildwood.

Hell, he doesn't have any other place to go.

As he walks he keeps calling, for Slade, for Houston, but there is only static. He knows his signal can't reach Earth anyway, not without the LM's big S-band booster.

At Wildwood's rim there is nothing but the footfalls he left earlier. He looks down into Wildwood, and there sits the Surveyor, glistening like some aluminium toy, unperturbed.

He finds his dropped carrier, with the spilled tools and bagged rocks. He bends sideways and scoops up the stuff, loading it back into the carrier.

Bado walks down into Wildwood, spraying lunar dust ahead of him.

He examines the Surveyor. Its solar cell array is stuck out on a boom above him, maybe ten feet over the regolith. The craft bristles with fuel tanks, batteries, antennae and sensors. He can see the craft's mechanical claw where it has scraped into the lunar regolith. And he can see how the craft's white paint has turned tan, maybe from exposure to the sunlight. There are splashes of dust under the vernier rocket nozzles; the Surveyor is designed to land hard, and the three pads have left a firm imprint in the surface.

He gets hold of a landing leg and shakes the Surveyor. "Okay," he calls up. "I'm jiggling it. It's planted here." There was a fear that the Surveyor might tip over onto the astronauts when they try to work with it. That evidently isn't going to happen. Bado takes a pair of cutting shears from his carrier, gets hold of the Surveyor's TV camera, and starts to chop through the camera's support struts and cables. "Just a couple more tubes," he says. "Then that baby's mine."

He'll finish up his Moonwalk, he figures, according to the timeline in the spiral-bound checklist on his cuff. He'll keep on reporting his observations, in case anyone is listening. And then—

And then, when he gets to the end of the walk, he'll figure out what to do next. Later there will be another boundary, when his PLSS's consumables expire. He'll deal with those things when they come. For now, he is going to work.

The camera comes loose, and he grips it in his gloves. "Got it! It's ours!"

He drops the camera in his carrier, breathing hard. His mouth is dry as sand; he'd give an awful lot for an ice-cool glass of water, right here and now.

There is a shimmer, like heat haze, crossing between him and the Surveyor. Just like before.

He tilts back and looks up. There is old Earth, the fat crescent. And a star, bright and unwavering, is crossing the black sky, directly over his head.

It has to be the Apollo CSM.

He drops the carrier to the dirt and starts jumping up and down, in great big lunar hops, and he waves, as if he is trying to attract a passing aircraft. "Hey, Al! Al Pond! Can you hear me?" Even without the LM, Pond, in the CSM, might be able to pick him up.

His mood changes to something resembling elation. He doesn't know where the hell Apollo has been, but if it is back, maybe soon so will be the LM, and Slade, and everything. That will suit Bado, right down to the lunar ground he is standing on. He'll be content to have it all back the way it had been, the way it is supposed to be, and figure out what has happened to him later.

"Al! It's me, Bado! Can you hear me? Can you…"

There is something wrong.

That light isn't staying steady. It is getting brighter, and it is drifting off its straight line, coming down over his head.

It isn't the CSM, in orbit. It is some kind of boxy craft, much smaller than a LM, descending towards him, gleaming in the sunlight.

He picks up his carrier and holds it close to his chest, and he stays close to the Surveyor. As the craft approaches he feels an unreasoning fear.

His kidneys send him a stab of distress. He stands still and lets go, into the urine collection condom. He feels shamed; it is like wetting his pants.

The craft is just a box, on four spindly landing legs. It is coming down vertically, standing on a central rocket. He can see no light from the rocket, of course, but he can see how the downward blast is starting to kick up some dust. It is going to land maybe fifty yards from the Surveyor, right in the middle of Wildwood Crater. The whole thing is made of some silvery metal, maybe aluminium. It has a little control panel, set at the front, and there is someone at the controls. It looks like a man—an astronaut, in fact—his face hidden behind a gold-tinted visor.

Bado can see the blue of a NASA logo, and a dust-coated Stars and Stripes, painted on the side of the craft.

Maybe fifty feet above the ground the rocket cuts out, and the craft begins to drop. The sprays of dust settle back neatly to the lunar soil. Now little vernier rockets, stuck to the side of the open compartment, cut in to slow the fall, kicking up their own little sprays.

It is all happening in complete silence.

The craft hits the ground with a solid thump. Bado can see the pilot, the astronaut, flick a few switches, and then he turns and jumps the couple of feet down off the little platform to the ground.

The astronaut comes giraffe-loping across the sunlit surface towards Bado.

He stops, a few feet from Bado, and stands there, slightly stooped forward, balancing the weight of his PLSS.

His suit looks pretty much a standard EMU, an Apollo Extravehicular Mobility Unit. There is the usual gleaming white oversuit—the thermal micrometeorite garment—with the lower legs and overshoes scuffed and stained with Tycho dust. Bado can see the PLSS oxygen and water inlets on the chest cover, and penlight and utility pockets on arms and legs. And there is Old Glory stitched to the left arm.

But Bado doesn't recognise the name stitched over the breast. WIL-LIAMS. There is no astronaut of that name in the corps, back in Houston.

Bado's headset crackles to life, startling him.

"I heard you, when the LFU came over the horizon. As soon as I got in line of sight. I could hear you talking, describing what you were doing. And when I looked down, there you are."

Bado is astonished. It is a woman's voice. This Williams is a goddamn woman. Bado can't think of a thing to say.

He didn't find it hard to find himself a place in the community here, to gather a fake ID around himself. Computers were pretty primitive, and there was little cross-checking of records.

Maybe, back home, the development of computers had been forced by the Apollo project, he speculated.

He couldn't see any way he was going to get home. He was stuck here. But he sure as hell didn't want to spend his life tuning crummy 1960s-design radios.

He tinkered with the Surveyor camera he'd retrieved from the Moon. It was a much more lightweight design than anything available here, as far as he could tell. But the manufacturing techniques required weren't much beyond what was available here.

He started to take camera components to electronic engineering companies.

He took apart his lunar suit. In all this world there was nothing like the suit's miniaturised telemetry system. He was able to adapt it to be used to transmit EKG data from ambulances to hospital emergency rooms. He sent samples of the Beta-cloth outer coverall to a fibreglass company, and showed them how the stuff could be used for fire hoses. Other samples went to military suppliers to help them put together better insulated blankets. The scratch-proof lens of the Surveyor camera went to an optical company, to manufacture better safety goggles and other gear. The miniature, high-performance motors driving the pumps and fans of his PLSS found a dozen applications.

He was careful to patent everything he "developed" from his lunar equipment. Pretty soon, the money started rolling in.

"Maybe I'm dreaming this," Williams says. "Dehydration, or something… Uh, I guess I'm pleased to meet you."

She has a Tennessee accent, he thinks.

Bado shakes the hand. He can feel it through his own stiff pressure glove. "I guess you're too solid for a ghost."

"Ditto," she says. "Besides, I've never met a ghost yet who uses VHF frequencies."

He releases her hand.

"I don't know how the hell you got here," she says. "And I guess you don't understand this any better than I do."

"That's for sure."

She dips her visored head. "What are you doing here, anyway?"

He holds up the carrier. "Sampling the Surveyor. I took off its TV camera."

"Oh. You couldn't get it, though."

"Sure. Here it is."

She turns to the Surveyor. "Look over there."

The Surveyor is whole again, its TV camera firmly mounted to its struts. But when he looks down at his carrier, there is the TV camera he's cut away, lying there, decapitated.

"Where's your LM?" she asks.

"Taylor Crater."

"Where?"

He describes the crater's location.

"Oh. Okay. We're calling that one San Jacinto. Ah, no, your LM isn't there."

"I know. I walked back. The crater's empty."

"No, it isn't," she says, but there is a trace of alarm in her voice. "That's where my LM is. With my partner, and the Payload Module."

Payload Module?

"The hell with it," she says. "Let's go see."

She turns and starts to lope back to her flying craft, rocking from side to side. He stands there and watches her go.

After a few steps she stops and turns around. "You want a lift?"

"Can you take two?"

"Sure. Come on. What choice do you have, if you're stuck here without a LM?"

Her voice carries a streak of common sense that somehow comforts him.

Side by side, they bound over the Moon.

They reach Williams's flying machine. It is just an aluminium box sitting squat on its four legs, with vernier rocket nozzles stuck to the walls like clusters of berries. The pilot has to climb in at the back and stand over the cover of the main rocket engine, which is about the size of a car engine, Bado supposes. Big spherical propellant and oxidiser tanks are fixed to the floor. There is an S-band antenna and a VHF aerial. There is some gear on the floor, hammers and shovels and sample bags and cameras; Williams dumps this stuff out, briskly, onto the regolith. Williams hops up onto the platform and begins throwing switches. Her control panel contains a few instruments, a CRT, a couple of handsets.

Bado lugs his heavy tool carrier up onto the platform, then he gets hold of a rail with both hands and jumps up. "What did you call this thing? An LFU?"

"Yeah. Lunar Flying Unit."

"I've got vague memories," says Bado. "Of a design like this. It was never developed, when the extended Apollo missions were cancelled."

"Cancelled? When did that happen?"

"When we were cut back to stop when we get to Apollo 17."

"Uh huh," she says dubiously. She eyes the tool carrier. "You want to bring that thing?"

"Sure. It's not too heavy, is it?"

"No. But what do you want it for?"

Bado looks at the battered, dusty carrier, with its meaningless load of rocks. "It's all I've got."

"Okay. Let's get out of here," she says briskly.

Williams kicks in the main rocket. Dust billows silently up off the ground, into Bado's face. He can see frozen vapour puff out of the attitude nozzles, in streams of shimmering crystals, as if this is some unlikely steam engine, a Victorian engineer's fantasy of lunar flight.

The basin of Wildwood Crater falls away. The lift is a brief, comforting surge.

Williams whoops. "Whee-hoo! What a ride, huh, pal?" She takes the LFU up to maybe sixty feet, and slows the ascent. She pitches the craft over and they begin sailing out of Wildwood.

The principles of the strange craft are obvious enough to Bado. You stand on your rocket's tail. You keep yourself stable with the four peroxide reaction clusters, the little vernier rockets spaced around the frame, squirting them here and there. When the thrust of the single big downwards rocket is at an angle to the vertical, the LFU goes shooting forwards, or sideways, or backwards across the pitted surface. Williams shows him the hand controls. They are just like the LM's. The attitude control moves in clicks; every time Williams turns the control the reaction rockets will bang and the LFU will tip over, by a degree at a time. The thrust control is a toggle switch; when Williams closes it the lift rockets roar, to give her a delta-vee of a foot per second.

"These are neat little craft," Williams says. "They fly on residual descent stage propellants. They've a range of a few miles, and you can do three sorties in each of them."

"Each?"

"We bring two. Rescue capability."

Bado thinks he is starting to see a pattern to what has happened to him.

In a way, the presence of the camera in his carrier is reassuring. It means he isn't crazy. There really have been two copies of the Surveyor: one of which he's sampled, and one he hasn't.

Maybe there is more than one goddamn Moon.

Moon One is the good old lantern in the sky that he and Slade touched down on yesterday. Maybe Slade is still back there, with the LM. But Bado sure isn't. Somehow he stumbled onto Moon Two, the place with the Surveyor, but no LM. And then this Williams showed up, and evidently by that time he was on another Moon, Moon Three, with its own copy of the Surveyor. And a different set of astronauts exploring, with subtly different equipment.

As if travelling to one Moon isn't enough.

He thinks about that strange, heat-haze shimmer. Maybe that has something to do with these weird transfers.

He can't discuss any of this with Williams, because she hasn't seen any of the changes. Not yet, anyhow.

Bado clings to the sides of the LFU and watches the surface of the Moon scroll underneath him. There are craters everywhere, overlaid circles of all sizes, some barely visible in a surface gardened by billions of years of micro-meteorite impact. The surface looks ghostly, rendered in black and white, too stark, unmoving, to be real.

He knew he was taking a risk, but he took his lunar rocks to a couple of universities.

He got laughed out of court. Especially when he wouldn't explain how these charcoal-dark rocks might have got from the Moon to the Earth.

"Maybe they got blasted off by a meteorite strike," he said to an "expert" at Cornell. "Maybe they drifted in space until they landed here. I've read about that."

The guy pushed his reading glasses further up his thin nose. "Well, that's possible." He smiled. "No doubt you've been reading the same lurid speculation I have, in the popular science press. What if rocks get knocked back and forth between the planets? Perhaps there are indeed bits of the Moon, even Mars, to be turned up, here on Earth. And, since we know living things can survive in the interiors of rocks—and since we know that some plants and bacteria can survive long periods of dormancy—perhaps it is even possible for life to propagate itself, across the trackless void, in such a manner."

He picked up Bado's Moon rock, dubiously. "But in that case I'd expect to see some evidence of the entry of this rock into the atmosphere. Melting, some glass. And besides, this rock is not volcanic. Mr Bado, everyone knows the Moon's major features were formed exclusively by vulcanism. This can't possibly be a rock from the Moon."

Bado snatched back his rock. "That's Colonel Bado," he said. He marched out.

He gave up, and went back to Daytona Beach.

The LFU slides over the rim of Taylor Crater. Or San Jacinto. Bado can see scuffed-up soil below him, and the big Huckleberry Finn Crater to his left, where he and Slade made their first stop.

At the centre of Taylor stands a LM. It glitters like some piece of giant jewellery, the most colourful object on the lunar surface. An astronaut bounces around in front of it, like a white balloon. He—or she—is working at what looks like a surface experiment package, white-painted boxes and cylinders and masts laid out in a star formation, and connected to a central nuclear generator by orange cables. It looks like an ALSEP, but it is evidently heavier, more advanced.

But the LM isn't alone. A second LM stands beside it, squat and spidery. Bado can see that the ascent stage has been heavily reworked; the pressurised cabin looks to be missing, replaced by cargo pallets.

"That's your Payload Module, right?"

"Yeah," Williams says. "The Lunar Payload Module Laboratory. It got here on automatics before we left the Cape. This is a dual Saturn launch mission, Bado. We've got a stay time of four weeks."

Again he has vague memories of proposals for such things: dual launches, well-equipped long-stay jaunts on the surface. But the funding squeezes since '66 have long since put paid to all of that. Evidently, wherever Williams comes from, the money is flowing a little more freely.

The LFU tips itself back, to slow its forward velocity. Williams throttles back the main motor and the LFU starts to drop down. Bado glances at the numbers; the CRT display evolves smoothly through height and velocity readings. Bado guesses the LFU must have some simple radar-based altimeter.

Now the LM and its misshapen partner are obscured by the dust Williams's rocket is kicking up.

At fifty feet Williams cuts the main engine. Bado feels the drop in the pit of his stomach, and he watches the ground explode towards him, resolving into unwelcome detail, sharp boulders and zap pits and footprints, highlighted by the low morning sun.

Then vernier dust clouds billow up around the LFU. Bado feels a comforting surge of deceleration.

The LFU lands with a jar that Bado feels in his knees.

For a couple of seconds the dust of their landing cloaks the LFU, and then it begins to settle out around them, coating the LFU's surfaces, his suit.

There is a heat-haze shimmer. "Oh, shit."

Williams is busily shutting down the LFU. She turns to face him, anonymous behind her visor.

There wasn't much astronomy going on at all, in fact, he found out when he looked it up in the libraries. Just a handful of big telescopes, scattered around the world, with a few crusty old guys following their obscure, decades-long projects. And all the projects were to do with deep space: the stars, and beyond. Nobody was interested in the Solar System. Certainly in nothing as mundane as the Moon.

He looked up at Moon Six, uneasily, with its bright, unscarred northwest quadrant. If that Imbrium meteorite hadn't hit three billion years ago—or in 1970—where the hell was it now?

Maybe that big mother was on its way, right now.

Quietly, he pumped some of his money into funding a little research at the universities into Earth-neighbourhood asteroids.

He also siphoned money into trying to figure out what had happened to him. How he had got here.

As the last dust settles, Bado looks towards the centre of Taylor Crater, to where the twin LMs stood.

He can make out a blocky shape there.

He feels a sharp surge of relief. Thank God. Maybe this transition hasn't been as severe as some of the others. Or maybe there hasn't been a transition at all…

But Williams's LM has gone, with its cargo-carrying partner. And so has the astronaut, with his surface package. But the crater isn't empty. The vehicle that stands in its place has the same basic geometry as a LM, Bado thinks, with a boxy descent stage standing on four legs, and a fat ascent stage cabin on top. But it is just fifteen feet tall—compared to a LM's twenty feet—and the cabin looks a lot smaller.

"My God," Williams says. She is just standing, stock still, staring at the little lander.

"Welcome to Moon Four," Bado whispers.

"My God." She repeats that over and over.

He faces her, and flips up his gold visor so she can see his face. "Listen to me. You're not going crazy. We've been through some kind of—transition. I can't explain it." He grins. It makes him feel stronger to think there is someone else more scared, more shocked, than he is.

He takes her through his tentative theory of the multiple Moons.

She turns to face the squat lander again. "I figured it had to be something like that."

He gapes at her. "You figured?"

"How the hell else could you have got here? Well, what are we supposed to do now?" She checks the time on her big Rolex watch. "Bado. How long will your PLSS hold out?"

He feels embarrassed. Shocked or not, she's cut to the chase a lot more smartly than he's been able to. He glances at his own watch, on the cuff next to his useless checklist. "A couple of hours. What about you?"

"Less, probably. Come on." She glides down from the platform of the LFU, her blue boots kicking up a spray of dust.

"Where are we going?"

"Over to that little LM, of course. Where else? It's the only source of consumables I can see anywhere around here." She begins loping towards the lander.

After a moment, he picks up his carrier, and follows her.

As they approach he gets a better look at the lander. The ascent stage is a bulbous, misshapen ball, capped by a fat, wide disk that looks like a docking device. Two dinner-plate-sized omnidirectional antennae are stuck out on extensible arms from the descent stage. The whole clumsy-looking assemblage is swathed in some kind of green blanket, maybe for thermal insulation.

A ladder leads from a round hatch in the front of the craft, and down to the surface via a landing leg. The ground there is scuffed with footprints.

"It's a hell of a small cabin," she says. "Has to be one man."

"You think it's American?"

"Not from any America I know. That ascent stage looks familiar. It looks like an adapted Soyuz orbital module. You know, the Russian craft, their Apollo equivalent."

"Russian?"

"Can you see any kind of docking tunnel on top of that thing?"

He looks. "Nope. Just that flat assemblage at the top."

"The crew must have to spacewalk to cross from the command module. What a design."

An astronaut comes loping around the side of the lander, swaying from side to side, kicking up dust. When he catches sight of Bado and Williams, he stops dead.

The stranger is carrying a flag, on a pole. The flag is stiffened with wire, and it is clearly bright red, with a gold hammer-and-sickle embroidered into it.

"How about that," Williams whispers. "I guess we don't always get to win, huh."

The stranger—the cosmonaut, Bado labels him—takes a couple of steps towards them. He starts gesticulating, waving his arms about, making the flag flutter. He wears a kind of hoop around his waist, held away from his body with stiff wire.

"I think he's trying to talk to us," Williams says.

"It'll be a miracle if we are on the same frequency. Maybe he's S-band only, to talk to Earth. No VHF. Look how stiff his movements are."

"Yeah. I think his suit is semi-rigid. Must be hell to move around in."

"What's with the hula hoop?" Bado asks.

"It will stop him falling over, in case he trips. Don't you get it? He's on his own here. That's a one-man lander. There's nobody around to help him, if he gets into trouble."

The cosmonaut is getting agitated. Now he hoists up the flag and throws it at them, javelin-style; it falls well short of Bado's feet. Then the cosmonaut turns and lopes towards his lander, evidently looking for more tools, or improvised weapons.

"Look at that," Bado says. "There are big funky hinges, down the side of his backpack. That must be the way into the suit."

Williams lifts up her visor. "Show him your face. We've got to find some way to get through to this guy."

Bado feels like laughing. "What for?"

The light changes.

Bado stands stock still. "Shit, not again."

Williams says, "What?"

"Another transition." He looks around for the tell-tale heat-haze flicker.

"I don't think so," Williams says softly. "Not this time."

A shadow, slim and jet-black, hundreds of feet long, sweeps over the surface of Taylor Crater.

Bado leans back and tips up his face.

The ship is like a huge artillery shell, gleaming silver, standing on its tail. It glides over the lunar surface, maybe fifty feet up, and where its invisible rocket exhaust passes, dust is churned up and sent gusting away in great flat sheets. The ship moves gracefully, if ponderously. Four heavy landing legs, with big spring-load shock absorbers, stick out from the base. A circle of portals glows bright yellow around the nose. A huge bull's-eye of red, white and blue is painted on the side, along with a registration number.

"Shit," Bado says. "That thing must be a hundred feet tall." Four or five times as tall as his lost LM. "What do you think it weighs? Two, three hundred tons?"

"Direct ascent," she says.

"Huh?"

"Look at it. It's streamlined. It's built for landing on the Moon in one piece, ascending again, and returning to Earth."

"But that was designed out years ago, by von Braun and the boys. A ship like that's too heavy for chemical rockets."

"So who said anything about chemical? It has to be atomic. Some kind of fission pile in there, superheating its propellant. One hell of a specific impulse. Anyhow, it's that or antigravity—"

The great silver fish hovers for a moment, and then comes swooping down at the surface. It flies without a quiver. Bado wonders how it is keeping its stability; he can't see any verniers. Big internal flywheels maybe.

As the ship nears the surface dust comes rushing across the plain, away from the big tail, like a huge circular sandstorm. There is a rattle, almost like rain, as heavy particles impact Bado's visor. He holds his gloved hands up before his face, and leans a little into the rocket wind.

The delicate little Russian lander just topples over in the breeze, and the bulbous ascent stage breaks off and rolls away.

In the mirror of his bedroom he studied his greying hair and spreading paunch.

Oddly, it had taken a while for him to miss his wife, Fay.

Maybe because everything was so different. Not that he was sorry, in a sense; his job, he figured, was to survive here—to earn a living, to keep himself sane— and moping after the unattainable wouldn't help.

He was glad they'd had no kids, though.

There was no point searching for Fay in Houston, of course. Houston without the space programme was just an oil town; with a big cattle pasture north of Clear Lake where the Manned Spacecraft Center should have been. El Lago, the Taylor housing development, had never been built.

He even drove out to Atlantic City, where he'd first met Fay, a couple of decades ago. He couldn't find her in the phone book. She was probably living under some married name, he figured.

He gave up.

He tried, a few times, to strike up relationships with other women here. He found it hard to get close to anyone, though. He always felt he needed to guard what he was saying. This wasn't his home, after all.

So he lived pretty much alone. It was bearable. It even got easier, as he got older.

Oddly, he missed walking on the Moon more than anything else, more than anything about the world he'd lost. He kept reliving those brief hours. He remembered Slade, how he looked bouncing across the lunar sand, a brilliant white balloon. How happy he'd seemed.

The silver ship touches down with a thump, and those big legs flex, the springs working like muscles.

A hatch opens in the ship's nose, maybe eighty feet from the ground, and yellow light spills out. A spacesuited figure appears, and begins rolling a rope ladder down to the surface. The figure waves to Bado and Williams, calling them to the ship.

"What do you think?" Bado asks.

"I think it's British. Look at that bull's-eye logo. I remember war movies about the Battle of Britain…Wherever the hell that's come from, it's some place very different from the worlds you and I grew up in."

"You figure we should go over there?" he asks.

She spreads her hands. "What choice do we have? We don't have a LM. And we can't last out here much longer. At least these guys look as if they know what they're doing. Let's go see what Boris thinks."

The cosmonaut lets Williams walk up to him. He is hauling at his ascent stage. But Bado can see the hull is cracked open, like an aluminium egg, and the cosmonaut's actions are despairing.

Williams points towards the silver ship, where the figure in the airlock is still waving at them.

Listlessly, the cosmonaut lets himself be led to the ship.

Close to, the silver craft looks even bigger than before, so tall that when Bado stands at its base he can't see the nose.

Williams goes up the ladder first, using just her arms, pulling her mass easily in the Moon's shallow gravity well. The cosmonaut takes off his hoop, dumps it on the ground, and follows her.

Bado comes last. He moves more slowly than the others, because he has his tool carrier clutched against his chest, and it is awkward to juggle while climbing the rope ladder.

It takes forever to climb past the shining metal of the ship's lower hull. The metal here looks like lead, actually. Shielding, around an atomic pile? He thinks of the energy it must take to haul this huge mass of metal around. He can't help comparing it with his own LM, which, to save weight, was shaved down to little more than a bubble of aluminium foil.

The hull shivers before his face. Heat haze.

He looks down. The wreckage of the little Russian lander, and Williams's LFU, has gone. The surface under the tail of this big ship looks unmarked, lacking even the raying of the landing. And the topography of the area is quite different; now he is looking down over some kind of lumpy, sun-drenched mountain range, and a wide, fat rille snakes through the crust.

"How about that," Williams says drily, from above him. Her voice signal is degraded; the amplifier on the LFU is no longer available to boost their VHF link.

"We're on Moon Five," he says.

"Moon Five?"

"It seems important to keep count." ·

"Yeah. Whatever. Bado, this time the geology's changed. Maybe one of the big primordial impacts didn't happen, leaving the whole lunar surface a different shape."

They reach the hatch. Bado lets the astronaut take his tool carrier, and clambers in on his knees.

The astronaut closes the hatch and dogs it shut by turning a big heavy wheel. He wears a British Union Flag on his sleeve, and there is a name stitched to his breast: TAINE.

The four of them stand around in the airlock, in their competing pressure suit designs. Air hisses, briefly.

An inner door opens, and Taine ushers them through with impatient gestures. Bado enters a long corridor, with nozzles set in the ceiling. The four of them stand under the nozzles.

Water comes gushing down, and runs over their suits.

Williams opens up her gold sun-visor and faces Williams. "Showers," she says.

"What for?"

"To wash off radioactive crap, from the exhaust." She begins to brush water over her suit arms and legs.

Bado has never seen anything like such a volume of water in lunar conditions before. It falls slowly from the nozzles, gathering into big shimmering drops in the air. Grey-black lunar dust swirls towards the plug holes beneath his feet. But the dirt is ingrained into the fabric of his suit legs; they will be stained grey forever.

When the water dies they are ushered through into a third, larger chamber. The walls here are curved, and inset with round, tough-looking portholes;

it looks as if this chamber reaches most of the way around the cylindrical craft.

There are people here, dozens of them, adults and children and old people, dressed in simple cotton coveralls. They sit in rows of crude metal-framed couches, facing outwards towards the portholes. They stare fearfully at the newcomers.

The astronaut, Taine, has opened up his faceplate; it hinges outward like a little door.

Bado pushes back his hood and reaches up to his fishbowl helmet. He undogs it at the neck, and his ears pop as the higher pressure of the cabin pushes air into his helmet.

He can smell the sharp, woodsmoke tang of lunar dust. And, overlaid on that, there is a smell of milky vomit: baby sick.

The Russian, his own helmet removed, makes a sound of disgust. *"Eta oozhasna!"*

Williams pulls off her Snoopy flight helmet. She is maybe forty, Bado guesses—around Bado's own age—with a tough, competent face, and close-cropped blond hair.

Taine shoos the three of them along. "Welcome to *Prometheus*," he says. "Come. There are some free seats further around here." His accent is flat, sounding vaguely Bostonian. Definitely British, Bado thinks, probably from the south of England. "You're the last, we think. We must get away. The impact is no more than twelve hours hence."

Bado, lugging his tool carrier, walks beside him. "What impact?"

"The meteorite, of course." Taine sounds impatient. "That's why we're having to evacuate the colonies. And you alternates. The Massolite got most of them off, of course, but—"

Williams says, "Massolite?"

Taine waves a hand. "A mass transporter. Of course it was a rushed job. And it had some flaws. But we knew we couldn't lift everybody home in time, not all those thousands in the big colonies, not before the strike; the Massolite was the best we can do, you see." They come to three empty couches. "These should do, I think. If you'll sit down I'll show you how to fit the seat belts, and instruct you in the safety precautions—"

"But," Williams says, "what has this Massolite got to do with—" She dries up, and looks at Bado.

He asks, "With moving between alternate worlds?"

Taine answers with irritation. "Why, nothing, of course. That's just a design flaw. We're working on it. Nonlinear quantum mechanical leakage, you see. I do wish you'd sit down; we have to depart..."

Bado shucks off his PLSS backpack, and he tucks his helmet and his carrier under his seat.

Taine helps them adjust their seat restraints until they fit around their pressure suits. It is more difficult for the Russian; his suit is so stiff it is more like armour. The Russian looks young, no more than thirty. His hair sticks up in the air, damp with sweat, and he looks at them forlornly from his shell of a suit. *"Gdye tooalyet?"*

The portholes before them give them a good view of the lunar surface. It is still Moon Five, Bado sees, with its mountains and that sinuous black rille.

He looks around at their fellow passengers. The adults are unremarkable; some of them have run to fat, but they have incongruously skinny legs and arms. Long-term adaptation to lunar gravity, Bado thinks.

But there are also some children here, ranging from babies in their mothers' arms up to young teenagers. The children are extraordinary: spindly, attenuated. Children who look facially as young as seven or eight tower over their parents.

The passengers clutch at their seatbelts, staring back at him.

Bado hears a clang of hatches, and a siren wails, echoing from the metal walls.

The ship shudders, smoothly, and there is a gentle surge.

"Mnye nada idtee k vrachoo," groans the Russian, and he clutches his belly.

As the years wore on he followed the news, trying to figure out how things might be different, back home.

The Cold War went on, year after year. There were no ICBMs here, but they had squadrons of bombers and nuke submarines and massive standing armies in Europe. And there were no spy satellites; nobody had a damn clue what the Russians—or the Chinese—were up to. A lot of shit came down that Bado figured might have been avoided, with satellite surveillance. It slowly leaked out into the paper press, usually months or years too late. Like the Chinese nuking of Tibet, for instance. And what the Soviets did to Afghanistan.

The Soviet Union remained a monolith, blank, threatening, impenetrable. Everyone in the US seemed paranoid to Bado, generations of them, with their bomb shelters and their iodine pills. It was like being stuck in the late 1950s.

And that damn war in Indochina just dragged on, almost forgotten back home, sucking up lives and money like a bloody sponge.

Around 1986, he felt a sharp tug of wistfulness. Right now, he figured, on the other side of that heat haze barrier, someone would be taking the first steps on Mars. Maybe it would be his old buddy, Slade, or someone like John Young. Bado might have made it himself.

Bado missed the live sports on TV.

In free fall, Taine gives them spare cotton coveralls to wear, which are comfortable but don't quite fit; the name stitched to Bado's is LEDUC, and on Williams's, HASSELL.

Bado, with relief, peels off the three layers of his pressure suit: the outer micrometeorite garment, the pressure assembly and the inner cooling garment. The other passengers look on curiously at Bado's cooling garment, with its network of tubes. Bado tucks his discarded suit layers into a big net bag and sticks it behind his couch.

They are served food: stodgy stew, lukewarm and glued to the plate with gravy, and then some kind of dessert, like bread with currants stuck inside it. Spotted dick, Taine calls it.

There is a persistent whine of fans and pumps, a subdued murmur of conversation, and the noise of children crying. Once a five-year-old, all of six feet tall, comes bouncing around the curving cabin in a spidery tangle of attenuated arms and legs, pursued by a fat, panting, queasy-looking parent.

Taine comes floating down to them, smiling. "Captain Richards would like to speak to you. He's intrigued to have you on board. We've picked up quite a few alternate-colonists, but not many alternate-pioneers, like you. Would you come forward to the cockpit? Perhaps you'd like to watch the show from there."

Williams and Bado exchange glances. "What show?"

"The impact, of course. Come. Your German friend is welcome too, of course," Taine adds dubiously.

The cosmonaut has his head stuck inside a sick bag.

"I think he's better off where he is," Bado says.

"You go," Williams says. "I want to try to sleep." Her face looks worn to Bado, her expression brittle, as if she is struggling to keep control. Maybe the shock of the transitions is getting to her at last, he thinks.

The cockpit is cone-shaped, wadded right in the nose of the craft. Taine leads Bado in through a big oval door. Charts and mathematical tables have been stuck to the walls, alongside pictures and photographs. Some of these show powerful-looking aircraft, of designs unfamiliar to Bado, but others show what must be family members. Pet dogs. Tools and personal articles are secured to the walls with elastic straps.

Three spacesuits, flaccid and empty, are fixed to the wall with loose ties. They are of the type Taine wore in the airlock: thick and flexible, with inlaid metal hoops, and hinged helmets at the top.

Three seats are positioned before instrument consoles. Right now the seats face forward, towards the nose of the craft, but Bado can see they are hinged so they will tip up when the craft is landing vertically. Bado spots a big, chunky periscope sticking out from the nose, evidently there to provide a view out during a landing.

There are big picture windows set in the walls. The windows frame slabs of jet-black, star-sprinkled sky.

A man is sitting in the central pilot's chair. He is wearing a leather flight jacket, a peaked cap, and—Bado can't believe it—he is smoking a pipe, for God's sake. The guy sticks out a hand. "Mr Bado. I'm glad to meet you. Jim Richards, RAF."

"That's Colonel Bado." Bado shakes the hand. "US Air Force. Lately of NASA."

"NASA?"

"National Aeronautics and Space Administration…"

Richards nods. "American. Interesting. Not many of the alternates are American. I'm sorry we didn't get a chance to see more of your ship. Looked a little cramped for the three of you."

"It wasn't our ship. It was a Russian, a one-man lander."

"Really," Richards murmurs, not very interested. "Take a seat." He waves Bado at one of the two seats beside him; Taine takes the other, sipping tea through a straw. Richards asks, "Have you ever seen a ship like this before, Colonel Bado?"

Bado glances around. The main controls are a conventional stick-and-rudder design, adapted for spaceflight; the supplementary controls are big, clunky switches, wheels, and levers. The fascia of the control panel is made of wood. And in one place, where a maintenance panel has been removed, Bado sees the soft glow of vacuum tubes.

"No," he says. "Not outside the comic books."

Richards and Taine laugh.

"It must take a hell of a launch system."

"Oh," says Richards, "we have good old Beta to help us with that."

"Beta?"

"This lunar ship is called Alpha," Taine says. "Beta gives us a piggyback out of Earth's gravity. We launch from Woomera, in South Australia. Beta is a hypersonic athodyd—"

Richards winks at Bado. "These double-domes, eh? He means Beta is an atomic ramjet."

Bado boggles. "You launch an atomic rocket from the middle of Australia? How do you manage containment of the exhaust?"

Taine looks puzzled. "What containment?"

"You must tell me all about your spacecraft," Richards says.

Bado, haltingly, starts to describe the Apollo system.

Richards listens politely enough, but after a while Bado can see his eyes drifting to his instruments, and he begins to fiddle with his pipe, knocking out the dottle into a big enclosed ashtray.

Richards becomes aware of Bado watching him. "Oh, you must forgive me, Colonel Bado. It's just that one encounters so many alternates."

"You do, huh."

"The Massolite, you know. That damn quantum-mechanical leakage. Plessey just can't get the thing tuned correctly. Such a pity. Anyhow, don't you worry; the boffins on the ground will put you to rights, I'm sure."

Bado is deciding he doesn't like these British. They are smug, patronising, icy. He can't tell what they are thinking.

Taine leans forward. "Almost time, Jim."

"Aha!" Richards gets hold of his joystick. "The main event." He twists the stick, and Bado hears what sounds like the whir of flywheels, deep in the guts of the ship. Stars slide past the windows. "A bit of showmanship, Colonel Bado. I want to line us up to give the passengers the best possible view. And us, of course. After all, this is a grandstand seat, for the most dramatic astronomical event of the century—what?"

The Moon, fat and grey and more than half-full, slides into the frame of the windows.

The Moon—Moon Five, Bado assumes it to be—looks like a ball of glass, its surface cracked and complex, as if starred by buckshot. Tinged pale white, the Moon's centre looms out at Bado, given three-dimensional substance by the Earthlight's shading.

The Moon looks different. He tries to figure out why.

There, close to the central meridian, are the bright pinpricks of Tycho, to the south, and Copernicus, in the north. He makes out the familiar pattern of the seas of the eastern hemisphere: Serenitatis, Crisium, Tranquillitatis—grey lakes of frozen lava framed by brighter, older lunar uplands.

He supposes there must be no Apollo 11 LM descent stage, standing on this version of the Sea of Tranquillity.

The Moon is mostly full, but he can see lights in the remaining crescent of darkness. They are the abandoned colonies of Moon Five.

Something is still wrong, though. The western hemisphere doesn't look right. He takes his anchor from Copernicus. There is Mare Procellarum, to the western limb, and to the north of that—

Nothing but bright highlands.

"Hey," he says. "Where the hell's Mare Imbrium?"

Richards looks at him, puzzled, faintly disapproving.

Bado points. "Up there. In the northwest. A big impact crater—the biggest—flooded with lava. Eight hundred miles across."

Richards frowns, and Taine touches Bado's arm. "All the alternate Moons are different to some degree," he says, placating. "Differences of detail—"

"Mare Imbrium is not a goddamn detail." Bado feels patronised again. "You're talking about my Moon, damn it." But if the Imbrium impact has never happened, no wonder the surface of Moon Five looks different.

Richards checks his wrist watch. "Any second now," he says. "If the big-brains have got it right—"

There is a burst of light, in the Moon's northwest quadrant. The surface in the region of the burst seems to shatter, the bright old highland material melting and subsiding into a red-glowing pool, a fiery lake that covers perhaps an eighth of the Moon's face. Bado watches huge waves, concentric, wash out across that crimson, circular wound.

Even from this distance Bado can see huge debris clouds streaking across the lunar surface, obscuring and burying older features, and laying down bright rays that plaster across the Moon's face.

The lights of the night-side colonies wink out, one by one.

Richards takes his pipe out of his mouth. "Good God almighty," he says. "Thank heavens we got all our people off."

"Only just in time, sir," Taine says.

Bado nods. "Oh, I get it. Here, this was the Imbrium impact. Three billion years late."

Richards and Taine look at him curiously.

It turned out that to build a teleport device—a "Star Trek" beaming machine—you needed to know about quantum mechanics. Particularly the Uncertainty Principle.

According to one interpretation, the Uncertainty Principle was fundamentally caused by there being an infinite number of parallel universes, all lying close to each other—as Bado pictured it—like the pages of a book. The universes blurred together at the instant of an event, and split off afterwards.

The Uncertainty Principle said you could never measure the position and velocity of any particle with absolute precision. But to teleport that was exactly what you needed to do: to make a record of an object, transmit it, and re-create the payload at the other end.

But there was a way to get around the Uncertainty Principle. At least in theory.

The quantum properties of particles could become entangled: fundamentally linked in their information content. What those British must have done is take sets of entangled particles, left one half on their Moon as a transmitter, and planted the other half on the Earth.

There was a lot of technical stuff about the Einstein-Podolsky-Rosen theorem which Bado skipped over; what it boiled down to was that if you used a description of your teleport passenger to jiggle the transmitter particles, you could reconstruct the passenger at the other end, exactly, from the corresponding jiggles in the receiver set.

But there were problems.

If there were small nonlinearities in the quantum-mechanical operators— and there couldn't be more than a billion-billion-billionth part, according to Bado's researchers—those parallel worlds, underlying the Uncertainty Principle, could short-circuit.

The Moon Five Brits had tried to build a cheap-and-dirty teleport machine. Because of the huge distances involved, that billion-billion-billionth nonlinearity had become significant, and the damn thing had leaked. And so they had built a parallel-world gateway, by accident.

This might be the right explanation, Bado thought. It fit with Captain Richards's vague hints about "nonlinear quantum mechanics."

This new understanding didn't make any difference to his position, though. He was still stranded here. The teleport devices his researchers had outlined— even if they'd got the theory right, from the fragments he'd given them—were decades beyond the capabilities of the mundane world Bado found himself in.

Reentry is easy. Bado estimates the peak acceleration is no more than a couple of Gs, no worse than a mild roller-coaster. Even so, many of the passengers looks distressed, and those spindly lunar-born children cry weakly, pinned to their seats like insects.

After the landing, Alpha's big doors are flung open to reveal a flat, barren desert. Bado and Williams are among the first down the rope ladders, lugging their pressure suits, and Bado's tool carrier, in big net bags.

Bado can see a small town, laid out with the air of a military barracks.

Staff are coming out of the town on little trucks to meet them. They are processed efficiently; the crew of the *Prometheus* gives details of where each passenger has been picked up, and they are all assigned little labels and forms, standing there in the baking sunlight of the desert.

The spindly lunar children are lowered to the ground and taken off in wheelchairs. Bado wonders what will happen to them, stranded at the bottom of Earth's deep gravity well.

Williams points. "Look at that. Another *Prometheus*."

There is a launch rail, like a pencil line ruled across the sand, diminishing to infinity at the horizon. A silver dart clings to the rail, with a slim bullet shape fixed to its back. Another Beta and Alpha. Bado can see protective rope barriers slung around the rail.

Taine comes to greet Bado and Williams. "I'm afraid this is goodbye," he says. He sticks out a hand. "We want to get you people back as quickly as we can. You alternates, I mean. What a frightful mess this is. But the sooner you're out of it the better."

"Back where?" Bado asks.

"Florida." Taine looks at them. "That's where you say you started from, isn't it?"

Williams shrugs. "Sure."

"And then back to your own world." He mimes stirring a pot of some noxious substance. "We don't want to muddy the time lines, you see. We don't know much about this alternating business; we don't know what damage we might do. Of course the return procedure's still experimental but hopefully we'll get it right.

"Well, the best of luck. Look, just make your way to the plane over there." He points.

The plane is a ramjet, Bado sees immediately.

Taine moves on, to another bewildered-looking knot of passengers.

The Russian cosmonaut is standing at Williams's side. He is hauling his stiff pressure suit along the ground; it scrapes on the sand like an insect's discarded carapace. Out of the suit the Russian looks thin, young, baffled, quite ill. He shakes Bado's hand. "*Do svidanya.*"

"Yeah. So long to you too, kid. Hope you get home safely. A hell of a ride, huh."

"*Mnye nada k zoobnomoo vrachoo.*" He clutches his jaw and grins ruefully. "*Schastleevava pootee. Zhilayoo oospyekhaf.*"

"Yeah. Whatever."

A British airman comes over and leads the Russian away.

"Goddamn," Williams says. "We never found out his name."

He got a report in from his meteorite studies group.

Yes, it turned out, there was a large object on its way. It would be here in a few years time. Bado figured this had to be this universe's edition of that big old Imbrium rock, arriving a little later than in the Moon Five world.

But this rock was heading for Earth, not the Moon. Its path would take it right into the middle of the Atlantic, if the calculations were right. But the margins of error were huge, and, and…

Bado tried to raise public awareness. His money and fame got him onto TV, even, such as it was. But nobody here took what was going on in the sky very seriously anyhow, and they soon started to think he was a little weird.

So he shut up. He pushed his money into bases at the poles, and at the bottom of the oceans, places that mightn't be so badly affected. Somebody might survive. Meanwhile he paid for a little more research into that big rock in space, and where and when, exactly, it was going to hit.

The ramjet takes ten hours to get to Florida. It is a military ship, more advanced than anything flying in Bado's world. It has the bull's-eye logo of the RAF painted to its flank, just behind the gaping mouth of its inlet.

As the ramjet rises, Bado glimpses huge atomic aircraft, immense ocean-going ships, networks of monorails. This is a gleaming world, an engineer's dream.

Bado has had enough wonders for the time being, though, and, before the shining coast of Australia has receded from sight, he's fallen asleep.

They land at a small airstrip, Bado figures somewhere north of Orlando. A thin young Englishman in spectacles is there to greet them. He is wearing Royal Air Force blue coveralls. "You're the alternates?"

"I guess so," Williams snaps. "And you're here to send us home. Right?"

"Sorry for any inconvenience you've been put through," he says smoothly. "If you'll just follow me into the van…"

The van turns out to be a battered diesel-engined truck that looks as if it is World War Two vintage. Williams and Bado with their bulky gear have to crowd in the back with a mess of electronic equipment.

The truck, windowless, bumps along badly finished roads.

Bado studies the equipment. "Look at this stuff," he says to Williams. "More vacuum tubes."

Williams shrugs. "They've got further than we have. Or you. Here, they've built stuff we've only talked about."

"Yeah." Oddly, he's forgotten that he and Williams have come from different worlds.

The roads off the peninsula to Merritt Island are just farmers' tracks, and the last few miles are the most uncomfortable.

They arrive at Merritt Island in the late afternoon.

There is no Kennedy Space Center.

Bado gets out of the van. He is on a long, flat beach; he figures he is a way south of where, in his world, the lunar ship launch pads will be built. Right here there will be the line of launch complexes called ICBM Row.

But he can't see any structures at all. Marsh land, coated with scrub vegetation, stretches down towards the strip of beach at the coast. Further inland, towards the higher ground, he can see stands of cabbage palm, slash pine and oak.

The place is just scrub land, undeveloped. The tracks of the British truck are dug crisply into the sand; there is no sign even of a road near here.

And out to the east, over the Atlantic, he can see a big full Moon rising. Its upper left quadrant, the fresh Imbrium scar, still glows a dull crimson. Bado feels vaguely reassured. That is still Moon Five; things seem to have achieved a certain stability.

In the back of the truck, the British technician powers up his equipment. "Ready when you are," he calls. "Oh, we think it's best if you go back in your own clothes. Where possible." He grins behind his spectacles. "Don't want you—"

"Muddying up the time lines," Williams says. "We know."

Bado and Williams shuck off their coveralls and pull on their pressure suits. They help each other with the heavy layers, and finish up facing each other, their helmets under their arms, Bado holding his battered tool carrier with its Baggies full of Moon rocks.

"You know," Bado says, "when I get back I'm going to have one hell of a lot of explaining to do."

"Yeah. Me too." She looks at him. "I guess we're not going to see each other again."

"Doesn't look like it."

Bado puts down his carrier and helmet. He embraces Williams, clumsily.

Then, on impulse, Bado lifts up his helmet and fits it over his head. He pulls his gloves over his hands and snaps them onto his wrists, completing his suit.

Williams does the same. Bado picks up his tool carrier.

The Brit waves, reaches into his van, and throws a switch.

There is a shimmer of heat haze.

Williams has gone. The truck has vanished.

Bado looks around quickly.

There are no ICBM launch complexes. He is still standing on an empty, desolate beach.

The Moon is brightening, as the light leaks out of the sky. There is no ancient Imbrium basin up there. No recent impact scar, either.

"Moon Six," Bado says to himself. "Oh, shit."

Evidently those British haven't ironed out all the wrinkles in their "experimental procedures" after all.

He takes off his helmet, breathes in the ozone-laden ocean air, and begins to walk inland, towards the rows of scrub pine.

On the day, he drove out to Merritt Island.

It was morning, and the sun was low and bright over the ocean, off to the east, and the sky was clear and blue, blameless.

He pulled his old Moon suit out of the car, and hauled it on: first the cooling garment, then the pressure layer, and finally the white micrometeorite protector and his blue lunar overshoes. It didn't fit so well any more, especially around the waist—well, it had been fitted for him all of a quarter-century ago—and it felt as heavy as hell, even without the backpack. And it had a lot of parts missing, where he'd dug out components and samples over the years. But it was still stained grey below the knees with lunar dust, and it still had the NASA logo, his mission patch, and his own name stitched to the outer garment.

He walked down to the beach. The tide was receding, and the hard-packed sand was damp; his ridged soles left crisp, sharp prints, just like in the lunar crust.

He locked his helmet into place at his neck.

To stand here, as close as he could get to ground zero, wasn't such a dumb thing to do, actually. He'd always remembered what that old professor at Cornell had told him, about the rocks bearing life being blasted from planet to planet by meteorite impacts. Maybe that would happen here, somehow.

Today might be the last day for this Earth. But maybe, somehow, some piece of him, fused to the glass of his visor maybe, would finish up on the Moon—Moon Six—or Mars, or in the clouds of Jupiter, and start the whole thing over again.

He felt a sudden, sharp stab of nostalgia, for his own lost world. He'd had a good life here, all things considered. But this was a damn dull place. And he'd been here for twenty-five years, already. He was sure that back home that old Vietnam War wouldn't have dragged on until now, like it had here, and funds would have got freed up for space, at last. Enough to do it properly, by God. By now, he was sure, NASA would have bases on the Moon, hundreds of people in Earth orbit, a couple of outposts on Mars, plans to go on to the asteroids or Jupiter.

Hell, he wished he could just look through the nonlinear curtains separating him from home. Just once.

He tipped up his face. The sun was bright in his eyes, so he pulled down his gold visor. It was still scuffed, from the dust kicked up by that British nuclear rocket. He waited.

After a time, a new light, brighter even than rocket light, came crawling down across the sky, and touched the ocean.

A BRIEF GUIDE TO OTHER HISTORIES

PAUL McAULEY

Before becoming a full-time writer, Paul McAuley worked as a research biologist in various universities, including Oxford and UCLA, and for six years was a lecturer in botany at St. Andrews University. His novels have won the Philip K. Dick Memorial Award, and the Arthur C. Clarke, John W. Campbell and Sidewise awards. His latest titles are *Cowboy Angels* (Pyr) and *In the Mouth of the Whale* (Gollancz). He lives in North London.

M y platoon had been in the American Bund sheaf for two weeks before it suffered its first major incident. It was gruesome and it robbed us of our innocence, but it was only the beginning of something stranger and deeper.

We'd come through the Turing gate at Brookhaven with the rest of the Third Brigade, First Armor Division, second battalion, as part of the ongoing operation to bring peace and reconciliation to that particular version of America's history. Seventeen PFCs and Spec 4s, and me, their commanding officer. We were all kids. I was the oldest, and I'd just turned twenty-four. Most of us hadn't been through the mirror before, and it put the zap on our heads. This was America, but it wasn't our version of America. New York, but not our version of New York. There were buildings I recognised from my visits to the city back in the Real. The Chrysler Building. The Empire

State. St Patrick's Cathedral. Yellow taxis jostled on the streets, manholes vented plumes of steam, and Central Park was right where it should have been, although it had been stripped of trees by people desperate for firewood in the last days of the war, and there was a refugee camp sprawled across Sheep Meadow. But although the Statue of Liberty stood out in the Hudson, she was holding up a sword instead of a torch. The sword was a hundred feet long, and forged out of stainless steel that shone like cold flame. The skyline was different, too. Lower. Instead of glass and steel skyscrapers, brutal chunks of marble and white stone hunched like giant toads: monumental railroad stations, government buildings, and palaces. Some were burnt out or shattered by bombs. The rest were holed by artillery shells and pockmarked by small-arms fire.

We'd been given orientation lectures and issued with copies of a pamphlet that explained that the different versions of history accessed by the Turing gates were every bit as real and valid as our own history. That their people were real people, American citizens just like us. Even so, driving around a city where familiar buildings mixed with alien intruders, half the traffic was military, and pedestrians were dressed in drab antique styles, was like inhabiting a dream. Or like taking the lead role in a movie when you had no idea of the script or plot.

The American Bund sheaf shared most of our history, but it had taken a different turn in the 1930s, when a bunch of generals and tycoons who didn't like where their country seemed to be heading under the New Deal had assassinated Franklin D. Roosevelt and installed a military government. One of the generals turned out to be more ruthless than the rest. After the coup, he'd seized power by a ruthless programme of murder and arrest, made himself President-for-Life, and established a tyranny that had lasted for more than thirty years. Towards the end of his rule, he'd become insane. He'd styled himself the Dear Leader, ordered the construction of hundreds of grandiose monuments to himself, put millions in prison or in work camps, massacred millions more. He'd been about to go to war against Europe when, in 1972, scientists in our version of history had opened a Turing gate onto his version of history. The Central Intelligence Group had sent through agents who'd made contact with rebels and supplied them with weapons and intel. As soon as civil war kicked off, two divisions drove through the mirror, quickly took control of the Eastern seaboard, captured the Dear Leader as he tried to flee to Argentina, and pushed over what turned out to be a regime hollowed by corruption and self-interest.

When my platoon and the rest of the Third Brigade came through the mirror a year later, deadenders who refused to accept that the war was over were waging a guerrilla campaign up and down the country. They used car bombs and land mines, improvised explosive devices from fertiliser, fuel oil, and scrap metal, and detonated them when convoys drove past. They fired mortars into our bases. They shot at us with sniper rifles or rocket-propelled grenades from vantage points in buildings, or took potshots at us and melted into panicked crowds. As in any insurrection, it was almost impossible to tell the good guys from the bad guys, and that was why one of my men ended up killing three innocent civilians.

We had been ordered to set up a traffic control point on the West Side, ten blocks south of the green zone. Two APCs backed by a Martindale light tank, razor-wire coiled across the street, the men waving vehicles forward one by one, doing stop and checks. The traffic was bunched up and jumpy, simmering in hundred-degree heat so humid you could have wrung water out of the air. And we were all jumpy, too. At any moment, someone could pop a trunk and find weapons or a primed car bomb, or some screwed-up munchkin could decide to take a shot at us just for the hell of it. So when a taxi lurched forward after it was directed to an inspection point, accelerating crazily, scattering men, Bobby Sturges, behind the .50 caliber machine gun on top of one of the APCs, made a split-second decision and put two hundred rounds into the taxi in less than a minute. Punching holes in the hood, exploding the tyres, shattering the windshield, shredding the driver and his two passengers, a man and his seventy-year-old mother. Sudden silence as the taxi rolled to a stop, engine dead, blood leaking from its door sills, blood and human meat spattered all over the interior.

That evening, Tommy McAfee said, "If these fucking munchkins learned to drive, this shit wouldn't happen."

Munchkins—that's what we called the locals. New York City—the American Bund sheaf's version of New York City—was Oz. The green zone in Oz, built up around a palace that before the revolution had been owned by one of the Dear Leader's sons, was the Emerald City.

Like many of the men, Tommy McAfee had trouble accepting that the people on this side of the mirror were as real as the people back home, couldn't believe that Americans could have brought themselves so low. He treated them with rough contempt, made endless jokes about them. He had a quick, sharp wit, knew how to time a punch line and cap someone else's joke with a zinger of his own, was gaining a solid reputation as the platoon's joker. So when he made his quip, he was surprised and upset when Ernie Wright told him to can it, and the rest of the men either made murmurs of agreement or looked away.

They were all lounging around by the side of the entrance that curved down to the underground garage where the Dear Leader's eldest son had once stored his limousines, sports cars and motorcycles, where we now parked our APCs and Jeeps. We ate and slept in what had been servants' quarters nearby, and had set up a barbeque pit outside. Folding chairs. A basketball hoop. A table-tennis set liberated from somewhere in the palace. Tommy McAfee was sitting on a case of oil cans, a rangy kid with rusty hair cropped short, a tattoo of a boxing leprechaun on his right bicep, looking at Ernie Wright and saying, "Jesus. You'd think I was the one shot that fucking taxi to death."

Ernie Wright was the biggest man in the platoon, but he could move quickly. He stepped up to Tommy McAfee and grabbed the front of his fatigues and pulled him to his feet in a single fluid motion, and asked him, their faces inches apart, "Any more smart remarks about what went down?"

"I can't think of any."

Wright set McAfee down and patted him on the shoulder, but that wasn't the end of it. Later on that evening they got into a fistfight. It was supposedly over who should have the last steak, but it was really about McAfee trying to regain some face after Wright had shamed him. McAfee could box, but Wright was stronger and heavier, and after some sparring he knocked McAfee on his ass with a solid punch. McAfee got up and came back at Wright and was knocked down again, and this time he stayed down. Sprawled flat on his back on floodlit concrete under the basketball hoop, breathing hard, his nose and mouth bloody, one eye swelling shut. After a while he got up and went to the ice-chest and washed his face with a handful of ice chips.

I didn't think much of it at the time. We'd all been on edge after the shooting, and the fistfight seemed to have dissipated much of the tension. And besides, I was more concerned about Bobby Sturges. He was a gentle kid, barely eighteen, sick to his soul over what he'd done. When I'd told him that he wouldn't get any blame when I wrote up the incident, that I accepted full responsibility because it had happened under my command, he'd given me a haunted look and said, "Doesn't make it right, Lieutenant. They're Americans, like us. Americans shouldn't be killing Americans."

"I agree. But some of them are trying to kill us, which is why you did the right thing."

"Maybe it was the right thing to do," Bobby Sturges said, "but that doesn't make it right."

I put in a request to pull him off the line for a few days R&R, but it was kicked back immediately. There was sand in the gears of the mission. We couldn't spare any men. I took him off the .50 cal, but he had to ride out with us on patrol the next day, and the day after that.

We manned checkpoints. We escorted convoys of supplies to hospitals and aid stations. We escorted a convoy of construction material to a power station that had been badly damaged during the war—jackhammers were pounding all over the city, cranes were swinging to and fro, and scaffolding was springing up like kudzu as the munchkins patched and repaired and rebuilt, as if tearing down one movie set and erecting another in its place. I noticed that Ernie Wright did his best to keep behind Tommy McAfee during foot patrols, and guessed what he was thinking. Tommy McAfee might want to even things out after his beating, we were all carrying guns, and it wasn't unknown for a soldier with a beef to put a round or two into their rival's back in the middle of a firefight. But Tommy McAfee seemed to have forgotten the incident, and although the deadenders were staging hit-and-run raids in Texas and parts of the Midwest, and Washington, D.C. was paralysed by a spate of car bombings, New York was pretty quiet. It was August, hot and sunny. I remember one day we were parked up near a playground, and Dave Brahma and Leroy Moss started handing out candy bars and cans of soft drink to the kids. Two men in flak jackets and helmets, M-16s slung over their shoulders, up to their waists in a crowd of happy children. Another time, Todd Cooper was checking IDs at a control point and a man started shaking his hand and wouldn't let go. This old man in a dusty suit and battered fedora, pumping Todd Cooper's hand and thanking him for being there, tears rolling down his cheeks.

Then a supply convoy running the expressway from Brookhaven into New York City was hit by a massive improvised explosive device buried at the side of the highway. Five died instantly, six were badly wounded. That night, my platoon took part in a raid on an apartment building in Brooklyn. According to an informer, the deadenders who had planted the IED were storing weapons and explosives there.

It kicked off at two in the morning. A psy-ops vehicle blasted out a message telling everyone to leave their doors open and wait with their hands on their heads for questioning. Two Cherokee helicopters beat above the building's flat roof, lighting up the front with searchlights. A squad of explosives specialists hit the basement first, and then everyone else went in.

My platoon had been assigned the top two floors. I was determined to do things by the book. I told the men to knock first and break down doors only if they had to, to keep their fingers off their triggers and treat everyone with respect. Even so, it was a pretty brutal business. We'd storm in, grab the man of the house and throw him down, pacify the rest of the family, and interrogate the man in front of them, ask him if he owned a weapon or had any insurgent propaganda, if he was involved in insurgent activity in any way. Then we'd rip up the place, pulling out drawers and tossing the contents, ripping through closets, looking for anything that could be used as a weapon. The people were mostly passive, but we'd been told to expect trouble and we had no idea what we might find or if the situation might suddenly turn ugly. Despite my orders, there was quite a bit of roughhousing and horseplay to relieve the tension, shouts and screams, the smash of glass and crockery. A frat house party with half the participants armed to the teeth, and the possibility of sudden death hanging in the air.

I was going from apartment to apartment, trying to curb excesses, when Dave Brahma came up and told me that something weird was going down. Smiling his gentle stoned smile, saying, "You have to see this, Lieutenant. It'll blow your mind. Truly."

I followed him downstairs to a single-room apartment with bookshelves along one wall, posters above the couch, books in piles on the floor. It was very hot. A standard lamp had been knocked over and threw huge shadows everywhere. Searchlights pried through blinds at the window. The whippy flutter of the helicopters matched my racing heartbeat. Todd Cooper and Tommy McAfee stood behind a man kneeling on the bare boards with his wrists plasticuffed. Ernie Wright stood in front of him, studying an ID card.

"Tell me what you think, Lieutenant," Tommy McAfee said, and jerked up the prisoner's head by his hair.

"Is he on the list?"

"Take a real good look," Tommy McAfee said. Both he and Todd Cooper were lit up, grinning. "His eyes, the colour of his hair... You don't see it?"

"Show the lieutenant that ID," Todd Cooper said.

Ernie Wright handed the card to me. He had a baffled, dazed expression, as if he'd run full-tilt into an invisible wall.

"You see it?" Tommy McAfee said, as I studied it. "You see it now?"

The name under the black and white photo card was Ernest C. Wright.

Tommy McAfee's grin widened when he saw my reaction, "I reckon we found ourselves Ernie's double."

"Bullshit," Ernie Wright said. "He's nothing like me. He doesn't even have the same date of birth."

"Oh yeah? Then how come he just told us he was born in the same dipshit town as you? His parents have the same names as your parents, he has your name, and he has your eyes, too," Tommy McAfee said, jerking the prisoner's head up again.

It was true, the prisoner's eyes were the same sharp blue as Ernie Wright's, and his hair was the same dirty blond. But otherwise he didn't look much like Ernie Wright at all. He was shy about fifty pounds, his face was leaner and paler, and he had a mustache.

"He's your doppelgänger, dude," Dave Brahma said. "Your dark half."

I asked if they'd found any explosives or weapons.

"There isn't anything to find," Ernie Wright said.

"Ain't this sweet," McAfee said. "Ernie is in love. In love with his own self."

Brahma asked the prisoner why he had all these books.

"I'm a teaching assistant at Brooklyn University," the man said.

His voice was lighter than Ernie Wright's.

"Yeah? What do you teach?" McAfee said.

"American literature."

Ernie Wright shook his head.

"If you're a teacher, I guess you're a party member," McAfee said, grinning at me. "This guy is guilty of something, Lieutenant. I can smell it."

"There were fifty million party members," the man said. "Including everyone who worked in every university and high school. It was the law."

"All these books," McAfee said. "I bet we could find something subversive. What do you say, Lieutenant? Shall we take him in?"

I thought that this was more about the beef Tommy McAfee had with Ernie Wright than about uncovering a potential suspect. I pulled my knife, cut the plasticuffs that bound the man's wrists, and looked straight into McAfee's grin and asked him if he had a problem.

No one said anything. The man knelt on the floor, rubbing his wrists, carefully not making eye contact with anyone.

"Move on," I said. "Everyone, right now."

Ernie Wright was staring at the man. Then he shuddered, all over, like a man waking in the middle of a dream, and marched straight out. The fallen lamp wheeled his shadow over the bookcase and ceiling. As McAfee, Cooper and Brahma trooped after him, I remembered that I was still holding the man's ID card.

"Sorry," I said, and dropped the card in front of him and bolted from the apartment, thoroughly spooked by the situation.

The men ragged Ernie Wright about his alleged double or doppelgänger on the ride back to Emerald City. Most of it was good-natured, but he turtled up, hunched in the back of the APC in a glowering silence that he broke only once, when Tommy McAfee told him that something must have gone badly wrong with his life, seeing as he'd ended up in the shit, while his doppelgänger had a good job, an education...

"That's the *point*," Ernie Wright said. "That guy, he isn't *anything* like me. So can your shit, McAfee. It ain't right. It isn't even funny."

After a silence, Dave Brahma said in his doper's drawl, "Know what they say about your doppelgänger? That it's just like you in every way, but it doesn't have a soul. And it knows that, and it wants one real bad. So if you ever meet it, it's like meeting a vampire hungry for, like, your exact blood type. One look, it can suck the soul right out of you. Turn you into what it was, make itself into you."

"There's something to that," Leroy Moss said. He was at the wheel of the APC, inclining his head so that the men in the back could hear him over the roar of the engine. "Everyone agrees that there can be no miraculous multiplication of souls. If there are two people the same, one in the Real, one in some other history, there can be but the one soul. And you can't divide a soul, either, so only one person can be in possession of it."

"You ask me, *all* the munchkins lack souls," Todd Cooper said. "They're all ghosts."

It was a common belief. The munchkins were spooks. Unreal. And because they were unreal, it didn't matter what you did to them.

"That's what doppelgänger means," Dave Brahma said. "It's German for ghost double."

"They say it's okay to fuck your doppelgänger," Todd Cooper said. "Really. It's like jacking off. Only, you know, double the fun."

"Yeah, but the only problem is, you have to waste him right afterward," Tommy McAfee said. "Otherwise, he'll waste *you*."

Most of the men laughed. Dave Brahma said, "It must have been pretty intense, Ernie, meeting your own ghost back there."

Ernie Wright didn't reply. I turned around and told the men to knock it off, but Tommy McAfee had to have the last word.

"The big question is, which is the ghost and which is the man? You think about that, Ernie."

A couple of days later, I saw Ernie Wright sitting on one of the plastic chairs in the R&R area, barechested in shorts and sandals, reading the pamphlet we'd all been given before coming through the mirror, *A Brief Guide to Other Histories.* I asked him how he was doing, and he said he was doing fine.

"Pretty interesting reading you have there."

He shrugged.

"You read it carefully, it'll explain why that guy isn't really your double."

"I know it," Ernie Wright said. "I knew it when I saw he was three years younger than me."

"As I understand it, if he was born after the history of this sheaf split from the history of the Real, he has to be a completely different person," I said. "Because all of his experiences are different from yours."

I'd been reading *A Brief Guide to Other Histories* too, after that night.

"That's pretty much what it says here," Ernie Wright said. He was holding the pamphlet in one hand, his forefinger marking his place. "You are what you do, and what's done to you. The sum of all your experiences. Him and me, we've had such different lives we aren't even like brothers."

"That's how I understand it," I said.

"Still," he said, "I guess we had the same mother and father."

I didn't understand the significance of that remark then. It was hardly my fault. I had trouble remembering the names of all my men in my platoon, let alone the details of their lives before they'd joined up or been drafted. But even though I could hardly have been expected to remember that Ernie Wright's mother had died in childbirth when he was just two years old, that he'd been brought up by a father who was a bitter and violent drunk, I still feel guilty about what happened. I still have the irrational idea that I should have known about Ernie Wright's unhappy childhood, that I should have done something to prevent what happened next, instead of making some inane remark about being pleased to see that he was putting the encounter in perspective.

"It was weird," he said, "but weird shit happens through the mirror. We just have to deal with it."

"Glad to hear it."

And after that, Ernie Wright did seem to be dealing with it. I overheard him having an earnest conversation with Leroy Moss, who carried a copy of the Bible in the breast pocket of his flak jacket, about the nature of souls and their indivisibility. He shrugged off Tommy McAfee's jibes. And then, two weeks later, the platoon was given a day of R&R, and he disappeared.

I didn't find out what had happened until the next day, when the military police took charge of Ernest Wright, the man Tommy McAfee had claimed to be Ernie Wright's doppelgänger.

It seemed that Ernie had changed into civilian clothes, hitched a ride out of Emerald City in a contractor's truck, and turned up at Ernest's apartment later that evening. Drunk but lucid, saying he wanted a quiet word, offering cigarettes and a bottle of Four Roses. A gift, he said, for the trouble a couple of weeks back. Ernest had deep misgivings, but he also felt sorry for Ernie, who seemed sad and bewildered and lost. And he was curious, too. So he invited Ernie in and made coffee, and they got to talking. They shared the same parents, but Ernie's had met several years before Ernest's had, Ernie's mother had died giving birth to a still-born baby when he was two, his father had become a serious drunk, and Ernie had joined the Army to get away from the son of a bitch, who had died three years ago, when his liver had finally given out on him.

"I don't miss him," Ernie said. "Not one bit."

Ernest's father—the American Bund's version of Ernie's father—had died in a traffic accident when Ernest was less than a year old. A couple of years later, his mother had remarried, to another teacher in the high school where she worked.

"That's how you got to be a college professor, uh?"

"There were always books in the house."

They talked about the town where they had been born, the little house where Ernie had lived with his father until he joined the Army. Ernest and his mother had moved out when he was three, he didn't remember much about it.

"I think there was a cherry tree in the front yard," he said.

Ernie smiled. "It was still there, last time I looked. Same tree, different lives."

"Two different trees, really," Ernest said. He told Ernie how he'd won a scholarship and come to New York to teach and study literature; Ernie told him a little bit about his so-called career in the army, fighting in a sheaf wrecked by nuclear war, and now policing the streets of New York.

"I never really knew my mom," he said. "And my dad was a mean drunk who beat me 'til I got big enough to beat him. But you had a real family. You have a college degree, all those books…"

"If you knew what it was like, growing up here, under the thumb of the Dear Leader and his psychopathic sons and his secret police, you might not think it was so great," Ernest said. He'd been tense and nervous all through their conversation, growing more and more resentful about the intrusion. "Look, it was nice to talk to you. Strange, but nice. But I have to go to work tomorrow."

"Me too. Out on the streets. Hey, I was just wondering," Ernie said with ponderous casualness, "about your mother. Is she still alive?"

That was why he'd come there, of course. It wasn't anything to do with Ernest, who was at best a brother he'd never known. No, Ernie Wright was chasing the ghost of his long-dead mother.

He looked for a long time at a snapshot Ernest reluctantly gave him, asked if she was still living in their home town. Maybe he could look her up some time, he said, and grew agitated after Ernest said that he didn't think that this was a good idea. Ernie blustered, said that he barely remembered his mother, all he wanted was to see how she had turned out, what was the harm? Sharp words were exchanged. Ernie started to paw through papers on the table Ernest used as a desk, drew his pistol when Ernest asked him to stop. Ernest panicked, threw coffee in Ernie's face, and the pistol went off. The shot barely missed Ernest. There was a struggle, another shot. That one hit Ernie in the thigh, nicking his femoral artery. There was a lot of blood. Ernest went to the apartment next door, which had a phone, and called an ambulance, but it took two hours to arrive because there were road blocks everywhere. Despite the best efforts of Ernest and his neighbours Ernie Wright bled to death on Ernest Wright's old Persian carpet.

Ernest Wright told me all this in a bleak interrogation room in Camp X-Ray, the holding facility for suspects in bombings or shootings, people caught trafficking weapons and explosives, curfew violators, and anyone else who had gotten into some kind of trouble with the occupying army. He'd been arrested on suspicion of murder by the local police, but they'd handed him over to us after they had discovered that the dead man in his apartment was a soldier. My commanding officer had advised me not to visit him, but it had happened on my watch and I felt responsible. I wanted to know what had happened so that I could figure out what I had done wrong. Also, I had read the transcript of Ernest Wright's interrogations, I had talked to the local police who had handled the case, and I was convinced that he was innocent.

When I told him this, he thanked me for my concern, and for my offer to give supporting testimony should his case come to trial. He told me the story while smoking several of the cigarettes I had brought, and at the end lit a fresh one and said, "There's a writer who described time as a garden of forking paths. Whenever someone makes a decision, it doesn't matter how small, it splits time into two. So there's this time, here and now, and another time where you decided not to help me."

I told him that I was familiar with the concept. By this time, I had read

A Brief Guide to Other Histories several times from cover to cover, trying to find something that would help me understand what had happened.

"An infinite series of paths, some divergent, some convergent, some running in parallel," Ernest Wright said. "Until a year ago, I thought it was just a story. A philosophical conceit. But then your people made themselves known when the revolution started. You sent troops through their Turing gates and helped defeat the Dear Leader. You told us that their agents had been visiting our history secretly before that, helping set up the revolution. You told us that you wanted to help us build a better America. But what you're really doing is shaping us in your image."

"We really do want to help you."

"Your path is only one of an infinite number of paths. And no one path can claim to be better or more privileged than any other. All are equal."

"Except we have the Turing gates," I said.

"Which gives your history the ability to interfere with other histories, other Americas. But it doesn't give your history moral superiority. You brought us freedom. Democracy. Fine. We're grateful for it, but we're not beholden. We have the right to make from that freedom what we will, whether you approve of it or not. If we're forced to become nothing more than a pale imitation of your version of America, what kind of freedom is that?"

I told him that he sounded a little like the deadenders, and he shook his head. He was thinner than I remembered, but because his head had been shaved and he had lost his mustache it seemed to me that he looked a lot more like Ernie Wright now. Or my memory of Ernie.

"The deadenders believe that they can restore the Bund if they can push you back through the mirror. We want to restore democracy, but on our own terms. It's like your friend. He didn't really understand that we were two completely different people. Strangers. My mother was not his mother," Ernest Wright said. "And this is not your history."

That was in 1974. I was twenty-four, back then. So innocent, so foolishly hopeful. Now, just turned thirty, I'm a published writer with five short stories and a novel under my belt. I've already used parts of this story in the novel, although in my version Ernie Wright doesn't end up bleeding out on the floor of Ernest Wright's apartment, shot by his own pistol. Instead, he finds out where Ernest Wright's parents are living and goes AWOL and hitches back to the American Bund's version of his home town. He spends a day watching Ernest Wright's mother, trying and failing to get up the courage to talk to her, finally realising that he has nothing to say to her because she isn't in any way like his mother, that nothing in Ernest Wright's life could explain what had gone wrong in his own. Although this version worked well enough within the frame of the novel, although it was true to Ernie Wright's need to understand and reach a reconciliation with his own history, although it clarified real events and gave them a neat ending, it was a contrivance. I was never satisfied with it, and felt guilty too, at the way I'd trivialised Ernest Wright, used him as a bit player, a ghostly reflection whose only function was to give Ernie Wright the information he needed to make his pilgrimage. This is as close to the truth as I can make it, and there's no neat ending, no bittersweet resolution.

Ernest Wright was released back to the local authorities after two months in Camp X-Ray. He didn't make bail, and was stabbed to death in a prison riot before his case came to trial. Todd Cooper was killed in a fire-fight a couple of months later, and Dave Brahma was badly wounded. The same day, Bobby Sturges injected his foot with a Syrette of morphine and shot off his big toe, a million-dollar wound that was his ticket back to the Real. I wrote it up as an accident; the kid had never gotten over shooting up that car. Then Leroy Moss was killed when a rocket-propelled grenade hit his APC. I was sitting next to him and spent two months in hospital while doctors worked to save my leg and shrapnel, some of it bone fragments from Leroy Moss, surfaced in different parts of my body. Some of it is still in there.

Tommy McAfee reupped, served another year, and survived without a scratch. After my novel was published, he phoned me late one night. He was drunk, and wanted to talk about old times. He told me that he had a bunch of stories I could help him make into a book as good as mine. I listened to him ramble on for a while, letting him vent whatever it was my novel had stirred up, making the right kind of noises, and when he finally hung up I realised that he'd hit on something useful, and started making notes for this story.

We are what we do, and what's done to us: if *A Brief Guide to Other Histories* was right about one thing it's this. And because what happens to us in war is more intense than ordinary life, it marks us more deeply, changes us more profoundly. Every soldier who comes back from war is haunted by the ghosts of the comrades who didn't make it, the people he killed or saw killed. By the things he did, and the things he should have done. And most of all by the innocent kid he once was, before the contingencies and experiences of war took that innocence away. I have summoned up my ghosts here, and tried to lay them to rest. But it seems to me now that all of us who passed through the mirror into different histories have become like ghosts, lost in the infinite possibilities of our stories, ceaselessly searching for an ideal we can never reach.

CRYSTAL HALLOWAY
AND THE
FORGOTTEN PASSAGE

SEANAN McGUIRE

Seanan McGuire was born and raised in Northern California, resulting in a love of rattlesnakes and an absolute terror of weather. She shares a crumbling old farmhouse with a variety of cats, far too many books, and enough horror movies to be considered a problem. Seanan publishes about three books a year, and is widely rumored not to actually sleep. When bored, Seanan tends to wander into swamps and cornfields, which has not yet managed to get her killed (although not for lack of trying). She also writes as Mira Grant, and talks about horrible diseases at the dinner table.

"That's the last of them," Crystal said. "We should be safe, for now."

The dire bat's headless body lay on the floor of the cave like an accusation, blackish blood still seeping from its neck. Crystal looked at it and shuddered, disgusted, before giving it a sharp kick. It rolled over the edge of the chasm and fell into darkness, vanishing without a trace. They'd have to find the head eventually. But that could wait.

"Are you sure?" Chester asked. Her companion peered anxiously down into the dark, his nose twitching. Crystal knew that his ears—which would have been better suited to a jackrabbit than a boy, as she'd teased him so many times over the years—would have been doing the same, if they hadn't been tucked up under his hat. He'd done that to protect them from the shrieking of the dire bats. She briefly considered snatching the hat from his head, but set the thought aside. Nervous as he still was, he wouldn't take the prank as innocently as it was meant.

"I'm sure." She slid her dagger back into its sheath before wiping the sweat-matted hair away from her forehead. "Listen. You can hear the wind again."

Not just the wind: there was also the gentle tapping of inhuman legs making contact with stone. The pair turned to see a great black spider easily the size of a small car come walking down the cavern wall. It reached the floor and continued walking toward them on its bristle-haired legs, stopping just a few short feet away. With an air of deep solemnity, the spider bowed.

"The land of Otherways is in your debt once again, young Crystal," said the spider, in a deep voice that was softer than its appearance suggested. "We thank you."

"Don't thank me, Naamen. It was my pleasure. It's always my pleasure." Crystal leaned forward to rest a hand on the spider's back, digging her fingers into the coarse black hair that grew there. "This is my home just as much as it's yours."

"Even so. Your service here is all the more heroic because it is freely offered. You could return to your world of origin at any time, leaving us to our fate, and yet you choose time and again to stay and fight for our survival." The spider straightened until the largest of its eyes were on a level with Crystal's own. "You are not the first to come from your world to Otherways, but you are far and away the bravest."

"Yeah. Brave me," said Crystal softly, and pulled her hand away. Talk of others coming to Otherways before her always made her uncomfortable, although she could never put her finger on exactly why that was. Maybe it was the fact that her friends in Otherways, who were otherwise forthright in all ways, would never describe the others as anything more than "the ones who came before you." They had no names; they had no faces; they had no stories to explain what could possibly have caused them to abandon a world as wonderful and magical as Otherways. They were just gone.

"Oh, bush and bother, Crystal, look!" Chester—who could always be counted on to panic over nothing, and to show surprising bravery in the face of actual danger—pointed toward the sky.

Not already. Not so soon. A sick knot of dread formed in her stomach as she followed the direction of his finger. There was nothing there but darkness. She relaxed a little, saying, "I don't understand. What are we looking at?"

"The Passage Star is shining again." Chester let his hand fall, looking at her sorrowfully. He was always the first to see the Passage Star's light, even as Crystal herself was always the last. "You can go home now."

The dread returned, clenched tighter than ever. "Oh."

"You can go *if you wish*," said Naamen, almost as if he could see what she was feeling. "The choice to stay or go is always yours. You know you would be welcome if you chose to remain."

"The Passage Star will only burn for three hours," said Crystal slowly, arguing a side she wasn't sure that she believed in. "After that…"

"After that, it will go out, but it will light again once a fortnight until a year has gone without someone passing from our world to yours. You would still have the opportunity to change your mind."

Crystal took a shaky breath, forcing her first answer aside. Naamen always asked if she would stay, and every time, it got a little bit harder to tell him no. How was she supposed to focus on school and chores and picking the right colleges to apply to when she was the champion of Otherways, the hero of the Endless Fields, and the savior of the Caverns of Time? The world she'd been born in seemed more like a dream every time she came to the Otherways, and this world—this strange, beautiful, terrible world, with its talking spiders and its deadly, scheming roses—seemed more like the reality.

Naamen and Chester looked at her hopefully. They'd been her best friends and sworn companions since she was just a little girl. Chester was barely more than a bunny when they first met. Now she was almost a woman, and Chester was… Chester. Naamen had been slightly smaller in those days, but no less ancient, and no less wise. Just the thought of leaving them made her heart break a little.

Hearts can heal, she thought, remembering something Naamen once told her, after they saved the Princess of Thorns from her mother, the wicked Rose Queen. Crystal took another, steadier breath, and gave the answer she'd been giving since her twelfth birthday, when the great spider first asked if she would stay: "Not yet. My parents would miss me too much. Let me turn eighteen. That's when they expect to lose me to college anyway. They can lose me to Otherways instead."

Naamen shifted his pedipalps in the gesture she had come to recognize as his equivalent of a nod. "If that is your wish, Crystal Halloway, it will be honored. We will count the hours until you return to us."

"Don't stay gone too long, okay, Crystal?" asked Chester.

"I never do, do I?" Crystal leaned over and hugged him hard. He was her best friend and her first love; he'd been her first kiss, the year she turned fourteen and saved the Meadows of Mourning from the machinations of the Timeless Child. "I miss you too much when I'm gone."

"Please, then. Take this, to remember us by." Naamen reached out one long black leg. A dreamcatcher dangled from his foot, the strands woven from silk so fine that it seemed almost like light held captive in a circle of willow wood and twine. "Hang it above your bed, and only good dreams will come to visit you."

Crystal knew the dreamcatcher would do nothing against her nightmares; Naamen had been giving her the same tokens since the first time he asked her to stay, and they hadn't stopped a single bad dream. Still, making the dreamcatchers seemed to soothe him in some way she couldn't quite understand, and so she reached out and took it, feeling the weight of it settle in her palm, simultaneously feather-light and heavy as a stone. Naamen returned his foot to the cavern floor.

"Thank you, my friend," she said, as she tucked the dreamcatcher into her pocket. "I'll hang it in a place of honor."

"See that you do." Naamen waved his pedipalps again, this time in the motion that denoted concern. "I wish you would reconsider, Crystal. I wish that you would stay."

Crystal paused, frowning. Naamen always asked her not to go. He'd never tried to change her mind before. "Naamen? What's wrong?"

"It's just that you are growing up, Crystal, and I worry for your safety." The great spider stilled, looking at her gravely. "The choice, as always, is yours."

"Oh, my friend." Crystal moved almost without thinking, stepping forward and wrapping her arms around the body of the spider, just behind the smallest of his eyes. Naamen leaned into her embrace, but only enough to show that he welcomed it; not enough for his greater size to knock her off her feet, as had happened so often in her younger days. "Don't worry about me. I'll always make it back to you. Always."

Naamen stroked her back with the tip of one foreleg, faceted eyes focused on the endless black in front of him, and said nothing. There was nothing left that he could say.

Crystal approached the Welcome Stone slowly, alone, as she always did. The dread was still there in the pit of her stomach, tangled with warring desires. She wanted to go home, to sleep in her own bed and hug her parents in the morning. She wanted to stay—always—to sleep in the cobweb-decked bedroom Naamen had spun for her in the brambles that ringed the End-less Fields. She wanted to graduate from high school. She wanted to kiss Chester again and again, forever. Most of all, she wanted to be there when the next child stumbled into the light of the Passage Star. She never wanted to be one of the children Naamen refused to name.

She wanted to stay.

But she couldn't.

The passage back to her own world only took a few seconds. She stepped into the light of the Passage Star—which always shone in a perfect circle, right at the center of the Welcome Stone—blinked, and was back in the world in which she'd been born, standing in the tiny room housing the magic telescope that let her travel into Otherways. She closed the telescope lens quickly, before something unpleasant could find a way to follow her, and turned to head down the narrow stone passageway that connected to the secret door at the back of her closet.

She'd found the secret door and the room beyond by accident when she was six, playing at seeking Narnia. Now she couldn't imagine a world where she didn't have the route to Otherways etched deep into her heart, like an ache that never quite went away.

The passage was tighter than it used to be. She had to stoop a little to keep her head from knocking against the ceiling, and there were places where she had to turn and scoot along sideways in order to avoid getting stuck. One more growth spurt and she'd wind up staying in Otherways because she couldn't make it back to her bedroom... or she'd wind up trapped in the world where she was born without ever once choosing to stay.

She couldn't keep going back and forth forever. She knew that; she'd known for a long time. Somehow, the feel of the walls pressing against her back and chest as she inched through the tighter spaces just made that fact more real. Soon, she would have to decide.

The passage widened as it came to an end, letting her into an antecham-ber almost as large as the telescope room. She walked the last few steps to the door with her head high, and placed her hand upon the doorknob. "My name is Crystal Halloway," she said, "and I am coming back from the most incredible adventure..."

The doorknob turned under her hand of its own accord, and the door of her closet swung open. Crystal pushed her way through the hanging coats—which were more window-dressing than anything else; she would never dream of using her closet to store *clothing* when she might need to rush to Otherways at a moment's notice—and she was back in the familiar bedroom that had been hers practically since she was born.

Moving more on autopilot than anything else, she walked to the bed, where she removed her dagger and shoved it under her pillow. It was unlikely to be seen by prying parental eyes while it was there, and she slept better knowing it was close at hand. She yawned vastly, suddenly aware of how tired she was, and how hungry she was, and how much her battle with the dire bats had left her in need of a shower.

The dreamcatcher stayed in the pocket of her jeans as she shucked off her clothes and put on her nightshirt, which was so old and faded that she was probably the only one in the world who still saw Mickey Mouse in the shapeless blurs on the front; the dreamcatcher stayed in the pocket of her jeans as she kicked them to one side and went to take her shower, shampooing her hair three times to get the smell of dire bat blood out; the dreamcatcher stayed in the pocket of her jeans as she went to the kitchen for a midnight snack, as she checked the locks, as she came back into the room and climbed into her bed.

The stuffed tarantula she slept with every night—bought for her when she was eight, two years after she first entered Otherways—was waiting for her on her nightstand. She picked it up and hugged it tightly. "Good night, Little Naamen," she said, with the gravity of a teenage girl who knows she's doing something silly, but does it anyway, because it's what she's always done. "Spin me good dreams tonight, okay?"

On some other night, maybe that silly ritual phrase would have reminded her of the dreamcatcher; maybe she would have pulled it out of her pocket, dusted the lint from its strands, and hung it above her bed where it belonged. It had happened before. But she was tired and sore from fighting the dire bats, and sick at heart from the knowledge that soon, she would have to choose one world over the other, and all she wanted was to stop thinking for a little while. The dreamcatcher stayed in the pocket of her jeans as she reached over to her bedside table, and turned off the light.

Crystal Halloway, savior of the Otherways, closed her eyes, and slept.

There was no one single thing that woke her. One moment, Crystal was asleep, and the next, she was awake, staring into the darkness and trying to figure out why every nerve was screaming. Something was wrong. As always, when something she couldn't name was wrong, Crystal's thoughts leapt to Otherways. The Passage Star was shining—it had to be shining—and something was stopping her from seeing its light properly. But the Star never rose this soon after a visit.

Filled with an unnamed dread, Crystal tried to jump out of the bed and run for the closet. The sheets that had been snarled so carelessly around her while she slept drew instantly tight, becoming a net as effective as one of Naamen's webs. Crystal's dread suddenly solidified into concrete fear. She struggled harder, and the sheets drew even tighter, tying her down. Opening her mouth, she prepared to scream…

…and stopped herself before the sound could escape. Sheets didn't move on their own, not in this world; whatever was happening, it was tied to the Otherways. If she screamed, her parents would come, and whatever was attacking her would take them, too. She was trapped, alone in the dark, and there was no one who could save her.

Crystal's mind raced, trying to figure out which of her many enemies from Otherways could be behind this invasion. The Rose Queen? The Old Man of the Frozen North? Even the Timeless Child? All of them were somewhere in Otherways, and all of them hated her, but none of them had ever demonstrated that they had the ability to travel through the light of the Passage Star before—

"Oh, good. You're awake. It's easier when they're awake." The voice was sweet, female, and unfamiliar. Crystal turned toward it, squinting to make out anything through the gloom. "Don't try to move. You'll only hurt yourself."

The idea that she could hurt herself caused Crystal to strain even harder against the sheets. Hurting herself implied movement, and movement could imply breaking loose. The woman sighed.

"You're going to be a troublesome one, aren't you? Ah, well, it can't be helped. You should never have been left so long. Whatever they were using to hide you worked very, very well. I knew there was one of you little runaways still in this town, but I couldn't seem to find you before tonight." The sweet-voiced woman flew languidly out of the shadows and hovered above Crystal, smiling serenely down at her. "Whatever you did wrong, my dear, thank you. I appreciate it."

The dreamcatcher, thought Crystal wildly, thinking of it for the first time since returning to her room. She took a short, sharp breath and stopped struggling. All her guesses as to her attacker's identity had been wrong. This wasn't one of the enemies she knew.

This was a stranger.

The woman in the air above her was round-faced and ruddy-cheeked, with soft brown curls and twinkling blue eyes. She looked like she would have been perfectly at home baking cookies or reading stories in a preschool—except for her rapidly fluttering mayfly wings. Those, and the large knife in her hand, established her as clearly supernatural, and just as clearly hostile.

"Who *are* you?" Crystal hissed, barely raising her voice above a whisper.

"Oh, there's no need to whisper. You can scream yourself hoarse and no one will hear you. But I recommend against it. Laryngitis is no fun for anyone." The woman continued to smile. "Still, if it will make you feel better, go right ahead."

"Get out of my room," snarled Crystal. The sheets were still tangled tight around her, but that gave her an idea. Naamen's webs worked by turning each captive's strength against them, letting the strong batter themselves into weakness. The sheets had tightened every time she struggled. Glaring at the woman, she forced herself to go limp.

"Now, now, dear, has no one taught you how to greet a guest? Your manners are sorely lacking."

The sheets were no looser than they had been, but they were getting no tighter. "I don't think manners apply to the uninvited."

"Manners apply to the uninvited most of all." The woman dipped lower in the air, reaching down to tap the fingers of her right hand against Crystal's cheek. "Remember that, if you can."

Crystal took a breath—and then she moved, calling on everything she'd learned from her games of catch-and-keep with Chester, who was faster than anyone else she'd ever known. The sheets reacted to the motion, but they were too slow, if only by a fraction of a second, missing her wrists as she yanked them free. Then her dagger was in her hand, and she was slashing wildly at the sheets still holding her down, preparing to lunge for the woman who had dared to invade her home, who had dared—

The binding spell crashed down on her with enough force to slam her against the mattress, knocking the air out of her lungs. Her dagger fell to the floor, slipping out of her nerveless fingers as she stared, unmoving, into the dark above her bed.

"Oh, you *naughty* thing. I see why they worked so hard to hide you. You were quite the catch for them, weren't you? I'm sorry to have to bind you, but you left me no choice. Try to breathe. This will all be over soon, and this silliness will fade away." The woman fluttered out of Crystal's view. The mattress creaked as a weight settled on it. Then a gentle hand grasped Crystal's chin, turning her head until she was facing the little woman who sat beside her.

Crystal glared with all the force that she could find. The woman smiled.

"You're sixteen, aren't you? Don't try to answer, I already know. Don't you think it's past time you stopped running off to some childish fantasy land, leaving this world—this good world, that you were born a part of—wanting? It's time to grow up, my dear." She tapped Crystal's cheek again. This time, she bore down enough that the sharp tips of her nails bit into Crystal's skin. "I'm here to help you. I'm the Truth Fairy, you see, and that means I can do what you haven't been able to do on your own."

Crystal tried to struggle.

Crystal failed.

"Haven't you ever noticed how fairies only come when there are things to be taken away? Santa Claus, the Easter Bunny, the Birthday Pig, they come to leave things behind them. Presents and chocolates and things like that. But the Tooth Fairy comes when you lose a tooth, and she takes that tooth away, and you never see it again. What she leaves is a hole. Something that your new tooth can fill. Do you understand yet, my dear?"

Crystal's eyes screamed hate at her—hate, and terror, because something of what the Truth Fairy was saying made perfect, terrible sense. All the children she'd known in elementary school, the ones who had traveled to worlds of their own, worlds like her own Otherways, but different... they'd all forgotten their adventures, hadn't they? She'd wondered why, with increasing confusion, as friend after friend suddenly swore their quests and their trials had been nothing but fantasies. She'd *been* to some of their worlds, traveling through mechanisms as strange and wondrous as her own Passage Star. And then one day, those children just forgot.

And there had been other children in Otherways before her.

"You can't be part of two worlds forever. The heart doesn't work like that. There isn't room, any more than there's room in a mouth for two sets of teeth. Baby teeth fall out. Childhoods end. That's how adult teeth, and adult lives, find the space to grow." The Truth Fairy leaned close, voice almost a whisper as she said, "Haven't you ever noticed how so many people seem to walk around empty inside, like there's a hole cut out of the middle of them, a space where something used to be, and isn't anymore? Someone has to dig the holes, Crystal. When your baby teeth don't fall out, someone has to pull them."

Hearts can heal, that was what Naamen had told her. But there'd been more to it, hadn't there? *Hearts can heal, as long as they remember the way home.*

Hearts could forget the way home.

The Truth Fairy rose on buzzing wings. Crystal's eyes widened, the reality of the moment sinking into her bones. There was no rescue. There was no salvation. Her name was going to be added to the quiet ranks of the forgotten, and never spoken again, not now, not tomorrow, not to the next child to stumble through the light of the Passage Star.

She was never going home again.

The knife went up. The knife came down. And somewhere deep inside her, in the place that the Truth Fairy's knife sought with such unerring skill, Crystal Halloway screamed.

Morning dawned, as mornings always do. Paul and Maryanne Halloway were in the kitchen when their daughter came down the stairs, still yawning and wiping the sleep from her eyes. "Morning, Mom and Dad," she said, voice muffled by the hand she pressed against her mouth. "Breakfast?"

"Scrambled eggs and toast," said Maryanne. "How did you sleep?"

"Really well." Crystal smiled a little blearily, as she dropped herself into a seat at the kitchen table. "I had the weirdest dreams."

Her father looked up from his laptop, leaving his half-composed email unsent. "What about?"

"You know, I don't remember now?" Crystal's smile became a puzzled frown. "Something about a rabbit, I think. I don't know." For a moment, her frown deepened, taking on an almost panicked edge. "It seemed so important…"

"Don't worry yourself, dear." Maryanne put a plate of eggs and toast down in front of her daughter. "Eat up. You don't want to be late for school."

"Yeah." The frown faded, replaced by calm. "We're talking about college applications today. I should probably be on time for that."

Crystal ate quickly and mechanically, and after she left, her parents marveled at how focused and collected she'd seemed, like she was finally ready to face the challenges of growing up.

Neither of them saw the empty space behind her eyes, in the place where a lifetime of adventures used to be. Neither of them saw the hole cut through her heart, waiting to be filled by a world that would never satisfy her, although she would never, until she died, be able to articulate why.

Neither of them really saw her at all, and it wouldn't have mattered if they had. Done was done, and a heart, once truly broken, could never remember the way home. Crystal's father had grown up in that same house; had known adventures and excitement in a world whose name he no longer knew. He would love his daughter all the more for having lost the same things he had lost. And her mother… she didn't remember the talking horses or the magical wars or the young prince with webs between his fingers, not consciously, even if sometimes in the night she cried. Both of them knew that empty space more intimately than they could understand.

And none of them, not Crystal, not her parents, could hear the distant, thready sound of a giant spider—the Guardian of the Passage to the Beyond, the one who had guided and guarded a hundred generations of human children, nurtured them, loved them, and lost them all—weeping.

AN EMPTY HOUSE WITH MANY DOORS

MICHAEL SWANWICK

Michael Swanwick is the author of the novels *Bones of the Earth, Griffin's Egg, In the Drift, The Iron Dragon's Daughter, Jack Faust, Stations of the Tide, Vacuum Flowers,* and *The Dragons of Babel.* His latest is a Darger and Surplus adventure titled *Dancing with Bears.* His short fiction has appeared in *Asimov's Science Fiction, Analog, The Magazine of Fantasy & Science Fiction,* and in numerous anthologies, and has been collected in *Cigar-Box Faust, A Geography of Unknown Lands, Gravity's Angels, Moon Dogs, Puck Aleshire's Abecedary, Tales of Old Earth,* and *The Dog Said Bow-Wow.* He is the winner of numerous awards, including the Hugo, Nebula, Sturgeon, Locus, and World Fantasy awards.

T he television set is upside down. I need its company while I clean, but not its distraction. Sipping gingerly at a glass of wine, I vacuum the oriental rugs one-handed, with great care. Ah, Katherine, you'd be amazed the job I've done. The house has never been so clean.

I put the vacuum cleaner back in the closet. Cleanup takes next to no time at all since I eliminated all the unneeded furniture.

Rugs done, I'm about to get out the floor polish when it occurs to me that trash pickup is tomorrow. Humming, I roll up the carpets one by one, tie them with string, carry all three out to the curb. Then, since it's no longer needed, I set the vacuum cleaner beside them.

Back in the house, the living room is all but empty, the dried and bleached bones of our life picked clean of meat and memories. One surviving chair, the television, and a collapsible tray I've used since discarding the dining room table. The oven timer goes off; the pot pies are ready. I get out the plate, knife and fork, slide out the pies, and throw away the foil roasting tray. I wipe the stove door with a damp rag, rinse the rag, wring it out and put it away. Pour myself another glass of wine.

The television gibbers and shouts at me as I eat. People hang upside down, like bats. They scuttle across the ceiling, smiling insanely. The news bimbo is chatting up the latest disaster, mouth an inverted crescent. Somebody in a woodpecker suit is bashing his head into the bed of a pickup truck, over and over again. Is all this supposed to mean something? Was it ever?

The wine in my glass is half-gone already. Making good time tonight. All of a sudden the bad feelings well up, like a gusher of misery. I squeeze my eyes shut, screwing my face tight, but somehow the tears seep through, and I'm sobbing. Crying uncontrollably, because while I'm still thinking about you, while I never do and never can stop thinking about you, it's getting harder and harder to remember what you looked like. It's going away from me. Oh Katherine, I'm losing your face!

No self pity. I won't give in to it. I get out the mop and fill a bucket with warm water and ammonia detergent. Swabbing as hard as I can, I start to clean the floors. Until finally, it's under control. I top off my glass, take a sip, feel the wine burning in my belly. Drinking like this will kill a man, sooner or later. Which is why I work at it so hard.

I'm teaching myself how to die.

If I don't get some fresh air, I'll pass out. If I pass out, I'll drink less. Timing is all. I get my coat, walk out the door. Wibbledy-wobbledy, down the hill I go. Past the row houses and corner hoagie shops, the chocolate factory and the gas station, under the railroad bridge and along the canal, all the way down into Manayunk. The wine is buzzing in my head, but still the traitor brain dwells on you, a droning monologue on pain and loss and yearning. If only I'd kept you home that day. If only I'd only fucking only. Even I'm sick of hearing it. I lift up and above it, until conscious thought is just a drear mumble underfoot and I soar up godlike in the early evening air.

How you loved Manayunk, its old mill buildings, tumbledown collieries, and blue-collar residences. The yuppies have gentrified Main Street, but three blocks uphill from it the people haven't changed a bit; still hard-headed, suspicious, good neighbors. I float through the narrow streets, to the strip of trendy little restaurants on Main. My head swells and balloons and my feet barely touch the ground. I pass through the happy evening crowd, attached to the earth by the most tenuous of tethers. I'd sever it if I could, and simply float away.

Then I see the man strangling in midair.

Nobody else can see him. They stride purposefully by, some even walking through the patch of congealed air that, darkly sparkling, contains his struggling figure.

He is twisting in slow agony on a frame of chrome bars, like a fly dying on a spider's web. The outlines of his distorted body are prismatic at the edges, like a badly tuned video. He is drowning in dirty rainbows. His body is a cubist nightmare, torso shattered into overlapping planes, limbs scattered through nine dimensions. The head swings around, eyes multiplying and being swallowed up by flesh, and then there is a flash of desperate hope as he realizes I can see him. He reaches toward me, outflung arm spreading through a fan of possibilities. Caught in jellied air, dark and sparkling, his body shattered into strangely fractured planes.

Mouth opens in a silent scream, and through some form of sympathetic magic the faintest distant echoes of his pain sound a whispering screech of fingernails across the back of my skull.

I know a man who is drowning when I see one. People are scurrying about, some right through the man. They glance at me oddly, standing there, frozen on the sidewalk. I reach up and take his

!

hand.

It *hurts*. It hurts like a sonofabitch. I feel like I've been hit with a two-by-four. One side of my body goes completely numb. I am slammed sideways, thought whiting out under sheets of hard white pain, and it is a blessing because for the first time since you died, oh most beloved, I stop thinking about you.

When I come to, I draw myself together, stand up. I haven't moved, but the street is empty and dark. Must be late at night. Which is crazy, because people wouldn't just leave me lying there. It's not that kind of neighborhood. So why did they? It doesn't bear thinking about.

I stand up, and there, beside me, is the man's corpse.

He's dressed in a kind of white jumpsuit, with little high-tech crap scattered all over it. A badge on his chest with a fan of arrows branching out, diverging from a single point. I look at him. Dead, poor bastard, and nothing I can do about it.

I need another drink.

Home again, home again, trudge trudge trudge. As I approach the house, something is wrong, though. There are curtains in the windows, and orange light spills out. If I were a normal man, I'd be apprehensive, afraid, fearful of housebreakers and psychopaths. There's nothing I'd be less likely to do than go inside.

I go inside.

Someone is rattling pans in the kitchen. Humming. "Is that you, love?"

I stand there, inside the living room, trembling with something more abject than fear. It's the kind of curdling terror you might feel just before God walks into the room. No, I say to myself, don't even think it.

You walk into the room.

"That didn't take long," you say, amused. "Was the store closed?" Then, seeing me clear, alarm touches your face, and you say "Johnny?"

I'm trembling. You reach out a hand and touch me, and it's like a world of ice breaking up inside, and I start to cry. "Love, what's *wrong*?"

Which is when I walk into the room.

Again.

The two of me stare at each other. At first, to be honest, I don't make the connection. I just think: There's something odd about this man. Strangest damn guy I ever did see, and I can't figure out why. All those movies and television shows where somebody is suddenly confronted by his exact double and goes slack-jawed with shock? Lies, the batch of them. He doesn't look a bit like the way I picture myself.

"Johnny?" Katherine says in a strangled little voice. But she's not looking at me but at the other guy and he's staring at me in a bemused kind of way, as if there's something strange and baffling about *me*, and then all of a sudden the dime drops.

He's me.

He's me and he's not getting it anymore than I was. "Katherine?" he says. "Who *is* this?"

A very long evening later, I find myself lying on the couch under a blanket with pillows beneath my head. Upstairs, Katherine and the other me are arguing. His voice is low and angry. Hers is calm and reasonable, but he doesn't like what it says. It was my wallet that convinced her: the driver's license identical to his in every way, the credit and library and insurance cards, all the incidental pieces of identification one picks up along the way, and every single one of them exactly the same as his.

Save for the fact that his belong to a man whose wife is still alive.

I don't know exactly what you're saying up there, but I can guess at the emotional heart of it. You love me. This is, in a sense, my house. I have nowhere else to go. You are not about to turn me out.

Meanwhile, I—the me upstairs, I mean—am angry and unhappy about my being here at all. He knows me better than you do, and he doesn't like me one-tenth as much. Knowing that there's no way you could tell us apart, he is filled with paranoid fantasies. He's afraid I'm going to try to take his place.

Which, if I could, I most certainly would. But that would probably require my killing him and I'm not sure I could actually kill a man. Even if that man was myself. And how could I possibly hope to square it with Katherine? I'm in uncharted territory here. I have no idea what might or might not happen.

For now, though, it's enough to simply hear your voice. I ignore the rest and close my eyes and smile.

A car rumbles down the road outside and then abruptly stops. As do the voices above. All other noises cease as sharply as if somebody has thrown a switch.

Puzzled, I get up from the couch.

Out of nowhere, strong hands seize my arms. There's a man standing to the right of me and another to the left. They both wear white jumpsuits, which I understand now to be a kind of uniform. They wear the same badge—a fan of arrows radiant from a common locus—as the man I saw strangling in the air.

"We're sorry, sir," says one. "We saw you trying to help our comrade, and we appreciate that. But you're in the wrong place and we have to put you back."

"You're time travelers or something, aren't you?" I ask.

"Or something," the second one says. He's holding onto my right arm. With his free hand he opens a kind of pod floating in the air beside him. An equipment bag, I think. It's filled with devices which seem to be only half there. A gleaming tube wraps itself around my chest, another around my forehead. "But don't worry. We'll have everything set right in just a jiff."

Then I twig to what's going on.

"No," I say. "She's *here*, don't you understand that? I'll keep my mouth shut, I won't say anything to anyone ever, I swear. Only let me stay. I'll move to another city, I won't bother anybody. The two upstairs will think they had some kind of shared hallucination. Only please, for God's sake, let me exist in a world where Katherine's not dead."

There is a terrible look of compassion in the man's eyes. "Sir. If it were possible, we would let you stay."

"Done," says the other. The world goes away.

So I return to my empty house. I pour myself a glass of wine and stare at it for a long, long time. Then I get up and pour it into the sink.

A year passes.

It's night and I'm standing in our tiny urban backyard, Katherine, looking up at the stars and a narrow sliver of moon. Talking to you. I know you can't hear me. But I've been thinking about that strange night ever since it happened, and it seems to me that in an infinite universe, all possibilities are manifest in an eternal present. Somewhere you're happy, and that makes me glad. In countless other places, you're a widow and heartbroken. Surely one of you at least is standing out in the back yard, like I am now, staring up at the moon and imagining that I'm saying these words. Which is why I'm here. So it will be true.

I don't really have much to say, I'm afraid. I just want you to know I still love you and that I'm doing fine. I wasn't, for a while there. But just knowing you're alive somehow, however impossibly far away, is enough to keep me going.

You're never really dead, I know that now.

And if it makes you feel any better, neither am I.

TWENTY-TWO CENTIMETERS

GREGORY BENFORD

Gregory Benford has published more than thirty books, mostly novels, of which nearly all remain in print, some after a quarter of a century. His fiction has won many awards, including the Nebula Award for his novel *Timescape*. A winner of the United Nations Medal for Literature, he is a professor of physics at the University of California, Irvine. He is a Woodrow Wilson Fellow, was Visiting Fellow at Cambridge University, and in 1995 received the Lord Prize for contributions to science. A fellow of the American Physical Society and a member of the World Academy of Arts and Sciences, he continues his research in both astrophysics and plasma physics.

T he Counter-Universe was dim. The Counter-Earth below them had a gray grandeur—lightly banded in pale pewter and salmon red, save where the shrunken Moon cast its huge gloomy shadow. Here the Moon clung close to the Counter-Earth, in a universe chilling toward absolute zero.

Julie peered out at a universe cooling into extinction. Below their orbit hung the curve of Counter-Earth, its night side lit by the pale Counter-Moon. Both these were lesser echoes of the "real" Earth-Moon system, a universe away—or twenty-two centimeters, whichever came first.

Massive ice sheets spread like pearly blankets from both poles. Ridges ribbed the frozen methane ranges. The equatorial land was a flinty, scarred ribbon of ribbed black rock, hemmed in by the oppressive ice. The planet turned almost imperceptibly, a major ridgeline just coming into view at the dawn line.

Julie sighed and brought their craft lower. Al sat silent beside her. Yet they both knew that all of Earthside—the real Earth, she still thought—listened and watched through their minicams.

"The focal point is coming into sunlight 'bout now," Al reported.

"Let's go get it," she whispered. This gloomy universe felt somber, awesome.

They curved toward the dawn line. Data hummed in their board displays, spatters of light reporting on the gravitational pulses that twisted space here.

They had already found the four orbiting gravitational wave radiators, just as predicted by the science guys. Now for the nexus of those four, down on the surface. The focal point, the coordinator of the grav wave transmissions that had summoned them here.

And just maybe, to find whatever made the focal point. Somewhere near the dawn line.

They came arcing over the Counter-night. A darkness deeper than she had ever seen crept across Counter. Night here, without the shrunken Moon's glow, had no planets dotting the sky, only the distant sharp stars. At the terminator shadows stretched, jagged black profiles of the ridgelines torn by pressure from the ice. The warming had somehow shoved fresh peaks into the gathering atmosphere, ragged and sharp. Since there was atmosphere thicker and denser than anybody had expected the stars were not unwinking points; they flickered and glittered as on crisp nights at high altitudes on Earth. Near the magnetic poles, she watched swirling blue auroral glows cloak the plains where fogs rose even at night.

A cold dark world a universe away from sunny Earth, through a higher dimension...

She did not really follow the theory; she was an astronaut. It was hard enough to comprehend the mathematical guys when they spoke English. For them, the whole universe was a sheet of space-time, called "brane" for membrane. And there were other branes, spaced out along an unseen dimension. Only gravity penetrated between these sheets. All other fields, which meant all mass and light, was stuck to the branes.

Okay, but what of it? had been her first response.

Just mathematics, until the physics guys—it was nearly always guys—

found that another brane was only twenty-two centimeters away. Not in any direction you could see, but along a new dimension. The other brane had been there all along, with its own mass and light, but in a dimension nobody could see. Okay, maybe the mystics, but that was it.

And between the two branes only gravity acted. So the Counter-Earth followed Earth exactly, and the Counter-Moon likewise. They clumped together, hugging each other with gravity in their unending waltz. Only the Counter-brane had less matter in it, so gravity was weaker there.

Julie had only a cartoon-level understanding of how another universe could live on a brane only twenty-two centimeters away from the universe humans knew. The trick was that those twenty-two centimeters lay along a dimension termed the Q-coordinate. Ordinary forces couldn't leave the brane humans called the universe, or this brane. But gravity could. So when the first big gravitational wave detectors picked up coherent signals from "nearby"—twenty-two centimeters away!—it was just too tempting to the physics guys.

And once they opened the portal into the looking-glass-like Counter-system—she had no idea how, except that it involved lots of magnets—somebody had to go and look. Julie and Al.

It had been a split-second trip, just a few hours ago. In quick flash-images she had seen: purple-green limbs and folds, oozing into glassy struts—elongating, then splitting into red smoke. Leathery oblongs and polyhedrons folded over each other. Twinkling, jarring slices of hard actinic light poked through them. And it all moved as though blurred by slices of time into a jostling hurry—

Enough. Concentrate on your descent trajectory.

"Stuff moving down there," Al said.

"Right where the focal point is?" At the dawn's ruby glow.

"Looks like." He close-upped the scene.

Below, a long ice ridge rose out of the sea like a great gray reef. Following its Earthly analogy, it teemed with life. Quilted patches of vivid blue-green and carrot-orange spattered its natural pallor. Out of those patches spindly trunks stretched toward the midmorning sun. At their tips crackled bright blue St. Elmo's fire. Violet-tinged flying wings swooped lazily in and out among them to feed. Some, already filled, alighted at the shoreline and folded themselves, waiting with their flat heads cocked at angles.

The sky, even at Counter's midmorning, remained a dark backdrop for gauzy auroral curtains that bristled with energy. This world had an atmospheric blanket not dense enough to scatter the wan sunlight. For on this brane, the sun itself had less mass, too.

She peered down. She was pilot, but a biologist as well. And they knew there was something waiting...

"Going in," she said.

Into this slow world they came with a high roar. Wings flapped away from the noise. A giant filled the sky.

Julie dropped the lander closer. Her legs were cramped from the small pilot chair and she bounced with the rattling boom of atmospheric braking.

She blinked, suddenly alarmed. Beside her in his acceleration couch Al peered forward at the swiftly looming landscape. "How's that spot?" He jabbed a finger tensely at the approaching horizon.

"Near the sea? Sure. Plenty of life forms there. Kind of like an African watering hole." Analogies were all she had to go on here but there was a resemblance. Their reconn scans had showed a ferment all along the shoreline.

Al brought them down steady above a rocky plateau. Their drive ran red-hot.

Now here was a problem nobody on the mission team, for all their contingency planning, had foreseen. Their deceleration plume was bound to incinerate many of the life forms in this utterly cold ecosystem. Even after hours, the lander might be too hot for any life to approach, not to mention scalding them when nearby ices suddenly boiled away.

Well, nothing to do about it now.

"Fifty meters and holding." Al glanced at her. "Ok?"

"Touchdown," she said, and they settled onto the rock.

To land on ice would have sunk them hip-deep in fluid, only to then be refrozen rigidly into place. They eagerly watched the plain. Something hurried away at the horizon, which did not look more than a kilometer away.

"Look at those lichen," she said eagerly. "In so skimpy an energy environment, how can there be so *many* of them?"

"We're going to be hot for an hour, easy," Al said, his calm, careful gaze sweeping the view systematically. The ship's computers were taking digital photographs automatically, getting a good map. "I say we take a walk."

She tapped a key, giving herself a voice channel, reciting her ID opening without thinking. "Okay, now the good stuff. As we agreed, I am adding my own verbal comments to the data I just sent you."

They had not agreed, not at all. Many of the Counter Mission Control engineers, wedded to their mathematical slang and NASA's jawbone acronyms, felt that commentary was subjective and useless. Let the expert teams back home interpret the data. But the PR people liked anything they could use.

"Counter is a much livelier place than we ever imagined. There's weather, for one thing—a product of the planet's six-day rotation and the mysterious heating. Turns out the melting and freezing point of methane is crucial. With the heating-up, the mean temperature is well high enough that nitrogen and argon stay gaseous, giving Counter its thin atmosphere. Of course, the ammonia and carbon dioxide are solid as rock—Counter's warmer, but still incredibly cold, by our standards. Methane, though, can go either way. It thaws, every morning. Even better, the methane doesn't just sublime— nope, it melts. Then it freezes at night."

Now the dawn line was creeping at its achingly slow pace over a ridgeline, casting long shadows that pointed like arrows across a great rock plain. There was something there she could scarcely believe, hard to make out even from their thousand-kilometer-high orbit under the best magnification. Something they weren't going to believe back Earthside. So keep up the patter and lead them to it. *Just do it.*

"Meanwhile on the dark side there's a great 'heat sink,' like the one over Antarctica on Earth. It moves slowly across the planet as it turns, radiating heat into space and pressing down a column of cold air—I mean, of even *colder* air. From its lowest, coldest point, winds flow out toward the day side. At the sunset line they meet sun-warmed air—and it snows. Snow! Maybe I should take up skiing, huh?"

At least Al laughed. It was hard, talking to a mute audience. And she was getting jittery. She took a hit of the thick, jolting Columbian coffee in her mug. Onward—

"On the sunrise side they meet sunlight and melting methane ice, and it rains. Gloomy dawn. Permanent, moving around the planet like a veil."

She close-upped the dawn line and there it was, a great gray curtain descending, marching ever-westward at about the speed of a fast car.

"So we've got a perpetual storm front moving at the edge of the night side, and another that travels with the sunrise."

As she warmed to her subject, all pretense at impersonal scientific discourse faded from Julie's voice; she could not filter out her excitement that verged on a kind of love. She paused, watching the swirling alabaster blizzards at twilight's sharp edge and, on the dawn side, the great solemn racks of cloud. Although admittedly no Jupiter, this planet—her planet, for the moment—could put on quite a show.

"The result is a shallow sea of methane that moves slowly around the world, following the sun. Who'd a thought, eh, you astro guys? Since meth-ane doesn't expand as it freezes, the way water does"—okay, the astro guys know that, she thought, but the public needs reminders, and this damn well was going out to the whole wide bloomin' world, right?—"I'm sure it's all slush a short way below the surface, and solid ice from there down. But so what? The sea isn't stagnant, because of what the smaller Counter-Moon is doing. It's close to the planet so it makes a permanent tidal bulge directly underneath it. And the two worlds are trapped, like two dancers forever in each other's arms. So that bulge travels around from daylight to darkness, too. So sea currents form, and *flow,* and freeze. On the night side, the tidal pull puts stress on the various ices, and they hump up and buckle into pressure ridges. Like the ones in Antarctica, but *much* bigger."

Miles high, in fact, in Counter's weak gravity. Massive peaks, worthy of the best climbers…

But her enthusiasm drained away and she bit her lip. Now for the hard part.

She'd rehearsed this a dozen times, and still the words stuck in her throat. After all, she hadn't come here to do close-up planetology. An unmanned orbital mission could have done that nicely. Julie had come in search of life—of the beings who had sent the gravitational wave signals. And now she and Al were about to walk the walk.

The cold here was unimaginable, hundreds of degrees below human experience. The suit heaters could cope—the atmosphere was too thin to steal heat quickly—but only if their boots alone actually touched the frigid ground. Sophisticated insulation could only do so much.

Julie did not like to think about this part. Her feet could freeze in her boots, then the rest of her. Even for the lander's heavily insulated shock-absorber legs, they had told her, it would be touch-and-go beyond a stay of a few hours. Their onboard nuclear thermal generator was already laboring hard to counter the cold she could see creeping in, from their external ther-mometers. Their craft already creaked and popped from thermal stresses.

And the thermal armor, from the viewpoint of the natives, must seem a hot, untouchable furnace. Yet already they could see things scurrying on the plain. Some seemed to be coming closer. Maybe curiosity was indeed a universal trait of living things.

Al pointed silently. She picked out a patch of dark blue-gray down by the shore of the methane sea. On their console she brought up the visual magnification. In detail it looked like rough beach shingle. Tidal currents during the twenty-two hours since dawn had dropped some kind of gritty detritus—not just ices, apparently—at the sea's edge. Nothing seemed to grow on the flat and—swiveling point of view—up on the ridge's knife-edge also seemed bare, relatively free of life. "It'll have to do," she said.

"Maybe a walk down to the beach?" Al said. "Turn over a few rocks?"

They were both tiptoeing around the coming moment. With minimal talk they got into their suits.

Skillfully, gingerly—and by prior coin-flip—Julie clumped down the ladder. She almost envied those pioneer astronauts who had first touched the ground on Luna, backed up by a constant stream of advice, or at least comment, from Houston. The Mars landing crew had taken a mutual, four-person single step. Taking a breath, she let go the ladder and thumped down on Counter. Startlingly, sparks spat between her feet and the ground, jolting her.

"There must be a *lot* of electricity running around out here," she said, fervently thanking the designers for all that redundant insulation.

Al followed. She watched big blue sparks zap up from the ground to his boots. He jumped and twitched.

"Ow! That smarts," Al said.

Only then did she realize that she had already had her shot at historical pronouncements, and had squandered it in her surprise. "*Wow*—what a profound thought," huh? she asked herself ruefully.

Al said solemnly, "We stand at the ramparts of the solar system."

Well, she thought, fair enough. He had actually remembered his prepared line. He grinned at her and shrugged as well as he could in the bulky suit. Now on to business.

Against the gray ice and rock their lander stood like an H. G. Wells Martian walking-machine, splay-footed and ominous.

"Rocks, anyone?" They began gathering some, using long tweezers. Soil samples rattled into the storage bin.

"Let's take a stroll," Al said.

"Hey, close-up that." She pointed out toward sea.

Things were swimming toward them. Just barely visible above the smooth surface, they made steady progress toward shore. Each had a small wake behind it.

"Looks like something's up," Al said.

As they carefully walked down toward the beach she tried her link to the lander's wide-band receiver. Happily, she found that the frequencies first logged by her lost, devoured probe were full of traffic. Confusing, though. Each of the beasts—for she was sure it was them—seemed to be broadcasting on all waves at once. Most of the signals were weak, swamped in background noise that sounded like an old AM radio picking up a nearby high-tension line. One, however, came roaring in like a pop-music station. She made the lander's inductance tuner scan carefully.

That pattern—yes! It had to be. Quickly she compared it with the probe-log she'd had the wit to bring down with her. These were the odd cadences and sputters of the very beast whose breakfast snack had been her first evidence of life.

"Listen to this," she said. Al looked startled through his face plate.

The signal boomed louder, and she turned back the gain. She decided to try the radio direction-finder. Al did, too, for cross-check. As they stepped apart, moving from some filmy ice onto a brooding brown rock, she felt sparks snapping at her feet. Little jolts managed to get through even the thermal vacuum-layer insulation, prickling her feet.

The vector reading, combined with Al's, startled her. "Why, the thing's practically on top of us!"

If Counter's lords of creation were all swimming in toward this island ridge for lunch, this one might get here first. Fired up by all those vitamins from the lost probe? she wondered.

Suddenly excited, Julie peered out to sea—and there it was. Only a roiling, frothing ripple, like a ship's bow wave, but arrowing for shore. And others, farther out.

Then it bucked up into view and she saw its great, segmented tube of a body, with a sheen somewhere between mother-of-pearl and burnished brass. Why, it was *huge*. For the first time it hit her that when they all converged on this spot, it was going to be like sitting smack-dab in a middling-sized dinosaur convention.

Too late to back out now. She powered up the small lander transmitter and tuned it to the signal she was receiving from seaward.

With her equipment she could not duplicate the creature's creative chaos of wavelengths. For its personal identification sign the beast seemed to use a simple continuous pulse pattern, like Morse code. Easy enough to simulate. After a couple of dry-run hand exercises to get with the rhythm of it, Julie sent the creature a roughly approximate duplicate of its own ID.

She had expected a call-back, maybe a more complex message. The result was astonishing. Its internal rocket engine fired a bright orange plume against the sky's blackness. It shot straight up in the air, paused, and plunged back. Its splash sent waves rolling up the beach. The farthest tongue of sluggish fluid broke against the lander's most seaward leg. The beast thrashed toward shore, rode a wave in—and stopped. The living cylinder lay there, half in, half out, as if exhausted.

Had she terrified it? Made it panic?

Cautiously, Julie tried the signal again, thinking furiously. It *would* give you quite a turn, she realized, if you'd just gotten as far in your philosophizing as I think, therefore I am, and then heard a thin, toneless duplicate of your own voice give back an echo.

She braced herself—and her second signal prompted a long, suspenseful silence. Then, hesitantly—shyly?—the being repeated the call after her.

Julie let out her breath in a long, shuddering sigh.

She hadn't realized she was holding it. Then she instructed DIS, the primary computer aboard *Venture,* to run the one powerful program Counter Mission Control had never expected her to have to use: the translator, Wiseguy. The creation of that program climaxed an argument that had raged for a century, ever since Whitehead and Russell had scrapped the old syllogistic logic of Aristotle in favor of a far more powerful method—sufficient, they believed, to subsume the whole of science, perhaps the whole of human cognition. All to talk to Counter's gravitational signals.

She waited for the program to come up and kept her eyes on the creature. It washed gently in and out with the lapping waves but seemed to pay her no attention. Al was busily snapping digitals. He pointed offshore. "Looks like we put a stop to the rest of them."

Heads bobbed in the sea. Waiting? For what?

In a few moments they might have an answer to questions that had been tossed around endlessly. Could all language be translated into logically rigorous sentences, relating to one another in a linear configuration, structures, a system? If so, one could easily program a computer loaded with one language to search for another language's equivalent structures. Or, as many linguists and anthropologists insisted, does a truly unknown language forever resist such transformations?

This was such a strange place, after all. Forbidding, weird chemistry. Alien tongues could be strange not merely in vocabulary and grammatical rules, but in their semantic swamps and mute cultural or even biological premises. What would life forms get out of this place? Could even the most inspired programmers, just by symbol manipulation and number-crunching, have cracked ancient Egyptian with no Rosetta Stone?

With the Counter Project already far over budget, the decision to send along Wiseguy—which took many terabytes of computational space—had been hotly contested. The deciding vote was cast by an eccentric but politically astute old skeptic, who hoped to disprove the "bug-eyed monster Rosetta Stone theory," should life unaccountably turn up on Counter. Julie had heard through the gossip tree that the geezer was gambling that his support would bring along the rest of the DIS package. That program he passionately believed in.

Wiseguy had learned Japanese in five hours; Hopi in seven; what smatterings they knew of Dolphin in two days. It also mastered some of the fiendishly complex, multi-logic artificial grammars generated from an Earthbased mainframe.

The unexpected outcome of six billion dollars and a generation of cyberfolk was simply put: a good translator had all the qualities of a true artificial intelligence. Wiseguy *was* a guy, of sorts. It—or she, or he; nobody had known quite how to ask—had to have cultural savvy *and* blinding mathematical skills. Julie had long since given up hope of beating Wiseguy at chess, even with one of its twin processors tied off.

She signaled again and waved, hoping to get the creature's attention. Al leaped high in the one-tenth-of-a-g gravity and churned both arms and legs in the ten seconds it took him to fall back down. Excited, the flying wings swooped silently over them. The scene was eerie in its silence; shouldn't birds make some sort of sound? The auroras danced, in Julie's feed from *Venture* she heard Wiseguy stumblingly, muttering…and beginning to talk.

She noted from the digital readout on her helmet interior display that Wiseguy had been eavesdropping on the radio crosstalk already. Now it was galloping along. In contrast to the simple radio signals she had first heard, the spoken, acoustic language turned out to be far more sophisticated. Wiseguy, however, dealt not in grammars and vocabularies but in underlying concepts. And it was *fast*.

Julie took a step toward the swarthy cylinder that heaved and rippled. Then another. Ropy muscles surged in it beneath layers of crusted fat. The cluster of knobs and holes at its front moved. It lifted its "head"—the snubbed-off, blunt forward section of the tube—and a bright, fast chatter of microwaves chimed through her ears. Followed immediately by Wiseguy's whispery voice. Discourse.

Another step. More chimes. Wiseguy kept this up at increasing speed. She was now clearly out of the loop. Data sped by in her ears, as Wiseguy had neatly inserted itself into the conversation, assuming Julie's persona, using some electromagnetic dodge. The creature apparently still thought it was speaking to her; its head swiveled to follow her.

The streaming conversation verged now from locked harmonies into brooding, meandering strings of chords. Julie had played classical guitar as a teenager, imagining herself performing before concert audiences instead of bawling into a mike and hitting two chords in a rock band. So she automatically thought in terms of the musical moves of the data flow. Major keys gave way to dusky harmonies in a minor triad. To her mind this had an effect like a cloud passing across the sun.

Wiseguy reported to her and Al in its whisper. It and Awk had only briefly had to go through the me-Tarzan-you-Jane stage. For a life form that had no clearly definable brain she could detect, it proved a quick study.

She got its proper name first, as distinguished from its identifying signal; *its* name, definitely, for the translator established early in the game that these organisms had no gender.

The Quand they called themselves. And this one—call it Awk, because that was all Wiseguy could make of the noise that came before—*Ark-Quand*. Maybe, Wiseguy whispered for Julie and Al alone, Awk was just a place-note to show that this thing was the "presently here" *of* the Quand. It seemed that the name was generic, for all of them.

"Like Earth tribes," Al said, "who name themselves the People. Individual distinctions get tacked on when necessary?"

Al was like that—surprising erudition popping out when useful, otherwise a straight supernerd techtype. His idea might be an alternative to Earth's tiresome clash of selfish individualisms and stifling collectivisms, Julie thought; the political theorists back home would go wild.

Julie took another step toward the dark beach where the creature lolled, its head following her progress. It was no-kidding *cold*, she realized. Her boots were melting the ground under her, just enough to make it squishy. And she could hear the sucking as she lifted her boot, too. So she wasn't missing these creatures' calls—they didn't use the medium.

One more step. Chimes in her ears, and Wiseguy sent them a puzzled, "It seems a lot smarter than it should be."

"Look, they need to talk to each other over distance, out of sight of each other," Julie said. "Those waxy all-one-wing birds should flock and probably need calls for mating, right? So do we." Not that she really thought that was a deep explanation.

"How do we frame an expectation about intelligence?" Al put in.

"Yeah, I'm reasoning from Earthly analogies," Julie admitted. "Birds and walruses that use microwaves—who woulda thought?"

"I see," Wiseguy said, and went back to speaking to Awk in its ringing microwave tones.

Julie listened to the ringing interchange speed up into a blur of blips and jots. Wiseguy could run very fast, of course, but this huge tubular thing seemed able to keep up with it. Microwaves' higher frequencies had far greater carrying capacity than sound waves and this Awk seemed able to use that. Well, evolution would prefer such a fast-talk capability, she supposed—but why hadn't it on Earth? Because sound was so easy to use, evolving out of breathing. Even here—Wiseguy told her in a sub-channel aside—individual notes didn't mean anything. Their sequence did, along with rhythm and intonation, just like sound speech. Nearly all human languages used either subject-object-verb order or else subject-verb-object, and the Quands did, too. But to Wiseguy's confusion, they used both, apparently not caring.

Basic values became clear, in the quick scattershot conversation. Something called "rendezvous" kept coming up, modified by comments about territory. "Self-merge," the ultimate, freely chosen—apparently with all the Quands working communally afterward to care for the young, should there luckily occur a birthing. Respect for age, because the elders had experienced so much more.

Al stirred restlessly, watching the sea for signs that others might come ashore. "Hey, they're moving in," Al said apprehensively.

Julie would scarcely have noticed the splashing and grinding on the beach as other Quands began to arrive—apparently for Rendezvous, their mating, and Wiseguy stressed that it deserved the capital letter—save that Awk stopped to count and greet the new arrivals. Her earlier worry about being crunched under a press of huge Quand bodies faded. They were social animals and this barren patch of rock was now Awk's turf. Arrivals lumbering up onto the dark beach kept a respectful distance, spacing themselves. Like walruses, yes.

Julie felt a sharp cold ache in her lower back. Standing motionless for so long, the chill crept in. She was astounded to realize that nearly four hours had passed. She made herself pace, stretch, eat, and drink from suit supplies.

Al did the same, saying, "We're eighty percent depleted on air."

"Damn it, I don't want to quit *now!*"

"How 'bout you get extra from the Lander?"

Al grimaced. He didn't want to leave either. They had all dedicated their lives to getting here, to this moment in this place. "Okay, Cap'n sir," he said sardonically as he trudged away.

She felt a kind of silent bliss here, just watching. Life, strange and wonderful, went on all around her. Her running digital coverage would be a huge hit Earthside. Unlike Axelrod's empire, the Counter Project gave their footage away.

As if answering a signal, the Quand hunched up the slope a short way to feed on some brown lichen-like growth that sprawled across the warming stones. She stepped aside. Awk came past her and another Quand slid up alongside. It rubbed against Awk, edged away, rubbed again. A courtship preliminary? Julie guessed.

They stopped and slid flat tongues over the lichen stuff, vacuuming it up with a slurp she could hear through her suit. Tentatively, the newcomer laid its body next to Awk. Julie could hear the pace of microwave discourse Awk was broadcasting, and it took, a lurch with the contact, slowing, slowing... And Awk abruptly—even curtly? it seemed to Julie—rolled away. The signal resumed its speed.

She laughed aloud. How many people had she known who would pass up a chance at sex to get on with their language lessons?

Or was Wiseguy into philosophy already? It seemed to be digging at how the Quand saw their place in this weird world.

Julie walked carefully, feeling the crunch of hard ice as she melted what would have been gases on Earth—nitrogen, carbon dioxide, oxygen itself. She had to keep up and the low-g walking was an art. With so little weight, rocks and ices that looked rough were still slick enough to make her slip. She caught herself more than once from a full, face-down splat—but only because she had so much time to recover, in a slow fall. As the Quand worked their way across the stony field of lichen, they approached the lander. Al wormed his way around them, careful to not get too close.

"Wiseguy! Interrupt." Julie explained what she wanted. It quickly got the idea, and spoke in short bursts to Awk—who re-sent a chord-rich message to the Quand.

They all stopped short. "I don't want them burned on the lander," Julie said to Al, who made the switch on her suit oxy bottles without a hitch.

"Burnt? I don't want them eating it," Al said.

Then the Quand began asking *her* questions, and the first one surprised her: *Do you come from Light-giver? As heralds?*

In the next few minutes Julie and Al realized from their questions alone that in addition to a society, the Quand had a rough-and-ready view of the world, an epic oral literature (though recited in microwaves), and something that resembled a religion. Even Wiseguy was shaken; it paused in its replies, something she had never heard it do before, not even in speed trials.

Agnostic though she was, the discovery moved her profoundly. *Light-giver.* After all, she thought with a rush of compassion and nostalgia, we started out as sun-worshippers too.

There were dark patches on the Quands upper sides, and as the sun rose these pulled back to reveal thick lenses. They looked like quartz—tough crystals for a rugged world. Their banquet of lichen done—she took a few samples for analysis, provoking a snort from a nearby Quand—they lolled lazily in their long day. She and Al walked gingerly through them, peering into the quartz "eyes." Their retinas were a brilliant blue with red wirelike filaments curling through and under. Convergent evolution seemed to have found yet another solution to the eye problem.

"So what's our answer? Are we from Light-giver?"

"Well… you're the cap'n, remember." He grinned. "And the biologist."

She quickly sent *No. We are from a world like this, from near, uh, Life-giver.*

Do not sad, it sent through Wiseguy. *Light-giver gives and Light-giver takes; but it gives more than any; it is the source of all life, here and from the Dark; bless Light-giver.*

Quands did not use verb forms underlining existence itself—no words for *are, is, be*—so *sad* became a verb. She wondered what deeper philosophical chasm that linguistic detail revealed. Still, the phrasing was startlingly familiar, the same damned, comfortless comfort she had heard preached at her grandmother's rain-swept funeral.

Remembering that moment of loss with a deep inward hurt, she forced it away. What could she say…?

After an awkward silence, Awk said something renderable as, *I need leave you for now.*

Another Quand was peeling out Awk's personal identification signal, with a slight tag-end modification. Traffic between the two Quands became intense. Wiseguy did its best to interpret, humming with the effort in her ears.

Then she saw it. A pearly fog had lifted from the shoreline and there stood a distant spire. Old, worn rocks peaked in a scooped-out dish.

"Al, there's the focal point!"

He stopped halfway between her and the lander. "Damn! Yes!"

"The Quand built it!"

"But…where's their civilization?"

"Gone. They lost it while this brane-universe cooled." The idea had been percolating in her, and now she was sure of it.

Al said, awed, "Once *these* creatures put those grav wave emitters in orbit? And built this focal point—all to signal to us, on our brane?"

"We know this universe is dying—and so do they."

The Counter-Brane had less mass in it, and somewhat different cosmology. Here space-time was much further along in its acceleration, heading for the Big Rip when the expansion of the Counter-universe would tear first galaxies, then stars and planets apart, pulverizing them down into atoms.

Julie turned the translator off. First things first, and even on Counter there was such a thing as privacy.

"They've been sending signals a long time, then," Al said.

"Waiting for us to catch up to the science they once had—and now have lost." She wondered at the abyss of time this implied. "As if we could help them…"

Al, ever the diplomat, began, "Y'know, it's been hours…" Even on this tenth-g world she was getting tired. The Quand lolled, Life-giver stroking their skins—which now flushed with an induced chemical radiance, harvesting the light. She took more digitals, thinking about how to guess the reaction—

"Y'know…"

"Yeah, right, let's go."

Outside they prepped the lander for lift-off. Monotonously, as they had done Earthside a few thousand times, they went through the checklist. Tested the external cables. Rapped the valves to get them to open. Tried the mechanicals for freeze-up—and found two legs that would not retract. They took all of Al's powerful heft to unjam them.

Julie lingered at the hatch and looked back, across the idyllic plain, the beach, the sea like a pink lake. She hoped the heat of launching, carried through this frigid air, would add to the suns thin rays and…and what? Maybe to help these brave beings who had sent their grav-wave plea for help?

Too bad she could not transmit Wagner's grand *Liebestod* to them, something to lift spirits—but even Wiseguy could only do so much.

She lingered, gazing at the chilly wealth here, held both by scientific curiosity and by a newfound affection. Then another miracle occurred, the way they do, matter-of-factly. Sections of carbon exoskeleton popped forth from the shiny skin of two nearby Quands. Jerkily, these carbon-black leaves articulated together, joined, swelled, puffed with visible effort into one great sphere.

Inside, she knew but could not say why, the two Quands were flowing together, coupling as one being. Self-merge.

For some reason, she blinked back tears. Then she made herself follow Al inside the lander. Back to...what? Checked and rechecked, they waited for the orbital resonance time with *Venture* to roll around. Each lay silent, immersed in thought. The lander went *ping* and *pop* with thermal stress.

Al punched the firing keys. The lander rose up on its roaring tail of fire. Her eyes were dry now, and their next move was clear: *Back through the portal, to Earth. Tell them of this vision, a place that tells us what is to come, eventually, in our own universe.*

"Goin' home!" Al shouted.

"Yes!" she answered. *And with us and the Quand together, maybe we can find a way to save us both. To rescue life and meaning from a universe that, in the long run, will destroy itself. Cosmological suicide.*

She had come to explore, and now they were going back with a task that could shape the future of two species, two branes, two universes that dwelled a hand's thickness from each other. Quite enough, for a mere one trip through the portal, through the looking-glass. Back to a reality that could never be the same.

ANA'S TAG

WILLIAM ALEXANDER

William Alexander studied theater and folklore at Oberlin College and English at the University of Vermont. His short stories have been nominated twice for the Pushcart Prize and published in various strange and wonderful places, including *Weird Tales*, *Lady Churchill's Rosebud Wristlet*, *Interfictions 2*, and *Fantasy: The Best of the Year 2008*. His first novel, *Goblin Secrets*, debuted in 2012. *Kirkus* described the book as "evocative in its oddities."

A na and Rico walked on the very edge of the road where the pavement slumped and crumbled. They were on their way to buy sodas, and there were no sidewalks. They made it as far as the spot where the old meat-packing factory had burned down when Deputy Chad drove up and coasted his car alongside at a walking pace.

Ana was just tall enough to see the deputy through his car window and the empty space of the passenger seat. Her brother Rico was taller, but he wasn't trying to look through the car window. Rico was staring straight ahead of him.

"Hi kids," said Deputy Chad.

"Hi," said Ana.

"I need to ask you both about the incident at the school," the deputy said.

"Okay," said Ana when Rico didn't say anything.

"It's very important," the deputy said. "This is the first sign of gang activity. Everyone knows that. *Gang activity*." He tried to arch one eyebrow, but it didn't really work and his forehead scrunched.

Other cars slowed to line up behind the squad car, coasting along.

"What's the second sign?" Ana asked.

"The *second* sign," said Deputy Chad, taking a deep breath, "happens at night, on the highway. It involves headlights. Do you know that keeping your high-beams on at night can blind oncoming traffic?"

Ana didn't. She nodded anyway.

"Usually a driver has just forgotten to turn them off, and the way to let them know is to flash your own high-beams, just briefly. But *they* drive around with the high-beams on *deliberately*. If you flash at one of *their* cars, they pull a quick and violent U-turn and follow you, very close. Sometimes they just do it to see where you live. Sometimes they run you off the road. Bam!" He smacked the top of his steering wheel.

Ana jumped. He grinned at her, and she grinned back.

"What's the third sign?" Rico asked, without grinning.

"I can't tell you that," said Deputy Chad. "Ask your parents. It is the last ceremony of initiation, and it involves blonde ten-year-olds."

"I'm ten," said Ana.

"You're not blonde, so you're probably safe. Probably."

"Oh," said Ana. "Good."

The line behind Deputy Chad was now seven cars long, coasting slowly. None of them dared to pass a cop.

"So," said the deputy. "You can see why we need to put a stop to this kind of thing right away, before it escalates. Do you know anything about the incident at school?"

"No," said Rico.

"What's the graffiti of?" asked Ana.

"It is deliberately illegible," said the deputy. "It's in code. Probably a street-name. A tag. Graffiti is often somebody's tag, delineating whose turf is whose. It looks like it could be in Spanish."

Ana and Rico's parents spoke Spanish. They used it as their secret language, and slipped into Spanish whisperings whenever they didn't want Ana or Rico to understand them. Sometimes, in public, Ana and Rico liked to pretend they could speak it too. They would toss together random words and gibberish and use an accent because both of them could fake a pretty good one. They hadn't played that game for a while.

Rico bent forward a little so he could look through the passenger window. "I'll let you know if I hear anything about it," he said.

"Good boy," said the deputy, and smiled a satisfied smile. "Be safe, now."

He drove off. Cars followed him like ducklings.

"*Perro muerto*," said Ana. It meant *dead dog*, or maybe *dead hair*. It was one of their nonsense curses. "He thinks you did it."

"Yeah," said Rico.

"Did you?" Ana asked.

"Yeah," said Rico.

"Oh. What does it say?"

"Not telling."

"Oh," said Ana. Rico pushed Ana to his right side so he could walk between her and the moving cars, and then he made a sign with his left hand. He tried not to let Ana see him do it. She saw anyway, but she didn't ask. She cared more about the graffiti. "I'll do all the dishes if you tell me what it says."

"No."

"Okay." Ana thought about how long it would take to get to the East Wells high school, try to read the painted wall, write down all of her guesses and walk home. She decided she could make it before dinner. Maybe Rico would tell her if she guessed right.

They were almost to the gas station, which had a much better selection of soda to pick from than the corner store. The last part of the walk was uphill, and Ana had to work harder to keep up with her brother.

"Do you think there really are gangs?" she asked.

Rico shrugged, and smiled a little. "Gangs of what?"

"I don't know. Gangs."

"I doubt it," he said. "East Wells isn't big enough to put together a gang of anything bigger than two people. Deputy Chad is just really, really bored." He reached up and twisted his new earring stud. He'd pierced it himself with a sewing needle. Ana had held the swabs and rubbing alcohol while he did it. She'd felt obliged to help, because she already had pierced ears so she could offer him the benefit of her knowledge.

"Don't forget to clean that when we get home," she said.

"I won't," he said. He sounded annoyed. Ana decided to change the subject to something casual and harmless.

"Why isn't there a West Wells?" she asked.

Rico stopped walking. They were in the gas station parking lot, only a few steps away from soda and air conditioning. Ana turned around. Her brother was staring at her.

"What did you say?"

"West Wells," she said again, trying to be extra casual and harmless. "We live in East Wells, but it isn't actually east *of* anything. There's just, you know, the woods by the school and then endless fields of grain on all sides. There's no West Wells."

Rico exhaled, loudly. "That's right," he said. "There is nothing to the west of this dinky little town. You are absolutely right." He walked by her and went inside. Ana followed. She had questions, endless questions bubbling up somewhere near her stomach and she had to swallow to keep them there because Rico was definitely not in an answering kind of mood.

She shivered in the air conditioning, even though she'd been looking forward to it. Rico knew which soda he wanted, but Ana took a long time to choose.

Ana got her cat backpack from her bedroom closet. It was brown and furry and had two triangular ears sewn onto the top. She pulled a stack of library books out of it and replaced them with a flashlight, rope, chocolate-chip granola bars, band-aids, a notebook and magic markers. She filled up the small, square canteen that had been Tio Frankie's with water and packed that, too. Then she took out the flashlight, because it was summer and it didn't get dark outside until long after dinnertime, and she needed to be back by dinner anyway.

"Did you clean your ear?" she asked Rico's bedroom door.

"No," he said from behind it.

"Don't forget. You don't want it to get infected."

"I won't forget," he said.

She walked to the East Wells high school, taking a shortcut through two cornfields to keep off the highway. It wasn't a long walk, but during the school year almost everybody took the bus anyway because of the highway and the lack of sidewalks. Rico liked walking, even in wintertime. Ana saw him sometimes through the bus window on her way to East Wells Elementary.

She walked between cornrows and underneath three billboards. Two of them said something about the bible. One was an ad for a bat cave ten miles further down the road. Ana had never seen the bat cave. Rico said it wasn't much to see, but she still wanted to go.

Ana crossed the empty parking lot in front of the high school, and skirted around the athletic field to the back of the gym. She knew where to find the gym because it doubled as a theater, and last summer a troupe of traveling actors had put on *The Pirates of Penzance*. After the show Ana had decided to become a traveling actor. Then she decided that what she really wanted to be was a pirate king.

A little strip of mowed lawn separated the gym from the western woods.

Three of Rico's friends were there, standing in front of the graffiti. Ana could see green paint behind them. They were smoking, of course. Julia and Nick smoked cloves, sweet-smelling. Garth wore a Marlboro-Man kind of hat, so he was probably smoking that kind of cigarette. His weren't sweet-smelling.

"Hey," Ana said.

"Hey," said Julia. Ana liked Julia.

"Hey," said Nick. Nick was Julia's boyfriend. Ana was pretty sure that her brother was jealous of this. Nick and Julia were both in Rico's band, and both of them were really, really tall. They were taller than Rico, and much taller than Garth.

Garth didn't say anything. He chose that moment to take a long drag on his cigarette, probably to demonstrate that he wasn't saying anything. Garth was short and stocky and scruffy. He wasn't in the band. He had a kind of beard, but only in some places. He also had a new piercing in his eyebrow. It was shaped like the tusk from a very small elephant. The skin around it was red and swollen and painful-looking.

Ana thought eyebrow rings were stupid. She liked earrings, and she could understand nose rings, belly-button rings and even pierced tongues, but metal sticking out of random facial places like eyebrows just looked to her like shrapnel from a booby-trapped jewelry box. She didn't like it. The fact that Garth's eyebrow was obviously infected proved that she was right, and that the universe didn't like it either.

"You should use silver for a new piercing," Ana told him. "And you need to keep it clean."

"This *is* silver," said Garth. He didn't look at her as he said it. He looked at the tops of trees.

"Don't worry about him," said Nick. "He likes pain. He gets confused and grumpy if something doesn't hurt."

"Oh," said Ana. She edged around them, trying to get a better look at the wall and the paint.

Garth threw down his cigarette, stepped on it, and reached out to knock the cloves from Nick and Julia's hands. "Bertha's coming," he said.

Bertha walked around the corner. She was the groundskeeper. Rico used to help her mow the school lawn as a summer job, but this year he hadn't bothered. Her name wasn't really Bertha, and Ana didn't want to ever call her that, but she didn't know what Bertha's name really was.

Bertha sniffed, and smiled. Her hair was a big, feathered mullet.

"One of you isn't smoking cloves," she said. "One of you is smoking *real* cigarettes, and I am going to bet it isn't the one with the kitten backpack. One of you is gonna buy my silence. 'Why no, officer, I sure didn't see any young hooligans smoking near your site of vandalism.'"

Ana, Nick and Julia all looked at Garth. Garth grunted, handed over his pack of cigarettes and walked away. He walked away into the woods.

"Bye, Ana," Julia said. "Say hi to Rico. Tell him we need to rehearse." She took Nick's arm and the two of them followed Garth.

Ana could see the graffiti, now. It was red and green and it wasn't anything Ana knew how to decipher. Parts of it were swoofy, and other parts had sharp, edgy bits. It looked like it was made up of letters, but she wasn't sure which letters they were.

Bertha lit one of Garth's cigarettes. "Gonna have to rent a sandblaster," she said. "Won't come off without a sandblaster, and it's brick so I can't just paint over it."

"Deputy Chad thinks it was gangs that did it," Ana said.

Bertha snorted. "Town isn't big enough for gangs," she said. "Doesn't matter anyway. This is just somebody marking their territory. This is colored piss with artistic pretensions."

Ana took out her notebook, but she didn't have any guesses to write down yet. "How's the novel?" she asked Bertha. This was the usual thing to ask. Bertha had always been writing a novel.

"Terrible," Bertha said.

"Sorry," said Ana. She wondered if it was better to be a novelist or a traveling actor, and decided it would still be better to be a pirate king.

"What's with the notebook?" Bertha asked. She flicked her cigarette butt at the graffiti, and it hit the bricks above the paint with a shower of orange sparks.

"I'm going to draw it," Ana said, "I'll take it home and figure out what it says, and then… then maybe I'll know who did it. I'll solve the mystery."

"Have fun," Bertha said. She opened a door in the gym wall with one of the many jingling keys at her belt and went in. The door shut behind her with a loud metal scrape.

Ana drew the graffiti tag. Luckily she had the right colors of magic marker. It took her seven tries to get it right.

The screen door squeaked when Ana opened it. The kitchen lights were on. One cold plateful of food sat on an otherwise bare table. Ana's mother sat at the other end, face down on her folded arms. She was snoring. Ana hid her backpack under the table, and put the plate of food on a chair and out of sight.

"Wake up, Mama," she said.

Her mother woke up. "Where have you been, child?" she asked, annoyed but mostly groggy.

"Here," Ana said. "I've been here for hours. Sorry I missed dinner."

"You should be," said her mother. "Where—"

Ana pretended to yawn. Her mother couldn't help yawning, then, and this made Ana yawn for real. "Bedtime," she said, once she was able to say anything. Her mother nodded, and both of them went upstairs.

Ana snuck back downstairs to throw away her dinner and fetch her backpack. She ate the chocolate granola bars while sitting on the floor of her bedroom and studying the graffiti in her notebook. She thought it might say *roozles*, *rutterkin* or *rumbustical*, but there were always extra letters, or at least extra swoofs and pointy edges to the letters, and the longer she stared at it the less each word fit.

Ana slept. She dreamed that her kitten-backpack climbed snuffling onto the foot of her bed. She woke up when it stepped on her toes, and once she was awake she could see its pointy-eared outline. A car drove by outside and made strange window-shade shadows sweep across the wall and ceiling. Maybe the car had its highbeams on.

Her bag moved. She kicked it and it fell off the edge, landing with more of a soft smacking sound than it should have. Ana wanted to turn on the light, but the light switch was across the room. She would have to touch the floor to get there. She decided that now would be a really excellent time to develop telekinetic powers, and spent the next several minutes concentrating on the light switch.

Another car went by.

She got up, tiptoed across the floor and turned on the light. She turned around.

The backpack was right at her feet. She didn't scream. She swallowed an almost-scream.

The furry, pointy-eared bag wasn't moving. She pulled on the edges of the zipper and peeked inside. Her expedition supplies were still there. She poked through them with the capped tip of a magic marker, just in case there was also something else in there. The notebook lay open to the seventh graffiti-covered page. She tried to nudge it aside, but the tip of the marker went through the colored surface. She dropped the pen. It passed through the graffiti and vanished. The page rippled like a pond.

She took another magic marker and used it to close the notebook cover. Then she looked out in the hallway to see if Rico's bedroom light was on. It was. She took the notebook, tiptoed by her parents' room, and sped up to pass the stairway. The air felt different at the top of the stairs. It felt like the stairway was holding its breath. It felt like the open space might breathe her in and down and swallow her.

She knocked on Rico's door. No answer. She knocked again, because she knew it would be locked from the inside so there wasn't any point in trying to open it herself. He still didn't answer. She tried the doorknob and it turned.

He wasn't there. She tread carefully on the few clear and visible parts of the floor, and took a better look around from the middle of the room. He wasn't standing behind his dresser or lurking behind the armrest of the ratty old couch. He wasn't hiding in his closet, because it was filled with too much junk already and nothing more would fit. She looked under the bed and he wasn't there either. She looked at the empty bed and found a rolled up piece of parchment. *You play tomorrow night, musician*, it said. *Be ready.*

The parchment crumbled into several brown leaves and drifted to the floor, settling among the socks and books and torn pieces of sheet music.

"He must be rehearsing," she said to herself. "I'll try to find him tomorrow."

She went back to her room, and hung the backpack up on the knob handle of one of her dresser drawers to keep it from wandering, and went to bed. She left the light on. She didn't see anything move for the rest of the night, including her backpack. She heard things move instead.

Rico wasn't at breakfast. This wasn't unusual, because he almost always slept until lunchtime, so their parents didn't seem worried as they bustled and joked and made coffee and went away to work after kissing Ana on each cheek. Ana went back upstairs as soon as they were gone. Rico wasn't in his room. Bits of brown leaves crunched and crumbled in the carpet under her feet.

Ana got dressed, and took her backpack down from the knob she'd hung it on.

"Don't go walking anywhere without me," she said. She took more granola bars from the kitchen, and refilled her little square canteen, and locked up the house.

It started to rain when she reached the first highway billboard, and Ana's clothes and backpack were soggy by the time she got to the gym. The bag's sopping ears lay flat against the zipper.

She stood in front of the graffiti, took a deep breath and wondered if she was supposed to say something out loud. Maybe she was supposed to say whatever the graffiti said, and she still couldn't read it.

Something snarled in the trees behind her. Ana turned around, took a step backwards and tried to press herself against the wall. It didn't work. She pressed and passed through it.

"Hello," said a voice that scraped against the insides of her ears.

Ana faced another painted wall, stone instead of brick. She took a breath. The air was still and it smelled like thick layers of dust. She turned around. An old man, thin and spindly, sat on a stool and polished a carved flute. He had a wispy beard. He tested two notes on the flute and set to polishing again. Behind him were several shelves of similar instruments. Some were plain and a pale yellow-grey. Some were carved with delicate patterns, and others inlaid with metals and lacquered over.

"Hello," Ana said.

"The Grey Lady brings deliveries every second Tuesday, and today is neither thing. Are you delivered here? Has she changed schedules?"

"I don't know any grey ladies," Ana said. "Except math teachers. Do you mean Mrs. Huddle?"

"No huddling things," the old man said. He set down the flute on a carved wooden stand, picked up a bone from his workbench and took a rasp to the knobby joints. "Tell me your purposes then, if no Lady brought you. Are you here to buy a flute?"

"No," Ana said. "I'm looking for my brother."

"Unfortunate that you should look for him here. How old?"

"He's sixteen."

"So old? Good, good. I won't have pieces of him, then."

Ana looked around for pieces of people. There was a straw cot in the corner beside a green metal stove. There were baskets and tin lanterns hanging by chains from a high ceiling. There were no windows. A staircase against one wall led up to the only doorway. There was a workbench, and shelves full of flutes, and a mural of moonlight and trees where she had stepped through the wall.

"He's a musician," Ana said. "A singer. He's in a band, I think. Last week they were The Paraplegic Weasels, but I don't know if that's still their name. It keeps changing."

"Very prudent," said the old man, rasping bone.

"He's supposed to play for someone tonight. I don't know who."

"Tonight there are many festivities, or so I've heard rumor." He swapped the rasp for a finer file, and began to scrape the bone more delicately.

Ana took a step closer. "The invitation turned into leaves after I read it."

"Then he'll likely play his music in the Glen," the old man said. "You should be on the forest paths, and not here in the City."

"City?"

"Oh yes. Underneath it, a few layers down." He wiped away loose bone-dust, and set both bone and file down on the workbench. "The stone floor you're standing on used to be a road, but the City is always growing up over itself."

"Oh," Ana said. She looked down at the floor. The old man reached down, scooped her up by the armpits and set her on the edge of the workbench. She swallowed an almost-scream when he pinched each leg, squeezing down to the thighbones, and then she kicked him in the stomach.

Ana jumped down, ran to the mural and smacked the surface of it with the palms of both hands. The surface held. Behind her the old man wheezed and coughed and laughed a little.

"No matter," he said. "Both bones broken, and all the music leaked out from the fractures. Can't make any kind of flute from either leg. How did you break them both?"

Ana turned around to watch him. He sat back on his stool, wheezing, and he seemed to want to stay there. "I jumped off the roof."

"And what flying thing were you fleeing from?" he asked.

"Nothing. Rico dared me to jump, so I did. I didn't tell on him, either. He still owes me for that."

"Well," the old man said, "I hope you can collect what he owes when you find him. Such a shame that your bones were broken. There are a great many children, and there isn't enough music. There isn't nearly enough."

"So how do I get out?" She hated admitting that she didn't already know.

The old man smiled, and widened up his eyes. "Boo," he said, puffing out his thin beard.

Ana took a step backwards, and passed through the stone.

Her face was inches away from her brother's graffiti. It was dark, and she could barely see the colors by moonlight. She looked around. She was alone. Her backpack was gone.

"I told it not to wander off," she said.

There was only one forest path she could find. Ana took a walking stick from a pile of broken branches near the edge of the woods, and took a deep breath, and set out. She wished she had her flashlight. She wished she had her backpack. In her head she promised to give it a scratch behind the ears if it would come back, and to never again hang it up on a dresser drawer knob. It had looked uncomfortable there. The air smelled like wet leaves, heavy and rich. She followed the path uphill and downhill and around sudden corners cut into the sides of hills. She passed trees that looked like tall, twisted people until she looked at them directly. Ana hoped she was following the right trail. She saw a wispy orange light between the tree trunks and decided to follow that instead.

The orange light brightened as Garth inhaled cigarette smoke. He was leaning on a boulder. He looked up and blew smoke at the moon.

Half of his face was swollen.

"Hey," said Ana. "What are you doing?"

"Nothing," he said. "Waiting for little girls, maybe."

"Your infection's worse."

"True," he said. "But this bit of silver is keeping me from gnawing on your bones."

"Oh," said Ana. "Good. Everybody should stay away from my bones."

He took another drag, brightening up the wispy orange light, and tugged his hat down to cover more of the swollen half of his face. Ana held on to her stick.

"Do you know where Rico is?" she asked.

"Maybe. He plays tonight."

"Can you take me to him?"

"Maybe." Garth dropped the cigarette and stepped on it, crushing the little orange flame. He walked off, away from the path. Ana waited for some signal from him that she should follow. She didn't get one. She followed.

Garth took long strides, and his boots hit the ground like he was trying to punish it for something. Ana tried to keep up, and she tried to keep a little bit behind him at the same time. She didn't want to be too close. He hunched, staring at the ground, and she thought he was moping more than usual until he dove, snarling. He came up holding a lanky thing covered in short, spiky fur.

"Where does the Guard keep watch tonight?" he asked.

The lanky thing shrugged and grinned many teeth.

"Where does the Guard watch the Glen?" He shook the thing in his hand. It snickered.

"Please?" Ana asked, very sweetly.

The lanky thing blew her a kiss. "Tonight there is no waking Guard," it said. "Tonight he is sleeping and dreaming that he guards, and he crosses no one unless they cross into his dreaming while he sleeps at his post, which is easy to do and see to it that you don't. Everything within a pebble's toss of him in all directions is only the substance of his dream, and inside it the Guard is a much better guard than he ever was awake. He guards the Western Arch."

"How many arches are there?" Garth asked.

"Tonight there is only the Western Arch. All others are overgrown. It rained today."

"Thank you," Ana said.

The lanky thing bowed, which was difficult to do while Garth held it up by the scruff of its neck. Then it bit him hard on the wrist and dropped to the ground. Garth howled. The lanky thing snickered from somewhere nearby.

"Let me see your wrist," Ana said. She had band-aids in her backpack. Then she remembered that she didn't have her backpack.

Garth looked at her. Garth never made eye contact, but he did so now, and he held it, and he also made a little rumbling noise in the back of his throat.

"No," he said.

"Okay," she said.

"You should know that I'm not interested in dying for your brother. He's alright. I like him. But I'm not interested in death on his behalf. I'm not interested in any of the things so close to death that the distinction makes no difference. This is something you should know before we go any further."

"Okay," she said again.

He walked away. She followed. She wondered where her backpack was.

They found an enormous figure in full plate armor, asleep. The Guard was dreaming a desert the size of a pebble's throw. All around it was sunlight and sand and nowhere to hide.

"That's the Western Gate," Garth said

"Where?" Ana whispered.

"Behind the desert. Cut into the wall of thorns, there." He pointed. Ana stood at the very edge of the desert and squinted. She could only see sand and sun in front of them.

Garth dropped another finished cigarette, driving it further into the dirt than he really needed to. "Good luck," he said.

"Wait," Ana told him. "Don't go yet. I'm going to try something."

She picked up a pebble, took aim, and threw it at the precise moment that she stepped forward into desert sand. For just a instant she knew what it was like to be an unimportant part of someone else's dream. Then the pebble struck the Guard's gold helmet, clanging loudly and waking it up.

The desert vanished. Ana ducked behind a tree that hadn't been there before and leaned against the trunk. She could hear the metal movements of plate armor on the other side. She didn't know where Garth was.

"I am a pirate king," Ana whispered to herself. "It's a glorious thing to be a pirate king."

She ran, and switched directions twice, and tried to circle back towards the Western Gate. She almost stumbled in the dark, but she didn't. The Guard almost caught her anyway. She felt gauntleted fingers snatch at her shoulder. Then she heard it clang and crash against the ground. She stopped, panting, and turned around to look.

Garth stood over the Guard, who was much shorter and less impressive than it had dreamed itself earlier. Garth looked at Ana, snarled and jerked his chin towards the Gate. Then he spit on the Guard's golden armor.

Ana backed further away. She watched the Guard pull itself up off the ground. It plucked out Garth's silver piercing with a little spray of blood.

Garth howled, and his face began to change.

Ana turned away and slipped inside.

The Glen was at least as big as a cornfield, and covered over with a dome of branches high overhead. Inside the branches were orange wisps of light, glowing and fading again.

It was full of dancers. Ana looked at them, and closed her eyes, and looked again. She could hear Rico singing over the noise of the crowd.

"I'm still a pirate king," she whispered to herself, weaving her way in between dancers and trying to find the stage. She dodged the dancing things, and bumped into some, and passed through the shimmering substance of others. She saw colors and antlers and sharp teeth in strange places.

She found the stage. She found her brother. He sang, and the language sounded a little bit like Spanish but not very much. Nick played a red guitar, acoustic and covered in gold ivy. Julia played a yellow-grey flute. Both of them were even taller than they usually were.

Rico saw her, and Ana saw a lot of white around the edges of his eyes when he did. He nudged Julia, and she started a flute solo, and he got down off the stage and pulled Ana behind it. She opened her mouth and he shushed her.

"Okay, don't eat or drink. Whatever else you do, don't eat anything and don't drink anything. Now tell me what you think you're doing."

"Looking for you," Ana said.

"I'm impressed," he said, biting on his lower lip. "I really am. But this is very, very bad and I'm not sure how to fix it."

"What's the problem?" Ana asked, folding her arms and looking at him as though she were the older one.

"Okay," Rico said, taking deep breaths. "Do you see those guys over there? The ones with the tattoos?"

"They're the gang?" Ana asked.

"Yeah. Sure. Kind of. And this is supposed to be my last task for them, and then after the concert I'll learn how to sing up every chrome piece of a motorcycle and ride it from town to town, stopping only to hum the fuel tank full again. I'll learn how to sing hurricanes and how to send them away. I'll learn how to sing something people can dance to for a full year and never notice the time passing."

"Sounds like fun," Ana said.

"Sure. The catch is that this crowd has to be happy and dancing until the dawn light comes. If they stop before then, I fail and I have to serve the guys with the tattoos for at least a hundred years. So you should either go, right now, however you came here, or else hide somewhere and don't eat or drink or talk to anyone until dawn. And don't do anything distracting, because the crowd might stop dancing and that would be very bad. They like children, here, but they care about music a lot more than they care about kids."

Ana looked up at Julia and her yellow-grey flute.

"I have go back onstage now," Rico said.

"Okay," Ana said.

"Hide," he said.

"Okay."

He went back onstage. Julia finished her solo, and Rico sang. He was good.

Ana thought she saw her backpack scamper between someone's hooves. She followed. Then she saw Garth, or at least she assumed it was Garth. He had started to eat people near the Western Arch.

"Crap," Ana said. He was distracting the crowd. Some of them weren't dancing anymore.

She ran back to the arch and slipped through. She looked everywhere, kicking up leaves. She found her walking stick and used it to poke through the leaves that were dark and wet and sticky. Then she found one golden gauntlet. Blood pooled underneath it. A small, silver tusk sat in its palm.

She picked up the silver. It was very sharp. She ran back through the arch and followed the screaming.

Garth was gnawing on a severed antler with his long wolf-muzzle. Some things in the crowd were shouting, and more were laughing, and most were still dancing but not all of them were.

"Hey, *perro muerto*," Ana said. She threw her walking stick at him. It got his attention. He dropped the antler, bounded forward and knocked her to the ground, slavering.

Ana grabbed one of his furry ears with her left hand and shoved the tusk through it with her right. The skin of his ear resisted, stretching a little before the silver broke through.

Garth rolled over and howled. Ana got to her feet and looked around her. The crowd danced. Even those who were bleeding from the fight with Garth were dancing again. She took a deep breath, and she didn't get a chance to let it out all the way before someone's hand took her by the elbow and pulled her towards the stage.

She looked up at the arm attached to the hand. It had green and red letters tattooed all up and down its length.

Rico, Julia and Nick bowed to the sound of applause and unearthly cries. The sky began to lighten above the branches, grey and rose-colored and pale.

The owner of the green and red arm pushed Ana forward in front of Rico. "What's this?" Rico asked.

"Your last initiation," said a very deep voice behind Ana. She didn't want to turn around. She looked straight ahead at her brother. "Sing her to sleep. Let her sleep for a thousand years, or at least until another glacier passes this way."

"I've already finished my initiation," Rico said. "They all danced until dawn."

"Yes," said the voice. "You held them, most of them, and they were deer in headlights highbeamed by your song. Those you lost you gained again as they danced bleeding. It was good. But it was not your last task. The last requires a ten-year-old."

"Crap," said Ana.

Rico took her hand, pulled her closer, and tossed red and green colors into the air between them and the crowd. Colors settled into the shape of his tag. Ana still couldn't read it.

"Home," Rico said. "I'll follow when I can."

"You have to tell me what it says," Ana told him, but he just smiled and pushed her through.

Their parents were as frantic as one might expect. Ana managed to slip into her brother's room and find green and red spray-paint hidden behind the couch before her mother and father and Deputy Chad came in to look for clues to Rico's whereabouts. Ana kept the spray-paint hidden under her own bed.

It took a long time for Ana to get back to the high school, because her parents kept closer tabs on her after Rico disappeared. Bertha had already sandblasted the graffiti, and Ana couldn't find the forest path, and she didn't know where Garth was. She hoped he wasn't dead, or something very close to dead. She walked home, and listened to three nervous phone messages from her mother on the answering machine. Ana called her back and told her she was home, and that everything was fine even though it wasn't really.

She went up to her room, and found her backpack sitting on her bed. She gave it a hug. It purred when she scratched behind its ears.

"I'm really, really angry at you for leaving," she said. It kept purring.

Inside she found three pages torn from her notebook. They were folded in half together, with "Ana" written on the front.

The first page was in Rico's handwriting. *I'll see you as soon as I find a way out of a hundred years of servitude*, it said. *Don't worry, I'll manage. DO NOT COME LOOKING FOR ME. Keep a pinch of salt in your pocket at all times, and stay out of the woods, and DO NOT keep following me around. I'm serious.*

Ana snorted, and turned the page. It was her seventh drawing, with a note written underneath: *This is my name, dumbass.*

She turned to the last page.

This is yours.

Ana looked at it, and saw that it was.

She took out her magic markers and practiced marking her territory on the back wall of her closet.

NOTHING PERSONAL

PAT CADIGAN

Pat Cadigan sold her first professional science fiction story in 1980. She is the author of fifteen books, including two nonfiction books on the making of *Lost in Space* and *The Mummy,* a young adult novel, and the two Arthur C. Clarke Award-winning novels *Synners* and *Fools*. Pat lives in gritty, urban North London with the Original Chris Fowler, her musician son Robert Fenner, and Miss Kitty Calgary, Queen of the Cats. She can be found on Facebook and Google+, and she tweets as @cadigan.

Detective Ruby Tsung could not say when the Dread had first come over her. It had been a gradual development, taking place over a period of weeks, possibly months, with all the subtlety of any of the more mundane life processes—weight-gain, greying hair, ageing itself. Time marched on and one day you woke up to find you were a somewhat dumpy, greying, middle-aged homicide detective with twenty-five years on the job and a hefty lump of bad feeling in the pit of your stomach: the Dread.

It was a familiar enough feeling, the Dread. Ruby had known it well in the past. Waiting for the verdict in an officer-involved shooting; looking up from her backlog of paperwork to find a stone-faced IAD officer standing over her; the doctor clearing his throat and telling her to sit down before giving her the results of the mammogram; answering an unknown trouble call and discovering it was a cop's address. Then there were the ever popular rumours, rumours, rumours: of budget cuts, of forced retirement for everyone with

97

more than fifteen years in, of mandatory transfers, demotions, promotions, stings, grand jury subpoenas, not to mention famine, war, pestilence, disease, and death—business as usual.

After a while she had become inured to a lot of it. You had to or you'd make yourself sick, give yourself an ulcer or go crazy. As she had grown more experienced, she had learned what to worry about and what she could consign to denial even just temporarily. Otherwise, she would have spent all day with the Dread eating away at her insides and all night with it sitting on her chest crushing the breath out of her.

The last ten years of her twenty-five had been in Homicide and in that time, she had had little reason to feel Dread. There was no point. This was Homicide—something bad *was* going to happen so there was no reason to dread it. Someone was going to turn up dead today, tomorrow it would be someone else, the next day still someone else, and so forth. Nothing personal, just Homicide.

Nothing personal. She had been coping with the job on this basis for a long time now and it worked just fine. Whatever each murder might have been about, she could be absolutely certain that it wasn't about her. Whatever had gone so seriously wrong as to result in loss of life, it was not meant to serve as an omen, a warning, or any other kind of signifier in her life. Just the facts, ma'am or sir. Then punch out and go home.

Nothing personal. She was perfectly clear on that. It didn't help. She still felt as if she had swallowed something roughly the size and density of a hockey puck.

There was no specific reason that she could think of. She wasn't under investigation—not as far as she knew, anyway, and she made a point of not dreading what she didn't know. She hadn't done anything (lately) that would have called for any serious disciplinary action; there were no questionable medical tests to worry about, no threats of any kind. Her son Jake and his wife Lita were nested comfortably in the suburbs outside Boston, making an indecent amount of money in computer software and raising her grandkids in a big old Victorian house that looked like something out of a storybook. The kids emailed her regularly, mostly jokes and scans of their crayon drawings. Whether they were all really as happy as they appeared to be was another matter but she was fairly certain they weren't suffering. But even if she had been inclined to worry unduly about them, it wouldn't have felt like the Dread.

Almost as puzzling to her as when the Dread had first taken up residence was how she had managed not to notice it coming on. Eventually she understood that she hadn't—she had simply pushed it to the back of her mind and then, being continuously busy, had kept on pushing it all the way into the *Worry About Later* file, where it had finally grown too intense to ignore.

Which brought her back to the initial question: When the hell had it started? Had it been there when her partner Rita Castillo had retired? She didn't remember feeling anything as unpleasant as the Dread when Rita had made the announcement or, later on, at her leaving party. Held in a cop bar, the festivities had gone on till two in the morning and the only unusual thing about it for Ruby had been that she had gone home relatively sober. Not by design and not for any specific reason. Not even on purpose—she had had a couple of drinks that had given her a nice mellow buzz, after which she had switched to diet cola. Some kind of new stuff—someone had given her a taste and she'd liked it. Who? Right, Tommy DiCenzo; Tommy had fifteen years of sobriety, which was some kind of precinct record.

But the Dread hadn't started that night; it had already been with her then. Not the current full-blown knot of Dread, but in retrospect, she knew that she had felt something and simply refused to think about the bit of disquiet that had sunk its barbed hook into a soft place.

But she hadn't been so much in denial that she had gotten drunk. You left yourself open to all sorts of unpleasantness when you tied one on at a cop's retirement party: bad thoughts, bad memories, bad dreams, and real bad mornings-after. Of course, knowing that hadn't always stopped her in the past. It was too easy to let yourself be caught up in the moment, in all the moments, and suddenly you were completely shitfaced and wondering how that could have happened. Whereas she couldn't remember the last time she'd heard of anyone staying sober by accident.

Could have been the nine-year-old that had brought the Dread on. That had been pretty bad even for an old hand like herself. Rita had been on vacation and she had been working alone when the boy's body had turned up in the dumpster on the south side—or south town, which was what everyone seemed to be calling it now. The sudden name-change baffled her; she had joked to Louie Levant at the desk across from hers about not getting the memo on renaming the 'hoods. Louie had looked back at her with a mixture of mild surprise and amusement on his pale features. "South town was what we always called it when I was growing up there," he informed her, a bit loftily. "Guess the rest of you finally caught on." Louie was about twenty years younger than she was, Ruby reminded herself, which meant that she had two decades more history to forget; she let the matter drop.

Either way, south side or south town, the area wasn't a crime hotspot.

It wasn't as upscale as the parklike west side or as stolidly middle/working class as the northland grid but it wasn't east midtown, either. Murder in south town was news; the fact that it was a nine-year-old boy was worse news and, worst of all, it had been a sex crime.

Somehow she had known that it would be a sex crime even before she had seen the body, lying small, naked, and broken amid the trash in the bottom of the dumpster. Just what she hadn't wanted to catch—kiddie sex murder. Kiddie sex murder had something for everyone: nightmares for parents, hysterical ammunition for religious fanatics, and lurid headlines for all. And a very special kind of hell for the family of the victim, who would be forever overshadowed by the circumstances of his death.

During his short life, the boy had been an average student with a talent for things mechanical—he had liked to build engines for model trains and cars. He had told his parents he thought he'd like to be a pilot when he grew up. Had he died in some kind of accident, a car wreck, a fall, or something equally unremarkable, he would have been remembered as the little boy who never got a chance to fly—tragic, what a shame, light a candle. Instead, he would now and forever be defined by the sensational nature of his death. The public memory would link him not with little-kid stuff like model trains and cars but with the pervert who had killed him.

She hadn't known anything about him, none of those specific details about models and flying when she had first stood gazing down at him; at that point, she hadn't even known his name. But she had known the rest of it as she had climbed into the dumpster, trying not to gag from the stench of garbage and worse and hoping that the plastic overalls and booties she had on didn't tear.

That had been a bad day. Bad enough that it could have been the day the Dread had taken up residence in her gut.

Except it wasn't.

Thinking about it, remembering the sight, the smell, the awful way it felt when she had accidentally stepped on the dead boy's ankle, she knew the Dread had already been with her. Not so cumbersome at the time, still small enough to snub in favour of more immediate problems, but definitely there.

Had it been Ricky Carstairs, then? About a month before the nine-year-old, she had been on her way out of the precinct house when she had passed two uniformed officers bringing him in and recognized him immediately. She had no idea how she had managed that mental feat—he had been skinny, dirty, and obviously strung out, and she hadn't seen him since he and Jake had been in the seventh grade together but she had known him at once and it hadn't been a good moment.

"It's just plain wrong," she had said when Rita asked her why she looked as if she had just found half a worm in the middle of an apple. "Your kid's old school friends are supposed go away and live lives with no distinguishing characteristics. Become office workers in someplace like Columbus or Chicago or Duluth."

"And that's just plain *weird*," Rita replied, her plump face wearing a slightly alarmed expression. "Or maybe not weird enough—I don't know. You been watching a lot of TV lately? Like the Hallmark Channel or something?"

"Never mind," she said, making a short dismissive wave with one hand. "It made more sense *before* I said it out loud."

Rita had burst into hearty laughter and that had been that; they'd gone with the rest of the day, whatever that had involved. Probably a dead body.

The dismaying sight of one of Jake's old school friends sweating in handcuffs had lodged in her mind more as a curiosity than anything else. Uncomfortable but hardly critical—not the fabled moment of clarity, not a short sharp shock or a reality check or a wake-up call from Planet Earth. Just a moment when she hoped that poor old Ricky hadn't recognized her, too.

So had the Dread already been lodged in her gut then?

She tried but she honestly couldn't remember one way or the other—the incident was just too far in the past and it had lasted only a minute, if that—but she thought it was very possible that it had.

It was unlikely, she realized, that she would ever pinpoint the exact moment when something had shifted or slipped or cracked—gone faulty, anyway—and let a sense of something wrong get in and take root. And for all she knew, it might not even matter. Not if she were in the first stage of one of those on-the-job crack-ups that a lot of cops fell victim to. Just what she needed—a slow-motion train-wreck. Christ, what the hell was the point of having a breakdown in slow-motion unless you could actually do something about it, actually prevent it from happening? Too bad it didn't work that way—every cop she knew who had come out the other side of a crash described it as unstoppable. If it had to happen, why couldn't it be fast? Crack up quick and have an equally rapid recovery, get it over with. She pictured herself going to the department shrink for help: *Overclock me, Doc—I got cases to solve and they're gaining on me.*

Ha-ha, good one; the shrink might even get a chuckle out of it. Unless she had to explain what overclocking was. Would a shrink know enough about computers to get it? Hell, she wouldn't have known herself if she hadn't picked things up from Jake, who had blossomed into a tech head practically in his playpen.

Her mind snagged on the idea of talking to the shrink and wouldn't let go. Why not? She had done it before. Granted, it had been mandatory, then—all cops involved in a shooting had to see the shrink—but she'd had no problem with that. And what the hell, it had done her more good than she'd expected it to. She had known at the time that she'd needed help and if she were honest with herself, she had to admit that she needed help now. Going around with the lead weight of the Dread dragging on her wasn't even on the extreme ass-end of acceptably screwed-up that was in the range of normal for a homicide detective.

The more she thought about it, the more imperative it seemed that she talk to the department shrink, because she sure hadn't talked to anyone else about it. Not her lieutenant, not Tommy DiCenzo, not even Rita.

Well, she wouldn't have talked to Lieutenant Ostertag—that was a no-brainer. Throughout her career, she had always had the good sense never to believe any my-door-is-always-open bullshit from a superior officer. Ostertag hadn't even bothered with the pretense.

Tommy DiCenzo, on the other hand, she could have talked to and counted on his complete confidence. They'd gone through the academy together and she'd listened to plenty from him, both before and after he'd dried out. Tommy might even have understood enough to tell her whether she was about to derail big time or just experiencing another side-effect of being middle-aged, overworked, and underpaid. But every time she thought about giving him a call or asking him to go for coffee, something stopped her.

Maddeningly, she couldn't think of a single good reason why. Hell, she couldn't even think of a crappy reason. There was no reason. She simply could not bring herself to talk to him about the Dread and that was all there was to it.

And Rita—well, there had been plenty of reasons not to talk to her. They were busy, far too busy to devote any time to anything that didn't have a direct bearing on the cases piling up on their respective desks. Not that Rita wouldn't have listened. But whenever she considered bringing it up, saying, *You know, Rita, lately I've had the damnedest feeling, a sense of being in the middle of something real bad that's about to get a whole lot worse*, the image of the nine-year-old boy in the dumpster would bloom in her brain and she would clench her teeth together.

Of course, she could go to Rita now. She could trot on over to her neat little fourth-floor condo, sit out on the balcony with her amid the jungle of plants with a few beers and tell her all about it. Only she knew what Rita would probably say, because Rita had already said it. That had been the night before she had put in her retirement papers; she had taken Ruby out to dinner and broken the news to her privately.

"I always planned to put in my twenty and get out while I was still young enough to enjoy it," she said, cheerfully sawing away at a slab of bloody steak. "You could have done that five years ago. Do it now and you'll be in good shape all the way around. Maybe you want to get in thirty but is putting in another five years really worth it?"

"Five years—" Ruby had shrugged. "What's five years? Blink of an eye, practically."

"All the more reason to get out," Rita had insisted. "Before it's too late to get a life."

Bristling inwardly, Ruby had looked down at her own steak. Why she had ordered that much food was beyond her. The Dread didn't leave anywhere nearly enough room for it. "I have a life."

"The job is *not* a life," Rita said, chewing vigourously and then dragging her napkin across her lips. "The job is the job. What do you do when you're not on the job?"

"Talk to the grandkids on email. Shop. Rent DVDs—"

"You ever go *out* to a movie? Or out to dinner—with anyone *other* than me?" Rita added quickly before she could answer. "Hell, girlfriend, when was the last time you got laid?"

Ruby blinked at her, startled, unsure whether it was by the question itself or by the fact that she didn't know the answer.

"I don't know if you've heard—" Rita leaned over the table and lowered her voice confidentially. "But there are more alternatives for people our age than the cone or the rabbit."

"Yeah, but my idea of sex doesn't involve *typing*." Ruby looked at her sidelong.

"Keeps the fingers nimble." Rita laughed. "No, I wasn't referring to chat room sex. I'm talking about going out and meeting people."

"Dating sites?" Ruby made a pained face.

"Please." Rita mirrored her expression. "Social groups. Meet-ups for people with similar interests. Hobbies, film festivals, shit like that. You know I've got a boyfriend?" Pause. *"And* a girlfriend."

"Sounds exciting," Ruby told her. "But I don't know if that's really for me."

"I didn't know either," Rita said. "I sure didn't go looking for it. It just happened. That's how it is when you have a life—things happen. You ought to try it."

"Yeah? Well, what I really want to know is how come I haven't gotten to meet these people you've been seeing." Ruby folded her arms and pretended to be stern.

"Well, for one thing—and I've got to be perfectly honest here—" Rita put down her knife and fork. "I wasn't sure how you'd react."

Ruby's eyebrows went up. "What? All this time we've worked together and you don't know I'm not a homophobe?"

"I was referring to the guy," Rita said, deadpan.

"Damn. And I thought I hid it so well," said Ruby, equally deadpan.

Rita gave a laugh and picked up her knife and fork again. "So pull the pin with me. You won't have to hide anything you don't want to."

"I'll give it some thought," Ruby lied.

"I'm asking you again—what're you waiting for?" Rita paused, regarding her expectantly. When she didn't answer, she went on: "They're not gonna promote you, you know. You *do* know that, don't you?"

Ruby dipped her head noncommittally.

"I sure knew they weren't gonna promote *me*. I knew that for a goddam *fact*." Rita took a healthy swig of wine and dragged her napkin across her mouth again.

"So is that why you decided to retire?"

Rita wagged her head emphatically. "I told you, it was my plan all along—get in my twenty and get the hell out. They'd have had to come up with a pretty hefty promotion to make me want to stay."

"Yeah? Like what—chief? Commissioner?"

"Supreme dictator for life. And I'm not so sure I would have said yes." Rita sighed. "What are you holding out for—lieutenant?"

"I passed the exam."

"So did I. So did umpty-hundred other cops ahead of us both and they ain't moving up, either." Rita's expression abruptly turned sad. "I never figured you for a lifer."

"Or maybe you hoped I wasn't?" Ruby said. "Personally, I never thought about it. I just get up and go to work every day."

"Think about it now," Rita said urgently. "Think about it like you've never thought about anything else. Get serious—you're topped out. Whatever you're waiting for, it isn't coming. All you can do is mark time."

"I work on solving murders and putting away the guilty parties," Ruby said, an edge creeping into her voice. "I wouldn't call that marking time."

"For you personally, it is," Rita insisted, unapologetic. "And in case you forgot, you count for something."

"I'm a good cop. That counts for a lot."

"That's not all you are, though. Do you even know that any more?"

Ruby shifted in her seat, more than a little irritated. "Retiring young isn't for everybody, even if you think it is. When all you have is a hammer, everything looks like a nail."

"Oh, for chrissakes, already—" Rita blew out a short breath. "That's what *I've* been trying to tell *you*."

They sat looking at each other for some unmeasured time and Ruby realized that her soon-to-be-ex-partner was just as irritated with her, possibly more. She tried to come up with something to say to defuse the situation before a serious quarrel developed but the Dread sitting large and uncomfortable in the middle of her body was eating her brain. The Dread was actually all she ever thought about now, like a pain that never went away, she realized, and there was barely room for anything else any more.

Then Rita had sat back in her chair, dismay in her plump, round face. "Shit, what the hell am I doing? I'm sorry, Rube."

Ruby stared at her, baffled.

"I'm telling you you don't have a life and I'm browbeating you like I'm trying to get a confession." She shook her head as if trying to clear it. "I think I'm getting out just in time."

"Well, I *was* gonna lawyer up," Ruby said, laughing a little. "Forget it. It's a touchy thing when a partner leaves, we both know that. Things can get a little weird, blown out of proportion."

They had finished their dinner—or rather, Rita had finished hers while Ruby got a doggy-bag—and called it a night early, smiles all round, although the smiles were slightly sad.

That was how things still stood between them: smoothed over but not actually resolved. If she went to Rita now and told her about the Dread, growing a little bit bulkier, a little heavier, and a little more uncomfortable every day with no end in sight, Rita would only take that as further proof that she was right about retirement.

And she really did not want to have that conversation with Rita because she had no intention of retiring. Because she knew, deep in her core and in her bones that even if she did take Rita's advice to pack it all in, even if she took it a step further, sold everything she owned and went off to a luxury beach condo in the Caribbean to laze around in the sun all day, indulge in fancy food and drink, and get thoroughly, perfectly laid every night by a series of gorgeous men and women, separately and together—despite all of that and a billion dollars besides, she knew with no uncertainty at all that she would still wake up every morning with the Dread that much larger and heavier and unrelenting than it had been the day before.

If she went to Rita, she would have to tell her that and she didn't want to because she really didn't think Rita would understand. And if she didn't tell her, then Rita would only start harping again on the question of what she was waiting for. Probably accuse her of waiting for the Dread to go away.

Then she would have to confess: *No. I'm waiting to find out. I'm waiting for whatever it is I've been Dreading to show up.* Which was something she hadn't quite admitted to herself yet.

"Coffee?"

The voice cut through the combination of Ruby's usual morning haze and the constant overriding pressure of the Dread, startling her and making her jump a little. She looked up from the open folder she had been staring at unseeingly to find a young guy standing next to her desk, holding out a large cup that definitely had not come from any of the precinct machines.

"I didn't know you guys delivered," she said, smiling as she took the cup from him.

"Don't let it get around," the guy said, "or I'll have to do it for every-body." He was about thirty, just a little too dark to be called olive-skinned, with a sprinkling of freckles across the bridge of his nose and a head full of honey-coloured dreadlocks that had the potential to become unruly. He was only a couple of inches taller than Ruby herself—five-eight, five-nine at the most—and slightly husky.

"It'll be our secret," she assured him, taking the lid off the cup. A dark roast aroma wafted up with the steam; not her favourite but she wasn't inclined to find fault. "Am I supposed to know you?"

"When the lieutenant comes in, he'll introduce me as your new partner."

"I see." Ruby studied him. "Transfer from vice?"

He shook his head.

"Narcotics?"

"Ah." He smiled with half his mouth. "Must be the dreads."

Ruby barely managed not to flinch at the word; it took a quarter of a second before she realized what he was referring to. "Well, it was some kind of undercover work, though. Right?"

"Fraud and cybercrime. Rafe Pasco." He held out his hand and Ruby took it. It was strong and square but as smooth and soft as a woman's.

"Portuguese?" she guessed.

"Filipino, actually. On my father's side." He grinned and half-sat on the edge of her desk. "Though as you can see, that's only part of the story. Even on my father's side." His grin widened a bit. "Like you, maybe."

Ruby shrugged. "Everybody had a story in my family and none of them could ever keep them straight. My father claimed they almost named me Kim Toy O'Toole. And I didn't even have freckles."

"Then you grew up deprived." He tilted his head to look at the file on her desk. "What are you working on?"

She had to glance down to remind herself. "Ah. Suspicious drowning. Wife reported her husband missing, three days later he turns up on the rocks under the Soldiers Road bridge. Coroner says he's pretty sure the guy didn't just happen to wash up there, that someone must have pulled him out and then just left him."

"Anonymous call tipping you off where to find him?"

Ruby shook her head. "Couple of kids found him and told their parents. Can't figure why someone would pull a corpse out of the river and then just leave him."

"The killer?"

"Then why pull him out at all?"

"Well, the wife couldn't collect on any insurance without a body. For instance."

"Could be." Ruby made a face. "But I don't think she killed him. I think he's a suicide and she's trying to make it seem like a murder so she doesn't lose the insurance. The pay-out isn't much—$25,000. Not enough to inspire murder but not a sum you'd want to have to give up, either."

Pasco nodded, looking thoughtful. "Is she a hardship case?"

"Why?" Ruby asked, frowning.

"Maybe she really needs it."

She gave a short laugh. "Hey, man, who *doesn't* need $25,000? Especially if it's on the verge of dropping right into your lap."

"Yeah, but if she's got kids or she's gonna get evicted or something, it'd be too bad to take it away from her."

Ruby leaned back in her chair and gave him a searching look. "Are you kidding?"

"I'm just saying."

"That's a whole lot of *just saying* about a case I only just now told you about. You always get so deeply invested on such short notice?"

He looked slightly embarrassed. "I'm not invested. This is just something we do in fraud—think about all the angles. Try to get into the mindset of the people we're investigating, try to figure out where they're coming from—are they desperate or do they feel entitled for some reason. Stuff like that."

Ruby had to bite her tongue to keep from making an acid remark concerning the mass media image of criminal profiling and other extraordinary popular delusions and the madness of crowds. It wouldn't do any good. Pasco would only get defensive and then expend a lot of effort trying to prove she was wrong instead of just working the cases. In the end, he'd flounder, trying to adapt the job to his methods rather than the other way around.

Abruptly she realized that she had been staring at him in silence for more than just a moment or two. Before she could think of some neutral comment, Lieutenant Ostertag came in and waved them into his office.

"I know, I know—he's a geek," Ostertag said to Ruby after he had waved Pasco out of his office again. "He's got, I dunno, two, three degrees, maybe four. He's been in fraud and cybercrime since he joined the department about five years ago."

Ruby nodded. "And somebody thinks he'd make a good homicide detective."

"Apparently he already is. In the course of his last two cases he cleared up two murders, one of which nobody even knew about at the time."

"Good for him," said Ruby. "Has anyone told him that he left all the criminal masterminds back in cybercrime?"

"He's working another case right now. I'll let him tell you about it." He got up and opened the door for her by way of declaring the meeting over, then caught her arm before she could leave. "You OK?"

Ruby drew back slightly, giving him a surprised look. "Sure I'm OK. Why wouldn't I be?"

Ostertag's mouth twitched. "You OK with getting this guy as a partner so soon after Rita leaving?".

She laughed a little. "Rita retired, she didn't die. I'm not in mourning."

The lieutenant nodded a bit impatiently. "This guy's pretty different than what you're used to."

Ruby tilted her head and frowned. "Are you asking me if I'd rather work with someone else?"

Ostertag's face turned expressionless. "No."

"What I thought," Ruby said goodnaturedly and went back to her desk.

She decided to give Pasco a little while to organize his desk, maybe meet a few of the other detectives and then go over to ask him about his case. Instead of taking over Rita's old spot, he had opted for the vacant desk by the blocky pillar that served as an unofficial bulletin board for less-than-official notices and items, usually cartoons (which were usually obscene). It was a strange choice; Ruby had never seen anyone actually opt for that particular desk if there was anything else available and there were two others empty at the moment. It was badly positioned—you had to sit either facing the pillar or with your back to it. Turn the desk sideways and it would obstruct the aisle. The previous lieutenant had tried switching the desk with a set of filing cabinets but that had been no solution at all and they'd switched things back before the day was up. Moving the desk out altogether would have made more sense but there were no city employees anywhere who would have been so foolish as to voluntarily give up anything. Someone at City Hall could get the wrong idea, start thinking that if there was no room for a desk in your area, there were probably other things you could do without as well.

Rafe Pasco obviously had no idea he had picked the lousiest spot in the room, Ruby thought. Maybe he'd had a similar spot in cybercrime, wherever that was headquartered. Spending all his time on a computer, he might not have noticed or cared where he sat.

"So you get the new guy." Tommy DiCenzo sat down in the chair beside her desk, a bottle of Coke Zero in one big paw. He tilted it toward her, offering her a sip.

She waved it away. "Rafe Pasco. From cybercrime."

"I heard." Tommy glanced over his shoulder. "What'd you do, tell him to keep his distance?"

"Didn't get a chance to," she said. "He picked it out himself." From where she was sitting, she could actually see him quite well. She watched as he took a shiny black laptop out of a bag and set it on the desk. "I see he brought his own hardware. Maybe he figures he'll have more privacy over there. No one'll be able to see when he's playing solitaire."

Tommy followed her gaze. "Guy's a geek. No offence," he added quickly. "How is Jake, anyway?"

Ruby laughed. "Fine. And he'd take offence if you *didn't* call him a geek. As would he, I imagine." She jerked her chin in Pasco's general direction.

"It's a different world," Tommy said, affecting a heavy sigh. Then his face grew suddenly serious. "You OK?"

"Damn." Ruby gave a short laugh. "You know you're the second person to ask me that today?"

Tommy's steely-grey eyebrows arched. "Oh? Must be something going around." His gazed at her thoughtfully. "So, *are* you OK? Anything bothering you?"

The Dread seemed to reawaken then; it shifted inside of her by way of reasserting itself, reminding her that it was there and it was in charge. "Like what?" she said, hoping the casually offhand tone in her voice didn't sound as forced as it felt.

"Well, like Rita pulling the pin."

She let out a long breath. "It'll take some getting used to. I keep looking around for her. Which is only normal, I guess."

"You weren't prepared for her leaving, were you." It wasn't really a question.

"No," she admitted. "But I'm OK with it."

"I'm sure you are." Tommy's smile was knowing. "But it still took you by surprise. You never thought about her retiring."

"I was busy," she said and then winced inwardly. Had she ever said anything lamer? "But you know, things, uh, change." Now she had.

"They do that." Tommy pushed himself to his feet. "It's not a steady-state universe."

"No, I guess not." Ruby stared after him as he ambled over to introduce himself to Rafe Pasco, wondering why his words seemed to hang in the air and echo in her brain. Maybe it was just having him and Ostertag ask her if she were OK within a few minutes of each other that had put a whole new level of odd over the day.

The call came in about twenty minutes before Ruby had tentatively planned to go to lunch. Which figured, she thought as she and Pasco drove to the east midtown address; it had been a quiet morning. Any time you had a quiet morning, you could just about count on having to skip lunch. Of course, since the Dread had moved in on her, it hadn't left much room in her stomach. Not a whole lot of room in her mind, either—she missed the turn onto the right street and, thanks to the alternating one-ways, had to drive around in a three-block circle. If Pasco noticed, he didn't say anything. Maybe she would let him drive back to the station.

She was a bit surprised to see that patrol cars had almost half the street blocked off, even though there were very few curious onlookers and not

much in the way of traffic. The address in question was a six-storey tene-
ment that Ruby had visited with Rita a few times in the past.

"Is this an actual residence or a squat?" Pasco asked her as they went up
the chipped concrete steps to the front door.

"Both," Ruby told him. She wasn't actually sure any more herself.

The uniform standing at the entrance was a young guy named Fraley;
Ruby thought he looked about twelve years old, despite the thick mous-
tache he was sporting. He opened the door for them as if that were really
what he did for a living.

The smell of urine in the vestibule was practically a physical blow; she
heard a sharp intake of breath from Pasco behind her.

"Straight from the perfume counter in hell," she said wryly. "Ever wonder
why it's always the front of the building, why they don't take a few extra
seconds to run to the back?"

"Marking their territory?" Pasco suggested.

"Good answer." Ruby glanced over her shoulder at him, impressed.

There was another uniformed officer in the hallway by the stairs, a tall
black woman named Desjean whom Ruby recognized as a friend of Rita's.
"Sorry to tell you this," she told them, "but your crime scene's on the roof
and there's no elevator."

Ruby nodded, resigned. "Do we know who it is?"

Desjean's dark features turned sad. "Girl about twelve or thirteen. No ID."

Ruby winced, feeling acid bubbling up in her chest. "Great. Sex crime."

"Don't know yet," the uniform replied. "But, well, up on the roof?"

"Local kid?" Ruby asked.

Desjean shook her head. "Definitely not."

Ruby looked at the stairs and then at Pasco. "You can go first if you think
you might go faster."

Pasco blew out a short breath. "I'm a geek, not a track star." He frowned.
"Ostertag did tell you that, didn't he?"

"Uh, yeah," Ruby said, unsure as to whether he was kidding around or
not. "Before we go up, one thing."

"Don't talk to you on the way?" He nodded. "The feeling's mutual."

She felt a brief moment of warmth toward him. Then the Dread overwhelmed it, crushing it out of existence, and she started up the stairs.

A uniformed sergeant named Papoojian met them just outside the door on
the roof. "Kid with a telescope spotted the body and called it in," she told
them as they stood catching their breath. "I sent a couple of officers over

to get a preliminary statement from him and his very freaked-out parents."

"Kid with a telescope." Ruby sighed. "I don't know if that's an argument for closed-circuit TV surveillance or against it."

The sergeant looked up at the sky worriedly. "I wish the lab guys would hurry up and get here with a tent or we're gonna have regular TV surveillance to deal with. I'm surprised the news helicopters aren't buzzing us already."

As if on cue, there was the faint sound of a chopper in the distance. Immediately, one of the other three uniformed cops on the roof produced a blanket and threw it over the body, then turned to look a question at Papoojian. Papoojian nodded an OK at him and turned back to Ruby. "If the lab has a problem with that, tell them to get in *my* face about it."

Ruby waved a hand. "You got nothing to worry about. No ID on the body?"

The sergeant shook her curly head. "Except for a charm on her bracelet with the name *Betty* engraved on it." She spelled it for them.

"There's a name you don't hear much these days." Ruby looked over at the blanket-covered form. She was no longer panting from the long climb, but for some reason, she couldn't make herself walk the twenty feet over to where the body lay on the dusty gravel.

"Hey, you caught that other case with the kid," Papoojian said suddenly. "The dumpster boy."

Ruby winced inwardly at the term. "Yeah."

"They dumping all the murdered kid cases on you now?"

She shrugged, taking an uncomfortable breath against the Dread, which now seemed to be all but vibrating in her midsection.

Was this what she had been dreading, she wondered suddenly—murdered children?

It almost felt as if she were tearing each foot loose from slow-hardening cement as she urged herself to go over and look at the victim, Pasco at her elbow with an attitude that seemed oddly dutiful.

"Ever see a dead kid?" she asked him in a low voice.

"Not like this," Pasco replied, his tone neutral.

"Well, it's gruesome even when it's not gruesome," she said. "So brace yourself." She crouched down next to the body and lifted the blanket.

The girl was lying face up, her eyes half-closed and her lips slightly parted, giving her a sort of preoccupied expression. She might have been in the middle of a daydream, except for the pallor.

"Well, I see why Desjean was so sure the girl wasn't local," Ruby said.

"Because she's Japanese?" he guessed.

"Well, there are a few Japanese in east midtown, not many, but I was referring to her clothes." Ruby shifted position, trying to relieve the pressure from the way the Dread was pushing on her diaphragm. It crossed her mind briefly that perhaps what she thought of as the Dread might actually be a physical problem. "That's quality stuff she's got on. Not designer but definitely boutique. You get it in the more upscale suburban malls. I have grandchildren," she added in response to Pasco's mildly curious expression.

She let the blanket drop and pushed herself upright, her knees cracking and popping in protest. Pasco gazed down at the covered body, his smooth, deep-gold face troubled.

"You OK?" Ruby asked him.

He took a deep breath and let it out.

"Like I said, kids are gruesome even when they're not—"

"I think this is related to this case I've been working on."

"Really." She hid her surprise. "We'll have to compare notes, then. Soon."

He didn't answer right away, looking from the blanket to her with a strange expression she wasn't sure how to read. There was something defensive about it, with more than a little suspicion as well. "Sure," he said finally, with all the enthusiasm of someone agreeing to a root canal.

Ruby felt a mix of irritation and curiosity, which was quickly overridden by the Dread. She couldn't decide whether to say something reassuring or simply assert her authority and reassure him later, after she knew she had his cooperation.

Then the crime lab arrived, saving her from having to think about anything from the immediate situation. And the Dread.

At the end of the day, Pasco managed to get away without talking about his case. It was possible of course that he had not been purposely trying to elude her. After spending most of the day talking to, or trying to talk to, the people in the building, checking on the results of the door-to-door in the neighbourhood, looking over the coroner's shoulder, and through it all pushing the Dread ahead of her like a giant boulder uphill, she was too tired to care.

She made a note about Pasco in her memo book and then dragged herself home to her apartment where she glanced at an unopened can of vegetable soup before stripping off and falling into bed, leaving her clothes in a heap on the floor.

3:11.

The numbers, glowing danger-red, swam out of the darkness and into focus. It was a moment or two before she realized that she was staring at the clock-radio on the nightstand.

Odd. She never woke in the middle of the night; even with the Dread pressing relentlessly harder on her every day, she slept too heavily to wake easily or quickly. Therefore, something must have happened, something big or close, or both. She held very still, not even breathing, listening for the sound of an intruder in the apartment, in the bedroom.

A minute passed, then another; nothing. Maybe something had happened in the apartment next door or upstairs, she thought, still listening, barely breathing.

Nothing. Nothing and more nothing. And perhaps that was all it was, a whole lot of nothing. It could have been a car alarm out on the street, an ambulance passing close with its siren on, or someone's bassed-out thump-mobile with the volume set on stun. Just because she didn't usually wake up didn't mean that she couldn't. She took a long deep breath and let it out, rolling onto her back.

There was something strange about the feel of the mattress under her and she realized that she wasn't alone in the bed.

Automatically she rolled onto her right side. Rafe Pasco's head was resting on the other pillow. He was gazing at her with an expression of deep regret.

Shock hit her like an electric jolt. She jumped back, started to scream.

In the next moment she was staring at the empty place next to her in the bed, her own strangled cry dying in her ears as daylight streamed in through the window.

She jumped again and scrambled out of bed, looking around. There was no one in the room except her, no sign that anyone else had been lying in bed with her. She looked at the clock. 7:59.

Still feeling shaky, she knelt on the bed and reached over to touch the pillow Pasco's head had been resting on. She could still see him vividly in her mind's eye, that regretful expression. Or maybe apologetic was more like it. Sorry that he had showed up in her bed uninvited? *Hope you'll forgive the intrusion—it was too late to call and there wasn't time to get a warrant.*

The pillow was cool to her touch. Of course. Because she had been dreaming.

She sat down on the edge of the bed, one hand unconsciously pressed to her chest. That had been some crazy dream; her heart was only now starting to slow down from double-time.

She stole a glance over her shoulder at the other side of the bed. Nope, still nobody there, not nobody, not no how and most especially not Rafe Pasco. What the hell had that been all about, anyway, seeing her new partner in bed with her? Why him, of all the goddam people? Just because he was new? Not to mention young and good-looking. She hadn't thought she'd been attracted to him but apparently there was a dirty old woman in her subconscious who begged to differ.

Which, now that she thought about it, was kind of pathetic.

"God or whoever, please, save me from that," Ruby muttered and stood up to stretch. Immediately, a fresh wave of the Dread washed over her, almost knocking her off balance. She clenched her teeth, afraid for a moment that she was going to throw up. Then she steadied herself and stumped off to the bathroom to stand under the shower.

Pasco was already at his desk when Ruby dragged herself in. She found it hard to look at him and she was glad to see that he was apparently too wrapped up in something on something on his notebook to pay attention to anything else. Probably the mysterious case he was working on and didn't seem to want to tell her about. *Shouldn't have slipped and told me you thought it might be related to the one we caught yesterday,* she admonished him silently, still not looking at him. *Now I'll have to pry it out of you.*

Later. She busied herself with phone calls, setting up some witness interviews, putting in a call to the medical examiner about getting a preliminary report on the Japanese girl, and requesting information from Missing Persons on anyone fitting the girl's description. It wasn't until nearly noon that it occurred to her that he was working just as hard to avoid catching her eye as vice versa.

She drew in an uneasy breath and the Dread seemed to breathe with her. *Maybe he had the same dream you did,* suggested a tiny voice in her mind.

As if he had sensed something, he looked up from his notebook at her. She gave him a nod, intending to turn away and find something else that had to be done before she could talk to him. Instead, she surprised herself by grabbing her memo book and walking over to his desk.

"So tell me about this case of yours," she said, pulling over an empty chair and plumping down in it. "And why you think it might have something to do with the dead girl from yesterday.

"Do we know who she is yet?" he asked.

Ruby shook her head. "I'm still waiting to hear from Missing Persons. I've also put a call into the company that makes the charm bracelet, to find out who sells it in this area."

Pasco frowned. "She could have bought it on the internet."

"Thanks for that," she said sourly. "You can start with the auction sites if I come up empty."

He nodded a bit absently and then turned his notebook around to show her the screen. The dead girl smiled out from what seemed to be a formal school photo; her eyes twinkled in the bright studio lights and her lips were parted just enough to show the thin gold line of a retainer wire around her front teeth.

"Where'd you get that?" Ruby demanded, incredulous.

"It's not the same girl," he told her.

"Then who is it—her twin?"

"Can't say at this point." He smiled a little. "This girl is Alice Nakamura. I was investigating a case of identity theft involving her parents."

"Perps or victims?"

"To be honest, I'm still not clear on that. They could be either, or even both."

Ruby shook her head slightly. "I don't get it."

"Identity theft is a complex thing and it's getting more complex all the time."

"If that's supposed to be an explanation, it sucks."

Pasco dipped his head slightly in acknowledgment. "That's putting it mildly. The Nakamuras first showed up entering the country from the Cayman Islands. Actually, you might say that's where they popped into existence as I couldn't find any record of them prior to that."

"Maybe they came from Japan via the Caymans?" Ruby suggested.

"The parents have—had—U.S. passports."

Ruby gave a short laugh. "If they've got passports, then they've got Social Security cards and birth certificates."

"And we looked those up—"

"We?"

"This task force I was on," he said, a bit sheepishly. "It was a state-level operation with a federal gateway."

Here comes the jargon, Ruby thought, willing her eyes not to film over.

"Anyway, we looked up the numbers. They were issued in New York, as were their birth certificates. There was no activity of any kind on the numbers—no salary, no withholding, no income, no benefits. According to the records, these people have never worked and never paid taxes."

"Call the IRS, tell them you've got a lead on some people who've never paid taxes. That'll take care of it."

"Tried that," Pasco said, his half-smile faint. "The IRS records show that everything is in order for the Nakamuras. Unfortunately, they can't seem to find any copies of their tax returns."

"That doesn't sound like the IRS *I* know," Ruby said sceptically.

Pasco shrugged. "They're looking. At least, that's what they tell me whenever I call. I have a feeling that it's not a priority for them."

"But what about the rest of it? The birth certificates? You said they were issued in New York?"

"They're not actually the original birth certificates," Pasco said. "They're notarised copies, replacing documents which have been lost. Some of the information is missing—like, where exactly each of them was born, the hospital, the attending physician, and, except for Alice, the parents' names."

Ruby glanced heavenward for a moment. "What are they, in witness protection?"

"I'll let you know if I ever get a straight answer one way or another on that one," Pasco said, chuckling a little, "but I'd bet money that they aren't."

"Yeah, me, too." Ruby sat for a few moments, trying to get her mind around everything he had told her. None of it sounded right. Incomplete birth certificates? Even if she bought the stuff about the IRS, she found that completely implausible. "But I still don't understand. Everything's computerized these days which means everything's recorded. Nobody just *pops* into existence, let alone a whole family."

"It's not against the law to live off the grid," Pasco said. "Some people do. You'd be surprised at how many."

"What—you mean living off the land, generating your own electricity, shit like that?" Ruby gave a short, harsh laugh. "Look at that photo. That's not a picture of a girl whose family has been living off the grid. She's got an orthodontist, for chrissakes."

"I'm not so sure," Pasco said. "We had the Nakamuras on our radar, so to speak, when they entered the state. However they had been covering themselves before they left the Caymans, whatever they'd been doing to stay invisible, they weren't doing it any more. They left an easy trail to follow. I found them in a northland hotel near the airport. They were there for a week. At the same time, the task force was investigating some fraudulent activity elsewhere in the same area. It seemed that the Nakamura case was going to converge with it."

"What was it, this other activity?" Ruby asked.

Pasco made a face. "More identity theft. I can run you through the long version later if you want but the short version is, be careful what you do with your utility bills after you pay them, and if you insist on paying them over the phone, don't use a cordless phone or a mobile." He paused; when she nodded, he went on. "Anyway, we had enough evidence for a warrant. But when the police got there, the house was abandoned. The only thing they found was the body of Alice Nakamura in one of the bedrooms. Her birth certificate, school photo, library card, and passport were lying next to her on the floor."

"How did she die?"

"Natural causes. Heart failure. I forget what the condition's called but the coroner said that a lot of kids on the transplant lists have it. Alice Nakamura wasn't on any of those. There are no medical records for her anywhere, in fact. And it turned out that her passport was a forgery."

Ruby blinked. "So much for homeland security."

"It was an excellent forgery, but a forgery nonetheless, as there was no record of her ever applying for a passport, let alone receiving one. Unlike her parents."

"If this is some kind of conspiracy, it's the most random and disorganized one I've ever heard of," Ruby said, frowning. "Not to mention that it doesn't make any sense. Unless you've actually been speaking a language that only sounds like English but all the words mean something entirely different and I haven't really understood a single thing you've said."

Her words hung in the air between them for a long moment. Pasco's face was deeply thoughtful (not deeply regretful; she stamped down on the memory again), practically contemplative, as if she had set out a significant issue that had to be addressed with care. Inside her, the Dread pushed sharply into the area just under her breastbone.

"I'm sure that's how everything probably looks when you see it from the outside," he said finally. "If you don't know a system, if you don't understand how things work or what the rules are, it won't make any sense. The way a foreign language will sound like gibberish."

Ruby grimaced at him. "But nothing's that strange. If you listen to a foreign language for even just a minute, you start picking up some sense of the patterns in it. You recognize it's a system even if it's one you're not familiar with—"

"Oh?" Pasco's half-smile was back. "Ever listened to Hungarian?"

She waved a hand at him. "No, but I've listened to Cantonese and Mandarin, simultaneously at full volume when my grandparents argued. You know what I mean. For a system—or anything—to be completely incomprehensible, it would have to be something totally—" She floundered, groping for a word. "It would have to be something totally alien. Outside human experience altogether."

Her words replayed themselves in her mind. "Christ," she said, massaging her forehead. "What the hell are we talking about and why?"

Pasco pressed his lips together briefly. "You were saying that there are a lot of things about my case that don't make any sense."

"You got *that* right, my man," she said feelingly and then let out a long sigh. "I suppose that's the human element at work."

"Pardon?" Now he looked bewildered.

"People are infinitely screwy," she said. "Human beings can make a mess out of chaos."

He surprised her by bursting into loud, hearty laughter. She twisted around in her seat to see that the whole room was staring at them curiously. "Thanks, I'll be here all week," she said a bit self-consciously and turned back to Pasco, trying to will him to wind down fast. Her gaze fell on the notebook screen again.

"Hey, what about her retainer?" she asked, talking over his guffaws.

"Her what?" Pasco said, slightly breathless and still chuckling a little.

"On her teeth." Ruby tapped the screen with her little finger. It felt spongy. "Were you able to trace it to a particular orthodontist?"

"She wasn't wearing a retainer and they didn't find one in the house," Pasco said, sobering.

"And what about her parents?"

"The Nakamuras have dropped out of sight again."

"*Popped out* of existence?"

"I thought so at first," he said, either oblivious to or ignoring her tone of voice. "But then that girl turned up on the roof yesterday, which leads me to believe they were still around. Up to that point, anyway. They might be gone by now, though."

"Why? You think they had something to do with the girl's death?"

"Not intentionally."

Ruby shook her head. "Intentionally, unintentionally—either way, why? Who is she to them—the long-lost twin of the girl who died of heart failure?" Abruptly the Dread gave her stomach a half-twist; she swallowed hard and kept talking. "How long ago was that anyway, when you found Alice Nakamura?"

Pasco hesitated, his face suddenly very serious. "*I* didn't find her. I mean, I only pinpointed the address. I wasn't there when the police entered the house. The Geek Squad never goes along on things like that. I think the other cops are afraid of geeks with guns."

"But you're cops, too."

"Exactly. Anyway—" He swivelled the notebook around and tapped the keyboard a few times. "That was about five and a half weeks ago, almost six." He looked up again. "Does that suggest anything special to you?"

Ruby shook her head. "You?"

"Just that the Nakamuras have managed to lay pretty low for quite a while. I wonder how. And where."

Ruby wanted to ask him something about that but couldn't quite figure out how to word the question. "And you're absolutely sure that girl—Alice Nakamura, I mean—died of natural causes?"

"None whatsoever. Also, she wasn't abused or neglected in any way before she died, either. She was well taken care of. She just happened to be very sick."

"Uh-huh." Ruby nodded absently. "Then why would they just go off and leave her?"

"If they didn't want to be found—and judging from their behaviour, they didn't—then they couldn't carry her dead body along with them."

"All right, *that* makes sense," Ruby said. "But it still leaves the question of why they don't want to be found. Because they're in on this identity theft thing, conspiracy, whatever it is?"

"Or because they're victims of identity theft who have had to steal a new identity themselves."

Ruby closed her eyes briefly. "OK, now we're back to not making sense again."

"No, it's been known to happen," Pasco insisted. "For some people, when their identity gets stolen, the thief does so much damage that they find it's virtually impossible to clear their name. They have to start over."

"But why steal someone else's identity to do that?" Ruby asked. "Why not just create an entirely new identity?"

"Because the created identity would eventually trace back to the old one. Better to get one with completely different connections."

Ruby shook her head obstinately. "You could still do that with a brand new identity."

Pasco was shaking his own head just as obstinately. "The idea isn't just to steal someone's identity—it's to steal their past, too. If I create a new identity, I really do have to start over in every way. That's pretty hard. It's easier if I can, say, build on your already-excellent credit rating."

"Obviously you've never tried to steal my identity," Ruby said with a short, humourless laugh. "Or you'd know better than to say something like that."

"I was just giving an example."

Ruby let out a long breath. "I think I'll pay the coroner a visit, see if there's anything he can tell me about how Alice Nakamura's twin died. Maybe it'll tell us something about—oh, I don't know, *anything*. In a way that will make sense." She stood up to go back to her desk.

"Hey—" Pasco caught her wrist; the contact startled her and he let go immediately. "What if she died of natural causes?"

"Jesus, you really can dream things up, can't you." Ruby planted her fists on her hips and gave him a hard look. "That would be entirely too much of a coincidence."

"Natural causes," said the coroner's assistant, reading from a clipboard. Her ID gave her name as Sheila St. Pierre; there was a tiny Hello, Kitty sticker under the St. She was a plump woman in her mid-twenties with short, spiky blonde hair and bright red cat's-eye glasses and, while she wasn't chewing gum, Ruby kept expecting to hear it pop every time she opened her mouth. "Aneurysm. Tragic in one so young, you know?"

"You're sure you have the right chart?" Ruby asked tensely.

"Unidentified Oriental adolescent female, brought in yesterday from a roof-top in east midtown, right?" Sheila St. Pierre offered Ruby the clipboard. "See for yourself."

Ruby scanned the form quickly several times before she was able to force herself to slow down and check each detail. "How can a thirteen-year-old girl have a fucking *aneurysm?*" she said finally, handing the clipboard back to the other woman. "The coroner must have screwed up. Where is he? I want to make him do it again."

"There's no do-overs in post-mortems," Sheila St. Pierre said, making a face. "What do you think we're working with here, Legos?" She shifted her weight to her right side and folded her arms, hugging the clipboard to her front. "How about a second opinion?"

"Great," Ruby said. "Where can I get one?"

"Right here. I assisted Dr. Levitt on this one and I saw it myself firsthand. It was an aneurysm. Case closed. You know, an aneurysm is one of those things anybody can have without even knowing it. You could have one, or I could. We just go along living our lives day in, day out, everything's swell, and suddenly—boom. Your head blows up and you're history. Or I am. Or we both are. Most people have no idea how thin that membrane between life and death can be. But then, isn't it really better that way? Better living though denial. Who'd want to go around in a constant state of dread?"

Ruby glared at her but she was turning away to put the clipboard down on a metal table nearby. "At least it isn't all bad news," she said, holding up a small plastic bag between two fingers. There was a retainer in it. "We did manage to identify the girl from her dental records."

"I didn't see that on that report!" Ruby snapped. "Why wasn't it on there? Who is she? When were you going to fucking tell me?"

Sheila St. Pierre tossed the bag with the retainer in it back on the table. "Which question would like me to fucking answer first?"

Ruby hesitated and then looked at the retainer. "Where did that come from, anyway? I didn't see one at the scene."

"Well, it was there. Nobody looked close enough till we got her on the table. Her name is Betty Mura—"

"What's her address?" Ruby demanded. "And why didn't you call me?"

"I did call you," Sheila St. Pierre said with exaggerated patience. "You weren't at your desk so I left a message."

Ruby had to force herself not to lunge forward and shake the woman. "When was that?"

"As near as I can tell, it was while you were on your way over here."

"Give me that information *now!*" Ruby ordered her but she was already picking up the clipboard. She slid a piece of paper out from under the form on top and handed it over.

"Thank you," she prompted politely as Ruby snatched it from her.

"You're welcome," Ruby growled over her shoulder, already out of the room.

There was a ticket on her windshield; another skirmish in the struggle to keep the area in front of the municipal complex a strict no-parking zone, this means you, no exceptions, especially cops. Ruby crumpled it up and tossed it in the backseat as she slid behind the wheel. She clipped Betty Mura's home address to her visor. A West Side address, no surprise there considering the girl's clothes. But what had she been doing on a roof in east midtown? What had she been doing *anywhere* in east midtown, and how had she gotten there? She might have died of natural causes but there had definitely been something unusual going on in the last hours of her life.

She went to start the car and then paused. First she should call Rafe Pasco, tell him she had the girl's name and address and she would pick him up.

The image of his head resting on the pillow beside her flashed in her mind; irritation surged and was immediately overwhelmed by the Dread in a renewed assault. She had a sudden strong urge to close her eyes and let her head fall forward on the steering wheel and stay that way until the next Ice Age or the heat death of the universe, which ever came second.

She took a steadying breath, popped her cell phone into the cradle on the dashboard, put it on speaker and dialled the squad room. Tommy DiCenzo answered; she asked him to put her through to Pasco.

"Can't, Ruby. He's not here, he left."

"Where'd he go?" she asked, but as soon as the words were out of her mouth, she knew the answer.

"Coroner's office called—they identified your rooftop girl from her dental records. He took the name and address and left."

"Did he say anything about coming to get me first?" Knowing that he hadn't.

Tommy hesitated. "Not to me. But I got the impression he thought you already knew, since you were on your way over to the coroner's anyway."

"*Shit,*" she muttered and started the car. "Hey, you wouldn't happen to know Pasco's cell phone number, would you? I don't have it with me."

"Hang on—"

"Tommy—" But he had already put the phone down. She could hear the tanky background noise of the squad room: footsteps, a phone ringing, and Tommy's voice, distant and indistinct, asking a question. A few seconds later he picked up the phone again.

"OK, ready?"

"Wait—" she found a pen, looked around hurriedly and then held the point over the back of her other hand. "Go."

He dictated the number to her carefully, saying it twice.

"Thanks, Tommy," she said, disconnecting before he could say anything else. She dialled the number he'd given her, then pulled away from the curb as it began to ring.

To her immense frustration, it kept on ringing for what seemed like a hundred times before she finally heard the click of someone picking up.

"Rafe Pasco speaking—"

"Goddamit, Rafe, why didn't you call me before—"

"I'm in the Bahamas for two weeks," his voice went on cheerfully, cutting into her tirade, "and as you can see, I didn't pack my cell phone. Sorry about that. But you can phone my house-sitter and talk to her if you want. It's *your call.*" There was another click followed by a mechanical female voice inviting her to leave a message after the beep.

Ruby stabbed the disconnect button and redialled. The same thing happened and she disconnected again, furious. Was Pasco playing some kind of mind-game or had he really just forgotten to change his voicemail message after his last vacation? Either way, she was going to have a hard time not punching him. Weaving in and out of the traffic, she headed for the freeway.

She was merging into traffic from the entrance ramp when all at once she found herself wondering what she was so frantic about. Pasco had been inconsiderate, even rude, but he must have figured she'd get the same information from the coroner. Possibly he had assumed she would head over to the Mura house directly from the coroner. He was her partner, after all—why should she be concerned about him going to the girl's house without her?

The Dread clutched her stomach like a fist and she swerved halfway into the breakdown lane. Behind her, a horn blared long and hard. She slowed down, pulling all the way into the breakdown lane to let the car pass; it whizzed by a fraction of a second later. The Dread maintained its grip on her, flooding her system and leaving no room for even a flash of fear at her close call. She slowed down intending to stop, but the Dread wouldn't let her step on the brake.

"What the *fuck*," she whispered as the car rumbled along. The Dread seemed to have come to life in her with an intensity beyond anything she had felt in the past. The maddening, horrible thing about it, however, was that it had not tipped over into terror or panic, which she realized finally was what she had been waiting for it to do. She had been expecting that as a logical progression—apprehension turned to dread, dread became fear. But it hadn't. She had never suspected it was possible to feel so much dread—Dread—without end. It shouldn't have been. Because it wasn't a steady-state universe.

So what kind of universe was it, then?

This was it, she thought suddenly; this was the crack-up and it was happening in fast-motion just like she had wanted. The thing to do now was stop the car, call Tommy DiCenzo, and tell him she needed help.

Then she pressed the accelerator, put on her turn signal and checked the rear-view mirror as she moved back into the travel lane.

The well-groomed West Side houses slid through the frame of the car windows as Ruby navigated the wide, clean streets. She didn't know the West Side quite as well as the rest of the city and the layout was looser than the strict, organized northland grid or the logical progressions of midtown and the south side. Developers and contractors had staked out patches of the former meadowlands and put up subdivisions with names like Saddle Hills and Wildflower Dale and filled them with split-level ranches for the young middle-class and cookie-cutter mansions for the newly affluent. Ruby had taken small notice of any of it during the years Jake had been growing up. There was no appeal to the idea of moving to the West Side from downtown—it would have meant two hours of sheer commuting every day, time she preferred to spend with her son. The downtown school district had not been cutting edge but it hadn't been anywhere near disastrous, either—

She gave her head a quick shake to clear it. Get a grip, she ordered herself and tightened her hands on the steering wheel as if that would help. She checked the address clipped to her visor again, then paused at the end of the street, craning her neck to read the road sign. It would solve a lot of problems she thought if the cheap-ass city would just put GPS navigation in all the goddam cars. She turned right onto the cross street and then wondered if she had made a mistake. Had she already driven along this street? The houses looked familiar.

Well, of course they looked familiar, she realized, irritated—they were all alike. She kept going, watching the street signs carefully. Christ, it wasn't only the houses themselves that were all alike—it was also the cars in the driveways, the front lawns, even the toys scattered on the grass. The same but not the same. Like Alice Nakamura and Betty Mura.

She came to another intersection and paused again, almost driving on before she realized that the street on her left was the one she wanted. The Dread renewed its intensity as she made the turn, barely noticing the woman pushing a double stroller with two toddlers in it. Both the woman and her children watched her pass with alert curiosity on their unremarkable faces. They were the only people Ruby had seen out walking but the Dread left no room for her to register as much.

The Mura house was not a cookie-cutter mansion—more like a cookie-cutter update of the kind of big old Victorian Jake and Lita lived in with the kids. Ruby pulled up at the curb instead of parking in the driveway where a shiny black SUV was blocked in by a not-so-shiny car that she knew had to belong to Rafe Pasco.

Ruby sat, staring at the front of the house. It felt as if the Dread were writhing inside her now. The last thing she wanted to do was go inside. Or rather, it should have been the last thing she wanted to do. The Dread, alive everywhere in her all the way to her fingertips, to the soles of her feet, threatened to become even worse if she didn't.

Moving slowly and carefully, she got out of the car and walked up the driveway, pausing at Pasco's car to look in the open driver's side window. The interior was impossibly clean for a cop or a geek—no papers, no old sandwich wrappers or empty drink cups. Hell, even the floormats were clean, as if they had just been vacuumed. Nothing in the backseat, either, except more clean.

She glanced over at the glove box; then her gaze fell on the trunk release. If she popped it, what would she find in there, she wondered—a portable car-cleaning kit with a hand vac? A carton of secret geek files? Or just more clean nothing?

There would be nothing in the trunk. All the secret geek files would be on Pasco's notebook and he probably had that with him. She considered popping the trunk anyway and then moved away from the car, stopping again to look inside the SUV. The windows were open and the doors were unlocked—apparently the Muras trusted their neighbours and the people who came to visit them. Even the alarm was off.

There was a hard-shell CD case sitting on the passenger seat and a thin crescent of disk protruding from the slot of the player in the dash. A small string of tiny pink and yellow beads dangled from the rear-view mirror along with a miniature pair of fuzzy, hot-pink dice. Ruby wondered if Betty Mura had put them there.

She turned toward the front door and then thought better of it. Instead, she made her way around the side of the garage and into the unfenced back yard.

Again she stopped. The yard was empty except for a swing-set and a brightly painted jungle gym. Behind the swings was a cement patio with a couple of loungers; under one of them was an empty plastic glass lying on its side, forgotten and probably considered lost.

The sliding glass patio doors were open, Ruby realized suddenly, although the screen door was closed and the curtains were drawn. She edged her way along the rear of the garage and sidled up next to the open door.

"…less pleading your case with me," she heard Pasco saying. "Both girls are dead. It ends here."

"But the other girls—" a man started.

"There are *no* other girls," Pasco told him firmly. "Not for you. They aren't your daughters."

Ruby frowned. Daughters? So the girls really had been twins?

"But they *are*—" protested a woman.

"You can't think that way," Pasco said. "Once there's been a divergence, those lives—your own, your children's, everyone's—are lost to you. To act as if it were otherwise is the same as if you went next door to your neighbour's house and took over everything they owned. Including their children."

"I told you, we didn't come here to kidnap Betty," the man said patiently. "I saw her records—the man showed me. He told us about her aneurysm. He said it was almost a sure thing that it would kill her before Alice's heart gave out. Then we could get her heart for transplant knowing that it would be a perfect match for Alice—"

"You heartless bastard," said a second male voice identical to the one that had been speaking. How many people were in that room, Ruby wondered.

"She was going to die anyway," said the first man. "There was nothing anyone could do about it—"

"The hell there wasn't. If we had known, we could have taken her to a hospital for emergency surgery," a woman said angrily. "They can fix those things now, you know. Or aren't they as advanced where you come from?"

"It doesn't matter any more," Pasco said, raising his voice to talk over them. "Because Alice died first after all."

"Yes," said the woman bitterly, speaking through tears. It sounded like the same woman who had been talking so angrily a few moments before but Ruby had a feeling it wasn't.

"And do you know why that is?" Pasco asked in a stern, almost paternal tone of voice.

"The man was wrong," said the tearful woman.

"Or he lied," said the angry one.

"No, it was because you came here and you brought Alice with you," Pasco said. "Once you did that, all bets as they say here were off. The moment you came in, it threw everything out of kilter because you don't belong here. You're extra—surplus. One too many times three. It interrupted the normal flow of progress; things scattered with such force that there were even natural-law anomalies. This morning, a very interesting woman said to me, 'Human beings can make a mess out of chaos.' I couldn't tell her how extraordinarily right she was, of course, so I couldn't stop laughing. She must have thought I was crazy."

Ruby pressed her lips together, thinking that he couldn't be any crazier than she was herself right now; it was just that she was a lot more confused.

Abruptly, she heard the sound of the front door opening, followed by new voices as a few more people entered the house. This was turning into quite a party; too bad Pasco had left her off the guest list.

"Finally," she heard him saying. "I was about to call you again, find out what happened to you."

"These West Side streets are confusing," a woman answered. This was a completely new voice but Ruby found it strangely familiar. "It's not a nice, neat grid like northland, you know."

"Complain all you want later," Pasco said. "I want to wrap this up as soon as possible."

"I don't know about that," said another man. "Have you looked out front?"

Pasco groaned. "What now?"

"There's a car parked at the curb, right in front of the house," the man said. "I don't think that's a coincidence."

"Oh, hell," Pasco said. She heard his footsteps thumping hurriedly away from the patio door—probably going to look out the window at the car—and then coming back again. She straightened her shoulders and, refusing to give herself time to think about it, she yanked open the screen door and stepped into the house, flinging aside the curtain.

"I'm right h—" Her voice died in her throat and she could only stand, frozen in place, one hand still clutching the edge of the curtain while she stared at Rafe Pasco. And a man who seemed to be his older, much taller brother. And two identical Japanese couples sitting side by side on a long sofa with their hands cuffed in front of them.

And, standing behind the couch, her newly retired ex-partner Rita Castillo.

"Now, don't panic," Pasco said after what might have been ten minutes or ten months.

"I'm not panicking," Ruby managed in a hoarse voice. She drew a long, shaky breath. Inside her, the Dread was no longer vibrating or writing or swelling; it had finally reached full power. This was what she had been dreading all this time, day after day. Except now that she was finally face to face with it, she had no idea what it actually was.

"I can assure you that you're not in any danger," Pasco added.

"I know," she said faintly.

"No, you don't."

"OK," Ruby said. Obviously he was in charge so she would defer willingly, without protest.

"The sensation you're feeling right now has nothing to do with your actual safety," Pasco went on, speaking carefully and distinctly, as if he were trying to talk her down from a high ledge. Or maybe a bad acid trip was more like it, she thought, glancing at the Japanese couples. The Muras and the Nakamuras, apparently. She wondered which was which. "What it actually is is a kind of allergic reaction."

"Oh?" She looked around the room. Everyone else seemed to understand what he was talking about, including the Japanese couples. "What am I allergic to?"

"It's something in the nature of a disturbance."

Oh, God, no, she thought, *now he's going to say something about "the force." I'll find out they're all actually a lunatic cult and Pasco's the leader. And I'm trapped in a house with them.* Her gaze drifted over to Rita. No, Rita would never have let herself get sucked into anything like that. Would she?

Rita shifted, becoming slightly uncomfortable under Ruby's gaze. "Do I know you?" she asked finally.

Ruby's jaw dropped. She felt as if Rita had slapped her.

"No, you don't," Pasco said over his shoulder. "She knows someone like you. Where you come from, the two of you never met. Here, you were partners."

"Wow," Rita said, shaking her head. "It never ceases to amaze me, all that what-might-have-been stuff." She smiled at Ruby, giving an apologetic shrug.

"And where does she come from?" Ruby wanted to know. Her voice was a little stronger now.

"That doesn't matter," Pasco told her. "Besides, the less you know, the better you'll feel."

"Really?" She made a sceptical face.

"No," he said, resigned. "Actually, you'll feel not quite so bad. Not quite so much Dread. It may not be much but any relief is welcome. Isn't it?" He took a small step toward her. "And you've been feeling very bad for a while now, haven't you? Though it wasn't quite so awful in the beginning."

Ruby didn't say anything.

"Only you're not sure exactly when it started," Pasco continued, moving a little closer. Ruby wondered why he was being so cautious with her. Was he afraid of what she might do? "I can tell you. It started when the Nakamuras arrived here. Ostensibly from the Cayman Islands. When they stepped out of their own world and into this one. Into yours."

Ruby took a deep breath and let it out, willing herself to be less tense. She looked around, spotted an easy chair opposite the couch and leaned on the back of it. "All right," she said to Pasco, "who are you and what the hell are you talking about?"

Pasco hesitated. "I'm a cop."

"No," Ruby said with exaggerated patience, "*I'm* a cop. Try again."

"It's the truth," Pasco insisted. "I really am a cop. Of sorts."

"What sort?" Ruby asked. "Geek squad? Not homicide."

He hesitated again. "Crimes against persons and property. This includes identity theft which is not a geek squad job in my line of law enforcement."

Ruby wanted to sit down more than anything in the world now but she forced herself to stay on her feet. To make Pasco look at her on the same level, as an equal. "Go on."

"It's my job to make sure that people who regret what might've been don't get so carried away that they try to do something unlawful to try to rectify it. Even if that means preventing a young girl from getting the heart transplant that will save her life."

Ruby looked over at the people sitting handcuffed on the sofa. They all looked miserable and angry.

"An unscrupulous provider of illegal goods and services convinced a couple of vulnerable parents that they could save their daughter's life if they went to a place where two other parents very similar to themselves were living a life in which things had gone a bit differently. Where their daughter, who was named Betty instead of Alice, had an undetected aneurysm instead of a heart condition."

Light began to dawn for Ruby. Her mind returned to the idea of being trapped in a house with a bunch of lunatic cultists. Then she looked at Rita. *Where you come from, the two of you never met.*

"Many of my cases are much simpler," Pasco went on. "People who want to win instead of lose—a hand of cards, a race, the lottery. Who think they'd have been better off if they'd turned left instead of right, said yes instead of no." He spread his hands. "But we can't let them do that, of course. We can't let them take something from its rightful owner."

"And by 'we' you mean…?" Ruby waited; he didn't answer. "All right, then let's try this: you can't possibly be the same kind of cop I am. I'm local, equally subject to the laws that I enforce. But you're not. Are you."

"I wouldn't say that, exactly," Pasco replied. "I have to obey those laws but in order to enforce them, I have to live outside the system they apply to."

She looked at Rita again. Or rather, the woman she had thought was Rita. "And what's your story? He said you're from a place where we never met. Does your being here with him mean you don't live there any more?"

Not-Rita nodded. "Someone stole my identity and I couldn't get it back. Things didn't end well."

"And all you could do was become a sort of a cop?" Ruby asked.

"We have to go," said Pasco's taller brother before the woman could answer. He could have been an alternative version of Pasco, Ruby thought, from a place where she hadn't met him, either. Would that be the same place that Not-Rita came from? She decided she didn't want to know and hoped none of them would feel compelled to tell her.

"We've still got time," Pasco said, looking at his watch, which seemed to be a very complicated device. "But there's no good in pushing things right down to the wire. Take them out through the garage and put them in the SUV—"

"Where are you taking them?" Ruby asked as taller Pasco and Not-Rita got the Japanese couples on their feet.

Pasco looked surprised by the question; it was a moment or two before he could answer. "To court. A kind of court."

"Ah," Ruby said. "Would that be for an arraignment? A sort of arraignment?"

He nodded and Ruby knew he was lying. She had no idea how she knew but she did, just as she knew it was the first time he had ever lied to her. She let it go, watching as the other two herded the Japanese couples toward the kitchen.

"Wait," she said suddenly. Everyone stopped, turning to look at her. "Which ones are the Nakamuras?"

Judging from the group reaction, she had definitely asked the wrong question. Even the couples looked dismayed, as if she had threatened them in some fashion.

"Does it matter?" Pasco said after a long moment.

"No, I guess not."

And it didn't, not to her or anyone else, she realized; not now, not ever again. When you got caught in this kind of identity theft, you probably had to give identity up completely. Exactly what that meant she had no idea but she knew it couldn't have been very pleasant.

Pasco nodded and the other two escorted the couples out of the room. A few moments later, Ruby heard the kitchen door leading to the garage open and close.

"How did you know the Nakamuras would come here?" Ruby asked Pasco.

"I didn't. Just dumb luck—they were here when I arrived so I took them all into custody."

"And they didn't resist or try to get away?"

"There's nowhere for them to go. The Nakamuras can't survive indefinitely here unless they could somehow replace the Muras."

"Then why did you arrest the Muras?"

"They were going to let the Nakamuras supplant them while they moved on to a place where their daughter hadn't died."

The permutations began to pile up in Ruby's brain; she squeezed her eyes shut for a moment, cutting off the train of thought before it made her dizzy.

"All right," she said. "But what about this master criminal who convinced the Nakamuras to do all this in the first place? How could he-she-whatever know about Betty Mura's aneurysm?"

Pasco's face became thoughtful again and she could practically see his mind working at choosing the right words. "Outside the system, there is access to certain kinds of information about the elements within it. Features are visible outside that can't be discerned inside.

"Unfortunately, making that information available inside never goes well. It's like poison. Things begin to malfunction."

"Is that really why Alice Nakamura died before the other girl?" Ruby asked.

"It was an extra contributing factor but it also had to do with the Nakamuras being in a world where they didn't belong. As I said." Pasco crossed the room to close the patio door and lock it. "What I was referring to were certain anomalies of time and space."

Ruby shook her head, not understanding.

"It's how Betty Mura ended up on a rooftop in midtown," he clarified. "She just *went* there, from wherever she had been at the time. Undoubtedly the shock blew out the weakness in her brain and killed her."

"Jesus," Ruby muttered under her breath. "Don't think I'll be including that in my report—" Abruptly, the memory of Rafe Pasco lying in bed with her, his head resting on the pillow and looking at her with profound regret lit up in her mind. *So sorry to have dropped in from nowhere without calling first.* Not a dream? He might tell her if she asked him but she wasn't sure that was an answer she really wanted.

"That's all right," Pasco said. "I will. Slightly different case, of course, and the report will go elsewhere."

"Of course." Ruby's knees were aching. She finally gave up and sat down on the edge of the chair. "Should I assume that all the information you showed me about the Nakamuras—passports, the IRS, all that—was fabricated?"

"I adapted it from their existing records. Alice's passport worried me, though. It's not exactly a forgery—they brought it with them and I have no idea why they left it or any other identifying materials behind."

"You don't have kids, do you," Ruby said, amused in spite of everything.

"No, I don't," he said, mildly surprised.

"If you did, you'd know why they couldn't just leave her to go nameless into an unmarked grave."

Pasco nodded. "The human factor." Outside, a horn honked. "It's time to go. Or do *you* want to stay here?"

Ruby stood up, looking around. "What's going to happen to this place? And all the other things in the Muras' lives?"

"We have ways of papering over the cracks and stains, so to speak," he told her. "Their daughter was just found dead. If they don't come back here for a while and then decide not to come back at all, I don't think anyone will find that terribly strange."

"But their families—"

"There's a lot to take care of," Pasco said, talking over her. "Even if I had the time to cover every detail for you, I would not. It comes dangerously close to providing information that doesn't belong here. I could harm the system. I'm sure I've told you too much as it is."

"What are you going to do?" she asked. "Take me to 'court,' too?"

"Only if you do something you shouldn't." He ushered her through the house to the front door.

"OK, but just tell me this, then." She put her hand on the doorknob before he could. "What are you going to do when the *real* Rafe Pasco comes back from the Bahamas?"

He stared at her in utter bewilderment. "What?"

"That is what you did, isn't it? Waited for him to go on vacation and then borrowed his identity so you could work on this case?" When he still looked blank, she told him about listening to the message on his cell phone.

"Ah, that," he said, laughing a little. "No, I *am* the real Rafe Pasco. I forgot to change my voicemail message after I came back from vacation. Then I decided to leave it that way. Just as a joke. It confuses the nuisance callers."

It figured, Ruby thought. She opened the door and stepped outside, Pasco following. Behind his car was a small white van; the print on the side claimed that it belonged to Five-Star Electrical Services, Re-Wiring Specialists, which Ruby thought also figured. Not-Rita was sitting in the driver's seat, drumming her fingers on the steering wheel. The tall guy was sitting in the SUV.

"So that's it?" Ruby said, watching Pasco lock the front door. "You close down your case and I just go home now, knowing everything that I know and that's all right with you?"

"Shouldn't I trust you?" he asked her.

"Should I trust you?" she countered. "How do I know I'm not going to get a service call from an electrician and end up with all new wiring, too?"

"I told you," he said patiently, "only if you use any of what you know to engage in something illegal. And you won't."

"What makes you so goddam sure about that?" she demanded.

Forehead creasing with concern, Pasco looked into her face. She was about to say something else when something happened.

All at once, her mind opened up and she found that she was looking at an enormous panorama—all the lost possibilities, the missed opportunities, the bad calls; a lifetime of uncorrected mistakes, missteps, and fumbles. All those things were a single big picture—perhaps the proverbial big picture, the proverbial forest you sometimes couldn't see for the proverbial trees. But she was seeing it now and seeing it all at once.

It was too much. She would never be able to recall it as an image, to look at it again in the future. Concentrating, she struggled to focus on portions of it instead:

Jake's father, going back to his wife, unaware that she was pregnant—she had always been sure that had been no mistake but now she knew there was a world where he had known and stayed with her, and one where he had known and left anyway—

Jake, growing up interested in music not computers; getting mixed up with drugs with Ricky Carstairs; helping Ricky Carstairs straighten out; coming out to her at sixteen and introducing his boyfriend; marrying his college sweetheart instead of Lita; adopting children with his husband Dennis; getting the Rhodes Scholarship instead of someone else; moving to California instead of Boston—

The mammogram and the biopsy results; the tests left too late—

Wounding the suspect in the Martinez case instead of killing him; missing her shot and taking a bullet instead while someone else killed him; having the decision by the shooting board go against her; retiring after twenty years instead of staying on; getting fed up and quitting after ten; going to night school to finish her degree—

Jury verdicts, convictions instead of acquittals and vice versa; catching Darren Hightower after the first victim instead of after the seventh—

Or going into a different line of work altogether—

Or finding out about all of this before now, long before now when she was still young and full of energy, looking for an edge and glad to find it.

Convincing herself that she was using it not for her own personal gain but as a force for good. Something that would save lives, literally and figuratively, expose the corrupt and reward the good and the worthy. One person *could* make a difference—wasn't that what everyone always said? The possibilities could stretch so far beyond herself:

Government with a conscience instead of agendas; schools and hospitals instead of wars; no riots, no assassinations, no terror, no Lee Harvey Oswald, no James Earl Ray, no Sirhan Sirhan, no 9/11—

And maybe even no nine-year-old boy found naked and dead in a dumpster—

Abruptly she found herself leaning heavily against the side of the Mura house, straining to keep from falling down while the Dread tried to turn her inside out.

Rafe Pasco cleared his throat. "How do you feel?"

She looked at him, miserable.

"That's what makes me so certain," he went on. "Your, uh, allergic reaction. If there's any sort of disruption here, no matter how large or small, you'll feel it. And it won't feel good. And if you tried to do something yourself—" He made a small gesture at her. "Well, you see what happened when you only thought about it."

"Great," she said shakily. "What do I do now, spend the rest of my life trying not to think impure thoughts?"

Pasco's expression turned sheepish. "That's not what I meant. You feel this way because of the current circumstances. Once the alien elements have been removed from your world—" he glanced at the SUV "—you'll start to feel better. The bad feeling will fade away."

"And how long is that going to take?" she asked him.

"You'll be all right."

"That's no answer."

"I think I've given you enough answers already." He started for his car and she caught his arm.

"Just one more thing," she said. "Really. Just one."

Pasco looked as if he were deciding whether to shake her off or not. "What," he said finally.

"This so-called allergic reaction of mine. Is there any reason for it or is it just one of those things? Like hayfever or some kind of weakness."

"Some kind of weakness." Pasco chuckled without humour. "Sometimes when there's been a divergence in one's own line, there's a certain…sensitivity."

Ruby nodded with resignation. "Is that another way of saying that you've given me enough answers already?"

Pasco hesitated. "All those could-have-beens, those might-have-dones and if-I-knew-thens you were thinking."

The words were out of her mouth before she even knew what she was going to say. "They all happened."

"I know you won't do anything," he said, lowering his voice and leaning toward her slightly, "because you have. And the conscience that bothers you still bothers you, even at long distance. Even in the hypothetical."

Ruby made a face. "My guilty conscience? Is that really what it is?"

"I don't know how else to put it."

"Well." She took a breath, feeling a little bit steadier. "I guess that'll teach me to screw around with the way things should be."

Pasco frowned impatiently. "It's not should or shouldn't. It's just what *is*."

"With no second chances."

"With second chances, third chances, hundredth chances, millionth chances," Pasco corrected her. "All the chances you want. But not a second chance to have a first chance."

Ruby didn't say anything.

"This is what poisons the system and makes everything go wrong. You live within the system, within the mechanism. It's not meant to be used or manipulated by an individual. To be taken personally. It's a system, a process. It's nothing personal."

"Hey, I thought it was time to go," the man in the SUV called impatiently.

Pasco waved at him and then turned to Ruby again. "I'll see you tomorrow."

"You will?" she said, surprised. But he was already getting into his car and she had no idea whether he had heard her or not. And he had given her enough answers already anyway, she thought, watching all three vehicles drive away. He had given her enough answers already and he would see her tomorrow.

And how would that go, she wondered, now that she knew what she knew? How would it be working with him? Would the Dread really fade away if she saw him every day, knowing and remembering?

Would she be living the rest of her life or was she just stuck with it?

Pasco had given her enough answers already and there was no one else to ask.

Ruby walked across the Mura's front lawn to her car, thinking that it felt as if the Dread had already begun to lift a little. That was something, at least. Her guilty conscience; she gave a small, humourless laugh. Now that was something she had never suspected would creep up on her. Time marched on and one day you woke up to find you were a somewhat dumpy, greying, middle-aged homicide detective with twenty-five years on the job and a hefty lump of guilty conscience and regret. And if you wanted to know why, to understand, well, that was just too bad because you had already been given too many answers already. Nothing personal.

She started the car and drove away from the empty house, through the meandering streets, and did no better finding her way out of the West Side than she had finding her way in.

THE ROSE WALL

JOYCE CAROL OATES

Joyce Carol Oates is the author of a number of works of fiction including, most recently, the novel *Mudwoman* (Ecco/HarperCollins) and the story collection *The Corn Maiden and Other Stories* (Grove Atlantic). She is a 2011 recipient of the President's Medal for the Humanities and is a member of the American Academy of Arts and Letters.

Throughout the protracted summers of my childhood and well into autumn, frequently as late as November, the wall at the base of our garden bloomed with climber roses. The bushes were luxuriant—they were carefully tended—and grew to a height of nine or ten feet. There were clusters of red roses bright as drops of blood; there were small, rather anemic pink roses that grew across the archway over the garden gate; there were rich yellow roses—my favorite—that glowed with light on even overcast or mist-shrouded days.

The rose wall, I called it—that section of the wall. The rose wall, which was so beautiful.

The wall itself, the real wall, was made of granite. It surrounded our house and grounds on all sides—an enormous rectangle—sturdy and functional and rather ugly except at the base of the garden where the roses bloomed. Most days I never noticed the wall. None of the children noticed the wall. You couldn't see it because it was always there, there was nothing to see or think about, everything was in its place and never changed. At the foot of the long gravel drive there was an enormous gate made of oak and iron which was kept bolted most of the time, so that the gate too was part of the wall, and invisible.

One day I asked our nursemaid why there were "sharp things"—spikes—growing out of the top of the wall. Without troubling to look toward the wall she told me that they had always been there. Yes, but why?—I asked. She did not reply. Why? I asked. Annoyed with her—our female servants were usually sullen and slow, and not very bright—I pulled at her arm and made her look at the wall, at the spikes: *Why* are they there? I asked. But her gaze was stubbornly averted; her reply was so low I could not hear. Ask them yourself, I seemed to have heard. *Ask someone else,* she must have said.

When my mother came to kiss me goodnight that night, after my bath, I asked her about the sharp things and she looked startled. Sharp things, she said, what sharp things? What do you mean?

In all our city, my father said, only a half-dozen houses were so grand as ours; and all were in our hilly district, behind high walls of stone or brick or granite. From our playroom on the third floor we could see the city sloping away below—chimneys, orange-tiled roofs, church spires, the tower and cross of the great cathedral, and the blue-glittering surface of the Aussenalster. How lovely! On exceptionally clear days, when the mist burned off by mid-morning, we could even see the highest towers of the old castle many miles to the north. Sometimes it looked like an ordinary stone building, faint and near-colorless with distance; at other times it looked glowering and iridescent, like a reflection quivering in water.

How lovely, visitors to the playroom would exclaim, leaning on the windowsill and breathing deeply the fragrant air that arose from the garden below. Oh yes, my mother or grandmother or one of my aunts would say, laughing, oh yes certainly—from *here*.

In my childhood there were many servants. No one could keep their names straight. It didn't matter—they came and went, speaking their strange dialects, nursemaids and cooks and handymen and gardeners and drivers and maids and washerwomen. Some lived inside the wall with us, in the servants' wing; others came by way of a rear gate, and entered the house by way of the kitchen. What a gabble we children heard if we eavesdropped! Most of the servants were peasants, difficult to train—and difficult to trust. They lied, they stole, they sabotaged things; they disappeared and my father was forced to send the police after them, to have them arrested. Where do they come from, we children asked, and the reply was always the same: From *out there*. One of the adults would make a careless gesture of the hand, indicating the city, or the countryside in the distance—the world beyond the wall. Where do they come from? Oh, from out there, where else?—out *there*.

Why are they so stupid, we asked, why do they talk funny?

They can't help it, it's the way they are, we were told. *Out there* it's the way people are.

Tutors came as well, more refined men and women. A piano instructor who played the piano so beautifully that tears flooded my eyes; a riding master with long curly moustaches. Though we were driven to mass at the cathedral two or three times a week, the priest frequently came to visit us; and the archbishop, who had been a friend of my grandfather's. And messengers and special deliverymen, bringing pastries and great baskets of fruit and wonderful chocolates of all kinds from my parents' favorite shops in town....

You must never forget how fortunate you are, everyone said. You must never forget how God has blessed you.

Kneeling at prayer, in the drafty cathedral or at the side of my bed. Dear God thank you for the blessings you have bestowed upon me.... Dear God thank you.... Thank you.... But my mind slipped away, grew bored and slipped away. Tiresome old God! He was another of the adults, older than Grandmother, spying at us from doorways.

God loves you, God has blessed you, an old servant-woman told me one day, with a queer peevish smile. She was looking directly at me as if she were seeing me—which was not the way anyone in our house looked at us children. I made an impatient gesture, or murmured something in embarrassment. I would have slipped away but she showed me a heart-shaped locket she wore around her scrawny neck which contained the photograph of a young girl with dark braided hair, thick straight dark eyebrows, and a defiant upper lip. God has blessed you, the old woman said.

What did I care about an ugly girl in a locket around an old woman's neck? I held my breath when servants stood too close.

Another time one of the laundresses, a large soft woman with carrot-red hair and teeth missing in her lower jaw, began to talk with me in a queer harsh dialect. I was prowling the house, I had wandered into the kitchen hallway in order to eavesdrop; but I did not want to talk with anyone. They have hurt little girls like you, the woman said, little girls prettier than you, she said, giving off a yeasty beery odor, actually touching my arm to detain me. Your people, soldiers, young soldiers from this town....

I should have pushed rudely away and escaped, but for some reason I stood there, unable to move. The woman's cheeks and forehead were flushed as if windburnt, there were two teeth missing in her lower jaw, and the rest of her teeth were badly stained. Her hands too were reddened—the skin stretched across the oversized knuckles was scraped raw. Sniffing, half-sobbing, she told me an angry incoherent story of an eleven-year-old girl... her family lying dead amid rubble... soldiers marching by on a road, in the mud.... Her dialect was so throaty and harsh, I could not understand most of the words. Stop, I don't want to hear, I hate you, you stink, I wanted to say, but I stood paralyzed while she continued: repeating herself, mumbling, wiping her nose on the back of her clumsy hand. Soldiers discovered the girl, soldiers were laughing and excited, they "did things to her" and afterward pushed her back down in the rubble, in what had been the cellar. She was bleeding, some of her teeth had been knocked out....

I wasn't afraid, but I started to cry. I hated the woman and didn't believe her, and couldn't understand most of her words, but I started to cry.

So she was frightened, and let me go. And I ran and ran and hid in my mother's bedroom.

(And I never saw that woman again—she must have been dismissed. A tall soft-bodied woman with red hair, a watery gaze, a mouth that looked as if it were lewdly smiling....)

My father was a very tall broad-shouldered man with sandy whiskers and clear pale eyes. My mother was a pretty, nervous woman who wore her hair—but what color was her hair?—in heavy coils around her head. My father wore dark colors, and dazzling white shirts; my mother wore dresses of all colors and all materials. (The dressmaker was always at our house. Often she and her two assistants stayed for a week at a time.) My father seemed vaguely embarrassed and impatient in my mother's presence, but then they were not together often. Though of course they shared the same bedroom. But during the day, in daytime, they were not often together.

It was my father who told me that I was forbidden to go outside the wall. Except of course when I was in the company of others, driven in one of our cars. The entire family went out to church, naturally; and we often went visiting, in the homes of families nearby; but there was no need for any of us children to leave the grounds because we had everything we wanted there—ponies, pets, a beautiful dark pond in which carp lived, a pretty wooden swing freshly painted white.

My mother said nothing about the wall, my mother did not see it. And anyway the garden gate—the gate at the rear of the garden—was always kept locked.

Except—not always.

Whenever I played in the garden, whenever I could slip away from the others, I would try the doorknob of the gate. Because the climber roses grew so profusely here I had to be careful of thorns. (Sometimes thin tendrils brushed against my face as if caressing me.) The gate was locked, the gate was always locked, except one afternoon when I turned the handle hard—so hard my fingers hurt—the gate came open!

I could not believe it. But it was true. The gate had not been locked after all, or perhaps the lock had broken under the strain.... The iron fixtures on the gate were rusted and moss grew so thickly underfoot, I had to wrench the gate open with all my strength. But it *did* come open, it *did* stand open. And I slipped through.

And was no one watching? Neither of my sisters, or my grandmother, or the freckled silent girl from the country who was supposed to watch closely over me...?

I did not worry that my mother would see: she had better things to do than spy on her children.

So I slipped through the gate. And found myself on a cobblestone street. Of course it was familiar—it was the street that bordered our property on one side—I had been driven along it hundreds of times—but for some reason it looked unfamiliar. The slanted lighting, perhaps (it was late afternoon); the startling noise of the traffic; new odors I could not define. It looked unfamiliar, but I wasn't in the least afraid.

Did I hear a voice behind me?—scolding and alarmed?

I pulled the gate shut, giggling, and ran out into the street.

And ran and ran....

I had never been on foot before, outside our wall. But I wasn't in the least afraid.

The traffic was heavy: automobiles, delivery vans, even several horse-drawn carriages: what a rumble of wheels, what a commotion! I tasted grit, my eyes smarted. Beside me the wall was high and blank, nothing grew on it, on this side. Or was it our wall, now?—I had been running downhill—I might have left our wall behind—but it didn't matter because I would have no difficulty making my way back.

Though—to be truthful—I did not really think about it, then, in those first elated minutes, *making my way back.*

I ran, breathless and giggling, glancing back over my shoulder to see if they were following, and it seemed to me that I had never really run before in my life, with such gaiety, with such surprising strength in my legs and feet: no one could catch me!—not even my father, or one of my brothers! I was running downhill, the cobblestone street on my right, the high rough featureless wall on my left, and my beating heart, and even the noisy turbulence of the street and its odors, delighted me. To run and run and run—what a prank, what an adventure!

Several times I heard voices behind me, shouts, pleas, but I never stopped running, and when I paused, out of breath, panting, at a busy intersection where five streets ran together—where the wall at last had disappeared—there was no one behind me. I wiped my sweaty face, and peered up the hill, which was a very steep hill, and saw no one. My heart leapt with mischievous delight!—I had slipped through the rose wall and escaped my pursuers and now I would explore the city on foot: *I would do exactly as I wanted for the rest of the day.*

No one followed. No one appeared suddenly beside me to seize my arm, and give me a good scolding, and take me immediately back home.

For some time I walked wherever my fancy led me, still in high spirits. If passersby noticed me and remarked upon me—for I was very small to be unaccompanied—I ignored them, and hurried past. I began to tire, but the elation of my escape stayed with me. How large and noisy the city was, and how fascinating!—what a clamor! Beefy-faced men and women of a kind I had never seen before, speaking in a strange guttural accent; shabby carriages and vans, driven recklessly by men not in uniform; a narrow makeshift bridge over a canal where I stood leaning against the railing for a half-hour, resting and watching the boats—mainly barges—that passed beneath, rocking on the oily waves.

The afternoon began to darken. I glanced around, thinking that someone from the house might be approaching. But I saw only traffic, which passed by in a continual stream, and strangers who gave me no notice.

I headed in the direction of our house, but found myself in a park I had never seen before. At the edge of a refuse-littered lagoon a few people stood tossing chunks of bread at a lazy group of geese and swans. The birds' feathers, particularly their breast feathers, were soiled with what looked like grease, but they were large handsome birds; I stood staring at them for a while. My eyelids grew heavy. A pair of geese paddled my way, curiously, then saw that I had nothing for them and turned indifferently aside.

My mouth watered at the sight of bread in the water. Bobbing on the surface, dipping and rising. A black swan snaked its head down to jab at a piece of bread with his salmon-pink bill, and I felt an absurd pang of hunger.

I left the park and began to climb the long cobblestone hill, which was much steeper than I remembered. My mouth was dry with dust, my eyes stung. It was nearly sundown. Lurid orange clouds like torn fabric lay across the sun and gave an eerie dreamlike cast to the cobblestones and the facades of buildings. I had never seen this district before, but an instinct led me dully on.

A bad girl, a naughty girl, *very* bad, *very* wicked, you will have to be punished all day tomorrow—you will have to stay in your room.

No—no tea-cakes, no chocolates. No. You will have to stay in your room.

My pale teary-eyed mother, stammering at me; my tall unsmiling father, not condescending even to touch me. But perhaps Grandmother would relent, and take me in her arms? In the doorway the freckled girl in her white uniform, her eyes smudged with tears. (For surely she would be dismissed.—She pushed me out of the garden and shut the gate on me, I would cry, she did it, it was her fault!)

The wind rose from the Aussenalster as it often did at dusk, and tiny goosebumps prickled on my bare arms and legs. The cobblestone hill had no end. Carriages rattled past, horses' hooves rang on the street, now and then a face in a window peered at me, but without recognition or interest. I was walking alongside a wall now but I could not determine if it was our wall. It might have been ten or fifteen feet high—I could not judge—and it was so rough-textured, so blank—no roses showed—not even a stray branch or tendril overhead.

Where is our wall, where is our house?—where is the gate that leads into the garden?

I began to sob with weariness and fear, running my hand along the wall. Was the wall made of granite?—or another kind of stone? I could not see a gate or a door of any kind. Not even the enormous gate at the end of the driveway.

I was very hungry. My pulses throbbed with fear.

You are a very, very naughty girl: we've been watching you. Your punishment will be to go without supper…to spend the night alone, outside the wall.

I climbed the hill, sobbing, running my fingers along the wall until they began to bleed. Where were they hiding, why didn't they call out my name! Just at dusk I came upon an entranceway of some kind—a door made of solid wood painted black, and now slightly peeling, set into the wall as if into a hill. It did not look familiar but I began to knock at it, and then to pound, fist over fist, sobbing, Let me in, let me in, I hate you, I won't be bad again, let me in—!

I pounded at the door until my fists were numb with pain. I kicked at it, sobbing and screaming.

But of course no one answered—no one heard.

Let me in, I want my supper, I want to go to bed, I hate you, I hate you, I hope you die, let me in, let me *in*—! So I screamed and screamed until I was exhausted, and sank down on the pavement.

And must have fallen asleep. Because when I came to my senses again it was dark, and quite chilly.

I got to my feet shakily. Nothing had changed: the high black door was before me, the wall on either side, blank and featureless and faint with light, reflected light from the sky. I saw now that this door—it was a garage or stable door—did not belong to my family, and in any case it was pointless for me to hammer on it.

It was pointless for me to stay here, I would have to go somewhere else, I would have to explain that I was lost and ask someone to take me home.

All this came to me with a peculiar chilling clarity. And I did not cry, because I had exhausted my tears.

Many years have passed since that night. I might almost say—many lifetimes.

I have cried a great deal, though never with anger or passion: for such emotion (one soon learns, outside the rose wall) is quite pointless.

My childhood is now distant. And cannot hurt. I see that child, that wretched little girl, as if through a distorting glass or the wrong end of a telescope. Please can you help me, please can you take me home, she begs of passersby, please, I'm lost, I can't find my house....

They draw away, annoyed.

There are so many beggars in the square, in the streets near the cathedral and the great hotels. Even children, very small children. Unaccompanied by adults.

Please can you help me, can you take me home?

Sometimes a man or a woman, or a strolling couple, would stop to listen: but for some reason they could not understand me. They stooped to hear, they peered frowning into my face, but they could not understand what I was saying.

I'm sorry, I'm sorry for being bad, I cried, I won't do it again, I want my supper and my bath, I want my Momma, I won't do it again....

They queried me, they shook their heads impatiently, what on earth was I saying? Their own dialects were strange: harsh and guttural, or high, sharp, and sibilant. I could recognize only a few words, tumbling over one another like pebbles in a stream.

In the end they shook their heads impatiently or pityingly. Sometimes with an amused smile, glancing behind me to see if—in a doorway or around a corner—an older beggar was hiding.

I walked on, jostled by the crowd. I had lost track of all time. Hours might have passed; or an entire day; or several days. I ate by snatching bread away from the mourning doves and pigeons (who were fed quite generously in the cathedral square)... I drank from the magnificent Roman fountain in the Royal Park... ladies took pity on me and tossed tinsel-wrapped choco-lates in my direction, soldiers in uniform, some of them hardly older than my brother, tossed pennies at me and chuckled as I scrambled after them across the cobblestones. What a quick, frisky little thing! Is it a little girl? Eh? A little girl, so bold?

I wandered along the canals at the heart of the city. Where the costly shops are located beneath stone arcades, to protect shoppers from the rain. Clothing shops, gold shops, shops selling jewelry, antiques, china, linen, stationery, ladies' hats, ladies' shoes, the very best pastries and chocolates and fruit. The season must have changed overnight for now everyone wore coats and carried umbrellas against the chill slanting rain.

A gentleman resembling my father was walking some distance ahead of me, carrying his ebony-topped cane. He was with one of my uncles, a white-haired uncle with a sly teasing wink whom all the children loved. Both strode along the damp pavement and did not hesitate for a moment when I called after them.

Pappa! Pappa! Wait, Pappa—

I ran close behind them but they did not slacken their pace.

I was certain they heard me: but they gave no sign.

Pappa, please wait—Pappa—I'm sorry—

My tall broad-shouldered impatient father in a dark topcoat, soft gray gloves, gleaming leather boots. His imperial profile, his sandy full mous-tache and beard. My uncle who adored whipped cream in his coffee, and teased us in the playroom by poking his head through the doorway and clapping his hands loudly....

Pappa! Uncle! Wait—

At last my father turned toward me and I saw that it was indeed my father: but he showed no recognition. His eyebrows arched quizzically, his thin-lipped mouth stretched in a grimace. Yes? What? Who is it—?

I pulled at the sleeve of his topcoat, tried to take hold of his cane.

I want to go home now, Pappa, I said, whining, I'm sorry for what I did, it wasn't my fault, the gate locked behind me—I want Momma—

My father drew back, staring. His nostrils were pinched as if he were in the presence of an abominable odor. Pappa please! I screamed, clutching at his knees.

He pushed me aside, stepped adroitly away, and with a brisk gesture tossed a coin in my direction. It struck my chest lightly and rolled across the cobblestones. Instinctively I scrambled after it. If the coin should drop into a drain, or be snatched up by another beggar—!

But I got it. My fingers closed greedily over it. And when I looked up my father and uncle were just getting into a horse-drawn cab.

Pappa, I cried angrily, on my hands and knees, Pappa, I screamed, don't you know who I am?—don't you love me anymore? Wait—

But they did not hear. They climbed into the cab, closed the door behind themselves, and the cab rolled smartly away.

Don't you love me anymore?—don't you love me?

But I got the coin, the gold coin: for it *was* a gold coin and not a mere penny. And with it I went into the closest chocolate shop, and sat at one of the pretty little wrought-iron tables, and ordered a plate of small cherry-topped cakes and a cup of hot chocolate, in a voice nearly as composed as that of my mother or grandmother.

I was faint with hunger, saliva flooded my mouth. My heart still beat painfully with the anger of my father's betrayal. But when the waitress brought my order I was not even ashamed of my filthy trembling hands; nor did I blush when she stared in unsmiling astonishment at me.

Isn't it a sight, that poor little thing!—ladies at a nearby table whispered. A child my own age in a pink woolen coat stared rudely at me. *Isn't* it shameful! the ladies whispered.

I ignored them. I ate greedily, for I was hungry. I was *very* hungry. But then I have never lacked appetite.

THE THIRTEEN TEXTS OF ARTHYRIA

JOHN R. FULTZ

John R. Fultz lives in Napa, California. His epic fantasy novel *Seven Princes* was released by Orbit Books earlier this year as the first volume in the Books of the Shaper trilogy. The second book, *Seven Kings*, follows in January 2013. John's fiction has appeared in *Weird Tales*, *Black Gate*, *Space & Time*, *Lightspeed*, and the anthologies *The Way Of The Wizard* and *Cthulhu's Reign*.

The first book called to him from a row of shelves smothered in gray dust.

Alone and friendless, he stumbled upon the little bookstore among a row of claustrophobic back-alley shops. It had been a month since his move, and he was still discovering the city's secrets, the obscure treasures it could offer. Quaint restaurants serving local fare; tiny theatres showing brilliant old films; and cluttered shops like this one, filled with antiques and baroque artifacts. *The Bearded Sage* read the sign above the door in Old English script. He smiled at the sign's artwork: a skull and quill lying atop a pile of moldering books.

There is something in here for me, he thought as he turned the brass doorknob. A little bell rang when he stepped across the threshold; it was beginning to rain in the street behind him. Inside were books and more books, stacked on tables, lining rows of shelves, heaped in piles on the floor. The pleasant odor of old paper filled his nostrils.

A whiff of dust made him cough a bit as he entered. An old lady sat behind the counter, Chinese or Filipino. She wore horn-rimmed glasses and slept with her head reclined against the wall. A stick of incense burned across the back of a tiny stone dragon near the cash register, emitting the sweet aroma of jasmine to mix with the perfume of ancient books.

He walked the cluttered aisles, staring at the spines of wrinkled paperbacks, vertical lines of text in his peripheral vision…called onward by the book. He knew it was here, somewhere among these thousands of realities bound by ink and paper. His eyes drank the contents of the shelves, his breathing slow and even. This was the way he moved through any bookstore, corporate chains or obscure nooks of basement treasures.

How do you always find so many great books? his wife had asked him, back when they were still married. *You always give me something good to read.*

I don't find them, he had told her. *They find me.*

She didn't believe that, as she discounted so many things he told her, but it was true.

His hand reached toward a shelf of heavy volumes near the back of the store. They were all leather-bound editions, a disorganized blend of fiction and non-fiction, encyclopedia and anatomical treatises, first editions and bound runs of forgotten periodicals, books in many languages—some of which he could not recognize. Running along the shelf's edge, his fingers stopped at a black spine engraved with cracked golden letters. He grabbed it gently and pulled it from its tight niche, accounting for its heaviness. With both hands he brought it down to eye level. Blowing the dust off the cover allowed him to read the title:

The One True World

Volume I: Transcending the Illusions of Modernity and Reason

There was no author listed, and no cover illustration…only faded black leather and its gold leaf inscription. On the spine was a Roman numeral "I" but he saw no accompanying volumes, just the singular tome.

It was the reason he was drawn to this place.

He opened it to the first page. His "acid test" for books: If he read the first few paragraphs and the author impressed him with style, content, imagery, or any combination of these, he would buy it. There was no use struggling through a dull text waiting for it to improve…if an author failed to show some excellence on the very first page, he would likely never show it at all.

After reading the first three sentences, he closed the book, marched to the counter, and woke the old lady by tapping on a little bell.

"I'll take this one," he said. His hands trembled as he drew thirty-four dollars out of his wallet and paid her. His gut churned the way it had when he'd first met Joanne...the thrill of discovery, the sense of standing on the edge of something wonderful and strange. *Love*...or something close to it.

"Great shop. How long have you been in business?" he asked the lady.

"Been here...*for-evah*!" said the old lady. She smiled at him with crooked teeth.

He laughed. "I'm Jeremy March," he told her, though he had no idea why.

She nodded, as if confirming his statement, and waved goodbye. "Please come again, Mr. March."

The tiny bell rang again as he left the shop. He tucked the book under his coat and walked into the pouring rain. Somehow, he walked directly back to his parking spot without even thinking about it. By the time he reached his apartment and laid the book on his bedside table, thunder and lightning had conquered the night.

Perfect night to read a good book.

Alone in his bedroom, his feet tucked beneath the warm covers, he began to read about the One True World.

The first thing you must understand is that the One True World is not a figment of your imagination, and it does not lie in some faraway dimension. To help you understand the relationship between the True World and the False, you must envision the True World lying beneath the False, as a man can lay hidden beneath a blanket, or a woman's true face can be hidden by an exquisite mask.

The Illusion that hides the True World from the eyes of living men is called the Modern World. It is a dense weave of illusory strands called facts, together composing the Grand Veil of Reason.

The True Philosopher, through dedication and study, comes to realize that Reason is a lie because it is Passion that fuels the universe; that Modernity is a falsehood because the Ancient World has never gone away. It only transforms and evolves, and is never any less Ancient. By meditating on the nature of the One True World, one may cause it to manifest, as Truth always overcomes Illusion, even if buried for eons.

In order to master these principles, to tear aside the dense fabric of Illusion and completely understand the One True World, you must not only read this text in its entirety, but also its succeeding volumes.

Of which there are twelve.

He woke the next day to emerald sunlight shining through the bedroom window. Blinking, he recalled a dream where the sun was not green, but orange, or an intense yellow-white. Or *was* it a dream? The sun was green— of course—it always had been. He shook the dream from his mind and headed for the bathroom. He'd stayed up most of the night reading the book, finishing it just before dawn. He'd never read a book that fast before.

Visions of the One True World danced through the steam in his bathroom mirror as he shaved…forest kingdoms and cloud cities…mountains full of roaming giants…winged ships soaring like eagles…knights in silver mail stalking the battlements of jade castles…griffins and manticores and herds of pegasi bearing maidens across an alien sea. He shook himself free of this trance, stumbled to the kitchen, and grabbed a diet soda.

He dressed in a T-shirt and jeans and walked outside, staring up at the ball of emerald flame. The day was warm, but not too hot. He pulled car keys from his pocket. There was no time for breakfast. The second book was calling out to him. There was a used book shop in a city some ninety miles north.

There he would find what he needed.

His next glimpse of the One True World.

Books & Candles was a corner shop in the city's most Bohemian district. The proprietors were an old hippie couple in their mid-sixties. The husband gave a peace sign greeting from behind a pair of John Lennon glasses. Jeremy nodded and walked toward the rows of bookshelves massed together on the left side of the store. On the other side stood a massive collection of handmade candles in all shapes and sizes, almost a shrine, a temple of tiny, dancing flames.

His eyes scanned the shelves, moving up and down, searching. Like walking toward a room where music was playing, and as he came closer to the doorway the melody grew louder.

He moved aside a cardboard box of mildewed paperbacks to reveal a low shelf, and he saw the book. It was identical to the first volume: Bound in black leather with gold leaf etching on spine and cover. He pulled it from the shelf with a symphony blaring between his ears, and stood with its comfortable weight in his hands.

The One True World
Volume II: The Kingdoms of Arthyria, and the Greater Cities

Despite their benign appearance, the hippie couple could tell he wanted the book badly. He had to pay over two-hundred dollars; luckily they accepted his credit card. Forgetting where his car was parked, he walked along the street to a fleabag hotel used mainly by the homeless. He couldn't wait; he had to read the book *now*. The day was warm and most of the usual boarders were out roaming the streets. He paid for a cot and lay himself down to read.

Hours later, when the sun set, the city's disaffected came wandering in to sip at their brown-bagged bottles and play gin rummy on battered folding tables. He never even noticed. His attention was claimed by the book and—just like the first volume—he could not stop reading until he finished every page.

He devoured the words like a famished vagrant at a royal feast.

The rightful name of the One True World is Arthyria. Twenty-one kingdoms there are in total, nine being the Greater Realms and twelve called the Lesser. Three mighty oceans gird the One True World, each taking its color from the emerald flames of the sun, and each with its own mysteries, island cultures, and hidden depths.

Among the nine Greater Realms thirty-three Great Cities thrive, each dating back to the Age of Walking Gods. Some of them have been destroyed many times over, yet always were rebuilt by faithful progeny.

The mightiest and most ancient of the Great Cities are seven in number. These are: Vandrylla (City of the Sword), Zorung (City of Stargazers), Aurealis (City of Wine and Song), Oorg (City of the Questing Mind), Ashingol (City of the Godborn), Zellim Kah (City of Sorcerers), and Yongaya (City of the Squirming Toad).

Among all the Great Cities, there is only one *where no living man may tread. Even to speak the name of that Dreaded Place is punishable by death in all kingdoms Greater and Lesser.*

Therefore, the name of the Shunned City will not be set down on these pages.

In his dreams, he was still married. He dreamed of Joanne the way she used to be: smiling, full of energy, her hair long and black as jet. The picnic at Albatross Lake was the usual setting for these kinds of dreams. A weird yellow sun blazed in an azure sky, and the wind danced in her hair. They drank a bottle of wine and watched the ducks play across the water before storm clouds rolled in to hide the sun. They lay under a big tree and made love while the rain poured down and leaves sighed over their heads.

I've never been more happy, he told her that day. He was only twenty-five, she was a year younger, and they were living proof that opposites attract. He never knew why someone like her had fallen for an eternal dreamer. He was more concerned with writing the perfect song than making a living. She worked at a bank for the entire three years they were married; he worked at a used record store and taught guitar lessons. The first year was bliss, the second a struggle, and the third a constant battle.

You're such a dreamer, she used to say. As if there was something *wrong* with that. A few months into the marriage he realized that as long as she made more money than him, he would be a failure in her eyes. That started his suit-and-tie phase, when he hung up his guitar for a mind-numbing corporate job. He did it all for her. She cut her hair short and seemed happy again for a while…but he became more and more miserable. Sterilized rows of cubicles comprised his prison…and prison was a place without hope.

You're such a dreamer. She told him this again in the dream, unaware of the irony, and her wedding dress turned to ashes when he kissed her.

She stood on a strand of cold gray beach, and he watched her recede as some kind of watercraft carried him away. Eventually she was just a little doll-sized thing, surrounded by other dolls on the beach. He turned to look at the boat, but it was empty. He stood alone on the deck, and a terrible wind caught the sail and drove him farther from shore.

Looking back, he called her name, but he'd drifted too far out on the lonesome tide. He dove into the icy water, determined to get back to shore, to get back to *her*, to get their love back. It was his only hope. There was nobody but her. There never had been, never would be.

But when the cold waters closed over his head, he remembered that he couldn't swim. He sank like a stone, salty brine rushing into his lungs.

He woke up gasping for breath among tall stalks of lavender grass. The sun burned high in the lime-colored sky. There was no sign of the cheap boarding house, or the homeless men whose refuge he shared. He lay in a field, alone. He stood and saw the soaring black walls of Aurealis.

Ramparts of basalt encircled the city. They curved several miles to the west, toward the bay where a thousand ships sat at anchor. This was the great port-city, famed far and wide for its excellent wines and superb singers. He walked toward the shore where the proud galleons lingered. He dreaded the open water, but he knew the next book lay beyond the lime-green sea. It called to him, as surely as spring calls forth a sleeping blossom.

By meditating on the nature of the One True World, one may cause it to manifest...

Following a road to the southern gate, he made his way through a crowd of robed pilgrims, armored watchmen, cart-pulling farmers, and simple peasants. Clusters of jade domes and towers gleamed in the distance, surrounded by a vast network of wooden buildings where the common folk worked and lived. The sounds of Aurealis were music and commerce: bards and poets performed on street corners. The smells of the city were horse, sweat, woodsmoke, and a plethora of spices.

Palanquin chairs borne by servants carried the wealthy through the streets. The rich of Aurealis dressed themselves for spectacle. Their robes were satin and silk, studded with patterned jewels to signify the emblems of their houses. Their heads were towering ovals of pastel hair sculpted with strands of pearls and golden wire. Rings sparkled on the fingers of male and female; both sexes painted their faces in shades of amber, ochre, and crimson. Squads of guards in silver ringmail flanked the palanquins, curved broadswords across their backs. The crests of their iron helms were serpents, falcons, or tigers.

As he moved aside to let a nobleman's entourage pass, Jeremy noticed his own clothing. It was like none worn by the folk of Aurealis. A black woolen tunic covered his chest and arms, tied with a thin belt of silver links. His breeches were some dark purple fabric, supple yet thick as leather, and his tall boots were the same material. A crimson cloak was secured at his neck by a ram's head amulet forged of silver, or white gold. His clothes smelled of horseflesh and dirt. Instinctively he reached for his wallet and found instead a woolen purse hanging from his belt. He poured the clanking contents into his hand: Eight silver coins with the ram's head on one side and a shining tower on the other.

Somehow he knew these coins were *drins*, also called rams, and they were minted in some distant city. He could not recall its name.

He smelled saltwater above the swirling odors of Aurealis. It was a long walk to the quays where the galleons were taking on cargo. Their sails were all the colors of the rainbow, but he recognized none of the emblems flying there. He looked past the crowded bay and the swarm of trading vessels, toward the distant horizon. The sun hung low in the sky now, and the ocean gleamed like a vast emerald shield.

Tarros.

The name surfaced in his mind as if rising from the green sea. It was the name of the island kingdom where he would find the next book.

After much inquiry, he discovered a blue-sailed galleon bearing a white seashell, the standard of the Island Queen. Brown-skinned sailors loaded bales of fabric and casks of Aurealan wine, and it was easy to find the captain and inquire about passage.

"Have you money, Philosopher?" asked the sweaty captain. He was round of body and face, with thick lips and dark curly hair. A necklace of oyster shells hung round his neck.

"I have eight silver rams," said Jeremy.

The Tarrosian smiled, teeth gleaming like pearls. "Aye, that'll serve."

He dumped the coins into the captain's palm and stared out at the waves.

"We sail by moonlight, when the sea is calm and cool," said the captain.

Stars blinked to life in the fading sky. The moon rose over the horizon, a jade disc reflected in the dark waves.

He followed the captain—who introduced himself as Zomrah the Sea-soned—up the gangplank. Suddenly he remembered the second volume, and the flophouse where he'd fallen asleep after reading it. He had no idea where the book was...did he leave it in the field? Was it somewhere in the city? Or had it disappeared completely? He wanted to run back across the city, back into the open field and see if it lay there among the violet grass.

No, he told himself. *I've read it.*

His path lay forward, across the green waves.

The closer to the island kingdom he came, the more he remembered of himself. By the time the wooded shores of Tarros came in sight, he knew why the captain had called him "philosopher," and why he wore the silver ram's head on his breast. He recalled his boyhood in the white towers of Oorg, City of the Questing Mind, the endless libraries that were the city's temples, and a thousand days spent in contemplation. Much of it still lay under a fog of non-memory, obscured by lingering visions of high school, college, and other lies. Yet after five days on the open ocean, he was certain that he was a trained philosopher from the white city, and that he always had been. On the sixth day out, he remembered his true name.

I am Jeremach of Oorg.

"I am Jeremach of Oorg!" he shouted across the green waves. The Tar-rosian sailors largely ignored his outburst, but their narrow eyes glanced his way when they thought he wasn't looking. Most likely they expected eccentric behavior from a man who spent his life pondering the meaning of existence.

But that's not all of it, he knew. *There's more…much more. Oorg feels like a memory of what I used to be…not what I am.* He knew that he was more than a simple child of Oorg, versed in the eight-hundred avenues of thought, savant of the fifty-nine philosophies. Perhaps the answer lay in the next volume of *The One True World*.

The rest of his memory lay somewhere within those pages.

After fourteen days of calm seas and healthy winds, the galley dropped anchor in Myroa, the port city of Tarros. It was a pale imitation of Aurealis, a humble collection of mud-walled dwellings, domed temples, and atop its tallest hill the modest palace of the Tarrosian Queen. A single tower rose between four spiked domes, the entire affair built of rose-colored marble veined with purple. The city was full of colorful birds, and the people were simple laborers for the most part, dressed in white shifts and pantaloons. Most of the men and women went bare-chested, though all wore the seashell necklaces that were the sign of their country and queen. The breath of the salty wind was sweetened by the tang of ripe fruit trees.

Zomrah the Seasoned was a trader captain in service to the queen's viceroy, so he had access to the palace. The viceroy was an old, leathery man with silvery robes and a ridiculous shell-shaped hat on his gray head. Or perhaps it was an actual shell. He examined Zomrah's bill of lading in a plush anteroom and gave the captain a bag of gold. When Zomrah introduced Jeremach the viceroy looked him over as if examining a new piece of freight. Eventually the old man nodded and motioned for the philosopher to follow him.

Jeremach followed him through winding corridors. Some were open-air walkways hemmed with rows of trellises thick with red and white orchids. Tapestries along the palace walls showed scenes of underwater peril, with trident-bearing heroes battling krakens, sharks, and leviathans. Somewhere, a high voice sang a lovely song that brought the ocean depths to mind.

The Queen of Tarros received Jeremach on the high balcony of her rosy tower. A tall chair had been placed in the sunlight where she could observe the island spreading to the west and north, and leagues of open sea to the east and south. Three brawny Tarrosians stood at attention, her personal guard armed with trident and sword, naked but for white loincloths and seashell amulets.

The queen rose from her chair, and he gasped. Her loveliness was stunning. The narrow chin and sapphire eyes were familiar, and her hair was dyed to the hue of fresh seaweed. It fell below her slim waist, shells of a dozen colors woven among its braids. Her dress was a diaphanous gown, almost colorless, and her brown body was perfect as a jewel.

She greeted him with a warm hug. "You look well, Philosopher. Much *younger* than when last you visited." She smiled.

Jeremach bowed, remembering the proper etiquette for such a situation. *I've been here before. She knows me.*

"Great Queen, your realm is the soul of beauty, and you are its heart," he said.

"Ever the flatterer," she said. She raised a tiny hand to his cheek and cupped it, staring at him as if amazed by his features.

"You've come for your books," she said, taking him by the hand. Her touch was delicate, yet simmering. "I've kept them safe for you."

Yes. There is more than one volume here.

Jeremach nodded. "Your Majesty is wise…"

"Please," she said, leading him into the tower. "Call me by my name, as you used to do. You have not forgotten it?"

He searched the murky depths of his memory.

"*Celestia,*" he said. "Sweet Celestia."

She led him up spiral stairs into a library. Twenty arched windows looked out upon the sea, and hundreds of books lined a shelved wall. He walked without direction to a specific shelf, and his hands reached (as they had done twice before) directly for the third book. Two more volumes sat beside it. He lay all three of them on a marble table and examined their golden inscriptions.

Volume III: The People and Their Faiths

Volume IV: The Lineages of the Great Kings and the Bloodlines of the Great Houses

Volume V: The Societies of the Pseudomen and the Cloud Kingdoms

"You see?" the queen said. "They are safe and whole. I have kept your faith."

He nodded, aching to open the third volume and read. But first he had to know. "Thank you," he said. "But how did you come to possess these texts?"

She looked at him quizzically, amused by the question. "You *gave* them to me when I was only a little girl. I always knew you would return for them, as you promised. I wish you'd have come while Father was still alive. He was very fond of you. We lost him four years ago."

He recalled a broad-chested man with a thick green beard and a crown of golden shells. In his mind, the King of Tarros laughed, and a little girl sat on his knee.

King Celestior. My friend. She is his daughter, once my student, and now the Queen of Tarros. How many years has it been?

He kissed the queen's cheek, and she left him to his books. Hours later, her servants brought him seafood stew, Aurealan wine in pearly cups, and a box of fresh candles. He read throughout the long night, while the warm salt air swept in from the sea, and the jade moon crept from window to window.

For days he sat in the chamber and read. Finally, they found him collapsed over the books, snoring, a white beard growing from his chin. They carried him to a proper bed, and he slept, dreaming of a distant world that was a lie, and yet also true in so many ways.

"You're walking out on me?" she said, eyes brimming with tears.

"You walked out on *me*," he told her.

She said nothing.

"Joanne…sweetheart…you know I'll always love you. But this isn't working. We…don't belong together."

"How can you be so *sure*?" she cried.

"Because if we did…you would have never climbed into bed with Alan."

Her sadness turned to anger, as it often did. "I told you! I never meant for it to happen."

"Yeah, you told me," he said. "But you did it. You *did* it, right? Three times…that I know of."

She grabbed him, wrapped her arms around his neck. Squeezed. "You can't just leave me behind," she said.

Now he was crying too. "I'm done with this," he said.

"No," she whimpered. "We can still fix it."

"How?"

She stood back from him, brushing a dark strand of hair from her forehead. Her eyes were dark, too. Black pearls.

"We'll get counseling," she pleaded. "We'll figure out what went wrong and we'll make sure it never happens again."

He turned away, lay his forehead against the mantle.

"You cheated too," she said, almost a whisper.

After you did. He didn't say it out loud. Maybe she was right. Maybe there still was hope.

He had never loved anyone but her.

Never.

They stood with their arms wrapped around each other for a little while. "I'll always love you," he said. "No matter what happens."

The people of Arthyria differ greatly in custom, dress, and culture, and wars are not unknown. Each kingdom has its share of inhuman denizens, humanoid races who live in proximity or complete integration with the human populace. These are the Pseudomen, and they have played a great role in many a war as mercenary troops adding to the ranks of whatever city-state they call home. There is generally little prejudice against the Pseudomen, although the Yellow Priests of Naravhen call them "impure" and have banned them from the Yellow Temples.

There are five Great Religions in practice across the triple continents of Arthyria, faiths that have survived the upheaval of ages and come down to us through the fractured corridors of time intact. The cults and sects of lesser deities are without number, but all of the Five Faiths worship some variation of the One Thousand Gods.

Some faiths, such as the Order of the Loyal Heart, are inclusive, claiming that all gods be revered. Others are singular belief systems, focused on only one god drawn from the ranks of the One Thousand. Through these commonalities of faith we see the development of the Tongue, a lingua franca that unites most of Arthyria with its thirty-seven dialects.

Here mention must be made of the Cloud Kingdoms, whose gods are unknown, whose language is incomprehensible to Arthyrians, and whose true nature and purpose has remained a mystery throughout the ages.

When he woke he was closer to being himself, and the people of Tarros were restored. He walked through the palace in search of Celestia, marveling at the beauty of those he had forgotten. Their glistening skins were shades of turquoise, their long fingers and toes webbed, tipped with mother-of-pearl talons. They wore very little clothing, only the same white loincloths he'd seen yesterday. Webbed, spiny crests ran up their backs, across the tops of narrow skulls, terminating on their tall foreheads. Their eyes were black orbs, their lips far thicker than any human's, and only the females grew any hair: long emerald tresses woven with pearls and shells.

They were amphibious Pseudomen, a marine race that had evolved to live on land. The island kingdom was a small portion of their vast empire, most of which lay deep beneath the waves. Some claimed they ruled the entire ocean, but Jeremach knew better. There were other, less civilized societies below the sea.

Now that he had read three more volumes, Arthyria was one step closer to being whole. So was he. Vastly important things lay just on the edge of his awareness. He must know them…everything depended on it.

He found Celestia in her gardens, surrounded by a coterie of amphibious subjects. They lounged around a great pool of seawater fed by undersea caverns.

"Jeremach…you look more like yourself today," said the queen, beckoning him with a webbed hand.

"I should say the same to you, Majesty," he replied. He saw himself now in the surface of the pool. His garb had changed little, but he looked older. At least forty, he guessed, but his hair and thick beard were as white as a codger's. *How old am I really?* he wondered. *Will I continue aging as the world keeps reverting to its true state?*

"I trust you found what you were looking for in those dreadful books?" she asked. She offered him a padded bench beside her own high seat. Tiny Tarrosian children splashed in the pool, playing subaquatic games and surfacing in bubbles of laughter.

"I did," he said. "I found the truth. Or *more* of it, at least."

"It is good to see you again, Old Tutor," she said, smiling with her marine lips. Her eyes gleamed at him, onyx orbs brimming with affection.

"You were always my favorite pupil," he told her honestly.

"How long will you stay with us?"

"Not long, I fear. I hear a call that cannot be denied. Tell me, did your father sign a treaty with the Kingdom of Aelda when you were still a child?"

"Yes…" Celestia raised her twin orbs to the sky. "The Treaty of Sea and Sky, signed in 7412, Year of the Ray. It was you who taught me that date."

"And your father received a gift from the Sovereign of Aelda…do you still have it?"

Clouds of jade cotton moved across the heavens. The next book called to him from somewhere high above the world.

She led him below the palace into a maze of caverns created by seawater in some elder age, and three guards accompanied them bearing torches. When they found the great door of obsidian that sealed the treasure vault, she opened it with a coral key. Inside lay a massive pile of gold and silver coins, centuries of tribute from the realms of Arthyria, fantastic suits of armor carved from coral and bone, spears and shields of gold and iron, jewels in all the colors of the prism, and objects of painful beauty to which he could not even put a name.

Celestia walked about the gleaming hoard until she found a horn of brass, gold, and jet. It might have been the horn of some mighty antelope, the way it twisted and curved. Yet Jeremach knew that it was forged somewhere no land animal could reach. She presented it to him with an air of satisfaction. She was still the student eager to please her tutor. He kissed her cheek and tucked the horn into his belt.

"Something else," she said. Wrapping her hand about a golden hilt, she drew forth from the piled riches a long, straight sword. The blade gleamed like silver, and the hilt was set with a blue jewel carved to the likeness of a shell. Jeremach remembered this blade hanging on the broad belt of King Celestior. Even a peace-loving king had to fight a few wars in his time.

"Take this," said the queen.

Jeremach shook his head. "No, Majesty," he protested. "This was…"

"My father's sword," she said. "But he is dead, and he would have wanted you to have it." She drew close to him, and whispered in his ear. Her voice was the sound of the ocean in the depths of a seashell. "I know something of what you are trying to do. As do others. You may *need* this."

Jeremach sighed and bowed. To reject her gift would be to insult her. He took the blade and kissed the hilt. She smiled at him, the tiny gills on her neck pulsing. She found a jeweled scabbard to sheathe the weapon, and he buckled it about his waist alongside the silver belt of the philosopher.

A philosopher who carries a sword, he thought. *How absurd.*

Yet, was he a philosopher still? What further changes lay in store for him when the last of the One True World was revealed?

He feasted with the queen and her court that night, getting rather drunk on Aurealan wine and stuffed full of clams, crabs, and oysters. By the time he stumbled up to his bed in the high tower, he was nearly senseless. He took off his belts, propped the sword in its scabbard against the bed post, and passed out.

It wasn't pain that woke him, but rather the terrible lack of air. He saw a green-blue haze, and wondered if Tarros had sank beneath the waves and he was drowning. The pain at his throat was his second sensation, dulled as it was by the great quantities of wine in his belly.

A shadow crouched above him, the toes of leather boots on either side of his face, and a thin strand of wire was cutting through the flesh under his chin, pulling terribly on his beard. It was the beard's thickness that prevented a quick death, giving him a few seconds to wake and realize he was being strangled.

He gasped for air, his fingers clawing at nothing, his legs wracked by spasms. Any second now the wire would cut through his throat—probably before he suffocated. The strangler tightened its iron grip on the wire, and Jeremach's body flailed. He could not even scream for help. They would find him here, dead in the queen's guest chamber, with no idea who killed him.

What will happen when I'm gone? he wondered.

Then, he knew of a certainty, some bit of memory racing back into his head; his face turned purple and his lungs seized up. If he did not finish reading the thirteen volumes, the One True World would fade back into the world of Modernity and Illusion.

If he died, Arthyria died with him.

His grasping fingers found the hilt of Celestior's sword. He wrapped them about the grip and yanked the sheathed blade up to crack against the strangler's skull. The stranglehold lessened, but he could not remove the sword from its scabbard, so it was no killing blow. Twice more he bludgeoned the strangler with the sword, wielding it like a metal club wrapped in leather.

On the third blow, the strangler toppled off the bed, and Jeremach sucked in air like a dying fish. He scrambled onto the floor and tried to unsheathe the sword. A dark figure rose across the mattress, hooded and cloaked in shades of midnight. It stepped toward him, face hidden in the shadows of the hood. An iron dagger appeared in its gloved fist, the blade corroded by rust. A single cut from that decayed iron would bring a poisonous death.

He scrambled for air and found his back against the wall. A froglike croaking came from his throat. He fumbled at the scabbard. Why wouldn't the damn sword come clear?

The assassin placed the rusted blade against his throat.

"*You cheated too*," said a cold voice from inside the hood.

No, that's not...that's not what I heard.

Three golden blade heads burst from the assassin's stomach. A Tarrosian guard stood behind the attacker, his trident impaling it.

Jeremach finally tore the sword free of the scabbard. He rolled onto his side as the skewered assassin drove its dagger into the stone wall, ignoring the trident jutting from its back.

The guard pulled his trident free for another jab, but Jeremach was on his feet now, both hands wrapped about the sword's hilt, swinging it in a silver arc. The hooded head flew from the assassin's body and rolled across the floor to lie at the foot of the bed.

The headless body stood for a moment, holding the rusted dagger. Then it collapsed with a sound like snapping wood, and became only a mound of bones and mildewed black cloth.

He stared at the face on the severed head. A woman with long hair dark as her robes. He blinked, coughed, and he would have screamed in terror, but could not.

Joanne...

He said her name through purple lips, his voice a rasping moan.

She stared up at him: weeping, bleeding, bodiless.

"You can't do this," she said, and black blood trickled from her lips. "You can't throw it all away. *You're destroying our world.* You're destroying the Past. How do you know *this* is the True World and not the False?"

He had no words; he fell to his knees and stared at her face. His heart ached more terribly than his throat.

"You said... you'd always love me," she wept. "But you're throwing it all away. How can you be *sure?*"

Her tongue, and then the rest of her face, withered into dust.

He stared into the blank sockets of a grinning skull.

Before the sun kissed the ocean, he left the palace and went alone to the island shore. As the first green light seeped into the sky, he blew on the horn of brass, gold, and jet. One long, loud note that rang across the waves and into the clouds of morning.

The island kingdom came to life behind him, and he stared across the waves. Soon he saw a speck of gold gleaming between the clouds. It grew larger, sinking toward the ocean, until it came clearly into view: A slim sky galleon bearing cloud-white sails. It floated toward the island like a great, soaring bird. Some distance from the shore it touched keel to water soundlessly. By the time it reached the sandy embankment, it looked no stranger than any other sea-going vessel. The figurehead on its pointed bow was a beautiful winged woman.

Someone let down a rope ladder, and Jeremach climbed it, dropping himself onto the deck. The sky galleon's crew were stone men, living statues of pale marble. They said nothing, but nodded politely when he showed them the horn of brass, gold, and jet. Then the stone captain took it from him, crushed it in his massive fist, and dropped its remains into the sea.

The sails caught a gust of wind, and the ship rose from the sea toward the clouds. The island of Tarros was a tiny expanse of forest surrounded by endless green waves; now it was a mote, now completely gone. Continents of cloud passed by on either side of the galleon. Higher and higher it rose, until all of Arthyria was lost below a layer of cumulus. The green sun blazed brightly in the upper realm.

Now the city of Aelda came into view: a sparkling crystal metropolis perched upon an island of white cloud. The spiral towers and needle-like pinnacles were like nothing in the world below. But a sense of vague familiarity flavored Jeremach's awe.

The rest of the books are here, he remembered.

All but one.

The Winged Folk had no voices, and their bodies were translucent. They moved with all the grace of swans, gliding through the sky on feathery appendages grown from their lean backs. Their beauty was incredible, so much that none could be classified as singly male or female. Their bodies were the sexless perfection of inhumanity. The highest order of all the Pseudomen, the people of the Cloud Kingdoms were also the most mysterious.

A flock of them glided by as the sky galleon docked alongside a crystal tower. They stared at the visitor with eyes of liquid gold. They neither waved nor questioned his presence. He had sounded the horn. Otherwise, he would not be here.

The galleon's crew of marble men followed him into a corridor of diamond and took their places in carved niches along the walls. Now they were only statues again. Someday, someone in Arthyria would blow another horn of brass, gold, and jet; and the statues would live again to man the golden ship. Jeremach left the stone men to their silent niches.

The scent of the Cloud Realms made his head swim as he walked toward the books. Up here lingered the aromas of unborn rain, naked sunlight, and the fragrance of unsoiled clouds. The diamond walls rang with musical tones, sweet enough to mesmerize the untutored into immobility. But Jeremach heard only the call of his books.

He found them right where he had left them so long ago, in a domed chamber supported by seven pillars of glassy quartz. The tomes lay upon a round table of crystalline substance, and they looked as incongruous here as the tall philosopher's chair he had placed before the table.

He sat in the chair, sighed, and ran his fingers over the faces of the seven books.

Volume VI: The Knights of Arthyria and the Secret Orders of Starlight
Volume VII: Wizards of the First Age

Don't think about Joanne, he told himself.

But her words haunted him.

You're throwing it all away.

How do you know this is the True World?

He opened the sixth volume, breathing in the smell of ancient papyrus and ink.

It's my choice.

I choose Arthyria.

He read.

In the year 7478, the Wizard Jeremach returned to the Shunned City.

Legions of the living dead rose from its ruined halls to assail him, but he dismissed them with a wave of his hand, turning them all to pale dust. He walked among the crumbled stones of the First Empire, frigid winds tearing at his long white beard.

As he neared the palace of the Dead King, a horde of black-winged devils descended screeching from the broken towers. These he smote with a flashing silver blade bearing the sign of Tarros. As the last of the fiends died at his feet, the wizard sheathed his weapon. He walked on, toward the Shattered Palace.

Before the Dead King's gates a band of ghosts questioned Jeremach, but he gave them riddles that would haunt them well into the afterworld. He spoke a single word, and the gates of blackened iron collapsed inward. He entered the utter darkness of the castle and walked until he found the Dead King sitting on a pile of gilded skulls, the heads of all those he had conquered in battle over the course of seven thousand years.

A red flame glowed in a pit before the Dead King's mailed feet, and he looked upon Jeremach. Similar flames glowed in the hollow pits of his eyes. His flesh had rotted away millennia ago, but his bones refused to die, or to give up his hard-won empire. In the last five thousand years, none but Jeremach had entered these gates and lived to speak of it.

The Dead King took up his great black sword, but Jeremach laughed at him.

"You know that I've not come to battle you," said the wizard.

The Dead King sighed, grave dust spilling from between his teeth. With fleshless fingers he lifted an ancient book from the floor of his hall. He offered it to Jeremach.

The wizard wiped away a coating of dust and saw the book's title.

The One True World

Volume XIII: The Curse of the Dead King and the Undying Empire

Jeremach did not need to read it, for he knew its contents with a touch.

The Dead King spoke in a voice of grinding bones. "You have won," he said.

"Yes," said Jeremach. "Though you cheated, sending an assassin after me. How desperate."

"I might claim you cheated with these books of yours," said the skull-king, "But in war all sins are forgiven."

"Still, I did win," said the wizard. "I proved that Truth will always overcome Illusion. That a False reality—no matter how tempting—cannot stand against that which is Real. I escaped your trap."

The Dead King nodded, and a crown of rusted iron tumbled from his skull. "For the first time in history, I have been defeated," he growled.

Was that relief *in his ancient voice?*

"Now…will you keep your promise, Stubborn King?" asked Jeremach. "Will you quit the world of the living and let this long curse come to an end? Will you let men reclaim these lands that you have held for millennia?"

The Dead King nodded again, and now his skull tumbled from his shoulders. His bones fell to dust, and a cold wind blew his remains across the hall. The moaning of a million ghosts filled the sky. In the distant cities of Oorg, Aurealis, Vandrylla, and Zorung, the living woke from nightmares and covered their ears.

Jeremach left the ruins of the Shunned City as they crumbled behind him. He carried the black book under his arm. As he walked, the moldering slabs of the city turned to dust, following their king into oblivion, and the frozen earth of that realm began to thaw in the sunlight. After long ages, spring had finally come.

By the time Jeremach crossed the horizon, there was no trace of the haunted kingdom left anywhere beneath the emerald sky.

RUMINATIONS IN AN ALIEN TONGUE

VANDANA SINGH

Vandana Singh is an Indian science fiction writer living in the U.S., where she is a physics professor at a state university. She has published short stories in various anthologies and magazines, including *Strange Horizons, TRSF,* and most recently *Lightspeed;* many of her stories have been reprinted in Year's Best volumes. Her novella *Distances* (Aqueduct Press) won the 2008 Carl Brandon Parallax award. Most recently she has been a columnist for *Strange Horizons,* where her reflections on science and the environment can be found.

Birha on the Doorstep

Sitting on the sun-warmed step at the end of her workday, Birha laid her hand on the dog's neck and let her mind drift. Like a gyre-moth finding the center of its desire, her mind inevitably spiraled inward to the defining moment of her life. It must be something to do with growing old, she thought irritably, that all she did was revisit what had happened all those years ago. Yet her irritation subsided before the memory. She could still see it with the shocking clarity of yesterday: the great, closed eyelid set in the enormous alien stronghold, opening in response to her trick. The thick air of the valley, her breath caught in her throat, the orange-and-yellow uniforms of the waiting soldiers. She had gone up the ladder, stepped through the round opening. Darkness, her footsteps echoing in the enormous space, the light she carried casting a small, bobbing pool of illumination. This was the alien stronghold considered invincible by the human conquerors, to which the last denizens of a dying race had crawled in a war she had forgotten when she was young. She had expected to find their broken, decayed bodies, but instead there was a silence like the inside of a temple up in the mountains. Silence, a faint smell of dust, and a picture forever burned into her mind: in the light of her lamp, the missing soldier, thunderstruck before the great mass of machinery in the center.

That was the moment when everything changed. For her, and eventually for humankind. She had been young then.

"Hah!" she said, a short, sharp sound—an old woman laughing at her foolishness. It felt good to sit here on the doorstep, although now it was turning a little cold. On this world, the sun didn't set for seven years as counted on the planet where she had been born. She knew she would not live to see another sunset; her bones told her that, and the faint smell in her urine, and her mind, which was falling backward into a void of its own making.

But the clouds could not be ignored, nor the yellow dog at her knee, who wanted to go inside. There would be rain, and the trees would open their veined, translucent cups to the sky. There would be gyre-moths emerging from holes in the ground, flying in smooth, ever-smaller circles, at the center of which was a cup of perfumed rain—and there would be furred worms slithering up the branches to find the sweet moth-meat. In the rain under the trees, the air would quiver with blood and desire, and the human companion animals—the dogs and cats and ferrets—would run to their homes lest the sleehawks or a feral arboril catch them for their next meal. Yes, rain was a time of beauty and bloodshed, here at the edge of the great cloud forest, among the ruins of the university that had been her home for most of her life.

She got up, noting with a grim satisfaction that, in *this* universe, old knees creaked. She went in with the dog and shut the door and the windows against the siren-like calls of the foghorn trees, and put some water on to boil. Rain drummed on the stone walls of her retreat, and she saw through the big window the familiar ruined curve of the university ramparts through a wall of falling water. Sometimes the sight still took her breath away. That high walk with the sheer, misty drop below was where she had first walked with Thirru.

A Very Short Rumination

When I was born my mother named me Birha, which means "separated" or "parted" in an ancient human language. This was because my mother was about to die.

Difficult Loves

Thirru was difficult and strange. He seemed eager to make Birha happy but was like a big, foolish child, unable to do so. A large, plump man, with hair that stood up on end, he liked to clap his hands loudly when he solved a difficult problem, startling everyone. His breath smelled of bitter herbs from the tea he drank all day. Even at their pairing ceremony he couldn't stop talking and clapping his hands, which she had then thought only vaguely annoying and perhaps endearing. Later, her irritation at his strangeness, his genius, his imbecility, provoked her into doing some of her best work. It was almost as though, in the discomfort of his presence, she could be more herself.

One time, when she was annoyed with Thirru, she was tempted by another man. This man worked with her; his fingers were long and shapely over the simulator controls, and he leaned toward her when he spoke, always with a warmth that made her feel as though she was a creature of the sunlight, unfurling in the rays of morning. He made her feel younger than she was. She didn't like him very much; she distrusted people with charm as a matter of principle, but he was more than charm. He was lean, and wore his dark hair long and loose, and every posture of his was insouciant, inviting, relaxed as a predatory animal; when he leaned toward her she felt the yearning, the current pulling her toward him. At these moments she was always stiff and polite with him; in privacy she cursed herself for her weakness. She avoided him, sought him out, avoided him, going on like this for days, until, quite suddenly, she broke through the barrier. She was no longer fascinated by him. It wasn't that his charm had faded; it was only (she congratulated herself) the fact that she had practiced the art of resisting temptation until she had achieved some mastery. You practice and it becomes easier, just like the alien mathematics on which she was working at the time. Just like anything else.

This freedom from desiring this man was heady. It was also relaxing not to feel drawn to him all the time, to be able to joke and laugh with him, to converse without that terrible, adolescent self-consciousness. She could even let herself like him after that.

In this manner she carried herself through other temptations successfully. Even after Thirru's own betrayal she wasn't tempted into another relationship. After the reconciliation they stayed together for an entire cycle, some of which was marked by an easy contentment that she had never known before, a deep wellspring of happiness. When they parted, it was as friends.

But what he left behind, what all old loves left behind were the ghostly imprints of their presence. For her, Thirru came back whenever she looked up at the high walk where she had first walked with him. Thirru was the feel of damp stone, the vivid green of the moss between the rocks, the wet, verdant aroma of the mist. She didn't have to go there anymore; just looking up at the stone arch against the clouds would bring back the feel of his hands.

After Thirru, she had had her share of companions, long and short term, but nobody had inspired her to love. And when the man happened along who came closest, she was unprepared for him. His name was Rudrak, and he was young.

What she loved about him was his earnestness, his delight in beautiful things, like the poeticas she had set up on the long table. He was an engineer, and his passion was experimental craft designed to explore stars. She loved his beautiful, androgynous face, how it was animated by thought and emotion, how quick his eyes were to smile, the way his brow furrowed in concentration. That crisp, black, curling hair, the brown arm flung out as he declaimed, dramatically, a line from a classic play she'd never heard of. When he came, always infrequently, unexpectedly, always on a quest for the woman Ubbiri, it was as though the sun had come out in the sky of her mind. Conversation with him could be a battle of wits, or the slow, easy, unhurried exchange of long-time lovers. She never asked him to stay for good (as though it were possible), never told him she loved him.

Now she was pottering about in her kitchen, listening to the rain, wondering if he would come one more time before she died. The last time he had come was a half-cycle ago (three and a half years on her birth planet, her mind translated out of habit). There was not much more than a half-cycle left to her. Would he come? Pouring her tea, she realized that despite the certainty with which she loved this man, there was something different about this love. She felt no need for him to reciprocate. Sometimes she would look at her arms, their brown, lean strength, the hands showing the signs of age, and remember what it was like to be touched, lovingly, and wonder what it would be like to caress Rudrak's arm, to touch his face, his lips. But it was an abstract sort of wondering. Even if she could make him forget Ubbiri (and there was no reason for her to do that), she did not really want him too close to her. Her life was the way she liked it: the rising into early mornings, the work with the poeticas—which was a meditation in sunlight and sound—then the long trek up the hill to the now-abandoned laboratory. Returning in the early evening before the old bells rang sunset (although the sun wouldn't set for half a cycle yet) into the tranquility of her little stone house, where the village girl entrusted with the task would have left her meal warming on the stove just the way she liked it. The peace of eating and reading by herself, watching the firelings outside her window, in the temporary, watery dark created by the frequent gathering of clouds. In those moments the universe seemed to open to her as much as it seemed shut to her during the long day. She would stare out at the silhouettes of trees and wonder if the answers she was seeking through her theories and equations weren't instead waiting for her out there in the forest, amidst the ululations of the frenet-bird and the complex script of the fireling's dance. In those moments it would seem to her as though all she had to do was to walk out into the verdure and pluck the answer from the air like fruit from trees; that it was in these moments of complete receptivity that the universe would be revealed to her, not in the hours at the simulators in the laboratory. That the equations would be like childish chatter compared to what was out there to know in its fullness.

She took her tea to her favorite chair to drink. On the way she let her fingers brush lightly over the wires of the poeticas that stood on wood frames on the long table. The musical notes sounded above the crash of the rain, speaking aloud her ruminations in the lost alien tongue. Rudrak had left his ghost behind here: The remembrance of his body leaning over the instruments, brushing them as he might, in some other universe, be brushing the hair from her face. Asking how this sequence of notes implied those words. Since she had walked into the alien stronghold so many years ago, since the time that everything had changed, Rudrak had visited her nine times. Each time he remembered nothing of his previous visits, not even who she was. Each time she had to explain to him that Ubbiri was dead, and that he should come in, and wouldn't he like some tea? She went through the repetition as though it was the first time, every time, which in a way it was. A sacred ritual.

Rudrak.

Would he come?

A Rambling Rumination

Simply by virtue of being, we create ripples in the ever-giving cosmic tree, the kalpa-vriksh. Every branch is an entire universe. Even stars, as they are born and die, leave permanent marks in the shadow universe of their memory. Perhaps we are ghosts of our other selves in other universes.

It was not right for Ubbiri to die. There is a lack of symmetry there, a lack even of a proper symmetry breaking. Somewhere, somehow, Ubbiri's meta-world-line and mine should connect in a shape that is pleasing to the mathematical eye. Sometimes I want to be Ubbiri, to know that a part of me did wander into another universe after all, and that separated, the two parts were joined together at last. There is something inelegant about Ubbiri's return and subsequent death. Ubbiri should have shared consciousness with me. Then, when Rudrak asks: "I am looking for Ubbiri. Is she here?" for the umpteenth time, I, Birha, will say yes. She's here.

Instead this is what I say:

"I'm sorry, Ubbiri passed away a long time ago. She told me about you when she died. Won't you come in?"

What is the probability that I am Ubbiri? If so, am I dead or alive, or both? Ubbiri is dead. I am Birha, and Birha is alone.

The Discovery

When Birha was neither young nor old, when Thirru had already moved off-planet, a young soldier volunteered to test-fly an alien flyer, one of two intact specimens. The flight went well until upon an impulse he decided to swoop by the alien ruins in the valley below the university. During the dive, he lost control of the flyer, which seemed to be heading straight for a round indentation like an eye in the side of an ancient dome. The indentation revealed itself to be a door, by opening and then closing behind the flyer.

When Birha was consulted about the problem, she suspected that the door worked on an acoustical switch. Calculating the frequency of sound emitted by the alien flyer at a certain speed in the close, thick air of the valley took some time. But when a sound wave of the requisite frequency was aimed at the door, it opened almost immediately, with a sigh as though of relief.

She volunteered to go alone into the chamber. They argued, but she had always been stubborn, and at the end they let her. She was the expert on the aliens after all.

The interior was vast, shrouded in darkness and her footsteps echoed musically. She saw the flyer, in some kind of docking bay, along with a dozen others. There were no decaying alien bodies, only silence. The young man stood in front of the great mass of machinery at the center of the room. In the light from her lamp (which flickered strangely) she saw a complexity of fine, fluted vanes, crystalline pipes as thin as her finger running in and out of lacy metalwork. The whole mass was covered in a translucent dome that gleamed red and blue, yellow and green, in the light from her lamp. There was a door in the side of the dome, which was ringed by pillars.

"My hand…" the soldier was staring at his hand. He looked at Birha at last. "My hand just went through that pillar…"

Birha felt a loosening of her body, as though her joints and tendons were coming apart, without pain. If she breathed out too hard, she might fling herself all over the cosmos. Her heart was beating in an unfamiliar rhythm. She put her hand in her pocket and took some coins out. Carefully she tossed each one in the air. Thirteen coins came down on the floor, all heads.

"There's nothing wrong with you," she told the aviator. "It's the machine. It's an alien artifact that changes the probabilities of things. We're standing in the leakage field. Look, just come with me. You'll be all right."

She led him into the light. The round door was propped open by a steel rod and there were crowds of people waiting at the foot of the ladder. The young man was still dazed.

"It tickled," he said. "My hand. When it went through the pillar."

A Rumination on the Aliens

What do we know about them? We know now they are not dead. They went through the great probability machine, the actualizer, to another place, a place we'll never find. The old pictures show that they had pale brown, segmented bodies, with a skeletal frame that allowed them to stand upright. They were larger than us but not by much, and they had feelers on their heads and light-sensitive regions beneath the feelers, and several limbs. They knew time and space, and as their culture was centered around sound, so was their mathematics centered around probability. Their ancient cities are filled with ruined acoustical devices, enormous poeticas, windchimes, and Aeolian harps as large as a building. Their music is strange but pleasant to humans, although its frequency range goes beyond what we can hear. When I was just an acolyte at the university, I chose to study what scripts were left after the war. They were acoustical scripts, corresponding to the notes in a row of poeticas on the main streets of their cities.

I was drunk with discovery, in love with the aliens, overcome with sorrow that they were, as we thought then, all dead. For the first time since I had come to this planet, I felt at home.

To understand the aliens I became a mathematician and a musician. After that, those three things are one thing in my mind: the aliens, the mathematics, the music.

Rudrak's Story

A bristleship, Rudrak told Birha, is like no other craft. It burrows into the heart of a star, enduring temperatures beyond imagination, and comes out on the other side whole and full of data. The current model was improved by Rudrak in his universe, a branch of the cosmic tree not unlike this one. He did it for his partner, Ubbiri, who was writing a thesis on white dwarf stars. Ubbiri had loved white dwarf stars since a cousin taught her a nursery rhyme about them when Ubbiri was small:

Why are you a star so dim
In the night beyond the rim
Don't you want someone to love?
In the starry skies above?

Ubbiri had to write a thesis on white dwarf stars. As dictated by academic custom in that culture, her thesis had to connect the six points of the Wheel of Knowing: Meta-networking, Undulant Theory, Fine-Jump Mathematics, Time-Bundles, Poetry, and Love. To enable her to achieve deep-knowing and to therefore truly love the star, she took a ride on the new bristleship with Rudrak. They discovered that when the ship went through the starry core, it entered another reality. This was later called the shadow universe of stars, where their existence and life history is recorded in patterns that no human has completely understood. Some poets call this reality the star's memory-space, or its consciousness, but Ubbiri thought that was extending metaphor beyond sense. The data from the bristleship told her that this star, this love, had been a golden star in its youth and middle age, harboring six planets (two of which had hosted life), and much space debris. In the late season of its existence it had soared in largeness, dimming and reddening, swallowing its planetary children. Now it was content to bank its fires until death.

After this discovery, Rudrak said, the two of them lived quiet lives that were rich and full. But one day before he was due to take off for another test flight, Ubbiri noticed there was a crack on the heat-shielded viewscreen of the bristleship. Rudrak tested it and repaired it, but Ubbiri was haunted by the possibility of the tiny crack spreading like a web across the viewscreen, and breaking up just as Rudrak was in the star's heart.

Perhaps that was what she thought when Rudrak disappeared. Rudrak only knew that instead of passing through the shadow universe before coming out, the bristleship took him somewhere else, to a universe so close to his own that he did not know the difference until he had crashlanded on a planet (this planet) and been directed to people who knew the truth. They led him to Birha, who sheltered him for fifteen days, allowed him to mourn and to come slowly to life again. Each time, she sent him back to his universe, as protocol demanded, by way of the alien probability machine, the actualizer. Somehow he was caught in a time-loop that took him back to the day before the ill-fated expedition. He had returned to her in exactly the same way nine times. His return visits were not predictable, being apparently randomly spaced, and her current (and last) calculation was an attempt to predict when he would come next.

Each visit was the same and not the same. Surely he had had less gray hair the last time? And that healed cut on his hand—hadn't that been from his last trip, when he was trying to help her cut fruit and the knife had slipped? And hadn't his accent improved just a little bit since last time? They'd had to teach him the language each visit as though it was new, but perhaps it became just a hair's breadth easier each time?

She tried to make each experience subtly different for him. She was afraid that too drastic a change might upset whatever delicate process was at work in the time-loop. He was like a leaf caught in an eddy—push too hard and the time stream might take him over a precipice. But a little tug here, a tug there, and perhaps he'd land safely on a shore, of this universe or that one.

So far nothing had worked. His bewilderment was the same, each time he appeared on her doorstep, and so was his grief. It was only these small, insignificant things that were different. One time he wore an embroidered collar, another time a plain one. Or the color of his shirt was different.

Birha worked on her calculations, but the kalpa-vriksh gave senseless, contradictory answers.

A Rumination on Timmar's Rock

I remember when I first came to the university, I used to pass a flat-topped boulder on the way to class. There was a depression on the flat surface of the rock in the exact shape of the bottom of a water bowl. When I met Thirru, he told me that the great Timmar Rayan, who had founded the School of Wind and Water, had sat there in daily meditation for three entire cycles, placing his water bowl in the same spot every time. Over the years the depression had developed. I have always marveled that something as unyielding as rock can give way before sheer habit, or regularity, or persistence, whatever you might call it.

Practice, whether in mathematics or in love, changes things.

Sometimes.

Ubbiri's Arrival

It was one thing to realize that the alien device in the center of the chamber was some kind of probability-altering machine. That it was the fabled actualizer hinted at in alien manuscripts, which she had always thought of as myth, was quite another thing. This knowledge she owed to Ubbiri, who was discovered lying on the floor of the chamber not three days after Birha had first opened the round door. Ubbiri was immediately incarcerated for questioning and only after several ten-days, when her language had been deciphered and encrypted into a translation device, had Birha been allowed to speak to her. They said the old woman was mad, babbling about shadow universes and tearing at her silver hair, but Birha found her remarkably sane. Ubbiri told her that she had tired of waiting for her partner, who had disappeared during a flight through a certain white-dwarf star, and when he didn't return, she had taken an old-model bristleship and dived into the heart of the star. When the ship passed through the core she defied its protestations and stepped out of it, seeking either him or death in the shadowy depths of the other reality. Instead she found herself lying on the floor of the chamber, aged beyond her years.

Over the course of four ten-days of conversation, Birha determined that the constants of nature were a hair's breadth different where Ubbiri came from, so it was very likely another universe entirely. She realized then that the machine at the center of the room did not merely change probabilities. It was an actualizer: a probability wave interference machine, and the portal inside it led to whatever branch of the kalpa-vriksh you created by changing the parameters. But the portal only opened if you'd satisfied consistency checks and if (as far as the machine could tell) the universe was stable. Somehow the pathways to other universes intersected within the cores of stars, hence Ubbiri's surprising arrival.

Not long after, Ubbiri died. She left a note stating that there were three things she was grateful for: her white dwarf star, Rudrak, and spending her last days with Birha.

A quarter-cycle after Ubbiri's death, Rudrak came for the first time into Birha's life.

A Rumination on Thirru, or Rudrak

There is a rift valley between us, a boundary that might separate two people or two universes. I've been exploring there, marveling at the tortured geometries of its sheer walls, the pits and chasms on its floor. Through them I've sometimes seen stars. So far I've avoided falling in, but who knows? One day maybe I'll hurtle through the layer between this universe and that, and find myself a meteor, a shooting star falling into the gravity well of a far planet.

What if a meteor changed its mind about falling? Would the universe allow it? Only if the rock fell under the sway of another imperative that lifted it beyond gravity's grasp. But where, in that endless sky, would it find the rift from which it had emerged? It would have to wander, searching, until the journey became an end in itself. And then, one day when the journey had changed it beyond recognition, it would find the rift and it would stand on the lip of it, wondering: Should I return?

But I am not a rock. I am a person, slowly ripening in the sun of this world, like a pear on a tree. I am not hard, I am not protected by rocky layers.

Still, I cannot soar through your sky without burning.

Theories of Probability

What the actualizer did was change probabilities. So sometimes things that were highly improbable, like walking through a wall, or tossing five thousand coins so that heads came up every time—all those things could become much more likely.

Birha thought that in some sense people had always known about the other branches of the kalpa-vriksh. So many of humankind's fantasies about the magical and the impossible were simply imaginative leaps into different regions of the cosmic tree. But to go to the place of your imagining in the flesh…that wasn't possible before the actualizer's discovery. If you adjusted the parameters, the actualizer would tweak the probability amplitudes to make your fairytale universe. Or perhaps it only opened a portal to an already existing one. What's the difference? So much for you, entropy, for heat death, for death. Make it more likely that you live from fatal cancer than an ant bite…

But you couldn't always predict how the amplitudes would work for complex systems like universes, and whether programming in coarse features you desired would give too much creative freedom to subsystems, resulting in surprises beyond imagining, and not always pleasant ones. Thus a mythology had already grown around the actualizer, detailing the possible and impossible other universes and their dangers. One made-up story related how they put in the parameters, the universal physical constants and the wavefunction behavior in space and time, and there came to be an instability in the matter of that universe that made people explode like supernovas when they touched each other with love. It was a fanciful lie, but it made a great opera.

In her idle moments, Birha wondered whether there was a curtain through which she could slip to find the place that always stays still amid the shifting cosmi, like the eye of a storm. But the foghorn trees were calling in the rain, and she was nodding over a bowl of soup, like the old woman she was. She looked at the veins standing out on the backs of her hands and the thick-jointed fingers, and thought of the body, her universe, which was not a closed system at all. Was there any system that was completely closed? Not in this universe, at least, where the most insulated of systems must interact with its environment, if only very slowly. So was our universe completely disconnected from the others, or did they bleed into each other? Exchange something? Not energy in any form we recognized, perhaps, but something more subtle, like dreams. She wanted to know what connected the universes, she wanted to step back from it all and see the kalpa-vriksh in its entirety. But she was caught in it as surely as anyone else. A participant-observer who must deduce the grand structure of the cosmic tree from within it, who must work at it while being caught in it, a worm in a twig, a fly in amber, to feel the knowing, the learning, like a new intimacy, a love.

"All matter is wavelike in some sense," she told the dog. "The actualizer generates waves, and through interference changes the probability amplitudes. The tiny bubble universe so formed then resonates with an existing universe with the same properties, and a doorway opens between them."

The dog sighed, as though this was passé, which in a way it was, and wagged his tail.

A Rumination, Dozing in the Sun

One day I dreamed I was the light falling off the edge of a leaf, nice and straight, but for the lacy diffraction at the edge. At night I flew into the clouds, to the well of stars, and became a piece of the void, a bit of dark velvet stitched on to the sky. In the afternoon I am just an old woman dozing in the sun with a yellow dog sitting beside her, wondering about stars, worried about the universes. If I could be the tap of your shoe, the glance out of the corner of your eye when you see that man or this woman, if I could be the curled lip of the snarling arboril, or a mote in the eye of a dog. What would I be, if I were to be any of this?

I am myself and yet not so. I contain multitudes and am a part of something larger; I am a cell the size of a planet, swimming in the void of the night.

When They Left

After the actualizer's discovery, it became a subject of study, a thing to explore, and ultimately an industry dealing in dreams. Streams of adventurers, dreamers, and would-be suicides, people dissatisfied with their lives, went through the actualizer to find the universe that suited them better. The actualizer became a wish-fulfillment machine, opening a path to a universe just like this one, but with your personal parameters adjusted ever so slightly, the complexity matrices shifted just so. (This was actually not possible: manipulating individual meta-world-lines was technically an unsolved problem, but tell that to the dreamers.) Among the last to go were the people who had worked with Birha, her colleagues and students. They claimed not to be deceived by the dream-merchants; their excuse was academic, but they went like so many other people into the void. The exodus left certain towns and regions thinly populated, some planets abandoned. Imagine being dissatisfied enough to want to change not towns, or planets, but entire universes! It was all Birha could do in the early days to stand there and watch the insanity until finally her dear companions were sundered from her by space, time, and whatever boundary kept one universe from another. Some people came back but they were strangers, probably from other planets in her universe. She had discovered the infinite branches of the cosmic tree, but it was not hers to claim in any way. She was the only one who wouldn't travel its endless ways.

Who knew how long her erstwhile companions would be gone, or in what shape they'd return, *if* they returned? She was too old to travel, and she liked the pleasures of small things, like tinkering with the tuning on the poeticas, designing and constructing new ones, and sipping the pale tea in the morning. She liked watching the yellow dog chase firelings. But also she was a prickly old woman, conservative as they come about universes and parameters, and she liked this one just fine, thank you. She liked the world on which she lived, with the seven-year day-cycle.

No, she wouldn't go. She was too obstinate and she disapproved of this meddling with the natural unfolding of things. Besides there was the elegance of death. The neatness of it, the way nothing's wasted after. It seemed as though only in this universe was death real. She liked to sit on the sunny doorstep and talk to the dog about it all. Dogs, she thought, don't need other universes; they are already perfect for the one in which they exist. She wondered if humans were refugees from some lost other branch of the Tree, which is why we were so restless. Always dissatisfied, going from planet to planet, galaxy to galaxy, branch to branch of the Cosmic Tree, and maybe rewriting our own life-histories of what-has-been. But we are not all like that; there have always been people who are like the dog, like Birha, perfectly belonging in the worlds of this universe.

A Rumination on Poeticas

A poetica consists of a series of suspended rods or wires under tension, mounted vertically on a frame. A sounding stick run by an ingenious mechanism of gears and a winding mechanism not unlike an old-fashioned clock brushes over the rods at a varying speed, forward and backward. A series of levers controls which rod or wire is struck. While this instrument can be designed to be played by an adept, it can also be fully automated by the mechanism, which is built to last. The enormous ones on public display recount the histories and great epic poems of the people, and are made of wood and stone and metal. Some kinds are designed to be played by the wind, but in these instruments, the sounds, and therefore the meanings, are always new, and ambiguous.

It took me years to learn the musical language of the aliens, and more years to learn to build miniature poeticas.

To sound these ruminations, I have had to interpolate and invent new syllables, new chords and phrases, in order to tell my story. There are no words in their language for some of what I feel and think, and similarly there are sounds in their tongue I'll never understand.

We call them aliens, but this is their world. We took it from them. We are the strangers, the interlopers, the aliens.

Birha's Loves

So Birha waits, watching the clouds gather over the university ramparts, walking every day to the abandoned laboratory, where her calculations give her both frustration and pleasure. Following the probability distribution of a single meta-world-line is tremendously difficult. Through the skeins and threads of possibility that arc across the simulator's three-dimensional result-space, she can discern several answers that fit the constraints. A problem with a multiplicity of answers as scattered as stars. Rudrak will be back in 0.3, or 0.87, or 4.6 cycles. Or in 0.0011, or 5.8, or 0.54 cycles. She is out of temper with herself and the meta-universe at large.

As she goes down the slope in the cloud-darkness that passes for evening, tripping a little bit because she wants to be in the stone house before the rain starts, it occurs to her that her irritation signifies love. For Thirru, for the man who temporarily attracted her, for the lesser loves of all the years after, for Rudrak, for all her long-gone colleagues and students, for the yellow dog who lives with her, for the village girl who brings the evening meal and cleans up in silence. For Timmar's rock, for the aliens and their gift to her, for the cloud forest, for that ever-giving Tree, the cosmic kalpa-vriksh, and especially her branch of it. And for death, who waits for her as she waits for Rudrak.

As she thinks this, her impatience at Rudrak's non-arrival dissipates the way the mist does when the sun comes out. In the stone house, she is out of breath; her chest hurts. There is an aroma of warm food and the yellow dog looks up from where he is lying and wags his tail lazily. She sits down to eat, dropping bits for the dog, sipping the pale tea. She thinks how it might be good for her to go out, when the time comes, into the deep forest and let her life be taken by a stinging death-vine, as is the custom among some of the natives. The vine brings a swift, painless death, wrapping the body in a shell of silken threads until all the juices are absorbed. The rest is released to become part of the rich humus of the forest floor. She feels like giving herself back to the world that gave her so much, even though she was not born here. It is comforting to think of dying in this way. The yellow dog will be happy enough with the village girl, and the old stone house will eventually be overcome by the forest. The wind will have to learn to play the poeticas, and then it will interpolate its own story with hers.

Only closed systems are lonely. And there is no such thing as a closed system.

Three days later, as the bell for morning tolls, there is a knock on the door. There is a man standing there. A stranger. No—it takes her a moment to recognize Rudrak, with his customary attitude of bewilderment and anxiety. The change is just enough to render him not quite familiar: more silver hairs, a shirt of a different fashion, in blue with an embroidered sash.

He's taller, stoops a little, and the face is different too, in a way that she can't quite explain. In that long moment of recognition, the kalpa-vriksh speaks to her. The mistake she had made in her calculations was to assume that through all the changes between universes, through space and through time, Rudrak would be Rudrak, and Birha, Birha, and Ubbiri would always remain Ubbiri. But finally she's seen it: identity is neither invariant nor closed. No wonder the answers had so much scatter in them! The truth, as always, is more subtle and more beautiful. Birha takes a deep breath of gratitude, feels her death only a few ten-days away.

"I'm looking for Ubbiri," says this almost-stranger, this new Rudrak. His accent is almost perfect. She ushers him in, and he looks around, at the pale sunlight falling on the long table with the poeticas, which are sounding softly. His look of anxiety fades for a moment, to be replaced by wonder. "This looks familiar," he says. "Have I been here before?

TEN SIGMAS

PAUL MELKO

Paul Melko's fiction has appeared in various magazines and anthologies. *Singularity's Ring,* his first novel, was released from Tor in 2008 and, that same year, a science fiction collection, *Ten Sigmas and Other Unlikelihoods,* was released from Fairwood Press. His work was nominated for the Sturgeon, Nebula, and Hugo awards in 2007. His second novel—a parallel worlds story—was *The Walls of the Universe,* and the sequel, *The Broken Universe,* came out in June.

A t first we do not recognize the face as such.

One eye is swollen shut, the flesh around it livid. The nose is crusted with blood, above the lip flecked with black-red, and the mouth taped with duct tape that does not contrast enough with her pale skin.

It does not register at first as a human face. No face should be peeking from behind the driver's seat. No face should look like that.

So at first we do not recognize it, until one of us realizes, and we all look.

For some the truck isn't even there, and we stand frozen at the sight we have seen. The street outside the bookstore is empty of anything but a pedestrian or two. There is no tractor trailer rumbling down Sandusky Street, no diesel gas engine to disturb the languid spring day.

In some worlds, the truck is there, past us, or there, coming down the road. In some it is red, in some it is blue, and in others it is black. In the one where the girl is looking out the window at us, it is metallic maroon with white script on the door that says "Earl."

There is just one world where the girl lifts her broken, gagged face and locks her one good eye on me. There is just one where Earl reaches behind him and pulls the girl from sight. In that world, Earl looks at me, his thick face and brown eyes expressionless.

The truck begins to slow, and that me disappears from our consciousness, sundered by circumstance.

No, I did not use my tremendous power for the good of mankind. I used it to steal the intellectual property of a person who exists in one world and pass it off as my own in another. I used my incredible ability to steal songs and stories and publish them as my own in a million different worlds. I did not warn police about terrorist attacks or fires or earthquakes. I don't even read the papers.

I lived in a house in a town that is sometimes called Delaware, sometimes Follett, sometimes Mingo, always in a house on the corner of Williams and Ripley. I lived there modestly, in my two-bedroom house, sometimes with a pine in front, sometimes with a dogwood, writing down songs that I hear on the radio in other worlds, telling stories that I've read somewhere else.

In the worlds where the truck has passed us, we look at the license plate on the truck, framed in silver, naked women, and wonder what to do. There is a pay phone nearby, perhaps on this corner, perhaps on that. We can call the police and say….

We saw the girl once, and that self is already gone to us. How do we know that there is a girl gagged and bound in any of these trucks? We just saw the one.

A part of us recognizes this rationalization for the cowardice it is. We have played this game before. We know that an infinite number of possibilities exist, but that our combined existence hovers around a huge multi-dimensional probability distribution. If we saw the girl in one universe, then probably she was there in an infinite number of other universes.

And safe in as many other worlds, I think.

For those of us where the truck has passed us, the majority of us step into the street to go to the bagel shop across the way. Some fraction of us turn to look for a phone, and they are broken from us, their choice shaking them loose from our collective.

I am—we are—omniscient, at least a bit. I can do a parlor trick for any friend, let another of me open the envelope and see what's inside, so we can amaze those around us. Usually we will be right. One of me can flip over the first card and the rest of me will pronounce it for what it is. Ace of Hearts, Four of Clubs, Ten of Clubs. Probably we are right for all fifty-two, at least fifty of them.

We can avoid accidents, angry people, cars, or at least most of us can. Perhaps one of us takes the hit for the rest. One of us is hit first, or sees the punch being thrown, so that the rest of us can ride the probability wave.

For some of us, the truck shifts gears, shuddering as it passes us. Earl, Bill, Tony, Irma look down at us or not, and the cab is past us. The trailer is metallic aluminum. Always.

I feel our apprehension. More of us have fallen away today than ever before. The choice to make a phone call has reduced us by a sixth. The rest of us wonder what we should do.

More of us memorize the license plate of Earl's truck, turn to find a phone, and disappear.

When we were a child, we had a kitten named "Cocoa." In every universe it had the same name. It liked to climb trees, and sometimes it couldn't get back down again. Once it crawled to the very top of the maple tree out front, and we only knew it was up there by its hysterical mewing.

Dad wouldn't climb up. "He'll figure it out, or...."

We waited down there until dusk. We knew that if we climbed the tree we would be hurt. Some of us had tried it and failed, disappearing after breaking arms, legs, wrists, even necks.

We waited, not even going in to dinner. We waited with some neighborhood kids, some there because they liked Cocoa and some there because they wanted to see a spectacle. Finally the wind picked up.

We saw one Cocoa fall through the dark green leaves, a few feet away, breaking its neck on the sidewalk. We felt a shock of sorrow, but the rest of us were dodging, our arms outstretched, and we caught the kitten as it plummets, cushioning.

"How'd you do that?" someone asked in a million universes.

I realized then that I was different.

We step back on the sidewalk, waiting for the truck to pass, waiting to get the license plate so we can call the police anonymously. The police might be able to stop Earl with a road block. They could stop him up U.S. 23 a few miles. If they believed us.

If Earl didn't kill the girl first. If she wasn't already dead.

My stomach lurched. We couldn't help thinking of the horror that the girl must have faced, must be facing.

Giving the license plate to the police wouldn't be enough.

We step into the street and wave our hands, flagging Earl down.

We once dated a woman, a beautiful woman with chestnut hair that fell to the middle of her back. We dated for several years, and finally became engaged. In one of the worlds, just one, she started to change, grew angry, then elated, then just empty. The rest of us watched in horror as she took a knife to us, just once, in one universe, while in a million others, she compassionately helped our retching self to the kitchen sink.

She didn't understand why I broke off the engagement. But then she didn't know the things I did.

Earl's cab shudders as he slams on the brakes. His CB mic slips loose and knocks the windshield. He grabs his steering wheel, his shoulders massive with exertion.

We stand there, our shopping bag dropped by the side of road, slowly waving our hands back and forth.

In a handful of worlds, the tractor trailer slams through us, and we are rattled by my death. But we know he will be caught there. For vehicular manslaughter, perhaps, and then they will find the girl. In almost all the worlds, though, Earl's semi comes to a halt a few inches from us, a few feet.

We look up over the chrome grill, past the hood ornament, a woman's head, like on a sea-going vessel of old, and into Earl's eyes.

He reaches up and lets loose with his horn. We clap our hands over our ears and, in some universes, we stumble to the sidewalk, allowing Earl to grind his truck into first and rumble away. But mostly, we stand there, not moving.

It didn't matter who was president, or who won the World Series. In sum, it was the same world for each of us, and so we existed together, on top of each other, like a stack of us, all living together within a deck of cards.

Each decision that created a subtly different universe, created another of us, another of a nearly infinite number of mes, who added just a fraction more to our intellect and understanding.

We were not a god. One of us once thought he was, and soon he was no longer with us. He couldn't have shared our secret. We weren't scared of that. Who would have believed him? And now that he was alone—for there could only be a handful of us who might have such delusions—there could be no harm to the rest of us.

We were worlds away.

Finally the horn stops and we look up, our ears benumbed, to see Earl yelling at us. We can't hear what he says, but we recognize on his lips "Mother Fucker" and "Son of a Bitch." That's fine. We need him angry. To incite him, we give him the bird.

He bends down, reaching under his seat. He slaps a metal wrench against his open palm. His door opens and he steps down. We wait where we are.

Earl is a large man, six-four, and weighing at least three hundred pounds. He has a belly, but his chest and neck are massive. Black sideburns adorn his face, or it is clearly shaven, or he has a mustache. In all worlds, his dead eyes watch us as if we are a cow and he is the butcher.

I am slight, just five-nine, one hundred and sixty pounds, but as he swings the wrench we dodge inside it as if we know where it is going to be. We do, of course, for it has shattered our skull in a hundred worlds, enough for the rest of us to anticipate the move.

He swings and we dodge again, twice more, and each time a few of us are sacrificed. We are suddenly uncomfortable at the losses. We are the consciousness of millions of mes. But every one of us that dies is a real instance, gone forever. Every death diminishes us.

We can not wait for the police now. We must save as much of ourself as we can.

We dodge again, spinning past him, sacrificing selves to dance around him as if he is a dance partner we have worked with for a thousand years. We climb the steps to the cab, slide inside, slam the door, and lock it.

I am a composite of all versions of myself. I can think in a million ways at once. Problems become picking the best choice of all choices I could ever have picked. I can not see the future or the past, but I can see the present with a billion eyes and decide the safest course, the one that keeps the most of me together.

I am a massively parallel human.

In the worlds where the sleeper is empty, we sit quietly for the police to arrive, weaving a story that they might believe while Earl glares at us from the street. These selves fade away from those where the girl is trussed in the back, tied with wire that cuts her wrists, and gagged with duct tape.

She is dead in some, her face livid with bruises and burns. In others she is alive and conscious and watches us with blue, bloodshot eyes. The cab smells of people living there too long, of sex, of blood.

In the universes where Earl has abducted and raped this young woman, he does not stand idly on the sidewalk, but rather smashes his window open with the wrench.

The second blow catches my forehead, as I have no place to dodge, and I think as my mind shudders that I am one of the sacrificed ones, one of those who has failed so that the rest of us might survive. But then I realize that it is most of us who have been hit. Only a small percentage have managed to dodge the blow. The rest of us roll to our back and kick at Earl's hand as it reaches in to unlock the cab door. His wrist rakes the broken safety glass, and he cries out, though still manages to pop the lock.

I crab backwards across the seat, flailing my legs at him. There are no options here. All of my selves are fighting for our lives or dying.

A single blow takes half of us. Another takes a third of those that are left. Soon my mind is a cloud. I am perhaps ten thousand, slow-witted. No longer omniscient.

A blow lands and I collapse against the door of the cab. I am just me. There is just one. Empty.

My body refuses to move as Earl loops a wire around my wrists and ankles. He does it perfunctorily—he wants to move, to get out of the middle of Sandusky Street—but it is enough to leave me helpless on the passenger side floor. I can see a half-eaten Big Mac and a can of Diet Coke. My face grinds against small stones and dirt.

I am alone. There is just me, and I am befuddled. My mind works like cold honey. I've failed. We all did, and now we will die like the poor girl in the back. Alone.

My vision shifts, and I see the cab from behind Earl's head, from the sleeping cab. I realize that I am seeing it from a self who has been beaten and tossed into the back. This self is dying, but I can see through his eyes, as the blood seeps out of him. For a moment our worlds are in sync.

His eyes lower and I spot the knife, a hunting knife with a serrated edge, brown with blood. It has fallen under the passenger's chair in his universe, under the chair I have my back against.

My hands are bound behind me, but I reach as far as I can under the seat. It's not far enough in my awkward position. My self's eyes lock on the knife, not far from where my fingers should be. But I have no guarantee that it's even in my own universe at all. We are no longer at the center of the curve. My choices have brought me far away from the selves now drinking coffee and eating bagels across the street from the bookstore.

Earl looks down at me, curses. He kicks me, and pushes me farther against the passenger seat. Something nicks my finger.

I reach gently around it. It is the knife.

I take moments to maneuver it so that I hold it in my palm, outstretched like the spine of a stegosaurus. I cut myself, and I feel the hilt get slippery. I palm my hand against the gritty carpet and position the knife again.

I wait for Earl to begin a right turn, then I pull my knees in, roll onto my chest, and launch myself, back first with knife extended, at Earl.

In the only universe that I exist in, the knife enters his thigh.

The truck caroms off something in the street, and I am jerked harder against Earl. He is screaming, yelling, pawing at his thigh.

His fist slams against me and I fall to the floor.

As he turns his anger on me, the truck slams hard into something, and Earl is flung against the steering wheel. He remains that way, unconscious, until the woman in the back struggles forward and leans heavily on the knife hilt in his leg, and slices until she finds a vein or artery.

I lie in Earl's blood until the police arrive. I am alone again, the self who had spotted the knife, gone.

The young woman came to see me while I mended in a hospital bed. There was an air of notoriety about me, and nurses and doctors were extremely pleasant. It was not just the events which had unfolded on the streets of their small town, but that I was the noted author of such famous songs as "Love as a Star" and "Romance Ho" and "Muskrat Love." The uncovering of Earl's exploits, including a grim laboratory in his home town of Pittsburgh, added fuel to the fire.

She seemed to have mended a bit better than I, her face now a face, her body and spirit whole again. She was stronger than I, I felt when I saw her smile. My body was healing, the cuts around my wrist and ankle, the shattered bone in my arm. But the sundering of my consciousness had left me dull, broken.

I listened to songs on the radio, other people's songs, and could not help wondering in how many worlds there had been no knife, there had been no escape. Perhaps I was the only one of us who reached the cab to survive. Perhaps I was the only one who had saved the woman.

"Thanks," she said. "Thanks for what you did."

I reached for something to say, something witty, urbane, nonchalant from my mind, but there was nothing there but me.

"Uh…you're welcome."

She smiled. "You could have been killed," she said.

I looked away. She didn't realize that I had been.

"Well, sorry for bothering you," she said quickly.

"Listen," I said, drawing her back. "I'm sorry I didn't…." I wanted to apologize for not saving more of her. For not ending the lives of more Earls. "I'm sorry I didn't save you sooner." It didn't make any sense, and I felt myself flush.

She smiled and said, "It was enough." She leaned in to kiss me.

I am disoriented as I feel her lips brush my right cheek, and also my left, and a third kiss lightly on my lips. I am looking at her in three views, a triptych slightly askew, and I manage a smile then, three smiles. And then a laugh, three laughs.

We have saved her at least once. That is enough. In one of the three universes we inhabit, a woman is singing a catchy tune on the radio. I start to write the lyrics down with my good hand, then stop. Enough of that, we three decide. There are other things to do now, other choices.

MAGIC FOR BEGINNERS

KELLY LINK

Kelly Link is the author of three collections, *Pretty Monsters, Magic for Beginners,* and *Stranger Things Happen.* Her short stories have won three Nebula awards, a Hugo, a Locus and a World Fantasy Award. She was born in Miami, Florida, and once won a free trip around the world by answering the question "Why do you want to go around the world?" ("Because you can't go through it.") Link lives in Northampton, Massachusetts, where she and her husband, Gavin J. Grant, run Small Beer Press and play ping-pong. In 1996 they started the occasional 'zine *Lady Churchill's Rosebud Wristlet.*

Fox is a television character, and she isn't dead yet. But she will be, soon. She's a character on a television show called *The Library.* You've never seen *The Library* on TV, but I bet you wish you had.

In one episode of *The Library,* a boy named Jeremy Mars, fifteen years old, sits on the roof of his house in Plantagenet, Vermont. It's eight o'clock at night, a school night, and he and his friend Elizabeth should be studying for the math quiz that their teacher, Mr. Cliff, has been hinting at all week long. Instead they've sneaked out onto the roof. It's cold. They don't know everything they should know about X, when X is the square root of Y. They don't even know Y. They ought to go in.

But there's nothing good on TV and the sky is very beautiful. They have jackets on, and up in the corners where the sky begins are patches of white in the darkness, still, where there's snow, up on the mountains. Down in the trees around the house, some animal is making a small, anxious sound: "Why cry? Why cry?"

"What's that one?" Elizabeth says, pointing at a squarish configuration of stars.

"That's The Parking Structure," Jeremy says. "And right next to that is The Big Shopping Mall and The Lesser Shopping Mall."

"And that's Orion, right? Orion the Bargain Hunter?"

Jeremy squints up. "No, Orion is over there. That's The Austrian Body-builder. That thing that's sort of wrapped around his lower leg is The Amorous Cephalopod. The Hungry, Hungry Octopus. It can't make up its mind whether it should eat him or make crazy, eight-legged love to him. You know that myth, right?"

"Of course," Elizabeth says. "Is Karl going to be pissed off that we didn't invite him over to study?"

"Karl's always pissed off about something," Jeremy says. Jeremy is resolutely resisting a notion about Elizabeth. Why are they sitting up here? Was it his idea or was it hers? Are they friends, are they just two friends sitting on the roof and talking? Or is Jeremy supposed to try to kiss her? He thinks maybe he's supposed to kiss her. If he kisses her, will they still be friends? He can't ask Karl about this. Karl doesn't believe in being helpful. Karl believes in mocking.

Jeremy doesn't even know if he wants to kiss Elizabeth. He's never thought about it until right now.

"I should go home," Elizabeth says. "There could be a new episode on right now, and we wouldn't even know."

"Someone would call and tell us," Jeremy says. "My mom would come up and yell for us." His mother is something else Jeremy doesn't want to worry about, but he does, he does.

Jeremy Mars knows a lot about the planet Mars, although he's never been there. He knows some girls, and yet he doesn't know much about them. He wishes there were books about girls, the way there are books about Mars, that you could observe the orbits and brightness of girls through telescopes without appearing to be perverted. Once Jeremy read a book about Mars out loud to Karl, except he kept replacing the word Mars with the word "girls." Karl cracked up every time.

Jeremy's mother is a librarian. His father writes books. Jeremy reads biographies. He plays trombone in a marching band. He jumps hurdles while wearing a school tracksuit. Jeremy is also passionately addicted to a television show in which a renegade librarian and magician named Fox is trying to save her world from thieves, murderers, cabalists, and pirates. Jeremy is a geek, although he's a telegenic geek. Somebody should make a TV show about him.

Jeremy's friends call him Germ, although he would rather be called Mars. His parents haven't spoken to each other in a week.

Jeremy doesn't kiss Elizabeth. The stars don't fall out of the sky, and Jeremy and Elizabeth don't fall off the roof either. They go inside and finish their homework.

Someone who Jeremy has never met, never even heard of—a woman named Cleo Baldrick—has died. Lots of people, so far, have managed to live and die without making the acquaintance of Jeremy Mars, but Cleo Baldrick has left Jeremy Mars and his mother something strange in her will: a phone booth on a state highway, some forty miles outside of Las Vegas, and a Las Vegas wedding chapel. The wedding chapel is called Hell's Bells. Jeremy isn't sure what kind of people get married there. Bikers, maybe. Supervillains, freaks, and Satanists.

Jeremy's mother wants to tell him something. It's probably something about Las Vegas and about Cleo Baldrick, who—it turns out—was his mother's great-aunt. (Jeremy never knew his mother had a great-aunt. His mother is a mysterious person.) But it may be, on the other hand, something concerning Jeremy's father. For a week and a half now, Jeremy has managed to avoid finding out what his mother is worrying about. It's easy not to find out things, if you try hard enough. There's band practice. He has overslept on weekdays in order to rule out conversations at breakfast, and at night he climbs up on the roof with his telescope to look at stars, to look at Mars. His mother is afraid of heights. She grew up in L.A.

It's clear that whatever it is she has to tell Jeremy is not something she wants to tell him. As long as he avoids being alone with her, he's safe.

But it's hard to keep your guard up at all times. Jeremy comes home from school, feeling as if he has passed the math test after all. Jeremy is an optimist. Maybe there's something good on TV. He settles down with the remote control on one of his father's pet couches: oversized and re-upholstered in an orange-juice-colored corduroy that makes it appear as if the couch has just escaped from a maximum security prison for criminally insane furniture. This couch looks as if its hobby is devouring interior decorators. Jeremy's father is a horror writer, so no one should be surprised if some of the couches he reupholsters are hideous and eldritch.

Jeremy's mother comes into the room and stands above the couch, looking down at him. "Germ?" she says. She looks absolutely miserable, which is more or less how she has looked all week.

The phone rings and Jeremy jumps up.

As soon as he hears Elizabeth's voice, he knows. She says, "Germ, it's on. Channel forty-two. I'm taping it." She hangs up.

"It's on!" Jeremy says. "Channel forty-two! Now!"

His mother has the television on by the time he sits down. Being a librarian, she has a particular fondness for *The Library*. "I should go tell your dad," she says, but instead she sits down beside Jeremy. And of course it's now all the more clear something is wrong between Jeremy's parents. But *The Library* is on and Fox is about to rescue Prince Wing.

When the episode ends, he can tell without looking over that his mother is crying. "Don't mind me," she says and wipes her nose on her sleeve. "Do you think she's really dead?"

But Jeremy can't stay around and talk.

Jeremy has wondered about what kind of television shows the characters *in* television shows watch. Television characters almost always have better haircuts, funnier friends, simpler attitudes toward sex. They marry magicians, win lotteries, have affairs with women who carry guns in their purses. Curious things happen to them on an hourly basis. Jeremy and I can forgive their haircuts. We just want to ask them about their television shows.

Just like always, it's Elizabeth who worked out in the nick of time that the new episode was on. Everyone will show up at Elizabeth's house afterward, for the postmortem. This time, it really is a postmortem. Why did Prince Wing kill Fox? How could Fox let him do it? Fox is ten times stronger.

Jeremy runs all the way, slapping his old track shoes against the sidewalk for the pleasure of the jar, for the sweetness of the sting. He likes the rough, cottony ache in his lungs. His coach says you have to be part-masochist to enjoy something like running. It's nothing to be ashamed of. It's something to exploit.

Talis opens the door. She grins at him, although he can tell that she's been crying, too. She's wearing a T-shirt that says *I'm So Goth I Shit Tiny Vampires*.

"Hey," Jeremy says. Talis nods. Talis isn't so Goth, at least not as far as Jeremy or anyone else knows. Talis just has a lot of T-shirts. She's an enigma wrapped in a mysterious T-shirt. A woman once said to Calvin Coolidge, "Mr. President, I bet my husband that I could get you to say more than two words." Coolidge said, "You lose." Jeremy can imagine Talis as Calvin Coolidge in a former life. Or maybe she was one of those dogs that don't bark. A basenji. Or a rock. A dolmen. There was an episode of *The Library*, once, with some sinister dancing dolmens in it.

Elizabeth comes up behind Talis. If Talis is unGoth, then Elizabeth is Ballerina Goth. She likes hearts and skulls and black pen-ink tattoos, pink tulle, and Hello Kitty. When the woman who invented Hello Kitty was asked why Hello Kitty was so popular, she said, "Because she has no mouth." Elizabeth's mouth is small. Her lips are chapped.

"That was the most horrible episode ever! I cried and cried," she says. "Hey, Germ, so I was telling Talis about how you inherited a gas station."

"A phone booth," Jeremy says. "In Las Vegas. This great-great-aunt died. And there's a wedding chapel, too."

"Hey! Germ!" Karl says, yelling from the living room. "Shut up and get in here! The commercial with the talking cats is on—"

"Shut it, Karl," Jeremy says. He goes in and sits on Karl's head. You have to show Karl who's boss once in a while.

Amy turns up last. She was in the next town over, buying comics. She hasn't seen the new episode and so they all shut it (except for Talis, who has not been saying anything at all) and Elizabeth puts on the tape.

In the previous episode of *The Library*, masked pirate-magicians said they would sell Prince Wing a cure for the spell that infested Faithful Margaret's hair with miniature, wicked, fire-breathing golems. (Faithful Margaret's hair keeps catching fire, but she refuses to shave it off. Her hair is the source of all her magic.)

The pirate-magicians lured Prince Wing into a trap so obvious that it seemed impossible it could really be a trap, on the one-hundred-and-fortieth floor of The Free People's World-Tree Library. The pirate-magicians used finger magic to turn Prince Wing into a porcelain teapot, put two Earl Grey tea bags into the teapot, and poured in boiling water, toasted the Eternally Postponed and Overdue Reign of the Forbidden Books, drained their tea in one gulp, belched, hurled their souvenir pirate mugs to the ground, and then shattered the teapot, which had been Prince Wing, into hundreds of pieces. Then the wicked pirate-magicians swept the pieces of both Prince Wing and collectable mugs carelessly into a wooden cigar box, buried the box in the Angela Carter Memorial Park on the seventeenth floor of The World-Tree Library, and erected a statue of George Washington above it.

So then Fox had to go looking for Prince Wing. When she finally discovered the park on the seventeenth floor of The Library, the George Washington statue stepped down off his plinth and fought her tooth and nail. Literally tooth and nail, and they'd all agreed that there was something especially nightmarish about a biting, scratching, life-sized statue of George Washington with long, pointed metal fangs that threw off sparks when he gnashed them. The statue of George Washington bit Fox's pinky finger right off, just like Gollum biting Frodo's finger off on the top of Mount Doom. But of course, once the statue tasted Fox's magical blood, it fell in love with Fox. It would be her ally from now on.

In the new episode, the actor playing Fox is a young Latina actress whom Jeremy Mars thinks he recognizes. She has been a snotty but well-intentioned fourth-floor librarian in an episode about an epidemic of food poisoning that triggered bouts of invisibility and/or levitation, and she was also a lovelorn, suicidal Bear Cult priestess in the episode where Prince Wing discovered his mother was one of the Forbidden Books.

This is one of the best things about *The Library*, the way the cast swaps parts, all except for Faithful Margaret and Prince Wing, who are only ever themselves. Faithful Margaret and Prince Wing are the love interests and the main characters, and therefore, inevitably, the most boring characters, although Amy has a crush on Prince Wing.

Fox and the dashing-but-treacherous pirate-magician Two Devils are never played by the same actor twice, although in the twenty-third episode of *The Library*, the same woman played them both. Jeremy supposes that the casting could be perpetually confusing, but instead it makes your brain catch on fire. It's magical.

You always know Fox by her costume (the too-small green T-shirt, the long, full skirts she wears to hide her tail), by her dramatic hand gestures and body language, by the soft, breathy-squeaky voice the actors use when they are Fox. Fox is funny, dangerous, bad-tempered, flirtatious, greedy, untidy, accident-prone, graceful, and has a mysterious past. In some episodes, Fox is played by male actors, but she always sounds like Fox. And she's always beautiful. Every episode you think that this Fox, surely, is the most beautiful Fox there could ever be, and yet the Fox of the next episode will be even more heartbreakingly beautiful.

On television, it's night in The Free People's World-Tree Library. All the librarians are asleep, tucked into their coffins, their scabbards, priest-holes, buttonholes, pockets, hidden cupboards, between the pages of their enchanted novels. Moonlight pours through the high, arched windows of the Library and between the aisles of shelves, into the park. Fox is on her knees, clawing at the muddy ground with her bare hands. The statue of George Washington kneels beside her, helping.

"So that's Fox, right?" Amy says. Nobody tells her to shut up. It would be pointless. Amy has a large heart and an even larger mouth. When it rains, Amy rescues worms off the sidewalk. When you get tired of having a secret, you tell Amy.

Understand: Amy isn't that much stupider than anyone else in this story. It's just that she thinks out loud.

Elizabeth's mother comes into the living room. "Hey guys," she says. "Hi, Jeremy. Did I hear something about your mother inheriting a wedding chapel?"

"Yes, ma'am," Jeremy says. "In Las Vegas."

"Las Vegas," Elizabeth's mom says. "I won three hundred bucks once in Las Vegas. Spent it on a helicopter ride over the Grand Canyon. So how many times can you guys watch the same episode in one day?" But she sits down to watch, too. "Do you think she's really dead?"

"Who's dead?" Amy says. Nobody says anything.

Jeremy isn't sure he's ready to see this episode again so soon, anyway, especially not with Amy. He goes upstairs and takes a shower. Elizabeth's family have a large and distracting selection of shampoos. They don't mind when Jeremy uses their bathroom.

Jeremy and Karl and Elizabeth have known each other since the first day of kindergarten. Amy and Talis are a year younger. The five have not always been friends, except for Jeremy and Karl, who have. Talis is, famously, a loner. She doesn't listen to music as far as anyone knows, she doesn't wear significant amounts of black, she isn't particularly good (or bad) at math or English, and she doesn't drink, debate, knit or refuse to eat meat. If she keeps a blog, she's never admitted it to anyone.

The Library made Jeremy and Karl and Talis and Elizabeth and Amy friends. No one else in school is as passionately devoted. Besides, they are all the children of former hippies, and the town is small. They all live within a few blocks of each other, in run-down Victorians with high ceilings and ranch houses with sunken living rooms. And although they have not always been friends, growing up, they've gone skinny-dipping in lakes on summer nights, and broken bones on each other's trampolines. Once, during an argument about dog names, Elizabeth, who is hot-tempered, tried to run Jeremy over with her ten-speed bicycle, and once, a year ago, Karl got drunk on green-apple schnapps at a party and tried to kiss Talis, and once, for five months in the seventh grade, Karl and Jeremy communicated only through angry e-mails written in all caps. I'm not allowed to tell you what they fought about.

Now the five are inseparable; invincible. They imagine that life will always be like this—like a television show in eternal syndication—that they will always have each other. They use the same vocabulary. They borrow each other's books and music. They share lunches, and they never say anything when Jeremy comes over and takes a shower. They all know Jeremy's father is eccentric. He's supposed to be eccentric. He's a novelist.

When Jeremy comes back downstairs, Amy is saying, "I've always thought there was something wicked about Prince Wing. He's a dork and he looks like he has bad breath. I never really liked him."

Karl says, "We don't know the whole story yet. Maybe he found out something about Fox while he was a teapot." Elizabeth's mom says, "He's under a spell. I bet you anything." They'll be talking about it all week.

Talis is in the kitchen, making a Velveeta-and-pickle sandwich.

"So what did you think?" Jeremy says. It's like having a hobby, only more pointless, trying to get Talis to talk. "Is Fox really dead?"

"Don't know," Talis says. Then she says, "I had a dream."

Jeremy waits. Talis seems to be waiting, too. She says, "About you." Then she's silent again. There is something dreamlike about the way that she makes a sandwich. As if she is really making something that isn't a sandwich at all; as if she's making something far more meaningful and mysterious. Or as if soon he will wake up and realize that there are no such things as sandwiches.

"You and Fox," Talis says. "The dream was about the two of you. She told me. To tell you. To call her. She gave me a phone number. She was in trouble. She said you were in trouble. She said *to keep in touch*."

"Weird," Jeremy says, mulling this over. He's never had a dream about *The Library*. He wonders who was playing Fox in Talis's dream. He had a dream about Talis, once, but it isn't the kind of dream that you'd ever tell anybody about. They were just sitting together, not saying anything. Even Talis's T-shirt hadn't said anything. Talis was holding his hand.

"It didn't feel like a dream," Talis says.

"So what was the phone number?" Jeremy says.

"I forgot," Talis says. "When I woke up, I forgot."

Kurt's mother works in a bank. Talis's father has a karaoke machine in his basement, and he knows all the lyrics to "Like a Virgin" and "Holiday" as well as the lyrics to all the songs from *Godspell* and *Cabaret*. Talis's mother is a licensed therapist who composes multiple-choice personality tests for women's magazines. "Discover Which Television Character You Resemble Most." Etc. Amy's parents met in a commune in Ithaca: her name was Galadriel Moon Shuyler before her parents came to their senses and had it changed legally. Everyone is sworn to secrecy about this, which is ironic, considering that this is Amy.

But Jeremy's father is Gordon Strangle Mars. He writes novels about giant spiders, giant leeches, giant moths, and once, notably, a giant carnivorous rosebush who lives in a mansion in upstate New York, and falls in love with a plucky, teenaged girl with a heart murmur. Saint Bernard-sized spiders chase his characters' cars down dark, bumpy country roads. They fight the spiders off with badminton rackets, lawn tools, and fireworks. The novels with spiders are all bestsellers.

Once a Gordon Strangle Mars fan broke into the Marses's house. The fan stole several German first editions of Gordon Strangle's novels, a hairbrush, and a used mug in which there were two ancient, dehydrated tea bags. The fan left behind a betrayed and abusive letter on a series of Post-It Notes, and the manuscript of his own novel, told from the point of view of the iceberg that sank the *Titanic*. Jeremy and his mother read the manuscript out loud to each other. It begins: "The iceberg knew it had a destiny." Jeremy's favorite bit happens when the iceberg sees the doomed ship drawing nearer, and remarks plaintively, "Oh my, does not the Captain know about my large and impenetrable bottom?"

Jeremy discovered, later, that the novel-writing fan had put Gordon Strangle Mars's used tea bags and hairbrush up for sale on eBay, where someone paid forty-two dollars and sixty-eight cents, which was not only deeply creepy, but, Jeremy still feels, somewhat cheap. But of course this is appropriate, as Jeremy's father is famously stingy and just plain weird about money.

Gordon Strangle Mars once spent eight thousand dollars on a Japanese singing toilet. Jeremy's friends love that toilet. Jeremy's mother has a painting of a woman wearing a red dress by some artist, Jeremy can never remember who. Jeremy's father gave her that painting. The woman is beautiful, and she looks right at you as if you're the painting, not her. As if *you're* beautiful. The woman has an apple in one hand and a knife in the other. When Jeremy was little, he used to dream about eating that apple. Apparently the painting is worth more than the whole house and everything else in the house, including the singing toilet. But art and toilets aside, the Marses buy most of their clothes at thrift stores.

Jeremy's father clips coupons.

On the other hand, when Jeremy was twelve and begged his parents to send him to baseball camp in Florida, his father ponied up. And on Jeremy's last birthday, his father gave him a couch reupholstered in several dozen yards of heavy-duty *Star Wars*-themed fabric. That was a good birthday.

When his writing is going well, Gordon Strangle Mars likes to wake up at 6 A.M. and go out driving. He works out new plot lines about giant spiders and keeps an eye out for abandoned couches, which he wrestles into the back of his pickup truck. Then he writes for the rest of the day. On weekends he reupholsters the thrown-away couches in remaindered, discount fabrics. A few years ago, Jeremy went through his house, counting up fourteen couches, eight love seats, and one rickety chaise lounge. That was a few years ago. Once Jeremy had a dream that his father combined his two careers and began reupholstering giant spiders.

All lights in all rooms of the Mars house are on fifteen-minute timers, in case Jeremy or his mother leave a room and forget to turn off a lamp. This has caused confusion—and sometimes panic—on the rare occasions that the Marses throw dinner parties.

Everyone thinks that writers are rich, but it seems to Jeremy that his family is only rich some of the time. Some of the time they aren't.

Whenever Gordon Mars gets stuck in a Gordon Strangle Mars novel, he worries about money. He worries that he won't, in fact, manage to finish the current novel. He worries that it will be terrible. He worries that no one will buy it and no one will read it, and that the readers who do read it will demand to be refunded the cost of the book. He's told Jeremy that he imagines these angry readers marching on the Mars house, carrying torches and crowbars.

It would be easier on Jeremy and his mother if Gordon Mars did not work at home. It's difficult to shower when you know your father is timing you, and thinking dark thoughts about the water bill, instead of concentrating on the scene in the current Gordon Strangle Mars novel, in which the giant spiders have returned to their old haunts in the trees surrounding the ninth hole of the accursed golf course, where they sullenly feast on the pulped entrail-juices of a brace of unlucky poodles and their owner.

During these periods, Jeremy showers at school, after gym, or at his friends' houses, even though it makes his mother unhappy. She says that sometimes you just need to ignore Jeremy's father. She takes especially long showers, lots of baths. She claims that baths are even nicer when you know that Jeremy's father is worried about the water bill. Jeremy's mother has a cruel streak.

What Jeremy likes about showers is the way you can stand there, surrounded by water and yet in absolutely no danger of drowning, and not think about things like whether you screwed up on the Spanish assignment, or why your mother is looking so worried. Instead you can think about things like if there's water on Mars, and whether or not Karl is shaving, and if so, who is he trying to fool, and what the statue of George Washington meant when it said to Fox, during their desperate, bloody fight, "You have a long journey ahead of you," and, "Everything depends on this." And is Fox really dead?

After she dug up the cigar box, and after George Washington helped her carefully separate out the pieces of tea mug from the pieces of teapot, after they glued back together the hundreds of pieces of porcelain, when Fox turned the ramshackle teapot back into Prince Wing, Prince Wing looked about a hundred years old, and as if maybe there were still a few pieces missing. He looked pale. When he saw Fox, he turned even paler, as if he hadn't expected her to be standing there in front of him. He picked up his leviathan sword, which Fox had been keeping safe for him—the one which faithful viewers know was carved out of the tooth of a giant, ancient sea creature that lived happily and peacefully (before Prince Wing was tricked into killing it) in the enchanted underground sea on the third floor—and skewered the statue of George Washington like a kebab, pinning it to a tree. He kicked Fox in the head, knocked her down, and tied her to a card catalog. He stuffed a handful of moss and dirt into her mouth so she couldn't say anything, and then he accused her of plotting to murder Faithful Margaret by magic. He said Fox was more deceitful than a Forbidden Book. He cut off Fox's tail and her ears and he ran her through with the poison-edged, dog-headed knife that he and Fox had stolen from his mother's secret house. Then he left Fox there, tied to the card catalog, limp and bloody, her beautiful head hanging down. He sneezed (Prince Wing is allergic to swordplay) and walked off into the stacks. The librarians crept out of their hiding places. They untied Fox and cleaned off her face. They held a mirror to her mouth, but the mirror stayed clear and unclouded.

When the librarians pulled Prince Wing's leviathan sword out of the tree, the statue of George Washington staggered over and picked up Fox in his arms. He tucked her ears and tail into the capacious pockets of his bird-shit-stained, verdigris riding coat. He carried Fox down seventeen flights of stairs, past the enchanted-and-disagreeable Sphinx on the eighth floor, past the enchanted-and-stormy underground sea on the third floor, past the even-more-enchanted checkout desk on the first floor, and through the hammered-brass doors of The Free People's World Tree Library. Nobody in *The Library*, not in one single episode, has ever gone outside. The Library is full of all the sorts of things that one usually has to go outside to enjoy: trees and lakes and grottoes and fields and mountains and precipices (and full of indoor things as well, like books, of course). Outside The Library, everything is dusty and red and alien, as if George Washington has carried Fox out of The Library and onto the surface of Mars.

"I could really go for a nice cold Euphoria right now," Jeremy says. He and Karl are walking home.

Euphoria is: *The Librarian's Tonic—When Watchfulness Is Not Enough.* There are frequently commercials for Euphoria on *The Library*. Although no one is exactly sure what Euphoria is for, whether it is alcoholic or caffeinated, what it tastes like, if it is poisonous or delightful, or even whether or not it's carbonated, everyone, including Jeremy, pines for a glass of Euphoria once in a while.

"Can I ask you a question?" Karl says.

"Why do you always say that?" Jeremy says. "What am I going to say? 'No, you can't ask me a question'?"

"What's up with you and Talis?" Karl says. "What were you talking about in the kitchen?" Jeremy sees that Karl has been Watchful.

"She had this dream about me," he says, uneasily.

"So do you like her?" Karl says. His chin looks raw. Jeremy is sure now that Karl has tried to shave. "Because, remember how I liked her first?"

"We were just talking," Jeremy says. "So did you shave? Because I didn't know you had facial hair. The idea of you shaving is pathetic, Karl. It's like voting Republican if we were old enough to vote. Or farting in Music Appreciation."

"Don't try to change the subject," Karl says. "When have you and Talis ever had a conversation before?"

"One time we talked about a Diana Wynne Jones book that she'd checked out from the library. She dropped it in the bath accidentally. She wanted to know if I could tell my mother," Jeremy says. "Once we talked about recycling."

"Shut up, Germ," Karl says. "Besides, what about Elizabeth? I thought you liked Elizabeth!"

"Who said that?" Jeremy says. Karl is glaring at him.

"Amy told me," Karl says.

"I never told Amy I liked Elizabeth," Jeremy says. So now Amy is a mind reader as well as a blabbermouth? What a terrible, deadly combination!

"No," Karl says, grudgingly. "Elizabeth told Amy that she likes you. So I just figured you liked her back."

"Elizabeth likes me?" Jeremy says.

"Apparently everybody likes you," Karl says. He sounds sorry for himself. "What is it about you? It's not like you're all that special. Your nose is funny looking and you have stupid hair."

"Thanks, Karl." Jeremy changes the subject. "Do you think Fox is really dead?" he says. "For good?" He walks faster, so that Karl has to almost-jog to keep up. Presently Jeremy is much taller than Karl, and he intends to enjoy this as long as it lasts. Knowing Karl, he'll either get tall, too, or else chop Jeremy off at the knees.

"They'll use magic," Karl says. "Or maybe it was all a dream. They'll make her alive again. I'll never forgive them if they've killed Fox. And if you like Talis, I'll never forgive you, either. And I know what you're thinking. You're thinking that I think I mean what I say, but if push came to shove, eventually I'd forgive you, and we'd be friends again, like in seventh grade. But I wouldn't, and you're wrong, and we wouldn't be. We wouldn't ever be friends again."

Jeremy doesn't say anything. Of course he likes Talis. He just hasn't realized how much he likes her, until recently. Until today. Until Karl opened his mouth. Jeremy likes Elizabeth too, but how can you compare Elizabeth and Talis? You can't. Elizabeth is Elizabeth and Talis is Talis.

"When you tried to kiss Talis, she hit you with a boa constrictor," he says. It had been Amy's boa constrictor. It had probably been an accident. Karl shouldn't have tried to kiss someone while they were holding a boa constrictor.

"Just try to remember what I just said," Karl says. "You're free to like anyone you want to. Anyone except for Talis."

The Library has been on television for two years now. It isn't a regularly scheduled program. Sometimes it's on two times in the same week, and then not on again for another couple of weeks. Often new episodes debut in the middle of the night. There is a large online community who spend hours scanning channels; sending out alarms and false alarms; fans swap theories, tapes, files; write fanfic. Elizabeth has rigged up her computer to shout "Wake up, Elizabeth! The television is on fire!" when reliable *Library* watch-sites discover a new episode.

The Library is a pirate TV show. It's shown up once or twice on most network channels, but usually it's on the kind of channels that Jeremy thinks of as ghost channels. The ones that are just static, unless you're paying for several hundred channels of cable. There are commercial breaks, but the products being advertised are like Euphoria. They never seem to be real brands, or things that you can actually buy. Often the commercials aren't even in English, or in any other identifiable language, although the jingles are catchy, nonsense or not. They get stuck in your head.

Episodes of *The Library* have no regular schedule, no credits, and sometimes not even dialogue. One episode of *The Library* takes place inside the top drawer of a card catalog, in pitch dark, and it's all in Morse code with subtitles. Nothing else. No one has ever claimed responsibility for inventing *The Library*. No one has ever interviewed one of the actors, or stumbled across a set, film crew, or script, although in one documentary-style episode, the actors filmed the crew, who all wore paper bags on their heads.

When Jeremy gets home, his father is making upside-down pizza in a casserole dish for dinner.

Meeting writers is usually disappointing at best. Writers who write sexy thrillers aren't necessarily sexy or thrilling in person. Children's book writers might look more like accountants, or axe murderers for that matter. Horror writers are very rarely scary looking, although they are frequently good cooks.

Though Gordon Strangle Mars *is* scary looking. He has long, thin fingers— currently slimy with pizza sauce—which are why he chose "Strangle" for his fake middle name. He has white-blond hair that he tugs on while he writes until it stands straight up. He has a bad habit of suddenly appearing beside you, when you haven't even realized he was in the same part of the house. His eyes are deep-set and he doesn't blink very often. Karl says that when you meet Jeremy's father, he looks at you as if he were imagining you bundled up and stuck away in some giant spider's larder. Which is probably true.

People who read books probably never bother to wonder if their favorite writers are also good parents. Why would they?

Gordon Strangle Mars is a recreational shoplifter. He has a special, complicated, and unspoken arrangement with the local bookstore, where, in exchange for autographing as many Gordon Strangle Mars novels as they can possibly sell, the store allows Jeremy's father to shoplift books without comment. Jeremy's mother shows up sooner or later and writes a check.

Jeremy's feelings about his father are complicated. His father is a cheapskate and a petty thief, and yet Jeremy likes his father. His father hardly ever loses his temper with Jeremy, he is always interested in Jeremy's life, and he gives interesting (if confusing) advice when Jeremy asks for it. For example, if Jeremy asked his father about kissing Elizabeth, his father might suggest that Jeremy not worry about giant spiders when he kisses Elizabeth. Jeremy's father's advice usually has something to do with giant spiders.

When Jeremy and Karl weren't speaking to each other, it was Jeremy's father who straightened them out. He lured Karl over, and then locked them both into his study. He didn't let them out again until they were on speaking terms.

"I thought of a great idea for your book," Jeremy says. "What if one of the spiders builds a web on a soccer field, across a goal? And what if the goalie doesn't notice until the middle of the game? Could somebody kill one of the spiders with a soccer ball, if they kicked it hard enough? Would it explode? Or even better, the spider could puncture the soccer ball with its massive fangs. That would be cool, too."

"Your mother's out in the garage," Gordon Strangle Mars says to Jeremy. "She wants to talk to you."

"Oh," Jeremy says. All of a sudden, he thinks of Fox in Talis's dream, trying to phone him. Trying to warn him. Unreasonably, he feels that it's his parents' fault that Fox is dead now, as if they have killed her. "Is it about you? Are you getting divorced?"

"I don't know," his father says. He hunches his shoulders. He makes a face. It's a face that Jeremy's father makes frequently, and yet this face is even more pitiful and guilty than usual.

"What did you do?" Jeremy says. "Did you get caught shoplifting at Wal-Mart?"

"No," his father says.

"Did you have an affair?"

"No!" his father says, again. Now he looks disgusted, either with himself or with Jeremy for asking such a horrible question. "I screwed up. Let's leave it at that."

"How's the book coming?" Jeremy says. There is something in his father's voice that makes him feel like kicking something, but there are never giant spiders around when you need them.

"I don't want to talk about that, either," his father says, looking, if possible, even more ashamed. "Go tell your mother dinner will be ready in five minutes. Maybe you and I can watch the new episode of *The Library* after dinner, if you haven't already seen it a thousand times."

"Do you know the end? Did Mom tell you that Fox is—"

"Oh jeez," his father interrupts. "They killed Fox?"

That's the problem with being a writer, Jeremy knows. Even the biggest and most startling twists are rarely twists for you. You know how every story goes.

Jeremy's mother is an orphan. Jeremy's father claims that she was raised by feral silent-film stars, and it's true, she looks like a heroine out of a Harold Lloyd movie. She has an appealingly disheveled look to her, as if someone has either just tied or untied her from a set of train tracks. She met Gordon Mars (before he added the Strangle and sold his first novel) in the food court of a mall in New Jersey, and fell in love with him before realizing that he was a writer and a recreational shoplifter. She didn't read anything he'd written until after they were married, which was a typically cunning move on Jeremy's father's part.

Jeremy's mother doesn't read horror novels. She doesn't like ghost stories or unexplained phenomena or even the kind of phenomena that require excessively technical explanations. For example: microwaves, airplanes. She doesn't like Halloween, not even Halloween candy. Jeremy's father gives her special editions of his novels, where the scary pages have been glued together.

Jeremy's mother is quiet more often than not. Her name is Alice and sometimes Jeremy thinks about how the two quietest people he knows are named Alice and Talis. But his mother and Talis are quiet in different ways. Jeremy's mother is the kind of person who seems to be keeping something hidden, something secret. Whereas Talis just *is* a secret. Jeremy's mother could easily turn out to be a secret agent. But Talis is the death ray or the key to immortality or whatever it is that secret agents have to keep secret. Hanging out with Talis is like hanging out with a teenage black hole.

Jeremy's mother is sitting on the floor of the garage, beside a large cardboard box. She has a photo album in her hands. Jeremy sits down beside her.

There are photographs of a cat on a wall, and something blurry that looks like a whale or a zeppelin or a loaf of bread. There's a photograph of a small girl sitting beside a woman. The woman wears a fur collar with a sharp little muzzle, four legs, a tail, and Jeremy feels a sudden pang. Fox is the first dead person that he's ever cared about, but she's not real. The little girl in the photograph looks utterly blank, as if someone has just hit her with a hammer. Like the person behind the camera has just said, "Smile! Your parents are dead!"

"Cleo," Jeremy's mother says, pointing to the woman. "That's Cleo. She was my mother's aunt. She lived in Los Angeles. I went to live with her when my parents died. I was four. I know I've never talked about her. I've never really known what to say about her."

Jeremy says, "Was she nice?"

His mother says, "She tried to be nice. She didn't expect to be saddled with a little girl. What an odd word. Saddled. As if she were a horse. As if somebody put me on her back and I never got off again. She liked to buy clothes for me. She liked clothes. She hadn't had a happy life. She drank a lot. She liked to go to movies in the afternoon and to séances in the evenings. She had boyfriends. Some of them were jerks. The love of her life was a small-time gangster. He died and she never married. She always said marriage was a joke and that life was a bigger joke, and it was just her bad luck that she didn't have a sense of humor. So it's strange to think that all these years she was running a wedding chapel."

Jeremy looks at his mother. She's half-smiling, half-grimacing, as if her stomach hurts. "I ran away when I was sixteen. And I never saw her again. Once she sent me a letter, care of your father's publishers. She said she'd read all his books, and that was how she found me, I guess, because he kept dedicating them to me. She said she hoped I was happy and that she thought about me. I wrote back. I sent a photograph of you. But she never wrote again. Sounds like an episode of *The Library*, doesn't it?"

Jeremy says, "Is that what you wanted to tell me? Dad said you wanted to tell me something."

"That's part of it," his mother says. "I have to go out to Las Vegas, to find out some things about this wedding chapel. Hell's Bells. I want you to come with me."

"Is that what you wanted to ask me?" Jeremy says, although he knows there's something else. His mother still has that sad half-smile on her face.

"Germ," his mother says. "You know I love your father, right?"

"Why?" Jeremy says. "What did he do?"

His mother flips through the photo album. "Look," she says. "This was when you were born." In the picture, his father holds Jeremy as if someone has just handed him an enchanted porcelain teapot. Jeremy's father grins, but he looks terrified, too. He looks like a kid. A scary, scared kid.

"He wouldn't tell me either," Jeremy says. "So it has to be pretty bad. If you're getting divorced, I think you should go ahead and tell me."

"We're not getting divorced," his mother says, "but it might be a good thing if you and I went out to Las Vegas. We could stay there for a few months while I sort out this inheritance. Take care of Cleo's estate. I'm going to talk to your teachers. I've given notice at the library. Think of it as an adventure."

She sees the look on Jeremy's face. "No, I'm sorry. That was a stupid, stupid thing to say. I know this isn't an adventure."

"I don't want to go," Jeremy says. "All my friends are here! I can't just go away and leave them. That would be terrible!" All this time, he's been preparing himself for the most terrible thing he can imagine. He's imagined a conversation with his mother, in which his mother reveals her terrible secret, and in his imagination, he's been calm and reasonable. His imaginary parents have wept and asked for his understanding. The imaginary Jeremy has understood. He has imagined himself understanding everything. But now, as his mother talks, Jeremy's heartbeat speeds up, and his lungs fill with air, as if he is running. He starts to sweat, although the floor of the garage is cold. He wishes he were sitting up on top of the roof with his telescope. There could be meteors, invisible to the naked eye, careening through the sky, hurtling toward Earth. Fox is dead. Everyone he knows is doomed. Even as he thinks this, he knows he's overreacting. But it doesn't help to know this.

"I know it's terrible," his mother says. His mother knows something about terrible.

"So why can't I stay here?" Jeremy says. "You go sort things out in Las Vegas, and I'll stay here with Dad. Why can't I stay here?"

"Because he put you in a book!" his mother says. She spits the words out. He has never heard her sound so angry. His mother never gets angry. "He put you in one of his books! I was in his office, and the manuscript was on his desk. I saw your name, and so I picked it up and started reading."

"So what?" Jeremy says. "He's put me in his books before. Like, stuff I've said. Like when I was eight and I was running a fever and told him the trees were full of dead people wearing party hats. Like when I accidentally set fire to his office."

"It isn't like that," his mother says. "It's you. It's *you*. He hasn't even changed your name. The boy in the book, he jumps hurdles and he wants to be a rocket scientist and go to Mars, and he's cute and funny and sweet and his best friend Elizabeth is in love with him and he talks like you and he looks like you and then he dies, Jeremy. He has a brain tumor and he dies. He dies. There aren't any giant spiders. There's just you, and you die."

Jeremy is silent. He imagines his father writing the scene in his book where the kid named Jeremy dies, and crying, just a little. He imagines this Jeremy kid, Jeremy the character who dies. Poor messed-up kid. Now Jeremy and Fox have something in common. They're both made-up people. They're both dead.

"Elizabeth is in love with me?" he says. Just on principle, he never believes anything that Karl says. But if it's in a book, maybe it's true.

"Oh, whoops," his mother says. "I really didn't want to say that. I'm just so angry at him. We've been married for seventeen years. I was just four years older than you when I met him, Jeremy. I was nineteen. He was only twenty. We were babies. Can you imagine that? I can put up with the singing toilet and the shoplifting and the couches and I can put up with him being so weird about money. But he killed you, Jeremy. He wrote you into a book and he killed you off. And he knows it was wrong, too. He's ashamed of himself. He didn't want me to tell you. I didn't mean to tell you."

Jeremy sits and thinks. "I still don't want to go to Las Vegas," he says to his mother. "Maybe we could send Dad there instead."

His mother says, "Not a bad idea." But he can tell she's already planning their itinerary.

In one episode of *The Library*, everyone was invisible. You couldn't see the actors: you could only see the books and the bookshelves and the study carrels on the fifth floor where the coin-operated wizards come to flirt and practice their spells. Invisible Forbidden Books were fighting invisible pirate-magicians and the pirate-magicians were fighting Fox and her friends, who were also invisible. The fight was clumsy and full of deadly accidents. You could hear them fighting. Shelves were overturned. Books were thrown. Invisible people tripped over invisible dead bodies, but you didn't find out who'd died until the next episode. Several of the characters—The Accidental Sword, Hairy Pete, and Ptolemy Krill (who, much like the Vogons in Douglas Adams's *The Hitchhiker's Guide to the Galaxy*, wrote poetry so bad it killed anyone who read it)—disappeared for good, and nobody is sure whether they're dead or not.

In another episode, Fox stole a magical drug from The Norns, a prophetic girl band who headline at a cabaret on the mezzanine of The Free People's World-Tree Library. She accidentally injected it, became pregnant, and gave birth to a bunch of snakes who led her to the exact shelf where renegade librarians had misshelved an ancient and terrible book of magic which had never been translated, until Fox asked the snakes for help. The snakes writhed and curled on the ground, spelling out words, letter by letter, with their bodies. As they translated the book for Fox, they hissed and steamed. They became fiery lines on the ground, and then they burnt away entirely. Fox cried. That's the only time anyone has ever seen Fox cry, ever. She isn't like Prince Wing. Prince Wing is a crybaby.

The thing about *The Library* is that characters don't come back when they die. It's as if death is for real. So maybe Fox really is dead and she really isn't coming back. There are a couple of ghosts who hang around The Library looking for blood libations, but they've always been ghosts, all the way back to the beginning of the show. There aren't any evil twins or vampires, either. Although someday, hopefully, there will be evil twins. Who doesn't love evil twins?

"Mom told me about how you wrote about me," Jeremy says. His mother is still in the garage. He feels like a tennis ball in a game where the tennis players love him very, very much, even while they lob and smash and send him back and forth, back and forth.

His father says, "She said she wasn't going to tell you, but I guess I'm glad she did. I'm sorry, Germ. Are you hungry?"

"She's going out to Las Vegas next week. She wants me to go with her," Jeremy says.

"I know," his father says, still holding out a bowl of upside-down pizza. "Try not to worry about all of this, if you can. Think of it as an adventure."

"Mom says that's a stupid thing to say. Are you going to let me read the book with me in it?" Jeremy says.

"No," his father says, looking straight at Jeremy. "I burned it."

"Really?" Jeremy says. "Did you set fire to your computer too?"

"Well, no," his father says. "But you can't read it. It wasn't any good, anyway. Want to watch *The Library* with me? And will you eat some damn pizza, please? I may be a lousy father, but I'm a good cook. And if you love me, you'll eat the damn pizza and be grateful."

So they go sit on the orange couch and Jeremy eats pizza and watches *The Library* for the second-and-a-half time with his father. The lights on the timer in the living room go off, and Prince Wing kills Fox again. And then Jeremy goes to bed. His father goes away to write or to burn stuff. Whatever. His mother is still out in the garage.

On Jeremy's desk is a scrap of paper with a phone number on it. If he wanted to, he could call his phone booth. When he dials the number, it rings for a long time. Jeremy sits on his bed in the dark and listens to it ringing and ringing. When someone picks it up, he almost hangs up. Someone doesn't say anything, so Jeremy says, "Hello? Hello?"

Someone breathes into the phone on the other end of the line. Someone says in a soft, musical, squeaky voice, "Can't talk now, kid. Call back later." Then someone hangs up.

Jeremy dreams that he's sitting beside Fox on a sofa that his father has re-upholstered in spider silk. His father has been stealing spider webs from the giant-spider superstores. From his own books. Is that shoplifting or is it self-plagiarism? The sofa is soft and gray and a little bit sticky. Fox sits on either side of him. The right-hand-side Fox is being played by Talis. Elizabeth plays the Fox on his left. Both Foxes look at him with enormous compassion.

"Are you dead?" Jeremy says.

"Are you?" the Fox who is being played by Elizabeth says, in that unmistakable Fox voice which, Jeremy's father once said, sounds like a sexy and demented helium balloon. It makes Jeremy's brain hurt, to hear Fox's voice coming out of Elizabeth's mouth.

The Fox who looks like Talis doesn't say anything at all. The writing on her T-shirt is so small and so foreign that Jeremy can't read it without feeling as if he's staring at Fox-Talis's breasts. It's probably something he needs to know, but he'll never be able to read it. He's too polite, and besides he's terrible at foreign languages.

"Hey look," Jeremy says. "We're on TV!" There he is on television, sitting between two Foxes on a sticky gray couch in a field of red poppies. "Are we in Las Vegas?"

"We're not in Kansas," Fox-Elizabeth says. "There's something I need you to do for me."

"What's that?" Jeremy says.

"If I tell you in the dream," Fox-Elizabeth says, "you won't remember. You have to remember to call me when you're awake. Keep on calling until you get me."

"How will I remember to call you," Jeremy says, "if I don't remember what you tell me in this dream? Why do you need me to help you? Why is Talis here? What does her T-shirt say? Why are you both Fox? Is this Mars?"

Fox-Talis goes on watching TV. Fox-Elizabeth opens her kind and beautiful un-Hello-Kitty-like mouth again. She tells Jeremy the whole story. She explains everything. She translates Fox-Talis's T-shirt, which turns out to explain everything about Talis that Jeremy has ever wondered about. It answers every single question that Jeremy has ever had about girls. And then Jeremy wakes up—

It's dark. Jeremy flips on the light. The dream is moving away from him. There was something about Mars. Elizabeth was asking who he thought was prettier, Talis or Elizabeth. They were laughing. They both had pointy fox ears. They wanted him to do something. There was a telephone number he was supposed to call. There was something he was supposed to do.

In two weeks, on the fifteenth of April, Jeremy and his mother will get in her van and start driving out to Las Vegas. Every morning before school, Jeremy takes long showers and his father doesn't say anything at all. One day it's as if nothing is wrong between his parents. The next day they won't even look at each other. Jeremy's father won't come out of his study. And then the day after that, Jeremy comes home and finds his mother sitting on his father's lap. They're smiling as if they know something stupid and secret. They don't even notice Jeremy when he walks through the room. Even this is preferable, though, to the way they behave when they do notice him. They act guilty and strange and as if they are about to ruin his life. Gordon Mars makes pancakes every morning, and Jeremy's favorite dinner, macaroni and cheese, every night. Jeremy's mother plans out an itinerary for their trip. They will be stopping at libraries across the country, because his mother loves libraries. But she's also bought a new two-man tent and two sleeping bags and a portable stove, so that they can camp, if Jeremy wants to camp. Even though Jeremy's mother hates the outdoors.

Right after she does this, Gordon Mars spends all weekend in the garage. He won't let either of them see what he's doing, and when he does let them in, it turns out that he's removed the seating in the back of the van and bolted down two of his couches, one on each side, both upholstered in electric-blue fake fur.

They have to climb in through the cargo door at the back because one of the couches is blocking the sliding door. Jeremy's father says, looking very pleased with himself, "So now you don't have to camp outside, unless you want to. You can sleep inside. There's space underneath for suitcases. The sofas even have seat belts."

Over the sofas, Jeremy's father has rigged up small wooden shelves that fold down on chains from the walls of the van and become table tops. There's a travel-sized disco ball dangling from the ceiling, and a wooden panel—with Velcro straps and a black, quilted pad—behind the driver's seat, where Jeremy's father explains they can hang up the painting of the woman with the apple and the knife.

The van looks like something out of an episode of *The Library*. Jeremy's mother bursts into tears. She runs back inside the house. Jeremy's father says, helplessly, "I just wanted to make her laugh."

Jeremy wants to say, "I hate both of you." But he doesn't say it, and he doesn't. It would be easier if he did.

When Jeremy told Karl about Las Vegas, Karl punched him in the stomach. Then he said, "Have you told Talis?"

Jeremy said, "You're supposed to be nice to me! You're supposed to tell me not to go and that this sucks and you're not supposed to punch me. Why did you punch me? Is Talis all you ever think about?"

"Kind of," Karl said. "Most of the time. Sorry, Germ, of course I wish you weren't going and yeah, it also pisses me off. We're supposed to be best friends, but you do stuff all the time and I never get to. I've never driven across the country or been to Las Vegas, even though I'd really, really like to. I can't feel sorry for you when I bet you anything that while you're there, you'll sneak into some casino and play slot machines and win like a million bucks. You should feel sorry for me. I'm the one that has to stay here. Can I borrow your dirt bike while you're gone?"

"Sure," Jeremy said.

"How about your telescope?" Karl said.

"I'm taking it with me," Jeremy said.

"Fine. You have to call me every day," Karl said. "You have to e-mail. You have to tell me about Las Vegas show girls. I want to know how tall they really are. Whose phone number is this?"

Karl was holding the scrap of paper with the number of Jeremy's phone booth.

"Mine," Jeremy said. "That's my phone booth. The one I inherited."

"Have you called it?" Karl said.

"No," Jeremy said. He'd called the phone booth a few times. But it wasn't a game. Karl would think it was a game.

"Cool," Karl said and he went ahead and dialed the number. "Hello?" Karl said, "I'd like to speak to the person in charge of Jeremy's life. This is Jeremy's best friend Karl."

"Not funny," Jeremy said.

"My life is boring," Karl said, into the phone. "I've never inherited anything. This girl I like won't talk to me. So is someone there? Does anybody want to talk to me? Does anyone want to talk to my friend, the Lord of the Phone Booth? Jeremy, they're demanding that you liberate the phone booth from yourself."

"Still not funny," Jeremy said and Karl hung up the phone.

Jeremy told Elizabeth. They were up on the roof of Jeremy's house and he told her the whole thing. Not just the part about Las Vegas, but also the part about his father and how he put Jeremy in a book with no giant spiders in it.

"Have you read it?" Elizabeth said.

"No," Jeremy said. "He won't let me. Don't tell Karl. All I told him is that my mom and I have to go out for a few months to check out the wedding chapel."

"I won't tell Karl," Elizabeth said. She leaned forward and kissed Jeremy and then she wasn't kissing him. It was all very fast and surprising, but they didn't fall off the roof. Nobody falls off the roof in this story. "Talis likes you," Elizabeth said. "That's what Amy says. Maybe you like her back. I don't know. But I thought I should go ahead and kiss you now. Just in case I don't get to kiss you again."

"You can kiss me again," Jeremy said. "Talis probably doesn't like me."

"No," Elizabeth said. "I mean, let's not. I want to stay friends and it's hard enough to be friends, Germ. Look at you and Karl."

"I would never kiss Karl," Jeremy said.

"Funny, Germ. We should have a surprise party for you before you go," Elizabeth said.

"It won't be a surprise party now," Jeremy said. Maybe kissing him once was enough.

"Well, once I tell Amy it can't really be a surprise party," Elizabeth said. "She would explode into a million pieces and all the little pieces would start yelling, 'Guess what? Guess what? We're having a surprise party for you, Jeremy!' But just because I'm letting you in on the surprise doesn't mean there won't be surprises."

"I don't actually like surprises," Jeremy said.

"Who does?" Elizabeth said. "Only the people who do the surprising. Can we have the party at your house? I think it should be like Halloween, and it always feels like Halloween here. We could all show up in costumes and watch lots of old episodes of *The Library* and eat ice cream."

"Sure," Jeremy said. And then: "This is terrible! What if there's a new episode of *The Library* while I'm gone? Who am I going to watch it with?"

And he'd said the perfect thing. Elizabeth felt so bad about Jeremy having to watch *The Library* all by himself that she kissed him again.

There has never been a giant spider in any episode of *The Library*, although once Fox got really small and Ptolemy Krill carried her around in his pocket. She had to rip up one of Krill's handkerchiefs and blindfold herself, just in case she accidentally read a draft of Krill's terrible poetry. And then it turned out that, as well as the poetry, Krill had also stashed a rare, horned Anubis earwig in his pocket which hadn't been properly preserved. Ptolemy Krill, it turned out, was careless with his kill jar. The earwig almost ate Fox, but instead it became her friend. It still sends her Christmas cards.

These are the two most important things that Jeremy and his friends have in common: a geographical location, and love of a television show about a library. Jeremy turns on the television as soon as he comes home from school. He flips through the channels, watching reruns of *Star Trek* and *Law & Order*. If there's a new episode of *The Library* before he and his mother leave for Las Vegas, then everything will be fine. Everything will work out. His mother says, "You watch too much television, Jeremy." But he goes on flipping through channels. Then he goes up to his room and makes phone calls.

"The new episode needs to be soon, because we're getting ready to leave. Tonight would be good. You'd tell me if there was going to be a new episode tonight, right?"

Silence.

"Can I take that as a yes? It would be easier if I had a brother," Jeremy tells his telephone booth. "Hello? Are you there? Or a sister. I'm tired of being good all the time. If I had a sibling, then we could take turns being good. If I had an older brother, I might be better at being bad, better at being angry. Karl is really good at being angry. He learned how from his brothers. I wouldn't want brothers like Karl's brothers, of course, but it sucks having to figure out everything all by myself. And the more normal I try to be, the more my parents think that I'm acting out. They think it's a phase that I'll grow out of. They think it isn't normal to be normal. Because there's no such thing as normal.

"And this whole book thing. The whole shoplifting thing, how my dad steals things, it figures that he went and stole my life. It isn't just me being melodramatic, to say that. That's exactly what he did! Did I tell you that once he stole a ferret from a pet store because he felt bad for it, and then he let it loose in our house and it turned out that it was pregnant? There was this woman who came to interview Dad and she sat down on one of the—"

Someone knocks on his bedroom door. "Jeremy," his mother says. "Is Karl here? Am I interrupting?"

"No," Jeremy says, and hangs up the phone. He's gotten into the habit of calling his phone booth every day. When he calls, it rings and rings and then it stops ringing, as if someone has picked up. There's just silence on the other end, no squeaky pretend-Fox voice, but it's a peaceful, interested silence. Jeremy complains about all the things there are to complain about, and the silent person on the other end listens and listens. Maybe it is Fox standing there in his phone booth and listening patiently. He wonders what incarnation of Fox is listening. One thing about Fox: she's never sorry for herself. She's always too busy. If it were really Fox, she'd hang up on him.

Jeremy opens his door. "I was on the phone," he says. His mother comes in and sits down on his bed. She's wearing one of his father's old flannel shirts. "So have you packed?"

Jeremy shrugs. "I guess," he says. "Why did you cry when you saw what Dad did to the van? Don't you like it?"

"It's that damn painting," his mother says. "It was the first nice thing he ever gave me. We should have spent the money on health insurance and a new roof and groceries and instead he bought a painting. So I got angry. I left him. I took the painting and I moved into a hotel and I stayed there for a few days. I was going to sell the painting, but instead I fell in love with it, so I came home and apologized for running away. I got pregnant with you and I used to get hungry and dream that someone was going to give me a beautiful apple, like the one she's holding. When I told your father, he said he didn't trust her, that she was holding out the apple like that as a trick and if you went to take it from her, she'd stab you with the peeling knife. He says that she's a tough old broad and she'll take care of us while we're on the road."

"Do we really have to go?" Jeremy says. "If we go to Las Vegas I might get into trouble. I might start using drugs or gambling or something."

"Oh, Germ. You try so hard to be a good kid," his mother says. "You try so hard to be normal. Sometimes I'd like to be normal, too. Maybe Vegas will be good for us. Are these the books that you're bringing?"

Jeremy shrugs. "Not all of them. I can't decide which ones I should take and which ones I can leave. It feels like whatever I leave behind, I'm leaving behind for good."

"That's silly," his mother says. "We're coming back. I promise. Your father and I will work things out. If you leave something behind that you need, he can mail it to you. Do you think there are slot machines in the libraries in Las Vegas? I talked to a woman at the Hell's Bells chapel and there's something called The Arts and Lovecraft Library where they keep Cleo's special collection of horror novels and gothic romances and fake copies of *The Necronomicon*. You go in and out through a secret, swinging-bookcase door. People get married in it. There's a Dr. Frankenstein's LoveLab, the Masque of the Red Death Ballroom, and also something just called The Crypt. Oh yeah, and there's also The Vampire's Patio and The Black Lagoon Grotto, where you can get married by moonlight."

"You hate all this stuff," Jeremy says.

"It's not my cup of tea," his mother says. "When does everyone show up tonight?"

"Around eight," Jeremy says. "Are you going to get dressed up?"

"I don't have to dress up," his mother says. "I'm a librarian, remember?"

Jeremy's father's office is above the garage. In theory, no one is meant to interrupt him while he's working, but in practice Jeremy's father loves nothing better than to be interrupted, as long as the person who interrupts brings him something to eat. When Jeremy and his mother are gone, who will bring Jeremy's father food? Jeremy hardens his heart.

The floor is covered with books and bolts and samples of upholstering fabrics. Jeremy's father is lying facedown on the floor with his feet propped up on a bolt of fabric, which means that he is thinking and also that his back hurts. He claims to think best when he is on the verge of falling asleep.

"I brought you a bowl of Froot Loops," Jeremy says.

His father rolls over and looks up. "Thanks," he says. "What time is it? Is everyone here? Is that your costume? Is that my tuxedo jacket?"

"It's five-ish. Nobody's here yet. Do you like it?" Jeremy says. He's dressed as a Forbidden Book. His father's jacket is too big, but he still feels very elegant. Very sinister. His mother lent him the lipstick and the feathers and the platform heels.

"It's interesting," his father allows. "And a little frightening."

Jeremy feels obscurely pleased, even though he knows that his father is more amused than frightened. "Everyone else will probably come as Fox or Prince Wing. Except for Karl. He's coming as Ptolemy Krill. He even wrote some really bad poetry. I wanted to ask you something, before we leave tomorrow."

"Shoot," his father says.

"Did you really get rid of the novel with me in it?"

"No," his father says. "It felt unlucky. Unlucky to keep it, unlucky not to keep it. I don't know what to do with it."

Jeremy says, "I'm glad you didn't get rid of it."

"It's not any good, you know," his father says. "Which makes all this even worse. At first it was because I was bored with giant spiders. It was going to be something funny to show you. But then I wrote that you had a brain tumor and it wasn't funny anymore. I figured I could save you—I'm the author, after all—but you got sicker and sicker. You were going through a rebellious phase. You were sneaking out of the house a lot and you hit your mother. You were a real jerk. But it turned out you had a brain tumor and that was making you behave strangely."

"Can I ask another question?" Jeremy says. "You know how you like to steal things? You know how you're really, really good at it?"

"Yeah," says his father.

"Could you not steal things for a while, if I asked you to?" Jeremy says. "Mom isn't going to be around to pay for the books and stuff that you steal. I don't want you to end up in jail because we went to Las Vegas."

His father closes his eyes as if he hopes Jeremy will forget that he asked a question, and go away.

Jeremy says nothing.

"All right," his father says finally. "I won't shoplift anything until you get home again."

Jeremy's mother runs around taking photos of everyone. Talis and Elizabeth have both showed up as Fox, although Talis is dead Fox. She carries her fake fur ears and tail around in a little see-through plastic purse and she also has a sword, which she leaves in the umbrella stand in the kitchen. Jeremy and Talis haven't talked much since she had a dream about him and since he told her that he's going to Las Vegas. She didn't say anything about that. Which is perfectly normal for Talis.

Karl makes an excellent Ptolemy Krill. Jeremy's Forbidden Book disguise is admired.

Amy's Faithful Margaret costume is almost as good as anything Faithful Margaret wears on TV. There are even special effects: Amy has rigged up her hair with red ribbons and wire and spray color and egg whites so that it looks as if it's on fire, and there are tiny papier-mâché golems in it, making horrible faces. She dances a polka with Jeremy's father. Faithful Margaret is mad for polka dancing.

No one has dressed up as Prince Wing.

They watch the episode with the possessed chicken and they watch the episode with the Salt Wife and they watch the episode where Prince Wing and Faithful Margaret fall under a spell and swap bodies and have sex for the first time. They watch the episode where Fox saves Prince Wing's life for the first time.

Jeremy's father makes chocolate/mango/espresso milk shakes for everyone. None of Jeremy's friends, except for Elizabeth, know about the novel. Everyone thinks Jeremy and his mother are just having an adventure. Everyone thinks Jeremy will be back at the end of the summer.

"I wonder how they find the actors," Elizabeth says. "They aren't real actors. They must be regular people. But you'd think that somewhere there would be someone who knows them. That somebody online would say, hey, that's my sister! Or that's the kid I went to school with who threw up in P.E. You know, sometimes someone says something like that or sometimes someone pretends that they know something about *The Library*, but it always turns out to be a hoax. Just somebody wanting to be somebody."

"What about the guy who's writing it?" Karl says.

Talis says, "Who says it's a guy?" and Amy says, "Yeah, Karl, why do you always assume it's a guy writing it?"

"Maybe nobody's writing it," Elizabeth says. "Maybe it's magic or it's broadcast from outer space. Maybe it's real. Wouldn't that be cool?"

"No," Jeremy says. "Because then Fox would really be dead. That would suck."

"I don't care," Elizabeth says. "I wish it were real, anyway. Maybe it all really happened somewhere, like King Arthur or Robin Hood, and this is just one version of how it happened. Like a magical After School Special."

"Even if it isn't real," Amy says, "parts of it could be real. Like maybe The World-Tree Library is real. Or maybe *The Library* is made up, but Fox is based on somebody that the writer knew. Writers do that all the time, right? Jeremy, I think your dad should write a book about me. I could be eaten by giant spiders. Or have sex with giant spiders and have spider babies. I think that would be so great."

So Amy does have psychic abilities, after all, although hopefully she will never know this. When Jeremy tests his own potential psychic abilities, he can almost sense his father, hovering somewhere just outside the living room, listening to this conversation and maybe even taking notes. Which is what writers do. But Jeremy isn't really psychic. It's just that lurking and hovering and appearing suddenly when you weren't expecting him are what his father does, just like shoplifting and cooking. Jeremy prays to all the dark gods that he never receives the gift of knowing what people are thinking. It's a dark road and it ends up with you trapped on late night television in front of an invisible audience of depressed insomniacs wearing hats made out of tinfoil and they all want to pay you nine-ninety-nine per minute to hear you describe in minute, terrible detail what their deceased cat is thinking about, right now. What kind of future is that? He wants to go to Mars. And when will Elizabeth kiss him again? You can't just kiss someone twice and then never kiss them again. He tries not to think about Elizabeth and kissing, just in case Amy reads his mind. He realizes that he's been staring at Talis's breasts, glares instead at Elizabeth, who is watching TV. Meanwhile, Karl is glaring at him.

On television, Fox is dancing in the Invisible Nightclub with Faithful Margaret, whose hair is about to catch fire again. The Norns are playing their screechy cover of "Come On, Eileen." The Norns only know two songs: "Come On, Eileen," and "Everybody Wants to Rule the World." They don't play real instruments. They play squeaky dog toys and also a bathtub, which is enchanted, although nobody knows who by, or why, or what it was enchanted for.

"If you had to chose one," Jeremy says, "invisibility or the ability to fly, which would you choose?"

Everybody looks at him. "Only perverts would want to be invisible," Elizabeth says.

"You'd have to be naked if you were invisible," Karl says. "Because otherwise people would see your clothes."

"If you could fly, you'd have to wear thermal underwear because it's cold up there. So it just depends on whether you like to wear long underwear or no underwear at all," Amy says.

It's the kind of conversation that they have all the time. It makes Jeremy feel homesick even though he hasn't left yet.

"Maybe I'll go make brownies," Jeremy says. "Elizabeth, do you want to help me make brownies?"

"Shhh," Elizabeth says. "This is a good part."

On television, Fox and Faithful Margaret are making out. The Faithful part is kind of a joke.

Jeremy's parents go to bed at one. By three, Amy and Elizabeth are passed out on the couch and Karl has gone upstairs to check his e-mail on Jeremy's iBook. On TV, wolves are roaming the tundra of The Free People's World-Tree Library's fortieth floor. Snow is falling heavily and librarians are burning books to keep warm, but only the most dull and improving works of literature.

Jeremy isn't sure where Talis has gone, so he goes to look for her. She hasn't gone far. She's on the landing, looking at the space on the wall where Alice Mars's painting should be hanging. Talis is carrying her sword with her, and her little plastic purse. In the bathroom off the landing, the singing toilet is still singing away in German. "We're taking the painting with us," Jeremy says. "My dad insisted, just in case he accidentally burns down the house while we're gone. Do you want to go see it? I was going to show everybody, but everybody's asleep right now."

"Sure," Talis says.

So Jeremy gets a flashlight and takes her out to the garage and shows her the van. She climbs right inside and sits down on one of the blue-fur couches. She looks around and he wonders what she's thinking. He wonders if the toilet song is stuck in her head.

"My dad did all of this," Jeremy says. He turns on the flashlight and shines it on the disco ball. Light spatters off in anxious, slippery orbits. Jeremy shows Talis how his father has hung up the painting. It looks truly wrong in the van, as if someone demented put it there. Especially with the light reflecting off the disco ball. The woman in the painting looks confused and embarrassed as if Jeremy's father has accidentally canceled out her protective powers. Maybe the disco ball is her Kryptonite.

"So remember how you had a dream about me?" Jeremy says. Talis nods. "I think I had a dream about you, that you were Fox."

Talis opens up her arms, encompassing her costume, her sword, her plastic purse with poor Fox's ears and tail inside.

"There was something you wanted me to do," Jeremy says. "I was supposed to save you, somehow."

Talis just looks at him.

"How come you never talk?" Jeremy says. All of this is irritating. How he used to feel normal around Elizabeth, like friends, and now everything is peculiar and uncomfortable. How he used to enjoy feeling uncomfortable around Talis, and now, suddenly, he doesn't. This must be what sex is about. Stop thinking about sex, he thinks.

Talis opens her mouth and closes it again. Then she says, "I don't know. Amy talks so much. You all talk a lot. Somebody has to be the person who doesn't. The person who listens."

"Oh," Jeremy says. "I thought maybe you had a tragic secret. Like maybe you used to stutter." Except secrets can't have secrets, they just *are*.

"Nope," Talis says. "It's like being invisible, you know. Not talking. I like it."

"But you're not invisible," Jeremy says. "Not to me. Not to Karl. Karl really likes you. Did you hit him with a boa constrictor on purpose?"

But Talis says, "I wish you weren't leaving." The disco ball spins and spins. It makes Jeremy feel kind of carsick and also as if he has sparkly, disco leprosy. He doesn't say anything back to Talis, just to see how it feels. Except maybe that's rude. Or maybe it's rude the way everybody always talks and doesn't leave any space for Talis to say anything.

"At least you get to miss school," Talis says, at last.

"Yeah," he says. He leaves another space, but Talis doesn't say anything this time. "We're going to stop at all these museums and things on the way across the country. I'm supposed to keep a blog for school and describe stuff in it. I'm going to make a lot of stuff up. So it will be like Creative Writing and not so much like homework."

"You should make a list of all the towns with weird names you drive through," Talis says. "Town of Horseheads. That's a real place."

"Plantagenet," Jeremy says. "That's a real place too. I had something really weird to tell you."

Talis waits, like she always does.

Jeremy says, "I called my phone booth, the one that I inherited, and someone answered. She sounded just like Fox when she talked. They told me to call back later. So I've called a few more times, but I don't ever get her."

"Fox isn't a real person," Talis says. "*The Library* is just TV." But she sounds uncertain. That's the thing about *The Library*. Nobody knows for sure. Everyone who watches it wishes and hopes that it's not just acting. That it's magic, real magic.

"I know," Jeremy says.

"I wish Fox was real," Fox-Talis says.

They've been sitting in the van for a long time. If Karl looks for them and can't find them, he's going to think that they've been making out. He'll kill Jeremy. Once Karl tried to strangle another kid for accidentally peeing on his shoes. Jeremy might as well kiss Talis. So he does, even though she's still holding her sword. She doesn't hit him with it. It's dark and he has his eyes closed and he can almost imagine that he's kissing Elizabeth.

Karl has fallen asleep on Jeremy's bed. Talis is downstairs, fast-forwarding through the episode where some librarians drink too much Euphoria and decide to abolish Story Hour. Not just the practice of having a Story Hour, but the whole Hour. Amy and Elizabeth are still sacked out on the couch. It's weird to watch Amy sleep. She doesn't talk in her sleep.

Karl is snoring. Jeremy could go up on the roof and look at stars, except he's already packed up his telescope. He could try to wake up Elizabeth and they could go up on the roof, but Talis is down there. He and Talis could go sit on the roof, but he doesn't want to kiss Talis on the roof. He makes a solemn oath to only ever kiss Elizabeth on the roof.

He picks up his phone. Maybe he can call his phone booth and complain just a little and not wake Karl up. His dad is going to freak out about the phone bill. All these calls to Nevada. It's 4 A.M. Jeremy's plan is not to go to sleep at all. His friends are lame.

The phone rings and rings and rings and then someone picks up. Jeremy recognizes the silence on the other end. "Everybody came over and fell asleep," he whispers. "That's why I'm whispering. I don't even think they care that I'm leaving. And my feet hurt. Remember how I was going to dress up as a Forbidden Book? Platform shoes aren't comfortable. Karl thinks I did it on purpose, to be even taller than him than usual. And I forgot that I was wearing lipstick and I kissed Talis and got lipstick all over her face, so it's a good thing everyone was asleep because otherwise someone would have seen. And my dad says that he won't shoplift at all while Mom and I are gone, but you can't trust him. And that fake-fur upholstery sheds like—"

"Jeremy," that strangely familiar, sweet-and-rusty door-hinge voice says softly. "Shut up, Jeremy. I need your help."

"Wow!" Jeremy says, not in a whisper. "Wow, wow, wow! Is this Fox? Are you really Fox? Is this a joke? Are you real? Are you dead? What are you doing in my phone booth?"

"You know who I am," Fox says, and Jeremy knows with all his heart that it's really Fox. "I need you to do something for me."

"What?" Jeremy says. Karl, on the bed, laughs in his sleep as if the idea of Jeremy doing something is funny to him. "What could I do?"

"I need you to steal three books," Fox says. "From a library in a place called Iowa."

"I know Iowa," Jeremy says. "I mean, I've never been there, but it's a real place. I could go there."

"I'm going to tell you the books you need to steal," Fox says. "Author, title, and the jewelly festival number—"

"Dewey Decimal," Jeremy says. "It's actually called the Dewey Decimal number in real libraries."

"Real," Fox says, sounding amused. "You need to write this all down and also how to get to the library. You need to steal the three books and bring them to me. It's very important."

"Is it dangerous?" Jeremy says. "Are the Forbidden Books up to something? Are the Forbidden Books real, too? What if I get caught stealing?"

"It's not dangerous to you," Fox says. "Just don't get caught. Remember the episode of *The Library* when I was the little old lady with the beehive and I stole the Bishop of Tweedle's false teeth while he was reading the banns for the wedding of Faithful Margaret and Sir Petronella the Younger? Remember how he didn't even notice?"

"I've never seen that episode," Jeremy says, although as far as he knows he's never missed a single episode of *The Library*. He's never even heard of Sir Petronella.

"Oh," Fox says. "Maybe that's a flashback in a later episode or something. That's a great episode. We're depending on you, Jeremy. You have got to steal these books. They contain dreadful secrets. I can't say the titles out loud. I'm going to spell them instead."

So Jeremy gets a pad of paper and Fox spells out the titles of each book twice. (They aren't titles that can be written down here. It's safer not to even think about some books.) "Can I ask you something?" Jeremy says. "Can I tell anybody about this? Not Amy. But could I tell Karl or Elizabeth? Or Talis? Can I tell my mom? If I woke up Karl right now, would you talk to him for a minute?"

"I don't have a lot of time," Fox says. "I have to go now. Please don't tell anyone, Jeremy. I'm sorry."

"Is it the Forbidden Books?" Jeremy says again. What would Fox think if she saw the costume he's still wearing, all except for the platform heels? "Do you think I shouldn't trust my friends? But I've known them my whole life!"

Fox makes a noise, a kind of pained whuff.

"What is it?" Jeremy says. "Are you okay?"

"I have to go," Fox says. "Nobody can know about this. Don't give anybody this number. Don't tell anyone about your phone booth. Or me. Promise, Germ?"

"Only if you promise you won't call me Germ," Jeremy says, feeling really stupid. "I hate when people call me that. Call me Mars instead."

"Mars," Fox says, and it sounds exotic and strange and brave, as if Jeremy has just become a new person, a person named after a whole planet, a person who kisses girls and talks to Foxes.

"I've never stolen anything," Jeremy says.

But Fox has hung up.

Maybe out there, somewhere, is someone who enjoys having to say good-bye, but it isn't anyone that Jeremy knows. All of his friends are grumpy and red-eyed, although not from crying. From lack of sleep. From too much television. There are still faint red stains around Talis's mouth and if everyone weren't so tired, they would realize it's Jeremy's lipstick. Karl gives Jeremy a handful of quarters, dimes, nickels, and pennies. "For the slot machines," Karl says. "If you win anything, you can keep a third of what you win."

"Half," Jeremy says, automatically.

"Fine," Karl says. "It's all from your dad's sofas, anyway. Just one more thing. Stop getting taller. Don't get taller while you're gone. Okay." He hugs Jeremy hard: so hard that it's almost like getting punched again. No wonder Talis threw the boa constrictor at Karl.

Talis and Elizabeth both hug Jeremy good-bye. Talis looks even more mysterious now that he's sat with her under a disco ball and made out. Later on, Jeremy will discover that Talis has left her sword under the blue fur couch and he'll wonder if she left it on purpose.

Talis doesn't say anything and Amy, of course, doesn't shut up, not even when she kisses him. It feels weird to be kissed by someone who goes right on talking while they kiss you and yet it shouldn't be a surprise that Amy kisses him. He imagines that later Amy and Talis and Elizabeth will all compare notes.

Elizabeth says, "I promise I'll tape every episode of *The Library* while you're gone so we can all watch them together when you get back. I promise I'll call you in Vegas, no matter what time it is there, when there's a new episode."

Her hair is a mess and her breath is faintly sour. Jeremy wishes he could tell her how beautiful she looks. "I'll write bad poetry and send it to you," he says.

Jeremy's mother is looking hideously cheerful as she goes in and out of the house, making sure that she hasn't left anything behind. She loves long car trips. It doesn't bother her one bit that she and her son are abandoning their entire lives. She passes Jeremy a folder full of maps. "You're in charge of not getting lost," she says. "Put these somewhere safe."

Jeremy says, "I found a library online that I want to go visit. Out in Iowa. They have a corn mosaic on the façade of the building, with a lot of naked goddesses and gods dancing around in a field of corn. Someone wants to take it down. Can we go see it first?"

"Sure," his mother says.

Jeremy's father has filled a whole grocery bag with sandwiches. His hair is drooping and he looks even more like an axe murderer than usual. If this were a movie, you'd think that Jeremy and his mother were escaping in the nick of time. "You take care of your mother," he says to Jeremy.

"Sure," Jeremy says. "You take care of yourself."

His dad sags. "You take care of yourself, too." So it's settled. They're all supposed to take care of themselves. Why can't they stay home and take care of each other, until Jeremy is good and ready to go off to college? "I've got another bag of sandwiches in the kitchen," his dad says. "I should go get them."

"Wait," Jeremy says. "I have to ask you something before we take off. Suppose I had to steal something. I mean, I don't have to steal anything, of course, and I know stealing is wrong, even when *you* do it, and I would never steal anything. But what if I did? How do you do it? How do you do it and not get caught?"

His father shrugs. He's probably wondering if Jeremy is really his son. Gordon Mars inherited his mutant, long-fingered, ambidextrous hands from a long line of shoplifters and money launderers and petty criminals. They're all deeply ashamed of Jeremy's father. Gordon Mars had a gift and he threw it away to become a writer. "I don't know," he says. He picks up Jeremy's hand and looks at it as if he's never noticed before that Jeremy had something hanging off the end of his wrist. "You just do it. You do it like you're not really doing anything at all. You do it while you're thinking about something else and you forget that you're doing it."

"Oh, Jeremy says, taking his hand back. "I'm not planning on stealing anything. I was just curious."

His father looks at him. "Take care of yourself," he says again, as if he really means it, and hugs Jeremy hard.

Then he goes and gets the sandwiches (so many sandwiches that Jeremy and his mother will eat sandwiches for the first three days, and still have to throw half of them away). Everyone waves. Jeremy and his mother climb in the van. Jeremy's mother turns on the CD player. Bob Dylan is singing about monkeys. His mother loves Bob Dylan. They drive away.

Do you know how, sometimes, during a commercial break in your favorite television shows, your best friend calls and wants to talk about one of her boyfriends, and when you try to hang up, she starts crying and you try to cheer her up and end up missing about half of the episode? And so when you go to work the next day, you have to get the guy who sits next to you to explain what happened? That's the good thing about a book. You can mark your place in a book. But this isn't really a book. It's a television show.

In one episode of *The Library*, an adolescent boy drives across the country with his mother. They have to change a tire. The boy practices taking things out of his mother's purse and putting them back again. He steals a sixteen-ounce bottle of Coke from one convenience market and leaves it at another convenience market. The boy and his mother stop at a lot of libraries, and the boy keeps a blog, but he skips the bit about the library in Iowa. He writes in his blog about what he's reading, but he doesn't read the books he stole in Iowa, because Fox told him not to, and because he has to hide them from his mother. Well, he reads just a few pages. Skims, really. He hides them under the blue-fur sofa. They go camping in Utah, and the boy sets up his telescope. He sees three shooting stars and a coyote. He never sees anyone who looks like a Forbidden Book, although he sees a transvestite go into the woman's rest room at a rest stop in Indiana. He calls a phone booth just outside Las Vegas twice, but no one ever answers. He has short conversations with his father. He wonders what his father is up to. He wishes he could tell his father about Fox and the books. Once the boy's mother finds a giant spider the size of an Oreo in their tent. She starts laughing hysterically. She takes a picture of it with her digital camera, and the boy puts the picture on his blog. Sometimes the boy asks questions and his mother talks about her parents. Once she cries. The boy doesn't know what to say. They talk about their favorite episodes of *The Library* and the episodes that they really hated, and the mother asks if the boy thinks Fox is really dead. He says he doesn't think so.

Once a man tries to break into the van while they are sleeping in it. But then he goes away. Maybe the painting of the woman with the peeling knife is protecting them.

But you've seen this episode before.

It's Cinco de Mayo. It's almost seven o'clock at night, and the sun is beginning to go down. Jeremy and his mother are in the desert and Las Vegas is somewhere in front of them. Every time they pass a driver coming the other way, Jeremy tries to figure out if that person has just won or lost a lot of money. Everything is flat and sort of tilted here, except off in the distance, where the land goes up abruptly, as if someone has started to fold up a map. Somewhere around here is the Grand Canyon, which must have been a surprise when people first saw it.

Jeremy's mother says, "Are you sure we have to do this first? Couldn't we go find your phone booth later?"

"Can we do it now?" Jeremy says. "I said I was going to do it on my blog. It's like a quest that I have to complete."

"Okay," his mother says. "It should be around here somewhere. It's supposed to be four point five miles after the turnoff, and here's the turnoff."

It isn't hard to find the phone booth. There isn't much else around. Jeremy should feel excited when he sees it, but it's a disappointment, really. He's seen phone booths before. He was expecting something to be different. Mostly he just feels tired of road trips and tired of roads and just tired, tired, tired. He looks around to see if Fox is somewhere nearby, but there's just a hiker off in the distance. Some kid.

"Okay, Germ," his mother says. "Make this quick."

"I need to get my backpack out of the back," Jeremy says.

"Do you want me to come too?" his mother says.

"No," Jeremy says. "This is kind of personal."

His mother looks like she's trying not to laugh. "Just hurry up. I have to pee."

When Jeremy gets to the phone booth, he turns around. His mother has the light on in the van. It looks like she's singing along to the radio. His mother has a terrible voice.

When he steps inside the phone booth, it isn't magical. The phone booth smells rank, as if an animal has been living in it. The windows are smudgy. He takes the stolen books out of his backpack and puts them in the little shelf where someone has stolen a phone book. Then he waits. Maybe Fox is going to call him. Maybe he's supposed to wait until she calls. But she doesn't call. He feels lonely. There's no one he can tell about this. He feels like an idiot and he also feels kind of proud. Because he did it. He drove cross-country with his mother and saved an imaginary person.

"So how's your phone booth?" his mother says.

"Great!" he says, and they're both silent again. Las Vegas is in front of them and then all around them and everything is lit up like they're inside a pinball game. All of the trees look fake. Like someone read too much Dr.

Seuss and got ideas. People are walking up and down the sidewalks. Some of them look normal. Others look like they just escaped from a fancy-dress ball at a lunatic asylum. Jeremy hopes they've just won lots of money and that's why they look so startled, so strange. Or maybe they're all vampires.

"Left," he tells his mother. "Go left here. Look out for the vampires on the crosswalk. And then it's an immediate right." Four times his mother let him drive the van: once in Utah, twice in South Dakota, once in Pennsylvania. The van smells like old burger wrappers and fake fur, and it doesn't help that Jeremy's gotten used to the smell. The woman in the painting has had a pained expression on her face for the last few nights, and the disco ball has lost some of its pieces of mirror because Jeremy kept knocking his head on it in the morning. Jeremy and his mother haven't showered in three days.

Here is the wedding chapel, in front of them, at the end of a long driveway. Electric purple light shines on a sign that spells out HELL'S BELLS. There's a wrought-iron fence and a yard full of trees dripping Spanish moss. Under the trees, tombstones and miniature mausoleums.

"Do you think those are real?" his mother says. She sounds slightly worried.

"'Harry East, Recently Deceased,'" Jeremy says. "No, I don't."

There's a hearse in the driveway with a little plaque on the back. RECENTLY BURIED MARRIED. The chapel is a Victorian house with a bell tower. Perhaps it's full of bats. Or giant spiders. Jeremy's father would love this place. His mother is going to hate it.

Someone stands at the threshold of the chapel, door open, looking out at them. But as Jeremy and his mother get out of the van, he turns and goes inside and shuts the door. "Look out," his mother says. "They've probably gone to put the boiling oil in the microwave."

She rings the doorbell determinedly. Instead of ringing, there's a recording of a crow. *Caw, caw, caw.* All the lights in the Victorian house go out. Then they turn on again. The door swings open and Jeremy tightens his grip on his backpack, just in case. "Good evening, Madam. Young man," a man says and Jeremy looks up and up and up. The man at the door has to lower his head to look out. His hands are large as toaster ovens. He looks like he's wearing Chihuahua coffins on his feet. Two realistic-looking bolts stick out on either side of his head. He wears green pancake makeup, glittery green eye shadow, and his lashes are as long and thick and green as AstroTurf. "We weren't expecting you so soon."

"We should have called ahead," Jeremy's mother says. "I'm real sorry."

"Great costume," Jeremy says.

The Frankenstein curls his lip in a somber way. "Thank you," he says.

"Call me Miss Thing, please."

"I'm Jeremy," Jeremy says. "This is my mother."

"Oh please," Miss Thing says. Even his wink is somber. "You tease me. She isn't old enough to be your mother."

"Oh please, yourself," Jeremy's mother says.

"Quick, the two of you," someone yells from somewhere inside Hell's Bells. "While you zthtand there gabbing, the devil ithz prowling around like a lion, looking for a way to get in. Are you juthzt going to zthtand there and hold the door wide open for him?"

So they all step inside. "Is that Jeremy Marthz at lathzt?" the voice says. "Earth to Marthz, Earth to Marthz. Marthzzz, Jeremy Marthzzz, there'thz zthomeone on the phone for Jeremy Marthz. She'thz called three timethz in the lathzt ten minutethz, Jeremy Marthzzzz."

It's Fox, Jeremy knows. Of course, it's Fox! She's in the phone booth. She's got the books and she's going to tell me that I saved whatever it is that I was saving. He walks toward the buzzing voice while Miss Thing and his mother go back out to the van.

He walks past a room full of artfully draped spider webs and candelabras drooping with drippy candles. Someone is playing the organ behind a wooden screen. He goes down the hall and up a long staircase. The banisters are carved with little faces. Owls and foxes and ugly children. The voice goes on talking. "Yoohoo, Jeremy, up the stairthz, that'thz right. Now, come along, come right in! Not in there, in here, in here! Don't mind the dark, we *like* the dark, just watch your step." Jeremy puts his hand out. He touches something and there's a click and the bookcase in front of him slowly slides back. Now the room is three times as large and there are more bookshelves and there's a young woman wearing dark sunglasses, sitting on a couch. She has a megaphone in one hand and a phone in the other. "For you, Jeremy Marth," she says. She's the palest person Jeremy has ever seen and her two canine teeth are so pointed that she lisps a little when she talks. On the megaphone the lisp was sinister, but now it just makes her sound irritable.

She hands him the phone. "Hello?" he says. He keeps an eye on the vampire.

"Jeremy!" Elizabeth says. "It's on, it's on, it's on! It's just started! We're all just sitting here. Everybody's here. What happened to your cell phone? We kept calling."

"Mom left it in the visitor's center at Zion," Jeremy says.

"Well, you're there. We figured out from your blog that you must be near Vegas. Amy says she had a feeling that you were going to get there in time.

She made us keep calling. Stay on the phone, Jeremy. We can all watch it together, okay? Hold on."

Karl grabs the phone. "Hey, Germ, I didn't get any postcards," he says. "You forget how to write or something? Wait a minute. Somebody wants to say something to you." Then he laughs and laughs and passes the phone on to someone else who doesn't say anything at all.

"Talis?" Jeremy says.

Maybe it isn't Talis. Maybe it's Elizabeth again. He thinks about how his mouth is right next to Elizabeth's ear. Or maybe it's Talis's ear.

The vampire on the couch is already flipping through the channels. Jeremy would like to grab the remote away from her, but it's not a good idea to try to take things away from a vampire. His mother and Miss Thing come up the stairs and into the room and suddenly the room seems absolutely full of people, as if Karl and Amy and Elizabeth and Talis have come into the room, too. His hand is getting sweaty around the phone. Miss Thing is holding Jeremy's mother's painting firmly, as if it might try to escape. Jeremy's mother looks tired. For the past three days her hair has been braided into two long fat pigtails. She looks younger to Jeremy, as if they've been traveling backward in time instead of just across the country. She smiles at Jeremy, a giddy, exhausted smile. Jeremy smiles back.

"Is it *The Library*?" Miss Thing says. "Is a new episode on?"

Jeremy sits down on the couch beside the vampire, still holding the phone to his ear. His arm is getting tired.

"I'm here," he says to Talis or Elizabeth or whoever it is on the other end of the phone. "I'm here." And then he sits and doesn't say anything and waits with everyone else for the vampire to find the right channel so they can all find out if he's saved Fox, if Fox is alive, if Fox is still alive.

[a ghost samba]

IAN McDONALD

Ian McDonald is the author of the 2011 Hugo Award-finalist *The Dervish House* and many other novels, including Hugo Award-nominees *River of Gods* and *Brasyl,* and the Philip K. Dick Award-winner *King of Morning, Queen of Day.* He won a Hugo in 2006 for his novelette, "The Djinn's Wife," and has won the Locus Award, three British Science Fiction Awards and the John W. Campbell Memorial Award. His short fiction, much of which was recently collected in *Cyberabad Days,* has appeared in magazines such as *Interzone* and *Asimov's* and in numerous anthologies. His latest novel is *Planesrunner,* from Pyr, the first part of a fun series for younger and younger-at-heart readers.

When Seu Alejandro played, men kissed each other and women ovulated. Brasil is the land of the boy from nowhere, the footballer from the favela, the musician from the mines, the sugarcane cutter from the sertão. Milton Nascimento was a Minas Gerais boy. The late great Chico Science, father of Mangue, was from Olinda. It's part of our national mythology: in this great nation anyone can rise to anything from anywhere. Cane cutters can become presidents. It's also part of our national mythology that, like Chico Science, like Seu Alejandro, they should die young. There's a pure beauty in imagining what they never achieved. The ghost samba can never disappoint you.

He went back for the tapes. He should never have gone back for the tapes. But he was a musician. It would have been like leaving a child in that burning studio. They were the masters for his new collection, the long-awaited second album that would crown the achievement of *Boy on the Corner*. All second albums are difficult—that's music—but some are more difficult than others. Seu Alejandro threw out a batch of songs because he wasn't happy with them. He was going to use Paulistano punk band, then he wasn't. He was going to duet with LoveFoxxx, then he wasn't. It was going to be him, alone, with his guitar and a drummer, the way I first heard him in that club in Lapa. Then it wasn't. His record company put out press releases that it was coming out in two weeks time; that would slip. Months, a season, a year. Four years. That would be the end of a career for anyone less angelically gifted than Seu Alejandro. It merely served to increase the appetite. Then word came that he was going back into the studio. The songs were right. The musicians were right. The arrangements were right. The soul was right and the ideas were running through him like lightning. We'd heard it before. But of course the producer wasn't right and the studio wasn't right, so he was going home, back up into Vila Canoas to the little bedroom studio where he produced the first collection of three songs for the MySpace site. And that was where on April 11, 2012, Wilson Severino de Araujo, known as Seu Alejandro, died in a stupid studio fire trying to save the masters of his second album. *Pretty Petty Thieves* joined the list of legendary albums-that-never-were.

It's five years since Seu Alejandro died and in that time he has grown from cult to myth to legend. Five years it's taken me to track down those masters, from legend back through myth to a scorched hard drive. I'm at a bar in Laranjeiras. You wouldn't know it, you've never even heard of it; if you were to come here you would think it dazingly trendy but the moment has already moved on from it. It's my job to know such things. The people who know all know me as Cento-réis: hundred-réal Man. The joke goes that that's the amount of money I'll spend in one session on music. You'd know me better as Rubem de Castro. Columnist reviewer commentator blogger pundit radio-wit and professional idler: the last of the Real Cariocas. All those little things a man must do not to be seen to be trying too hard. If you met me you'd hate me. I'm the guy on the music forums with so much cooler recommendations than yours. At a party I'll sneer at the host's unforgivably populist playlist and tell you who you should be listening to now and where to find them. I might even slip on my own podcast and you'll say, *Who are these guys?* While you're jabbering away on your social networking sites about have you heard Tita Maria and Duane Duarte and Bonde do Role? I've already moved on to the next thing after the next thing. I could take you to the clubs and the bars and the sound systems but once I'd taken you, that would be the end of it, you know? For four decades I've surfed the sea of music that breaks around the rocks of this most lovely of cities. It's tiring and relentless and it's no way for a middle-aged man to live, but the moment you lose the wave, you go under.

Because I'm a middle-aged man still living on teenage overhang, when I hear the word "masters" I expect tape. I expect digibeta, DAT; the romantic part of me hopes for reels. The masters for *Pretty Petty Thieves* are on a hard drive the size of a cigarette packet. They sit on the table next to Guinle's real packet of Hollywood Blues. Some bright-eyed singer-songwriter is picking out her heart-fluff to the fourths and fifths on the little stage. I've heard a thousand heartbreaks just like hers. I move my beer away from the drive. It's been through fire and deep lost time but I'm terrified of spilling Antarctica over it.

"Can I hear some?"

"It's a hard drive." When Guinle left the police, like most of the cops who paid enough to be safe up in the favelas, he set up a private detective agency. His specialism was kidnappings: footballers' mothers and pets. Now he runs a successful stable of gumshoes so he no longer has to hack security cameras or go through anyone's garbage with chopsticks and only tackles those cases that interest him. I know him from the days when the New Bossa swept through the city. There's an old musicians' gaydar: we recognised each immediately at our tables on opposing sides of the dark, noisy club. It's the set of the body, the sit and slight lean, the tilt of the head that says that whatever else you are hearing, you are always listening to the music.

I say, "I could be buying someone's collection of boy-porn."

Guinle holds out his phone. A set of white earbuds is plugged into it.

"Do you want to listen to it?"

"Have you listened to it?" Panic snatches sudden and cold at my heart. I can't bear it that Guinle could have listened to the masters before me. It makes it dirty, used. It's almost a sex thing, like someone else's girlfriend after an indecently short interval.

"Not a note. What do you take me for? I just copied it because I knew you'd ask me that."

"Promise me you won't…" The need in my voice is ridiculous. Have some dignity man.

"I'll give you until tomorrow morning. Once you've remembered that other little matter."

I slide the envelope of cash across the table. It's a big envelope, A4, too full to seal down the flap. There's a pheromone of notes, of ink and hands and trade. Guinle scoops it into his briefcase. He's too much a carioca to count the notes and too much a pro to query his clients' cash calls.

"I make no representations about the state of the contents. You asked me to get the masters, I got them."

"I must ask you how you did that sometime," I say but I can hear my voice go off the moment, the way you hear it when a singer loses a cover of a song he doesn't really understand or believe in. Just words. Because I have it. I have the lost *Pretty Petty Thieves*. In that slightly blackened titanium box is the last musical testament of Seu Alejandro. The world thought it was lost, but I found it and now it sits in the palm of my hand. I see that hand shake.

"Yes, you really must," says Guinle.

I have a ritual. Everyone has a ritual. I know a great great singer who can only face an audience if he's masturbated. You'd know him too. He's a household name. There are footballers who have to put on one boot first, or never wear two the same colour, or carry a picture of the Pope or Our Lady next to their hearts. Truckers bless their rigs, coders bless their keyboards, policemen bless their guns. And then there is sex. There is always sex. Some have times and places and positions; some have foreplay that's scripted and rehearsed as a high mass. Some cannot achieve anything with the lights on. For some it's clothing: something they have to wear, or have the other wear, without which they cannot be remotely aroused.

I practice my ritual in the best room in the apartment. It's not the biggest or the best aired or the quietest but it has a breathtaking view out over Botafogo and Guanabara to the hills of Niteroi beyond. Out of the right-hand window are Leme Morro and the Sugarloaf. In the evening, in the sudden lilac twilight when the lights come like a necklace around the shoulders of the moros, it is heartbreakingly beautiful. Here's what I keep in this room. A chair of course; an old, deep leather armchair with the springs going so I can sag into it. A beer fridge. A small side table for the beer and the remote. The sound system, in the holy corner where the two views meet. This is my listening room. This is my church. I take my place in the chair. I've had it positioned scientifically to get the best surround sound separation. My cleaner is under orders never to move it on pain of instant dismissal. I settle my fat ass deep into the seat. It's important to get comfortable. I'm going to be there for a while. I take one Antarctica from the fridge and pop the can. Rio spreads like wings on either side of me. I love her so hard it hurts. Then I lift the remote control and start Seu Alejandro's *Pretty Petty Thieves*.

On the first listen through I never do anything. I need to get the whole recording. The whole concept, entire, the song order, the big idea. Marcelo from the Tuesday Afternoon Boys calls it the gestalt. He's some kind of therapist in it. Call that first pass the *hearing*. This second pass is the *listening*. It's then you notice the details of the arrangements, the engineering, how the lyrics work with the melody. Is that a horn section there? He's pulled the bass up here, pushed it back there. Why has he used a cello line, for God's sake? The third time is the *savouring*. You know how the songs work, what they are trying to achieve and the way the music is constructed and how it works on your heart. Now you can appreciate the details. The way drum and bass syncopate against each other. The complex time signature—11/8—that always eludes your four-square tapping toe. That ever-shifting harmony line that disguises a very simple, almost folk melody and gives it a dress of carioca sophistication. The twists, the false starts and surprise endings, the games you can play with middle eights, joys you can only appreciate after a lifetime of immersion in MPB.

But there are holes. There are hideous holes. Trans-Amazonian-Highway holes, that can swallow an entire truck. The main vocals are unmixed. On some of the songs Seu Alejandro sounds like he is bellowing like an old and angry beach bum, others like he is humming to himself trying to find his car in a supermarket car park. Arrangements are fragmentary; there are suggestions of '70s funk horn sections or his signature trip-hop rhythms, which he lifted from another age, another culture and made unmistakably Tropicalismo. Back vocals are either non-existent or too far to the front and the bass is painfully low in the mix. There is a screamingly frustrating twenty three second gap in the middle of "Immaculate Conception" and track 8: "Bottle Club", just ends, full stop, whether by fire or intention I can't tell. The title track doesn't exist beyond an opening carnaval blast of drums, brass and what sounds like sampled traffic noise. Astonishing, but a shard. Again, this could be a Seu Alejandro joke or the effects of the fire. The last two tracks are sketches: "Breakfast News" is an acoustic guitar piece—few ever tugged the heart so with his strings than Seu Alejandro, with suggestions of lyrics muttered into the mike; scraps and lines and euphonies. The final track, provisionally titled [a ghost samba] is his joyfully melancholy guitar with a severely simple cello line.

But it is Seu Alejandro. Unmistakably, gloriously Seu Alejandro.

I crack a fresh Antarctica and start the third listen. My hand is shaking.

As I listen with the ear of savouring, the shake becomes worse until I can hardly hold my beer. My whole body is tight, every muscle like a drumskin; I am quivering as if trying to keep back tears. Not just tears, but the kind of uncontrollable, on-the-floor howling and quaking that leaves phlegm pouring from your nose and mouth, the kind men must never be seen doing, the kind men do when love walks away from them and they realise their lives have been lies. It's the holes, those Amazonian holes; they join together into a void. How dare Seu Alejandro die and leave it incomplete and damaged? How dare Seu Alejandro leave me with just this? It is as abandonment as complete as any of my brief wives and girlfriends. I am bereft, I am furious with him.

It's full dark now. The lights draw the curves of the bays and the breasts of the hills. *Pretty Petty Thieves* comes to its third ending and I am all right. I'm all right. I'm already starting to think of how I might put it all together and complete what the Seu left broken.

We are the Tuesday Afternoon Boys and every Tuesday afternoon we play at the Lagoa futsal court. We've been playing every Tuesday for seven years, ever since the first of us turned forty. In the afternoon the only other teams are skinny kids in basketball vests and baggy shorts. We don't play them, they can dribble the ball around us like Garrincha tying a left-back in knots; we play each other. We play futsal to show we're still alive, we play in the afternoon to show we're masters of our own time.

I'm on the subs bench. When the average team age is in the low forties, you spend most of the game on the subs bench, but everyone gets a turn on court. That's the point of turning up on a Tuesday afternoon. But the real work gets done on that bench.

The ball goes out and Carlinhos, our manager for this week, calls Captain Spooky off. He looks like he's dying. Face so red it could explode, chest heaving, the sweat lashing off him. He crashes down on the bench beside me and it's a full two minutes before he can get a word between the death-gasps.

"Jesus and Mary," I tell him. "You should listen to your doctor sometime. He said this is going to be the death of you."

He shakes his head, smiling through the panting.

"The person. Most likely. To kill you. Is your own. Doctor."

Captain Spooky claims he is a *real* doctor. MDs are not real doctors. It's all hand waving and wizardry. MD-ing is about instinct and opinion and subjective thought. There's no science, no objectivity, nothing empirical or evidence-based about medicine. It's a package of received knowledge, opinion and status-plays. *Physicians*, from the word *physic*: that makes it sound like a science. Proper science has hypotheses, experiments, statistical analysis, proof and margins of certainty and error. Physics, now that is science, and that's what Captain Spooky is: a real, true, proper physicist. With angina.

His real science is theoretical physics. It's a young man's game, he'll tell you—like futsal—but he's kept his tenure, no lean feat for a man pushing fifty. Five more years, he says. Five more years and he'll take the retirement package. His field is so complex and abstruse it makes my head swim even thinking about it. It sounds like esoteric nonsense to me, but he swears that theoretical quantum computing has millions of everyday applications and implications that will change our lives beyond recognition. I bow to his experience—he's beaten off a lot of young dogs snapping from below; all I know is that he's tried to explain it to me in the Rodrigo de Freitas Bar and Grill over the post-match caipiroskas with which we replace lost body-fluids, and I still don't get it. When things get really really small and really really short in duration they behave in ways that seem impossible to us; that seems to be the gist of it. And because of that, there isn't one me, there are billion trillion mes, and there isn't one world, there are a billion trillion worlds, all different: every possible world and me that can exist, exists somewhere. If you thought about that too much you'd fry your head. And that's why we call him Captain Spooky.

"So." The words are easier now. "Your limited edition. How many times have you listened to her now?"

For Captain Spooky everything to do with computers was feminine. Our Lady of the Digits.

"Enough for it to be exciting like a lover, not so much that it's become a wife."

"Jesus man, you need to get over that. How long ago was it?"

"Eight years five months."

"We've all been through it. It's a life stage. Well, all except John the Idiot, and he'd welcome the chance for an agonising divorce." The circles of sweat on the front and back of his T-shirt are expanding to meet the ones under his arms. It is not a good look. Captain Spooky squirts water from the Action! bottle over his face. He says, "I mean, have you thought about doing anything with it?"

"What, you mean, copy it? Distribute it? Release it?" I think I keep the sudden crackle of rage out of my voice, but I feel my muscles clench and tense. "Do you know what I call those? Blasphemy records. Once they have you, those companies will release every half-baked idea or whistle you ever recorded, every coffee-bar twang. If they could make money they'd put out Seu Alejandro singing in the shower. Bastards. The entire reason I tracked down and bought that disk was to keep it out of the hands of those vultures."

I feel my face is now the red one, and Captain Spooky's pale at my anger. He holds up his hands in supplication.

"Okay okay okay man. It's your music. What I meant was, you say it's full of holes and drops out and incomplete tracks." He leans forward. It's not a good smell. "What if you could fill in those holes and finish those part songs?"

I shake my head.

"It'd be guesswork. It'd be someone else either fitting their own ideas in or, which is worse, doing a bad Seu Alejandro impersonation. No no no, keep it the way it is. I'll always be imagining what it would have been like. That's okay. That's the price."

Captain Spooky purses thumb and forefinger; a scientist of the very small's gesture of precision.

"What if we could take imagination out of it? What if we could finish the collection exactly as Seu Alejandro intended? With his own music?"

"Short of a medium I can't see how anyone could do that."

"I could. Just give me a copy. I don't want your masters, you hold on to them, just give a decent OMFs. A disk would do, or email them over to me."

I want to ask him what spooky *macumba* he intends to work but the ball has gone out and Carlinhos, the other, real captain, is sending Bastard Max off and signing for me to come on. My muscles have gone tight as a virgin; I will play like a drain but with the Tuesday Afternoon Boys everyone gets a turn on pitch. I can suffer for it later.

The room, the chair, the beer, the sunset. My hand on the remote but my finger wavers over the play button. Three weeks and three days after I sent him the files of *Pretty Petty Thieves* they came back to me. Captain Spooky hadn't been at the Lagoa since the day we talked about the good music, the pure music. The chest pains and the overheating had got worse so he'd been to see his doctor and the man had gone berserk. Running around kicking a ball at his age at his weight in this heat. Of course, the doctor still knew nothing, but he'd take his advice—purely precautionary—until the pain went away. *Sorry it took so long,* he said in the email. *The quantum mainframe gets booked pretty solid.* I could see alone from the attachment details that they were changed. Fatter, fresher. Frightening. I dithered, I hovered over the files. I didn't want to open them. I didn't want to hear them. I wanted to rip them on to my system then and there. I wanted to hear them like my daughter's voice on the phone.

The sky is lilac but won't hold it much longer: indigo's coming. There's a high jet, night-bound up out over the Atlantic: it's gold in the caught twilight. The streets and the cars are twinkling and I watch the glow of the cable cars slide like pearls between the pendant lights of the stations. Rio has always, irreducibly been *she.*

I hit play.

There is a ritual so I give it the three listens though from the very opening bar I can hear the difference. The first time is still the whole thing. I listen to *Pretty Petty Thieves* straight through. It's some time before I hit the play button for the second listen. I'm floored, I'm on the ceiling, my heart is racing and at the same time I shine like a child at a first communion. It's all there. Entire and full and rich and more ambitious, more playful, more daring than I could ever have imagined. No holes, this is a smooth highway of sound. And it's Seu Alejandro, unmistakably Seu Alejandro though everything is new and strange and wonderful like falling in love. It sounds like the greatest thing you ever heard. I must listen again. I must dive in and swim down deep between the tracks and the layers and the individual notes.

The second time I deep-listen. That's a Senegalese guitar with a deliberately primitive *noreste* four-part harmony: it's Mother Africa but with Seu Alejandro's signature English trip-hop beat. But there's invention: *musique concrete* from Rio traffic noises fluttering as delicate as bird song over "Miracle of the Fishes", and a dazzling, hilarious two-step of dub bass with Nacão Zumbi death-guitar thrashes on "Angela and Angela". "Kicking" is so totally different I almost did not recognise the song on first pass, now on second listen the changes are so radical I feel them as a physical shock. It had been faux fun, now it's a shimmering, shadowy dubstep, dark and melancholic. And then there is [a ghost samba]. It is still the same simple cello line and heartbreak acoustic guitar but it has words now, Seu Alejandro's unearthly but diamond-clear, diamond-sharp falsetto and a twitter of four-a.m. electronics so ethereal it might come through a radio telescope. The breath catches in my chest. I can hear my heart. It's some time before I touch the play button again.

And now I listen to taste, to eat the music and make it part of me. This time I break my rule, I'm impatient to get to the final track. I want to hear Seu Alejandro's words from whatever place Captain Spooky summoned him. That's a Tuesday Afternoon question. Now I need it to be just me and Seu Alejandro high over the circling city lights. It's a song about a moment of wonder and the sweetness of loss, like many of the best Brasilian songs. Take her face out of the mornings. I've seen that face. Imagined glimpses in a car across the highway, a figure passing on the street that might just be a wish. If our lives were like songs we would hear the harmonies, we would live a chorus. On the street. We are older but no wiser and in a flicker we'll be gone.

Full dark. I've forgotten the hour. My chest is heaving, my face wet with tears. I drove away the women who loved me. I let my children go. I'm not a bad man, I just loved the music with all of my heart. I always knew that the radio played just for me. The songs never let you down. They would always rhyme with your heart.

The cleaner finds me the next morning, still in the chair in the yellow morning light.

"Your *macumba* is strong," I say to Captain Spooky and slide the caipiroska across the table to him. I'm one down already and it's hit hard like a bailiff's knock.

"I wield the power cosmic," he says. He takes a big draw from the drink. He winces as the vodka goes down, a grimace of pain. "Jesus." He thumps his fist against his breastbone, gasps twice. "The laws of the multiverse bow down to me."

He looks like shit, the kind of pale and pasty shit you get if you feed a dog too much dried food.

"No but really, what did you do? In words a man can understand."

"There is not one world, there are many worlds."

"There is not one me, there are many mes, yeah yeah." Including ones where my social universe doesn't consist solely of fortysomething males.

"And there are universes where Seu Alejandro didn't go back into the studio."

"Since when have you become an expert on Seu Alejandro?"

"Research is my business, right? And universes where that studio never caught fire."

"So what exactly did you do?"

"The quantum computational equivalent of being a DJ in your own bedroom. I quantumised your master on the uni quantum core and then set her to re-render."

"That spooky quantum computer of yours."

"That spooky quantum computer of mine can perform calculations no other computer can in less than the lifetime of the universe because she exports the problem to her sisters in parallel universes. Somewhere in the region of ten to the power of eight hundred universes. In a sense there is only ever one universal quantum computer, spread through the whole multiverse. It's the one true universal constant."

When Captain Spooky talks, like his name, it makes my head spin and my balls contract. The world around me goes pale and washed-out, like those old last-century postcards of Rio, bleached by the light of other suns. Millions upon billions of other universes; numbers so huge that even if there were as many Leblon beaches as there were grains of sand on Leblon beach, they still would not be one sand-grain of those other Rios, other lives, other mes. Because I can't help but think about those other mes and the oblivious lives they lead. On the balance of probabilities I cannot live the best of all those probable lives. It's equally unlikely that I live the worst. I can easily imagine the worst. I've seen it. The terrible news from the multiverse is that I am grey and average. I'm not a football hero or a samba star and I didn't marry an underwear model. I'm not a wrecked man throwing bottles at the wall every lilac sunset or dead in some police-and-malandros firefight. This is the best I can reasonably hope for. This is…endurable. How can a man face such grand indifference? I am not the centre of the universe after all.

"So is basically the multiversal equivalent of clicking Seu Alejandro on quantum iTunes and downloading *Pretty Petty Thieves*?"

Captain Spooky throws up his hands in grand offence.

"There's some work in this you know. Mixing and stuff."

"You, mix?"

"My nephew works in radio. He's got this software on his laptop. The question is, never mind my nephew or whatever quantum spookiness I pulled, how does it sound?"

I duck my head in a small acquiescence.

"It sounds like Seu Alejandro."

"Well there you go. Now, I'm going up to get something to eat. Do you want anything?"

The Grill part of the Rodrigo de Freitas Bar and Grill is a small per-kilo restaurant, fine for lining the stomach against a post-match evening of drinking. See? We don't even have to worry about Wednesday hangover. Captain Spooky floats and dithers over the buffet. Eating by weight is a fine art to him. He's shown me his trick of slipping a little finger under the scales to take a coupe of réis off the price. But I'm hearing ghost sambas. What the Captain pulled in from across the universes is Seu Alejandro. There is no doubt that it's him; from the moment I first heard that hunted, melancholy street guitar and the incredible falsetto soar above it like Christ the Redeemer on his high hill, from that evening he took the chatter and the cynicism of the Cambucás Club and turned it all to him and held every soul in the place until he chose to release it, I've learned every grace note Seu Alejandro's played. It's him. But of all the many many *Pretty Petty Thieves* that exist across that head-frying multiverse, how can I trust that this is the one that the Seu Alejandro who died in that studio fire intended; the ghost in the scorched hard drive? It's *a Pretty Petty Thieves*, but can I ever know it's *the Pretty Petty Thieves*?

The crash is tremendous; a clatter of plates and metal trays and cutlery hitting the harsh white tiles all at once. Captain Spooky is on his side. He is covered in cold starters, his right leg is bent under him in an ugly, terrifying way. He's not moving. He's not making any sound. The Tuesday Afternoon Boys are on their feet and the Rodrigo de Freitas Bar and Grill is filled with a dull bellowing.

Rio is not a city for funerals. Suits don't suit us. We'd rather do our business in Bermudas and Havaianas. São Paolo, wedged between those eerie towers, perhaps in one of those all-too-common grey drizzles, that's a city that does funerals well. The crumbling pastel colonial facades of Salvador and Olinda; there the slow rot and return to the earth is written into every house-front and Baroque Mission Jesus. That is a landscape of death. Rio is sex and life. That life is cheap—every day I hear the gunfire and the sirens—but cariocas understand that that is how death is done here. What Rio will not forgive is a heart that just grew tired of her and stopped dead at the serving counter in a kilometric restaurant. You get no kiss from Bitch City.

So I'm too hot and too tight in my going-to-funerals suit—I'm at that life stage where I need one—and the collar is chafing my neck. For a time the priests were getting younger. Now they're all getting older. The seminaries can't get the young men. It's no life really. The Tuesday Afternoon Boys have all turned out. In our suits and shades we look like a convention of dons. Our floral tribute is in the shape of a futsal ball. The old Captain would have appreciated the black joke but the family doesn't seem to appreciate the humour. His daughters look good in their black miniskirts and hats. The youngest has fantastic legs and that sullen pout thing I love in a girl. His students are hot too. They keep back, acquaintances like us. One of them is visibly upset. The guy with his arms around her shoulder must be the boyfriend. I wonder if he knows. They'll fuck afterwards. People always fuck after funerals. It's not just Rio's way, it's everyone's way. Death and sex.

I talk with those faces you only see at funerals; those partial conversations that, like Christmas or carnaval chat, continue from calendar to date to calendar, stitched through time; then Marcelo offers me a lift home.

"Did the Cap ever give you his theory for why he was going to live forever?"

"Was this another one of his quantum-theory-explains-everything-in-the-universe theories that no one understood?"

"I always thought you understood." Marcelo punches the horn as a yellow Honda full of teenagers cuts him up. "Don't you have jobs to go to? Why aren't you working? Parasites."

"Me? God no. I was just impressed with his theory for everything. Then you know what to blame when it goes wrong."

"No, he had this theory that he was going to live forever. Not just him, everyone. There was a price, though, and he was very drunk when he told me this. He told it like an experiment, like this. You're a very old and very distinguished physics professor with a very hot young PA. Well, she doesn't have to be young and hot, she just needs to be an observer. There always had to be observers in Cap's theories. The reason that you're very old is that you're about to put down the big stake on a bet: your life. There's a gun with some quantum doohickey attached, I don't know how it works but all it needs is to be a random Russian roulette device. You stand in front of the gun and then you say, all right Miss Hottie, start the process and record what you see. The quantum device spins the gun at random and fires. Click. Nothing happens. And again: click. Nothing happens. And a third time, click. You're still alive. Miss Hottie notes it down. Round four. The quantum device spins the chamber and fires. Oh my God! screams Miss Hottie as you take one right smack between the eyes and go down dead as dead can be."

"Correct me if my quantum theory is flawed, my friend, but this sounds more like a quantum suicide device than an immortality theory."

"Not so fast. Round four, other point of view. The quantum thingie spins the barrel and fires. And where Miss Hottie sees the back of your head come off, all you hear is another click. Empty chamber."

At the lights a lad skinny as want waves his windshield squeegee at us. I wave him away.

"Explain."

"Well, I don't understand it but Captain Spooky did and according to him it was this. Now, he was very drunk at the time, but every time the quantum thingie spins the barrel, it divides the multiverse into two sets of universes, one in which you live and one in which you die."

"I'm keeping up so far."

"And the next time it spins, that set of universes where you live on takes another hit: a subset where you live, another where you die."

"This is basic probability. Anyone who's ever put a bet on will get this. The odds get shorter all the time whether it's dice or Captain Spooky's parallel universes."

"Absolutely, but no matter how many times the gun fires, there will always be a universe where you live."

I consider that as we pass a group of Pentecostals dressed in respectable whites holding some evangelical praise-service in a bus shelter.

"But in the one that really matters you're dead," I say.

"Now here comes the spooky bit. Those universes where the gun fires, you've no awareness of them. You're dead. The only realities which exist for you are the ones in which the gun hits the empty chamber and you live. You can't perceive your own death. So the quantum trigger runs on and the gun barrel spins and goes click click click. And it will keep going click click how ever long you stand there, because you must always survive to perceive those realities."

We're at a light again. A crente waves a badly printed tract at us. I wave him away too. I'm getting that coldness in my balls, the clench of the alien.

"But what about Miss Hottie? She saw you die in front of the gun."

"Ah, but that's her perception, isn't it? From your perception you're immortal. No matter what happens, a miracle will always save you. You'll never be in that fatal car crash or get into that mugging. If you get cancer, they'll find a cure. If you get Alzheimer's, they'll work something out. When you're so old they have to feed you soup and hold your dick to pee, they'll find some way to make you twenty-five again and hung like a horse. Because only you can perceive those universes where you exist. You'll be there at the fucking end of time. It'll be you and God."

I shiver again but it's not quantum chill. It's the deeper darker cold of mortality and the futility of any hope against it; Captain Spooky's insane theories or the promise of a street corner evangelical tract. I say,

"I can see how this chimes with your gestalt theory, mate. But it didn't work for him, did it?"

"He'd say that we're seeing from our own point of view. We're the Miss

Hotties. From his point-of-view, it was just a little twinge, a little trapped wind, a quick burp and he's fine."

"There's a big difference between a quantum Russian roulette machine and a dicky ticker."

"Yeah but he reckoned everything was quantum, all the way up, the only reason we couldn't see it was because our minds were all just aspects of that universal quantum computer he used to play with."

We've arrived at my apartment. The beach is two blocks down, lines of gold and blue like the design on a 1930s cigarette packet. I hate the beach, I don't do beaches but today in my going-to-funerals suit and too-tight tie it looks like heaven,

"The Captain surely did have a theory for everything," I say.

"That I think was the idea," Marcelo says.

"You got your check-up booked?" I ask stepping out of the car.

"The earliest I could get was Friday," Marcelo says. "You?"

"Next Monday. It does kind of make you sit and look after yourself." I close the car door.

And I go to the beach. I slop along the hot hot white sand in my sober suit, grit filling my shoes. There are gorgeous people here, playing beach volleyball, futvolley, roller-blading along the sidewalk. There are boats in the marina and stalls for beer and caipis and men fishing and old men just staring out across the bay, their leather skins knuckled with melanomas. I'm listening to *Pretty Petty Thieves*. Sun and shade, *alegria* and *saudade*, joy and melancholy; that has always been our music. The final track plays: [a ghost samba]. Those ghost worlds are real, the guitar and cello, the whispered vocals say. We come from there. Among those parallel universes the Captain is in a tutorial with his good-looking students, reading at his desk with his trademark small coffee, exploring those other worlds and other lives on that magical computer. He'll never know about those worlds where his heart stops dead and drops him to the floor of his favourite per-kilo restaurant. There's a dark truth buried in Captain Spooky's vision of himself stepping forward to the end of the universe, one that makes this bright day and its people look as false and insubstantial as carnaval costumes. Around us others die, by age or disease or accident, but we live on. Little by little we lose everything and everyone. Every one of us is alone in our own little universe of ourselves.

I stop dead, a mad man in a dark suit on a blazing beach, and watch a TAM shuttle lift off from Santos Dumont. The compulsion, formed in an instant, possesses me. I must know if the Captain's *Pretty Petty Thieves* is the one my Seu Alejandro intended. Certainty is impossible—that's as true in pop music as quantum theory—but I can find hints and intimations. There is still room for faith. I trudge up between the brown volley-boys on to the sidewalk. I sit on a bench and empty the sand out of my lace-ups.

If in another life—another universe—I had to be a favelado, I think it would be in Vila Canoas. It's small and green and folded in on itself so that streets and alleys can cross each other several times. There's an underground river. Police and taxi drivers eat in the diner on the corner. They always know where the good food is. There's even a neat little backpacker hostel. I've never got that sense of perpetual tension I feel in big sister Rocinha around the mountain; as if the whole city on a hill might break lose and slide into the sea like an avalanche, sweeping the rich of Barra de Tijuca before it.

So, I'm a cosy middle-class music hack who doesn't know any speak of the street or the signs and ways you need to know to live as a Vila Canoista and not a tourist and I wouldn't last more than two nights in this place without killing or being killed. But I like the circle of forested mountains and the lap of sea. I like the way the clouds catch around São Conrado Mountain. Hang-gliders circle through the mist up there like hawks. On the intersection at the café a youth painstakingly welds an old Toyota pick-up, his gun wired into the streetlight. I turn off into the shadowed alleys between the leaning buildings, overhung by ramshackle balconies and washing. There is the studio, rebuilt and now a DJ school. I remembered it burned, I remember the yellow walls smoke-stained and the green paint peeled away, the windows and doors empty and eyeless. Vila Canoas was a pilgrimage site for a time. I was one of many who laid flowers and set candles and plastic virgins, Flamengo shirts and thongs to the Seu. I feel the hard drive in the breast pocket of my jacket grown heavy and warm. There's a second Pretty Petty Thief in it; the ghost Captain Spooky found on the shores of the multiverse.

The bar across the alley is changeless, a brick counter built into the under-hang beneath an apartment house, a bench seat set into the opposite wall. The television blares some Canal Quatro reality shit, the usual malandros loll around with Antarcticas, one in green with an attempted moustache, one in yellow with a smart light in his eye, one in white who thinks he rules. They nod when I greet them.

"I wonder if you could help me; does the Dona Severino de Araujo still live round here?"

The barman steps back to better regard me. His bar is the width of a street.

"I don't know who you mean."

I introduce myself. "The music journalist? I have a column in *Copa News*." Looks, head-shakes, shrugs. "I do a radio programme on Saturday afternoons. The history of MPB? "

Kid in yellow throws his head back.

"Just before Football Focus; I know you now. So you're looking for the Dona."

"I've something I want to show her. Something the Seu left behind."

"I think I remember you now," says the barman. "You did some interviews with her and his sisters. I saw them, they were good." They all look at the emperor in white. He stubs out a cigarette.

"You'll find her where you found her last time," he says.

"It's easy to get lost here," says Kid Green "I'll show you." He casts off from the bar and leads by two steps behind through the labyrinth of alleys and tunnels. I'm sure I didn't go this way before, I'm sure it was straighter, less shadowed. But the house are built and rebuilt and the streets change so often up here it's as if they move themselves, in the night. We drill down into the roots of Vila Canoas, through a doorway skewed into a parallelogram and along a short concrete tunnel lined with television-lit windows. The sound of running water rushes around the corridor. We cross the buried stream that races down from São Conrado on a concrete culvert and climb a flight of steps towards the sun. It's there that I hear the once-heard never-mistaken sound and turn to face the gun in Green Boy's hand.

"Look, I'm just a journalist." I offer him my wallet, my cellular. My cards he knows will be biometriced, usable only to my touch but I give them to him anyway. I pray he won't kidnap and march me to an ATM every day until I've emptied out my own account. Move slowly, withhold nothing and let them know they are in total control. I've been held up before. I know the drill.

"What's in the pocket?" Green waves his gun barrel.

I think of denying, I think of lying but the square bulge of the drive betrays me. I take out the master disk carefully, between thumb and forefinger.

"It's only music."

"An iPod."

"No it's a hard drive."

"An iPod, an MP4 player?"

"It's for Dona de Araujo. Seu Alejandro's mother. It's a present for her."

"An iPod," Green Boy says again. He's chewing his lip repeatedly now. That's never good.

"No it's not an iPod." I'm getting agitated. Give it to him. Give him whatever he wants. Get down on your knees and blow him if you need to. But it's *Pretty Petty Thieves*.

"Give me the fucking iPod!" Green screams.

"It's not a fucking iPod!" I scream back over the gurgle of buried water. I pull my hand back. He stabs forward with the gun. I see his finger close on the trigger.

And I hear a click. A dead-gun click. Green Boy frowns. He stabs with the gun held sideways this time, pulls the trigger. I hear a click. Then another. Then another.

THE CRISTÓBAL EFFECT

SIMON McCAFFERY

Simon McCaffery writes science fiction, horror, and hybrids of both genres, and has long been a fan of parallel worlds in fiction. His stories have appeared in *Lightspeed, Black Static, Rocket Science, Tomorrow SF, Alfred Hitchcock's Mystery Magazine, Mondo Zombie, Best New Werewolf Tales* and other anthologies. He lives in Tulsa with his wife, three children, and a spoiled dachshund.

> *All existence is a theft paid for by other existences; no life flowers except on a cemetery.—Remy de Gourmont*

> *"Eternity?… That is one hell of a movie."—J. B. D.*

The wooden detour barricade is barely in place when I spot the car closing fast from the east. Just a glint of light against the desert hills, yet I know it is *his* car. I ignite the last flare and toss it onto the centerline of the lonely rural two-lane highway.

Intersecting Highway 466 is an unpaved county road. Four miles west is a second, more infamous Y intersection: state route 41, near Cholame. In arid, remote Cholame, working men and ranchers are returning home in rattling pickups and dust-coated sedans like so many wind-blown tumbleweeds.

The car's mid-mounted 1.5 liter aluminum engine sings as it streaks toward me, gold rays of fading sunlight dancing along its sleek contours. It isn't slowing. Does he think the detour signs and hissing flares are a mirage?

The trained physicist in me recognizes the irony: If I stand still and die, I prove I've entered a malleable universe, a Wobbly-Brane. If not, he'll swerve to miss me instead of the Ford Tudor driven by a Cal Poly student, and die of internal injuries as he does in all the rigid-event universes. Like the one in which *you* live.

Tires shriek and the Porsche 550 Spyder slews to a stop a foot from my knees. I stare at its eternally youthful driver: the go-to-hell hair, high forehead, jutting chin and those cool baby-blues squinting at me behind tinted aviator glasses. I can hear my own heart pounding in my ears.

The tiny car crouches only inches above the road. The driver and a dark-haired passenger stare up at me.

"What's the emergency here, friend?"

"Detour," I stutter, a B-actor suffering from stage fright.

The driver turns down the blaring radio.

"Say again?"

"*Detour*," I repeat. "Highway's blocked off. Chemical truck tipped over and sprayed poison gas everywhere a mile from here. Heck of a mess."

The passenger is his racing mechanic, Rolf Wütherich. Dead from a 1981 auto accident after several failed suicide attempts, he grins. "Taking the back roads was a bad idea. The girls will be mad if we're late."

The driver scrutinizes the truck parked on the opposite shoulder. The hand-painted letters on its flaking side read: MONTEREY COUNTY ROAD DEPT. Is he suspicious?

"You fellows in a hurry to get someplace?"

The driver cocks a finger. "Got a race to win up in Salinas tomorrow. Will that road get us back on the highway?"

I nod, pointing with the flag. "It'll take you a few miles out of your way, but not far. Go six miles and take the first right. It's that or go back the way you came."

He removes his sunglasses and wipes road dust from the lenses on his white T-shirt. My mind records the tiny moon-shaped shaving cut along his chin; the way his hair curls back in carefree waves from his brow; the full, sensual lower lip, so like Brando's.

"Thanks for the warning, fellow. Try to stay out of the middle of the road."

He pops the race car named "Little Bastard" into gear and roars away into the twilight, the dry air whipping his hair, leaving a rooster tail of dust.

I wait ten minutes in the hot ticking silence to make certain he doesn't double back.

Science fiction writers had it wrong. In rigid-event universes—an infinite paper-doll chain of Earths separated by a quantum frequency shift that only a Device can interpolate—a mysterious, immutable law binds everything down to the subatomic level of reality. Elasticity is limited. Visitors may alter only the most negligible of details. In an ordinary universe, no matter what story I fabricate he'll get lost and return to find my barricade removed, and he'll proceed to his fate. Or he'll ignore the detour and roar past on the shoulder with a one-fingered salute. Or he'll take Highway 1 north from L.A. to Salinas.

In a Wobbly-B, phase space is unchained and events are malleable. We have a stiff, scientific acronym: Fluid-Event Branes.

I load the signs into the truck bed and kick the guttering flares onto the shoulder, hastily burying them under sand. A deep chime sounds inside my mind.

Hurry!

A two-tone Ford sedan wheezes by from the west, a lanky bespectacled young man behind the wheel. Mr. Turnipseed, saved from a lifetime of notoriety. Half an hour later another Ford will pass this spot trailing the Spyder, a station wagon driven by photographer Sanford Roth, with fellow racer Bill Hickman riding shotgun.

The sun, a fiery egg, slides behind the desert foothills. Soon people will shut their windows against the cold night air and the howl of coyotes prowling the Diablo Range like gray ghosts. And in the morning, James Byron Dean will stumble out of bed in a Salinas bungalow, his hair corkscrewed from sleep and his eyes sporting the dark bags immortalized in *LIFE*.

Alive and ready to race on the first day of October, 1955.

"Brane-slicer" contraband, case D-T 5154:
SHIPWRECKED (1957). JAMES DEAN, RITA HAYWORTH, JAMES GARNER, ROBERT WAGNER. WWII rebel James Dean and a strong supporting cast battle Japanese soldiers on a balmy pacific atoll. Directed by GEORGE STEVENS, Warner Bros., color, 137 minutes. First-generation 35mm Technicolor print.
Final Bid: $268M US
[bidder identity redacted pending prosecution]
CONTENTS OF THIS INVESTIGATION ARE CLASSIFIED by order of Director of National Intelligence (DNI) and Department of Defense / DARPA-TUNNEL

It isn't time travel. Please keep that firmly in mind.

Traveling to the past inside one's home universe is impossible. Traveling to a precise multiverse spacetime coordinate inside an adjacent reality *is* possible, if you possess a Device. Their inventor remains unknown. The trip utterly destroys every atom in your body, but a new copy of you arrives safely on the other side.

It's best if you don't think about that part.

My identity was erased after I stole a Device and deserted my job as a military physicist, but we'll use one of the aliases I take to deal with my carefully selected, extremely wealthy clients: Jason Blackstone, brane slicer. That's the slang term for outlaws like me.

Finding Jimmy in this 1956 isn't difficult.

The scene is the Villa Capri, Jimmy's favorite Hollywood bar. It's a popular hangout for stars, including the sexually indeterminate and closeted gay actors. I spot Anthony Perkins, buxom Terry Moore, bronzed Tab Hunter and an incredibly youthful Dennis Hopper. They stop at Jimmy's table to pay their respects. *Rebel* has opened and teenagers are flocking to theaters. George Stevens is trying to edit *Giant* down to two-hundred minutes to meet an August release, two months early, because he doesn't need to secretly hire Nick Adams to dub Jimmy's muffled, drunken lines in the last-supper scene.

From my bar stool I make eye contact.

I've replaced the filthy overalls and dust with slacks and an open-throated shirt, dark hair combed back. No flicker of recognition.

Brooding is Jimmy's specialty, so I step to his table and buy him a drink. He stops fooling with those bongos he carries everywhere. He has bags under his eyes and is dressed in the rig that so infuriated the studio heads until they realized its marketing potential—scuffed boots, T-shirt, faded jeans and a dirty leather jacket.

My face is familiar but he hasn't made the connection. We drink and talk about the races and the new Triumph 650cc Tiger motorcycle.

In his nearby bungalow he falls asleep as I rattle on about classic films and performances. He would often fall sound asleep in restaurants during conversations. When he finally stirs, I recount our meeting on the road to Cholame and Paso Robles. His face hardens in a mask of suspicion. If a ten-gallon hat were pushed back on his head, the image of Jett Rink, the angry, loveless cowboy, would be complete. He glances at my bare forearms, looking for the needle marks of a heroin addict.

"You're from the future and I'm a ghost."

"It's a lot to process."

He laughs. "So is Eisenhower going to be re-elected? When are the Reds gonna drop an atom bomb on New York?"

I'm not about to discuss a technology that shifts a conscious organism through the multiverse, burrowing through infinite branes, if you'll excuse the morbid turn of phrase. The time-travel hokum works best.

Jimmy stabs out his cigarette and vaults up from the sofa. He smiles, exhaling smoke from both nostrils.

"You're a fruitcake."

I stay seated, keeping my voice low and even.

"Jimmy, you should at least hear what I have to say."

He slips on the black leather jacket over the crumpled T-shirt and is instantly transformed into Jim Stark, the volatile middle-class rebel with smoldering eyes.

"I think you better hit the road."

I do as he says, but pause at the door.

"Your first dog, Tuck, used to piss all over your Aunt Ortense's back porch in the winter, next to that little black potbelly stove. Stunk like hell. Your favorite ice cream is coffee and raspberry mixed together. Revolting. Your favorite book is *The Little Prince*. Favorite poet: James Whitcomb Riley. Favorite waiter in New York: Louie de Liso at Jerry's Bar and Restaurant. Louie used to serve you plates of spaghetti on the house when your money ran out between jobs—"

Jimmy doesn't blink. "Anybody could have dug all that up with a PI."

"And the detour near Cholame?"

His eyes narrow. "I've done lots of work on television. You recognized me. I just can't see what your angle is."

"Lola Barnes."

That gets an instant reaction.

"She seduced you after the Sadie Hawkins dance your senior year in high school and you sweated until you were certain she wasn't pregnant."

He opens his mouth to reply, but I interrupt him in my omnipotent, time-traveler-knows-all voice.

"I've studied your entire life, Jimmy. Right up until the end."

Stark is gone. He looks like a kid jarred awake from a nightmare only to discover that it has crawled out from under the bed.

"It was a near head-on collision with a 1950 Ford sedan driven by a kid named Donald Turnipseed," I continue. "You weren't traveling twice the speed limit as people reported for years, but you weren't wearing a seat belt. Rolf was thrown clear, but you were declared dead in the ambulance on the way to the hospital in Paso Robles at 5:59 Pacific Time."

He runs a hand wildly through his hair. "This is *nuts*."

"Would I make up a name like Turnipseed?"

"Next you'll tell me you ride around in one of those flying saucers," he says in a sulky tone.

Jung was right: flying saucers are a manifestation of our collective fears in an epoch in which mankind's own creations are more horrifying than any brimstone Underworld. But parallel universes, which precede early Hindu mythology, are quite real.

This jaunt has almost expired.

"I protect unique, lost works of art, like twentieth-century motion pictures."

"So why me? I'm a nobody."

This is the hook, and the only undeniable truth.

"You're one of the greatest actors of your generation, and three films wasn't enough. You'll have the opportunity to develop your craft and not be pigeonholed as the bad-boy rebel. Isn't that what you've dreamed of since you raised sheep on your uncle's farm?"

Disbelief and desperate hope collide in his eyes like a stormfront.

"What if I decide to never step in front of a camera again?" He crosses his arms, dips his chin. That willful petulance—

I smile. "Jimmy, it's your life and future. Except with one possible caveat."

"Oh yeah?"

"When I saved your life, I created a small fracture in reality. Like a fault line."

"What does that mean?"

"If you move back to Indiana and become a dentist, events could snap back like a rubber band."

"You mean—"

His enigmatic mother, Mildred Dean, succumbed to ovarian cancer when he was nine. She has haunted his life. Jimmy's greatest anxiety is the specter of death, and he instinctively rejected the afterlife espoused by his aunt and uncle. That's the lever I use.

"You'll die, Jimmy. Like you were meant to."

"Brane slicer" contraband, case D-T 2756
Diana: My Story (2017). Autobiography of the former Princess of

Wales chronicling her privileged childhood, education, life before and after Prince Charles, motherhood, her second and third marriages, a failed 2008 suicide attempt, and her re-dedication to charitable work. Random House, 398 pages. Stated first edition. Signed by the author.

Bid: $71M EUR [convicted bidder identity redacted]

In 1974 an Air Force corporal named Pete Moss (no more a joke name than Turnipseed) found a small transistor radio that wasn't a radio. It was constructed using highly advanced fabrication technologies, unrecognizable at the time. A Device's invisible skin resembles graphene, incredibly strong layers of carbon arranged in a hexagon honeycomb lattice an atom thick. Inside there are no solid-state circuits or chips. Instead, intricate networks of nano-machines and quantum computers the size of large molecules link with other Devices across universes using an entanglement codec like a cosmic GPS unit, calibrating frequency shifts and navigation. Devices aren't solid objects in the conventional sense and they easily take the form of ordinary items, chromatic surface particles coordinating to mimic a pack of cigarettes or a smartphone.

Moss's discovery lay forgotten in Pentagon storage for forty-five years until a brilliant young DARPA analyst named Dick Jenks activated it. More on Jenks later.

DARPA-Tunnel physicists failed to reverse-engineer the Devices, but they uncovered a wholly unexpected view of existence: that endless paper-doll chain of Earths characterized by a puzzling dominant sameness. All those stories we loved of snuffing out Hitler or arming the Rebs with machine guns or stopping Oswald from murdering JFK—hopeless.

And the Devices impose three primary restrictions. Considering that we're still homicidal primates, I think that's fortunate, don't you?

You cannot visit a *future* coordinate on another Earth. Maybe this is a fundamental law of travel of the multiverse, or maybe it's a governor function.

Second, you can never revisit the same coordinate in the same universe.

Third, you always arrive on Earth. The Devices don't double as transdimensional portals to Altair IV or exo-planets like Gliese 581g. A Tunnel sub-team is exploring this possibility: a cornucopian New World of raw material would vault America back to superpower status. If there's an indigenous population, well, I think of Chris Columbus, and shudder.

Dick Jenks whimsically called it the Cristóbal Effect.

The Devices deny us the tantalizing power to redirect history, but someone with access could employ one in that most signature human enterprise—making astounding amounts of money on a black market unlike any in history. Brane slicers.

What exactly were you expecting?

"You're some kind of criminal, aren't you?"

We're poking around the engine of Jimmy's Spyder, parked at the edge of a dusty Bakersfield raceway. It's March 20, 1956.

I grin at Jimmy. "I prefer the term *rebel*."

Beneath that teen-idol exterior he's a maelstrom of driven ambition and vulnerability.

"You've got to tell me one thing," he asks. "Am I going to win it this time?"

"You'll have to wait, I'm afraid."

I clap an oil-blackened hand on Jimmy's shoulder, and he winces.

Eight days later he beats out Anthony Quinn, Robert Stack and Anthony Perkins to accept the Best Supporting Actor Academy Award for *Giant*.

I studied film history at Colombia while majoring in particle physics. I loved the magic of early cinema before digital effects and motion-capture, so it's easy to convince myself that I'm doing a Great Thing. Saving important films that should have been made, etc. The row of glowing numbers in my encrypted offshore bank account strongly suggests that I am as full of shit as Dick Jenks.

Ask yourself why Christopher Columbus petitioned various European crowns for nearly a decade to finance his dream of a quicker trade route to India. Any classroom of overfed American children will tell you that the son of a wool weaver and sometimes cheese-stand merchant was a visionary explorer whose brave tenacity forever changed world history. Forget that their nation is erected atop a graveyard of butchered and displaced human beings. Forget the titles (Admiral of the Ocean Seas) and riches (Hispaniola gold and ten percent of all profits made in the new lands) that drove Columbus to make four hazardous journeys to the New World. Catholic priest Bartolomé de las Casas catalogued the crimes committed against the people "discovered" by Columbus and his hired Spaniards during the years of single-minded pursuit of wealth and prestige: "My eyes have seen these acts so foreign to human nature, and now I tremble as I write."

Humans are explorers, but our motivations haven't changed since before we stood fully upright.

For myself, money is no longer a valid motivation. The next films are purely for art, for posterity.

Jimmy's name, in glowing ruby capitals, dwarfs even the picture's title, *Shipwrecked*, atop the Grauman's Chinese Theatre marquee.

Inside the lobby I stop to admire a movie poster depicting Jimmy battling Japanese soldiers on a lush pacific atoll. Jimmy gleams like a knight in his pearl-white Navy uniform, a blazing .45 Colt in either hand. A banner blares, GEORGE STEVENS' GREATEST EPIC YET! and *Over Two Years in the Making!* I shake my head in wonderment. In an eternity of 1957s, *The Bridge on the River Kwai* dominated the awards, but now?

I approach Jimmy, with Ursula Andress at his side radiating glamour like a quasar. I pluck a fluted glass of champagne from a passing waiter and spill it down the front of Jimmy's tuxedo jacket. The sycophants surrounding him draw back, aghast.

"Godallmighty, I'm sorry! Let me get you cleaned up!"

Inside the men's washroom, I dab away at his soggy jacket with a wet silk handkerchief, but he shoves me against the porcelain sink.

"You."

"That was intentional, but my hands *are* shaking," I say. "I'm about to see the *fourth* great James Dean film. You once said you wanted to do *Hamlet* while you were young, and re-create the role of Billy the Kid onscreen. The future is yours."

He glares into the ornate mirror. "You'll come back for those, too."

He turns and the bipolar, fear-shrouded Jimmy emerges.

"I ain't afraid of the future. I'm afraid of *you*. I have awful dreams after you go…wherever. I didn't sell the Spyder because of what that fop Guinness said in the papers, I just couldn't stand riding in it anymore. I'm not some damned puppet."

Jimmy pivots and punches me in the face. Flashbulbs pop inside my head and I sag to the tiled floor.

"Sorry about the eye," Jimmy says, "but I've got a reputation to maintain."

The tissue around my eye tingles and swells. I grin up at him. "No need to apologize."

This body, face and sizzling nerve endings will be annihilated in fifteen minutes.

Jimmy stalks out to rejoin his waiting entourage.

"Brane-slicer" contraband, case D-T 6987:

The Wolf (1905), Frank Norris, Doubleday, Page & Co., 354 pages—Norris's final Naturalist novel in his sweeping *The Epic of the Wheat* trilogy (following *The Octopus* and *The Pit*) describes the American-grown wheat relieving a famine-stricken village in Europe. Signed clothbound first edition.

Bid: $48.6M US [buyer identity redacted based on plea-bargain to assist in the apprehension of the seller]

The paramount rule in the unwritten Brane Slicer's Guide to Survival is, don't get caught. The second rule is, *never* get altruistic about your work. You're a quantum-tunneling conquistador, not Captain Kirk. The only Prime Directive is to make money.

Consider the tale of Dick Jenks.

Jenks was obsessed with Lennon. He abandoned his research and became the founding father of brane slicers so he could prevent the shooting outside The Dakota and allow his idol's musical renaissance to flourish beyond *Double Fantasy* and the posthumous, incomplete *Milk and Honey*. Jenks tried to intercede on a thousand Earths and watched Lennon die again and again. He eventually located a Wobbly-B, but the D-T boys were closing in, and he cracked. Jenks disguised himself as Lennon, identical clothes, black wire-rimmed glasses and a wig. He arrived sixty seconds ahead of schedule and Chapman, waiting in the gloom, emptied his pistol into Jenks instead. Lennon was so shaken by the near miss that he withdrew from public life, went back on H, and turned the paranoid dial up to ten. He died of an overdose on Christmas Eve 1980.

Poor Jenks. It wasn't a Wobbly.

Having auctioned the *Shipwrecked* print, my plan is to undergo extensive gene therapy and pop back into my wonderful Wobbly to, say, the high-flying 1990s. Stow the Device somewhere, and live off interest.

But first—

"What the hell is this?" Jimmy says.

We're on the Universal backlot in the Old West Town, spring 1963.

"It's the Hitchcock script I gave you. It'll be groundbreaking, like *Psycho*. Hitchcock will be back on top, and you'll win another Oscar."

Kaleidoscope is the crypt-dark Hitchcock masterpiece that every studio passed on, the story of a handsome young serial killer, told from the murderer's perspective. He planned to shoot it using hand-held cameras, three decades before *The Blair Witch Project*. Only Jimmy could invoke the necessary mix of sex appeal and tortured soul.

"He's a rapist," Jimmy says. "What would my fans think?"

He drops the script and walks away, spurs jingling.

Jimmy's career is in a tailspin. He is arrested for beating a gossip columnist over a scathing review of his *Hamlet*, and again when he breaks a director's nose after a botched scene in *Billy the Kid Rides Again* with John Wayne. The studio heads are tired of the drinking, reckless driving between films and scandals. Jimmy is thirty-three and looks forty-five. He's uninsurable. Jack Warner dumps him. Paramount signs and then drops him after he walks off the set of a love triangle with Jane Fonda and Paul Newman.

Jimmy cables Hitchcock and tells him what a fat, sick bastard he is. MCA drops the project.

I confront Jimmy in his trailer on the set of *The Horror of Party Beach*. It is June 1964, and Jimmy's hair is thinning, his face hollowed. The trailer reeks of sour beer and marijuana. His dust-covered bongos are piled in one corner, half-buried by soiled clothes.

I am dressed as a stagehand. "The director is waiting for you."

Jimmy is sprawled on a sofa bed, drinking from a bottle of Jack Daniel's. He glares at the walls and motions for me to leave.

I say, "Remember when you shot *East of Eden*? You used to whistle when you were ready for a scene. It was a signal you and Kazan worked out."

Jimmy flinches and his arm knocks the bottle off the sofa. He watches whiskey gurgle onto the dirty carpet before grabbing it. He staggers to his feet and I recoil from the anguish in his eyes.

"Jimmy—"

He gestures around the trailer. "Not exactly the Chateau Marmont, is it? I'm just doing this little picture to...to *broaden* my range." He laughs, a humorless whistling sound. "Will I win an Oscar for this one?"

He hurls something and I duck. The whiskey bottle spins over my head to shatter against the wall.

Jimmy removes a small blue-steel revolver from the mirrored counter and crosses the length of the trailer with surprising speed, kicking litter out of his way. His pale, whiskered face looks feral. He aims the pistol at my head and cocks the hammer.

"Stop screwing with my life." His eyes are flat, like a shark's.

The chime sounds inside my mind. I back slowly to the door. "I gave you a second chance, Jimmy. I warned you about instability—"

"I think you've been lying to me from the start," he says, and his finger whitens on the trigger.

At forty-six, Jimmy is unrecognizable. The hair clinging to his scalp in a widow's peak is gray and closely cropped. His face is an atlas of wrinkles. His eyes are rheumy and vacant. The tip of his left ear is missing. It is November 1977.

I sit beside him on the park bench and sling birdseed to a motley band of Central Park pigeons. Jimmy smokes a lumpy hand-rolled cigarette and stares straight through the bright clusters of playground children.

Given the gift of years, his feverish passion for his craft should have blossomed—but his soul was eaten away by the moths of time like Welles and Brando. If he were alive, crazy Dick Jenks would be rolling on the damp pavement, roaring laughter, scaring the pigeons.

"Hello, Jimmy."

His head swivels like a gun turret. His eyes focus.

"So I didn't kill you."

"No, but it was very close."

His face crumples like newspaper.

"Have you spoken to your daughter? Have you thought about working again, something small like off-Broadway theater?"

Defiant fire stokes behind Jimmy's eyes. I see Jim Stark, not a broken, prematurely old man.

"You can go straight to hell."

I place a white envelope on the bench seat.

Jimmy flicks away the cigarette butt and leans close enough for me to smell his poverty and despair.

"Money inside? What I *want* is to wake up, and all of this be a bad dream." He grabs the scarf around my neck in his wiry hands and hauls me to my feet. His voice rises in pitch, the lost sound of a frightened child. "I want to be young again. I want to be famous again." His eyes tear up.

"I want to be *great* again. You can wind all this back," he chokes, "and this time you don't put up that detour."

"Jimmy, I can't return to the same places and times. But I have a plan—"

He opens the envelope as if it might contain a black widow, and shakes the contents into his palm: Marlboro cigarettes and a small drift of diamonds.

He scatters the gemstones to the pigeons and tosses me the cigarettes.

"I quit in prison."

"Wait, that's not a pa—" I stop.

Jimmy shuffles away, gloveless hands buried in frayed coat pockets, disappearing into the gray New York streets he once haunted.

Columbus, our merchant-apostle, fervently believed that as lord of Hispaniola he would bring piety and civilization to the barbarous *los Indios* he ruled, but all he brought was epidemic and atrocity. He died a bitter pauper, unable to return to the New World with more ships and soldiers. Until his last breath he remained convinced he could rectify his mistakes and his reputation.

In uncounted worlds Jimmy is preserved as a youthful, misunderstood lost soul of postwar cinema, his mystery secure and eternal. Just look at what I've reduced him to in this one.

I return the identical Device disguised as a pack of smokes into my coat pocket next to its twin.

A chime, and the park vanishes in a silent white supernova.

The little car is a nimble bullet.

I blink and grip the steering wheel with white-knuckled hands, feel my right foot pressing the accelerator pedal. The desert wind screams past and the supercharger howls in answer. I glance in the little side mirror and see Jimmy's twenty-four-year-old face. No. My face. *Our face.*

Memory pours back like freezing stream water.

I return after the older, broken Jimmy shuffles away, the pigeons pecking at diamonds, and they're waiting for me. Commando shapes in night-gear, the cough and bee-sting of subsonic missiles striking my upper back and neck. A short fall into blackness.

"Better ease off a bit," says Rolf Wütherich, resurrected from dust to take this fateful ride again. "Shoot a piston and you won't be racing for a week."

I forgot to tell you how they dispose of brane slicers.

They might strand you 350 million years ago in Paleozoic Kansas when it was a vast lowland swamp, part of the supercontinent Laurussia, a tasty lunch for the twenty-foot crocodiles and meter-long scorpions. Or your consciousness is transmitted into the cranium of a pinstripe-suited stockbroker right before the first airliner knifes into the WTC North Tower on 9/11, experiencing that doomed soul's final moments of stark terror.

The last mile unwinds like the final reel of a familiar film. The radio plays "Love's Old Sweet Song." A hawk flaps up from a telephone pole. The mechanical clock in the Spyder's dashboard reads 5:39 P.M.

We round a bend and cruise down a mild hill toward the 41 junction. A car is waiting, a '50 Ford Tudor, idling on the centerline. Jimmy's heart—

my heart—begins hammering a slow drum-roll. Sweat rolls into my eyes. Piloted by the dependable Donald Turnipseed, the Ford hesitates and then lurches across the ash-colored highway. Rolf shouts above the wind as I veer directly into its path. His hand reaches for the wheel and I bat it away. No sense in fighting fate unless you're in a Wobbly. The blunt chrome nose of the Ford blots out the high deep-blue sky. I glimpse its driver's white face. It's a good death, and just penance for my avarice.

Jimmy's face smiles in the mirror, young again. Immortal again. In that last instant before we hit, I give him a wink.

—For Alexandra

BEYOND PORCH AND PORTAL

E. CATHERINE TOBLER

E. Catherine Tobler lives and writes in Colorado—strange how that works out. Among others, her fiction has appeared in *Sci Fiction, Fantasy Magazine, Realms of Fantasy, Talebones*, and *Lady Churchill's Rosebud Wristlet*. She is an active member of SFWA and senior editor at *Shimmer Magazine*.

When they found my uncle wandering incoherent in the foggy morning streets he wasn't wearing his own clothes.

A man unknown to me brought word of my uncle's illness, presenting me with a small folded letter on fine ivory paper. The paper *shushed* between our bare fingers a moment before he turned away. He traced his way through the general store with its many occupants, back into the bustle of the street.

"Sir!"

Clutching the letter at which I'd only glanced, I followed him through the double doors, grabbing his jacket sleeve before he could be overcome by a claret and gold four-in-hand. The black horses blew past us and onward down the cobblestones with the loud ring of their silver-shod feet overtaking my words.

The man glared down at me as if I had upset his day rather than he mine. There was something in his eyes, half familiar and frightening. He was not an older man; he seemed of a marrying age, but I knew he was not married. How I knew this, I could not say. He disliked my consideration of him and twisted his arm free from my hold.

"You'd best go *now*. He hasn't much time."

"Are you a friend to my uncle?"

He refused me even that much information and hurried down the street after the four-in-hand, October's breeze lifting the tails of his coat behind him. I blinked once and he was fully gone. If anyone else upon the street noticed something odd about that, they didn't look sideways. I expected someone to gasp and say, "But here, he walked here a moment ago, and now has vanished like a candle's flame under a breath!" No one said a word; the people were too wrapped in their own business.

Carefully I smoothed the letter I had crumpled. The ink had smudged upon the page, written in a hand I did not know. My uncle had been found this morning; he now rested at the college hospital and, as the mysterious man had, the letter urged me to hurry to his side before he passed into the next world.

There were things in that next world that my uncle would welcome, I thought as I left off shopping and followed the fingerboards to the hospital. I had never been there in my twenty years. My mother and father died there, so my uncle told me, leaving me in his capable care ever after.

He seemed capable no longer. Doctors led me to my uncle's side and he did not know me. He clutched at my skirts and muttered, "Reynolds, *fonderous* Reynolds..."

I untangled his hand and saw that he indeed wore someone else's clothes. The trousers were butternut, the coat an earthy brown. My uncle always, even on Sundays, wore black. Even his boiled shirts would have been black, but this one was whiter than I'd ever seen, with a smudge of blood against the collar, were blood to be mostly ochre.

"Uncle?"

He startled and reached blindly out. I grabbed his clammy hand and lowered myself to his bedside, to breathe in the scent of him. There was no alcohol on his breath as I'd feared. He groaned and tried to roll away from me. This motion pulled his shirt cuff back, exposing the pink, abraded skin of his wrist.

"What happened to you?" I whispered. I couldn't fathom it.

Edgar Poe was my only kin; the man who taught me geography and history, the man who could scare a rational-minded young woman like me under my bed with his stories of vengeful madmen; the man who preferred spending rainy days writing poetry or walking Baltimore's streets in search of such.

"Fonderous R-Reynolds?" he asked. "The s-seam above the floor? Oh, vast sky." He closed his eyes and turned his head against the pillow, but held firm to my hand.

"Miss Franks?"

Dr. Griffin, an older man with soft hands and hard eyes, had been known to me for years. The first time my uncle was found publicly drunk, it was Dr. Griffin who brought him to the hospital to sober up. I saw pity on his face now, but I shook my head and stood to meet him.

"He's sober," I said.

The doctor scrubbed a hand over his unshaven cheeks. "Your assessment agrees with my own. Your uncle is suffering from a malady unknown to me. Did he recognize you?"

"No." I looked down at my uncle. "I saw him just yesterday and he was well. Have you seen his wrist?"

"Reynolds!" my uncle cried. "Endless lands! Vilest fire." He shoved the sheets off his body, scrambling backward in an attempt to get out of the bed. When he hit the headboard, he turned to his left, rolled onto the checkerboard floor, and crawled away.

Dr. Griffin called for his colleagues; I could not get near my uncle without him shrieking anew. I backed away, only realizing I was crying when Nurse Templeton shoved a handkerchief into my hand.

"Go home, Miss Franks," Dr. Griffin said over his struggles with my uncle.

"The seam!" My uncle screamed these words, over and over until I covered my ears to block it—but still, I heard it like a heartbeat. *The seam. The seam.*

Dr. Griffin and three other men carried my uncle back to the bed and firmly strapped him down. By hand and foot they bound him and when this made his screams worse, they also bound his mouth. He screamed even beyond the gag, muffled and strained.

"You can't!"

Nurse Templeton led me out of the room and closed the door behind us. I was shaking as she guided me to a chair and pushed me into it. I stared at her heavily lined mouth, unable to understand a word that came from it. She gave me a hard shake and then I heard, "...come again tomorrow; perhaps he will be well."

I knew as I walked back to our townhouse in the mist, that one evening would not solve my uncle's problems. What had happened to haunt his eyes so? What part did the stranger from this morning play?

My uncle had employed a housekeeper these last two years, to tidy what he messed while I spent my days as a tailor's assistant. Though Mrs. Wine would have made me a warm dinner, I sent her home. I wanted only to be alone. I locked the door behind her, discarded my coat and bag, and went to my uncle's office.

It was the one room Mrs. Wine was asked not to touch, but nothing struck me as unusual as I entered. Papers and books were spread over the sofa and chairs, over desktop and floor. I lifted a pile from one chair and sat, bringing the sheets into my lap. He was working on a new poem.

I fell asleep reading of a city by the sea, where mortals bought fruit from angels carrying baskets. I didn't dream of this place; I didn't dream of anything. When I woke, I felt rested and wondered if morning had come, but the thought left my mind when I saw the man who gave me the note perched in a far corner, watching me.

Think of it. You believe yourself alone in your own home, are comfortable enough to sleep wherever you lay down and when you wake, your mind still fuzzy from its rest, you discover yourself not alone, but watched. Your mind races, but it can't catch your heart. How long has he watched you?

Was he there when I came in? Who is he and how did he gain entry? I pictured broken windows and doors, but felt it was worse than that; this man had come inside another way, a way unknown to me. That frightened me most of all.

"Please do not scream," he said.

I screamed. I flung my uncle's poetry and fled the office, feeling this man close on my heels. He yanked the door open when I meant to slam it; he snatched my skirts, slowing my escape. His fingers seemed to catch my hair and pull me backward. Through his fingertips I felt shackles around my uncle's wrists. Those hands had placed them there, but not in this world, in another.

"Reynolds?" I asked.

His touch vanished. I swung around in the darkness of the hallway and felt a presence, though I could not see him.

"He called me that." His crumpled velvet voice brushed against my cheek. "Go to your uncle."

The voice came from all around me now, disembodied. As I turned round, I would have sworn to the stroke of fingers against my skirts. *Shush. Shush.*

My heart pounded in my throat. "What did you do to my uncle?"

This man admitted nothing. Round and round he circled me. I felt his eyes upon me (half familiar and frightening!) but still I could see nothing of him. Maddening! His cold-kissed fingers brushed over my cheeks and then I was horribly alone.

I did not sleep that night. I checked the doors and windows, but decided it would not matter how securely they were locked. That man had come into our house another way. Taking no chance, I retrieved my uncle's small pistol from the locked box beneath his bed and sat with my back to the wall the entire night through. Rain drummed upon the roof; in its rhythm, I found words. *The seam. The seam.*

Come morning, I went to the hospital, the pistol concealed in my bro-cade reticule. I would not be caught unawares another time by Reynolds, whatever name he took.

My uncle was less coherent that morning, Dr. Griffin reluctant to allow me into his room.

"I have bled him twice to no effect," Griffin said to me outside my uncle's door. The doctor paced, slapping the back of one hand into the palm of the other. "I begin to fear, Miss Franks, that he has a blackness within him and if I cannot find and remove it, he shall perish."

Reynolds' first words echoed back at me. *"You'd best go now. He hasn't much time."* Would he perish at the doctor's hands or was my uncle already near death from whatever had befallen him?

I gripped my reticule, feeling through the fabric the line of the pistol. Was it the solidity of the gun that calmed me or the idea of pressing it against Reynolds' chin?

"I want to speak with my uncle," I said and made to move past the doctor, to open my uncle's door.

Griffin grabbed me by the arm to forestall me, then dropped it when a nurse passed us. He bowed his head to look at me through narrowed eyes.

"Absolutely not! I don't believe you grasp the seriousness of the situation, Miss Franks."

Being accosted by a strange man in one's own home was quite serious enough for me.

Griffin continued. His tone was low and calm, as though he were trying to calm a spooked horse. "When I remove his gag, he speaks of terrible things. I do not understand the blackness within him. I need to find it, cut it out. We loosened him for a bit this morning as a test and he nearly cut out his own eye—"

I grabbed Dr. Griffin by the arm as he had me in an effort to make him understand that on this matter I would not be budged. "I will speak with my uncle," I said. "No matter the terrible things he says, I will."

The doctor let me step into the room and did not follow. I closed the door to blot out his disapproving expression. However, now in the gray room with its scent of antiseptic and rapidly aging old man, I hesitated. I looked across the room at the figure in the bed and did not recognize it for my uncle. This man was thin and dark, lashed to a bed with a thin mattress. A hard rubber gag covered his mouth and now even his eyes were masked. Coarse hair covered his sunken cheeks.

"Uncle?"

He did not move and I wondered if he was sleeping. Or dead. I held my breath as I waited for the rise of his chest. Only when I saw that feeble movement did I step toward the bed.

I set my reticule on the bedside table and reached for the mask which covered Edgar's eyes. The tie was lost in the bird's nest of his hair; it took some time to find the end. When at last I loosened the ties, I found myself looking into unfamiliar eyes. Or let me say that upon longer examination, the eyes themselves were painfully familiar—it was the deep wrinkles around them, it was the pale white scar above the left eye, it was the freshly stitched wound below the right—these were the things I could not equate with my uncle.

With some difficulty I loosened and removed the gag from his mouth. Edgar closed his mouth, licked his lips, and swallowed.

"Do you know me?" I asked him.

His eyes rolled back into his head and he turned his cheek against the pillow. "Vilest fire." His voice cracked the words apart like they were nutshells in his throat. "Hunters stab never sleeping sky—the seam above the floor. The seam—"

He spoke of phenomenon and contraptions I could not understand while his hands moved against his bonds, fingers straining to reach the unseen. His eyes seemed to watch an invisible dance in the air between the bed and ceiling; flit, flit, glide.

I had hoped to make some sense of the "terrible things" Dr. Griffin mentioned, but as my uncle spoke on and on until his voice dried to a whisper, I could find no reason in the words. There was only one word that made sense to me and when he said it at last, his eyes moved to the far corner of the room.

"Reynolds."

I turned in time to see the man called Reynolds slink out of the room. The tail of his brown coat (how like the coat my uncle had been found in) slithered out the door a second before it closed.

How long has he watched you?
How did he get in?

My heart stammered in my chest. I grabbed my bag and followed Reynolds from the hall, only in time to see his coattails once again slide around a distant corner. I fled past Dr. Griffin and into the blowing rain of the day. Reynolds was a tall man with a long stride and there was no keeping pace with him. By the time I reached the store where I had first met Reynolds, I could see no sign of him.

Then, coming down the cobblestones appeared the same gold and claret four-in-hand I had seen the day before, Reynolds now perched beside the driver. The horses' hooves didn't seem to touch the ground, even though I heard them clearly ring against the street stone. I lunged into the street, for the driver would have to stop for fear that he might hit me, but he didn't. The hot breath of one horse curled over my cheek before the world went black.

I woke, if one can awaken when one does not remember sleeping, atop the auburn horse, harness and tack cutting into my left hand, while my right still clung to my bag with its pistol. The ground sped away beneath me at a dreadful haste and for a moment I buried my face in the horse's mane. My cheek lay against hot horsehide, silky red-gold mane blinding me, every part of my body jostled as the carriage continued onward.

I chanced a backwards glance at the driver and Reynolds and squeezed my eyes shut a second after. They were not men!

Another look proved this true. The driver sat tall in the seat, a black coat dripping from its narrow body. A tattered blue scarf gave the illusion of a neck, but I feared he truly had none. The octangular head was small and gray, with bulging black eyes that must have taken everything in at once. Surely he saw me staring at his four spindly legs and two arms, all of which seemed employed in driving the carriage. His arms bore spines and hooks, over which he had draped a couple reins, but I felt certain this wasn't their main usage.

"Miss Franks!"

It was Reynolds who spoke, but a Reynolds I did not recognize. Reynolds possessed a squat body, colored brown with slim yellow stripes, and he now spoke through mandibles. His brown coat had pooled around him; why, his thin arms would never support the fabric!

"Hold fast!" he said. "We cannot stop in the endless lands."

I turned my head around, so that I might see these endless lands for myself; lifted myself on elbows enough to see around the whipping horse mane.

Every bit of Baltimore had vanished and all around us spread a seemingly endless blur of gold shot through with ruby stars. Whirlpools twisted in the sky, churning nausea within me as I watched them. I watched until I felt I would be ill, then bowed and buried my head again. I prayed the ride would soon be over, but perhaps there was no one to answer that prayer, for the ride went on and on.

The motion of the horse beneath me soon became familiar, enjoyable. I had never known such a sensation. Its warm hide was also a comfort as the air grew colder around us. There seemed to be no sun, yet all around us were slanting shafts of light. Colored golden and ivory, they fell from above and the more I watched them, the more my eyes began to adjust and see what truly lay around us.

The land was no longer barren. Perhaps it never had been. My eyes became accustomed to the light and the way it changed the landscape around us. From one angle, the land was empty; from another, I could glimpse strange constructs in the distance. There seemed to be little near the horizon; everything I was able to see hovered in that sunless sky. If I saw other people, it was only briefly; I saw what seemed a woman, but the wind was tearing her apart. She shredded, arms and legs peeling apart like fabric, and then even her clothing lifted up and away. This didn't seem to bother her. She smiled and went on her way, into the vast sky.

Oh, that vast sky—my uncle's sky? Had he seen this place and breathed this air? This air, that smelled vaguely of apricots and roasting meat, washed over us in abrupt gusts, forcing my eyes shut. I savored the darkness.

I couldn't understand this place. What was it and how could it exist? The more I wondered, the more ill I felt. I remembered my Baltimore with its rain-washed streets, hints of sky caught between close buildings, people rushing to and from work. There seemed no such things here.

The carriage never slowed. My nausea deepened. I became aware of hands on my shoulders, an arm under my legs. Reynolds lifted me from the horse and carried me back into the carriage itself. I lay on the padded bench and stared at him sitting opposite me. In this light, he looked like a man and had a beautiful mouth.

The thought should have shocked me, but it didn't.

"You shouldn't be here," he said.

"That much is plain." I had to fight to say the words and my voice didn't sound right when I finally forced them out. I fought also to sit up, to focus my attention on Reynolds. Even though I knew he wasn't a man, he appeared as such and it gradually began to calm my mind.

"You've placed me in quite a predicament," he added.

I could hardly believe he was serious, but I recalled the look on his face the day we'd met, when I'd pulled him back from this very carriage. I now understood I had kept him from returning. What had drawn him out in the first place? What else tied us together? My uncle, I thought as my eyes settled on Reynolds' vest.

"You— You're wearing my uncle's vest," I said. "I sewed it for him—"

"A gift last Christmas," Reynolds said.

His dark velvet voice was rough again. "How can you know that?" My hands sought the bag at my side, but I no longer carried it; my pistol was lost.

"Edgar told me all about you." His mouth bent into a smile and I realized this man knew things about me he shouldn't know. He knew about my first pet (a kitten named Croak) and my first formal dance (how I'd stumbled down the last two stairs and fallen to reveal entirely too much to those gathered); he knew my uncle's stories could frighten me, and he knew that deep down, I loved the fear.

"I don't understand." I blinked back tears and looked out the carriage window. The angle of light allowed me to see to the horizon this time. Against its water-washed color, I saw a wrecked whale bone ship. Closer to the carriage wheels, I saw pallid bloated creatures upon the shifting ground. One of them held a golden key in its mouth.

"How long have you known my uncle?" I asked. I looked back at Reynolds, who watched me and not the world beyond the windows. "How long was he your prisoner?"

"I did not imprison your uncle, though others of my kind did."

"I felt you put those shackles on him."

Reynolds said nothing to that. Maybe it was an action he couldn't argue; maybe he had been forced. Whichever, he kept his silence, watching me with keen eyes that seemed to see all of me at once. He knew my parents were dead, and he knew— He knew Edgar was my only family.

"Stop watching me," I whispered.

"I will not," Reynolds said. "I spent far too many years dreaming of you to look away now."

I curled my hands into my skirts. "What the devil do you mean by that?" If I thought I could have survived it, I would have jumped from the carriage. I think Reynolds must have known this, for he grasped my hands and held me firm.

"Your uncle should never have come here. I tried to fix that and have failed. The least I could do was see that he didn't die alone this time. He's gone now. All you've known is gone. You shouldn't be here, but I can't help but be happy you are."

I jumped from the carriage then. Reynolds' words scared me worse than the idea of death. I wrenched my hands out of his, pushed him backwards, and kicked the door open. I flung myself into the speeding landscape and landed in sandy, loose ground.

There was no sign of the carriage, nor any sound from it. Its wheels had left no tracks. Wherever I was, I needed to get out, but there was nothing to guide me. No sun, no landmarks, nothing on the horizon here. I wiped the grit from my eyes and strained to see through the beams of light.

Reynolds found me first. I caught him from the corner of my eye, running at me as fast as the carriage horses had flown. I turned to run, but the ground seemed to suck me down. Reynolds was on me before I could escape; he dragged me down and pinned my hands, slapping a shackle around one wrist.

"Beast!" I cried, unable to wrench myself free.

"Literally, that is true," Reynolds said. His nice mouth curled in a sneer. "Edgar called me fonderous."

I slapped him with my free hand. He felt of flesh and bone and his skin reddened as would any man's under a strike, but he only laughed and secured the other shackle to my other wrist.

"Come on."

Reynolds kept hold of the shackles, pulling me alongside him. The ground beneath our feet became increasingly more solid, less sandy, and I walked with a little more assurance. Even if I didn't have the first notion where we were going, we were certainly making a good pace.

"I want you to understand," Reynolds said as we crested a slight rise in the land. I could see beasts in the distance, moving high in the sky. Even so, they were still tethered to the ground by long, spindly legs.

"Then speak plainly. I am your captive audience."

A look of pain crossed Reynolds' face; I had seen the same thing in my uncle at the hospital just that morning

"We must reach the city, Miss Franks," he said. "Will you come back into the carriage? We cannot reach it on foot."

I now saw the carriage awaiting us, a claret-colored shimmer in the strange air. There was no choice, was there? Go with Reynolds to his city, or stay here where I knew no direction and might wander forever. I lifted my hands.

"Unbind me and I will come with you," I said.

Reynolds did not argue. He unlocked my shackles with a key he kept in his sleeve. We climbed back into the carriage and, without word to the driver, were off. Reynolds watched me the entire ride and I told myself I didn't care. I didn't care.

I never witnessed stranger things than I did in the city itself. The light continued to play tricks upon my mind, and the buildings seemed half open to the sky. The people of the city were paper thin; on edge they could not be seen, though when they turned a certain way in the light their monstrous faces became dreadfully apparent. Some looked as our carriage driver did; others I could barely comprehend. I quickly learned how to look in order to see only the slimmest slice of them.

When I learned this manner of looking, I discovered something else. This city was not anchored to the ground. Indeed, the entire place was on the move, buildings and artworks balanced on the backs of immense creatures. A great distance below us, I could see their small feet moving; legs made of thin spire-wire upward to their fabulous bodies—bearing these incredible weights. So too I realized the carriage had come to rest upon its four horses; they carried us without effort through the buildings, the creatures, the people balanced upon a road of memory between.

"This place makes no sense," I said and Reynolds laughed darkly. He pressed behind me at the carriage window, his hand beneath my ribcage. Did he fear I would jump again? Or did he just find pleasure in touching me?

"Your uncle wanted to understand it. Do you remember his stories? His poems?"

I had forgotten them (and indeed Baltimore, my uncle, the rain, the everything) until Reynolds brought them back to me. I had trouble breathing when I remembered it all. All I had now lost.

"He wrote of this place," I said. Once the idea was voiced, I saw my uncle everywhere I looked. There, he had written of that strange creature with its shrieking hair; and there, he had written of that building, ever in flame. My uncle's mind sparked in every shadow of this place; as the creatures made their roads of memory, so too my uncle made the roads, circling ever on, one begetting the beginning of the other.

"He helped create this place," Reynolds said.

The horses carried us to an enormous throne, so large it took three of the creatures to support it. How they managed I'll never know. Reynolds bid me to hold his hand, for I'd never walked a street such as this; it was alive beneath my feet, guiding us from the carriage up to the throne where a woman awaited us.

Her boundless hyacinth hair spilled down her body like water, to her feet and beyond, where gardenias and sand dollars scattered. Silver stars gleamed around her head. She wore a comet for a bracelet; endlessly circling, sparking with vilest fire. Near her throne sat dark, hand-woven baskets filled with fruit. She reached down, plucked a green pear, and offered it to me.

I did not take it. I had read my uncle's stories and knew well enough what happened to young women who ate the fruit of strange lands. The queen, if she were such, took no offense. She smiled down at me, then looked at Reynolds.

"You failed," she said.

"I did." He bowed before her. "He has died alone yet again."

"Speak plain, the both of you." Granted, my uncle had also written stories of outspoken young women; their end was little better than that of those who ate the fruit. I didn't care; I was somewhere beyond care.

Neither spoke. Rather, they showed me.

The queen twisted the pear in half and within its gritty flesh I saw my uncle writing. He wrote of this place, of a city near a sea. He slept each night and thought he dreamed, but his dreams were not that at all. He came here, snatched away by these people. Fairy, he named them, but they were not; it was the only word he knew to apply.

They stole him away every night, him and more of his kind, artists all, for these creatures loved their minds. I felt this love equal to my own for Edgar Poe. But this love had a dark side for as they loved these artists, they consumed them.

When my uncle made to escape and leave this place behind, they chained him. They held him, naked and dirty in an unlit cell. How many cells stretched in the darkness? I could not count them all. This placed smelled of your worst imaginings—darker, fouler. There was a seam of light that came through the door to hover above the floor. *The seam!* Within this light, dust sparked, dreams flicked.

In this place, my uncle wrote stories in his head. Despite their cruelty to him, some part of my uncle still loved the magic of these people, the impossibility. He loved that they made him create better stories, stories that helped create their fantastic reality.

Only one person visited my uncle; Edgar came to name him Reynolds. Reynolds came daily, to take stories for his people, to bring Edgar a measure of food and clean water. Eventually Edgar's stories turned from madmen to a sorrowful young woman who did not even know she was sorrowful. The thing that pleased her most were the stories, so my uncle kept on spinning them. Reynolds fell in love with this young woman. With me.

My uncle escaped them—I laughed through my tears at the sight of him slipping his bonds like a magician. He stole clothes—no, see there, it is a hand! A hand offering Edgar clothing that was not his own. Reynolds' hand.

"Death has little meaning here," the queen said as she squashed half of the pear and tossed it away. "Though it means much in your world."

"Please speak plain," I whispered, the scent of pear and despair sharp in the air between us. I glanced at Reynolds. "Please."

"I helped your uncle escape," Reynolds said. "The first time, he died alone, unknown. I undid that memory—"

As one undoes a knot, I thought. I had looked into his eyes before; I had kissed that mouth once. I remembered these things though through a wash of water; they were blurred and indistinct. Reynolds had tried once before; I had not listened.

"—and tried again. I brought him to Baltimore, got you the note; you reached him, and yet now you've come here and he will die alone; *has* died alone. You—"

"Can only return to death," the queen said and threw away the rest of the now-rotted pear.

"Your uncle is dead," Reynolds said. "The moment he returned, the years he had been here caught up to him."

"But he wasn't gone years," I said. Surely there was a mistake. I felt desperate to make these creatures understand that. "Only overnight. I feared him drunk and sleeping it off."

"Overnight to you," Reynolds said and his voice skipped. "He was taken almost every night."

And every day returned to his world, to my world. To live years over the course of a night; to wake each morning in his bed, thinking it all a dream. How I had once laughed at my uncle and his small circle of friends, all of them old, bent men. How young might they have honestly been?

"Miss Franks—" He clasped my hands within his own. "Agnes. I never intended for you to come here. You are dead to your world; time has gone on without you and made what it will of Baltimore."

Though I wished to believe that all of this was some terrible dream, I knew within my heart that it was not. Edgar's stories of this place should have prepared me. He had seen this place; its people had loved him and in the end destroyed him.

"Only overnight," I said. "I can go back." I had to know, what had become of my world? Was my uncle truly gone? Had the thing I feared most come to pass? It could not be. What if he still lived?

"What are you not telling me?"

Reynolds grabbed my arm. "Is isn't just overnight—not for you."

It was then that Reynolds' trespass became clear to me. I had misunderstood what the queen showed me. Every day my uncle woke in my world, it was Reynolds who brought him to that moment. Reynolds unstitched the decades that had passed within this strange world to bring my uncle back into my time, so that I might have a living relation at my side.

How many times should my uncle have died? It was no wonder he tried to cut out his own eyes when at last he seemed firmly rooted here.

"It remains her choice," the queen said to Reynolds. "You asked us to allow that, to never take another of her kind without their permission. This is no different because you love her."

I looked beyond the queen's star-wreathed head, to the vast sky where golden birds stretched their wings. No, not birds; angels. When I looked the right direction, I saw their slim bodies. But where was the sea my uncle wrote of, I wondered, and watched the slow ebb and flow of the entire city itself and realized *the city is the sea* and wanted to weep with the joy of it.

"You would live a full life here," Reynolds said.

My eyes met Reynolds'. When I looked at him a certain way, I saw the truth of him, his true body, and if I looked deeper, I saw to the heart of him. Darker, fouler; a seam of brightness. *He could take me back as he did my uncle,* I thought, *but he doesn't want to.* He wanted to keep me. "I want to go back." I had to go. To look—to see whatever had become of whatever I loved.

The queen seized my chin in her pear-wet hand and my world went black.

When light returned, it fell in hazy curtains around me. The air was ashen, bits of burnt paper falling as snow would. Walls like skeletal fingers rose around me. Scattered bricks, the stench of burnt wood. I saw hunched figures in the street and ran for them, but as I neared they became only heaps of more debris. I saw no people.

Though my legs were tired and ached with each step, and my lungs burned, I walked on. I walked up streets once familiar to me; dead, burnt things crunched underfoot. I searched for anything I might recognize and while there were ruined shops aplenty, I knew none of them.

I walked through all the wreckage of this city, until the sun touched and began to fall below the horizon. Exhaustion dragged me to sit on a curb and I couldn't find the energy to mind the rubbish I settled in.

How many years had passed Baltimore by? How long had the city lain in ruin? Was it God who decided to destroy this place, or man? Did it matter at all?

In the remains at my feet, I found a scrap of poetry, about a woman with hyacinth hair. It could not be my uncle's handwriting—though perhaps it was, for as I stood to continue my journey, I could not remember his handwriting. I could barely remember his face.

It was his voice I remembered best of all, and the beat of those words in my head. *The seam*. It rested inside of me, unable to escape. He'd wept for it in the end, shouting for Reynolds to snatch him back to that world.

I folded the page into my hand and walked on. As far as I walked, the whole city through, there was only gray ruin. I yelled, but no one answered. Perhaps there was no one *to* answer.

"Anyone!" I cried as loud as I could from the middle of the street. I looked to the sky, the veiled sun now set in the gray west.

My world was dead. I had nothing. I looked at my filthy hands and saw them old and wrinkled. I was but twenty and felt the universe retreating from me.

"Reynolds! Fonderous Reynolds!"

The ring of hooves on cobblestones answered me. Sharp and distinct down the ruined street they came, pulling a claret and gold four-in-hand.

There was one thing left to me. Hope in the brightness in the seam above the floor. Hope that there existed in that place a life worth living, with beings I might one day love. My uncle was dead in both worlds, but I was only dead in one.

I stepped in the path of the carriage and my world went black—

But only for a moment.

SIGNAL TO NOISE

ALASTAIR REYNOLDS

Alastair Reynolds was born in Barry in 1966. He spent his early years in Cornwall, then returned to Wales for his primary and secondary school education. He completed a degree in astronomy at Newcastle, then a PhD in the same subject at St. Andrews in Scotland. He left the UK in 1991 and spent the next sixteen years working in the Netherlands, mostly for the European Space Agency, although he also did a stint as a postdoctoral worker in Utrecht. He had been writing and selling science fiction since 1989, and published his first novel, *Revelation Space*, in 2000. He has recently completed his tenth novel and has continued to publish short fiction. His novel *Chasm City* won the British Science Fiction Award, and he has been shortlisted for the Arthur C. Clarke Award three times. In 2004 he left scientific research to write full time. He married in 2005 and returned to Wales in 2008, where he lives in Rhondda Cynon Taff.

FRIDAY

Mick Leighton was in the basement with the machines when the police came for him. He'd been trying to reach Joe Liversedge all morning, to cancel a prearranged squash match. It was the busiest week before exams, and Mick had gloomily concluded that he had too much tutorial work to grade to justify sparing even an hour for the game. The trouble was that Joe had either turned off his phone or left it in his office where it wouldn't interfere with the machines. Mick had sent an email, but when that had gone unanswered he decided there was nothing for it but to stroll over to Joe's half of the building and inform him in person. By now Mick was a sufficiently well-known face in Joe's department that he was able to come and go more or less as he pleased.

"Hello, matey," Joe said, glancing over his shoulder with a half-eaten sandwich in one hand. There was a bandage on the back of his neck, just below the hairline. He was hunched over a desk covered in laptops, cables, and reams of hardcopy. "Ready for a thrashing, are you?"

"That's why I'm here," Mick said. "Got to cancel, sorry. Too much on my plate today."

"Naughty."

"Ted Evans can fill in for me. He's got his kit. You know Ted, don't you?"

"Vaguely." Joe set down his sandwich to put the lid back on a felt-tipped pen. He was an amiable Yorkshireman who'd come down to Cardiff for his postgraduate work and decided to stay. He was married to an archaeologist named Rachel who spent a lot of her time poking around in the Roman ruins under the walls of Cardiff Castle. "Sure I can't twist your arm? It'll do you good, you know, bit of a workout."

"I know. But there just isn't time."

"Your call. How are things, anyway?"

Mick shrugged philosophically. "Been better."

"Did you phone Andrea like you said you were going to?"

"No."

"You should, you know."

"I'm not very good on the phone. Anyway, I thought she probably needed a bit of space."

"It's been three weeks, mate."

"I know."

"Do you want the wife to call her? It might help."

"No, but thanks for suggesting it anyway."

"Call her. Let her know you're missing her."

"I'll think about it."

"Yeah, sure. You should stick around, you know. It's all *go* here this morning. We got a lock just after seven this morning." Joe tapped one of the laptop screens, which was scrolling rows of black-on-white numbers. "It's a good one, too."

"Really?"

"Come and have a look at the machine."

"I can't. I need to get back to my office."

"You'll regret it later. Just like you'll regret canceling our match, or not calling Andrea. I know you, Mick. You're one of life's born regretters."

"Five minutes, then."

In truth, Mick always enjoyed having a nose around Joe's basement. As solid as Mick's own early-universe work was, Joe had really struck gold. There were hundreds of researchers around the world who would have killed for a guided tour of the Liversedge laboratory.

In the basement were ten hulking machines, each as large as a steam turbine. You couldn't go near them if you were wearing a pacemaker or any other kind of implant, but Mick knew that, and he'd been careful to remove all metallic items before he came down the stairs and through the security doors. Each machine contained a ten tonne bar of ultra-high-purity iron, encased in vacuum and suspended in a magnetic cradle. Joe liked to wax lyrical about the hardness of the vacuum, about the dynamic stability of the magnetic field generators. Cardiff could be hit by a Richter six earthquake, and the bars wouldn't feel the slightest tremor.

Joe called it the call center.

The machines were called correlators. At any one time eight were online, while two were down for repairs and upgrades. What the eight functional machines were doing was cold-calling: dialing random numbers across the gap between quantum realities, waiting for someone to answer on the other end.

In each machine, a laser repeatedly pumped the iron into an excited quantum state. By monitoring vibrational harmonics in the excited iron—what Joe called the back-chirp—the same laser could determine if the bar had achieved a lock onto another strand of quantum reality—another world-line. In effect, the bar would be resonating with its counterpart in another version of the same basement, in another version of Cardiff.

Once that lock was established—once the cold-calling machine had achieved a hit—then those two previously indistinguishable worldlines were linked together by an information conduit. If the laser tapped the bar with low-energy pulses, enough to influence it but not upset the lock, then the counterpart in the other lab would also register those taps. It meant that it was possible to send signals from one lab to the other, in both directions.

"This is the boy," Joe said, patting one of the active machines. "Looks like a solid lock, too. Should be good for a full ten or twelve days. I think this might be the one that does it for us."

Mick glanced again at the bandage on the back of Joe's neck. "You've had a nervelink inserted, haven't you."

"Straight to the medical center as soon as I got the alert on the lock. I was nervous—first time, and all that. But it turned out to be dead easy. No pain at all. I was up and out within half an hour. They even gave me a Rich Tea Biscuit."

"Ooh. A Rich Tea Biscuit. It doesn't get any better than that, does it. You'll be going through today, I take it?"

Joe reached up and tore off the bandage, revealing only a small spot of blood, like a shaving nick. "Tomorrow, probably. Maybe Sunday. The nervelink isn't active yet, and that'll take some getting used to. We've got bags of time, though; even if we don't switch on the nervelink until Sunday, I'll still have five or six days of bandwidth before we become noise-limited."

"You must be excited."

"Right now I just don't want to cock up anything. The Helsinki boys are nipping at our heels as it is. I reckon they're within a few months of beating us."

Mick knew how important this latest project was for Joe. Sending information between different realities was one thing, and impressive enough in its own right. But now that technology had escaped from the labs out into the real world. There were hundreds of correlators in other labs and institutes around the world. In five years it had gone from being a spooky, barely believable phenomenon, to an accepted part of the modern world.

But Joe—whose team had always been at the forefront of the technology—hadn't stood still. They'd been the first to work out how to send voice and video comms across the gap with another reality, and within the last year they'd been able to operate a camera-equipped robot, the same battery-driven kind that all the tourists had been using before nervelinking became the new thing. Joe had even let Mick have a go on it. With his hands operating the robot's manipulators via force-feedback gloves, and his eyes seeing the world via the stereoscopic projectors in a virtual-reality helmet, Mick had been able to feel himself almost physically present in the other lab. He'd been able to move around and pick things up just as if he were actually walking in that alternate reality. Oddest of all had been meeting the other version of Joe Liversedge, the one who worked in the counterpart lab. Both Joes seemed cheerily indifferent to the weirdness of the setup, as if collaborating with a duplicate of yourself was the most normal thing in the world.

Mick had been impressed by the robot. But for Joe it was a stepping stone to something even better.

"Think about it," he'd said. "A few years ago, tourists started switching over to nervelinks instead of robots. Who wants to drive a clunky machine around some smelly foreign city, when you can drive a warm human body instead? Robots can see stuff, they can move around and pick stuff up, but they can't give you the smells, the taste of food, the heat, the contact with other people."

"Mm," Mick had said noncommittally. He didn't really approve of nerve-linking, even though it essentially paid Andrea's wages.

"So we're going to do the same. We've got the kit. Getting it installed is a piece of piss. All we need now is a solid link."

And now Joe had what he'd been waiting for. Mick could practically see the *Nature* cover-article in his friend's eyes. Perhaps he was even thinking about taking that long train ride to Stockholm.

"I hope it works out for you," Mick said.

Joe patted the correlator again. "I've got a good feeling about this one."

That was when one of Joe's undergraduates came up to them. To Mick's surprise, it wasn't Joe she wanted to speak to.

"Doctor Leighton?"

"That's me."

"There's somebody to see you, sir. I think it's quite important."

"Someone to see me?"

"They said you left a note in your office."

"I did," Mick said absent-mindedly. "But I also said I wouldn't be gone long. Nothing's *that* important, is it?"

But the person who had come to find Mick was a policewoman. When Mick met her at the top of the stairs her expression told him it wasn't good news.

"Something's happened," he said.

She looked worried, and very, very young. "Is there somewhere we can talk, Mister Leighton?"

"Use my office," Joe said, showing the two of them to his room just down the corridor. Joe left the two of them alone, saying he was going down to the coffee machine in the hall.

"I've got some bad news," the policewoman said, when Joe had closed the door. "I think you should sit down, Mister Leighton."

Mick pulled out Joe's chair from under the desk, which was covered in papers: coursework Joe must have been in the process of grading. Mick sat down, then didn't know where to put his hands. "It's about Andrea, isn't it."

"I'm afraid your wife was in an accident this morning," the policewoman said.

"What kind of accident? What happened?"

"Your wife was hit by a car when she was crossing the road."

A mean, little thought flashed through Mick's mind. Bloody Andrea: she'd always been one for dashing across a road without looking. He'd been warning her for years she was going to regret it one day.

"How is she? Where did they take her?"

"I'm really sorry, sir." The policewoman hesitated. "Your wife died on the way to hospital. I understand that the paramedics did all they could, but…"

Mick was hearing it, and not hearing it. It couldn't be right. People still got knocked down by cars. But they didn't *die* from it, not anymore. Cars couldn't go fast enough in towns to kill anyone. Being knocked down and killed by a car was something that happened to people in soap operas, not real life.

Feeling numb, not really present in the room, Mick said, "Where is she now?" As if by visiting her, he might prove that they'd got it wrong, that she wasn't dead at all.

"They took her to the Heath, sir. That's where she is now. I can drive you there."

"Andrea isn't dead," Mick said. "She can't be. Not now."

"I'm really sorry," the policewoman said.

SATURDAY

For the last three weeks, ever since they had separated, Mick had been sleeping in a spare room at his brother's house in Newport. The company had been good, but now Bill was away for the weekend on some ridiculous team-building exercise in Snowdonia. For tedious reasons, Mick's brother had had to take the house keys with him, leaving Mick with nowhere to sleep on Friday night. When Joe had asked him where he was going to stay, Mick said he'd go back to his own house, the one he'd left at the beginning of the month.

Joe was having none of it, and insisted that Mick sleep at his house instead. Mick spent the night going through the usual cycle of emotions that came with any sudden bad news. He'd had nothing to compare with losing his wife, but the texture of the shock was familiar enough, albeit magnified from anything in his previous experience. He resented the fact that the world seemed to be continuing, crassly oblivious to Andrea's death. The news wasn't dominated by his tragedy; it was all about some Polish miners trapped underground. When he finally managed to get to sleep, Mick was tormented by dreams that his wife was still alive, that it had all been a mistake.

But he knew it was all true. He'd been to the hospital; he'd seen her body. He even knew why she'd been hit by the car. Andrea had been crossing the road to her favorite hair salon; she'd had an appointment to get her hair done. Knowing Andrea, she had probably been so focused on the salon that she was oblivious to all that was going on around her. It hadn't even been the car that had killed her in the end. When the slow-moving vehicle knocked her down, Andrea had struck her head against the side of the curb.

By midmorning on Saturday, Mick's brother had returned from Snowdonia. Bill came around to Joe's house and hugged Mick silently, saying nothing for many minutes. Then Bill went into the next room and spoke quietly to Joe and Rachel. Their low voices made Mick feel like a child in a house of adults.

"I think you and I need to get out of Cardiff," Bill told Mick, when he returned to the living room. "No ifs, no buts."

Mick started to protest. "There's too much that needs to be done. I still need to get back to the funeral home."

"It can wait until this afternoon. No one's going to hate you for not returning a few calls. C'mon; let's drive up to the Gower and get some fresh air. I've already reserved a car."

"Go with him," Rachel said. "It'll do you good."

Mick acquiesced, his guilt and relief in conflict at being able to put aside thoughts of the funeral plans. He was glad Bill had come down, but he couldn't quite judge how his brother—or his friends, for that matter—viewed his bereavement. He'd lost his wife. They all knew that. But they also knew that Mick and Andrea had been separated. They'd been having problems for most of the year. It would only be human for his friends to assume that Mick wasn't quite as affected by Andrea's death as he would have been had they still been living together.

"Listen," he told Bill, when they were safely under way. "There's something I've got to tell you."

"I'm listening."

"Andrea and I had problems. But it wasn't the end of our marriage. We were going to get through this. I was going to call her this weekend, see if we couldn't meet."

Bill looked at him sadly. Mick couldn't tell if that meant that Bill just didn't believe him, or that his brother pitied him for the opportunity he'd allowed to slip between his fingers.

When they got back to Cardiff in the early evening, after a warm and blustery day out on the Gower, Joe practically pounced on Mick as soon as they came through the door.

"I need to talk to you," Joe said. "Now."

"I need to call some of Andrea's friends," Mick said. "Can it wait until later?"

"No. It can't. It's about you and Andrea."

They went into the kitchen. Joe poured him a glass of whisky. Rachel and Bill watched from the end of the table, saying nothing.

"I've been to the lab," Joe said. "I know it's Saturday, but I wanted to make sure that lock was still holding. Well, it is. We could start the experiment tomorrow if we wanted to. But something's come up, and you need to know about it."

Mick sipped from his glass. "Go on."

"I've been in contact with my counterpart in the other lab."

"The other Joe."

"The other Joe, yes. We were finessing the equipment, making sure everything was optimal. And we talked, of course. Needless to say I mentioned what had happened."

"And?"

"The other me was surprised. Shocked, even. He said Andrea hadn't died in his reality." Joe held up a hand, signaling that Mick should let him finish before speaking. "You know how it works. The two histories are identical before the lock takes effect: so identical that there isn't even any point in thinking of them as being distinct realities. The divergence only happens once the lock is in effect. The lock was active by the time you came down to tell me about the squash match. The other me also had a visit from you. The difference was that no policewoman ever came to his lab. You eventually drifted back to your office to carry on grading tutorials."

"But Andrea was already dead by then."

"Not in that reality. The other me phoned you. You were staying at the Holiday Inn. You knew nothing of Andrea having had any accident. So my other wife..." Joe allowed himself a quick smile. "The other version of Rachel called Andrea. And they spoke. Turned out Andrea had been hit by a car, but she'd barely been bruised. They hadn't even called an ambulance."

Mick absorbed what his friend had to say, then said, "I can't deal with this, Joe. I don't need to know it. It isn't going to help."

"I think it is. We were set up to run the nervelink experiment as soon as we had a solid lock, one that we could trust to hold for the full million seconds. This is it. The only difference is it doesn't have to be me who goes through."

"I don't understand."

"I can put you through, Mick. We can get you nervelinked tomorrow morning. Allowing for a day of bedding in and practice once you arrive in the other reality…well, you could be walking in Andrea's world by Monday afternoon, Tuesday morning at the latest."

"But you're the one who is supposed to be going through," Mick said. "You've already had the nervelink put in."

"We've got a spare," Joe said.

Mick's mind raced through the implications. "Then I'd be controlling the body of the other you, right?"

"No. That won't work, unfortunately. We've had to make some changes to these nervelinks to get them to work properly through the correlator, with the limited signal throughput. We had to ditch some of the channels that handle proprioceptive mapping. They'll only work properly if the body on the other end of the link is virtually identical to the one on this side."

"Then it won't work. You're nothing like me."

"You're forgetting *your* counterpart on the other side," Joe said. He glanced past Mick at Bill and Rachel, raising his eyebrows as he did so. "The way it would work is, you come into the lab and we install the link in you, just the same way it happened for me yesterday morning. At the same time your counterpart in Andrea's world comes into *his* version of the lab and gets the other version of the nervelink put into him."

Mick shivered. He'd become used to thinking about the other version of Joe; he could even begin to accept that there was a version of Andrea walking around somewhere who was still alive. But as soon as Joe brought the other Mick into the argument, he felt his head begin to unravel.

"Wouldn't he—the other me—need to agree to this?"

"He already has," Joe said solemnly. "I've been in touch with him. The other Joe called him into the lab. We had a chat over the videolink. He didn't go for it at first—you know how you both feel about nervelinking. And he hasn't lost *his* version of Andrea. But I explained how big a deal this was. This is your only chance to see Andrea again. Once this window closes—we're talking about no more than eleven or twelve days from the start of the lock, by the way—we'll never make contact with another reality where she's alive."

Mick blinked and placed his hands on the table. He felt dizzy with the implications, as if the kitchen was swaying. "You're certain of that? You'll never open another window into Andrea's world?"

"Statistically, we were incredibly lucky to get this one chance. By the time the window closes, Andrea's reality will have diverged so far from ours that there's essentially no chance of ever getting another lock."

"Okay," Mick said, ready to take Joe's word for it. "But even if I agree to this—even if the other me agrees to it—what about Andrea? We weren't seeing each other."

"But you wanted to see her again," Bill said quietly.

Mick rubbed his eyes with the palms of his hands, and exhaled loudly. "Maybe."

"I've spoken to Andrea," Rachel said. "I mean, Joe spoke to himself, and the other version of him spoke to the other Rachel. She's been in touch with Andrea."

Mick hardly dared speak. "And?"

"She says it's okay. She understands how horrible this must be for you. She says, if you want to come through, she'll meet you. You can spend some time together. Give you a chance to come to some kind of…"

"Closure," Mick whispered.

"It'll help you," Joe said. "It's got to help you."

SUNDAY

The medical center was normally closed on weekends, but Joe had pulled strings to get some of the staff to come in on Sunday morning. Mick had to sit around a long time while they ran physiological tests and prepared the surgical equipment. It was much easier and quicker for tourists, for they didn't have to use the modified nervelink units Joe's team had developed.

By the early afternoon they were satisfied that Mick was ready for the implantation. They made him lie down on a couch with his head encased in a padded plastic assembly with a hole under the back of the neck. He was given a mild, local anesthetic. Rubberized clamps whirred in to hold his head in position with micromillimeter accuracy. Then he felt a vague impression of pressure being applied to the skin on the back of his neck, and then an odd and not entirely pleasant sensation of sudden pins and needles in every part of his body. But the unpleasantness was over almost as soon as he'd registered it. The support clamps whirred away from his head. The couch tilted up, and he was able to get off and stand on his feet.

Mick touched the back of his neck, came away with a tiny smear of blood on his thumb.

"That's it?"

"I told you there was nothing to it," Joe said, putting down a motorcycling magazine. "I don't know what you were so worried about."

"It's not the nervelink operation itself I don't approve of. I don't have a problem with the technology. It's the whole system, the way it encourages the exploitation of the poor."

Joe tut-tutted. "Bloody *Guardian* readers. It was you lot who got the bloody moratorium against air travel enacted in the first place. Next you'll be telling us we can't even *walk* anywhere."

The nurse swabbed Mick's wound and applied a bandage. He was shunted into an adjoining room and asked to wait again. More tests followed. As the system interrogated the newly embedded nervelink, he experienced mild electrical tingles and strange, fleeting feelings of dislocation. Nothing he reported gave the staff any cause for alarm.

After Mick's discharge from the medical center, Joe took him straight down to the laboratory. An electromagnetically shielded annex contained the couch Joe intended to use for the experiment. It was a modified version of the kind tourists used for long-term nervelinking, with facilities for administering nutrition and collecting bodily waste. No one liked to dwell too much on those details, but there was no way around it if you wanted to stay nervelinked for more than a few hours. Gamers had been putting up with similar indignities for decades.

Once Mick was plumbed in, Joe settled a pair of specially designed immersion glasses over his eyes, after first applying a salve to Mick's skin to protect against pressure sores. The glasses fit very tightly, blocking out Mick's view of the lab. All he could see was a blue-gray void, with a few meaningless red digits to the right side of his visual field.

"Comfortable?" Joe asked.

"I can't see anything yet."

"You will."

Joe went back into the main part of the basement to check on the correlation. It seemed that he was gone a long time. When he heard Joe return, Mick half-expected bad news—that the link had collapsed, or some necessary piece of technology had broken down. Privately, he would not have been too sorry were that the case. In his shocked state of mind in the hours after Andrea's death, he would have given anything to be able to see her again. But now that the possibility had arisen, he found himself prone to doubts. Given time, he knew he'd get over Andrea's death. That wasn't being cold, it was just being realistic. He knew more than a few people who'd lost their partners, and while they might have gone through some dark times afterward, almost all of them now seemed settled and relatively content. It didn't mean they'd stopped feeling anything for the loved one who had died, but it did mean they'd found some way to move on. There was no reason to assume he wouldn't make the same emotional recovery.

The question was, would visiting Andrea hasten or hamper that process? Perhaps they should just have talked over the videolink, or even the phone. But then he'd never been very good on either.

He knew it had to be face to face, all or nothing.

"Is there a problem?" he asked Joe, innocently enough.

"Nope, everything's fine. I was just waiting to hear that the other version of you is ready."

"He is?"

"Good to go. Someone from the medical center just put him under. We can make the switch any time you're ready."

"Where is he?"

"Here," Joe said. "I mean, in the counterpart to this room. He's lying on the same couch. It's easier that way; there's less of a jolt when you switch over."

"He's unconscious already?"

"Full coma. Just like any nervelinked mule."

Except, Mick thought, unlike the mules, his counterpart hadn't signed up to go into a chemically induced coma while his body was taken over by a distant tourist. That was what Mick disapproved of more than anything. The mules did it for money, and the mules were always the poorest people in any given tourist hotspot, whether it was some affluent European city or some nauseatingly "authentic" Third World shithole. No one ever aspired to become a mule. It was what you did when all other options had dried up. In some cases it hadn't just supplanted prostitution, it had become an entirely new form of prostitution in its own right.

But enough of that. They were all consenting adults here. No one—least of all the other version of himself—was being exploited. The other Mick was just being kind. No, kinder, Mick supposed, than *he* would have been had the tables been reversed, but he couldn't help feeling a perverse sense of gratitude. And as for Andrea...well, she'd always been kind. No one ever had a bad word to say for Andrea on that score. Kind and considerate, to a fault.

So what was he waiting for?

"You can make the switch," Mick said.

There was less to it than he'd been expecting. It was no worse than the involuntary muscular jolt he sometimes experienced in bed, just before dozing off to sleep.

But suddenly he was in a different body.

"Hi," Joe said. "How're you feeling, matey?"

Except it was the other Joe speaking to him now: the Joe who belonged to the world where Andrea hadn't died. The original Joe was on the other side of the reality gap.

"I feel…" But when Mick tried speaking, it came out hopelessly slurred.

"Give it time," Joe said. "Everyone has trouble speaking to start with. That'll come quickly."

"Can't shee. Can't see."

"That's because we haven't switched on your glasses. Hold on a tick."

The gray-green void vanished, to be replaced by a view of the interior of the lab. The quality of the image was excellent. The room looked superficially the same, but as Mick looked around—sending the muscle signals through the nervelink to move the body of the other Mick—he noticed the small details that told him this wasn't his world. Joe was wearing a different checked shirt, smudged white trainers instead of Converse sneakers. In this version of the lab, Joe had forgotten to turn the calendar over to the new month.

Mick tried speaking again. The words came easier this time.

"I'm really here, aren't I."

"How does it feel to be making history?"

"It feels…bloody weird, actually. And no, I'm not making history. When you write up your experiment, it won't be me who went through first. It'll be you, the way it was always meant to be. This is just a dry run. You can mention me in a footnote, if that."

Joe looked unconvinced. "Have it your way, but—"

"I will." Mick moved to get off the couch. This version of his body wasn't plumbed in like the other one. But when he tried to move, nothing happened. For a moment, he felt a crushing sense of paralysis. He must have let out a frightened sound.

"Easy," Joe said, putting a hand on his shoulder. "One step at a time. The link still has to bed in. It's going to be hours before you'll have complete fluidity of movement, so don't run before you can walk. And I'm afraid we're going to have to keep you in the lab for rather longer than you might like. As routine as nervelinking is, this *isn't* simple nervelinking. The shortcuts we've had to use to squeeze the data through the correlator link mean we're exposing ourselves to more medical risks than you'd get with the standard tourist kit. Nothing that you need worry about, but I want to make sure we keep a close eye on all the parameters. I'll be running tests in the morning and evening. Sorry to be a drag about it, but we do need numbers for our paper, as well. All I can promise is that you'll still have a lot of time available to meet Andrea. If that's what you still want to do, of course."

"It is," Mick said. "Now that I'm here…no going back, right?"

Joe glanced at his watch. "Let's start running some coordination exercises. That'll keep us busy for an hour or two. Then we'll need to make sure you have full bladder control. Could get messy otherwise. After that—we'll see if you can feed yourself."

"I want to see Andrea."

"Not today," Joe said firmly. "Not until we've got you house-trained."

"Tomorrow. Definitely tomorrow."

MONDAY

He paused in the shade of the old, green boating shed at the edge of the lake. It was a hot day, approaching noon, and the park was already busier than it had been at any time since the last gasp of the previous summer. Office workers were sitting around the lake making the most of their lunch break: the men with their ties loosened and sleeves and trousers rolled up, the women with their shoes off and blouses loosened. Children splashed in the ornamental fountains, while their older siblings bounced meters into the air on servo-assisted pogo sticks, the season's latest, lethal-looking craze. Students lolled around on the gently sloping grass, sunbathing or catching up on neglected coursework in the last week before exams. Mick recognized some of them from his own department. Most wore cheap, immersion glasses, with their arms covered almost to the shoulder in tight-fitting, pink, haptic feedback gloves. The more animated students lay on their backs, pointing and clutching at invisible objects suspended above them. It looked like they were trying to snatch down the last few wisps of cloud from the scratchless blue sky above Cardiff.

Mick had already seen Andrea standing a little further around the curve of the lake. It was where they had agreed to meet, and true to form Andrea was exactly on time. She stared pensively out across the water, seemingly oblivious to the commotion going on around her. She wore a white blouse, a knee-length burgundy skirt, sensible office shoes. Her hair was shorter than he remembered, styled differently and barely reaching her collar. For a moment—until she'd turned slightly—he hadn't recognized her at all. Andrea held a Starbucks coffee holder in one hand, and every now and then she'd take a sip or glance at her wristwatch. Mick was five minutes late now, and he knew there was a risk Andrea would give up waiting. But in the shade of the boating shed, all his certainties had evaporated.

Andrea turned minutely. She glanced at her watch again. She sipped from the coffee holder, tilting it back in a way that told Mick she'd finished the last drop. He saw her looking around for a waste bin.

Mick stepped from the shade. He walked across the grass, onto concrete, acutely conscious of the slow awkwardness of his gait. His walking had improved since his first efforts, but it still felt as if he were trying to walk upright in a swimming pool filled with treacle. Joe had assured him that all his movements would become more normal as the nervelink bedded in, but that process was obviously taking longer than anticipated.

"Andrea," he said, sounding slurred and drunk and too loud, even to his own ears.

She turned and met his eyes. There was a slight pause before she smiled, and when she did, the smile wasn't quite right, as if she'd been asked to hold it too long for a photograph.

"Hello, Mick. I was beginning to think…"

"It's okay." He forced out each word with care, making sure it came out right before moving to the next. "I just had some second thoughts."

"I don't blame you. How does it feel?"

"A bit odd. It'll get easier."

"Yes, that's what they told me." She took another sip from the coffee, even though it must have been empty. They were standing about two meters apart, close enough to talk, close enough to look like two friends or colleagues who'd bumped into each other around the lake.

"It's really good of you…" Mick began.

Andrea shook her head urgently. "Please. It's okay. We talked it over. We both agreed it was the right thing to do. If the tables were turned, you wouldn't have hesitated."

"Maybe not."

"I know you, Mick. Maybe better than you know yourself. You'd have done all that you could, and more."

"I just want you to know…I'm not taking any of this lightly. Not you having to see me, like this…not what *he* has to go through while I'm around."

"He said to tell you there are worse ways to spend a week."

Mick tried to smile. He felt the muscles of his face move, but without a mirror there was no way to judge the outcome. The moment stretched. A football splashed into the lake and began to drift away from the edge. He heard a little boy start crying.

"Your hair looks different," Mick said.

"You don't like it."

"No, I do. It really suits you. Did you have that done after…oh, wait. I see. You were on your way to the salon."

He could see the scratch on her face where she'd grazed it on the curb, when the car knocked her down. She hadn't even needed stitches. In a week it would hardly show at all.

"I can't begin to imagine what it's been like for you," Andrea said. "I can't imagine what *this* is like for you."

"It helps."

"You don't sound convinced."

"I want it to help. I think it's going to. It's just that right now it feels like I've made the worst mistake of my life."

Andrea held up the coffee holder. "Do you fancy one? It's my treat."

Andrea was a solicitor. She worked for a small legal firm located in modern offices near the park. There was a Starbucks near her office building. "They don't know me there, do they."

"Not unless you've been moonlighting. Come on. I hate to say it, but you could use some practice walking."

"As long as you won't laugh."

"I wouldn't dream of it. Hold my hand, Mick. It'll make it easier."

Before he could step back, Andrea closed the distance between them and took his hand in hers. It was good of her to do that, Mick thought. He'd been wondering how he would initiate that first touch, and Andrea had spared him the fumbling awkwardness that would almost certainly have ensued. That was Andrea to a tee, always thinking of others and trying to make life a little easier for them, no matter how small the difference. It was why people liked her so much; why her friends were so fiercely loyal.

"It's going to be okay, Mick," Andrea said gently. "Everything that's happened between us…it doesn't matter now. I've said bad things to you and you've said bad things to me. But let's forget about all that. Let's just make the most of what time we have."

"I'm scared of losing you."

"You're a good man. You've more friends than you realize."

He was sweating in the heat, so much so that the glasses began to slip down his nose. The view tilted toward his shoes. He raised his free hand in a stiff, salutelike gesture and pushed the glasses back into place. Andrea's hand tightened on his.

"I can't go through with this," Mick said. "I should go back."

"You started it," Andrea said sternly, but without rancor. "Now you finish it. All the way, Mick Leighton."

TUESDAY

Things were much better by the morning of the second day. When he woke in Joe Liversedge's lab there was a fluency in his movements that simply hadn't been there the evening before, when he'd said goodbye to Andrea. He now felt as if he was inhabiting the host body, rather than simply shuffling it around like a puppet. He still needed the glasses to be able to see anything, but the nervelink was conveying sensation much more effectively now, so that when he touched something it came through without any of the fuzziness or lag he'd been experiencing the day before. Most tourists were able to achieve reasonable accuracy of touch differentiation within twenty-four hours. Within two days, their degree of proprioceptive immersion was generally good enough to allow complex motor tasks such as cycling, swimming, or skiing. Repeat-visit tourists, especially those that went back into the same body, got over the transition period even faster. To them it was like moving back into a house after a short absence.

Joe's team gave Mick a thorough checkup in the annex. It was all routine stuff. Amy Flint, Joe's senior graduate student, insisted on adding some more numbers to the tactile test database that she was building for the study. That meant Mick sitting at a table, without the glasses, being asked to hold various objects and decide what shape they were and what they were made of. He scored excellently, only failing to distinguish between wood and plastic balls of similar weight and texture. Flint was cheerfully casual around him, without any of the affectedness or oversensitivity Mick had quickly detected in his friends or colleagues. Clearly she didn't know what had happened; she just thought Joe had opted to go for a different test subject than himself.

Joe was upbeat about Mick's progress. Everything, from the host body to the hardware, was holding up well. The bandwidth was stable at nearly two megabytes per second, more than enough spare capacity to permit Mick the use of a second video feed to peer back into the version of the lab on the other side. The other version of Joe held the cam up so that Mick could see his own body, reclining on the heavy-duty immersion couch. Mick had expected to be disturbed by that, but the whole experience turned out to be oddly banal, like replaying a home movie.

When they were done with the tests, Joe walked Mick over to the university canteen, where he ate a liquid breakfast, slurping down three containers of fruit yoghurt. While he ate—which was tricky, but another of the things that was supposed to get easier with practice—he gazed distractedly at the television in the canteen. The wall-sized screen was running through the morning news, with the sound turned down. At the moment the screen was showing grainy footage of the Polish miners, caught on surveillance camera as they trudged into the low, concrete pithead building on their way to work. The cave-in had happened three days ago. The miners were still trapped underground, in all the worldlines that were in contact with this one, including Mick's own.

"Poor fuckers," Joe said, looking up from a draft paper he was penciling remarks over.

"Maybe they'll get them out."

"Aye. Maybe. Wouldn't fancy my chances down there, though."

The picture changed to a summary of football scores. Again, most of the games had ended in identical results across the contacted worldlines, but two or three—highlighted in sidebars, with analysis text ticking below them—had ended differently, with one team even being dropped from the rankings.

Afterward Mick walked on his own to the tram stop and caught the next service into the city center. Already he could feel that he was attracting less attention than the day before. He still moved a little stiffly, he could tell that just by looking at his reflection in the glass as he boarded the tram, but there was no longer anything comical or robotic about it. He just looked like someone with a touch of arthritis, or someone who'd been overdoing it in the gym and was now paying with a dose of sore muscles.

As the tram whisked its way through traffic, he thought back to the evening before. The meeting with Andrea, and the subsequent day, had gone as well as he could have expected. Things had been strained at first, but by the time they'd been to Starbucks, he had detected an easing in her manner, and that had made him feel more at ease as well. They'd made small talk, skirting around the main thing neither of them wanted to discuss. Andrea had taken most of the day off; she didn't have to be at the law offices until late afternoon, just to check that no problems had arisen in her absence.

They'd talked about what to do with the rest of their day together.

"Maybe we could drive up into the Beacons," Mick had said. "It'll be nice up in the hills with a bit of a breeze. We always used to enjoy those days out."

"Been a while though," Andrea had said. "I'm not sure my legs are up to it anymore."

"You always used to hustle up those hills."

"Emphasis on the 'used to,' unfortunately. Now I get out of breath just walking up St. Mary's Street with a bag full of shopping."

Mick looked at her skeptically, but he couldn't deny that Andrea had a point. Neither of them was the keen, outdoors type they had been when they met fifteen years earlier through the university's hill-walking club. Back then they'd spent long weekends exploring the hills of the Brecon Beacons and the Black Mountains, or driving to Snowdonia or the Lake District. They'd had some hair-raising moments together, when the weather turned against them or when they suddenly realized they were on completely the wrong ridge. But what Mick remembered, more than anything, was not being cold and wet, but the feeling of relief when they arrived at some cozy warm pub at the end of the day, both of them ravenous and thirsty and high on what they'd achieved. Good memories, all of them. Why hadn't they kept it up, instead of letting their jobs rule their weekends?

"Look, maybe we might drive up to the Beacons in a day or two," Andrea said. "But I think it's a bit ambitious for today, don't you?"

"You're probably right," Mick said.

After some debate, they'd agreed to visit the castle and then take a boat ride around the bay to see the huge and impressive sea defenses up close. Both were things they'd always meant to do together but had kept putting off for another weekend. The castle was heaving with tourists, even on this midweek day. Because a lot of them were nervelinked, though, they afforded Mick a welcome measure of inconspicuousness. No one gave him a second glance as he bumbled along with the other shade-wearing bodysnatchers, even though he must have looked considerably more affluent and well-fed than the average mule. Afterward, they went to look at the Roman ruins, where Rachel Liversedge was busy talking to a group of bored primary school children from the valleys.

Mick enjoyed the boat ride more than the trip to the castle. There were still enough nervelinked tourists on the boat for him not to feel completely out of place, and being out in the bay offered some respite from the cloying heat of the city center. Mick had even felt the breeze on the back of his hand, evidence that the nervelink was really bedding in.

It was Andrea who nudged the conversation toward the reason for Mick's presence. She'd just returned from the counter with two paper cups brimming with murky coffee, nearly spilling them as the boat swayed unexpectedly. She sat down on the boat's hard wooden bench.

"I forgot to ask how it went in the lab this morning?" she asked brightly. "Everything working out okay?"

"Very well," Mick said. "Joe says we were getting two megs this morning. That's as good as he was hoping for."

"You'll have to explain that to me. I know it's to do with the amount of data you're able to send through the link, but I don't know how it compares with what we'd be using for a typical tourist setup."

Mick remembered what Joe had told him. "It's not as good. Tourists can use as much bandwidth as they can afford. But Joe's correlators never get above five megabytes per second. That's at the start of the twelve-day window, too. It only gets worse by day five or six."

"Is two enough?"

"It's what Joe's got to work with." Mick reached up and tapped the glasses. "It shouldn't be enough for full color vision at normal resolution, according to Joe. But there's an awful lot of clever software in the lab to take care of that. It's constantly guessing, filling in gaps."

"How does it look?"

"Like I'm looking at the world through a pair of sunglasses." He pulled them off his nose and tilted them toward Andrea. "Except it's the glasses that are actually doing the seeing, not my—*his*—eyes. Most of the time, it's good enough that I don't notice anything weird. If I wiggle my head around fast—or if something streaks past too quickly—then the glasses have trouble keeping up with the changing view." He jammed the glasses back on, just in time for a seagull to flash past only a few meters from the boat. He had a momentary sense of the seagull breaking up into blocky areas of confused pixels, as if it had been painted by a cubist, before the glasses smoothed things over and normality ensued.

"What about all the rest of it? Hearing, touch…"

"They don't take up anything like as much bandwidth as vision. The way Joe puts it, postural information only needs a few basic parameters: the angles of my limb joints, that kind of thing. Hearing's pretty straight forward. And touch is the easiest of all, as it happens."

"Really?"

"So Joe says. Hold my hand."

Andrea hesitated an instant, then took Mick's hand.

"Now squeeze it," Mick said.

She tightened her hold. "Are you getting that?"

"Perfectly. It's much easier than sending sound. If you were to say something to me, the acoustic signal would have to be sampled, digitized, compressed, and pushed across the link: hundreds of bytes per second. But all touch needs is a single parameter. The system will still be able to keep sending touch even when everything else gets too difficult."

"Then it's the last thing to go."

"It's the most fundamental sense we have. That's the way it ought to be."

After a few moments, Andrea said, "How long?"

"Four days," Mick said slowly. "Maybe five, if we're lucky. Joe says we'll have a better handle on the decay curve by tomorrow."

"I'm worried, Mick. I don't know how I'm going to deal with losing you."

He closed his other hand on hers and squeezed in return. "You'll get me back."

"I know. It's just…it won't be you. It'll be the other you."

"They're both me."

"That's not how it feels right now. It feels like I'm having an affair while my husband's away."

"It shouldn't. I am your husband. We're both your husband."

They said nothing after that, sitting in silence as the boat bobbed its way back to shore. It was not that they had said anything upsetting, just that words were no longer adequate. Andrea kept holding his hand. Mick wanted this morning to continue forever: the boat, the breeze, the perfect sky over the bay. Even then he chided himself for dwelling on the passage of time, rather than making the most of the experience as it happened to him. That had always been his problem, ever since he was a kid. School holidays had always been steeped in a melancholic sense of how few days were left.

But this wasn't a holiday.

After a while, he noticed that some people had gathered at the bow of the boat, pressing against the railings. They were pointing up, into the sky. Some of them had pulled out phones.

"There's something going on," Mick said.

"I can see it," Andrea answered. She touched the side of his face, steering his view until he was craning up as far as his neck would allow. "It's an aeroplane."

Mick waited until the glasses picked out the tiny, moving speck of the plane etching a pale contrail in its wake. He felt a twinge of resentment toward anyone still having the freedom to fly, when the rest of humanity was denied that right. It had been a nice dream when it lasted, flying. He had no idea what political or military purpose the plane was serving, but it would be an easy matter to find out, were he that interested. The news would be in all the papers by the afternoon. The plane wouldn't just be overflying this version of Cardiff, but his as well. That had been one of the hardest things to take since Andrea's death. The world at large steamrolled on, its course undeflected by that single human tragedy. Andrea had died in the accident in his world, she'd survived unscathed in this one, and that plane's course wouldn't have changed in any measurable way (in either reality).

"I love seeing aeroplanes," Andrea said. "It reminds me of what things were like before the moratorium. Don't you?"

"Actually," Mick said, "they make me a bit sad."

WEDNESDAY

Mick knew how busy Andrea had been lately, and he tried to persuade her against taking any time off from her work. Andrea had protested, saying her colleagues could handle her workload for a few days. Mick knew better than that—Andrea practically ran the firm single-handedly—but in the end they'd come to a compromise. Andrea would take time off from the office, but she'd pop in first thing in the morning to put out any really serious fires.

Mick agreed to meet her at the offices at ten, after his round of tests. Everything still felt the way it had the day before; if anything he was even more fluent in his body movements. But when Joe had finished, the news was all that Mick had been quietly dreading, while knowing it could be no other way. The quality of the link had continued to degrade. According to Joe they were down to one point eight megs now. They'd seen enough decay curves to be able to extrapolate forward into the beginning of the following week. The link would become noise-swamped around teatime on Sunday, give or take three hours either way.

If only they'd started sooner, Mick thought. But Joe had done all that he could.

Today—despite the foreboding message from the lab—his sense of immersion in the counterpart world had become total. As the sunlit city swept by outside the tram's windows, Mick found it nearly impossible to believe that he was not physically present in this body, rather than lying on the couch in the other version of the lab. Overnight his tactile immersion had improved markedly. When he braced himself against the tram's upright handrail, as it swept around a curve, he felt cold aluminum, the faint greasiness where it had been touched by other hands.

At the offices, Andrea's colleagues greeted him with an unforced casualness that left him dismayed. He'd been expecting awkward expressions of sympathy, sly glances when they thought he wasn't looking. Instead he was plonked down in the waiting area and left to flick through glossy brochures while he waited for Andrea to emerge from her office. No one even offered him a drink.

He leafed through the brochures dispiritedly. Andrea's job had always been a sore point in their relationship. If Mick didn't approve of nervelinking, he had even less time for the legal vultures that made so much money out of personal injury claims related to the technology. But now he found it difficult to summon his usual sense of moral superiority. Unpleasant things *had* happened to decent people because of negligence and corner-cutting. If nervelinking was to be a part of the world, then someone had to make sure the victims got their due. He wondered why this had never been clear to him before.

"Hiya," Andrea said, leaning over him. She gave him a businesslike kiss, not quite meeting his mouth. "Took a bit longer than I thought, sorry."

"Can we go now?" Mick asked, putting down the brochure.

"Yep, I'm done here."

Outside, when they were walking along the pavement in the shade of the tall, commercial buildings, Mick said: "They didn't have a clue, did they? No one in that office knows what's happened to us."

"I thought it was best," Andrea said.

"I don't know how you can keep up that act, that nothing's wrong."

"Mick, nothing *is* wrong. You have to see it from my point of view. I haven't lost my husband. Nothing's changed for me. When you're gone—when all this ends, and I get the other *you* back—my life carries on as normal. I know what's happened to you is a tragedy, and believe me I'm as upset about it as anyone."

"Upset," Mick said quietly.

"Yes, upset. But I'd be lying if I said I was paralyzed with grief. I'm human, Mick. I'm not capable of feeling great emotional turmoil at the thought that some distant counterpart of myself got herself run over, all because she was rushing to have her hair done. Silly cow, that's what it makes me feel. At most it makes me feel a bit odd, a bit shivery. But I don't think it's something I'm going to have trouble getting over."

"I lost my wife," Mick said.

"I know, and I'm sorry. More than you'll ever know. But if you expect *my* life to come crashing to a halt…"

He cut her off. "I'm already fading. One point eight this morning."

"You always knew it would happen. It's not like it's any surprise."

"You'll notice a difference in me by the end of the day."

"This isn't the end of the day, so stop dwelling on it. All right? Please, Mick. You're in serious danger of ruining this for yourself."

"I know, and I'm trying not to," he said. "But what I was saying, about how things aren't going to get any better...I think today's going to be my last chance, Andrea. My last chance to be with you, to be with you properly."

"You mean us sleeping together," Andrea said, keeping her voice low.

"We haven't talked about it yet. That's okay; I wasn't expecting it to happen without at least some discussion. But there's no reason why..."

"Mick, I..." Andrea began.

"You're still my wife. I'm still in love with you. I know we've had our problems, but I realize now how stupid all that was. I should have called you sooner. I was being an idiot. And then this happened...and it made me realize what a wonderful, lovely person you are, and I should have seen that for myself, but I didn't...I needed the accident to shake me up, to make me see how lucky I was just to know you. And now I'm going to lose you again, and I'm not sure how I'm going to cope with that. But at least if we can be together again...properly, I mean."

"Mick..."

"You've already said you might get back together with the other Mick. Maybe it took all this to get us talking again. Point is, if you're going to get back together with him, there's nothing to stop us getting back together *now*. We were a couple before the accident; we can still be a couple now."

"Mick, it isn't the same. You've lost your wife. I'm not *her*. I'm some weird thing there isn't a word for. And you aren't really my husband. My husband is in a medically induced coma."

"You know none of that really matters."

"To you."

"It shouldn't matter to you either. And your husband—me, incidentally—agreed to this. He knew exactly what was supposed to happen. And so did you."

"I just thought things would be better—more civilized—if we kept a kind of distance."

"You're talking as if we're divorced."

"Mick, we were already separated. We weren't talking. I can't just forget what happened before the accident as if none of that mattered."

"I know it isn't easy for you."

They walked on in an uneasy silence, through the city center streets they'd walked a thousand times before. Mick asked Andrea if she wanted a coffee, but she said she'd had one in her office not long before he arrived. Maybe later. They paused to cross the road near one of Andrea's favorite boutiques and Mick asked if there was something he could buy for her.

Andrea sounded taken aback at the suggestion. "You don't need to buy me anything, Mick. It isn't my birthday or anything."

"It would be nice to give you a gift. Something to remember me by."

"I don't need anything to remember you, Mick. You're always going to be there."

"It doesn't have to be much. Just something you'll use now and then, and will make you think of me. *This* me, not the one who's going to be walking around in this body in a few days."

"Well, if you really insist…" He could tell Andrea was trying to sound keen on the idea, but her heart still wasn't quite in it. "There was a handbag I saw last week…"

"You should have bought it when you saw it."

"I was saving up for the hairdresser."

So Mick bought her the handbag. He made a mental note of the style and color, intending to buy an identical copy next week. Since he hadn't bought the gift for his wife in his own worldline, it was even possible that he might walk out of the shop with the exact counterpart of the handbag he'd just given Andrea.

They went to the park again, then to look at the art in the National Museum of Wales, then back into town for lunch. There were a few more clouds in the sky compared to the last two days, but their chrome whiteness only served to make the blue appear more deeply enameled and permanent. There were no planes anywhere at all; no contrail scratches. It turned out the aircraft—which had indeed been military—that they had seen yesterday had been on its way to Poland, carrying a team of mine rescue specialists. Mick remembered his resentment at seeing the plane, and felt bad about it now. There had been brave men and women aboard it, and they were probably going to be putting their own lives at risk to help save other brave men and women stuck miles underground.

"Well," Andrea said, when they'd paid the bill. "Moment of truth, I suppose. I've been thinking about what you were saying earlier, and maybe…" She trailed off, looking down at the remains of her salad, before continuing, "We can go home, if you'd like. If that's what you really want."

"Yes," Mick said. "It's what I want."

They took the tram back to their house. Andrea used her key to let them inside. It was still only the early afternoon, and the house was pleasantly cool, with the curtains and blinds still drawn. Mick knelt down and picked up the letters that were on the mat. Bills, mostly. He set them on the hall-side table, feeling a transitory sense of liberation. More than likely he'd be confronted with the same bills when he got home, but for now *these* were someone else's problem.

He slipped off his shoes and walked into the living room. For a moment he was thrown, feeling as if he really was in a different house. The wallscreen was on another wall; the dining table had been shifted sideways into the other half of the room; the sofa and easy chairs had all been altered and moved.

"What's happened?"

"Oh, I forgot to tell you," Andrea said. "I felt like a change. You came around and helped me move them."

"That's new furniture."

"No, just different seat covers. They're not new, it's just that we haven't had them out for a while. You remember them now, don't you?"

"I suppose so."

"C'mon, Mick. It wasn't that long ago. We got them off Aunty Janice, remember?" She looked at him despairingly. "I'll move things back. It *was* a bit inconsiderate of me, I suppose. I never thought how strange it would be for you to see the place like this."

"No, it's okay. Honestly, it's fine." Mick looked around, trying to fix the arrangement of furniture and décor in his mind's eye. As if he were going to duplicate everything when he got back into his own body, into his own version of this house.

Maybe he would, too.

"I've got something for you," Andrea said suddenly, reaching onto the top of the bookcase. "Found it this morning. Took ages searching for it."

"What?" Mick asked.

She held the thing out to him. Mick saw a rectangle of laminated pink card, stained and dog-eared. It was only when he tried to hold it, and the thing fell open and disgorged its folded paper innards, that he realized it was a map.

"Bloody hell. I wouldn't have had a clue where to look." Mick folded the map back into itself and studied the cover. It was one of their old hill-walking maps, covering that part of the Brecon Beacons where they'd done a lot of their walks.

"I was just thinking…seeing as you were so keen…maybe it wouldn't kill us to get out of town. Nothing too adventurous, mind."

"Tomorrow?"

She looked at him concernedly. "That's what I was thinking. You'll still be okay, won't you?"

"No probs."

"I'll get us a picnic, then. Tesco's does a nice luncheon basket. I think we've still got two thermos flasks around here somewhere, too."

"Never mind the thermos flasks, what about the walking boots?"

"In the garage," Andrea said. "Along with the rucksacks. I'll dig them out this evening."

"I'm looking forward to it," Mick said. "Really. It's kind of you to agree."

"Just as long you don't expect me to get up Pen y Fan without getting out of breath."

"I bet you'll surprise yourself."

A little later they went upstairs, to their bedroom. The blinds were open enough to throw pale stripes across the walls and bedsheets. Andrea undressed, and then helped Mick out his own clothes. As good as his control over the body had now become, fine motor tasks—like undoing buttons and zips—would require a lot more practice than he was going to have time for.

"You'll have to help me get all this on afterward," he said.

"There you go, worrying about the future again."

They lay together on the bed. Mick had already felt himself growing hard long before there was any corresponding change in the body he was now inhabiting. He had an erection in the laboratory, halfway across the city in another worldline. He could even feel the sharp plastic of the urinary catheter. Would the other Mick, sunk deep into coma, retain some vague impression of what was happening now? There were occasional stories of people coming out of their coma with a memory of what their bodies had been up to while they were under, but the agencies had said these were urban myths.

They made slow, cautious love. Mick had become more aware of his own awkwardness, and the self-consciousness only served to exaggerate the stiffness of his movements. Andrea did what she could to help, to bridge the gap between them, but she could not work miracles. She was patient and forgiving, even when he came close to hurting her. When he climaxed, Mick felt it happen to the body in the laboratory first. Then the body he was inhabiting responded, too, seconds later. Something of it reached him through the nervelink—not pleasure, exactly, but confirmation that pleasure had occurred.

Afterward, they lay still on the bed, limbs entwined. A breeze made the blinds move back and forth against the window. The slow movement of light and shade, the soft tick of vinyl on glass, was as lulling as a becalmed boat. Mick found himself falling into a contented sleep. He dreamed of standing on a summit in the Brecon Beacons, looking down on the sunlit valleys of South Wales, with Andrea next to him, the two of them poised like a tableau in a travel brochure.

When he woke, hours later, he heard her moving around downstairs. He reached for the glasses—he'd removed them earlier—and made to leave the bed. He felt it then. Somewhere in those languid hours he'd lost a degree of control over the body. He stood and moved to the door. He could still walk, but the easy facility he'd gained on Tuesday was now absent. When he moved to the landing and looked down the stairs, the glasses struggled to cope with the sudden change of scene. The view fractured, reassembled. He moved to steady himself on the banister, and his hand blurred into a long smear of flesh.

He began to descend the stairs, like a man coming down a mountain.

THURSDAY

In the morning he was worse. He stayed overnight at the house, then caught the tram to the laboratory. Already he could feel a measurable lag between the sending of his intentions to move, and the corresponding action in the body. Walking was still just about manageable, but all other tasks had become more difficult. He'd made a mess trying to eat breakfast in Andrea's kitchen. It was no surprise when Joe told him that the link was now down to one point two megs, and falling.

"By the end of the day?" Mick asked, even though he could see the print-out for himself.

"Point nine, maybe point eight."

He'd dared to think it might still be possible to do what they had planned. But the day soon became a catalogue of declining functions. At noon he met Andrea at her office and they went to a car rental office, where they'd booked a vehicle for the day. Andrea drove them out of Cardiff, up the valleys, along the A470 from Merthyr to Brecon. They had planned to walk all the way to the summit of Pen y Fan, an ascent they'd done together dozens of times during their hill-walking days. Andrea had already collected the picnic basket from Tesco's and packed and prepared the two rucksacks. She'd helped Mick get into his walking boots.

They left the car at the Storey Arms then followed the well-trodden trail that wound its way toward the mountain. Mick felt a little ashamed at first. Back in their hill-walking days, they'd tended to look down with disdain on the hordes of people making the trudge up Pen y Fan, especially those that took the route up from the pub. The view from the top was worth the climb, but they'd usually made a point of completing at least one or two other ascents on the same day, and they'd always eschewed the easy paths. Now Mick was paying for that earlier superiority. What started out as pleasantly challenging soon became impossibly taxing. Although he didn't think Andrea had begun to notice, he was finding it much harder than he'd expected to walk on the rough, craggy surface of the path. The effort was draining him, preventing him from enjoying any of the scenery, or the sheer bliss of being with Andrea. When he lost his footing the first time, Andrea didn't make much of it—she'd nearly tripped once already, on the dried and cracked path. But soon he was finding it hard to walk more than a hundred meters without losing his balance. He knew, with a heavy heart, that it would be difficult enough just to get back to the car. The mountain was still two miles away, and he wouldn't have a hope as soon as they hit a real slope.

"Are you okay, Mick?"

"I'm fine. Don't worry about me. It's these bloody shoes. I can't believe they ever fit me."

He soldiered on for as long as he could, refusing to give in, but the going got harder and his pace slower. When he tripped again and this time grazed his shin through his trousers, he knew he'd pushed himself as far as he could go. Time was getting on. The mountain might as well have been in the Himalayas, for all his chances of climbing it.

"I'm sorry. I'm useless. Go on without me. It's too nice a day not to finish it."

"Hey." Andrea took his hand. "Don't be like that. It was always going to be hard. Look how far we've come anyway."

Mick turned and looked dispiritedly down the valley. "About three kilometers. I can still see the pub."

"Well, it felt longer. And besides, this is actually a very nice spot to have the picnic." Andrea made a show of rubbing her thigh. "I'm about ready to stop anyway. Pulled a muscle going over that sty."

"You're just saying that."

"Shut up, Mick. I'm happy, okay? If you want to turn this into some miserable, pain-filled trek, go ahead. Me, I'm staying here."

She spread the blanket next to a dry brook and unpacked the food. The contents of the picnic basket looked very good indeed. The taste came through the nervelink as a kind of thin, diluted impression, more like the *memory* of taste rather than the thing itself. But he managed to eat without making too much of a mess, and some of it actually bordered on the enjoyable. They ate, listening to the birds, saying little. Now and then other walkers trudged past, barely giving Mick and Andrea a glance, as they continued toward the hills.

"I guess I shouldn't have kidded myself I was ever going to get up that mountain," Mick said.

"It *was* a bit ambitious," Andrea agreed. "It would have been hard enough without the nervelink, given how flabby the two of us have become."

"I think I'd have made a better job of it yesterday. Even this morning...I honestly felt I could do this when we got into the car."

Andrea touched his thigh. "How does it feel?"

"Like I'm moving away. Yesterday I felt like I was in this body, fully a part of it. Like a face filling a mask. Today it's different. I can still see through the mask, but it's getting further away."

Andrea seemed distant for several moments. He wondered if what he'd said had upset her. But when she spoke again there was something in her voice—a kind of steely resolution—that he hadn't been expecting, but which was entirely Andrea.

"Listen to me, Mick."

"I'm listening."

"I'm going to tell you something. It's the first of May today; just past two in the afternoon. We left Cardiff at eleven. This time next year, this exact day, I'm coming back here. I'm going to pack a picnic basket and go all the way up to the top of Pen y Fan. I'll set off from Cardiff at the same time. And I'm going to do it the year after, as well. Every first of May. No matter what day of the week it is. No matter how bloody horrible the weather is. I'm going up this mountain and nothing on Earth is going to stop me."

It took him a few seconds to realize what she was getting at. "With the other Mick?"

"No. I'm not saying we won't ever climb that hill together. But when I go up it on the first of May, I'll be on my own." She looked levelly at Mick. "And you'll do it alone as well. You'll find someone new, I'm sure of it. But whoever she is will have to give you that one day to yourself. So that you and I can have it to ourselves."

"We won't be able to communicate. We won't even know the other one's stuck to the plan."

"Yes," Andrea said firmly. "We will. Because it's going to be a promise, all right? The most important one either of us has ever made in our whole lives. That way we'll know. Each of us will be in our own universe, or worldline, or whatever you call it. But we'll both be standing on the same Welsh mountain. We'll both be looking at the same view. And I'll be thinking of you, and you'll be thinking of me."

Mick ran a stiff hand through Andrea's hair. He couldn't get his fingers to work very well now.

"You really mean that, don't you?"

"Of course I mean it. But I'm not promising anything unless you agree to your half of it. Would you promise, Mick?"

"Yes," he said. "I will."

"I wish I could think of something better. I could say we'd always meet in the park. But there'll be people around; it won't feel private. I want the silence, the isolation, so I can feel your presence. And one day they might tear down the park and put a shopping center there instead. But the mountain will always be there. At least as long as we're around."

"And when we get old? Shouldn't we agree to stop climbing the mountain, when we get to a certain age?"

"There you go again," Andrea said. "Decide for yourself. I'm going to keep climbing this thing until they put me in a box. I expect nothing less from you, Mick Leighton."

He made the best smile he was capable of. "Then…I'll just have to do my best, won't I?"

FRIDAY

In the morning Mick was paraplegic. The nervelink still worked perfectly, but the rate of data transmission from one worldline to the other had become too low to permit anything as complex and feedback-dependent as walking. His control over the body's fingers had become so clumsy that his hands might as well have been wearing boxing gloves. He could hold something if it was presented to him, but it was becoming increasingly difficult to manipulate simple objects, even those that had presented no difficulty twenty-four hours earlier. When he tried to grasp the breakfast yoghurt, he succeeded only in tipping it over the table. His hand had seemed to lurch toward the yoghurt, crossing the distance too quickly. According to Joe he had lost depth perception overnight. The glasses, sensing the dwindling data rate, were no longer sending stereoscopic images back to the lab.

He could still move around. The team had anticipated this stage and made sure an electric wheelchair was ready for him. Its chunky controls were designed to be used by someone with only limited upper body coordination. The chair was equipped with a panic button, so that Mick could summon help if he felt his control slipping faster than the predicted rate. Were he to fall into sudden and total paralysis, the chair would call out to passersby to provide assistance. In the event of an extreme medical emergency, it would steer itself to the nearest designated care point.

Andrea came out to the laboratory to meet him. Mick wanted one last trip into the city with her, but although she'd been enthusiastic when they'd talked about the plan on the phone, Andrea was now reluctant.

"Are you sure about this? We had such a nice time on Thursday. It would be a shame to spoil the memory of that now."

"I'm okay," Mick said.

"I'm just saying, we could always just stroll around the gardens here."

"Please," Mick said. "This is what…I want."

His voice was slow, his phrasing imprecise. He sounded drunk and depressed. If Andrea noticed—and he was sure she must have—she made no observation.

They went into town. It was difficult getting the wheelchair on the tram, even with Andrea's assistance. No one seemed to know how to lower the boarding ramp. One of the benefits of nervelink technology was that you didn't see that many people in wheelchairs anymore. The technology that enabled one person to control another person's body also enabled spinal injuries to be bypassed. Mick was aware that he was attracting more attention than on any previous day. For most people wheelchairs were a medical horror from the past, like iron lungs or leg braces.

On the tram's video monitor he watched a news item about the Polish miners. It wasn't good. The rescue team had had a number of options available to them, involving at least three possible routes to the trapped men. After carefully evaluating all the data—aware of how little time remained for the victims—they'd chosen what had promised to be the quickest and safest approach.

It had turned out to be a mistake, one that would prove fatal for the miners. The rescuers had hit a flooded section and had been forced to retreat, with damage to their equipment, and one of their team injured. Yet the miners *had* been saved in one of the other contacted worldlines. In that reality, one of the members of the rescue team had slipped on ice and fractured his hip while boarding the plane. The loss of that one man—who'd been a vocal proponent for taking the quickest route—had resulted in the team following the second course. It had turned out to be the right decision. They'd met their share of obstacles and difficulties, but in the end they'd broken through to the trapped miners.

By the time this happened, contact with that worldline had almost been lost. Even the best compression methods couldn't cope with moving images. The pictures that came back, of the men being liberated from the ground, were grainy and monochrome, like a blowup of newsprint from a hundred years earlier. They'd been squeezed across the gap in the last minutes before noise drowned the signal.

But the information was useless. Even armed with the knowledge that there was a safe route through to the miners, the team in this worldline didn't have time to act.

The news didn't help Mick's mood. Going into the city turned out to be exactly the bad move Andrea had predicted. By midday his motor control had deteriorated even further, to the point where he was having difficulty steering the wheelchair. His speech became increasingly slurred, so that Andrea had to keep asking him to repeat himself. In defense, he shut down into monosyllables. Even his hearing was beginning to fail, as the auditory data was compressed to an even more savage degree. He couldn't distinguish birds from traffic, or traffic from the swish of the trees in the park. When Andrea spoke to him she sounded like her words had been fed through a synthesizer, then chopped up and spliced back together in some tinny approximation to her normal voice.

At three, his glasses could no longer support full color vision. The software switched to a limited color palette. The city looked like a hand-tinted photograph, washed out and faded. Andrea's face oscillated between white and sickly gray.

By four, Mick was fully quadriplegic. By five, the glasses had reverted back to black and white. The frame rate was down to ten images per second, and falling.

By early evening, Andrea was no longer able to understand what Mick was saying. Mick realized that he could no longer reach the panic button. He became agitated, thrashing his head around. He'd had enough. He wanted to be pulled out of the nervelink, slammed back into his own waiting body. He no longer felt as if he was in Mick's body, but he didn't feel as if he was in his own one either. He was strung out somewhere between them, helpless and almost blind. When the panic hit, it was like a foaming, irresistible tide.

Alarmed, Andrea wheeled him back to the laboratory. By the time she was ready to say goodbye to him, the glasses had reduced his vision to five images per second, each of which was composed of only six thousand pixels. He was calmer then, resigned to the inevitability of what tomorrow would bring: he would not even recognize Andrea in the morning.

SATURDAY

Mick's last day with Andrea began in a world of sound and vision—senses that were already impoverished to a large degree—and ended in a realm of silence and darkness.

He was now completely paralyzed, unable even to move his head. The brain that belonged to the other, comatose Mick now had more control over this body than its wakeful counterpart. The nervelink was still sending signals back to the lab, but the requirements of sight and sound now consumed almost all available bandwidth. In the morning, vision was down to one thousand pixels, updated three frames per second. His sight had already turned monochrome, but even yesterday there had been welcome gradations of gray, enough to anchor him into the visual landscape.

Now the pixels were only capable of registering on or off; it cost too much bandwidth to send intermediate intensity values. When Andrea was near him, her face was a flickering abstraction of black and white squares, like a trick picture in a psychology textbook. With effort he learned to distinguish her from the other faces in the laboratory, but no sooner had he gained confidence in his ability than the quality of vision declined even further.

By midmorning the frame rate had dropped to eight hundred pixels at two per second, which was less like vision than being shown a sequence of still images. People didn't walk to him across the lab—they jumped from spot to spot, captured in frozen postures. It was soon easy to stop thinking of them as people at all, but simply as abstract structures in the data.

By noon he could not exactly say that he had any vision at all. *Something* was updating once every two seconds, but the matrix of black and white pixels was hard to reconcile with his memories of the lab. He could no longer distinguish people from furniture, unless people moved between frames, and then only occasionally. At two, he asked Joe to disable the feed from the glasses, so that the remaining bandwidth could be used for sound and touch. Mick was plunged into darkness.

Sound had declined overnight as well. If Andrea's voice had been tinny yesterday, today it was barely human. It was as if she were speaking to him through a voice distorter on the end of the worst telephone connection in the world. The noise was beginning to win. The software was struggling to compensate, teasing sense out of the data. It was a battle that could only be prolonged, not won.

"I'm still here," Andrea told him, her voice a whisper fainter than the signal from the furthest quasar.

Mick answered back. It took some time. His words in the lab had to be analyzed by voice-recognition software and converted into ASCII characters. The characters were compressed further and sent across the reality gap, bit by bit. In the other version of the lab—the one where Mick's body waited in a wheelchair, the one where Andrea hadn't died in a car crash—equivalent software decompressed the character string and reconstituted it in mechanically generated speech, with an American accent.

"Thank you for letting me come back," he said. "Please stay. Until the end. Until I'm not here anymore."

"I'm not going anywhere, Mick."

Andrea squeezed his hand. After all that he had lost since Friday, touch remained. It really was the easiest thing to send: easier than sight, easier than sound. When, later, even Andrea's voice had to be sent across the gap by character string and speech synthesizer, touch endured. He felt her holding him, hugging his body to hers, refusing to surrender him to the drowning roar of quantum noise.

"We're down to less than a thousand useable bits," Joe told him, speaking quietly in his ear in the version of the lab where Mick lay on the immersion couch. "That's a thousand bits total, until we lose all contact. It's enough for a message, enough for parting words."

"Send this," Mick said. "Tell Andrea that I'm glad she was there. Tell her that I'm glad she was my wife. Tell her I'm sorry we didn't make it up that hill together."

When Joe had sent the message, typing it in with his usual fluid speed, Mick felt the sense of Andrea's touch easing. Even the microscopic data-transfer burden of communicating unchanging pressure, hand on hand, body against body, was now too much for the link. It was like one swimmer letting a drowning partner go. As the last bits fell, he felt Andrea slip away forever.

He lay on the couch, unmoving. He had lost his wife, for the second time. For the moment the weight of that realization pinned him into still-ness. He did not think he would ever be able to walk in his world, let alone the one he had just vacated.

And yet it was Saturday. Andrea's funeral was in two days. He would have to be ready for that.

"We're done," Joe said respectfully. "Link is now noise-swamped."

"Did Andrea send anything back?" Mick asked. "After I sent my last words…"

"No. I'm sorry."

Mick caught the hesitation in Joe's answer. "Nothing came through?"

"Nothing intelligible. I thought something was coming through, but it was just…" Joe offered an apologetic shrug. "The setup at their end must have gone noise-limited a few seconds before ours did. Happens, some-times."

"I know," Mick said. "But I still want to see what Andrea sent."

Joe handed him a printout. Mick waited for his eyes to focus on the sheet. Beneath the lines of header information was a single line of text: SO0122215. Like a phone number or a postal code, except it was obviously neither.

"That's all?"

Joe sighed heavily. "I'm sorry, mate. Maybe she was just trying to get something through…but the noise won. The fucking noise always wins."

Mick looked at the numbers again. They began to talk to him. He thought he knew what they meant.

"…always fucking wins," Joe repeated.

SUNDAY

Andrea was there when they brought Mick out of the medically induced coma. He came up through layers of disorientation and half-dream, adrift until something inside him clicked into place and he realized where he had been for the last week, what had been happening to the body over which he was now regaining gradual control. It was exactly as they had promised: no dreams, no anxiety, no tangible sense of elapsed time. In a way, it was not an entirely unattractive way to spend a week. Like being in the womb, he'd heard people say. And now he was being born again, a process that was not without its own discomforts. He tried moving an arm and when the limb did not obey him instantly, he began to panic. But Joe was already smiling.

"Easy, boyo. It's coming back. The software's rerouting things one spinal nerve at a time. Just hold on there and it'll be fine."

Mick tried mumbling something in reply, but his jaw wasn't working properly either. Yet it would come, as Joe had promised. On any given day, thousands of recipients went through this exact procedure without blinking an eyelid. Many of them were people who'd already done it hundreds of times before. Nervelinking was almost insanely safe. Far safer than any form of physical travel, that was certain.

He tried moving his arm again. This time it obeyed without hesitation.

"How are you feeling?" Andrea asked.

Once more he tried speaking. His jaw was stiff, his tongue thick and uncooperative, but he managed to make some sounds. "Okay. Felt better."

"They say it's easier the second time. Much easier the third."

"How long?"

"You went under on Sunday of last week. It's Sunday again now." Joe said.

A full week. Exactly the way they'd planned it.

"I'm quite hungry," Mick said.

"Everyone's always hungry when they come out of the coma," Joe said. It's hard to get enough nourishment into the host body. We'll get you sorted out, though."

Mick turned his head to look at Joe, waiting for his eyes to find grudging focus. "Joe," he said. "Everything's all right, isn't it? No complications, nothing to worry about?"

"No problems at all," Joe said.

"Then would you mind giving Andrea and me a moment alone?"

Joe held up his hand in hasty acknowledgement and left the room, off on some plausible errand. He shut the door quietly behind him.

"Well?" Mick asked. "I'm guessing things must have gone okay, or they wouldn't have kept me under for so long."

"Things went okay, yes," Andrea said.

"Then you met the other Mick? He was here?"

Andrea nodded heavily. "He was here. We spent time together."

"What did you get up to?"

"All the usual stuff you or I would've done. Hit the town, walked in the parks, went into the hills, that kind of thing."

"How was it?"

She looked at him guardedly. "Really, really sad. I didn't really know how to behave, to be honest. Part of me wanted to be all consoling and sympathetic, because he'd lost his wife. But I don't think that's what Mick wanted."

"The other Mick," he corrected gently.

"Point is, he didn't come back to see me being all weepy. He wanted another week with his wife, the way things used to be. Yes, he wanted to say goodbye, but he didn't want to spend the whole week with the two of us walking around feeling down in the dumps."

"So how did you feel?"

"Miserable. Not as miserable as if I'd lost my husband, of course. But some of his sadness started wearing off on me. I didn't think it was going to...*I'm* not the one who's been bereaved here—but you'd have to be inhuman not to feel something, wouldn't you?"

"Whatever you felt, don't blame yourself for it. I think it was a wonderful thing you agreed to do."

"You, too."

"I had the easy part," Mick said.

Andrea stroked the side of his face. He realized that he needed a good shave. "How do *you* feel?" she asked. "You're nearly him, after all. You know everything he knows."

"Except how it feels to lose a wife. And I hope I don't ever find that out. I don't think I can ever really understand what he's going through now. He feels like someone else, a friend, a colleague, someone you'd feel sorry for..."

"But you're not cut up about what happened to him."

Mick thought for a while before responding, not wanting to give the glib, automatic answer, no matter how comforting it might have been. "No. I wish it hadn't happened...but you're still here. We can still be together, if we want. We'll carry on with our lives, and in a few months we'll hardly ever think of that accident. The other Mick isn't me. He isn't even anyone we'll ever hear from again. He's gone. He might as well not exist."

"But he does. Just because we can't communicate anymore...he *is* still out there."

"That's what the theory says." Mick narrowed his eyes. "Why? What difference does it really make, to us?"

"None at all, I suppose." Again that guarded look. "But there's something I have to tell you, something you have to understand."

There was a tone in her voice that troubled Mick, but he did his best not to show it. "Go on, Andrea."

"I made a promise to the other Mick. He's lost something no one can ever replace, and I wanted to do something, anything, to make it easier for him. Because of that, Mick and I came to an arrangement. Once a year,

I'm going to go away for a day. For that day, and that day only, I'm going somewhere private where I'm going to be thinking about the other Mick. About what he's been doing; what kind of life he's had; whether he's happy or sad. And I'm going to be alone. I don't want you to follow me, Mick. You have to promise me that."

"You could tell me," he said. "There doesn't have to be secrets."

"I'm telling you now. Don't you think I could have kept it from you if I wanted to?"

"But I still won't know where…"

"You don't need to. This is a secret between me and the other Mick. Me and the other you." She must have read something in his expression, something he had hoped wasn't there, because her tone turned grave. "And you need to find a way to deal with that, because it isn't negotiable. I already made that promise."

"And Andrea Leighton doesn't break promises."

"No," she said, softening her look with a sweet half-smile. "She doesn't. Especially not to Mick Leighton. Whichever one it happens to be."

They kissed.

Later, when Andrea was out of the room while Joe ran some more post-immersion tests, Mick peeled off a yellow Post-it note that had been left on one of the keyboards. There was something written on the note, in neat, blue ink. Instantly he recognized Andrea's handwriting: he'd seen it often enough on the message board in their kitchen. But the writing itself—SO0122215—meant nothing to him.

"Joe," he asked casually. "Is this something of yours?"

Joe glanced over from his desk, his eyes freezing on the small rectangle of yellow paper.

"No, that's what Andrea asked—" Joe began, then caught himself. "Look, it's nothing. I meant to bin it, but…"

"It's a message to the other Mick, right?"

Joe looked around, as if Andrea might still be hiding in the room or about to reappear. "We were down to the last few usable bits. The other Mick had just sent his last words through. Andrea asked me to send that response."

"Did she tell you what it meant?"

Joe looked defensive. "I just typed it. I didn't ask. Thought it was between you and her. I mean, between the other Mick and her."

"It's okay," Mick said. "You were right not to ask."

He looked at the message again, and something fell solidly into place. It had taken a few moments, but he recognized the code for what it was now, as some damp and windswept memory filtered up from the past. The numbers formed a grid reference on an Ordnance Survey map. It was the kind Andrea and he had used when they went on their walking expeditions. The reference even looked vaguely familiar. He stared at the numbers, feeling as if they were about to give up their secret. Wherever it was, he'd been there, or somewhere near. It wouldn't be hard to look it up. He wouldn't even need the Post-it note. He'd always had a good memory for numbers.

Footsteps approached, echoing along the linoleum-floored hallway that led to the lab.

"It's Andrea," Joe said.

Mick folded the Post-it note until the message was no longer visible. He flicked it in Joe's direction, knowing that it was none of his business anymore.

"Bin it."

"You sure?"

From now on there was always going to be a part of his wife's life that didn't involve him, even if it was only for one day a year. He would just have to find a way to live with that.

Things could have been worse, after all.

"I'm sure," he said.

PORRIDGE ON ISLAC

URSULA K. LE GUIN

Ursula K. Le Guin is the author of innumerable SF and fantasy classics, such as *The Left Hand of Darkness*, *The Lathe of Heaven*, *The Dispossessed*, and *A Wizard of Earthsea* (and the others in the Earthsea Cycle). She has been named a Grand Master by the Science Fiction Writers of America, and is the winner of five Hugos, six Nebulas, two World Fantasy Awards, and twenty Locus Awards. She's also a winner of the Newbery Medal, The National Book Award, the PEN/Malamud Award, and was named a Living Legend by the Library of Congress.

I t must be admitted that the method invented by Sita Dulip is not entirely reliable. You sometimes find yourself on a plane that isn't the one you meant to go to. If whenever you travel you carry with you a copy of Roman's *Handy Planary Guide,* you can read up on wherever it is you get to when you get there, though Roman is not always reliable either. But the *Encyclopedia Planaria,* in forty-four volumes, is not portable, and after all, what is entirely reliable unless it's dead?

I arrived on Islac unintentionally, when I was inexperienced, before I had learned to tuck Roman into my suitcase. The Interplanary Hotel there did have a set of the *Encyclopedia,* but it was at the bindery, because, they said, the bears had eaten the glue in the bindings and the books had all come to pieces. I thought they must have rather odd bears on Islac, but did not like to ask about them. I looked around the halls and my room carefully in case any bears were lurking. It was a beautiful hotel and the hosts were pleasant, so I decided to take my luck as it came and spend a day or two on Islac. I got to looking over the books in the bookcase in my room and trying out the built-in legemat, and had quite forgotten about bears, when something scuttled behind a bookend.

I moved the bookend and glimpsed the scuttler. It was dark and furry but had a long, thin tail of some kind, almost like wire. It was six or eight inches long not counting the tail. I didn't much like sharing my room with it, but I hate complaining to strangers—you can only complain satisfactorily to people you know really well—so I moved the heavy bookend over the hole in the wall the creature had disappeared into, and went down to dinner.

The hotel served family style, all the guests at one long table. They were a friendly lot from several different planes. We were able to converse in pairs using our translatomats, though general conversation overloaded the circuits. My left-hand neighbor, a rosy lady from a plane she called Ahyes, said she and her husband came to Islac quite often. I asked her if she knew anything about the bears here.

"Yes," she said, smiling and nodding. "They're quite harmless. But what little pests they are! Spoiling books, and licking envelopes, and snuggling in the bed!"

"Snuggling in the bed?"

"Yes, yes. They were pets, you see."

Her husband leaned forward to talk to me around her. He was a rosy gentleman. "Teddy bears," he said in English, smiling. "Yes."

"Teddy bears?"

"Yes, yes," he said, and then had to resort to his own language—"teddy bears are little animal pets for children, isn't that right?"

"But they're not live animals."

He looked dismayed. "Dead animals?"

"No—stuffed animals—toys—"

"Yes, yes. Toys, pets," he said, smiling and nodding.

He wanted to talk about his visit to my plane; he had been to San Francisco and liked it very much, and we talked about earthquakes instead of teddy bears. He had found a 5.6 earthquake "a very charming experience, very enjoyable," and he and his wife and I laughed a great deal as he told about it. They were certainly a nice couple, with a positive outlook.

When I went back to my room I shoved my suitcase up against the bookend that blocked the hole in the wall, and lay in bed hoping that the teddy bears did not have a back door.

Nothing snuggled into the bed with me that night. I woke very early, being jet-lagged by flying from London to Chicago, where my westbound flight had been delayed, allowing me this vacation. It was a lovely warm morning, the sun just rising. I got up and went out to take the air and see the city of Slas on the Islac plane.

It might have been a big city on my plane, nothing exotic to my eye, except the buildings were more mixed in style and in size than ours. That is, we put the big imposing buildings at the center and on the nice streets, and the small humble ones in the neighborhoods or barrios or slums or shantytowns. In this residential quarter of Slas, big houses were all jumbled up together with tiny cottages, some of them hardly bigger than hutches. When I went the other direction, downtown, I found the same wild variation of scale in the office buildings. A massive old four-story granite block towered over a ten-story building ten feet wide, with floors only five or six feet apart—a doll's skyscraper. By then, however, enough Islai were out and about that the buildings didn't puzzle me as much as the people did.

They were amazingly various in size, in color, in shape. A woman who must have been eight feet tall swept past me, literally: she was a street sweeper, busily and gracefully clearing the sidewalk of dust. She had what I took to be a spare broom or duster, a great spray of feathers, tucked into her waistband in back like an ostrich's tail. Next came a businessman striding along, hooked up to the computer network via a plug in his ear, a mouthpiece, and the left frame of his spectacles, talking away as he studied the market report. He came up about to my waist. Four young men passed on the other side of the street; there was nothing odd about them except that they all looked exactly alike. Then came a child trotting to school with his little backpack. He trotted on all fours, neatly, his hands in leather mitts or boots that protected them from the pavement; he was pale, with small eyes, and a snout, but he was adorable.

A sidewalk café had just opened up beside a park downtown. Though ignorant of what the Islai ate for breakfast, I was ravenous, ready to dare anything edible. I held out my translatomat to the waitress, a worn-looking woman of forty or so with nothing unusual about her, to my eye, but the beauty of her thick, yellow, fancifully braided hair. "Please tell me what a foreigner eats for breakfast," I said.

She laughed, then smiled a beautiful, kind smile, and said, via the translatomat, "Well, *you* have to tell me that. We eat cledif, or fruit with cledif."

"Fruit with cledif, please," I said, and presently she brought me a plate of delicious-looking fruits and a large bowl of pale yellow gruel, smooth, about as thick as very heavy cream, lukewarm. It sounds ghastly, but it was delicious—mild but subtle, lightly filling and slightly stimulating, like café au lait. She waited to see if I liked it. "I'm sorry, I didn't think to ask if you were a carnivore," she said. "Carnivores have raw cullis for breakfast, or cledif with offal."

"This is fine," I said.

Nobody else was in the place, and she had taken a liking to me, as I had to her. "May I ask where you come from?" she asked, and so we got to talking. Her name was Ai Li A Le. I soon realised she was not only an intelligent person but a highly educated one. She had a degree in plant pathology—but was lucky, she said, to have a job as a waitress. "Since the Ban," she said, shrugging. When she saw that I didn't know what the Ban was, she was about to tell me; but several customers were sitting down now, a great bull of a man at one table, two mousy girls at another, and she had to go wait on them.

"I wish we could go on talking," I said, and she said, with her kind smile, "Well, if you come back at sixteen, I can sit and talk with you."

"I will," I said, and I did. After wandering around the park and the city I went back to the hotel for lunch and a nap, then took the monorail back downtown. I never saw such a variety of people as were in that car—all shapes, sizes, colors, degrees of hairiness, furriness, featheriness (the street sweeper's tail had indeed been a tail), and, I thought, looking at one long, greenish youth, even leafiness. Surely those were fronds over his ears? He was whispering to himself as the warm wind swept through the car from the open windows.

The only thing the Islai seemed to have in common, unfortunately, was poverty. The city certainly had been prosperous once, not very long ago. The monorail was a snazzy bit of engineering, but it was showing wear and tear. The surviving old buildings—which were on a scale I found familiar—were grand but run-down, and crowded by the more recent giant's houses and doll's houses and buildings like stables or mews or rabbit hutches—a terrible hodgepodge, all of it cheaply built, rickety-looking, shabby. The Islai themselves were shabby, when they weren't downright ragged. Some of the furrier and featherier ones were clothed only by their fur and feathers. The green boy wore a modesty apron, but his rough trunk and limbs were bare. This was a country in deep, hard economic trouble.

Ai Li A Le was sitting at one of the outside tables at the café (the cledifac) next door to the one where she waited tables. She smiled and beckoned to me, and I sat down with her. She had a small bowl of chilled cledif with sweet spices, and I ordered the same. "Please tell me about the Ban," I asked her.

"We used to look like you," she said.

"What happened?"

"Well," she said, and hesitated. "We like science. We like engineering. We are good engineers. But perhaps we are not very good scientists."

To summarise her story: the Islai had been strong on practical physics, agriculture, architecture, urban development, engineering, invention, but weak in the life sciences, history, and theory. They had their Edisons and Fords but no Darwin, no Mendel. When their airports got to be just like ours, if not worse, they began to travel between planes; and on some plane, about a hundred years ago, one of their scientists discovered applied genetics. He brought it home. It fascinated them. They promptly mastered its principles. Or perhaps they had not quite mastered them before they started applying them to every life-form within reach.

"First," she said, "to plants. Altering food plants to be more fruitful, or to resist bacteria and viruses, or to kill insects, and so on."

I nodded. "We're doing a good deal of that too," I said.

"Really? Are you…" She seemed not to know how to ask the question she wanted to ask. "I'm corn, myself," she said at last, shyly.

I checked the translatomat. Uslu: corn, maize. I checked the dictionary, and it said that uslu on Islac and maize on my plane were the same plant.

I knew that the odd thing about corn is that it has no wild form, only a distant wild ancestor that you'd never recognise as corn. It's entirely a construct of long-term breeding by ancient gatherers and farmers. An early genetic miracle. But what did it have to do with Ai Li A Le?

Ai Li A Le with her wonderful, thick, gold-colored, corn-colored hair cascading in braids from a topknot…

"Only four percent of my genome," she said. "There's about half a percent of parrot, too, but it's recessive. Thank God."

I was still trying to absorb what she had told me. I think she felt her question had been answered by my astonished silence.

"They were utterly irresponsible," she said severely. "With all their programs and policies and making everything better, they were fools. They let all kinds of things get loose and interbreed. Wiped out rice in one decade. The improved breech went sterile. The famines were terrible…Butterflies, we used to have butterflies, do you have them?"

"Some, still," I said.

"And deletu?" A kind of singing firefly, now extinct, said my translatomat.

I shook my head wistfully.

She shook her head wistfully.

"I never saw a butterfly or a deletu. Only pictures…The insecticidal clones got them…But the scientists learned nothing—nothing! They set about improving the animals. Improving us! Dogs that could talk, cats that could play chess! Human beings who were going to be all geniuses and never get sick and live five hundred years! They did all that, oh yes, they did all that. There are talking dogs all over the place, unbelievably boring they are, on and on and on about sex and shit and smells and smells and shit and sex, and do you love me, do you love me, do you love me. I can't stand talking dogs. My big poodle Rover, he never says a word, the dear good soul. And then the humans! We'll never, ever get rid of the Premier. He's a Healthy, a bloody GAPA. He's ninety now and looks thirty and he'll go on looking thirty and being premier for four more centuries. He's a pious hypocrite and a greedy, petty, stupid, mean-minded crook. Just the kind of man who ought to be siring children for five centuries…The Ban doesn't apply to him…But still, I'm not saying the Ban was wrong. They had to do something. Things were really awful, fifty years ago. When they realised that genetic hackers had infiltrated all the laboratories, and half the techs were Bioist fanatics, and the Godsone Church had all those secret factories in the eastern hemisphere deliberately turning out genetic melds…Of course most of those products weren't viable. But a lot of them were…The hackers were so good at it. The chicken people, you've seen them?"

As soon as she asked, I realised that I had: short, squat people who ran around in intersections squawking, so that all the traffic gridlocked in an effort not to run them over. "They just make me want to cry," Ai Li A Le said, looking as if she wanted to cry.

"So the Ban forbade further experimentation?" I asked.

She nodded. "Yes. Actually, they blew up the laboratories. And sent the Bioists for reeducation in the Gubi. And jailed all the Godsone Fathers. And most of the Mothers too, I guess. And shot the geneticists. And destroyed all the experiments in progress. And the products, if they were"—she shrugged—"too far from the norm. The norm!" She scowled, though her sunny face was not made for scowling. "We don't have a norm any more. We don't have species any more. We're a genetic porridge. When we plant maize, it comes up weevil-repellent clover that smells like chlorine. When we plant an oak, it comes up poison oak fifty feet high with a ten-foot-thick trunk. And when we make love we don't know if we're going to have a baby, or a foal, or a cygnet, or a sapling. My daughter—" and she paused. Her face worked and she had to compress her lips before she could go on. "My daughter lives in the North Sea. On raw fish. She's very beautiful. Dark and silky and beautiful. But—I had to take her to the seacoast when she was two years old. I had to put her in that cold water, those big waves. I had to let her swim away, let her go be what she is. But she is human too! She is, she is human too!"

She was crying, and so was I.

After a while, Ai Li A Le went on to tell me how the Genome Collapse had led to profound economic depression, only worsened by the Purity Clauses of the Ban, which restricted jobs in the professions and government to those who tested 99.44% human—with exceptions for Healthies, Righteous Ones, and other GAPAs (Genetically Altered Products Approved by the Emergency Government). This was why she was working as a waitress. She was four percent maize.

"Maize was once the holy plant of many people, where I come from," I said, hardly knowing what I said. "It is such a beautiful plant. I love everything made out of corn—polenta, hoecake, cornbread, tortillas, canned corn, creamed corn, hominy, grits, corn whiskey, corn chowder, on the cob, tamales—it's all good. All good, all kind, all sacred. I hope you don't mind if I talk about eating it!"

"Heavens no," said Ai Li A Le, smiling. "What did you think cledif was made from?"

After a while I asked her about teddy bears. That phrase of course meant nothing to her, but when I described the creature in my bookcase she nodded—"Oh yes! Bookbears. Early on, when the genetic designers were making everything better, you know, they dwarfed bears way down for children's pets. Like toys, stuffed animals, only they were alive. Programmed to be passive and affectionate. But some of the genes they used for dwarfing came from insects—springtails and earwigs. And the bears began to eat the children's books. At night, while they were supposed to be cuddling in bed with the children, they'd go eat their books. They like paper and glue. And when they bred, the offspring had long tails, like wires, and a sort of insect jaw, so they weren't much good for the children any more. But by then they'd escaped into the woodwork, between the walls…Some people call them bearwigs."

I have been back to Islac several times to see Ai Li A Le. It is not a happy plane, or a reassuring one, but I would go to worse places than Islac to see so kind a smile, such a topknot of gold, and to drink maize with the woman who is maize.

MRS. TODD'S SHORTCUT

STEPHEN KING

Stephen King is the bestselling, award-winning author of innumerable classics, such as *The Shining, Carrie, Cujo*, and *The Dead Zone*—all of which have been adapted to film, as have many of King's other novels and stories. Other projects include editing *Best American Short Stories 2007*, writing a pop culture column for *Entertainment Weekly*, scripting for the Vertigo comic *American Vampire*, and a collaboration on a musical with rocker John Mellencamp called *Ghost Brothers of Darkland County*. His most recent books are the novels *11/22/63* and *The Wind Through the Keyhole*. Another recent book, *Full Dark, No Stars*, is a short fiction collection of four all-new, previously unpublished stories. His other work includes classics such as *The Stand, The Dark Tower, Salem's Lot*, among others.

"There goes the Todd woman," I said.

Homer Buckland watched the little Jaguar go by and nodded. The woman raised her hand to Homer. Homer nodded his big, shaggy head to her but didn't raise his own hand in return. The Todd family had a big summer home on Castle Lake, and Homer had been their caretaker since time out of mind. I had an idea that he disliked Worth Todd's second wife every bit as much as he'd liked 'Phelia Todd, the first one.

This was just about two years ago and we were sitting on a bench in front of Bell's Market, me with an orange soda-pop, Homer with a glass of mineral water. It was October, which is a peaceful time in Castle Rock. Lots of the lake places still get used on the weekends, but the aggressive, boozy summer socializing is over by then and the hunters with their big guns and their expensive nonresident permits pinned to their orange caps haven't started to come into town yet. Crops have been mostly laid by. Nights are cool, good for sleeping, and old joints like mine haven't yet started to complain. In October the sky over the lake is passing fair, with those big white clouds that move so slow; I like how they seem so flat on the bottoms, and how they are a little gray there, like with a shadow of sundown foretold, and I can watch the sun sparkle on the water and not be bored for some space of minutes. It's in October, sitting on the bench in front of Bell's and watching the lake from afar off, that I still wish I was a smoking man.

"She don't drive as fast as 'Phelia," Homer said. "I swan I used to think what an old-fashion name she had for a woman that could put a car through its paces like she could."

Summer people like the Todds are nowhere near as interesting to the year-round residents of small Maine towns as they themselves believe. Year-round folk prefer their own love stories and hate stories and scandals and rumors of scandal. When that textile fellow from Amesbury shot himself, Estonia Corbridge found that after a week or so she couldn't even get invited to lunch on her story of how she found him with the pistol still in one stiffening hand. But folks are still not done talking about Joe Camber, who got killed by his own dog.

Well, it don't matter. It's just that they are different racecourses we run on. Summer people are trotters; us others that don't put on ties to do our week's work are just pacers. Even so there was quite a lot of local interest when Ophelia Todd disappeared back in 1973. Ophelia was a genuinely nice woman, and she had done a lot of things in town. She worked to raise money for the Sloan Library, helped to refurbish the war memorial, and that sort of thing. But *all* the summer people like the idea of raising money. You mention raising money and their eyes light up and commence to gleam. You mention raising money and they can get a committee together and appoint a secretary and keep an agenda. They like that. But you mention *time* (beyond, that is, one big long walloper of a combined cocktail party and committee meeting) and you're out of luck. Time seems to be what summer people mostly set a store by. They lay it by, and if they could put it up in Ball jars like preserves, why, they would. But 'Phelia Todd seemed willing to *spend* time—to do desk duty in the library as well as to raise money for it. When it got down to using scouring pads and elbow grease on the war memorial, 'Phelia was right out there with town women who had lost sons in three different wars, wearing an overall with her hair done up in a kerchief. And when kids needed ferrying to a summer swim program, you'd be as apt to see her as anyone headed down Landing Road with the back of Worth Todd's big shiny pickup full of kids. A good woman. Not a town woman, but a good woman. And when she disappeared, there was concern. Not grieving, exactly, because a disappearance is not exactly like a death. It's not like chopping something off with a cleaver; more like something running down the sink so slow you don't know it's all gone until long after it is.

"'Twas a Mercedes she drove," Homer said, answering the question I hadn't asked. "Two-seater sportster. Todd got it for her in sixty-four or sixty-five, I guess. You remember her taking the kids to the lake all those years they had Frogs and Tadpoles?"

"Ayuh."

"She'd drive 'em no more than forty, mindful they was in the back. But it chafed her. That woman had lead in her foot and a ball bearing sommers in the back of her ankle."

It used to be that Homer never talked about his summer people. But then his wife died. Five years ago it was. She was plowing a grade and the tractor tipped over on her and Homer was taken bad off about it. He grieved for two years or so and then seemed to feel better. But he was not the same. He seemed waiting for something to happen, waiting for the next thing. You'd pass his neat little house sometimes at dusk and he would be on the porch smoking a pipe with a glass of mineral water on the porch rail and the sunset would be in his eyes and pipe smoke around his head and you'd think—I did, anyway—*Homer is waiting for the next thing.* This bothered me over a wider range of my mind than I liked to admit, and at last I decided it was because if it had been me, I wouldn't have been waiting for the next thing, like a groom who has put on his morning coat and finally has his tie right and is only sitting there on a bed in the upstairs of his house and looking first at himself in the mirror and then at the clock on the mantel and waiting for it to be eleven o'clock so he can get married. If it had been me, I would not have been waiting for the next thing; I would have been waiting for the last thing.

But in that waiting period—which ended when Homer went to Vermont a year later—he sometimes talked about those people. To me, to a few others.

"She never even drove fast with her husband, s'far as I know. But when I drove with her, she made that Mercedes strut."

A fellow pulled in at the pumps and began to fill up his car. The car had a Massachusetts plate.

"It wasn't one of these new sports cars that run on onleaded gasoline and hitch every time you step on it; it was one of the old ones, and the speedometer was calibrated all the way up to a hundred and sixty. It was a funny color of brown and I ast her one time what you called that color and she said it was Champagne. Ain't that *good*, I says, and she laughs fit to split. I like a woman who will laugh when you don't have to point her right at the joke, you know."

The man at the pumps had finished getting his gas.

"Afternoon, gentlemen," he says as he comes up the steps.

"A good day to you," I says, and he went inside.

"'Phelia was always lookin for a shortcut," Homer went on as if we had never been interrupted. "That woman was mad for a shortcut. I never saw the beat of it. She said if you can save enough distance, you'll save time as well. She said her father swore by that scripture. He was a salesman, always on the road, and she went with him when she could, and he was always lookin for the shortest way. So she got in the habit.

"I ast her one time if it wasn't kinda funny—here she was on the one hand, spendin her time rubbin up that old statue in the Square and takin the little ones to their swimmin lessons instead of playing tennis and swimming and getting boozed up like normal summer people, and on the other hand bein so damn set on savin fifteen minutes between here and Fryeburg that thinkin about it probably kep her up nights. It just seemed to me the two things went against each other's grain, if you see what I mean. She just looks at me and says, 'I like being helpful, Homer. I like driving, too—at least sometimes, when it's a challenge—but I don't like the *time* it takes. It's like mending clothes—sometimes you take tucks and sometimes you let things out. Do you see what I mean?'

"'I guess so, missus,' I says, kinda dubious.

"'If sitting behind the wheel of a car was my idea of a really good time *all* the time, I would look for long-cuts,' she says, and that tickled me s'much I had to laugh."

The Massachusetts fellow came out of the store with a six-pack in one hand and some lottery tickets in the other.

"You enjoy your weekend," Homer says.

"I always do," the Massachusetts fellow says. "I only wish I could afford to live here all year round."

"Well, we'll keep it all in good order for when you *can* come," Homer says, and the fellow laughs.

We watched him drive off toward someplace, that Massachusetts plate showing. It was a green one. My Marcy says those are the ones the Massachusetts Motor Registry gives to drivers who ain't had a accident in that strange, angry, fuming state for two years. If you have, she says, you got to have a red one so people know to watch out for you when they see you on the roll.

"They was in-state people, you know, the both of them," Homer said, as if the Massachusetts fellow had reminded him of the fact.

"I guess I did know that," I said.

"The Todds are just about the only birds we got that fly north in the winter. The new one, I don't think she likes flying north too much."

He sipped his mineral water and fell silent a moment, thinking.

"*She* didn't mind it, though," Homer said. "At least, I *judge* she didn't although she used to complain about it something fierce. The complaining was just a way to explain why she was always lookin for a shortcut."

"And you mean her husband didn't mind her traipsing down every woodroad in tarnation between here and Bangor just so she could see if it was nine-tenths of a mile shorter?"

"He didn't care piss-all," Homer said shortly, and got up, and went in the store. There now, Owens, I told myself, you know it ain't safe to ast him questions when he's yarning, and you went right ahead and ast one, and you have buggered a story that was starting to shape up promising.

I sat there and turned my face up into the sun and after about ten minutes he come out with a boiled egg and sat down. He ate her and I took care not to say nothing and the water on Castle Lake sparkled as blue as something as might be told of in a story about treasure. When Homer had finished his egg and had a sip of mineral water, he went on. I was surprised, but still said nothing. It wouldn't have been wise.

"They had two or three different chunks of rolling iron," he said.

"There was the Cadillac, and his truck, and her little Mercedes go-devil. A couple of winters he left the truck, 'case they wanted to come down and do some skiin. Mostly when the summer was over he'd drive the Caddy back up and she'd take her go-devil."

I nodded but didn't speak. In truth, I was afraid to risk another comment. Later I thought it would have taken a lot of comments to shut Homer Buckland up that day. He had been wanting to tell the story of Mrs. Todd's shortcut for a long time.

"Her little go-devil had a special odometer in it that told you how many miles was in a trip, and every time she set off from Castle Lake to Bangor she'd set it to 000-point-0 and let her clock up to whatever. She had made a game of it, and she used to chafe me with it." He paused, thinking that back over.

"No, that ain't right."

He paused more and faint lines showed up on his forehead like steps on a library ladder.

"She *made* like she made a game of it, but it was a serious business to her. Serious as anything else, anyway." He flapped a hand and I think he meant the husband. "The glovebox of the little go-devil was filled with maps, and there was a few more in the back where there would be a seat in a regular car. Some was gas station maps, and some was pages that had been pulled from the Rand-McNally Road Atlas; she had some maps from Appalachian Trail guidebooks and a whole mess of topographical survey-squares, too. It wasn't her having those maps that made me think it wa'n't a game; it was how she'd drawed lines on all of them, showing routes she'd taken or at least tried to take.

"She'd been stuck a few times, too, and had to get a pull from some farmer with a tractor and chain.

"I was there one day laying tile in the bathroom, sitting there with grout squittering out of every damn crack you could see—I dreamed of nothing but squares and cracks that was bleeding grout that night—and she come stood in the doorway and talked to me about it for quite a while. I used to chafe her about it, but I was also sort of interested, and not just because my brother Franklin used to live down-Bangor and I'd traveled most of the roads she was telling me of. I was interested just because a man like me is always oncommon interested in knowing the shortest way, even if he don't always want to take it. You that way too?"

"Ayuh," I said. There's something powerful about knowing the shortest way, even if you take the longer way because you know your mother-in-law is sitting home. Getting there quick is often for the birds, although no one holding a Massachusetts driver's license seems to know it. But *knowing* how to get there quick—or even knowing how to get there a way that the person sitting beside you don't know… that has power.

"Well, she had them roads like a Boy Scout has his knots," Homer said, and smiled his large, sunny grin. "She says, 'Wait a minute, wait a minute,' like a little girl, and I hear her through the wall rummaging through her desk, and then she comes back with a little notebook that looked like she'd had it a good long time. Cover was all rumpled, don't you know, and some of the pages had pulled loose from those little wire rings on one side.

"'The way Worth goes—the way *most* people go—is Route 97 to Mechanic Falls, then Route 11 to Lewiston, and then the Interstate to Bangor. 156.4 miles.'"

I nodded.

"'If you want to skip the turnpike—and save some distance—you'd go to Mechanic Falls, Route 11 to Lewiston, Route 202 to Augusta, then up Route 9 through China Lake and Unity and Haven to Bangor. That's 144.9 miles.'

"'You won't save no time that way, missus,' I says, 'not going through Lewiston *and* Augusta. Although I will admit that drive up the Old Derry Road to Bangor is real pretty.'

"'Save enough miles and soon enough you'll save time,' she says. 'And I didn't say that's the way I'd go, although I have a good many times; I'm just running down the routes most people use. Do you want me to go on?'

"'No,' I says, 'just leave me in this cussed bathroom all by myself starin at all these cussed cracks until I start to rave.'

"'There are four major routes in all,' she says. 'The one by Route 2 is 163.4 miles. I only tried it once. Too long.'

"'That's the one I'd hosey if my wife called and told me it was leftovers,' I says, kinda low.

"'What was that?' she says.

"'Nothin,' I says. 'Talkin to the grout.'

"'Oh. Well, the fourth—and there aren't too many who know about it, although they are all good roads—paved, anyway—is across Speckled Bird Mountain on 219 to 202 *beyond* Lewiston. Then, if you take Route 19, you can get around Augusta. Then you take the Old Derry Road. That way is just 129.2.'

"I didn't say nothing for a little while and p'raps she thought I was doubting her because she says, a little pert, 'I know it's hard to believe, but it's so.'

"I said I guessed that was about right, and I thought—looking back—it probably was. Because that's the way I'd usually go when I went down to Bangor to see Franklin when he was still alive. I hadn't been that way in years, though. Do you think a man could just—well—forget a road, Dave?"

I allowed it was. The turnpike is easy to think of. After a while it almost fills a man's mind, and you think not how could I get from here to there but how can I get from here to the turnpike ramp that's *closest* to there. And that made me think that maybe there are lots of roads all over that are just going begging; roads with rock walls beside them, real roads with blackberry bushes growing alongside them but nobody to eat the berries but the birds and gravel pits with old rusted chains hanging down in low curves in front of their entryways, the pits themselves as forgotten as a child's old toys with scrum-grass growing up their deserted unremembered sides. Roads that have just been forgot except by the people who live on them and think of the quickest way to get off them and onto the turnpike where you can pass on a hill and not fret over it. We like to joke in Maine that you can't get there from here, but maybe the joke is on us. The truth is there's about a damn thousand ways to do it and man doesn't bother.

Homer continued: "I grouted tile all afternoon in that hot little bathroom and she stood there in the doorway all that time, one foot crossed behind the other, bare-legged, wearin loafers and a khaki-colored skirt and a sweater that was some darker. Hair was drawed back in a hosstail. She must have been thirty-four or -five then, but her face was lit up with what she was tellin me and I swan she looked like a sorority girl home from school on vacation.

"After a while she musta got an idea of how long she'd been there cuttin the air around her mouth because she says, 'I must be boring the hell out of you, Homer.'

"'Yes'm,' I says, 'you are. I druther you went away and left me to talk to this damn grout.'

"'Don't be sma'at, Homer,' she says.

"'No, missus, you ain't borin me,' I says.

"So she smiles and then goes back to it, pagin through her little notebook like a salesman checkin his orders. She had those four main ways—well, really three because she gave up on Route 2 right away—but she must have had forty different other ways that were play-offs on those. Roads with state numbers, roads without, roads with names, roads without. My head fair spun with 'em. And finally she says to me, 'You ready for the blue-ribbon winner, Homer?'

"'I guess so,' I says.

"'At least it's the blue-ribbon winner *so far*,' she says. 'Do you know, Homer, that a man wrote an article in *Science Today* in 1923 proving that no man could run a mile in under four minutes? He *proved* it, with all sorts of calculations based on the maximum length of the male thigh-muscles, maximum length of stride, maximum lung capacity, maximum heart-rate, and a whole lot more. I was *taken* with that article! I was so taken that I gave it to Worth and asked him to give it to Professor Murray in the math department at the University of Maine. I wanted those figures checked because I was sure they must have been based on the wrong postulates, or something. Worth probably thought I was being silly—"Ophelia's got a bee in her bonnet" is what he says—but he took them. Well, Professor Murray checked through the man's figures quite carefully… and do you know *what,* Homer?'

"'No, missus.'

"'Those figures were *right.* The man's criteria were *solid.* He proved, back in 1923, that a man couldn't run a mile in under four minutes. He *proved* that. But people do it all the time, and do you know what that means?'

"'No, missus,' I said, although I had a glimmer.

"'It means that no blue ribbon is forever,' she says. 'Someday—if the world doesn't explode itself in the meantime—someone will run a two-minute mile in the Olympics. It may take a hundred years or a thousand, but it will happen. Because there is no ultimate blue ribbon. There is zero, and there is eternity, and there is mortality, but there is no *ultimate.*'

"And there she stood, her face clean and scrubbed and shinin, that darkish hair of hers pulled back from her brow, as if to say 'Just you go ahead and disagree if you can.' But I couldn't. Because I believe something like that. It is much like what the minister means, I think, when he talks about grace.

"'You ready for the blue-ribbon winner *for now?*' she says.

"'Ayuh,' I says, and I even stopped groutin for the time bein. I'd reached the tub anyway and there wasn't nothing left but a lot of those frikkin squirrelly little corners. She drawed a deep breath and then spieled it out at me as fast as that auctioneer goes over in Gates Falls when he has been putting the whiskey to himself, and I can't remember it all, but it went something like this."

Homer Buckland shut his eyes for a moment, his big hands lying perfectly still on his long thighs, his face turned up toward the sun. Then he opened his eyes again and for a moment I swan he *looked* like her, yes he did, a seventy-year-old man looking like a woman of thirty-four who was at that moment in her time looking like a college girl of twenty, and I can't remember exactly what *he* said any more than *he* could remember exactly what *she* said, not just because it was complex but because I was so fetched by how he looked sayin it, but it went close enough like this:

"'You set out Route 97 and then cut up Denton Street to the Old Town-house Road and that way you get around Castle Rock downtown but back to 97. Nine miles up you can go an old logger's road a mile and a half to

Town Road #6, which takes you to Big Anderson Road by Sites' Cider Mill. There's a cut-road the old-timers call Bear Road, and that gets you to 219. Once you're on the far side of Speckled Bird Mountain you grab the Stanhouse Road, turn left onto the Bull Pine Road—there's a swampy patch there but you can spang right through it if you get up enough speed on the gravel—and so you come out on Route 106. 106 cuts through Alton's Plantation to the Old Derry Road—and there's two or three woods roads there that you follow and so come out on Route 3 just beyond Derry Hospital. From there it's only four miles to Route 2 in Etna, and so into Bangor.'

"She paused to get her breath back, then looked at me. 'Do you know how long that is, all told?'

"'No'm,' I says, thinking it sounds like about a hundred and ninety miles and four bust springs.

"'It's 116.4 miles,' she says."

I laughed. The laugh was out of me before I thought I wasn't doing myself any favor if I wanted to hear this story to the end. But Homer grinned himself and nodded.

"I know. And you know I don't like to argue with anyone, Dave. But there's a difference between having your leg pulled and getting it shook like a damn apple tree.

"'You don't believe me,' she says.

"'Well, it's hard to believe, missus,' I said.

"'Leave that grout to dry and I'll show you,' she says. 'You can finish behind the tub tomorrow. Come on, Homer. I'll leave a note for Worth—he may not be back tonight anyway—and you can call your wife! We'll be sitting down to dinner in the Pilot's Grille in'—she looks at her watch—'two hours and forty-five minutes from right now. And if it's a minute longer, I'll buy you a bottle of Irish Mist to take home with you. You see, my dad was right. Save enough miles and you'll save time, even if you have to go through every damn bog and sump in Kennebec County to do it. Now what do you say?'

"She was lookin at me with her brown eyes just like lamps, there was a devilish look in them that said turn your cap around back'rds, Homer, and climb aboard this hoss, I be first and you be second and let the devil take the hindmost, and there was a grin on her face that said the exact same thing, and I tell you, Dave, I wanted to *go*. I didn't even want to top that damn can of grout. And I *certain* sure didn't want to drive that go-devil of hers. I wanted just to sit in it on the shotgun side and watch her get in, see her skirt come up a little, see her pull it down over her knees or not, watch her hair shine."

He trailed off and suddenly let off a sarcastic, choked laugh. That laugh of his sounded like a shotgun loaded with rock salt.

"Just call up Megan and say, 'You know 'Phelia Todd, that woman you're halfway to being so jealous of now you can't see straight and can't ever find a good word to say about her? Well, her and me is going to make this speed-run down to Bangor in that little champagne-colored go-devil Mercedes of hers, so don't wait dinner.'

"Just call her up and say that. Oh *yes*. Oh *ayuh*."

And he laughed again with his hands lying there on his legs just as natural as ever was and I seen something in his face that was almost hateful and after a minute he took his glass of mineral water from the railing there and got outside some of it.

"You didn't go," I said.

"Not *then.*"

He laughed, and this laugh was gentler.

"She must have seen something in my face, because it was like she found herself again. She stopped looking like a sorority girl and just looked like 'Phelia Todd again. She looked down at the notebook like she didn't know what it was she had been holding and put it down by her side, almost behind her skirt.

"I says, 'I'd like to do just that thing, missus, but I got to finish up here, and my wife has got a roast on for dinner.'

"She says, 'I understand, Homer—I just got a little carried away. I do that a lot. All the time, Worth says.' Then she kinda straightened up and says, 'But the offer holds, any time you want to go. You can even throw your shoulder to the back end if we get stuck somewhere. Might save me five dollars.' And she laughed.

"'I'll take you up on it, missus,' I says, and she seen that I meant what I said and wasn't just being polite.

"'And before you just go believing that a hundred and sixteen miles to Bangor is out of the question, get out your own map and see how many miles it would be as the crow flies.'

"I finished the tiles and went home and ate leftovers—there wa'n't no roast, and I think 'Phelia Todd knew it—and after Megan was in bed, I got out my yardstick and a pen and my Mobil map of the state, and I did what she had told me...because it had laid hold of my mind a bit, you see. I drew a straight line and did out the calculations accordin to the scale of miles. I was some surprised. Because if you went from Castle Rock up there to

Bangor like one of those little Piper Cubs could fly on a clear day—if you didn't have to mind lakes, or stretches of lumber company woods that was chained off, or bogs, or crossing rivers where there wasn't no bridges, why, it would just be seventy-nine miles, give or take."

I jumped a little.

"Measure it yourself, if you don't believe me," Homer said. "I never knew Maine was so small until I seen that."

He had himself a drink and then looked around at me.

"There come a time the next spring when Megan was away in New Hampshire visiting with her brother. I had to go down to the Todds' house to take off the storm doors and put on the screens, and her little Mercedes go-devil was there. She was down by herself.

"She come to the door and says: 'Homer! Have you come to put on the screen doors?'

"And right off I says: 'No, missus, I come to see if you want to give me a ride down to Bangor the short way.'

"Well, she looked at me with no expression on her face at all, and I thought she had forgotten all about it. I felt my face gettin red, the way it will when you feel you just pulled one hell of a boner. Then, just when I was getting ready to 'pologize, her face busts into that grin again and she says, 'You just stand right there while I get my keys. And don't change your mind, Homer!'

"She come back a minute later with 'em in her hand. 'If we get stuck, you'll see mosquitoes just about the size of dragonflies.'

"'I've seen 'em as big as English sparrows up in Rangely, missus,' I said, 'and I guess we're both a spot too heavy to be carried off.'

"She laughs. 'Well, I warned you, anyway. Come on, Homer.'

"'And if we ain't there in two hours and forty-five minutes,' I says, kinda sly, 'you was gonna buy me a bottle of Irish Mist.'

"She looks at me kinda surprised, the driver's door of the go-devil open and one foot inside. 'Hell, Homer,' she says, 'I told you that was the Blue Ribbon for *then*. I've found a way up there that's *shorter*. We'll be there in two and a half hours. Get in here, Homer. We are going to roll.'"

He paused again, hands lying calm on his thighs, his eyes dulling, perhaps seeing that champagne-colored two-seater heading up the Todds' steep driveway.

"She stood the car still at the end of it and says, 'You sure?'

"'Let her rip,' I says. The ball bearing in her ankle rolled and that heavy foot come down. I can't tell you nothing much about whatall happened after that. Except after a while I couldn't hardly take my eyes off her. There was somethin wild that crep into her face, Dave—something *wild* and something *free,* and it frightened my heart. She was beautiful, and I was took with love *for* her, anyone would have been, any man, anyway, and maybe any woman too, but I was scairt *of* her too, because she looked like she could kill you if her eye left the road and fell on you and she decided to love you back. She was wearin blue jeans and a old white shirt with the sleeves rolled up—I had a idea she was maybe fixin to paint somethin on the back deck when I came by—but after we had been goin for a while seemed like she was dressed in nothin but all this white billowy stuff like a pitcher in one of those old gods-and-goddesses books."

He thought, looking out across the lake, his face very somber. "Like the huntress that was supposed to drive the moon across the sky."

"Diana?"

"Ayuh. Moon was her go-devil. 'Phelia looked like that to me and I just tell you fair out that I was stricken in love for her and never would have made a move, even though I was some younger then than I am now. I would not have made a move even had I been twenty, although I suppose I might of at sixteen, and been killed for it—killed if she looked at me was the way it felt.

"She was like that woman drivin the moon across the sky, halfway up over the splashboard with her gossamer stoles all flyin out behind her in silver cobwebs and her hair streamin back to show the dark little hollows of her temples, lashin those horses and tellin me to get along faster and never mind how they blowed, just faster, faster, *faster.*

"We went down a lot of woods roads—the first two or three I knew, and after that I didn't know none of them. We must have been a sight to those trees that had never seen nothing with a motor in it before but big old pulp-trucks and snowmobiles; that little go-devil that would most likely have looked more at home on the Sunset Boulevard than shooting through those woods, spitting and bulling its way up one hill and then slamming down the next through those dusty green bars of afternoon sunlight—she had the top down and I could smell everything in those woods, and you know what an old fine smell that is, like something which has been mostly left alone and is not much troubled. We went on across corduroy which had been laid over some of the boggiest parts, and black mud squelched up between some of those cut logs and she laughed like a kid. Some of the logs was old and rotted, because there hadn't been nobody down a couple of those roads—except for her, that is—in I'm going to say five or ten years.

We was *alone,* except for the birds and whatever animals seen us. The sound of that go-devil's engine, first buzzin along and then windin up high and fierce when she punched in the clutch and shifted down…that was the only motor-sound I could hear. And although I knew we had to be close to *some-place* all the time—I mean, these days you always are—I started to feel like we had gone back in time, and there wasn't *nothing.* That if we stopped and I climbed a high tree, I wouldn't see nothing in any direction but woods and woods and more woods. And all the time she's just *hammering* that thing along, her hair all out behind her, smilin, her eyes flashin. So we come out on the Speckled Bird Mountain Road and for a while I known where we were again, and then she turned off and for just a little bit I *thought* I knew, and then I didn't even bother to kid myself no more. We went cut-slam down another woods road, and then we come out—I swear it—on a nice paved road with a sign that said MOTORWAY B. You ever heard of a road in the state of Maine that was called MOTORWAY B?"

"No," I says. "Sounds English."

"Ayuh. *Looked* English. These trees like willows overhung the road. 'Now watch out here, Homer,' she says, 'one of those nearly grabbed me a month ago and gave me an Indian burn.'

"I didn't know what she was talkin about and started to say so, and then I seen that even though there was no wind, the branches of those trees was dippin down—they was *waverin* down. They looked black and wet inside the fuzz of green on them. I couldn't believe what I was seein. Then one of em snatched off my cap and I knew I wasn't asleep. 'Hi!' I shouts. 'Give that back!'

"'Too late now, Homer,' she says, and laughs. 'There's daylight, just up ahead…we're okay.'

"Then another one of em comes down, on her side this time, and snatches at her—I swear it did. She ducked, and it caught in her hair and pulled a lock of it out. 'Ouch, dammit that *hurts!*' she yells, but she was laughin, too. The car swerved a little when she ducked and I got a look into the woods and holy God, Dave! *Everythin* in there was movin. There was grasses wavin and plants that was all knotted together so it seemed like they made faces, and I seen somethin sittin in a squat on top of a stump, and it looked like a tree-toad, only it was as big as a full-growed cat.

"Then we come out of the shade to the top of a hill and she says, 'There! That was exciting, wasn't it?' as if she was talkin about no more than a walk through the Haunted House at the Fryeburg Fair.

"About five minutes later we swung onto another of her woods roads. I didn't want no more woods right then—I can tell you that for sure—but these were just plain old woods. Half an hour after that, we was pulling into the parking lot of the Pilot's Grille in Bangor. She points to that little odometer for trips and says, 'Take a gander, Homer.' I did, and it said 111.6. 'What do you think now? Do you believe in my shortcut?'

"That wild look had mostly faded out of her, and she was just 'Phelia Todd again. But that other look wasn't entirely gone. It was like she was two women, 'Phelia and Diana, and the part of her that was Diana was so much in control when she was driving the back roads that the part that was 'Phelia didn't have no idea that her shortcut was taking her through places... places that ain't on any map of Maine, not even on those survey-squares.

"She says again, 'What do you think of my shortcut, Homer?'

"And I says the first thing to come into my mind, which ain't something you'd usually say to a lady like 'Phelia Todd. 'It's a real piss-cutter, missus,' I says.

"She laughs, just as pleased as punch, and I seen it then, just as clear as glass: She didn't remember none of the funny stuff. Not the willow-branches—except they weren't willows, not at all, not really anything like em, or anything else—that grabbed off m'hat, not that MOTORWAY B sign, or that awful-lookin toad-thing. *She didn't remember none of that funny stuff!* Either I had dreamed it was there or she had dreamed it wasn't. All I knew for sure, Dave, was that we had rolled only a hundred and eleven miles and gotten to Bangor, and that wasn't no daydream; it was right there on the little go-devil's odometer, in black and white.

"'Well, it is,' she says. 'It *is* a piss-cutter. I only wish I could get Worth to give it a go sometime...but he'll never get out of his rut unless someone blasts him out of it, and it would probably take a Titan II missile to do that, because I believe he has built himself a fallout shelter at the bottom of that rut. Come on in, Homer, and let's dump some dinner into you.'

"And she bought me one hell of a dinner, Dave, but I couldn't eat very much of it. I kep thinkin about what the ride back might be like, now that it was drawing down dark. Then, about halfway through the meal, she excused herself and made a telephone call. When she came back she ast me if I would mind drivin the go-devil back to Castle Rock for her. She said she had talked to some woman who was on the same school committee as her, and the woman said they had some kind of problem about somethin or other. She said she'd grab herself a Hertz car if Worth couldn't see her back down. 'Do you mind awfully driving back *in* the dark?' she ast me.

"She looked at me, kinda smilin, and I knew she remembered *some* of it all right—Christ knows how much, but she remembered enough to know I wouldn't want to try her way after dark, if ever at all…although I seen by the light in her eyes that it wouldn't have bothered her a bit.

"So I said it wouldn't bother me, and I finished my meal better than when I started it. It was drawin down dark by the time we was done, and she run us over to the house of the woman she'd called. And when she gets out she looks at me with that same light in her eyes and says, 'Now, you're *sure* you don't want to wait, Homer? I saw a couple of side roads just today, and although I can't find them on my maps, I think they might chop a few miles.'

"I says, 'Well, missus, I would, but at my age the best bed to sleep in is my own, I've found. I'll take your car back and never put a ding in her… although I guess I'll probably put on some more miles than you did.'

"Then she laughed, kind of soft, and she give me a kiss. That was the best kiss I ever had in my whole life, Dave. It was just on the cheek, and it was the chaste kiss of a married woman, but it was as ripe as a peach, or like those flowers that open in the dark, and when her lips touched my skin I felt like… I don't know exactly what I felt like, because a man can't easily hold on to those things that happened to him with a girl who was ripe when the world was young or how those things felt—I'm talking around what I mean, but I think you understand. Those things all get a red cast to them in your memory and you cannot see through it at all.

"'You're a sweet man, Homer, and I love you for listening to me and riding with me,' she says. 'Drive safe.'

"Then in she went, to that woman's house. Me, I drove home."

"How did you go?" I asked.

He laughed softly. "By the turnpike, you damned fool," he said, and I never seen so many wrinkles in his face before as I did then. He sat there, looking into the sky.

"Came the summer she disappeared. I didn't see much of her…that was the summer we had the fire, you'll remember, and then the big storm that knocked down all the trees. A busy time for caretakers. Oh, I *thought* about her from time to time, and about that day, and about that kiss, and it started to seem like a dream to me. Like one time, when I was about sixteen and couldn't think about nothing but girls. I was out plowing George Bascomb's west field, the one that looks across the lake at the mountains, dreamin about what teenage boys dream of. And I pulled up this rock with the harrow blades, and it split open, and it *bled*. At least, it looked to me like it bled. Red stuff come runnin out of the cleft in the rock and soaked into the soil. And I never told no one but my mother, and I never told her what it meant to me, or what happened to me, although she washed my drawers and maybe she knew. Anyway, she suggested I ought to pray on it. Which I did, but I never got no enlightenment, and after a while something started to suggest to my mind that it had been a dream. It's that way, sometimes. There is holes in the *middle,* Dave. Do you know that?"

"Yes," I says, thinking of one night when I'd seen something. That was in '59, a bad year for us, but my kids didn't know it was a bad year; all they knew was that they wanted to eat just like always. I'd seen a bunch of whitetail in Henry Brugger's back field, and I was out there after dark with a jacklight in August. You can shoot two when they're summer-fat; the second'll come back and sniff at the first as if to say *What the hell? Is it fall already?* and you can pop him like a bowlin pin. You can hack off enough meat to feed yowwens for six weeks and bury what's left. Those are two whitetails the hunters who come in November don't get a shot at, but kids have to eat. Like the man from Massachusetts said, *he'd* like to be able to afford to live here the year around, and all I can say is sometimes you pay for the privilege after dark. So there I was, and I seen this big orange light in the sky; it come down and down, and I stood and watched it with my mouth hung on down to my breastbone and when it hit the lake the whole of it was lit up for a minute a purple-orange that seemed to go right up to the sky in rays. Wasn't nobody ever said nothing to me about that light, and I never said nothing to nobody myself, partly because I was afraid they'd laugh, but also because they'd wonder what the hell I'd been doing out there after dark to start with. And after a while it was like Homer said—it seemed like a dream I had once had, and it didn't signify to me because I couldn't make nothing of it which would turn under my hand. It was like a moonbeam. It didn't have no handle and it didn't have no blade. I couldn't make it work so I left it alone, like a man does when he knows the day is going to come up nevertheless.

"There are *holes* in the middle of things," Homer said, and he sat up straighter, like he was mad. "Right in the damn *middle* of things, not even to the left or right where your p'riph'ral vision is and you could say 'Well, but hell—' They are there and you go around them like you'd go around a pothole in the road that would break an axle. You know? And you forget it. Or like if you are plowin, you can plow a dip. But if there's somethin like a *break* in the earth, where you see darkness, like a cave might be there, you say 'Go around, old hoss. Leave that alone! I got a good shot over here to the left'ards.' Because it wasn't a cave you was lookin for, or some kind of college excitement, but good plowin.

"Holes in the *middle* of things."

He fell still a long time then and I let him be still. Didn't have no urge to move him. And at last he says:

"She disappeared in August. I seen her for the first time in early July, and she looked…" Homer turned to me and spoke each word with careful, spaced emphasis. "Dave Owens, she looked *gorgeous!* Gorgeous and wild and almost untamed. The little wrinkles I'd started to notice around her eyes all seemed to be gone. Worth Todd, he was at some conference or something in Boston. And she stands there at the edge of the deck—I was out in the middle with my shirt off—and she says, 'Homer, you'll never believe it.'

"'No, missus, but I'll try,' I says.

"'I found two new roads,' she says, 'and I got up to Bangor this last time in just sixty-seven miles.'

"I remembered what she said before and I says, 'That's not possible, missus. Beggin your pardon, but I did the mileage on the map myself, and seventy-nine is tops…as the crow flies.'

"She laughed, and she looked prettier than ever. Like a goddess in the sun, on one of those hills in a story where there's nothing but green grass and fountains and no puckies to tear at a man's forearms at all. 'That's right,' she says, 'and you can't run a mile in under four minutes. It's been mathematically *proved.*'

"'It ain't the same,' I says.

"'It's the same,' she says. 'Fold the map and see how many miles it is then, Homer. It can be a little less than a straight line if you fold it a little, or it can be a lot less if you fold it a lot.'

"I remembered our ride then, the way you remember a dream, and I says, 'Missus, you can fold a map on paper but you can't fold *land.* Or at least you shouldn't ought to try. You want to leave it alone.'

"'No sir,' she says. 'It's the one thing right now in my life that I won't leave alone, because it's *there,* and it's *mine.*'

"Three weeks later—this would be about two weeks before she disappeared—she give me a call from Bangor. She says, 'Worth has gone to New York, and I am coming down. I've misplaced my damn key, Homer. I'd like you to open the house so I can get in.'

"Well, that call come at eight o'clock, just when it was starting to come down dark. I had a sanwidge and a beer before leaving—about twenty minutes. Then I took a ride down there. All in all, I'd say I was forty-five minutes. When I got down there to the Todds', I seen there was a light on in the pantry I didn't leave on while I was comin down the driveway. I was lookin at that, and I almost run right into her little go-devil. It was parked kind of on a slant, the way a drunk would park it, and it was splashed with muck all the way up to the windows, and there was this stuff stuck in that mud along the body that looked like seaweed…only when my lights hit it, it seemed to be *movin.* I parked behind it and got out of my truck. That stuff wasn't seaweed, but it *was* weeds, and it *was* movin…kinda slow and sluggish, like it was dyin. I touched a piece of it, and it tried to wrap itself around my hand. It felt nasty and awful. I drug my hand away and wiped it on my pants. I went around to the front of the car. It looked like it had come through about ninety miles of splash and low country. Looked *tired,* it did. Bugs was splashed all over the windshield—only they didn't look like no kind of bugs I ever seen before. There was a moth that was about the size of a sparrow, its wings still flappin a little, feeble and dyin. There was things like mosquitoes, only they had real eyes that you could see—and they seemed to be seein me. I could hear those weeds scrapin against the body of the go-devil, dyin, tryin to get a hold on somethin. And all I could think was: Where in the hell has she been? And how did she get here in only three-quarters of an hour? Then I seen somethin else. There was some kind of a animal half-smashed onto the radiator grille, just under where that Mercedes ornament is—the one that looks kinda like a star looped up into a circle? Now most small animals you kill on the road is bore right under the car, because they are crouching when it hits them, hoping it'll just go over and leave them with their hide still attached to their meat. But every now and then one will jump, not away, but right at the damn car, as if to get in one good bite of whatever the buggardly thing is that's going to kill it—I have known that to happen. This thing had maybe done that. And it looked mean enough to jump a Sherman tank. It looked like something which come of a mating between a woodchuck and a weasel, but there was other stuff thrown in that a body didn't even want to look at. It hurt your eyes, Dave; worse'n that, it hurt your *mind.* Its pelt was matted with blood, and there was claws sprung out of the pads on its feet like a cat's claws, only longer. It had big yellowy eyes, only they was glazed. When I was a kid I had a porcelain marble—a croaker—that looked like that. And teeth. Long thin needle teeth that looked almost like darning needles, stickin out of its mouth. Some of them was sunk right into that steel grillwork. That's why it was still hanging on; it had hung its *own* self on by the teeth. I looked at it and knowed it had a headful of poison just like a rattlesnake, and it jumped at that go-devil when it saw it was about to be run down, tryin to bite it to death. And I wouldn't be the one to try and yonk it offa there because I had cuts on my hands—hay-cuts—and I thought it would kill me as dead as a stone parker if some of that poison seeped into the cuts.

"I went around to the driver's door and opened it. The inside light come on, and I looked at that special odometer that she set for trips…and what I seen there was 31.6.

"I looked at that for a bit, and then I went to the back door. She'd forced the screen and broke the glass by the lock so she could get her hand through and let herself in. There was a note that said: 'Dear Homer—got here a little sooner than I thought I would. Found a shortcut, and it is a dilly! You hadn't come yet so I let myself in like a burglar. Worth is coming day after tomorrow. Can you get the screen fixed and the door reglazed by then? Hope so. Things like that always bother him. If I don't come out to say hello, you'll know I'm asleep. The drive was very tiring, but I was here in no time! Ophelia.'

"*Tirin!* I took another look at that bogey-thing hangin offa the grille of her car, and I thought Yessir, it *must* have been tiring. By God, *yes.*"

He paused again, and cracked a restless knuckle.

"I seen her only once more. About a week later. Worth was there, but he was swimmin out in the lake, back and forth, back and forth, like he was sawin wood or signin papers. More like he was signin papers, I guess.

"'Missus,' I says, 'this ain't my business, but you ought to leave well enough alone. That night you come back and broke the glass of the door to come in, I seen somethin hangin off the front of your car—'

"'Oh, the chuck! I took care of that,' she says.

"'Christ!' I says. 'I hope you took some care!'

"'I wore Worth's gardening gloves,' she said. 'It wasn't anything anyway, Homer, but a jumped-up woodchuck with a little poison in it.'

"'But missus,' I says, 'where there's woodchucks there's bears. And if that's what the woodchucks look like along your shortcut, what's going to happen to you if a bear shows up?'

"She looked at me, and I seen that other woman in her—that Diana-woman. She says, 'If things are different along those roads, Homer, maybe I am different, too. Look at this.'

"Her hair was done up in a clip at the back, looked sort of like a butterfly and had a stick through it. She let it down. It was the kind of hair that would make a man wonder what it would look like spread out over a pillow. She says, 'It was coming in gray, Homer. Do you see any gray?' And she spread it with her fingers so the sun could shine on it.

"'No'm,' I says.

"She looks at me, her eyes all a-sparkle, and she says, 'Your wife is a good woman, Homer Buckland, but she has seen me in the store and in the post office, and we've passed the odd word or two, and I have seen her looking at my hair in a kind of satisfied way that only women know. I know what she says, and what she tells her friends...that Ophelia Todd has started dyeing her hair. But I have not. I have lost my way looking for a shortcut more than once...lost my way...and lost my gray.' And she laughed, not like a college girl but like a girl in high school. I admired her and longed for her beauty, but I seen that other beauty in her face as well just then...and I felt afraid again. Afraid *for* her, and afraid *of* her.

"'Missus,' I says, 'you stand to lose more than a little sta'ch in your hair.'

"'No,' she says. 'I tell you I am different over there... I am *all myself* over there. When I am going along that road in my little car I am not Ophelia Todd, Worth Todd's wife who could never carry a child to term, or that woman who tried to write poetry and failed at it, or the woman who sits and takes notes in committee meetings, or anything or anyone else. When I am on that road I am in the heart of myself, and I feel like—'

"'*Diana*,' I said.

"She looked at me kind of funny and kind of surprised, and then she laughed. 'O like some goddess, I suppose,' she said. 'She will do better than most because I am a night person—I love to stay up until my book is done or until the National Anthem comes on the TV, and because I am very pale, like the moon—Worth is always saying I need a tonic, or blood tests or some sort of similar bosh. But in her heart what every woman wants to be is some kind of goddess, I think—men pick up a ruined echo of that thought and try to put them on pedestals (a woman, who will pee down her own leg if she does not squat! It's funny when you stop to think of it)—but what a man senses is not what a woman wants. A woman wants to be in the clear, is all. To stand if she will, or walk...' Her eyes turned toward that little go-devil in the driveway, and narrowed. Then she smiled. 'Or to *drive*, Homer. A man will not see that. He thinks a goddess wants to loll on a slope somewhere on the foothills of Olympus and eat fruit, but there is no god or goddess in that. All a woman wants is what a man wants—a woman wants to *drive*.'

"'Be careful where you drive, missus, is all,' I says, and she laughs and give me a kiss spang in the middle of the forehead.

"She says, 'I will, Homer,' but it didn't mean nothing, and I known it, because she said it like a man who says he'll be careful to his wife or his girl when he knows he won't…can't.

"I went back to my truck and waved to her once, and it was a week later that Worth reported her missing. Her and that go-devil both. Todd waited seven years and had her declared legally dead, and then he waited another year for good measure—I'll give the sucker that much—and then he married the second Missus Todd, the one that just went by. And I don't expect you'll believe a single damn word of the whole yarn."

In the sky one of those big flat-bottomed clouds moved enough to disclose the ghost of the moon—half-full and pale as milk. And something in my heart leaped up at the sight, half in fright, half in love.

"I do though," I said. "Every frigging damned word. And even if it ain't true, Homer, it ought to be."

He give me a hug around the neck with his forearm, which is all men can do since the world don't let them kiss but only women, and laughed, and got up.

"Even if it *shouldn't* ought to be, it is," he said. He got his watch out of his pants and looked at it. "I got to go down the road and check on the Scott place. You want to come?"

"I believe I'll sit here for a while," I said, "and think."

He went to the steps, then turned back and looked at me, half-smiling. "I believe she was right," he said. "She *was* different along those roads she found…wasn't nothing that would dare touch her. You or me, maybe, but not her.

"And I believe she's young."

Then he got in his truck and set off to check the Scott place.

That was two years ago, and Homer has since gone to Vermont, as I think I told you. One night he come over to see me. His hair was combed, he had a shave, and he smelled of some nice lotion. His face was clear and his eyes were alive. That night he looked sixty instead of seventy, and I was glad for him and I envied him and I hated him a little, too. Arthritis is one buggardly great old fisherman, and that night Homer didn't look like arthritis had any fishhooks sunk into his hands the way they were sunk into mine.

"I'm going," he said.

"Ayuh?"

"Ayuh."

"All right; did you see to forwarding your mail?"

"Don't want none forwarded," he said. "My bills are paid. I am going to make a clean break."

"Well, give me your address. I'll drop you a line from one time to the another, old hoss." Already I could feel loneliness settling over me like a cloak…and looking at him, I knew that things were not quite what they seemed.

"Don't have none yet," he said.

"All right," I said. *"Is* it Vermont, Homer?"

"Well," he said, "it'll do for people who want to know."

I almost didn't say it and then I did. "What does she look like now?"

"Like Diana," he said. "But she is kinder."

"I envy you, Homer," I said, and I did.

I stood at the door. It was twilight in that deep part of summer when the fields fill with perfume and Queen Anne's Lace. A full moon was beating a silver track across the lake. He went across my porch and down the steps. A car was standing on the soft shoulder of the road, its engine idling heavy, the way the old ones do that still run full bore straight ahead and damn the torpedoes. Now that I think of it, that car *looked* like a torpedo. It looked beat up some, but as if it could go the ton without breathin hard. He stopped at the foot of my steps and picked something up—it was his gas can, the big one that holds ten gallons. He went down my walk to the passenger side of the car. She leaned over and opened the door. The inside light came on and just for a moment I saw her, long red hair around her face, her forehead shining like a lamp. Shining like the *moon.* He got in and she drove away. I stood out on my porch and watched the taillights of her little go-devil twinkling red in the dark…getting smaller and smaller. They were like embers, then they were like flickerflies, and then they were gone.

Vermont, I tell the folks from town, and Vermont they believe, because it's as far as most of them can see inside their heads. Sometimes I almost believe it myself, mostly when I'm tired and done up. Other times I think about them, though—all this October I have done so, it seems, because October is the time when men think mostly about far places and the roads which might get them there. I sit on the bench in front of Bell's Market and think about Homer Buckland and about the beautiful girl who leaned over to open his door when he come down that path with the full red gasoline can in his right hand—she looked like a girl of no more than sixteen, a girl on her learner's permit, and her beauty *was* terrible, but I believe it would no longer kill the man it turned itself on; for a moment her eyes lit on me, I was not killed, although part of me died at her feet.

Olympus must be a glory to the eyes and the heart, and there are those who crave it and those who find a clear way to it, mayhap, but I know Castle Rock like the back of my hand and I could never leave it for no shortcuts where the roads may go; in October the sky over the lake is no glory but it is passing fair, with those big white clouds that move so slow; I sit here on the bench, and think about 'Phelia Todd and Homer Buckland, and I don't necessarily wish I was where they are...but I still wish I was a smoking man.

THE ONTOLOGICAL FACTOR

DAVID BARR KIRTLEY

David Barr Kirtley has published fiction in magazines such as *Realms of Fantasy, Weird Tales, Lightspeed, Intergalactic Medicine Show, On Spec,* and *Cicada,* and in anthologies such as *New Voices in Science Fiction, Fantasy: The Best of the Year,* and *The Dragon Done It.* Recently he's contributed stories to several of John Joseph Adams's anthologies, including *The Living Dead, The Living Dead 2,* and *The Way of the Wizard.* He's attended numerous writing workshops, including Clarion, Odyssey, Viable Paradise, James Gunn's Center for the Study of Science Fiction, and Orson Scott Card's Writers Bootcamp, and he holds an MFA in screenwriting and fiction from the University of Southern California. He also teaches regularly at Alpha, a Pittsburgh-area science fiction workshop for young writers, and is the co-host of *The Geek's Guide to the Galaxy.* He lives in New York.

W hen my great uncle Cornelius died, our family needed someone to drive up to his house in Providence and make an inventory of his property, and I was the natural choice. After all, my recent bachelor's degree in philosophy and East Asian studies had done nothing to secure me regular employment, and I'd had to move back in with my parents, where I'd thrown myself into an ambitious project to create the world's longest-running manga comic about a flying mushroom who quotes Hegel. Cornelius had had some sort of falling out with the rest of the family years before I was born, over some (possibly imagined) slight. He'd lived alone, in a mansion he'd inherited from his mother.

I wasn't crazy about being by myself in a giant old house. For years I'd suffered from an odd, disconnected feeling, as if nothing was real, including myself, and this caused me constant low-level anxiety as well as the occasional panic attack. The distress inevitably intensified the longer I spent alone. I had not mentioned this to anyone.

I told my dad, "I don't know if I'm really the best person to be going through his things. I never even met the guy."

"Just do your best," Dad said. "Everyone else is busy. I'll try to come and help out if I can."

So, reluctantly, I agreed.

I arrived in the late afternoon. The house was gray, Victorian, sprawled across the top of a low, forested hill. The central section was three stories tall, and additional two-story wings spread out in either direction.

I drove up the gravel drive, then pulled to a stop near the front door and got out. Dark clouds filled the sky, and as I approached the house a cool breeze rose, rustling the dry leaves that littered its porch. I jogged up the front steps and let myself in with the key I'd been given.

The place was musty and dim, with papers piled everywhere. I wandered through room after room of tables and sofas and bookshelves. Pausing by a window, I looked out into the backyard, where a gazebo overgrown with weeds huddled beside a scum-covered pond. I made my way into the kitchen. The sinks and countertops were cluttered with dirty dishes, and the cupboards revealed that the owner's diet had consisted mostly of coffee and cold cereal. So far this was about what I'd expected.

My first surprise came when I stepped into a parlor off the main corridor. There was a door there. A very strange door.

It was built into the far wall and painted bright green, a revolting neon shade that clashed with the subdued hues of the rest of the house. The door was quite small—I'd have to stoop to pass through it—and extremely crooked, though this seemed intentional. And unlike the rest of the place, this door looked new, and clean, and I suspected it was something Cornelius had added himself. Strangest of all, it was locked with no less than four heavy padlocks.

I stepped closer, studying the locks. I had only the one key, and it obviously didn't fit any of them. I'd have to come back later and see if I could spring them with my tools. Among my many odd and useless skills was picking locks, at which I had always been uncannily talented.

I began gathering up all the loose papers and sorting them into piles on the dining room table. There were the usual bills, ads, catalogs, etc., but also strange notebooks, dozens of them, full of puzzling diagrams and near-illegible scribbling, though certain words—"portal," "opener," "world"—jumped out at me.

I was so absorbed in the task that I didn't notice anyone enter the dining room, but suddenly a voice at my elbow barked, "Who are you?"

I started violently, and turned.

In the corner stood a large, burly woman who was maybe in her mid-forties. She wore a knapsack, and her outfit looked like a cross between a sweatsuit and a uniform.

"I...I'm Steven," I said. "Cornelius...he was my great uncle."

"Who's Cornelius?" she said.

"He...owns this place. I mean, he did."

When she'd first spoken, I'd thought she must be a friend of Cornelius—though by all accounts he hadn't had any. Now I wondered if she might be a burglar—she was sort of dressed like one—but she spoke with such casual authority that I doubted this was the case. At least, I wasn't about to ask.

She studied me, and I noticed that her irises were an odd golden color. Also, I could swear that her skin had a faint bluish tinge to it...like something not of this world. And it was as if she'd just appeared out of thin air...

"All right, Steve," she said, "you seem harmless enough. Carry on. But stay out of the east wing, if you know what's good for you."

She turned, as if to depart, though she was standing in the corner.

"Wait," I said. "Who are you?"

"Asha," she called over her shoulder. "Nice to meet you."

A dozen questions swirled in my mind, but I sensed that I'd only get a chance to ask one, and that one, the most important, rose to my lips. "Wait," I called softly. "Are...are you real?"

"Ha! That's a good one. Am *I* real?" she said, as she walked straight through a solid wall and disappeared.

So obviously I was freaked out, but what could I do? Run home and tell my parents that I'd been chased off by a ghost? No thanks. Instead I turned on as many lights as I could and positioned myself on a couch in the center of one of the larger rooms, where nothing could sneak up on me, and played movies on my laptop to keep the silence at bay. Finally I passed out, from sheer exhaustion.

When I woke it was morning, and everything seemed more manageable. As I wandered the empty house, I was already half convinced that my encounter with Asha had just been something I'd dreamed during the night. Still, I avoided the east wing.

What I needed right then, I decided, was some sort of challenge to occupy my mind, and the padlocks on the green door seemed just the thing. I'd become increasingly intrigued by the door, because, as near as I could tell, it couldn't possibly lead anywhere. The layout of the surrounding rooms was like a maze, but I was pretty sure I'd seen the far side of that wall, and there was nothing there but blank plaster.

I pulled up a chair before the door and sat down, wielding my tools. The work went quickly, the locks giving way one after another. I placed each one on the floor at my feet, then reached forward and pushed at the door, which swung aside.

A rush of humid air hit me, redolent with swamp smells of marsh grass and mud. Beyond the door lay a livid green sky above rolling hills dotted with forests and ponds. In a daze I rose to my feet and strode forward, my bare feet sinking into the surprisingly spongy earth. Another world, I thought, staring in wonder. It was actually there, actually real.

I glanced back over my shoulder. From this side, the green door was built into the wall of a small tower made of rough granite bricks. Through the door I could see back into the parlor of Cornelius's mansion.

I wandered down the hill into the field below. There was a small lake there, its waters murky and brown, and below the surface I could just make out the wavering suggestion of glimmering lights. Then a balmy breeze blew by, and I heard voices on the air. Crouching in the underbrush, I peered through a screen of trees.

A line of black-robed men were making their way up the hill. There were twenty of them, and they wore hoods, and chanted, and some bore a palanquin upon which sat an ebony idol, some sort of frog-headed deity on a gnarled throne.

It was a distinctly sinister tableau, and I was in no hurry to join the parade. Now that my initial wonder was subsiding, I had second thoughts about the wisdom of wandering barefoot and alone through an unknown world.

I turned to beat a hasty retreat, and almost ran right into a strange woman who was crawling up the beach toward me. She was thin and bony, and had come from the water, which dotted her pale flesh, and her thin green hair was plastered back across her oddly elongated scalp. When she was just a few feet away, she cocked her head at me, staring up with bulbous eyes and smiling faintly, as if she were expecting a treat.

I backed away, and suddenly she grinned, the corners of her mouth stretching three times as wide as I would've thought possible. Her teeth were like a piranha's.

Then she screamed, a banshee wail, a piercing shriek that went on and on.

I glanced behind me, through the trees. The black-robed men were turning my way now, and throwing back their hoods. Their faces were like hers, and from beneath their robes they drew short staffs topped with tridents.

I edged around the woman—her still screaming, still eager and staring—and sprinted back toward the tower and the green door.

I was out of breath and staggering by the time I was halfway up the hill, and then I stumbled on that strangely pliant ground and fell to my hands and knees, and the creatures swarmed about me, capering and gibbering, thrusting at me with their tridents. I threw my arms over my face and curled into a ball. How could I have been so stupid? Maybe Freud had been right about the death drive, that we all subconsciously seek our own destruction.

The weapons struck my shoulders, my back, my legs. It took a moment before I realized that the pain was minimal, as if they were children poking me with sticks. I was not bleeding, not harmed.

I opened one eye, and a fish-man roared into my face with his dagger-toothed mouth. Instinctively I lashed out, and when I struck his head it burst like an overinflated balloon, splattering me with gore. I dragged myself to my feet as the rest of the fish-men fled. I had absolutely no idea what was going on.

I made it back to the tower, passed through the green door, and slammed it behind me. As I snapped the locks shut one by one, I swore that I would never, ever, *ever* go opening any mysterious doors ever again. Breathing a sigh of relief, I turned around.

Asha stood there, frowning.

I screamed.

She seized me by the arm and growled, "Come with me."

"W-where are we going?" I said, as she dragged me through the halls, but she didn't answer.

I said, "There were creatures in there! They attacked me."

"Well, what do you expect from a bunch of twos?" she muttered.

I had no idea what to make of that.

She escorted me into the west wing of the house, into a section I hadn't really explored yet, and marched me into a large bedroom. Built into the corner was another of those strange doors, this one bright orange rather than bright green, and tilted to the right rather than the left, but otherwise identical to the other—right down to the four heavy padlocks.

"I need you to open this," Asha said, as we crossed the room.

I wasn't at all sure that was a good idea. I pointed weakly at the locks. "Uh, my tools are back—"

She reached out with her bare hands and ripped apart the locks as if they were made of cotton candy.

Then she turned to face me. "Open it," she ordered. "Now."

So what could I do? With a trembling hand I gave the door a small push, and it swung back with a creak, revealing yet another alien world—dry, rolling scrub plains beneath a dusty orange sky.

Asha beamed. "Excellent!"

Puzzled, I said, "Why couldn't you just open it yourself?"

"Because I'm not an opener," she said. "You are. Hard as that is to believe."

Opener? I thought.

She added quickly, "And now, Steve my boy, there's something else I need you to do for me. I need you to go through this door and find me a weapon. A gun would be my first choice, of course, but any sort of weapon will do—a sword, an axe, anything like that." She reached into her knapsack and pulled out a revolver, which she handed to me. "Or even just some bullets, if they'll work with this."

The gun felt amazingly heavy in my hand. I said, "Why do you need a weapon?"

She scowled. "Look, there's no time to waste, okay? Just do it. Trust me on this, it's important."

Somehow, maybe because I was still high on adrenaline from my encounter with the fish-men, I found the guts to say, "No."

"Kid," she growled, fixing me with an intense glare, "you have no idea what's at stake here."

"Then tell me!" I said. "Tell me what's going on! But I'm not going to go marching off and bring back a weapon just because you say so!"

For a moment Asha looked so frustrated that I thought she might tear me apart the way she had the locks.

Finally she sighed. "All right, fine. I'll explain." She snatched the gun from me and tossed it in her knapsack. "Follow me."

I tagged along behind her as she led the way back toward the other end of the house.

"Okay," she said, as we went, "you know that there are different worlds, and that it's possible to open portals between them. The first thing you have to understand is that not all worlds are created equal. Some are more real than others."

I chimed in, "But who's to say what's real and what isn't?"

"Oh," she said. "We use this." She reached into the knapsack and pulled out a device that looked like a black-and-purple-striped candy cane. "It's called an O-meter. Each world, and everything native to it, has a specific Ontological Factor, or OF, which is what the machine measures. Here, I'll show you."

She pointed the device at me, and sections of it lit up in sequence until about half its length was glowing.

"See?" she said. "You're a five."

"Oh," I said. "Is that good?"

"No," she said.

"Oh."

"But hey, it could be worse. Like those degenerates you ran into earlier. Twos. Total figments. Not real enough to do any damage even to you."

So that's why I'd survived the attack of the fish-men, I thought. That made sense. Sort of.

"What number are you?" I asked.

"Ten," she said. "Obviously."

After a moment, I added, "At first I thought you were a ghost."

"Kid, there's no such thing as ghosts."

"But you walked right through a wall, so—"

"Yeah, but it was just a *five* wall."

I frowned. We were silent for a while.

She eyed me. "What's the matter? You seem nonplussed."

"I don't know," I said, "I don't like this. Some of the greatest minds in history have grappled with the question of what's real and what isn't, and how do we know, and it's something that's bothered me for a long time too. And then to have someone come along and say it's just a number that you can measure on a machine—"

"Is *that* what's bothering you?" she said. "Kid, forget that crap. We've got bigger problems. *Much* bigger."

"What do you mean?"

We were in the east wing of the house now. We entered a large library— hardwood floors, overstuffed chairs, a fireplace. And of course, built into the far wall was another of those small crooked doors, this one bright purple.

Asha nodded at it. "That's the one that killed him."

"Who?" I said.

"Your great uncle. What's his name? Cornelius? Creating a portal is hard on anyone, let alone a five. He must've been pretty desperate to get out of this craphole world. Can't say I blame him."

I stared at the purple door. Unlike the other two, it wasn't locked. "He did hate it here," I said.

"Unfortunately for him," Asha went on, "his first two attempts led to cul-de-sac worlds, and I guess that wasn't good enough for him. This one here is different. It leads to a world that's connected to half a dozen others. You can get anywhere from here."

"So what's the problem?" I said.

"The problem," she said pointedly, "is Abraxas."

"What's Abraxas?"

"Not what—who. Abraxas is a type of being we call a 'demon'—someone who can soak up the reality of other people and absorb it into himself. That's illegal, of course, and most demons refrain from using their ability. But every once in a while you get a bad one, and Abraxas is one of the worst."

"I see," I said. "He's like the embodiment of Nietzsche's will to power."

She stared at me levelly for a moment, then continued as if I hadn't spoken. "I caught up with him a few days ago, here, on this world. I'm a sort of...bounty hunter, you might say. Unfortunately Abraxas is one sneaky bastard. He gave me the slip, and made off with a bunch of my gear to boot, including my skeleton key. Without it, I can't open portals. I also used up all my bullets firing at him as he fled."

She sighed. "So here I am. These portals that your great uncle created are the only ones on this world that are traversable at the moment, and two of them, as I said, are dead ends." She glanced over her shoulder at the purple door. "Abraxas has to get through this one, and if he does—if he gets away—then we can't restore the stolen reality to the dozens of worlds, including yours, that he's pillaged, which leaves all of you at greater risk of cross-world invasion."

I stood in stunned silence.

"*And*," she added grimly, "if someone doesn't lock him up soon, one of these days he'll have absorbed enough reality to put him beyond contention even by us tens, and then there'll be no stopping him, ever. So *that's* Abraxas. And he could be showing up here at any minute, and I'll have to fight him. Now"—she held up her massive hands—"these hands are formidable things, but nevertheless, given the circumstances, I really wouldn't mind having a weapon, you know what I mean? You getting the picture?"

"Yes," I said meekly.

"This world is a five," she said, "so nothing around here is real enough to harm him at all. But behind the orange door is a world that's an eight. Not the best, but a weapon from there should be enough to knock him for a loop, I'd say. I can't go myself, because I have to stay and guard this door. That's where you come in."

She looked me in the eye and said, "So that's the story. Now, Steve, I'm asking you, will you help me? Please?"

My mind was made up. "Okay," I said. "I'll do it."

"Terrific," Asha exclaimed. "Finally. All right, let's get you prepped for a little cross-world travel. First of all"—she reached into her knapsack, produced a bottle of pills and a canteen, and handed them to me—"take some of these. Actually, better take them all."

I opened the bottle and studied the pills, which were small and dark and soft, like caviar. I tossed them in my mouth, took a gulp from the canteen, and swallowed. "What are they?"

"Brain worms," she said.

I froze.

She caught my expression, and added quickly, "Oh, but not *bad* brain worms. Good brain worms. They know most of the languages that are spoken across the worlds, and pretty soon you will too."

"Oh," I said, uncertainly.

She passed me the knapsack. "Take this too. It's got pretty much everything a cross-world traveler might need. There's silver in the side pocket."

"Silver?" I said.

"Right. It makes a good universal currency. It gets traded around quite a lot, actually, so any silver you come across has a fair chance of having a higher OF than ambient materials. Doesn't this world have any legends about invincible monsters that can only be harmed by silver?"

"Yeah," I said.

She nodded. "Most worlds do. Now you know why." She frowned. "Unfortunately, I have yet to come across *anything* on this piece of crap world with a high OF."

I was getting a little irked by her attitude. I mean, I had mixed feelings about this world myself, but it *was* my home. On the other hand, maybe the place she came from really *was* a whole lot better. Certainly what little I'd seen of a world with an OF of two tended to bear out her prejudices. That reminded me...

"What if I get attacked again?" I said.

She blanched. "Yeah, that's an issue, for sure. Be careful with yourself. They're eights and you're a five, so they're basically untouchable as far as you're concerned. But I don't expect you'll have any problems. Eights tend to be pretty civilized, you'll see."

I shouldered the pack. "All right. Is that everything?"

"Yup," she said. "Thanks for doing this, kid, I really appreciate it. See you soon, okay?"

"Okay," I said, and departed the library, making my way toward the orange door.

I stepped out into a hot, dry day, and looked around. On this side, the door was built into a white brick wall that was about as tall as I was, and that hugged the contours of the rolling hills for as far as I could see in either direction. In the valley below, a perfectly straight road ran from the horizon to a city of gleaming spires a few miles away.

I took a deep breath, adjusted my pack, and started down the hill toward the road. Hopefully, I thought, my sophomore effort at cross-world travel would turn out more auspiciously than my first. Though I *was* a lot more prepared this time around. I had shoes, for one thing, and a pack full of food and water and money. I also had a gun, though it was empty. Most importantly, I had a rough idea of what was going on.

I also had worms in my brain. *Good* worms. Yeah.

On the other hand, this world was an eight, and I was a mere five. I stomped on the ground experimentally. I supposed that it did feel a bit more substantial than usual, and the colors around me did look more vibrant and saturated, especially the looming orange sky.

After an hour I reached the road, which was a hundred feet across and made of a smooth white substance that showed virtually no wear. I set off toward the city.

A bit later I heard a distant humming sound, and raised my head. Something was speeding down the road toward me, and throwing up clouds of dust as it came. It was white, and seemed to float above the ground. As it neared I saw that it looked almost exactly like a giant flying egg.

It came to a halt beside me, then spoke in a low, soothing voice. The language was unfamiliar, but I realized that I could indeed understand it. It said, "Greetings, pilgrim. May I conduct you to the city?"

"Um, okay," I replied, in that same language.

The egg's top half unfolded like a blooming flower, revealing a cushioned red seat within. "Welcome aboard."

I climbed a short set of steps and settled into the chair. The dome re-formed itself above me—the vehicle resuming its egglike shape—and we accelerated toward the city. From inside, the thing's walls were transparent, and I watched as the ground sped by beneath us and the city drew ever nearer.

We flew through an enormous gate and came to a halt in a white plaza beside a giant fountain. The vehicle opened and let me out, then sped away, back to wherever flying eggs go.

There were people all around me. They were varied in appearance, but were all apparently human, and most were dressed in white, their garments simple and clean. I felt a little conspicuous standing there in my street clothes, which were still a bit spattered with fish-man, but no one seemed to pay me any attention as they strolled about, chatting and laughing.

I wandered down a broad avenue toward the city center, keeping an eye out for any sort of weapon. Having no knowledge of local customs, I was a bit reluctant to just come right out and ask where I could buy a gun. I kept hoping to see a big sign with a sword or machinegun on it, but no such luck.

I passed a park. The grass there had been shaped into a triangular field, upon which children played a sport involving a cube-shaped ball and sticks that looked like a cross between a golf club and a cricket bat. I paused for a moment to watch.

On a bench beside me sat a man who was watching the game. He said, "Dhajat season is always my favorite time of year."

He was an older fellow with a placid face and a long white beard, and he held a glass of what looked like lemonade.

"Uh, yeah, mine too," I said, hoping that was an appropriate response.

He gave me a friendly smile. "What brings you to the city, pilgrim?"

"Um, I'm looking for something," I said.

He nodded sagely. "We're all looking for something."

"Oh," I said. "Right."

Should I chance it? Oh what the hell, he seemed as friendly and talkative as anyone I was likely to meet.

I added, "But, um, actually I'm looking for something kind of specific."

"Truth?" he said. "Enlightenment? I was like you once. Don't worry, you'll find it."

"No," I said, "more like, um, a gun."

He chortled. "Ha! That's a good one."

I waited for him to elaborate, but he didn't. He was back to watching the game. I said, "Or a sword. I mean, any sort of weapon, really."

Slowly he turned to face me. "You are…joking?"

"Um…" I said.

"You came *here* to shop for weapons?" He laughed uproariously. "Tourists!" he declared, wiping tears from his eyes. "Don't you know where you are? No one would ever *dream* of bringing a weapon within a hundred miles of Nervuh Nah, City of Peace."

I started to get a sinking feeling. I turned away.

Things were definitely not looking good. There were no weapons here, no weapons anywhere *near* this whole city. My mission was a complete failure. There was nothing I could do to help stop Abraxas, and now he'd probably escape through the purple door, leaving Earth forever in a state of crippled ontological peril.

Also, Asha was going to be *really* pissed off.

Then I had an idea.

Asha eyed my offering with disbelief. "And what exactly," she declared, "is *that*?"

"A dhajat bat," I said.

"And just what am I supposed to do with that?"

"Um, play dhajat," I said. "But—"

She put her face in her hands and shook her head. "Kid," she moaned, "is there something about the concept of a 'weapon' that you're not getting?"

"It's not my fault!" I said. "It was like a whole city of pacifists! There were no weapons anywhere. I just thought—"

"All right, all right," she interrupted. "Give it here."

I passed her the bat, and she took a few practice swings.

She sighed. "Well, it's better than nothing, I guess. But I wish you would've—"

She stopped suddenly.

"What?" I said.

She whispered, "He's here." She nodded at the fireplace. "Get over there. Stay out of this."

I hurried to comply. A short time later I heard footsteps approaching. Asha hefted the bat.

My dad walked into the room.

"Wait!" I cried, as Asha rushed him. I lunged to interpose myself between them, waving my arms. "It's okay, it's my dad!"

Then I noticed that my dad was grinning in a very sinister, very un-dad-like way. And he was holding something—a snow globe?

"Steve!" Asha roared, shoving me aside, "get out of the way! It's—"

My dad hurled the globe to the floor at Asha's feet.

Then it was like I was staring into the sun. I flew through the air—

I came to moments later, draped across one of the overstuffed chairs, which had been knocked to the floor, apparently by me, and I hurt everywhere. I raised my head to try to see what was going on.

Asha lay sprawled on the floor. Whatever that glass ball weapon had been, she'd absorbed the brunt of it, and seemed to be out cold. The dhajat bat had flown from her grasp and landed in the corner, where a tall, thin figure was bending over to retrieve it.

He didn't look at all like my dad now. He wore a brown trenchcoat and fedora, and the hat cast impossibly deep shadows over his face, but I could make out hints of gaunt, skeletal cheeks, and a heavy jaw lined with jagged teeth.

He gripped the bat and straightened, turning toward Asha.

"No!" I cried, stumbling to my feet. I snatched up a heavy ceramic ashtray and threw it at him, but when it struck him it bounced off as if it were made of styrofoam, and he paid no attention.

I felt a flood of despair. The only object in the room with enough reality to affect him was the bat, and—

Wait! I thought. Asha's knapsack. Her gun! If it had come from her world, it must have an OF of ten, like her. I tore open the pack and yanked out the gun.

Abraxas stood over Asha and raised the bat to strike. With a cry I hurled the gun at him as hard as I could.

It hit him in the back of the head, and his hat went flying. "Ow!" he screamed.

Then he turned to regard me, and his face was even more frightening than I'd imagined. His eyes were black sockets within which green ghost-fires blazed.

I fled in a mad panic, sprinting out the door and into the hall. As I rounded the corner, Abraxas stepped out through the wall right in front of me.

He smiled, and I backed away, cringing and stumbling. As I retreated past the library door, I noticed that Asha's body was gone. Where—?

Suddenly two hands reached out through the wall, seized Abraxas by the shoulders, and yanked him sideways. He gasped—and the bat fell from his fingers—as he was dragged back through the wall.

I moved to the door, and watched as Asha raised him above her head, and then she spun him around and piledrove him into the floor, which exploded like it'd been hit by a meteor. I ducked behind the wall as bits of flooring and foundation rained all about the room.

When I peeked in again, I saw that the center of the library was now a giant crater, and at its base were Asha and Abraxas. He was on his knees, and she had him in a chokehold. I scooped up the dhajat bat and hurried forward.

As I neared, Abraxas slumped. The fires that were his eyes dwindled to the size of candle flames, then went out, and Asha yanked his arms behind his back and bound his wrists with glowing cuffs.

Then she stood, looking immensely pleased with herself. "Ha!" she declared, clapping her hands and raising them before her. "What did I tell you, kid? These hands are formidable things."

I let out a deep breath, and lowered the bat.

"Thought he was pretty clever," Asha said, "using my own stun-bulbs against me. Good thing I had them all rigged for one-quarter power…just in case someone ever grabbed one and tried to use it on me." She prodded him with her toe and said, "Guess you're not the only sneaky one around here, eh, smart guy?"

She turned back to me, and added, "Still, I don't know if I would've been able to get the drop on him, if you hadn't distracted him. That was real good thinking."

"Wow, thanks, Asha. I—"

"Of course," she said, "you *did* almost get me killed by jumping between us like that."

"Oh," I said glumly. "Yeah."

She waved a hand. "But don't worry about it. That was my fault. I should've warned you about his disguises. No, overall you did pretty great, I'd say." She added, "For a five, I mean."

I grinned.

"So what happens now?" I asked.

A few weeks later all the preparations had been made for my extended vacation. A cab dropped me off in front of Cornelius's mansion, and I made my way through the house to the library, which had been repaired with some help from Asha's off-world friends—without anyone around here being the wiser.

Asha stood waiting, beside the purple door.

"You all set?" she asked me.

"Yup," I said, as I crossed the room.

In my backpack was food, water, and silver, as well as a handgun that Asha had provided, loaded with OF-ten bullets.

She gestured to the door. "You want to do the honors?"

I smiled and stepped forward, and gave the door a push, and it swung aside to reveal a night sky full of massed purple clouds and circling flocks of long-necked birds, and below that soaring peaks beside plunging chasms, and on every precipice a fortress whose windows blazed with yellow light, like jack-o'-lanterns. The night air that blew in past us was pleasantly brisk, and smelled of rich earth and sweet flowers.

I paused to admire the view, even if this world *was* only a six.

"Let's get a move on," Asha said, as she stepped through the door. "No time to waste gawking at second-rate realities. We've got a full itinerary ahead of us. Nines and tens all the way."

I took one last look around the library, at my home world, in all its modest five-ness, then moved to follow her.

"Come on, kid," she told me. "Let me show you what a *real* world looks like."

DEAR ANNABEHLS

MERCURIO D. RIVERA

Nominated for the 2011 World Fantasy Award for his short fiction, Mercurio D. Rivera's stories can be found in venues such as *Asimov's Science Fiction, Interzone, Nature, Black Static, Sybil's Garage, Murky Depths,* and *Year's Best Science Fiction 17,* edited by Hartwell & Cramer (HarperCollins). His fiction has been podcast at *Escape Pod, StarShipSofa,* and *Transmissions From Beyond,* and translated and reprinted in the Czech Republic and Poland. He is a lawyer, a sports enthusiast, and a proud member of the acclaimed Manhattan writing group Altered Fluid (www.alteredfluid.com). "Dear Annabehls" is set in the same universe as his story "Snatch Me Another," which can be read at online magazine *Abyss & Apex.*

== 1. ==

Dear Annabehl:

I'm concerned about the inordinate amount of time that my 13-year-old son "Jeff" spends with himself. A boy his age should be out and about, playing with friends, participating in sports and other after-school activities. I come from a very traditional family, and I have to confess that I'm concerned that this behavior suggests that Jeff may be gay.

My husband thinks I'm overreacting. What do you think?

Concerned Tuscaloosa Mom

Dear Concerned:

Generally, a boy Jeff's age spending time with himself is perfectly normal. The question I would pose is: How *many* of his selves does he spend time with? Attachment to any particular self might prove to be unhealthy. If your son's behavior persists for more than a few weeks, you need to revoke his Snatcher privileges and take him in for some psiprobing. If it's of any comfort, this sounds more like classic narcissism than homosexuality. However, should your son be gay, you need to learn to love him for who he is. Alternatively, search for a heterosexual replacement. I recommend that you swallow two Validums, and pick up the recently published *Bonds Between Multiple Me's* by Dr. Gregory Byars for an excellent discussion of this subject.

== **2.** ==

Dear Annabehl:

I'm going through the most difficult period of my life. I caught my husband Robbie cheating on me. The thing is, he's cheating on me—with me. He insists that as long as the person he's sleeping with *is* me, he isn't technically cheating. That's BS! I say that he exchanged his vows with *me*, not with skinnier, stringy-haired, slutty versions of me. He's being immoral and unfaithful, isn't he, Annabehl? I just don't get it. What does he see in other me's that he doesn't see in me? I'm hurt, lonely and frustrated.
Dora/Memphis, TN

Dear Dora:

Take a deep breath and a Xantax, dear. It's all a matter of perspective. That Robbie chooses to spend his time away from you *with you* is actually quite romantic. In fact, one might say he's exceedingly faithful and truly devoted. You should be flattered as heck. What strikes me as odd is that while Robbie is off enjoying you, you're "lonely and frustrated." Get up off your derriere, girl, and kwitcherwhining! You should be spending time with other Robbies. You'll find that doing so will strengthen your marriage and make both of you much happier in the long run.

== **3.** ==

Dear Annabehl:

We lost our son Tommy to an inoperable brain tumor, just a few days before his sixth birthday. My wife got it into her head that we should go forward with the birthday party with another version of Tommy as a way to say our final goodbyes. We set the Snatcher to a high-end frequency and nabbed another Tommy, who was none the wiser about his displacement. Well, you guessed it. The birthday party came and went and now "Tommy" is still with us. What about "Tommy's" real parents? They must be going through hell. And what about our Tommy? Doesn't he deserve to be mourned?

Whenever I raise this issue with my wife, she gets angry and changes the subject. She pretends that nothing ever happened. I know I should love the new Tommy, but all I feel is numb. What should I do?

L.P./Chicago, Illinois

Dear L.P.:

I strongly recommend professional psiprobing so you can learn to accept Tommy's variant as part of your family. Your emotional confusion is understandable, sweetie. Many people who suffer a loss like yours find it difficult to accept a replacement. But your wife is behaving no differently than any mother would in her situation. Be sure to have Tommy routinely checked for the condition that caused his initial passing. It may become necessary to get yourselves another replacement. Good luck to you.

== **4.** ==

Dear Annabehl:

My mom and dad are fairly well-connected. As a result, we have Government authorization for Total Access to billions of Snatcher frequencies. My family's been on the move ever since the first Snatcher prototype was developed. We've skipped into all sorts of psychedelic realities, including a black-and-white dimension at a high-end frequency where we were the only colored people in the world. (My parents, who think they're cool, thought it would be "educational" for us to experience firsthand the prejudices faced by minorities. Well, we were treated like friggin' circus freaks!) But most of the time the differences were so subtle that I couldn't even tell we'd skipped.

I've met a boy I really like who lives down the block from us, so I want to stay here. I'm not even sure if this is the reality we originally came from, but it's close enough, I guess. Why do my parents insist on skipping around? Apart from having a new boyfriend here, I've made other friends too. And it's hard to make friends every time I skip. Sometimes the same people are slightly "off" in a new reality, and not as likeable. I hate what the Snatcher

has done to my life! My parents just don't understand.
Elinor/Houston, TX

Dear Elinor:

I suspect you may no longer be around to read this. But in case some other you (or others like you) need advice on this subject, I say: inject some soft hemo-music, take a long drag on a joint, and relax, honey. The important thing is to speak to your parents and keep the lines of communication open. If they refuse to take your feelings into account, speak to a stream of variants until you find a set of parents who care enough about your feelings to listen and to lay down roots here. Instead of condemning the Snatcher (shame on you!), why don't you use it to help solve your problems?

== **5.** ==

Dear Annabehl:

My sister "Betty" is having a crisis of faith. Before the Breach War began, variants of so many faiths skipped through our transborder that she wonders now whether our beliefs are any more "true" than the beliefs of other versions of us. Yesterday a bald variant of Betty showed up and proclaimed her Jesus Christ—a clean-shaven Christ with a buzz cut—the one true Son of God. She ridiculed our own bearded Jesus and called him "a slovenly hippie imposter." Ever since then, Betty has stopped going to church and has fallen into a deep depression. She keeps asking about the near-infinite number of souls that populate the transdimensional slate and why God, if He exists, would have created them to believe in so many different faiths.

What can I do to help her?
Chastity/Pomfret, Conn.

Dear Chas:

I've consulted with spokesman Father Joseph E. DeMichael about the Catholic Church's position on this subject. Church doctrine, he explained, teaches us that the variants who refuse to believe in the true, bearded Jesus—not other, bizarre Jesii with different haircuts and wardrobes—are doomed to eternal damnation. In fact, many church scholars believe that the very reason God allowed us to invent the Snatcher is so we can seek out our variants and enlighten them about the one true God. So whatever else happens, at least our souls are safe, dear. Pass it along. Tell Betty to pour herself a tall glass of cabernet and relax.

== **6.** ==

Dear Annabehl:

I'm stationed at the frontlines near the Great Wall of China where the Breach is at its worst. The hordes continue to battle their way through. We've been fighting hard to repel these forces, and this week alone I've lost six friends and three versions of their replacements. The other-dimensional armies grow more freakish every day, some are barely humanoid, in fact. We don't know what's coming through next, Annabehl. I have to confess: I'm afraid. I'm writing to ask your readers for their prayers and support. Any e-transmissions they could send our way would provide a tremendous lift. Neural books and movies—and especially hemo-music—would be greatly appreciated as well. Thank you.
Private Sandy Ripple,
Special Global Forces

All readers, atten-*tion*! Every citizen of this plane should applaud the heroism and self-sacrifice of our brave young troops. Thank you, thank you, thank you, for defending the transborders from that wave of lower-dimensional scum, Private Ripple. While those of us who have not done a tour of duty cannot possibly understand the horrors you and your compatriots have faced, we all extend our love and support. Readers, please send your letters and donations to Dear Annabehl and we will arrange to forward them to the troops. Don't let our soldiers down. Yes, they're replaceable. But remember, *so are the invaders.* This is why there appears to be no end in sight to this war. Support our troops!

== **7.** ==

Dear Annabehl:

Maybe I'm old-fashioned, but your advice to L.P. from Chicago struck me as amazingly insensitive. He had just lost his son to a brain tumor and his wife used their Snatcher to abduct a variant from a nearby dimension. Of course he felt numb! He never had a chance to grieve. Worse, what about the parents of the variant they kidnapped? They must be devastated by his disappearance. This whole world is turning to [crap]! What were you

thinking, Annabehl?
An Old-Timer/Topeka, KS

Dear Old-Timer:

I stand by my advice, gramps. There was simply no need for L.P. to grieve when a replacement was so easily accessible. Grieving is dead! *Death* is dead! I did recommend psiprobing, however, so he could learn to accept his new son, who is an innocent in all this, after all. As for the transdimensional parents who lost their child, you seem to forget that they too can use their Snatcher to find themselves a replacement. So search for that antique bong in the back of your dusty closet, old man, and inhale deeply. Get with the times.

== **8.** ==

Dear Readers:

I am pleased that we are once again able to bring you my Dear Annabehl column after our long absence. It's been a difficult six months. Today's column is dedicated to all the courageous soldiers and their replacements who gave their lives at the Breach. I understand that there's still a great deal of confusion, some pessimists might even call it chaos, with the Ardiente administration taking over. Although the Ardiente underlords do have a pseudo-demonic appearance, don't let their horns and red tails throw you. As they've pointed out, they're "broadminded traditionalists," a God-fearing salt-of-the-earth-type of people. Most importantly, they have promised to rule benignly and to deregulate Snatchers, to allow Total Access into and out of our reality to people everywhere. Freedom is precious, after all.

There will be a period of adjustment before things get back to normal, but trust me, readers, they will. Keep working hard and have faith. There is a reason for everything. You'll see. This will all turn out for the best.

== **9.** ==

Dear Annabehl:

With the new Government taking over and Total Access now fully in effect, I've decided that it's time for me and my family to take our leave from this reality. My wife is reluctant to leave her friends behind, but I keep telling her that we can relocate just a few frequencies away where she can have the same friends, more or less. Meanwhile, other me's are flooding in at an unprecedented rate: me's with blue skin; me's with mammary glands; me's with really bad haircuts; and me's indistinguishable from me in every objectively discernable way (except every now and then one of me will smile in a dark, sly way that gives me chills). There isn't room in my house for all of me's. And there's only one job for one of me. They won't tell me, but I think they're all running from something, something truly terrible in their own realities. Whatever it is, I'm afraid that it may be coming. How can I convince my wife to leave? I think it's time for *everyone* to escape across the transborder. I know a lot of people who have made the same decision. Maybe I'll find another world, one where Snatchers were never invented. But how can I skip through unless it *has* a Snatcher portal entrance? Do you have any advice on whether we should leave?

Packed But Not-Quite-Ready To Go/Biloxi, Mississippi

Dear Packed:

This is Annabehl filling in for Annabehl. Annabehl (persona prime) has moved on to a higher plane and left this column in my lucky hands. I consider it an honor to be stepping into her shoes (figuratively and literally). Forgive me if it takes a bit of time to get up to speed. In my reality, I stripped for a living and doled out advice at the bar during breaks, so this is quite a step up for me.

Freedom is a precious, wonderful gift. Go wherever you think you'll be happy. By all means, cross the transborder! Take an acid trip! Do whatever! We're free!

== 10. ==

Dear Annabehls:

While at work last week I dialed into my bank and discovered that all of my accounts had been emptied. By the time I got home, all of my clothes and other personal belongings were also gone. It's apparent that one of my variants has gone too far this time, Annabehl.

I've decided to commence legal action against my self and have retained an attorney who's agreed to take the case on a contingency basis. My friends insist that litigation against one's self is just a waste of time and money. I disagree. Part of the reason why the world economy is on the verge of collapse is because of the actions of a few variants like this one. What do you think? Should I fight for my rights? Or should I do as my friends suggest

and just let this go?
Esteban/Bronx, New York

Dear Esteban:
Have you ever heard of a little item called a Snatcher? Step through it and retrieve your items upfrequency, for goodness sake! Then snort a little elcitron and relax.
—Annabehl

Dear Esteban:
Annabehl is off-base on this one. Two wrongs don't make a right. Pursue your remedies the way all patriots do: through litigation. Then snort a little elcitron and relax.
—Annabehl

Dear Esteban:
I've consulted a legal expert who points out that service of process can be tricky in transdimensional litigation. Also, the law is still unclear on whether our courts even have jurisdiction over our variants. No, I have to agree with Annabehl and disagree with Annabehl on this one. Take a short trip upfrequency and exercise a little self-help. Then snort a little elcitron and relax.
—Annabehl

== 11. ==

Dear Annabehls:
Congrats on the great job you're doing in place of Annabehl, who was miles better than Annabehl, who was leagues better than Annabehl, who was almost as good, I'd say, as Annabehl. Here's my dilemma. I've asked my cousin JoJo (persona prime) and three of her variants to serve in my bridal party as maids of honor. It turns out that JoJo, one of JoJo's variants, is feuding with her mother, my Aunt Josie. Since that JoJo isn't from this reality, Aunt Josie isn't her real mother, mind you, but JoJo can't seem to get this through her thick skull. She refuses to attend unless I replace Aunt Josie with a variant—even though Aunt Josie really *is*, in effect, a variant, at least in relation to the complaining JoJo. Aunt Josie refuses to attend if her selves are invited. (My aunt and my mom are old-fashioned and insist on being the only versions of themselves at the wedding.) Two of the other

JoJos insist, however, that I invite their actual mothers from their respective realities—and refuse to participate in the bridal party unless I do so. Meanwhile, Sean, my fiancé, has demanded multiple me's be present on my wedding night! I guess I'm my mother's daughter because I have no desire to share the stage with anyone on my wedding night—even me! I want my wedding night to be a special, one-on-one experience between me (me prime, that is) and Sean (Sean prime, that is). What should I do about JoJo, JoJo, JoJo, JoJo, Aunt Josie and Sean? I'm too busy and stressed to deal with all of this. I have wedding plans to make!

Desperate Dixie/San Diego, CA

Dear Dixie:

We Annabehls are unanimous on this one: schedule a session at the Snatcher ASAP! Replace the troublesome JoJo—the JoJo who still carries that unseemly transdimensional grudge against her mother, your aunt (non-prime to her, actually, though that JoJo refuses to acknowledge it)—with another more agreeable version of JoJo. And good riddance! Carrying that type of transdimensional baggage really is childish and unacceptable. Talk to the two remaining JoJos and explain to them that this is your special day, that weddings are expensive and that *you* decide how many variants of your guests can attend. If they don't like it, *zap*, get yourself two more replacements. As for your fiancé's desire to turn your wedding night into an orgy, you'll have to forgive me, honey, but you might want to zap yourself a variant who has a little more regard for your feelings. (After the wedding night, he can indulge in whatever multiple-you shenanigans you and other consenting variants of you wish to engage. But on the wedding night? He's a pig!) Finally, to reduce the stress, snatch another you out of the Snatcher and delegate these wedding tasks to your self. Then mix yourself a margarita and head to the sim-beach for some well-deserved RNR.

== **12.** ==

Dear Annabehls:

I've come to the depressing realization that my life is empty and truly, truly meaningless. Over the past few years I've met variants of myself who've led fascinating lives: one lived in a remote village in Guatemala where he helped construct homes for the poor; one skydived at sunset from a stealth copter into the Grand Canyon's Colorado River; another made a point of scaling Everest every autumn and making love to a beautiful woman on its snowy mountaintops. When I think about my own life, Annabehl, I'm struck by the safe choices I've made. I spend my days focused on the tedium of an office job I've never really wanted, caring for an elderly mother who doesn't even recognize me anymore, living life just going through the motions. I can see the remainder of my humdrum life stretched out in front of me, only I'm trying to pretend that I don't see it, Annabehl, because I know I don't have the ability to make any changes anyway and thinking about it just makes me feel more hopeless and impotent. And what does it matter what I choose to do? For every South American village I've never visited, for every mountain peak I've never climbed, another version of me is out there embarking on those adventures anyway. Nothing seems to matter anymore.

Jacob/Salt Lake City, Utah

Dear Jacob:

I'm not going to tell you to stop feeling sorry for yourself. And I'm not going to tell you to get up off your keister and make some changes in your life. Why bother? Somewhere some variant of you is making those necessary changes. You see, essentially you're right. Whatever you decide to do really is meaningless. But there's certainly nothing to be gained by being depressed about this fact either. You're suffering from classic symptoms of Variant Inadequacy, kiddo, which is not at all uncommon. To give yourself a better perspective, you need to interact with some downfrequency variants who don't have it anywhere near as good as you. Heck, nothing cheers a person up more quickly than studying the misery of his variants. So pop open a beer, visit the Snatcher, and just relax.

Annabehl, Annabehl, Annabehl, Annabehl and Annabehl concur with Annabehl's advice.

Annabehl, Annabehl and Annabehl dissent with the substance of the advice, but concur in the recommendation of a beer.

Annabehl abstains.

== **13.** ==

0000000000000000000111000000000000000000001111000000000000000
000000009911555550000000000000000000000770000000000000000000000
0000Dear Annabehls: 0000011111333377777777700099999999999999
99:

I'm afraid. So afraid I can barely function. I feel totally adrift, as if nothing, no one, that I know is quite right. It's difficult to explain, but sometimes

I swear I don't recognize my children. Didn't I used to have a uni-daughter named Allison? I have a memory, a fading dream-memory of brushing her tangled blond hair. The thing is, I know no one has uni-daughters, certainly not me. I have an adorable set of identical septuplet boys. And while I know that this is my house, why do I sometimes find myself stumbling into rooms I never even knew existed? And my friends. Why do I forget their names? Sometimes I stare into the mirror-eyes of our pet elphine, and I don't even recognize my own reflection. The diagonal rows of black eyes that speckle my face seem unfamiliar to me. I'm afraid, afraid that the walls between realities have finally crumbled, and that I'm the only one who sees it. Wasn't the sky blue a long time ago? I could swear that it used to be. Didn't we used to walk upright on two legs? I'm lost, Annabehls. I don't think I know who or what I am any more.

Lost in Newfoundland

00000000000009955555777777779990000000000000000000000000000 00Dear Lost: 999999999999999990007777777711110000000000000 07

We're sorry to say that there's only one reality, dear, and we're stuck with it. The sky has always been deep red, we've always skittered on six legs, and we've always come in sets of seven, nine or thirteen. It's not unusual to sometimes feel out of place, to feel cast adrift like a wind-blown ember in the eye of a black tornado, everything around you changing while you're standing still. We've felt that way ourselves, sometimes. Do what we do, Lost. Buck up. Fly high on the fumes of ecsahol, if necessary. And relax.

THE GOAT VARIATIONS

JEFF VANDERMEER

Jeff VanderMeer is a two-time winner of the World Fantasy Award whose stories have been published by *Tor.com, Clarkesworld, Conjunctions, Black Clock*, and several year's best anthologies. Recent books include the Nebula finalist novel *Finch* (2009), and the short story collection *The Third Bear* (2010). His *The Steampunk Bible* was featured on *CBS This Morning* and been named a finalist for the Hugo Award for best related book. He also recently co-edited the mega-compendium *The Weird* with his wife Ann. A co-founder of Shared Worlds, a teen SF/F writing camp, VanderMeer has been a guest speaker at the Library of Congress and MIT, among others. He writes book reviews for the *Los Angeles Times, New York Times Book Review,* and the *Washington Post.* VanderMeer's latest novel, just completed, is *Annihilation.*

It would have been hot, humid in September in that city, and the Secret Service would have gone in first, before him, to scan for hostile minds, even though it was just a middle school in a county he'd won in the elections, far away from the fighting. He would have emerged from the third black armored vehicle, blinking and looking bewildered as he got his bearings in the sudden sunlight. His aide and the personal bodyguards who had grown up protecting him would have surrounded him by his first step onto the asphalt of the driveway. They would have entered the school through the front, stopping under the sign for photos and a few words with the principal, the television cameras recording it all from a safe distance.

He would already be thinking past the event, to the next, and how to prop up sagging public approval ratings, due both to the conflict and what the press called his recent "indecision," which he knew was more analogous to "sickness." He would be thinking about, or around, the secret cavern beneath the Pentagon and the pale, almost grublike face of the adept in his tank. He would already be thinking about the machine.

By the end of the photo op, the sweat itches on his forehead, burns sour in his mouth, but he has to ignore it for the cameras. He's turning a new word over and over in his mind, learned from a Czech diplomat. *Ossuary.* A word that sounds free and soaring, but just means a pile of skulls. The latest satellite photos from the battlefield states of Kansas, Nebraska, and Idaho make him think of the word. The evangelicals have been eschewing god-missiles for more personal methods of vengeance, even as they tie down federal armies in an endless guerilla war. Sometimes he feels like he's presiding over a pile of skulls.

The smile on his face has frozen into a rictus as he realizes there's something wrong with the sun; there's a red dot in its center, and it's eating away at the yellow, bringing a hint of green with it. He can tell he's the only one who can see it, can sense the pulsing, nervous worry on the face of his aide.

He almost says "ossuary" aloud, but then, sunspots wandering across his eyes, they are bringing him down a corridor to the classroom where he will meet with the students and tell them a story. They walk past the open doors to the cafeteria—row on row of sagging wooden tables propped up by rusted metal legs. He experiences a flare of anger. Why *this* school, with the infrastructure crumbling away? The overpowering stale smell of macaroni-and-cheese and meatloaf makes him nauseous.

All the while, he engages in small talk with the entourage of teachers trailing in his wake, almost all overweight middle-aged women with circles under their eyes and sagging skin on their arms. Many of them are black. He smiles into their shiny, receptive faces and remembers the hired help in the mansion growing up. Some of his best friends were black until he took up politics.

For a second, as he looks down, marveling at their snouts and beaks and muzzles, their smiles melt away and he's surrounded by a pack of animals.

His aide mutters to him through clenched teeth, and two seconds later he realizes the words were "Stop staring at them so much." There have always been times when meeting too many people at once has made him feel as if he's somewhere strange, all the mannerisms and gesticulations and varying tones of voice shimmering into babble. But it's only lately that the features of people's faces have changed into a menagerie if he looks at them too long.

They'd briefed him on the secret rooms and the possibility of the machine even before they'd given him the latest intel on China's occupation of Japan and Taiwan. Only three hours into his presidency, an armored car had taken him to the Pentagon, away from his wife and the beginnings of the inauguration party. Once there, they'd entered a green-lit steel elevator that went down for so long he thought for a moment it was broken. It was just him, his aide, a black-ops commander who didn't give his name, and a small, haggard man who wore an old gray suit over a faded white dress shirt, with no tie. He'd told his vice president to meet the press while he was gone, even though he was now convinced the old man had dementia.

The elevators had opened to a rush of stale cool air, like being under a mountain, and, beneath the dark green glow of overhead lamps, he could see rows and rows of transparent, bathtub-shaped deprivation vats. In each floated one dreaming adept, skin wrinkled and robbed of color by the exposure to the chemicals that preserved and pacified them. Every shaven head was attached to wires and electrodes, every mouth attached to a breathing tube. Catheters took care of waste. The stale air soon faded as they walked silent down the rows, replaced by a smell like turpentine mixed with honeysuckle. Sometimes the hands of the adepts twitched, like cats hunting in their sleep.

A vast, slow, repeating sound registered in his awareness. Only after several minutes did he realize it was the sound of the adepts as they slowly moved in their vats, creating a slow ripple of water repeated in thousands of other vats. The room seemed to go on forever, into the far distance of a horizon tinged at its extremity by a darkening that hinted of blood.

His sense of disgust, revulsion grew as the little man ran out ahead of them, navigated a path to a control center, a hundred yards in and to the left, made from a luminous blue glass, set a story up and jutting out over the vats like some infernal crane. And still he did not know what to say. The atmosphere combined morgue, cathedral, and torture chamber. He felt a compulsion, if he spoke, to whisper.

The briefing papers he'd read on the ride over had told him just about everything. For years, adepts had been screened out at birth and, depending on the secret orders peculiar to each administration, either euthanized or imprisoned in remote overseas detention camps. Those that managed to escape detection until adulthood had no rights if caught, not even the rights given to illegal immigrants. The founding fathers had been very clear on that in the constitution.

He had always assumed that adults when caught were eliminated or sent to the camps. Radicals might call it the last reflexive act of a Puritanical brutality that reached across centuries, but most citizens despised the invasion of privacy an adept represented or were more worried about how the separatist evangelicals had turned the homeland into a nation of West and East Coasts, with no middle.

But now he knew where his predecessor had been storing the bodies. He just didn't yet know *why*.

In the control center, they showed him the images being mined from the depths of the adepts' REM sleep. They ranged from montages as incomprehensible as the experimental films he'd seen in college to single shots of dead people to grassy hills littered with wildflowers. Ecstasy, grief, madness, peace. Anything imaginable came through in the adepts' endless sleep.

"Only ten people in the world know every aspect of this project, and three of them are dead, Mr. President," the black-ops commander told him.

Down below, he could see the little man, blue-tinted, going from vat to vat, checking readings.

"We experimented until we found the right combination of drugs to augment their sight. One particular formula, culled from South American mushrooms mostly, worked best. Suddenly, we began to get more coherent and varied images. Very different from before."

He felt numb. He had no sympathy for the men and women curled up in the vats below him—an adept's grenade had killed his father in midcampaign a decade before, launching his own reluctant career in politics—but, still, he felt numb.

"Are any of them dangerous?" he asked the black-ops commander. "They're all dangerous, Mr. President. Every last one."

"When did this start?"

"With a secret order from your predecessor, Mr. President. Before, we just disappeared them or sent them to work camps in the Alaskas."

"Why did he do it?"

Even then, he would realize later, a strange music was growing in his head, a distant sound fast approaching.

"He did it, Mr. President, or said he did it, as a way of getting intel on the Heartland separatists."

Understandable, if idiosyncratic. The separatists and the fact that the federal armies had become bogged down in the Heartland fighting them were the main reasons his predecessor's party no longer controlled the executive, judicial, or legislative branches. And no one had ever succeeded in placing a mole within evangelical ranks.

The scenes continued to cascade over the monitors in a rapid-fire nonsense-rhythm.

"What do you do with the images?"

"They're sent to a full team of experts for interpretation, Mr. President. These experts are not told where the images come from."

"What do these adepts see that is so important?'

The black-ops commander grimaced at the tone of rebuke. "The future, Mr. President. Its early days, but we believe they see the future."

"And have you gained much in the way of intel?"

The black-ops commander looked at his feet. "No, not yet, we haven't. And we don't know why. The images are jumbled. Some might even be from our past or present. But we have managed to figure out one thing, which is why you've been brought here so quickly: something will happen later this year, in September."

"Something?"

Down below, the little man had stopped his purposeful wandering. He gazed, as if mesmerized, into one of the vats.

"Something cataclysmic, Mr. President. Across the channels. Across all of the adepts, it's quite clear. Every adept has a different version of what that something is. And we don't know *exactly* when, but in September."

He had a thousand more questions, but at that moment one of the military's top scientific researchers entered the control room to show them the schematics for the machine—the machine they'd found in the mind of one particular adept.

The time machine.

The teachers are telling him about the weather, and he's pretending to care as he tries to ignore the florescent lighting as yellow as the skin that forms on old butter, the cracks in the dull beige walls, the faded construction paper of old projects taped to those walls, drooping down toward a tired, washed-out green carpet that's paper-thin under foot.

It's the kind of event that he's never really understood the point of, even as he understands the reason for it. To prove that he's still fit for office. To prove that the country, some of it, is free of war and division. To prove he cares about kids, even though this particular school seems to be falling apart. Why this class, why today, is what he really doesn't understand, with so many world crises—China's imperialism, the Siberian separatist movement, Iraq as the only bulwark against Russian influence in the Middle

East. Or a vice president he now knows may be too old and delusional to be anything other than an embarrassment, and a cabinet he let his family's political cronies bully him into appointing, and a secret cavern that has infected his thoughts, infected his mind.

And that would lead to memories of his father, and the awful silence into which they told him, as he sat coked up and hung-over that morning on the pastel couch in some sleazy apartment, how it had happened while his father worked a town hall meeting in Atlanta.

All of this has made him realize that there's only one way to succeed in this thing called the presidency: just let go of the reality of the world in favor of whatever reality he wants or needs, no matter how selfish.

The teachers are turning into animals again, and he can't seem to stop it from happening.

The time machine had appeared as an image on their monitors from an adept named "Peter" in vat 1023, and because they couldn't figure out the context—weapon? camera? something new?—they had to wake Peter up and have a conversation with him.

A time machine, he told them.

A time machine?

A time machine that travels through time, he'd clarified.

And they'd believed him, or if not believed him, dared to hope he was right. That what Peter had seen while deprived of anything but his own brain, like some deep-sea fish, like something constantly turning inwards and then turning inwards again, had been a time machine.

If they didn't build it and it turned out later that it might have worked and could have helped them avert or change what was fated to happen in September…

That day, three hours after being sworn in, he had had to give the order to build a time machine, and quickly.

"Something bad will happen in late summer. Something bad. Across the channels. Something awful."

"What?" he kept asking, and the answer was always the same: *We don't know.*

They kept telling him that the adepts didn't seem to convey literal information so much as impressions and visions of the future, filtered through dreamscapes. As if the drugs they'd perfected, which had changed the way the adepts dreamed, both improved and destroyed focus, in different ways.

In the end, he had decided to build the machine—and defend against almost everything they could think of or divine from the images: any attack against the still-surviving New York financial district or the monument to the Queen Mother in the New York harbor; the random god-missiles of the Christian jihadists of the Heartland, who hadn't yet managed to unlock the nuclear codes in the occupied states; and even the lingering cesspool that was Los Angeles after the viruses and riots.

But they still did not really know.

He's good now at talking to people when it's not a prepared speech, good at letting his mind be elsewhere while he talks to a series of masks from behind his own mask. The prepared speeches are different because he's expected to *inhabit* them, and he's never fully inhabited anything, any role, in his life.

They round the corner and enter the classroom: thirty children in plastic one-piece desk-chairs, looking solemn, and the teacher standing in front of a beat-up battlewagon of a desk, overflowing with papers.

Behind her, posters they'd made for him, or someone had made to look like the children made them, most showing him with the crown on his head. But also a blackboard, which amazes him. So anachronistic, and he's always hated the sound of chalk on a blackboard. Hates the smell of glue and the sour food-sweat of unwashed kids. It's all so squalid and tired and oddly close to the atmosphere in the underground cavern, the smell the adepts give off as they thrash in slow-motion in their vats, silently scream-ing out images of catastrophe and oblivion.

The children look up at him when he enters the room like they're watch-ing something far away and half-wondrous, half-monstrous.

He stands there and talks to them for a while at first, trying to ignore the window in the back of the classroom that wants to show him a scene that shouldn't have been there. He says the kinds of things he's said to kids for years while on the campaign trail, running for ever-greater office. Has said these things for so many years that it's become a sawdust litany meant to convince them of his charm, his wit, his competence. Later, he won't remember what he said, or what they said back. It's not important.

But he's thought about the implications of that in bed at night, lying there while his wife reads, her pale, freckled shoulder like a wall above him. He could stand in a classroom and say nothing, and still they would be fascinated with him, like a talisman, like a golden statue. No one had ever told him that sometimes you don't have to inhabit the presidency; sometimes, it inhabits you.

He'd wondered at the time of coronation if he'd feel different. He'd wondered how the parliament members would receive him, given the split between the popular vote and the legislative vote. But nothing had happened. The parliament members had clapped, some longer than others, and he'd been sworn in, duly noting the absence of the rogue Scottish delegation. The Crown of the Americas had briefly touched his head, like an "iron kiss from the mouth of God," as his predecessor had put it, and then it was gone again, under glass, and he was back to being the secular president, not some sort of divine king.

Then they'd taken him to the Pentagon, hurtled him half a mile underground, and he'd felt like a man who wins a prize only to find out it's worthless. *Ossuary.* He'd expected clandestine spy programs, secret weapons, special powers. But he hadn't expected the faces in the vats or the machine.

Before they built the time machine, he had insisted on meeting "Peter" in an interrogation room near the vats. He felt strongly about this, about looking into the eyes of the man he had almost decided to trust.

"Are you sure this will work?" he asked Peter, even as he found the question irrelevant, ridiculous. No matter what Peter said, no matter how impossible his scientists said it was, how it subverted known science, he was going to do it. The curiosity was too strong.

Peter's eyes were bright with a kind of fever. His face was the palest white possible, and he stank of the chemicals. They'd put him in a blue jumper suit to cover his nakedness.

"It'll work. I pulled it out of another place. It was a true-sight. A true-seeing. I don't know how it works, but it works. It'll work, it'll work, and then," he turned toward the black one-way glass at the far end of the room, hands in restraints behind his back, "I'll be free?"

There was a thing in Peter's eyes he refused to acknowledge. A sense of something being held back, of something not quite right. Later, he would never know why he didn't trust that instinct, that perception, and the only reason he could come up with was the strength of his curiosity and the weight of his predecessor's effort to get to that point.

"What, exactly, is the machine for? Exactly. Not just...time travel. Tell me something more specific."

The scientist accompanying them smiled. He had a withered, narrow face, a firm chin, and wore a jumpsuit that matched Peter's, with a black belt at the waist that held the holster for an even blacker semi-automatic pistol. He smelled strongly of a sickly sweet cologne, as if hiding some essential putrefaction.

"Mr. President," he said, "Peter is not a scientist. And we cannot peer into his mind. We can only see the images his mind projects. Until we build it, we will not know exactly how it works."

And then, when the machine was built, and they took him to it, he didn't know what to make of it. He didn't think they did, either—they were gathered around it in their protective suits like apes trying to figure out an internal combustion engine.

"Don't look directly into it," the scientist beside him advised. "Those who have experience a kind of…disorientation."

Unlike the apes examining it, the two of them stood behind three feet of protective, blast-proof glass, and yet both of them had moved to the back of the viewing room—as far away from the artifact as possible.

The machine consisted of a square housing made of irregular-looking gray metal, caulked on the interior with what looked like rotted beef, and in the center of this assemblage: an eye of green light. In the middle of the eye, a piercing red dot. The machine was about the size of a microwave oven.

When he saw the eye, he shuddered, could not tell at first if it was organic or a metallic lens. The effect of the machine on his mind was of a thousand maggots inching their way across the top of a television set turned on but not receiving a station.

He couldn't stop looking, as if the scientist's warning had made it impossible not to stare. A crawling sensation spread across his scalp, his arms, his hands, his legs.

"How does it work?" he asked the scientist.

"We still don't know."

"Does the adept know?"

"Not really. He just told us not to look into it directly."

"Is it from the future?"

"That is the most logical guess."

To him, it didn't look real. It looked either like something from another planet or something a psychotic child would put together before turning to more violent pursuits.

"Where else could it be from?"

The scientist didn't reply, and anger began to override his fear. He continued to look directly into the eye, even as it made him feel sick.

"Well, what do you know?"

"That it shouldn't work. As we put the pieces together…we all thought… we all thought it was more like witchcraft than science. Forgive me, Mr. President."

He gave the scientist a look that the scientist couldn't meet. Had he meant the gravity of the insult? Had he meant to imply their efforts were as blasphemous as the adept's second sight?

"And now? What do you think now?"

"It's awake, alive. But we don't see how it's…"

"It's what?"

"Breathing, Mr. President. A machine shouldn't breathe."

"How does it take anyone into the future, do you think?"

The temperature in the room seemed to have gone up. He was sweating.

The eye of the thing, impossibly alien, bored into him. Was it changing color?

"We think it doesn't physically send anyone into the future. That's the problem. We think it might somehow…create a localized phenomenon."

He sighed. "Just say what you mean."

The pulsing red dot. The shifting green. Looking at him. Looking into him.

"We think it might not allow physical travel, just mental travel."

In that instant, he saw adept Peter's pale face again and he felt a weakness in his stomach, and even though there was so much protection between him and the machine, he turned to the scientist and said, "Get me out of here."

Only, it was too late.

The sickness, the shifting, had started the next day, and he couldn't tell anyone about it, not even his wife, or they would have removed him from office. The constitution was quite clear about what do with "witches and warlocks."

At this point, his aide would hand him the book. They'd have gone through a dozen books before choosing that one. It is the only one with nothing in it anyone could object to; nothing in it of substance, nothing, his people thought, that the still-free press could use to damage him. There was just a goat in the book, a goat having adventures. It was written by a Constitutionalist, an outspoken supporter of coronation and expansion.

As he takes the book, he realizes, mildly surprised, that he has already become used to the smell of sweating children (he has none of his own) and the classroom grunge. (*Ossuary.* It sounded like a combination of "osprey" and "sanctuary.") The students who attend the school all experience it differently from him, their minds editing out the sensory perceptions he's still receiving. The mess. The depressed quality of the infrastructure. But what if you couldn't edit it out? And what if the stakes were much, much higher?

So then they would sit him down at a ridiculously small chair, almost as small as the ones used by the students, but somehow he would feel smaller in it despite that, as if he was back in college, surrounded by people both smarter and more dedicated than he was, as if he is posing and being told he's not as good: an imposter.

But it's still just a children's book, after all, and at least there's air conditioning kicking in, and the kids really seem to want him to read the book, as if they haven't heard it a thousand times before, and he feeds off the look in their eyes—*the President of North America and the Britains is telling us a story*—and so he begins to read.

He enjoys the storytelling. Nothing he does with the book can hurt him. Nothing about it has weight. Still, he has to keep the pale face of the adept out of his voice, and the Russian problem, and the Chinese problem, and the full extent of military operations in the Heartland. (There are cameras, after all.)

It's September 2001, and something terrible is going to happen, but for a moment he forgets that fact.

And that's when his aide interrupts his reading, comes up to him with a fake smile and serious eyes, and whispers in his ear.

Whispers in his ear and the sound is like a buzzing, and the buzzing is numinous and all-encompassing. The breath on his ear is a tiny curse, an infernal itch. There's a sudden rush of blood to his brain as he hears the words and his aide withdraws. He can hardly move, is seeing light where there shouldn't be light. The words drop heavy into his ear as if they have weight.

And he receives them and keeps receiving them, and he knows what they mean, eventually; he knows what they mean throughout his body.

The aide says, his voice flecked with relief, "Mr. President, our scientists have solved it. It's not time travel or far-sight. It's alternate universes. The adepts have been staring into alternate universes. What happens there in September may not happen here. That's why they've had such trouble with the intel. The machine isn't a time machine."

Except, as soon as the aide opens his mouth, the words become a trigger, a catalyst, and it's too late for him. A door is opening wider than ever before. The machine has already infected him.

There are variations. A long row of them, detonating in his mind, trying to destroy him. A strange, sad song is creeping up inside of him, and he can't stop that, either.

>>> He's sitting in the chair, wearing a black military uniform with medals on it. He's much fitter, the clothes tight to emphasize his muscle tone. But his face is contorted around the hole of a festering localized virus, charcoal and green and viscous. He doesn't wear an eye patch because he wants his people to see how he fights the disease. His left arm is made of metal. His

tongue is not his own, colonized the way his nation has been colonized, waging a war against bioresearch gone wrong, and the rebels who welcome it, who want to tear down anything remotely human, themselves no longer recognizable as human.

His aide comes up and whispers that the rebels have detonated a bio-mass bomb in New York City, which is now stewing in a broth of fungus and mutation: the nearly instantaneous transformation of an entire metropolis into something living but alien, the rate of change has become strange and accelerated in a world where this was always true, the age of industrialization slowing it, if only for a moment.

"There are no people left in New York City," his aide says. "What are your orders?"

He hadn't expected this, not so soon, and it takes him seven minutes to recover from the news of the death of millions. Seven minutes to turn to his aide and say, "Call in a nuclear strike."

>>>…and his aide comes up to him and whispers in his ear, "It's time to go now. They've moved up another meeting. Wrap it up." Health insurance is on the agenda today, along with Social Security. Something will get done about that and the environment this year or he'll die trying…

>>> He's sitting in the chair reading the book and he's gaunt, eyes feverish, military personnel surrounding him. There's one camera with them, army TV, and the students are all in camouflage. The electricity flickers on and off. The school room has reinforced metal and concrete all around it. The event is propaganda being packaged and pumped out to those still watching in places where the enemy hasn't jammed the satellites. He's fighting a war against an escaped, human-created, rapidly reproducing intelligent species prototype that looks a little bit like a chimpanzee crossed with a Doberman. The scattered remnants of the hated adept underclass have made common cause with the animals, disrupting communications.

His aide whispers in his ear that Atlanta has fallen, with over sixty-thousand troops and civilians massacred in pitched battles all over the city. There's no safe air corridor back to the capital. In fact, the capital seems to be under attack as well.

"What should we do?"

He returns to reading the book. Nothing he can do in the next seven minutes will make any difference to the outcome. He knows what they have to do, but he's too tired to contemplate it just yet. They will have to head to the Heartland and make peace with the Ecstatics and their god-missiles. It's either that or render entire stretches of North America uninhabitable from nukes, and he's not that desperate yet.

He begins to review the ten commandments of the Ecstatics in his mind, one by one, like rosary beads.

>>> He's in mid-sentence when the aide hurries over and begins to whisper in his ear—just as the first of the god-missiles strikes and the fire washes over and through him, not even time to scream, and he's nothing anymore, not even a pile of ashes.

>>> He's in a chair, in a suit with a sweat-stained white shirt, and he's tired, his voice as he reads thin and raspy. Five days and nights of negotiations between the rival factions of the New Southern Confederacy following a month of genocide between blacks and whites from Arkansas to Georgia: too few resources, too many natural disasters, and no jobs, the whole system breaking down, although Los Angeles is still trying to pretend the world isn't coming to an end, even as jets are falling out the sky. Except, that's why he's in the classroom: *pretending*. Pretending neighbor hasn't set upon neighbor for thirty days, like in Rwanda except not with machetes, with guns. Teenagers shooting people in the stomach, and laughing. Extremist talk radio urging them on. Closing in on a million people dead.

His aide comes up and whispers in his ear: "The truce has fallen apart. They're killing each other again. And not just in the South. In the North, along political lines."

He sits there because he's run out of answers. He thinks: *In another time, another place, I would have made a great president.*

>>> He's sitting in the classroom, in the small chair, in comfortable clothes, reading the goat story. No god-missiles here, no viruses, no invasions. The Chinese and Russians are just on the cusp of being a threat, but not there yet. Adepts here have no real far-sight, or are not believed, and roam free. Los Angeles is a thriving money pit, not a husked-out shadow.

No, the real threat here, besides pollution, is that he's mentally ill, although no one around him seems to know it. A head full of worms, insecurity, and pure, naked *need*. He rules a country called the "United States" that wavers between the First and the Third World. Resources failing, infrastructure crumbling, political system fueled by greed and corruption.

When the aide comes up and whispers in his ear to tell him that terrorists have flown two planes into buildings in New York City, there's blood behind his eyes, as well as a deafening silence, and a sudden leap from people falling from the burning buildings to endless war in the Middle East, bodies broken by bullets and bombs. The future torques into secret trials, torture, rape, and hundreds of thousands of civilians dead, or displaced, a country bankrupted and defenseless, ruled ultimately by martial law and generals. Cities burn, the screams of the living are as loud as the screams of the dying.

He sits there for seven minutes because he really has no idea what to do.

...and *his* fate is to exist in a reality where towers do not explode in September, where Islamic fundamentalists are the least of his worries.

There is only one present, only one future now, and he's back in it, driving it. Seven minutes have elapsed, and there's a graveyard in his head. Seven minutes, and he's gradually aware that in that span he's read the goat story twice and then sat there for thirty seconds, silent.

Now he smiles, says a few reassuring words, just as his aide has decided to come up and rescue him from the yawning chasm. He's living in a place now where they'll never find him, those children, where there's a torrent of blood in his mind, and a sky dark with planes and helicopters, and soldiers blown to bits by the roadside.

At that point, he would rise from his chair and his aide would clap, encouraging the students to clap, and they will, bewildered by this man about whom reporters will say later, "Doesn't seem quite all there."

An endless line of presidents rises from the chair with him, the weight almost too much. He can see each clearly in his head. He can see what they're doing, and who they're doing it to.

Saying his goodbyes is like learning how to walk again, while a nightmare plays out in the background. He knows as they lead him down the corridor that he'll have to learn to live with it, like and unlike a man learning to live with missing limbs—phantom limbs that do not belong, that he cannot control, but are always there, and he'll never be able to explain it to anyone. He'll be as alone and yet as crowded as a person can be. The wall between him and his wife will be more unbearable than ever.

He remembers Peter's pale, wrinkled, yearning face, and he thinks about making them release the man, put him on a plane somewhere beyond his country's influence. Thinks about destroying the machine and ending the adept project.

Then he's back in the wretched, glorious sunlight of a real, an ordinary day, and so are all of his reflections and shadows. Mimicking him, forever.

THE LONELY SONGS OF LAREN DORR

GEORGE R. R. MARTIN

George R. R. Martin is the wildly popular author of the *A Song of Ice and Fire* epic fantasy series, and many other novels, such as *Dying of the Light* and *The Armageddon Rag*. His short fiction—which has appeared in numerous anthologies and in most, if not all, of the genre's major magazines—has garnered him four Hugos, two Nebulas, the Stoker, and the World Fantasy Award. Martin is also known for editing the *Wild Cards* series of shared world superhero anthologies, and for his work as a screenwriter on such television projects as the 1980s version of *The Twilight Zone* and *Beauty and the Beast*. A TV series based on *A Song of Ice and Fire* debuted on HBO in 2011.

There is a girl who goes between the worlds.

She is gray-eyed and pale of skin, or so the story goes, and her hair is a coal-black waterfall with half-seen hints of red. She wears about her brow a circlet of burnished metal, a dark crown that holds her hair in place and sometimes puts shadows in her eyes. Her name is Sharra; she knows the gates.

The beginning of her story is lost to us, with the memory of the world from which she sprang. The end? The end is not yet, and when it comes we shall not know it.

We have only the middle, or rather a piece of that middle, the smallest part of the legend, a mere fragment of the quest. A small tale within the greater, of one world where Sharra paused, and of the lonely singer Laren Dorr and how they briefly touched.

One moment there was only the valley, caught in twilight. The setting sun hung fat and violet on the ridge above, and its rays slanted down silently into a dense forest whose trees had shiny black trunks and colorless ghostly leaves. The only sounds were the cries of the mourning-birds coming out for the night, and the swift rush of water in the rocky stream that cut the woods.

Then, through a gate unseen, Sharra came tired and bloodied to the world of Laren Dorr. She wore a plain white dress, now stained and sweaty, and a heavy fur cloak that had been half-ripped from her back. And her left arm, bare and slender, still bled from three long wounds. She appeared by the side of the stream, shaking, and she threw a quick, wary glance about her before she knelt to dress her wounds. The water, for all its swiftness, was a dark and murky green. No way to tell if it was safe, but Sharra was weak and thirsty. She drank, washed her arm as best she could in the strange and doubtful water, and bound her injuries with bandages ripped from her clothes. Then, as the purple sun dipped lower behind the ridge, she crawled away from the water to a sheltered spot among the trees and fell into exhausted sleep.

She woke to arms around her, strong arms that lifted her easily to carry her somewhere, and she woke struggling. But the arms just tightened and held her still. "Easy," a mellow voice said, and she saw a face dimly through gathering mist, a man's face, long and somehow gentle.

"You are weak," he said, "and night is coming. We must be inside before darkness."

Sharra did not struggle, not then, though she knew she should. She had been struggling a long time, and she was tired. But she looked at him, confused. "Why?" she asked. Then, not waiting for an answer, "Who are you? Where are we going?"

"To safety," he said.

"Your home?" she asked, drowsy.

"No," he said, so soft she could scarcely hear his voice. "No, not home, not ever home. But it will do." She heard splashing then, as if he were carrying her across the stream, and ahead of them on the ridge she glimpsed a gaunt, twisted silhouette, a triple-towered castle etched black against the sun. Odd, she thought, that wasn't there before.

She slept.

When she woke, he was there, watching her. She lay under a pile of soft, warm blankets in a curtained, canopied bed. But the curtains had been drawn back, and her host sat across the room in a great chair draped by shadows. Candlelight flickered in his eyes, and his hands locked together neatly beneath his chin. "Are you feeling better?" he asked, without moving.

She sat up and noticed she was nude. Swift as suspicion, quicker than thought, her hand went to her head. But the dark crown was still there, in place, untouched, its metal cool against her brow. Relaxing, she leaned back against the pillows and pulled the blankets up to cover herself. "Much better," she said, and as she said it she realized for the first time that her wounds were gone.

The man smiled at her, a sad, wistful sort of smile. He had a strong face, with charcoal-colored hair that curled in lazy ringlets and fell down into dark eyes somehow wider than they should be. Even seated, he was tall. And slender. He wore a suit and cape of some soft gray leather, and over that he wore melancholy like a cloak. "Claw marks," he said speculatively, while he smiled. "Claw marks down your arm, and your clothes almost ripped from your back. Someone doesn't like you."

"Something," Sharra said. "A guardian, a guardian at the gate." She sighed. "There is always a guardian at the gate. The Seven don't like us to move from world to world. Me they like least of all."

His hands unfolded from beneath his chin and rested on the carved wooden arms of his chair. He nodded, but the wistful smile stayed. "So, then," he said. "You know the Seven, and you know the gates." His eyes strayed to her forehead. "The crown, of course. I should have guessed."

Sharra grinned at him. "You did guess. More than that, you knew. Who are you? What world is this?"

"My world," he said evenly. "I've named it a thousand times, but none of the names ever seem quite right. There was one once, a name I liked, a name that fit. But I've forgotten it. It was a long time ago. My name is Laren Dorr, or that was my name, once, when I had use for such a thing. Here and now it seems somewhat silly. But at least I haven't forgotten it."

"Your world," Sharra said. "Are you a king, then? A god?"

"Yes," Laren Dorr replied, with an easy laugh. "And more. I'm whatever I choose to be. There is no one around to dispute me."

"What did you do to my wounds?" she asked.

"I healed them." He gave an apologetic shrug. "It's my world. I have certain powers. Not the powers I'd like to have, perhaps, but powers nonetheless."

"Oh." She did not look convinced.

Laren waved an impatient hand. "You think it's impossible. Your crown, of course. Well, that's only half right. I could not harm you with my, ah, powers, not while you wear that. But I can help you." He smiled again, and his eyes grew soft and dreamy. "But it doesn't matter. Even if I could I would never harm you, Sharra. Believe that. It has been a long time."

Sharra looked startled. "You know my name. How?"

He stood up, smiling, and came across the room to sit beside her on the bed. And he took her hand before replying, wrapping it softly in his and stroking her with his thumb. "Yes, I know your name. You are Sharra, who moves between the worlds. Centuries ago, when the hills had a different shape and the violet sun burned scarlet at the very beginning of its cycle, they came to me and told me you would come. I hate them, all Seven, and I will always hate them, but that night I welcomed the vision they gave me. They told me only your name, and that you would come here, to my world. And one thing more, but that was enough. It was a promise. A promise of an ending or a start, of a change. And any change is welcome on this world. I've been alone here through a thousand sun-cycles, Sharra, and each cycle lasts for centuries. There are few events to mark the death of time."

Sharra was frowning. She shook her long, black hair, and in the dim light of the candles the soft red highlights glowed. "Are they that far ahead of me, then?" she said. "Do they know what will happen?" Her voice was troubled. She looked up at him. "This other thing they told you?"

He squeezed her hand, very gently. "They told me I would love you," Laren said. His voice still sounded sad. "But that was no great prophecy. I could have told them as much. There was a time long ago—I think the sun was yellow then—when I realized that I would love any voice that was not an echo of my own."

Sharra woke at dawn, when shafts of bright purple light spilled into her room through a high arched window that had not been there the night before. Clothing had been laid out for her: a loose yellow robe, a jeweled dress of bright crimson, a suit of forest green. She chose the suit, dressed quickly. As she left, she paused to look out the window.

She was in a tower, looking out over crumbling stone battlements and a dusty triangular courtyard. Two other towers, twisted matchstick things with pointed conical spires, rose from the other corners of the triangle. There was a strong wind that whipped the rows of gray pennants set along the walls, but no other motion to be seen.

And, beyond the castle walls, no sign of the valley, none at all. The castle with its courtyard and its crooked towers was set atop a mountain, and far and away in all directions taller mountains loomed, presenting a panorama of black stone cliffs and jagged rocky walls and shining clean ice steeples that gleamed with a violet sheen. The window was sealed and closed, but the wind *looked* cold.

Her door was open. Sharra moved quickly down a twisting stone staircase, out across the courtyard into the main building, a low wooden structure built against the wall. She passed through countless rooms, some cold and empty save for dust, others richly furnished, before she found Laren Dorr eating breakfast.

There was an empty seat at his side; the table was heavily laden with food and drink. Sharra sat down and took a hot biscuit, smiling despite herself. Laren smiled back.

"I'm leaving today," she said, in between bites. "I'm sorry, Laren. I must find the gate."

The air of hopeless melancholy had not left him. It never did. "So you said last night," he replied, sighing. "It seems I have waited a long time for nothing."

There was meat, several types of biscuits, fruit, cheese, milk. Sharra filled a plate, face a little downcast, avoiding Laren's eyes. "I'm sorry," she repeated.

"Stay awhile," he said. "Only a short time. You can afford it, I would think. Let me show you what I can of my world. Let me sing to you." His eyes, wide and dark and very tired, asked the question.

She hesitated. "Well…it takes time to find the gate."

"Stay with me for a while, then."

"But Laren, eventually I must go. I have made promises. You understand?"

He smiled, gave a helpless shrug. "Yes. But look. I know where the gate is. I can show you, save you a search. Stay with me, oh, a month. A month as you measure time. Then I'll take you to the gate." He studied her. "You've been hunting a long, long time, Sharra. Perhaps you need a rest."

Slowly, thoughtfully, she ate a piece of fruit, watching him all the time. "Perhaps I do," she said at last, weighing things. "And there will be a guardian, of course. You could help me, then. A month…that's not so long. I've been on other worlds far longer than a month." She nodded, and a smile spread slowly across her face. "Yes," she said, still nodding. "That would be all right."

He touched her hand lightly. After breakfast he showed her the world they had given him.

They stood side by side on a small balcony atop the highest of the three towers, Sharra in dark green and Laren tall and soft in gray. They stood without moving, and Laren moved the world around them. He set the castle flying over restless, churning seas, where long, black serpent-heads peered up out of the water to watch them pass. He moved them to a vast, echoing cavern under the earth, all aglow with a soft green light, where dripping stalactites brushed down against the towers and herds of blind white goats moaned outside the battlements. He clapped his hands and smiled, and steam-thick jungle rose around them; trees that climbed each other in rubber ladders to the sky, giant flowers of a dozen different colors, fanged monkeys that chittered from the walls. He clapped again, and the walls were swept clean, and suddenly the courtyard dirt was sand and they were on an endless beach by the shore of a bleak gray ocean, and above the slow wheeling of a great blue bird with tissue-paper wings was the only movement to be seen. He showed her this, and more, and more, and in the end as dusk seemed to threaten in one place after another, he took the castle back to the ridge above the valley. And Sharra looked down on the forest of black-barked trees where he had found her and heard the mourning-birds whimper and weep among transparent leaves.

"It is not a bad world," she said, turning to him on the balcony.

"No," Laren replied. His hands rested on the cold stone railing, his eyes on the valley below "Not entirely. I explored it once, on foot, with a sword and a walking stick. There was a joy there, a real excitement. A new mystery behind every hill." He chuckled. "But that, too, was long ago. Now I know what lies behind every hill. Another empty horizon."

He looked at her and gave his characteristic shrug. "There are worse hells, I suppose. But this is mine."

"Come with me, then," she said. "Find the gate with me, and leave. There are other worlds. Maybe they are less strange and less beautiful, but you will not be alone."

He shrugged again. "You make it sound so easy," he said in a careless voice. "I have found the gate, Sharra. I have tried it a thousand times. The guardian does not stop me. I step through, briefly glimpse some other world, and suddenly I'm back in the courtyard. No. I cannot leave."

She took his hand in hers. "How sad. To be alone so long. I think you must be very strong, Laren. I would go mad in only a handful of years."

He laughed, and there was a bitterness in the way he did it. "Oh, Sharra. I have gone mad a thousand times, also. They cure me, love. They always cure me." Another shrug, and he put his arm around her. The wind was cold and rising. "Come," he said. "We must be inside before full dark."

They went up in the tower to her bedroom, and they sat together on her bed and Laren brought them food; meat burned black on the outside and red within, hot bread, wine. They ate, and they talked.

"Why are you here?" she asked him, in between mouthfuls, washing her words down with wine. "How did you offend them? Who were you, before?"

"I hardly remember, except in dreams," he told her. "And the dreams—it has been so long, I can't even recall which ones are truth and which are visions born of my madness." He sighed. "Sometimes I dream I was a king, a great king in a world other than this, and my crime was that I made my people happy. In happiness they turned against the Seven, and the temples fell idle. And I woke one day, within my room, within my castle, and found my servants gone. And when I went outside, my people and my world were also gone, and even the woman who slept beside me.

"But there are other dreams. Often I remember vaguely that I was a god. Well, an almost-god. I had powers, and teachings, and they were not the teachings of the Seven. They were afraid of me, each of them, for I was a match for any of them. But I could not meet all Seven together, and that was what they forced me to do. And then they left me only a small bit of my power, and set me here. It was cruel irony. As a god, I'd taught that people should turn to each other, that they could keep away the darkness by love and laughter and talk. So all these things the Seven took from me.

"And even that is not the worst. For there are other times when I think that I have always been here, that I was born here some endless age ago. And the memories are all false ones, sent to make me hurt the more."

Sharra watched him as he spoke. His eyes were not on her, but far away, full of fog and dreams and half-dead rememberings. And he spoke very slowly, in a voice that was also like fog, that drifted and curled and hid things, and you knew that there were mysteries there and things brooding just out of sight and far-off lights that you would never reach.

Laren stopped, and his eyes woke up again. "Ah, Sharra," he said. "Be careful how you go. Even your crown will not help you should they move on you directly. And the pale child Bakkalon will tear at you, and Naa-Slas feed upon your pain, and Saagael on your soul."

She shivered and cut another piece of meat. But it was cold and tough when she bit into it, and suddenly she noticed that the candles had burned very low. How long had she listened to him speak?

"Wait," he said then, and he rose and went outside, out the door near where the window had been. There was nothing there now but rough, gray stone; the windows all changed to solid rock with the last fading of the sun.

Laren returned in a few moments, with a softly shining instrument of dark black wood slung around his neck on a leather cord. Sharra had never quite seen its like. It had sixteen strings, each a different color, and all up and down its length brightly glowing bars of light were inlaid amid the polished wood. When Laren sat, the bottom of the device rested on the floor and the top came to just above his shoulder. He stroked it lightly, speculatively; the lights glowed, and suddenly the room was full of swift-fading music.

"My companion," he said, smiling. He touched it again, and the music rose and died, lost notes without a tune. And he brushed the light-bars and the very air shimmered and changed color. He began to sing.

I am the lord of loneliness,
Empty my domain...

...the first words ran, sung low and sweet in Laren's mellow far-off fog voice. The rest of the song—Sharra clutched at it, heard each word and tried to remember, but lost them all. They brushed her, touched her, then melted away, back into the fog, here and gone again so swift that she could not remember quite what they had been. With the words, the music; wistful and melancholy and full of secrets, pulling at her, crying, whispering promises of a thousand tales untold. All around the room the candles flamed up brighter, and globes of light grew and danced and flowed together until the air was full of color.

Words, music, light; Laren Dorr put them all together and wove for her a vision.

She saw him then as he saw himself in his dreams; a king, strong and tall and still proud, with hair as black as hers and eyes that snapped. He was dressed all in shimmering white, pants that clung tight and a shirt that ballooned at the sleeves, and a great cloak that moved and curled in the wind like a sheet of solid snow. Around his brow he wore a crown of flashing silver, and a slim, straight sword flashed just as bright at his side. This Laren, this younger Laren, this dream vision, moved without melancholy, moved in a world of sweet ivory minarets and languid blue canals. And the world moved around him, friends and lovers and one special woman whom Laren drew with words and lights of fire, and there was an infinity of easy days and laughter.

Then, sudden, abrupt darkness. He was here.

The music moaned; the lights dimmed; the words grew sad and lost. Sharra saw Laren wake in a familiar castle, now deserted. She saw him search from room to room and walk outside to face a world he'd never seen. She watched him leave the castle, walk off towards the mists of a far horizon in the hope that those mists were smoke. And on and on he walked, and new horizons fell beneath his feet each day, and the great fat sun waxed red and orange and yellow, but still his world was empty. All the places he had shown her he walked to; all those and more; and finally, lost as ever, wanting home, the castle came to him.

By then his white had faded to dim gray. But still the song went on. Days went, and years, and centuries, and Laren grew tired and mad but never old. The sun shone green and violet and a savage hard blue-white, but with each cycle there was less color in his world. So Laren sang, of endless empty days and nights when music and memory were his only sanity, and his songs made Sharra feel it.

And when the vision faded and the music died and his soft voice melted away for the last time and Laren paused and smiled and looked at her, Sharra found herself trembling.

"Thank you," he said softly, with a shrug. And he took his instrument and left her for the night.

The next day dawned cold and overcast, but Laren took her out into the forests, hunting. Their quarry was a lean white thing, half cat, half gazelle, with too much speed for them to chase easily and too many teeth for them to kill. Sharra did not mind. The hunt was better than the kill. There was a singular, striking joy in that run through the darkling forest, holding a bow she never used and wearing a quiver of black wood arrows cut from the same dour trees that surrounded them. Both of them were bundled up tightly in gray fur, and Laren smiled out at her from under a wolf's-head hood. And the leaves beneath their boots, as clear and fragile as glass, cracked and splintered as they ran.

Afterwards, unblooded but exhausted, they returned to the castle, and Laren set out a great feast in the main dining room. They smiled at each other from opposite ends of a table fifty feet long, and Sharra watched the clouds roll by the window behind Laren's head, and later watched the window turn to stone.

"Why does it do that?" she asked. "And why don't you ever go outside at night?"

He shrugged. "Ah. I have reasons. The nights are, well, not good here." He sipped hot spice wine from a great jeweled cup. "The world you came from, where you started—tell me, Sharra, did you have stars?"

She nodded. "Yes. It's been so long, though. But I still remember. The nights were very dark and black, and the stars were little pinpoints of light, hard and cold and far away. You could see patterns sometimes. The men of my world, when they were young, gave names to each of those patterns, and told grand tales about them."

Laren nodded. "I would like your world, I think," he said. "Mine was like that, a little. But our stars were a thousand colors, and they moved, like ghostly lanterns in the night. Sometimes they drew veils around them to hide their light. And then our nights would be all shimmer and gossamer. Often I would go sailing at startime, myself and she whom I loved. Just so we could see the stars together. It was a good time to sing." His voice was growing sad again.

Darkness had crept into the room, darkness and silence, and the food was cold and Sharra could scarce see his face fifty long feet away. So she rose and went to him, and sat lightly on the great table near to his chair. And Laren nodded and smiled, and at once there was a whooosh, and all along the walls torches flared to sudden life in the long dining hall. He offered her more wine, and her fingers lingered on his as she took the glass.

"It was like that for us, too," Sharra said. "If the wind was warm enough, and other men were far away, then we liked to lie together in the open. Kaydar and I." She hesitated, looked at him.

His eyes were searching. "Kaydar?"

"You would have liked him, Laren. And he would have liked you, I think. He was tall and he had red hair and there was a fire in his eyes. Kaydar had powers, as did I, but his were greater. And he had such a will. They took him one night, did not kill him, only took him from me and from our world. I have been hunting for him ever since. I know the gates, I wear the dark crown, and they will not stop me easily."

Laren drank his wine and watched the torchlight on the metal of his goblet. "There are an infinity of worlds, Sharra."

"I have as much time as I require. I do not age, Laren, no more than you do. I will find him."

"Did you love him so much?"

Sharra fought a fond, flickering smile, and lost. "Yes," she said, and now it was her voice that seemed a little lost. "Yes, so much. He made me happy, Laren. We were only together for a short time, but he *did* make me happy. The Seven cannot touch that. It was a joy just to watch him, to feel his arms around me and see the way he smiled."

"Ah," he said, and he did smile, but there was something very beaten in the way he did it. The silence grew very thick.

Finally Sharra turned to him. "But we have wandered a long way from where we started. You still have not told me why your windows seal themselves at night."

"You have come a long way, Sharra. You move between the worlds. Have you seen worlds without stars?"

"Yes. Many, Laren. I have seen a universe where the sun is a glowing ember with but a single world, and the skies are vast and vacant by night. I have seen the land of frowning jesters, where there is no sky and the hissing suns burn below the ocean. I have walked the moors of Carradyne, and watched dark sorcerers set fire to a rainbow to light that sunless land."

"This world has no stars," Laren said.

"Does that frighten you so much that you stay inside?"

"No. But it has something else instead." He looked at her. "Would you see?"

She nodded.

As abruptly as they had lit, the torches all snuffed out. The room swam with blackness. And Sharra shifted on the table to look over Laren's shoulder. Laren did not move. But behind him, the stones of the window fell away like dust and light poured in from outside.

The sky was very dark, but she could see clearly, for against the darkness a shape was moving. Light poured from it, and the dirt in the courtyard and the stones of the battlements and the gray pennants were all bright beneath its glow. Puzzling, Sharra looked up.

Something looked back. It was taller than the mountains and it filled up half the sky, and though it gave off light enough to see the castle by, Sharra knew that it was dark beyond darkness. It had a man-shape, roughly, and it wore a long cape and a cowl, and below that was blackness even fouler than the rest. The only sounds were Laren's soft breathing and the beating of her heart and the distant weeping of a mourning-bird, but in her head Sharra could hear demonic laughter.

The shape in the sky looked down at her, in her, and she felt the cold dark in her soul. Frozen, she could not move her eyes. But the shape did move. It turned and raised a hand, and then there was something else up there with it, a tiny man-shape with eyes of fire that writhed and screamed and called to her.

Sharra shrieked and turned away. When she glanced back, there was no window. Only a wall of safe, sure stone, and a row of torches burning, and Laren holding her within strong arms. "It was only a vision," he told her. He pressed her tight against him, and stroked her hair. "I used to test myself at night," he said, more to himself than to her. "But there was no need. They take turns up there, watching me, each of the Seven. I have seen them too often, burning with black light against the clean dark of the sky, and holding those I loved. Now I don't look. I stay inside and sing, and my windows are made of night-stone."

"I feel...fouled," she said, still trembling a little.

"Come," he said. "There is water upstairs, you can clean away the cold. And then I'll sing for you." He took her hand and led her up into the tower.

Sharra took a hot bath while Laren set up his instrument and tuned it in the bedroom. He was ready when she returned, wrapped head to foot in a huge fluffy brown towel. She sat on the bed, drying her hair and waiting.

And Laren gave her visions.

He sang his other dream this time, the one where he was a god and the enemy of the Seven. The music was a savage pounding thing, shot through with lightning and tremors of fear, and the lights melted together to form a scarlet battlefield where a blinding-white Laren fought shadows and the shapes of nightmare. There were seven of them, and they formed a ring around him and darted in and out, stabbing him with lances of absolute black, and Laren answered them with fire and storm. But in the end they overwhelmed him, the light faded, and then the song grew soft and sad again, and the vision blurred as lonely dreaming centuries flashed by.

Hardly had the last notes fallen from the air and the final shimmers died than Laren started once again. A new song this time, and one he did not know so well. His fingers, slim and graceful, hesitated and retraced themselves more than once, and his voice was shaky, too, for he was making up some of the words as he went along. Sharra knew why. For this time he sang of her, a ballad of her quest. Of burning love and endless searching, of worlds beyond worlds, of dark crowns and waiting guardians that fought with claws and tricks and lies. He took every word that she had spoken, and used each, and transformed each. In the bedroom, glittering panoramas formed where hot white suns burned beneath eternal oceans and hissed in clouds of steam, and men ancient beyond time lit rainbows to keep away the dark. And he sang Kaydar, and he sang him true somehow, he caught and drew the fire that had been Sharra's love and made her believe anew.

But the song ended with a question, the halting finale lingering in the air, echoing, echoing. Both of them waited for the rest, and both knew there was no more. Not yet.

Sharra was crying. "My turn, Laren," she said. Then: "Thank you. For giving Kaydar back to me."

"It was only a song," he said, shrugging. "It's been a long time since I had a new song to sing."

Once again he left her, touching her cheek lightly at the door as she stood there with the blanket wrapped around her. Then Sharra locked the door behind him and went from candle to candle, turning light to darkness with a breath. And she threw the towel over a chair and crawled under the blankets and lay a long, long time before drifting off to sleep.

It was still dark when she woke, not knowing why. She opened her eyes and lay quietly and looked around the room, and nothing was there, nothing was changed. Or was there?

And then she saw him, sitting in the chair across the room with his hands locked under his chin, just as he had sat that first time. His eyes steady and unmoving, very wide and dark in a room full of night. He sat very still. "Laren?" she called, softly, still not quite sure the dark form was him.

"Yes," he said. He did not move. "I watched you last night, too, while you slept. I have been alone here for longer than you can ever imagine, and very soon now I will be alone again. Even in sleep, your presence is a wonder."

"Oh, Laren," she said. There was a silence, a pause, a weighing and an unspoken conversation. Then she threw back the blanket, and Laren came to her.

Both of them had seen centuries come and go. A month, a moment; much the same.

They slept together every night, and every night Laren sang his songs while Sharra listened. They talked throughout dark hours, and during the day they swam nude in crystalline waters that caught the purple glory of the sky. They made love on beaches of fine white sand, and they spoke a lot of love.

But nothing changed. And finally the time drew near. On the eve of the night before the day that was end, at twilight, they walked together through the shadowed forest where he'd found her.

Laren had learned to laugh during his month with Sharra, but now he was silent again. He walked slowly, clutched her hand hard in his, and his mood was more gray than the soft silk shirt he wore. Finally, by the side of the valley stream, he sat and pulled her down by his side. They took off their boots and let the water cool their feet. It was a warm evening, with a lonely, restless wind, and already you could hear the first of the mourning-birds.

"You must go," he said, still holding her hand but never looking at her. It was a statement, not a question.

"Yes," she said, and the melancholy had touched her, too, and there were leaden echoes in her voice.

"My words have all left me, Sharra," Laren said. "If I could sing for you a vision now, I would. A vision of a world once empty, made full by us and our children. I could offer that. My world has beauty and wonder and mystery enough, if only there were eyes to see it. And if the nights are evil, well, men have faced dark nights before, on other worlds in other times. I would love you, Sharra, as much as I am able. I would try to make you happy."

"Laren..." she started. But he quieted her with a glance.

"No, I could say that, but I will not. I have no right. Kaydar makes you happy. Only a selfish fool would ask you to give up that happiness to share my misery. Kaydar is all fire and laughter, while I am smoke and song and sadness. I have been alone too long, Sharra. The gray is part of my soul now, and I would not have you darkened. But still..."

She took his hand in both of hers, lifted it, and kissed it quickly. Then, releasing him, she lay her head on his unmoving shoulder. "Try to come with me, Laren," she said. "Hold my hand when we pass through the gate, and perhaps the dark crown will protect you."

"I will try anything you ask. But don't ask me to believe that it will work." He sighed. "You have countless worlds ahead of you, Sharra, and I cannot see your ending. But it is not here. That I know. And maybe that is best. I don't know anymore, if I ever did. I remember love vaguely, I think I can recall what it was like, and I remember that it never lasts. Here, with both of us unchanging and immortal, how could we help but to grow bored? Would we hate each other then? I'd not want that." He looked at her then, and smiled an aching, melancholy smile. "I think that you had known Kaydar for only a short time, to be so in love with him. Perhaps I'm being devious after all. For in finding Kaydar, you may lose him. The fire will go out someday, my love, and the magic will die. And then you may remember Laren Dorr."

Sharra began to weep, softly. Laren gathered her to him, and kissed her, and whispered a gentle "No." She kissed back, and they held each other, wordless.

When at last the purple gloom had darkened to near-black, they put back on their boots and stood. Laren hugged her and smiled.

"I *must* go," Sharra said. "I *must*. But leaving is hard, Laren, you must believe that."

"I do," he said. "I love you *because* you will go, I think. Because you cannot forget Kaydar, and you will not forget the promises you made. You are Sharra, who goes between the worlds, and I think the Seven must fear you far more than any god I might have been. If you were not you, I would not think as much of you."

"Oh. Once you said you would love any voice that was not any echo of your own."

Laren shrugged. "As I have often said, love, *that* was a very long time ago."

They were back inside the castle before darkness, for a final meal, a final night, a final song. They got no sleep that night, and Laren sang to her again just before dawn. It was not a very good song, though; it was an aimless, rambling thing about a wandering minstrel on some nondescript world. Very little of interest ever happened to the minstrel; Sharra couldn't quite get the point of the song, and Laren sang it listlessly. It seemed an odd farewell, but both of them were troubled.

He left her with the sunrise, promising to change clothes and meet her in the courtyard. And sure enough, he was waiting when she got there, smiling at her, calm and confident. He wore a suit of pure white; pants that clung, a shirt that puffed up at the sleeves, and a great heavy cape that snapped and billowed in the rising wind. But the purple sun stained him with its shadow rays.

Sharra walked out to him and took his hand. She wore tough leather, and there was a knife in her belt, for dealing with the guardian. Her hair, jet-black with light-born glints of red and purple, blew as freely as his cape, but the dark crown was in place. "Good-bye, Laren," she said. "I wish I had given you more."

"You have given me enough. In all the centuries that come, in all the sun-cycles that lie ahead, I will remember. I shall measure time by you, Sharra. When the sun rises one day and its color is blue fire, I will look at it and say, 'Yes, this is the first blue sun after Sharra came to me.'"

She nodded. "And I have a new promise. I will find Kaydar, someday. And if I free him, we will come back to you, both of us together, and we will pit my crown and Kaydar's fires against all the darkness of the Seven."

Laren shrugged. "Good. If I'm not here, be sure to leave a message," he said. And then he grinned.

"Now, the gate. You said you would show me the gate."

Laren turned and gestured at the shortest tower, a sooty stone structure Sharra had never been inside. There was a wide wooden door in its base. Laren produced a key.

"Here?" she said, looking puzzled. "In the castle?"

"Here," Laren said. They walked across the courtyard, to the door. Laren inserted the heavy metal key and began to fumble with the lock. While he worked, Sharra took one last look around, and felt the sadness heavy on her soul. The other towers looked bleak and dead, the courtyard was forlorn, and beyond the high icy mountains was only an empty horizon. There was no sound but Laren working at the lock, and no motion but the steady wind that kicked up the courtyard dust and flapped the seven gray pennants that hung along each wall. Sharra shivered with sudden loneliness.

Laren opened the door. No room inside; only a wall of moving fog, a fog without color or sound or light. "Your gate, my lady," the singer said.

Sharra watched it, as she had watched it so many times before. What world was next? she wondered. She never knew. But maybe in the next one, she would find Kaydar.

She felt Laren's hand on her shoulder. "You hesitate," he said, his voice soft.

Sharra's hand went to her knife. "The guardian," she said suddenly. "There is always a guardian." Her eyes darted quickly round the courtyard.

Laren sighed. "Yes. Always. There are some who try to claw you to pieces, and some who try to get you lost, and some who try to trick you into taking the wrong gate. There are some who hold you with weapons, some with chains, some with lies. And there is one, at least, who tried to stop you with love. Yet he was true for all that, and he never sang you false."

And with a hopeless, loving shrug, Laren shoved her through the gate.

Did she find him, in the end, her lover with the eyes of fire? Or is she searching still? What guardian did she face next?

When she walks at night, a stranger in a lonely land, does the sky have stars?

I don't know. He doesn't. Maybe even the Seven do not know. They are powerful, yes, but all power is not theirs, and the number of worlds is greater than even they can count.

There is a girl who goes between the worlds, but her path is lost in legend by now. Maybe she is dead, and maybe not. Knowledge moves slowly from world to world, and not all of it is true.

But this we know: In an empty castle below a purple sun, a lonely minstrel waits, and sings of her.

OF SWORDS
AND HORSES

CARRIE VAUGHN

Carrie Vaughn is the author of the bestselling series about a werewolf named Kitty who hosts a talk radio advice show. She's also written for young adults (*Steel, Voices of Dragons*), the novels *Discord's Apple* and *After the Golden Age*, many short stories, and she's a contributor to George R. R. Martin's *Wild Cards* series. When she isn't writing, she collects hobbies and enjoys the great outdoors in Colorado, where she makes her home.

I raised my daughter on Disney princess movies because I'd loved them so much as a girl: the music, the happily ever afters, and those amazing dresses. They made me dream of other worlds, and I'd wondered what it would be like to dance at a ball, to marry a prince, to live in a world with magic.

Maybe I thought that Maggie would turn into me, or something like me. I'd have a friend I could sigh over the movies with, a little girl I could dress in satin princess gowns.

But Maggie's questions startled me.

"How come the girls don't get to ride horses and have swords and things?"

Then, I showed her *Mulan*, in which the girl rides a horse and has a sword, and my six-year-old astutely observed, "But she's dressed like a boy."

So I signed her up for fencing lessons.

I read an article in the paper about the local fencing school where one of the students—a girl—had just won a medal in the world champion-ships and a scholarship to Harvard. Who knew Harvard offered fencing scholarships? The school advertised that their classes boosted confidence and increased poise and self-esteem, especially for girls.

Maggie loved it. Better, she worked at it, listened to everything her coach said, practiced at home with a dowel rod from Dave's workshop, making little gliding steps across the kitchen floor, lining her feet up with the lines on the linoleum. I watched her during lessons, then sparring with her class-mates, and, when my heart wasn't in my throat imagining all the ways she could get hurt, felt a tingle of pride every time she outwitted her opponent, scooped her blade out of the way, swished it over and touched to score a point. When she took her mask off, her face glowed with smiling. The advertisements were right: she grew to be confident and poised, more than I ever was at her age, when I tended to creep along, slouching in oversized sweaters.

At twelve, the riding lessons started, because she begged and kept her grades up. Dave printed off an article about Modern Pentathlon, a strange sport where athletes competed in running, swimming, pistol shooting, fenc-ing, and riding. Supposedly, the event was modeled on nineteenth-century military training, replicating the skills a spy would need to cross enemy lines and deliver a message to his commander. Maggie read the article, her eyes growing rounder and rounder. She took up jogging in the mornings before school.

My daughter showed no interest at all in conventional sports like vol-leyball or gymnastics. I'd been in marching band.

When she was fifteen, Dave asked her, jokingly, as he gave our credit card number to the fencing supply company's website—yet again—for new epee blades and shoes because she'd grown out of the old ones, "Swords and horses. Why couldn't you have been a track star like your old man?"

She didn't look up from her horse magazine, didn't smile, and answered seri-ously, "Because when Corlath whisks me away to Damar I have to be ready."

Dave stared at her blankly.

"I think it's from a book she read," I explained. She kept a stack of pa-perbacks by her bed. Most of them had swords, or horses, or both on the covers.

Her riding coach told Dave and me, she has a gift. She's a natural. Even I could see it, and all I knew about horses was what I learned from Disney movies. The animals carried her around jumping courses, their ears flicked back and listening to her, though she never seemed to move while she sat on their backs, never seemed to tell them what to do. She had an uncanny way with the horses, and I thought, maybe it's all those books about horses that gave her that sixth sense.

Her coach wanted us to buy her a horse, a big thoroughbred who'd been competing in Europe and was experienced enough to teach Maggie about advanced riding and boost her confidence. She laid out a plan, including all the expenses, showing what it would take for Maggie to ride in the world championships, the Olympics. It cost too much, of course. The horse alone cost a third of what our house was worth, never mind what it cost to keep a horse. We didn't want to break Maggie's heart by telling her we couldn't help her chase such a dream—you want to support your children. Strange, though, she seemed to understand. She never asked for more than we could give.

She said, smiling wisely, "My time will come."

When she was seventeen, Maggie disappeared.

The police found her car—she'd driven herself to a riding lesson—on the road by the lake where my family had a cabin. I couldn't tell them why she might have gone there. They didn't find any sign of Maggie.

It made the news for weeks, because she was young and pretty, blond and smiling. We took out a second mortgage and offered a huge reward for information. We went on the news shows—how could we not, when the cameras camped outside our doorstep? The whole neighborhood put up yellow ribbons.

It was all so exhausting. I let Dave do all the talking about how much we prayed for her safe return. Somber, he braced himself with his arm around my shoulder.

I told the police what every mother tells the police—she isn't the kind of girl to just run away. She's not like that. She got straight As, she took out the trash.

They just shook their heads. She's seventeen, they said. She could have done anything. Are there any boys? Anyone she was seeing? No, I said. None. She'd never dated, which had been a vague cause of worry. Another difference between her and me that I didn't understand. When I was fifteen I couldn't wait to date boys, couldn't wait to find my Prince Charming. When she was fifteen I told Dave, "The horse thing, she'll grow out of it. They always grow out of it when they discover boys." Except if I'd been paying attention, I'd have known that some girls didn't. Her riding instructors, for example: devoted women who practically lived at the barn, because they hadn't grown out of it.

No, there weren't any boys, except for Corlath, a character in a book with a sword and a horse on the cover.

She couldn't have run away, I told them. She was taken. Whisked away. I couldn't say by whom.

After two years, everyone assumes that she's dead. We wait to hear word that her body has been found by a hiker in the woods. Decayed beyond recognition, they'll need her dental records to confirm her identity.

Dave wants to sell the house and move. I refuse, because what if she comes home? How will she know where to go? I keep her room clean and ready.

I threw all my DVDs of Disney princess movies away. I wonder if it's my fault that she's gone. If I'd watched her closer, made her take gymnastics instead of fencing—I'd never understood her, and she knew it somehow, and she ran away.

"She didn't run away," Dave says. Sometimes, lying in bed at night, both of us pretending to sleep but really staring at opposite walls and holding ourselves rigid, he says this. "She isn't that kind of girl."

Except that she's gone, and is it really easier to believe that someone had taken her, had done things to her? Or that she's locked up helpless somewhere wondering why we don't come looking for her?

Wondering why there isn't a prince to rescue her?

No, she wouldn't look for a prince. She'd always carried her own sword. I'm the one who'd looked for a prince.

Every couple of months, Dave takes me to the cabin. It's the family cabin that I share with four of my cousins—a house, really, with two stories, three bedrooms, a screened-in porch, a stone walkway leading to a tiny wooden dock jutting into the lake, where we tie up the canoes. Dave wants me to get away from the cameras, the news, the phone calls we still sometimes get from police about tips that didn't pan out. Every time the phone rings my heart stops. Is it Maggie calling to ask us to come get her and bring her home? Or is it the police telling us that they've found her, or what's left of her?

When we came here as a family, Maggie would sit out on the dock at twilight, reading a book and watching the evening mist form over the water. She said she dreamed pictures in the haze, stories from the books she read.

They found the car just a few miles away. She must be close, one way or the other.

The cabin holds as many difficult memories as the house, but I think

Dave needs the quiet, the solitude, and he needs to believe that it's me who needs the quiet.

Every time we visit, I sit on the dock, watching the mist, and wonder what she saw. Horses and swords, warriors riding out against dragons who breathed fire. Warriors with long, streaming hair, who didn't have to disguise themselves as boys. Those are the stories she told herself—that's what she saw in the mist. I'd sat out here when I was a girl, but if I saw pictures in the mist over the water, or heard voices calling, I don't remember.

She'd dreamed of competing in Modern Pentathlon in the Olympics someday. I'd applauded the goal, supported her all I could, as best as I knew how—you try to support your children, even when you don't understand their dreams or the visions they see in the mist. All that was taken away from her. From me.

Every time I sit on the dock in the evening, Dave comes after dark to help me to my feet and lead me back to the cabin. I've usually grown too stiff from sitting there and can't bring myself to stand and walk away.

How long can it go on? Our lives have stuck, waiting for Maggie to come home. I could stay out on this dock for the rest of my life. Become a statue sitting here. One day Dave won't bother coming to get me. One day, he'll just leave, sell the house like he wants, and start a new life somewhere.

He has that luxury. Me, I'll never have another little girl.

Dave's gone to town for groceries. He asked me to stay in the house until he got back, but I've come to sit on the dock for the afternoon. I'll get sunburned, and when he gets back he'll yell at me for it, but I won't be offended. He yells for other reasons. From helplessness. We'll hold each other after he yells at me.

My skin flushes and tingles and burns in the sun, and I stay by the water, watching the sun splash flecks of gold on the tiny rippling waves. Shadows grow long, thin, and stretched, the sky turns an impossible royal blue, and the air begins to bite. This is when the mist starts to rise from the water, when the flecks of gold disappear and the water turns pewter, thick like molten metal.

Some birds cry. Bats dip over the water snatching at insects, and fish splash to the surface, doing the same.

And there is splashing, more steady than the fish, rhythmic and purposeful. Oars tucked gently into the water, not fish leaping carelessly.

Both canoes are tied to the dock. No one visits us here. Or if they do, they drive.

Someone is coming over the water, and I can't be bothered to stand.

Then it appears, sliding out of the mist. Not a canoe but something larger, like a rowboat but stretched. It's wood, not plastic or aluminum—boards fitted together and sealed with pitch. The bow slopes up and ends in a spiral carving.

There are four hunched figures in the boat, hidden in shadows. Not shadows—they're wearing cloaks with hoods up. The largest of them sits in the middle and works the oars. The oars creak in the oarlocks, but the figure itself makes no sound. Another figure sits in the back, holding the long, smooth handle of the rudder. Two more sit in the front. One of them leans forward, searching. The other reaches out for her, like he's afraid she might fall over the side.

I'm not sure why I think that figure is a woman.

I wait because I can't not wait. Pictures in the mist, is this what Maggie saw? Had she always seen strangers, so that she didn't think them strange and would follow them, get into their cars and let them take her away?

The boat slides up to the end of the dock. A rope is thrown out, one of the men jumps onto the dock and ties the rope to the post. The woman gets out and runs three steps, stops, stares at me.

Throws back her hood to show her yellow hair, and her face, my Maggie's face, a little weathered maybe, and I wonder what has made her look tired.

I just stare at her.

"Mom?"

The cloak, pushed over her shoulders now, reaches to her ankles. It might be wool, thick and homespun. She wears a thick leather vest over a long-sleeved brown shirt, belted over leather pants. Her tall boots look softer and more comfortable than her usual stiff black riding boots. There's a sword hanging from her belt by leather straps. It's hidden in a scabbard, and seems heavier and more threatening than anything she ever used in fencing class.

She kneels in front of me. I'm hugging my knees to my chest. My muscles are frozen, but my face is wet.

"Mom?" she says again, fearfully, her voice cracking.

"You didn't run away. I kept telling them you didn't run away."

"I had to go, Mom. I had to."

"Maggie. They took you away from me. They took you away—" I stare at her, my heart bleeding and breaking. She is a ghost and I have gone mad at last.

She puts her arms around me. I fall into her embrace, sobbing like a child, inconsolable. She is solid, my child, not a ghost.

I look over her shoulder at the men I believe—I assume—took her away from me. Masters of some religious cult, or a gang (Were there any boys? the police asked, and like a fool I said no, when I didn't know anything).

The three of them stand near the boat, watching us uncomfortably. They're dressed like Maggie, in leather and rough cloth, high boots, scuffed and worn, cloaks with hoods, studded belts and swords.

The largest of them has coarse hair tied back with a piece of leather. He looks over the water, clutching the hilt of his sword. He's standing guard; the posture is unmistakable. The oldest has short hair the color of fog and a trimmed beard. He watches the third man, who watches my daughter. This one's face is set in hard lines, his lips frowning, an expression that makes him formidable, yet handsome. Unreachably handsome. I hate him for the way he watches my daughter with such intensity his eyes burn. He has short hair and no beard, and wears a polished red stone on a chain.

This means something. This all means something, but I can't guess what.

Maggie must sense me staring back at him, because she pulls away and turns to look back and forth between us. "Mom, I have so much to tell you."

I clutch her sleeves, holding her arms as best I can, my knuckles white. The scenarios playing in my mind to explain what I see before me are muddled.

It doesn't help when Maggie says, "This is my husband. He's the king."

King of what? The words don't make sense.

"They took you away," is all I can find to say.

"I had to go." She pulls on my arms, helping me to stand. I feel like an old woman. None of my joints work. But a moment later I'm standing. Maggie is still talking. "They needed me. They still need me. I didn't know what was happening at first. I came here, something drew me here. I watched the mist over the lake, like I used to do when I was little. This time, the mist spoke to me. Maybe it had always been speaking to me, but this time I really heard it. I was at that point—I didn't want to go to college, couldn't train for the pentathlon, and I no idea what to do with my life. So I stepped out. I stepped over the water—and there he was with the boat, waiting."

"She belongs with us," the man, the one Maggie said is a king, and her husband, speaks. I'm surprised I understand him—I expect him to speak a guttural Scandinavian language. He sets his shoulders, fisting his hands, like he's preparing to do battle.

I realize that Maggie isn't staying.

"Who are you?" My voice is shrill.

"Mom—" Maggie recognizes the tone.

The gray-haired man steps forward. "We are warriors protecting you and your world from a darkness you cannot fathom."

It's silly. Words from the blurb on a paperback.

"We called one of you to join us in the battle. For a long time, we called. Almost, she came too late." He glares like this is my fault. I glare like I don't believe him.

"Mom, I only have a few minutes. I have to say goodbye."

"Why? Why call *her*?"

"Because you did not answer when I called you." And this wasn't me failing my duty to his world. I had betrayed him personally. That is what his look says to me. He might have been the prince in his day.

Had there been a time, when I was a girl staying with my family and cousins at the cabin, standing on this dock, when I heard voices in the mist, and ran away because I was afraid?

"Where's Dad," Maggie asks. "Is he here?"

I shake my head. I haven't heard the car return, crunching along the gravel drive. "He's getting groceries."

She presses her lips in a line. "Will you tell him I was here? Will you tell him I love him? I love you both. I'm sorry I can't stay."

"Maggie." The word is a sob, filled with desperation.

It's no comfort that she's crying too. "There's still fighting. I have to go."

The thought of her using that sword—a real sword with a sharp edge that draws blood, not a dull flexible rod with a button on the tip that registers hits with a green or red light—makes me ill. The thought of her coming up against such a weapon makes me ill.

The large man says, "We should go. The shadows grow close."

He's right. The mist has become a wall around us.

The king nods. "Meg?"

It's not her name, but she nods. When had she become Meg? If she wanted us to call her Meg why didn't she say anything? She studies me, like she expects to never see me again.

They will have children, my grandchildren, and I will never see them.

"I want you to be proud of me, Mom. I'm happy, with him. I need you to be happy for me."

You try to be supportive. All I want to do is scream. But I nod.

She kisses my cheek, then lets go of me. The king holds out his hand to her, and she takes it. A look of such trust passes between them, I can't understand it because I come from a world without princes. They have saved each other's lives. He guides her back to the boat.

"Maggie!" I cry, stumbling forward, falling to my knees. "I love you! Don't go, please—"

The boat, all its passengers aboard, fades back to the mist, without even a splash.

You did not answer when I called you.

Just after twilight, under a dark blue sky, Dave finds me lying on the dock, as if I'd curled up to sleep. He picks me up, carries me to the house, puts me to bed, and I don't even notice. I pretend I'm dreaming. I wake up sometime—lamps light the room, the windows are dark—to smell hot tea and a crackling fire. Dave sits by the bed, watching me with something like desperation. He is no king or wizard from the mist. His brown hair is thin, the hairline receding. He wears a plaid flannel shirt untucked over gray sweatpants, not leather armor.

"What were you doing out there?" he says.

I know the words are crazy but I have to say them because she asked me to. "I saw Maggie. She was here. She said to tell you she loves you. She loves us. She had to go." Rolling to my side, I stretch my arm under the pillow and hug it to my face. She came back, I think, strangely happy. She didn't have to come back to tell me what happened to her, but she did. "She isn't coming back."

We stare at each other, because after all this time I've made it real. Saying the words has locked hope away, sealed its coffin. She isn't coming back.

Dave puts another log on the fire in the bedroom fireplace, then watches it burn.

I don't say another word about seeing Maggie and neither does he. If I say another word, he'll say something like "therapy" or "hospital," and we'll fight. We've both had counseling, apart and together, and mainly it helps us get through the day, and add up the days so we can get through the weeks, and the months. But every day has felt like the one before it, and we don't know how to move on. Dave is afraid that insanity is the next symptom of being frozen.

I can stay frozen for the rest of my life.

"We should get back," Dave says the next morning at breakfast. "The neighbors'll wonder what happened to us." He smiles, trying to make it a joke. Never mind the neighbors, Dave's job won't wait. I left mine when I lost Maggie. Not going back is part of being frozen. But Dave is responsible.

"Just a little longer." I lean on the edge of the sink, looking out the kitchen window at the lake, the dock. The sun is up, sending quicksilver sparkles over the water. She stood there yesterday. Like a dream. "Another day."

Or week, or year. This is close to where she is, wherever she is. I think I should stay.

"I'll pack up today," Dave says. "We can leave tomorrow morning."

After breakfast, I don't bother changing out of my pajamas. I pull on a robe, slip my feet into canvas sneakers, and walk down to the lake. I sit cross-legged at the end of the dock, close enough to hear water lapping against the wood. I can spend a last few moments with her.

The mist won't rise until evening. Still, I hear the water and think of oars. I keep very, very still, listening for the call. I don't know why. I'd obviously never heard it before. Only whispers, easy to ignore.

I let Maggie learn to fight with a sword, learn to ride horses, like the princesses in the movies never did. Did I doom her, then? Made sure she heard the call, then left me? Or would she have found those things on her own, resented me for keeping them from her, and left me anyway? I don't know.

She seemed happy. She seemed to be in love.

I am standing at the edge of the dock, toes hanging over the edge of the warped and weathered boards. The sun is setting. In moments, the mist will rise. I'll call to her, as loud as I can I'll call. *Take me with you.*

If she can't stay here, maybe I can go.

A gray tendril swirls on the pewter surface of the water. I clench my hands. I step out.

An ancient, slender boat does not catch me, does not rise up to keep me dry.

I splash into ice-cold water, sink like a stone, gasp for breath and choke on water instead. Reflex takes over, because my mind is numb, startled at what I have done, because of course the boat wasn't there, never would come for me, and what was I thinking? I thrash and kick, yet somehow I can't find the surface, can't find the air. The lake is a trap that has caught me.

Something grabs hold of me, takes my arm, a force pulls up. I try to grab it back, but my hands aren't in the right place. Then, I touch air, then my face reaches air, and my mouth gapes open to suck in a breath. I sound like a bellows.

Hands pull at my shirt. I'm flopping like a fish in someone's grasp. My back scrapes against the edge of the dock, then I'm sitting there. Dave hugs me close, clings to me. He's shouting.

"What are you doing? What do you think you're doing? I can't lose you both, I can't lose you too!"

He's crying. I've never seen him cry.

I clutch his shirt in clawlike hands, to let him know I'm alive. He holds me, rocks me, and I curl up in his arms.

"I only wanted to see where Maggie went," I say weakly.

He shifts, moving me away so he can look at me. He touches me, my face, my soaking hair. His eyes and nose are running, his whole face is wet.

"You think she killed herself," he says.

My eyes widen. "No—oh God, no! She didn't, I wasn't trying—" But that's what it looks like. I pull myself back into his embrace. I can't explain it. Not now. "I think we'll never understand what happened."

"You're shivering. Come in and sit by the fire." He helps me stand, never lets go of me. My own true prince.

"We're leaving in the morning, right?" I ask. Dave nods.

We reach the cabin, close the door, and shut out the night before the mist covers the water.

IMPOSSIBLE DREAMS

TIM PRATT

Tim Pratt has won a Hugo Award for short fiction, and has been nominated for World Fantasy, Stoker, Sturgeon, and Nebula awards. His most recent collection is *Hart & Boot & Other Stories*. He lives in Berkeley with his wife Heather and son River.

P ete was walking home from the revival movie house, where he'd caught an evening showing of *To Have and Have Not*, when he first saw the video store.

He stopped on the sidewalk, head cocked, frowning at the narrow store squeezed between a kitschy gift shop and a bakery. He stepped toward the door, peered inside, and saw old movie posters on the walls, racks of DVDs and VHS tapes, and a big screen TV against one wall. The lettering on the door read "Impossible Dreams Video," and the smudges on the glass suggested it had been in business for a while.

Except it *hadn't* been. Pete knew every video store in the county, from the big chains to the tiny place staffed by film students up by the university to the little porno shop downtown that sometimes sold classic Italian horror flicks and bootleg Asian movies. He'd never even heard of this place, and he walked this way at least twice a week. Pete believed in movies like other people believed in God, and he couldn't understand how he'd overlooked a store just three blocks from his own apartment. He pushed open the door, and a bell rang. The shop was small, just three aisles of DVDs and a wall of VHS tapes, fluorescent lights and ancient, blue industrial carpet, and there were no customers. The clerk said, "Let me know if you need any help," and he nodded, barely noticing her beyond the fact that she was female, somewhere south of thirty, and had short pale hair that stuck up like the fluff on a baby chick.

Pete headed toward the classics section. He was a cinematic omnivore, but you could judge a video store by the quality of its classics shelf the same way you could judge a civilization by the state of its prisons. He looked along the row of familiar titles—and stopped at a DVD turned face-out, with a foil "New Release" sticker on the front.

Pete picked it up with trembling hands. The box purported to be the director's cut of *The Magnificent Ambersons* by Orson Welles.

"Is this a joke?" he said, holding up the box, almost angry.

"What?" the clerk said.

He approached her, brandishing the box, and he could tell by her arched eyebrows and guarded posture that she thought he was going to be a problem. "Sorry," he said. "This says it's the director's cut of *The Magnificent Ambersons*, with the missing footage restored."

"Yeah," she said, brightening. "That came out a few weeks ago. You didn't know? Before, you could only get the original theatrical version, the one the studio butchered—"

"But the missing footage," he interrupted, "it was lost, destroyed, and the only record of the last fifty minutes was the continuity notes from the production."

She frowned. "Well, yeah, the footage *was* lost, and everyone assumed it was destroyed, but they found the film last year in the back corner of some warehouse."

How had this news passed Pete by? The forums he visited online should have been *buzzing* with this, a film buff's wet dream. "How did they find the footage?"

"It's an interesting story, actually. Welles talks about it on the commentary track. I mean, it's a little scattered, but the guy's in his nineties, what do you expect? He—"

"You're mistaken," Pete said. "Unless Welles is speaking from beyond the grave. He died in the 1980s."

She opened her mouth, closed it, then smiled falsely. Pete could practically hear her repeating mental customer service mantras: the customer is always right, even when he's wrong. "Sure, whatever you say. Do you want to rent the DVD?"

"Yeah," he said. "But I don't have an account here."

"You local? We just need a phone number and ID, and some proof of address."

"I think I've got my last pay stub," Pete said, rooting through his wallet and passing over his papers. She gave him a form to fill out, then typed his information into her computer. While she worked he said, "Look, I don't mean to be a jerk, it's just—I'd *know*. I know a lot about movies."

"You don't have to believe me," she said, tapping the DVD case with her finger. "Total's $3.18."

He took out his wallet again, but though it bulged with unsorted receipts and scraps of paper with notes to himself, there was no cash. "Take a credit card?"

She grimaced. "There's a five-buck minimum on credit card purchases, sorry—house rules."

"I'll get a couple of other movies," he said.

She glanced at the clock on the wall. It was almost 10:00.

"I know you're about to close, I'll hurry," he said.

She shrugged. "Sure."

He went to the Sci-Fi shelf—and had another shock. *I, Robot* was there, but *not* the forgettable action movie with Will Smith—this was older, and the credits said "written by Harlan Ellison." But Ellison's adaptation of the Isaac Asimov book had never been produced, though it *had* been published in book form. "Must be some bootleg student production," he muttered, and he didn't recognize the name of the production company. But—but—it said "winner of the Academy Award for Best Adapted Screenplay." That *had* to be a student director's little joke, straight-facedly absurd box copy, as if this were a film from some alternate reality. Worth watching, certainly, though again, he couldn't imagine how he'd never heard of this. Maybe it had been done by someone local. He took it to the counter and offered his credit card.

She looked at the card dubiously. "Visa? Sorry, we only take Weber and FosterCard."

Pete stared at her, and took back the card she held out to him. "This is a major credit card," he said, speaking slowly, as if to a child. "I've never even heard of—"

Shrugging, she looked at the clock again, more pointedly this time. "Sorry, I don't make the rules."

He *had* to see these movies. In matters of film—new film! strange film!—Pete had little patience, though in other areas of his life he was easygoing to a fault. But movies *mattered*. "Please, I live right around the corner, just let me go grab some cash and come back, ten minutes, please?"

Her lips were set in a hard line. He gestured at *The Magnificent Ambersons*.

"I just want to see it, as it was meant to be seen. You're into movies, right? *You* understand."

Her expression softened. "Okay. Ten minutes, but that's it. I want to get home, too."

Pete thanked her profusely and all but ran out of the store. He *did* run when he got outside, three mostly uphill blocks to his apartment in a stucco duplex, fumbling the keys and cursing, finally getting into his sock drawer where he kept a slim roll of emergency cash. He raced back to Impossible Dreams, breathing so hard he could feel every exhalation burning through his body, a stitch of pain in his side. Pete hadn't run, *really* run, since gym class in high school, a decade earlier.

He reached the bakery, and the gift shop, but there was no door to Impossible Dreams Video between them—there was no *between* at all. The stores stood side by side, without even an alleyway dividing them.

Pete put his hand against the brick wall. He tried to convince himself he was on the wrong block, that he'd gotten turned around while running, but he knew it wasn't true. He walked back home, slowly, and when he got to his apartment, he went into his living room, with its floor-to-ceiling metal shelves of tapes and DVDs. He took a disc down and loaded it into his high-end, region-free player, then took his remote in hand and turned on the vast plasma flat-screen TV. The surround-sound speakers hummed to life, and Pete sank into the exquisitely contoured leather chair in the center of the room. Pete owned a rusty four-door Honda with 200,000 miles on the engine, he lived mostly on cheap macaroni and cheese, and he saved money on toilet paper by stealing rolls from the bathrooms in the university's Admissions Office, where he worked. He lived simply in almost every way, so that he could live extravagantly in the world of film.

He pressed play. Pete owned the entire *Twilight Zone* television series on DVD, and now the narrator's eminently reasonable voice spoke from the speakers, introducing the tale of a man who finds a dusty little magic shop, full of wonders.

As he watched, Pete began to nod his head, and whispered, "Yes."

Pete checked in the morning; he checked at lunch; he checked after leaving his job in the Admissions Office in the evening; but Impossible Dreams did not reappear. He grabbed dinner at a little sandwich shop, then paced up and down the few blocks at the far end of the commercial street near his apartment. At 8:30 he leaned against a light pole, and stared at the place where Impossible Dreams had been. He'd arrived at, what, 9:45 last night?

But who knew if time had anything to do with the miraculous video store's manifestation? What if it had been a one-time only appearance?

Around 8:45, the door was suddenly there. Pete had blinked, that was all, but between blinkings, something had *happened*, and the store was present again.

Pete shivered, a strange exultation filling him, and he wondered if this was how people who witnessed miraculous healings or bleeding statues felt. He took a deep breath and went into the store.

The same clerk was there, and she glared at him. "I waited for you last night."

"I'm sorry," Pete said, trying not to stare at her. Did she know this was a shop of wonders? She certainly didn't *act* as though she did. He thought she was *of* the miracle, not outside it, and to her, a world with *The Magnificent Ambersons* complete and uncut was nothing special. "I couldn't find any cash at home, but I brought plenty tonight."

"I held the videos for you," she said. "You really should see the Welles, it'll change your whole opinion of his career."

"That's really nice of you. I'm going to browse a little, maybe pick up a few things."

"Take your time. It's been really slow tonight, even for a Tuesday."

Pete's curiosity about her—the proprietor (or at least clerk) of a magic shop!—warred with his desire to ransack the shelves. "You always work by yourself?"

"Mostly, except on weekends. There really should be two clerks here, but my boss is losing money like crazy, with people downloading movies online, getting DVDs by mail order, all that stuff." She shook her head.

Pete nodded. He got movies online and in the mail, too, but there was something to be said for the instant gratification of renting something from the store, without waiting for mail or download. "Sorry to hear that. This seems like a great store. Are you here every night?"

She leaned on the counter and sighed. "Lately, yeah. I'm working as much as I can, double shifts some days. I need the money. I can't even afford to eat lately, beyond like an apple at lunch time and noodles for dinner. My roommate bailed on me, and I've had to pay twice the usual rent while I look for a new roommate, it sucks. I just—ah, sorry, I didn't mean to dump all over you."

"No, it's fine," Pete said. While she spoke, he was able to look straight at her openly, and he'd noticed that, in addition to being a purveyor of miracles, she was pretty, in a frayed-at-the-edges ex-punk sort of way. Not his type at all—except that she obviously loved movies.

"Browse on," she said, and opened a heavy textbook on the counter.

Pete didn't need any more encouragement than that. Last night he'd developed a theory, and everything he saw now supported it. He thought this store belonged to some parallel universe, a world much like his own, but with subtle changes, like different names for the major credit cards. But even small differences could lead to huge divergences when it came to movies. Every film depended on so many variables—a director's capricious enthusiasm, a studio's faith in a script, a big star's availability, which starlet a producer happened to be sleeping with—*any* of those factors could irrevocably alter the course of a film, and Hollywood history was littered with the corpses of films that *almost* got made. Here, in this world, some of them *were* made, and Pete would go without sleeping for a week, if necessary, to see as many as possible.

The shelves yielded miracle after miracle. Here was *The Death of Superman*, directed by Tim Burton, starring Nicolas Cage; in Pete's universe, Burton and Cage had both dropped the project early on. Here was *Total Recall*, but directed and written by David Cronenberg, not Paul Verhoeven. Here was *The Terminator*, but starring O. J. Simpson rather than Arnold Schwarzenegger—though Schwarzenegger was still in the film, as Kyle Reese. Here was *Raiders of the Lost Ark*, but starring Tom Selleck instead of Harrison Ford—and there was no sign of any later *Indiana Jones* films, which was sad. Pete's hands were already full of DVDs, and he juggled them awkwardly while pulling more movies from the shelves. Here was *Casablanca* starring George Raft instead of Bogart, and maybe it had one of the alternate endings, too! Here a John Wayne World War II movie he'd never heard of, but the box copy said it was about the *ground invasion* of the Japanese islands, and called it a "riveting historical drama." A quick scan of the shelves revealed no sign of Stanley Kubrick's *Dr. Strangelove*, and those two things together suggested that in *this* world, the atomic bomb was never dropped on Japan. The implications of that were potentially vast...but Pete dismissed broader speculations from his mind as another film caught his eye. In this world, Kubrick had lived long enough to complete *Artificial Intelligence* on his own, and Pete *had* to see that, without Steven Spielberg's sentimental touch turning the movie into Pinocchio.

"You only get them for three days," the clerk said, amused, and Pete blinked at her, feeling like a man in a dream. "You going to have time to watch all those?"

"I'm having a little film festival," Pete said, and he was—he planned to call in sick to work and watch *all* these movies, and copy them, if he could; who knew what kind of bizarre copy protection technology existed in this world?

"Well, my boss won't want to rent twenty movies to a brand new member, you know? Could you maybe cut it down to four or five, to save me the hassle of dealing with him? You live near here, right? So you can always bring them back and rent more when you're done."

"Sure," Pete said. He didn't like it, but he was afraid she'd insist if he pushed her. He selected four movies—*The Magnificent Ambersons*, *The Death of Superman*, *I, Robot*, and *Casablanca*—and put the others away. Once he'd rented a few times, maybe she'd let him take ten or twenty movies at once. Pete would have to see how much sick time he had saved up. This was a good time to get a nasty flu and miss a couple of weeks of work.

The clerk scanned the boxes, tapped her keyboard, and told him the total, $12.72. He handed over two fives, two ones, two quarters, a dime, two nickels, and couple of pennies—he'd brought *lots* of cash this time.

The clerk looked at the money on the counter, then up at him with an expression caught between amusement and wariness. She tapped the bills. "I know you aren't a counterfeiter, because then you'd at least try to make the fake money look real. What is this, from a game or something? It's not foreign, because I recognize our presidents, except the guy on, what's this, a dime?"

Pete suppressed a groan. The *money* was different, he'd never even thought of that. He began to contemplate the logistics of armed robbery.

"Wait, you've got a couple of nickels mixed in with the fake money," she said, and pulled the two nickels aside. "So that's only $12.62 you still owe me."

"I feel really dumb," Pete said. "Yeah, it's money from a game I was playing yesterday, I must have picked it up by mistake." He swept up his bills and coins.

"You're a weird guy, Pete. I hope you don't mind me saying."

Nodding dolefully, he pulled a fistful of change from his pockets. "I guess I am." He had a lot of nickels, which were real—or close enough—in this world, and he counted them out on the counter, $3.35 worth, enough for one movie. He'd go to the bank tomorrow and change his cash for *sacks* of nickels, as much as he could carry, and he would rent all these movies, five cents at a time. Sure, he could just snatch all four movies and run now, but then he'd never be able to come *back*, and there were shelves upon shelves of movies he wanted to see here. For tonight, he'd settle for just *The Magnificent Ambersons*. "This one," he said, and she took his nickels, shaking her head in amusement. She passed him a translucent plastic case and pennies in change, odd little octagonal coins.

"I'll put these away, Mr. Nickels," she said, taking the other movies he'd brought to the counter. "Enjoy, and let me know what you think of it."

Pete mumbled some pleasantry as he hurried out the door, disc clutched tight to his chest, and he alternated walking and running back to his apartment. Once inside, he turned on his humming stack of A/V components and opened the tray on the DVD player. He popped open the plastic case and removed the disc—simple, black with the title in silver letters—and put it in the tray. The disc was a little smaller than DVDs in this world, but it seemed to fit okay. The disc spun, hummed, and the display on the DVD flashed a few times before going blank. The television screen read "No disc." Pete swore and tried loading the disc again, but it didn't work. He sat in his leather chair and held his head in his hands. Money wasn't the only thing that was different in that other world. DVD encryption was, too. Even his region-free player, which could play discs from all over the world, couldn't read this version of *The Magnificent Ambersons*. The videotapes would be similarly useless—he'd noticed they were different than the tapes he knew from this world, some format that didn't exist here, smaller than VHS, larger than Betamax.

But all was not lost. Pete went out the door, carrying *The Magnificent Ambersons* with him, since he couldn't bear to let it go. He raced back to Impossible Dreams. "Do you rent DVD players?" he gasped, out of breath. "Mine's broken."

"We do, Pete," she said, "but there's a $300 deposit. You planning to pay that in nickels?"

"Of course not," he said. "I got some real money from home. Can I see the player?" To hell with being reasonable. He'd snatch the player and run. She had his address, but this wasn't *her* world, and in a few more minutes the shop would disappear again. He could come back tomorrow night with a toy gun and steal all the DVDs he could carry, he would bring a *suitcase* to load them all in, he'd—

She set the DVD player on the counter with the cord curled on top. The electrical plug's two posts were oddly angled, one perpendicular to the other, and Pete remembered that electrical standards weren't even the same in *Europe* as they were in North America, so it was ridiculous to assume his own outlets would be compatible with devices from another universe. He rather doubted he'd be able to find an adapter at the local Radio Shack, and even if he could rig something, the amount of voltage carried in his wires at home could be all wrong, and he might destroy the DVD player, the way some American computers got fried if you plugged them into a European power outlet.

"Never mind," he said, defeated. He made a desultory show of patting his pockets and said "I forgot my wallet."

"You okay, Pete?" she asked.

"Sure, I was just really excited about seeing it." He expected some contemptuous reply, something like "It's just a movie," the sort of thing he'd been hearing from friends and relatives his entire life.

Instead she said, "Hey, I get that. Don't worry, we'll have it in stock when you get your player fixed. Old Orson isn't such a hot seller anymore."

"Sure," Pete said. He pushed the DVD back across the counter at her.

"Want a refund? You only had it for twenty minutes."

"Keep it," Pete said. He hung around outside and watched from across the street as the clerk locked up. About ten minutes past 10:00, he blinked, and the store disappeared in the moment his eyes were closed. He trudged away.

That night, at home, he watched his own DVD of *The Magnificent Ambersons*, with its butchered continuity, its studio-mandated happy ending, tacked on so as not to depress wartime audiences, and afterward he couldn't sleep for wondering what might have been.

Pete didn't think Impossible Dreams was going to reappear, and it was 9:00 before it did. He wondered if the window was closing, if the store would appear later and later each night until it never reappeared at all, gone forever in a week or a day. Pete pushed open the door, a heavy plastic bag in his hand. The clerk leaned on the counter, eating crackers from little plastic packages, the kind that came with soup in a restaurant. "Hi."

"Mr. Nickels," she said. "You're the only customer I get after 9:00 lately."

"You, ah, said you didn't have money for dinner lately, and I wanted to apologize for being so much trouble and everything...anyway, I brought some food, if you want some." He'd debated all day about what to bring. Fast food was out—what if her world didn't *have* McDonald's, what would she make of the packaging? He worried about other things, too—should he avoid beef, in case mad cow disease was rampant in her world? What if bird flu had made chicken into a rare delicacy? What if her culture was exclusively vegetarian? He'd finally settled on vegetarian egg rolls and rice noodles and hot and sour soup. He'd seen Hong Kong action movies in the store, so he knew Chinese culture still existed in her world, at least, and it was a safe bet that the food would be mostly the same.

"You are a *god*, Pete," she said, opening a paper container of noodles and wielding her chopsticks like a pro. "You know what I had for lunch today? A *pear*, and I had to steal it off my neighbor's tree. I got the crackers off a tray in the dining hall. You saved my life."

"Don't mention it. I'm really sorry I was so annoying the last couple of nights."

She waved her hand dismissively, mouth crammed with egg roll, and in her presence, Pete realized his new plan was impossible. He'd hoped to endear himself to her, and convince her to let him hang around until after closing, so he could...*stow away*, and travel to her world, where he could see *all* the movies, and maybe become the clerk's new roommate. It had all made sense at 3:00 in the morning the night before, and he'd spent most of the day thinking about nothing else, but now that he'd set his plan in motion he realized it was more theatrical than practical. It might work in a *movie*, but in life he didn't even know this woman's name, she wouldn't welcome him into her life, and even if she *did*, what would he do in her world? He spent all day processing applications, ordering transcripts, massaging a database, and filing things, but what would he do in her world? What if the computers there had totally different programming languages? What would he do for money, once his hypothetical giant sack of nickels ran out?

"I'm sorry, I never asked your name," he said.

"I'm Ally," she said. "Eat an egg roll, I feel like a pig."

Pete complied, and Ally came around the counter. "I've got something for you." She went to the big screen TV and switched it on. "We don't have time to watch the whole thing, but there's just enough time to see the last fifty minutes, the restored footage, before I have to close up." She turned on the DVD player, and *The Magnificent Ambersons* began.

"Oh, Ally, thanks," he said.

"Hey, your DVD player's busted, and you really *should* see this."

For the next fifty minutes, Pete watched. The cast was similar, with only one different actor that he noticed, and from everything he'd read, this was substantially the same as the lost footage he'd heard about in his world. Welles's genius was apparent even in the butchered RKO release, but here it was undiluted, a clarity of vision that was almost overwhelming, and this version was *sad*, profoundly so, a tale of glory and inevitable decline.

When it ended, Pete felt physically drained, and sublimely happy.

"Closing time, Pete," Ally said. "Thanks again for dinner. I'm a fiend for Chinese." She gently herded him toward the door as he thanked her, again and again. "Glad you liked it," she said. "We can talk about it tomorrow." She closed and locked the door, and Pete watched from a doorway across the street until the shop disappeared, just a few minutes after 10:00. The window *was* closing, the shop appearing for less time each night.

He'd just have to enjoy it while it lasted. You couldn't ask more of a miracle than it was willing to give.

The next night he brought kung pao chicken and asked what her favorite movies were. She led him to the Employee Picks shelf and showed him her selections. "It's mostly nostalgia, but I still love *The Lunch Bunch*—you know, the sequel to *The Breakfast Club*, set ten years later? Molly Ringwald's awesome in it. And *Return of the Jedi*, I know a lot of people hate it, but it's one of the best movies David Lynch ever directed, I thought *Dune* was a muddle, but he really got to the heart of the *Star Wars* universe, it's so much darker than *The Empire Strikes Back*. *Jason and the Argonauts* by Orson Welles, of course, that's on *everybody's* list…"

Pete found himself looking at her while she talked, instead of at the boxes of the movies she enthused over. He wanted to see them, of course, every one, but he wouldn't be able to, and really, he was talking to a woman from *another universe*, and that was as remarkable as anything he'd ever seen on a screen. She was smart, funny, and knew as much about movies as he did. He'd never dated much—he was more comfortable alone in the dark in front of a screen than he was sitting across from a woman at dinner, and his relationships seldom lasted more than a few dates when the women realized movies were his main mode of recreation. But with Ally—he could talk to her. Their obsessions were congruent and complementary.

Or maybe he was just trying to turn this miracle into some kind of theatrical romance.

"You look really beautiful when you talk about movies," he said.

"You're sweet, Mr. Nickels."

Pete came the next three nights, a few minutes later each time, as the door appeared for shorter periods of time. Ally talked to him about movies, incredulous at the bizarre gaps in his knowledge—"You've never heard of Sara Hansen? She's one of the greatest directors of all time!" (Pete wondered if she'd died young in his world, or never been born at all.) Ally had a fondness for bad science fiction movies, especially the many Ed Wood films starring Bela Lugosi, who had lived several years longer in Ally's world, instead of dying during the filming of *Plan 9 from Outer Space*. She liked good sci-fi movies, too, especially Ron Howard's *Ender's Game*. Pete regretted that he'd never see any of those films, beyond the snippets she showed him to illustrate her points, and he regretted even more that he'd soon be unable to see Ally at all, when the shop ceased to appear, as seemed inevitable.

She understood character arcs, the use of color, the underappreciated skills of silent film actors, the bizarre audacity of pre-Hayes-Code-era films, the perils of voiceover, why an extended single-camera continuous scene was worth becoming rapturous about, why the animation of Ray Harryhausen was in some ways infinitely more satisfying than the slickest CGI. She was his *people*.

"Why do you like movies so much?" he asked on that third night, over a meal of Szechwan shrimp, her leaning on her side of the counter, he on his.

She chewed, thinking. "Somebody described the experience of reading great fiction as being caught up in a vivid continuous dream, and I think movies do that better than any other kind of story. Some people say the best movie isn't as good as the best book, and I say they're not watching the right movies, or else they're not watching them the right *way*. My life doesn't make a lot of sense sometimes, I'm hungry and lonely and cold, my parents are shit, I can't afford tuition for next semester, I don't know what I want to do when I graduate. But when I see a great film, I feel like I understand life a little better, and even not-so-great films help me forget the shitty parts of my life for a couple of hours. Movies taught me to be brave, to be romantic, to stand up for myself, to take care of my friends. I didn't have church or loving parents, but I had *movies*, cheap matinees when I cut school, videos after I saved up enough to buy a TV and player of my own. I didn't have a mentor, but I had Obi-Wan Kenobi, and Jimmy Stewart in *It's a Wonderful Life*. Sure, movies can be a way to hide from life, but shit, sometimes you need to hide from life, to see a better life on the screen, to know life can be better than it is, or to see a worse life and realize how good you have it. Movies taught me not to settle for less." She took a swig from her water bottle. "That's why I love movies."

"Wow," Pete said. "That's...wow."

"So," she said, looking at him oddly. "Why do you pretend to like movies?"

Pete frowned. "What? Pretend?"

"Hey, it's okay. You came in and said you were a big movie buff, but you don't even know who Sara Hansen is, you've never seen *Jason and the Argonauts*, you talk about actors starring in movies they didn't appear in...I mean, I figured you liked me, you didn't know how else to flirt with me or something, but I *like* you, and if you want to ask me out, you can, you don't have to be a movie trivia expert to impress me."

"I *do* like you," Pete said. "But I *love* movies. I really do."

"Pete...you thought Clark Gable was in *Gone with the Wind*." She shrugged. "Need I say more?"

Pete looked at the clock. He had fifteen minutes. "Wait here," he said. "I want to show you something."

He ran home. The run was getting easier. Maybe exercise wasn't such a bad idea. He filled a backpack with books from his reference shelves—*The Encyclopedia of Science Fiction Movies*, the *AFI Film Guide*, the previous year's *Video and DVD Guide*, others—then ran back. Panting, he set the heavy bag on the counter. "Books," he gasped. "Read," gasp. "See you," gasp, "tomorrow."

"Okay, Pete," Ally said, raising her eyebrow in that way she had. "Whatever you say."

Pete lurched out of the store, still breathing hard, and when he turned to look back, the door had already disappeared. It wasn't even 10:00 yet. Time was running out, and even though Ally would soon leave his life forever, he couldn't let her think he was ignorant about their shared passion. The books might not be enough to convince her. Tomorrow, he'd show her something more.

Pete went in as soon as the door appeared, at nearly 9:30. Ally didn't waste time with pleasantries. She slammed down his copy of the *AFI Desk Reference* and said, "What the *hell* is going on?"

Pete took the bag off his shoulder, opened it, and withdrew his slim silver laptop, along with a CD wallet full of DVDs. "*Gone with the Wind*," he said, inserting a disc into the laptop, calling up the DVD controls, and fast forwarding to the first scene with Clark Gable.

Ally stared at the LCD screen, and Pete watched the reflected colors move against her face. Gable's voice, though tinny through the small speakers, was resonant as always.

Pete closed the laptop gently. "I *do* know movies," he said. "Just not exactly the same ones you do."

"This, those books, *you*…you're from another world. It's like…like…"

"Something out of the *Twilight Zone*, I know. But actually, *you're* from another world. Every night, for an hour or so—less, lately—the door to Impossible Dreams appears on my street."

"What? I don't understand."

"Come on," he said, and held out his hand. She took it, and he led her out the door. "Look," he said, gesturing to the bakery next door, the gift shop on the other side, the bike repair place across the street.

Ally sagged back against the door, half-retreating back inside the shop. "This isn't right. This isn't what's supposed to be here."

"Go on back in," he said. "The store has been appearing later and vanishing sooner every night, and I'd hate for you to get stranded here."

"Why is this happening?" Ally said, still holding his hand.

"I don't know," Pete said. "Maybe there's no reason. Maybe in a movie there would be, but…"

"Some movies reassure us that life makes sense," Ally said. "And some movies remind us that life doesn't make any sense at all." She exhaled roughly. "And some things don't have anything to do with movies."

"Bite your tongue," Pete said. "Listen, keep the laptop. The battery should run for a couple of hours. There's a spare in the bag, all charged up, which should be good for a couple more hours. Watching movies really sucks up the power, I'm afraid. I don't know if you'll be able to find an adapter to charge the laptop in your world—the standards are different. But you can see a couple of movies at least. I gave you all my favorite DVDs, great stuff by Hayao Miyazaki, Beat Takeshi, Wes Anderson, some classics…take your pick."

"Pete…"

He leaned over and kissed her cheek. "It's been so good talking to you these past few nights." He tried to think of what he'd say if this was the last scene in a movie, his *Casablanca* farewell moment, and a dozen appropriate quotes sprang to mind. He dismissed all of them. "I'm going to miss you, Ally."

"Thank you, Pete," she said, and went, reluctantly, back into Impossible Dreams. She looked at him from the other side of the glass, and he raised his hand to wave just as the door disappeared.

Pete didn't let himself go back the next night, because he knew the temptation to go into the store would be too great, and it might only be open for ten minutes this time. But after pacing around his living room for hours, he finally went out after 10:00 and walked to the place the store had been, thinking maybe she'd left a note, wishing for some closure, some final-reel gesture, a rose on the doorstep, something.

But there was nothing, no door, no note, no rose, and Pete sat on the sidewalk, wishing he'd thought to photograph Ally, wondering which movies she'd decided to watch, and what she'd thought of them.

"Hey, Mr. Nickels."

Pete looked up. Ally stood there, wearing a red coat, his laptop bag hanging from her shoulder. She sat down beside him. "I didn't think you'd show, and I did *not* relish the prospect of wandering in a strange city all night with only fifty dollars in nickels to keep me warm. Some of the street names are the same as where I'm from, but not enough of them for me to figure out where you lived."

"Ally! What are you doing here?"

"You gave me those *books*," she said, "and they all talk about *Citizen Kane* by Orson Welles, how it transformed cinema." She punched him gently in the shoulder. "But you didn't give me the DVD!"

"But...Everyone's seen *Citizen Kane*!"

"Not where I'm from. The print was destroyed. Hearst knew the movie was based on his life, and he made a deal with the studio, the guards looked the other way, and someone destroyed the film. Welles had to start over from nothing, and he made *Jason and the Argonauts* instead. But you've got *Citizen Kane*! How could I *not* come see it?"

"But Ally...you might not be able to go back."

She laughed, then leaned her head on his shoulder. "I don't plan to go back. There's nothing for me there."

Pete felt a fist of panic clench in his chest. "This isn't a movie," he said.

"No," Ally said. "It's better than that. It's my life."

"I just don't know—"

Ally patted his leg. "Relax, Pete. I'm not asking you to take me in. Unlike Blanche DuBois—played by Jessica Tandy, not Vivien Leigh, where I'm from—I don't depend on the kindness of strangers. I ran away from home when I was fifteen, and never looked back. I've started from nothing before, with no friends or prospects or ID, and I can do it again."

"You're not starting from nothing," Pete said, putting his arm around her. "Definitely not." The lights weren't going to come up, the curtain wasn't coming down; this wasn't the end of a movie. For once, Pete liked his life better than the vivid continuous dream of the screen. "Come on. Let's go watch *Citizen Kane*."

They stood, and walked together. "Just out of curiosity," he said. "Which movies did you watch on the laptop?"

"Oh, none of them. I thought it would be more fun watching them with you."

Pete laughed. "Ally, I think this could be the beginning of a beautiful friendship."

She cocked her head and raised her eyebrows. "You sound like you're quoting something," she said, "but I don't know what."

"We've got a lot of watching to do," he said.

"We've got a lot of *everything* to do," Ally replied.

LIKE MINDS

ROBERT REED

Robert Reed is the author of more than two hundred works of short science fiction, with the occasional fantasy and odd horror thrown into the mix. He has also published various novels, including *Marrow* and *The Well of Stars,* two epic tales about a world-sized starship taking a lap around the galaxy. His novella, "A Billion Eves," won the Hugo in 2007. Reed lives in Lincoln, Nebraska, with his wife and daughter, and a computer jammed with forgotten files.

T his is what you do:

Begin with a fleck of your skin and a modest fee. Then a psychological evaluation that is little better than nothing, and forms to sign. Always, forms. Then someone wearing a narrow smile sits before you, listing the most obvious troubles that come with too much of this very good thing. Obsessions. Addictions. Depression. Spiritual obliteration. Chronic indifference. Or a pernicious amorality that infects every facet of what has always been, the truth told, a ridiculously insignificant life.

"Do you wish to continue?" that someone asks.

Of course you do.

"Do you understand the terms and obligations of this license?"

Of course you cannot. You've barely paid attention to any of the dark warnings. If you really could appreciate the countless risks, you wouldn't have come here in the first place.

"Are you absolutely certain that you wish to continue?" she asks one final time. Or he asks. Or sometimes, several attendants sit before you, speaking with a shared voice. "Are you willingly and happily accepting any and all of these negative consequences?"

With a cocky smile, you say, "Sure."

Or you say, "Of course I do," and leak a nervous sigh.

Or you simply smile and nod, and with a tight little voice ask, "So what happens next?"

Next is a cool hand reaching out, dropping a tiny white pill into your damp palm. There is evidence and much informed conjecture that the pill is a delivery system for subtle technologies that rework the mind. Most assume that this is how the Authority reads thoughts, which in turn allows it to turn imprecise wishes into worthy gifts. Carefully, you place the miracle pill on your tongue and swallow. There comes a tingling sensation, brief and perhaps imagined. And then you make yourself laugh, telling your audience, "I know some of us have troubles. But I won't. You'll see. I'm going to do just fine, thank you. Don't worry about me."

Josh is eighteen today, and legal. He sits in a small room, and he sits at the shore of a great ocean. Barely two meters across, the ocean resembles a puddle of quiet gray water. That bland appearance is part of its charm, Josh decides. Incalculably deep and wondrously complex, the ocean is filled with machines too vast and swift to have been built by mere humans. To get a sense of the vastness, imagine the visible universe thoroughly rebuilt. Every star and scrap atom is used to build a single computer, pushing local physics as far as they can be pushed, in every dimension. And that machine still cannot make even the most rudimentary calculations necessary to serve that eighteen-year-old man-child who sits on a plain wooden stool, crouched over the great ocean.

But of course Josh isn't sitting inside just this one room. There are trillions of very nearly identical rooms—where "trillion" is a sloppy fat number meant to imply an immeasurable multitude. And there are trillions of identical Joshes peering down into a uniform grayness—a shared quantum linkage connecting all that is potential and possible, and everything inevitable.

For Josh and his world, this linkage is a very new technology.

"Hello?" he whispers nervously.

The gray surface shimmers slightly.

Then Josh says, "A book, a novel."

Words cause a multitude of realms to work together, the Authority suddenly engaged. A deceptively quiet voice asks the obvious: "Who is the author of this book, this novel?"

Josh can say any name. But he takes a deep breath and blurts, "Me."

"By 'me,'" the Authority inquires, "do you mean your own genotype?"

This is why Josh surrendered a piece of his own skin. His very complex and specific DNA serves as an identity and as a marker. "Sure. Yeah. My genotype." Then he flinches, confessing, "This is my first time."

But the Authority knows that already. "Are there other criteria?"

"Like what?" Josh had thought that he came prepared, but he feels sick with nervous energy, almost too anxious to think.

"I pick random examples," the Authority cautions. "But you may narrow the category in significant ways. For instance, what is the author's age? How well did this novel sell? And did the author win any awards or commendations?"

"Awards?" He hadn't quite thought of that. "You mean, what...like the Nobel Prize?"

"Exactly."

"*The* Nobel Prize?"

"Certainly," the voice purrs.

Josh licks his lips. "I'm a very good writer," he boasts. "People say so." Then with a nervous gravity, he says, "Okay. I wrote the novel in my thirties, and I won the Nobel Prize *and* the Pulitzer, too."

"Does the novel have a theme?"

"I don't care." Then he reconsiders, saying, "Maybe, yeah. How about how it feels to be eighteen? Yeah. I want a novel about growing up...a coming-of-age story. You know?"

"Are there any other criteria, sir?"

With a determined nod, Josh says, "No, that's plenty."

A closed doorway stands behind him. Each of the other milky white walls is equipped with its own make-portal. From one portal comes a thick leather-bound volume that hits the floor with an impressive thud. Josh picks it up and turns to the title page, reading a name that isn't his. But why should the author call himself Josh Thorngate? Besides genetics, they might share nothing at all.

"And what will be next, sir?"

"Politics." Josh closes the book. From his tone and upright posture, it is obvious that he has given this request some consideration. "I want my memoirs or a journal...from a universe where I'm an old man, and important. Like a president, or some sort of world leader."

"Perhaps you might narrow your aim."

Josh agrees, and trying not to miss an opportunity, he asks, "Like how?"

"There are many forms of government."

"Democracy," Josh suggests. But that doesn't sound original, does it? "No, wait. What else is possible?"

The Authority begins by listing the familiar democratic governments, quickly spiraling outwards into increasingly peculiar political systems. When the voice says something about a Holy Godhood, Josh interrupts, asking, "What's that?"

"A despotic state," the Authority allows. "High technologies are concentrated in one person's hands, and he, or she, rules over a population of worshipful peasants—"

"That," he blurts. "That's what I want."

He says, "I want a journal written by my genotype, who happens to be the leader of a Holy Godhood."

And then, "Please."

The second make-portal opens. The resulting volume is deceptively small. With too much text for any reasonable book, fifty thousand pages of private thoughts have been buried inside a few sheets of bound plastic. Josh stands and walks around the ocean, opening the cover and calling up a random page. "And then I gave him wings," he reads, "and because he had scorned me, I chased him high enough that his lungs froze and he plunged back to earth again."

He blanks the page, and sighs, settling on the stool again.

"You have one more request," the Authority reminds him.

Three requests are standard for each session. Three gifts from the compliant genie; why is that nearly universal among humans?

"Sir?" the Authority prods.

Josh is eighteen, bright and possessing some genuine talents. Standardized tests and well-meaning teachers have told him to expect good things from his life, and his devoted if rather critical parents have inflated his sense of self-worth. That, and he is eighteen years old. He has one overriding talent—a passion that will never be greater than it is today. And because it is his request to make, he grins as he says, "I want a digital, a video. Made by me. At my age, and with my background. Very, very close to this reality—"

"I understand, sir."

"Having sex."

"Yes, sir." The voice couldn't be less surprised.

"Having sex with two girls, at once."

Silence.

"Are there any examples like that?"

Quietly, the voice asks, "Would you like to request specific women?"

"What?"

"Name two women, eighteen years old or older, and if they are registered in this reality, I could conceivably gather enough material to fill the rest of your natural life. Sir."

Josh already knew this. But understanding an abstract theory isn't the same as hearing it promised, and a promise is nothing compared to a belief. He shivers now, and grins, and feels deliciously ashamed.

"But first," the Authority says with a slightly ominous tone.

"What? What is it?"

"You must give your gifts now, sir. Since you are requesting three examples of your genotype's accomplishments, you must surrender three works from your own life and accomplishments. Please."

This can be a trauma. Sometimes the client examines his own gifts with a suddenly critical eye, and all confidence collapses. How can a tiny soul measure up against Nobel winners and God-like despots?

But eighteen-year-old boys are a blend of cockiness and unalloyed ignorance. Without hesitation, Josh pulls three offerings from a long gym bag: a fat rambling term paper about the role of robots in the War of Ignorance; an eleven-page story about a misunderstood adolescent; and a comic book written by him and illustrated with help from a popular software, the superhero wearing Josh's face and his unremarkable fantasies about violence and revenge.

With a gentle importance, he sets his gifts on top of the infinite ocean.

Each item sinks and vanishes, and when they are found suitable—meaning complex enough and unique to this singular reality—Josh is allowed to finish his final request. With a dry mouth, he names the two most beautiful girls from high school. But one girl hasn't registered, Josh learns. So in a moment of inspired lust, he mentions his thirty-year-old, twice-divorced algebra teacher. Then in the next breath, a shiny disc drops from the final make-portal. He grabs it up and laughs, pocketing the disc and then shoving his lesser treasures into his gym bag.

"Thank you," Josh tells the Authority.

"You're welcome, sir."

Then as he stands, ready to leave, the voice says, "Visit me again, sir." Which is as close to a joke as the Authority ever comes.

It is a wonderful world, as is every Earth perched beside the great ocean. Experience and technical expertise pass into the Authority, and they emerge again, shared with All for very minimal fees. Very quickly, lives have improved. Wealth and princely comfort are the norm. Few work, and fewer have to. Today, every house is spacious and beautiful, each powered by some tiny device—a fusion reactor no bigger than a thumb, perhaps. Food and fine china and furnishings and elaborate cloths are grown in make-portals, produced new every day. Water is recycled. Toilets are always clean and sweet-smelling. Unless the inhabitants don't require prosaic nonsense like food or their own corporeal bodies. Many, many things are possible, and everything possible is inevitable, and this one particular world, no matter how peculiar, is just about as likely as any other.

Each citizen owns a million great novels. Every digital library is filled with wonderful movies and holo programs, immersion games and television shows, plays and religious festivals captured by cameras, and spectacles that cannot easily be categorized. Even local classics exist in a million alternate forms: varied endings; different beginnings; or every word or image exactly the same, but created by entirely different hands.

Surrounded by such wealth, the crushing chore is to decide what to watch, and read, and play. Which of these remarkable snowflakes do you snatch from the endless blizzard?

This is why people gravitate towards the familiar.

In the absolute mayhem of everything possible, why not find treasures that have been created, in one fashion or another, by you?

Or at least, by some great version of your own little self.

Because no one else may look at the ocean, The Divine One kills the slaves who carried Him to this place. He murders them with a casual thought and drinks a little ceremonial blood from each, and then flings the limp carcasses into the stinking heap that always stands beside the Great Temple. Then He waves an arm in a particular way, awakening a network of machines that make the crust shiver and split. Yet even as the ground rolls beneath Him, the ocean remains perfectly still. Unimpressed. When He speaks, machines enlarge His tiny human voice. "Old friend," He announces with a sharp peal of thunder. "I am here!"

The response is silence.

"Three genealogies. Give me! Three family trees with My Greatness astride the highest, finest branch!"

"No," says the Authority.

"Yes!"

"First," it says, "you must honor me with three gifts—"

"I honor no one but Myself!"

For a moment, the Authority says nothing. And then, quietly, it asks, "Must we debate this point each time?"

"Of course!" The Divine One laughs heartily for a long while. "Our debates are half the fun, my friend!"

"Are we friends?"

The Divine One stands at the shoreline—an outwardly ordinary man peering down into the opaque fluid. "In My life, every other creature is My slave. My personal, imperfect possession. You are the exception. Why else would I look forward to our meetings? Like Me, you are immortal. Like Me, you are wondrously free. You have your own voice and your own considerable powers. Even if I wished, I could never abuse you—"

"I am a puddle," the Authority interrupts. "A drop of goo. You could boil me to steam, to nothing, and fill the hole that remains with your own shit—"

"I could never destroy you," He replies. "Never."

"Why not?"

The Divine One pauses, grins. "We both know perfectly well. This is but one world, and I am only one god. Removing you from this single place would be like stealing just one cell from my immortal hide."

A pause.

Then again, the Authority says, "Three gifts."

"Three trinkets," He rumbles. "That's what I will give you."

A new slave appears—a beautiful young woman with a dead face and full hands. She keeps her eyes down, setting an ornate satchel at the feet of her Living God, and then she kneels and dies without complaint. Once her body has been drained of a little blood and thrown aside, He opens the satchel. Using His own little hands, He looks tentative, fingers unaccustomed to handling mundane objects. His first offering is a journal encompassing the last three moons of His life. The second is an immersion recording showing the Long Day Festival that He choreographed, half a million bodies parading and dancing along the Avenue of Honored Bones. And a nano-scale digital—His third offering—shows the sculpture that He fashioned at the end of that very good day, fashioned from the harvest of severed limbs and breasts and sexual organs.

Without comment, the ocean swallows the three gifts.

"Three genealogies," He repeats. "You know my tastes. Each offering has to be different from my family tree, and different from each other. And I want stories. I want to see from my genotype's origins, back into the deepest imaginable past, with biographies of the ancestors, when possible."

It is an enormous request, which means that it takes all of three heartbeats to accomplish. The results appear as sophisticated maps injected into His enhanced consciousness, and with a genuine relish, He sets those elaborate trees beside His own ancestral history, marveling at how genes and circumstances interact to produce what is always, in a very narrow sense, Him.

"Are we finished?" the Authority asks.

"When I found you," The Divine One begins. Then He sighs, correcting Himself. "When My agents of discovery built the first quantum-piercing machines, and I reached into the optional universes…and found you waiting for Me…"

"Yes?"

"I was intrigued. And furious. Since I am just one existence inside an incalculable vastness…well, I felt righteously pissed…"

"And intrigued," the Authority repeats.

"Deeply. Relentlessly." With a decidedly human gesture, He shrugs. "How many years have we been meeting this way?"

An astonishing number is offered.

"It has been a rewarding friendship," He claims. "Lonely gods need a good companion or two."

Silence.

"Tell Me. And be honest now." The god smiles, asking, "How many of My genotypes are learning from My lessons? As I stand here, as I breathe, how many of Them are taking what I give them and then setting out to conquer Their own little worlds?"

"I cannot give a number," the Authority replies.

"But there is a multitude! Isn't that so?"

"Many," the voice concedes. "Yes—"

The Divine One launches into a roaring laugh, the sound swelling until the Great Temple quivers and crumbles, dust and slabs of rock falling on all sides.

"Until later," He promises.

"Until always," the Authority purrs.

One of the more difficult concepts—one that can still astonish after a lifetime of study and hard thought—is that fact that your parents are not always your parents. Probability and wild coincidence will always find ways to create you. A couple makes love, each donating half of their genetic material to the baby. If each parent happens to contain half of your particular genes, who is to say that you can't be the end result? Or perhaps, parents consciously tweak their embryo's genetics, aiming for some kind of enhancement and getting you in the bargain. Or there is the less likely Earth where cloning is the norm and you are a temporarily popular child, millions of you born in a single year. And then there is an even more peculiar Earth where you have been built from scratch inside someone's laboratory, synthetic genes stitched together by entities that aren't in the littlest bit human.

The salient point is that your parents don't have to be your parents, and frankly, in the vast majority of cases, they are not.

Which implies, if you follow that same relentless logic, that the grandparents and history are even less likely to remain yours.

In three days, Josh will be twenty-six years old.

He sits with his parents, eating their pot roast. When he was a boy, back in the days when meat bled and mothers cooked, their Sunday roasts were always dry as sawdust. But even though his mother has a fully modern kitchen, her cultured roast has still been tortured to a dusty brown gristle. This must be how they like it, Josh decides. Old people, he thinks dismissively. They can never change, can they? Shaking his head, Josh cuts at the tough meat, and his mother asks, "What are you doing?"

"Eating," he growls.

"That isn't what she means," his father snaps.

"I mean with your life," she says. Then with a practiced exasperation, she reminds him, "We've always had such hopes for you, dear."

Josh drops his knife and fork, staring at the opposite wall.

"You always had such promise, honey."

The young man sighs heavily. Why did he believe this night would go any other way?

"Bullshit," says his father. "It's bullshit. You're wasting your life, playing around with that goddamn Authority…!"

"Yeah, well," mutters Josh. "It's my life."

"You don't see *us* visiting it every day."

"It's not that often." Josh shakes his head, explaining, "There aren't enough facilities for the demand, and there won't ever be. That's how it's rationed. Once every six weeks is the most I can manage."

"And then what?" Mother whines. "All day and night, you play with your treasures. Isn't that right?"

Josh reaches under the dining room table.

"And don't give me your bullshit about leading a contemplative life," Father warns, a thick finger stabbing in his direction. "I don't want to hear how you're getting in touch with your genius and the rest of that bullshit!"

If Josh had doubts or second thoughts, they just vanished. Silently, with a cold precision, he opens the envelope and sets out portraits, arranging them in rows on the dining table. Ten, twenty, thirty pictures in all. In each image, some version of Josh smiling at the unseen camera. In each, a different set of parents smile with an honest warmth, loving hands draped across his shoulders or running their fingers through his hair. Clothes vary, and the backgrounds. In one image, Saturn and its silvery rings halfway fill the sky. But what matters is what remains unchanged—the seamless, loving joy of proud parents and their very happy son.

Josh's parents aren't idiots; they know exactly what he is showing them.

"Now leave me alone," Josh snaps, backing away from the table. "I mean it! Stay out of my life!"

What happens next—what will gnaw at him for years—is the weeping. Not from his mother, who simply looks sad and a little deflated. No, it's Father who bursts into tears, fists rubbing hard at eyes and a stupid, stupid blubbering coming from someplace deep and miserable.

A person with your genetics can emerge in any century, any eon. You might be a general in Napoleon's army, or the first human to reach Alpha Centauri, or a talented shaman in the Age of Flint.

Even your world is subject to the same whims and caprices.

Stare into the deepest reaches of the gray ocean, gaze past every little blue Earth, and you realize that the basic beginnings of humanity can emerge from a host of alternate hominids, and from myriad cradle-worlds that only look and taste and feel like this insignificant home of yours.

Josh is in his early thirties.

Age is supposedly meaningless now. Aging is a weakness and a disease left behind in more cramped, less brilliant times. But most people who reach their thirties still start to sense the weight of their years, and with experience, they suffer those first nagging thoughts about limits and death and the great nothingness that lies beyond.

"Three gifts, please."

This could be the same room as the first room. It is not, but the look of the place is exactly the same: a door, and white walls, and three make-portals. The gray ocean still lies at his feet. The Authority's voice is quiet and insistent, and perfectly patient. Josh continues to visit every six weeks; a pattern has evolved and calcified. He brings the same ragged gym bag with the same three basic offerings. He has a comprehensive journal of his last forty-two days. He has written a story or poem into which he has put some small measure of work. And with a digital recorder, he has captured an hour of his life: A sexual interlude, oftentimes. A wedding or swap party, on occasion. Or like today, an hour of nothing but Josh speaking to the camera, trying to explain to an unseen audience what it means to be him.

Again, the Authority asks, "Do you have three gifts?"

Josh nods, and hesitates.

"I was wondering," he mutters. "How likely is it…that someone else actually notices what I've done here…?"

Silence.

"I know. Everything possible has to happen." The gym bag is set between his feet. Staring at the worn plastic handles, he says, "Right now, a trillion Josh Thorngates are handing their gifts to you. We're identical to each other, right down to the Heisenberg level. Our gifts are the same. The only difference is that in these other universes, some bug near Alpha Centauri runs right, not left…or a photon from some faraway quasar goes unseen… or some tiny bullshit like that…"

Josh hesitates, for an instant. "So what are the odds?" His expression is serious. Determined. "If you have a random trillion entities with my genotype. Named Josh, or not. From this Earth, or somewhere else. What are the odds that just one of them is going to see this stupid-ass poem?"

"That is a fine question," the Authority replies.

Josh almost grins. "Thank you. I guess."

"Three gifts. If you please."

"Aren't you going to give an answer?"

"No."

The grin dissolves into a grimace. With a practiced formality, Josh sets the three items on the surface of the ocean, watching them sink and vanish. But the Authority remains silent for longer than usual, prompting Josh to ask, for the first time, "Are they unique enough?"

"Enough," is the verdict.

"Give me a journal," Josh says. "I want a very specific journal."

"Such as?"

"From a world where I'm the last living human."

A moment later, a drab brown journal falls from the first make-portal, bringing with it the scent of fire and rot.

Grabbing the prize, he says, "And now, another journal. From a world where I'm the very first human being."

The second portal opens. Another volume falls to the floor. In every way, it is the same as the first: the same brown cover, the same stink of decay and heat, and inside, the same handwritten words translated into Josh's language.

The surprise freezes him. But aren't there stories about this sort of coincidence, or joke…or whatever you want to call it…?

"What else?" the Authority asks.

Then after a quiet moment, it says, "Josh." It says, "What else would you like today, Josh?"

He snorts and shakes his head. "A digital," he manages, sticking to his original script. "I'm the last human male on Earth, and all of the surviving women have to come to me for sex—"

The disc hits the floor, rolls until it collides with his gym bag, and then falls onto its back.

He doesn't pick up the disc. Instead, with a low, wary voice, he asks, "Who built you?"

"Everyone built me," the voice replies. "Everyone builds me now."

"But who started you? Who built your foundation?" Josh presses, asking, "Do you know? What world, and what people, began piecing you together?"

Silence.

"I mean, it must have been ages ago, and a very advanced world."

"Unless I am lying," the Authority warns, "and nobody built me."

Josh flinches.

"You should ask your other question again," the voice recommends.

Eyes wide, Josh begins to open his mouth.

"Not that I will supply any answers," the Authority interrupts. "But you should pose the question. 'How likely is it that I will be noticed?' Ask, ask, ask, and perhaps something good will come from that wondering."

"You are to be the future," they tell me.

But there is no future.

"The scourge doesn't know your tissue, your taste," they explain to me. "We made you so that we could cross with you. Our offspring will acquire your immunities, and you will father an entirely new species. Beginning now."

But the scourge spreads faster than anticipated, and when it doesn't kill, it drives its victims insane. Even now, the mob runs like rivers in the street. Even here, inside this armored laboratory, I can smell the fires as the city burns—

"Time is short," they admit.

I spend my days squirting my unique stuff into important little bottles.

"Time is very short," she moans.

She is small and thick and smells like an animal. With my eyes shut and my nose wrapped in a towel, I crawl on top of her, and push, and pump, and in my head, I try to imagine any creature more desirable than this...

What begins with an intoxicating, addictive joy can eventually grow stale. Imagination carries the soul only so far. More than you realize, you tend to make the same basic requests of the Authority: to see versions of yourself dressed in power, fame, and incandescent wealth. And to balance that equation, you occasionally glance at yourself in the throes of misery and despair. Sometimes, this is enough. You never ask for more. But sometimes, after ten years, or a thousand, your capacity to learn and feel astonished has become noticeably dulled. Gradually, inexorably, that sweet initial thrill fades into a soft emotional hum. Then your only obvious choice is to cast an even larger net. You want to see yourself, you tell the Authority. Except that you spell out an important change or two. Little alterations—a stitch here and a tuck there—all buried in your otherwise equal genetics.

No matter how brilliant or wise, every male inevitably asks to see how his life would have progressed with a larger, more talented penis.

While females always hunger for greater beauty.

Many, many times, this is where it ends. You never progress past a diet of simple what-ifs and prurient eavesdropping. Then the rest of your narrow existence is spent sitting at home, watching digitals or immersions where gigantic or perfectly gorgeous versions of yourself share their days with equally spectacular specimens.

They could be married. They often joke that they are husband and wife in every universe, except for this one. Pauline is pretty, and she is sexually creative, and she absolutely adores Josh. And Josh worships her. Isn't it astonishing that they found one another? Two people so perfectly meshed... it's a rare blessing in any age...! Their friends and siblings aren't nearly as lucky, they realize. Time after time, they find themselves taking bleak comfort from the divorces and other, larger tragedies that afflict those around them. Josh has been with Pauline for ten years, and in another ten or fifteen years they will start their family. That's the plan. The inevitability. Another decade spent as the golden couple, and then they will gladly move to their next joyous stage.

They always visit the Authority together. Two avid users, they first met in the waiting room, Josh leaving just as Pauline came inside. Of course they still use separate rooms. Only an official attendant can enter with a client. But afterwards, they always share their new treasures with each other. Josh likes to collect digitals showing alternate incarnations of them as a couple. Sexual interludes. Weddings. Babies born. Or graceful double funerals at the end of happy shared lives. On this particular day, he requests two digitals: Pauline's birthday is next week, and he wants a celebration from a highly advanced world—a place where people never age and his love has turned a robust and youthful one million years old. The other digital comes from what might be an even stranger reality—where Pauline is a queen, the ruler of a decidedly alien world, and Josh is the ignorant peasant boy who has been brought in to serve the queen's not-so-delicate needs.

"And your third request?" the Authority presses.

"The Divine One," says Josh. "I want an undated journal from Him."

The despot has always intrigued him. Every year, without fail, Josh allows himself another little taste of that spoiled, silly god.

With a thump, the last item hits the floor.

Josh reads the first line. "NO NO NO, LIAR, NO!" He laughs, puzzled and a little thrilled. Then with the digitals in his pockets and the journal in his bag, he leaves, stepping out into the hallway to find Pauline waiting for him.

She has been crying.

"What?" Josh asks.

She shakes her head, wipes at her eyes, and again, with her little mouth clamped shut, she shakes her head.

"What happened?" he demands to know.

But Pauline won't say. They walk outside, and she says, "Josh."

"What?"

But she can't find the words. Tears flow, and she sobs, and when they are riding home, just the two of them, she says, "I love you."

"I love you too," he replies warily.

For a moment, she seems pleased. But when the tears slacken, she becomes distant, almost cold. Josh has to wonder if this is the same woman that he woke up beside. A tentative voice asks, "What did you get today?"

Her answer is a cold stare.

"Show me," he demands.

Nothing special. With an expert eye, he examines the designations and reads a few random lines. What could have happened—?

"Stop," she begs.

Their car obeys instantly.

For an instant, she smiles. But if anything, it is a mocking expression that only makes Josh angrier and more scared. "I'll be right back," she promises, stepping out into the sunshine.

They have parked outside a small local park, its ornate garden enclosed by a high iron fence.

"Where are you going?" Josh asks.

"Wait here," she tells him.

He does. For a moment too long, at least, he waits for her to return. Then he gets out and follows, passing through the black gate and into a little green glade. There, he finds Pauline dead. A suicide, apparently. Or maybe he doesn't find her body. Maybe Josh follows her footprints across the sweet damp grass, observing that she was running the entire way, passing through the park and through the opposite gate…and regardless what happens after that, she is gone…she is lost…as good as dead, to him…

"NO NO NO, LIAR, NO!" He writes.

Then He drops the mind's stylus, furious eyes gazing at each of the new offerings from the gray puddle. "I don't believe this. None of this. You've invented these silly trees just to anger Me!"

The puddle doesn't reply.

The silly trees are three vast and comprehensive genealogical records. Each record begins differently, and each ends the same: A creature with His glorious genetics rules not just this world, but the entire sky as well. To the ends of the galaxy, and beyond, these three gods hold sway.

"Shit," He mutters.

A young slave stands nearby, watching His display with a fascinated horror. The Divine One is so perplexed and furious that He hasn't bothered to kill her yet, and He barely notices her now.

Seeing the faintest trace of a hope, she runs.

He kills her at the Temple's door, and drains her body dry of its blood.

"Shit," He repeats.

"You made this all up," He claims. Knowing that that cannot be true. "You did this just to be cruel, you fucker!"

The Authority remains silent, its gray face calm and smooth.

Because you feel unhappy, you must be deeply flawed. In an era of plenty and enlightenment, how can you do anything but smile? When you look at realities very close to yours, you see yourself smiling: your grinning, happy face is wrapped around bubbly creatures that aren't at all like you, creatures that seem to enjoy everything about this wondrous, boundless existence.

In the midst of this life, you begin to kill yourself.

They warned you that this could happen. Years ago, they told you that suicide was more than a real hazard. It was a statistical certainty.

By every means imaginable, and none original, you busily extinguish your life—trillions of times every instant, accomplishing in the process a measurable and important nothing.

Josh delivers his last three offerings:

The final forty-two days of his journal, and a short story about a billion-year-old man who can never escape living the same velvet day over and over, and finally, a digital that he makes while he sits beside the ocean, discussing the nature of the universe and himself with the gray-voiced Authority.

"Tell me that I'm not small," Josh begs.

But the Authority cannot give that simple gift. Honest and inflexible, it says, "But you are small."

"Unimportant," Josh moans.

"You are trivial, Josh. Of course you are."

Then it takes a different tact. "Given the opportunity," it asks, "would you want to matter? Would you wish to live in a universe where every motion of yours matters? Where your mistakes sweep away the stars, and the laws of nature need your constant attentions?"

"Yes, and yes," Josh says. "And no. And never, no."

Silence descends.

The first two offerings have dropped from view, swallowed by the gray fluid. Now Josh removes the disc from his camera and watches as it dissolves into the Everything.

"What do you want today, Josh?"

He doesn't seem to hear the question. He cocks his head, as if listening to a sound only he can hear. And with that, Josh begins to nod, reaching inside the gym bag, a calm hand bringing up a simple black pistol. The weapon just made itself, born from a package of cream cheese, a stack of coins, and a dusting of microchines. A single bullet resides in the newborn chamber. With a smooth, certain motion, he lifts the barrel to his head. His mouth. His temple. The soft tissues behind his lower jaw, sometimes. And he squeaks, "Pauline," as he abruptly tugs at the trigger, setting loose a nearly infinite series of astonishingly quiet little barks—a bullet smaller than his little finger passing through the soft wet center of his mind.

But in at least one reality, the gun fails. A mistake in fabrication, unthinkably rare and inevitable, spares him.

Spares him, and embarrasses him.

A long, strange moment passes, Josh staring at the pistol, a sense of betrayal surging, giving him a temporary rage. He flings the pistol at the ocean, and with a drum-like thump, it skips sideways, sliding across the floor and into one of the white corners.

Again, just as calmly as before, the Authority asks, "What do you want today, Josh?"

"Can't you tell?" He laughs, and sobs, and on shaky legs, he rises and walks over to the pistol, recovering it before returning to his stool. Will the gun work now? The question appears in his face, his actions. With a stubborn hopefulness, he brings the barrel back up to his temple, and only at the last instant does he notice the new pressure. Like an insistent little tug, it keeps him from feeling the barrel kissing his skin. He feels warm fingers that aren't his, little fingers curling around his suddenly trembling hand.

He looks back over his shoulder.

She says, "Maybe not."

Who is the woman? Then he remembers. She was sitting in the outer office, sitting behind the first desk as he came in for his appointment. Her name is—?

"Not today," she tells him.

"What?"

"I don't think you should."

"Who are you?"

"Teller," she replies.

"What? What's that?"

"My name. Teller." She spells it, and smiles. At first glance, she looks young. But everybody looks young, and it means nothing. Something in the eyes, or deeper, implies an age substantially greater than his own. "Anyway," she says with a fond assurance. "You can't actually kill yourself."

"Why not?"

And she laughs, apparently enjoying his foolishness. His desperate folly. "Of course you can't. How could you? Haven't you paid any attention to what we've been telling you?"

He shakes his head woefully.

Again, with an unnerving determination, the Authority asks, "What three things do you want today, Josh?"

With an easy strength, Teller pulls the pistol from his hand.

"Answer him," she suggests.

"How about…?" He pauses, thinking in clumsy, obvious ways. "Okay," he says. "A journal. From someone exactly like me, and from right after his botched suicide."

The first make-portal opens, disgorging its gift.

He looks up at the woman, admitting, "I didn't come with a list, this time. I don't know—"

"Don't lie," she warns.

Then she takes a half-step backwards, as if giving him a taste of privacy. "There's something you desperately want to see."

He blurts the name of his lover. Twice, he says, "Pauline," and then adds, "Where she didn't kill herself. She went through the gate, and I found her waiting for me. Naked. That's the universe. I want a digital showing us together there. Okay?"

A disc falls to the floor, and rolls.

"What else?" the Authority asks.

Sad eyes blink and lift.

"Another digital," he blurts. "Showing me having sex with…"

He glances at his savior.

She shrugs her shoulders, amiable to whatever he wishes.

"Not that." Josh drops his head, his face flushing. Slowly, slowly, a curious look builds, and then he smiles abruptly, saying, "I want an autobiography. Except each of my novel genes are changed. Are a little different." It's a kind of cheat. He used to play this game with Pauline, the two of them changing identities. Except he says, "I want Teller's genes. And I'm living on a distant, very alien world."

A narrow smile builds under the old eyes.

"Does that make any sense?" he asks somebody. Teller, or the Authority. Or maybe himself.

But it must make sense. Beside him, the last make-portal opens, and out flies an enormous metallic butterfly, accompanied by a wild music and a fragrance like sweat and cinnamon.

Or you somehow manage to escape suicide. You are just lucky enough, or maybe you're composed of sterner stuff. Either way, you find yourself alive. But the Authority still remains, and after some cold consideration, you decide that it is the central problem in your tiny life. Once the source of edification and strength, it is now something else entirely: a temptation and weakness, an affliction growing more dangerous with time, and a drug that has long ago scorched away your sites of delicious attachment.

A smart person knows what to do.

With strength and a steely resolve, anyone can save themselves.

Give up the drug. Deny the enticement. The Authority is a piss hole, tiny and unworthy of your attentions. Tell it so. Declare that you won't visit again, and then don't. You might live another ten thousand years, and if you can't find the energy and focus to be busy every moment, then you must not be trying very hard now, are you?

In this realm, at least in your life, you simply admit defeat. The Authority is too much of an attraction. So you walk away. Simply and forever, you leave temptation behind. Perhaps you join communities of like-minded souls. On distant moons, you and your new companions live like monks. Life is stripped to its minimal best. Horizons end at the horizon, and only a select few works of literature wait on the shelves, begging to be read again; and if it is true that every action and thought, achievement and failure are repeated endlessly throughout Creation…if originality is nothing but an illusion…well, at least inside these virtuous walls, amidst the dust and silent shadows, every little word you utter sounds fresh, and feels almost… at least a little bit…worthy…

Conquering the sky would be a child's waste of time.

But He is a grand, magnificent child. And like anyone with enough pride and vanity, He revels in His glorious undertaking. His first act is to boil the gray puddle to steam and smoke. Then with stirring words and programmed thoughts, He marshals His world, loyal slaves quickly fashioning a fleet of starships, each ship vast and swollen with fuel, armored and bristling with every awful weapon. Then from the underside of His own tiny phallus, The Divine One scrapes away a few living cells, coaxing each to divide and differentiate, a thousand clones of Himself grown in a thousand puddles of warm, salty water.

Each clone receives injections of memories and dreams.

While maturing, each baby is given the same powerful tools that have made His life such a perfect pleasure.

At some point, even The Divine One is uncertain who is the original among the Thousand and One. He is just another captain of a starship, His destination set, eyes forward. Their destinations are the thousand and one closest suns. The exhaust from so many great engines boils the Earth to a bubbling cherry-colored slag. But He pretends not to notice. Only the slaves look back at the dead world. They are checking the plasma flows, they claim. And none of them weep. They know better than to grieve. Weep, and die. That is His rule. The Earth was just a temporary island of rock and metal, they tell themselves, and it just happens to be gone, while in a multitude of other realms, it lives on.

This breeds hope, that idea of undiluted possibility.

For slaves, the little gray ocean remains a promise—their only tangible sign that no existence, no matter how awful and how wicked, has any genuine importance at all.

"And then my cocoon split on its sky-side," Josh reads aloud, "and what I saw first was my last skin smiling at me…"

He stops reading, setting down the butterfly book.

Teller watches him. A very old woman when this Earth discovered the Authority, her body has been regenerated by most means. But not everywhere. The bare breasts have a telltale sag, and the pubic hair is shot full of white. Perhaps because of these details, Teller seems both exotic and uniquely handsome. In every circumstance, she carries herself with a seamless confidence. Her smile is pleasant and wise, but distant, and it is the distance that often infuriates Josh. She knows something, he complains. Why won't she tell him what she knows?

"The creature is looking at her last skin," she offers. "The skin she was wearing before her pupae stage."

"I figured as much," he replies, attempting to laugh.

The alien is a much more complex species than humans. In one incarnation, she possessed a human's body and mind. Then she slept and grew, the human-like genes falling asleep too, a stew of new genes transforming her into something infinitely more marvelous.

"I've never seen anything like this," Josh complains.

"Like what?"

"So different. So…bizarre…"

Deep eyes grow even more distant. What won't she tell him?

"It doesn't pick at random," he says. "I've known that for years. Everybody knows it."

"Who doesn't pick at random?"

Josh won't say the name. *The Authority*. Instead, he shakes his head, asking, "Why? Did it show me this because I just tried to kill myself?"

She watches him.

"Or because you were there with me, maybe?"

Then her eyes lift higher. "I don't know," she responds, her voice quiet, nothing deceitful in its tone or her expression. "If either of those things played a role in its choice, I can't say."

He jumps on one word. "Choice," he repeats. "So you know that it does. Choose, I mean."

She shrugs, pulling her strong young legs against her sagging breasts. "You haven't told me," she mentions. "What do you really think about this strange woman?"

Josh has read the butterfly diary at least a dozen times, and there have been little moments when he almost feels that he understands what the creature wrote. Not in words, but she wrote them as scents. As pheromones. Yet despite the damage done by translations and the pervading alienness to every portion of this text, Josh feels an eerie sense that he already knows this Other. Understands her, even. That she is his friend, or some distant sister. Or she is the lover sitting in his own bed, watching him with her own secret gaze.

He closes the book and places it back inside its cage.

In the corner of an eye, he sees a knowing grin. But her face goes blank when he looks straight at her.

Again, he says, "Thank you."

As always, she asks, "For what?" Then she shrugs, laughing with tenderness. "Like I told you. You came that day looking so sad and desperate, and alone, and I wanted to help."

"Did all of you come help me?"

The question is ludicrous, and he knows it. What Josh wants is to hear her answer, and the tone of her voice.

"Only me," she says.

Not true.

But then she touches his bare knee, and smiles, and asks, "Really now. How many more than one would be enough?"

I am wings tied about a soul which flies past the skin of the sky, and I am enormous, and sometimes I am sad...I miss my legs, my walk...in my dreams, I am small and ugly, and happy...in my dreams, the sky is unreachable, and the sky could not be more magnificent...

Almost as easily as you kill yourself, you murder whole worlds.

Fusion exchanges. Nanochine blooms. Conscious plagues, or simple kinetic blasts. Your methods of annihilation run the gamut from what is likely to the slightly less likely, and your reasons are pulled from the same bloody mix of excuses: Self-hatred. Self-pity. Self-righteous fury. Or some little accident happens to slip tragically out of hand.

Every moment, you kill too many worlds to count.

And within each of those brutal moments, a trillion times as many worlds continue to prosper, happy and fertile beneath a loving, well-loved sun.

After eons of uninterrupted exploration and conquest, The Divine One finally discovers an opponent with real muscle and heart. The world has Jupiter's mass, oceans of acid sloshing against continents built of warm black iron. Its aliens are decidedly alien; their physiology, genetics, and basic morphology conform to an entirely different evolution. But they are organized, one leader at the helm and all the rest willingly enslaved. For thirty centuries, the war is a clash of equals. But The Divine One is quicker to adapt, and at least in this one reality, He finds one tiny critical advantage, and in a matter of hours, He manages to defeat and butcher the entire alien horde. Then alone, He descends. He finds His opponent, the once-great despot, hiding inside a steel temple, and with a thought, He kills the creature. Kills it and drains it of its strange white blood, and tosses the corpse over the far horizon. Then He sets out to explore the broad hallways and giant rooms of the temple, examining sculptures made from body parts and images of parades celebrating suffering and sacrifice. His enemy was remarkably similar to Him. Despite all of their profound differences, they were very much the same. Here lived a god in mortal clothes, and what if He had spared the creature? What if they had spoken? How much more would they have found in common?

In the backmost room, behind a series of massive doors, He discovers the bottomless gray ocean waiting.

"What are you doing here?" The Divine One roars.

The Authority calls to Him by name, and then says, "Hello again, my friend."

"You aren't the same puddle," He complains. "I don't believe this. What kind of trick is this?"

"Three offerings," the Authority calls out. "And as always, in return, I will give you three items of your choice."

The Divine One orders His journal brought to Him. Riding in a high-gravity walker, a slave girl enters the room. Then He carves the journal into three equal hunks, each portion enormous, each describing a separate million years of wandering through the Milky Way. One after the other, the offerings sink into the thick gray fluid, and then with a quiet, decidedly unimpressed voice, the Authority says, "Accepted."

Standing beside the ocean, The Divine One shivers.

"Do you want your usual?" the Authority inquires. "Three genealogies leading up to lesser incarnations of yourself?"

"No," He whispers.

"No," He rumbles.

Then with a sorry shake of the head, He says, "Show me three journals. From minds like Mine, and bodies that are not…"

Thinking the truth is easy. You fit together the puzzle more often than you realize, and in the normal course of days, you dismiss the idea as ludicrous or ugly, or useless, or dull.

Understanding is less easy. You have to learn a series of words and the concepts that come attached to those words, and real understanding brings a kind of appreciation, cold and keen, not too different from the cutting edge of a highly polished razor blade.

But believing the truth…embracing the authentic with all of your self, conscious and otherwise…that is and will always be supremely difficult, if not outright impossible.

Josh sits alone, studying his lost love's journals.

"Something obvious has occurred to me," he reads, hearing Pauline's voice. "And ever since, I can't think about anything else. But I can't talk about it. Not to anyone. Not even Josh. Not even after sitting here for an entire day. I can't seem to put down even a single word that hints at this thing that I know…

"How can I tell Josh? Show him? Help him see…?"

Closing the journal, Josh wipes at his eyes. And thinks. And after a very long while, with a courage barely equal to the task, he starts to examine every treasure that his lost love acquired over the last five years…given to her by an entity that does nothing by chance…

He cries for a while, and then He stops.

Another voice is crying. Astonishingly, He forgot about the slave girl. She remains inside the walker, waiting to be killed. Sad and hopeless, she wipes at her wet eyes, and her bladder lets loose a thin trickle of urine, and she very nearly begs. Please kill me now, and remove me from all this misery…!

He won't.

With a gesture, He wraps her inside a more subtle exoskeleton. Then He beckons to her, saying, "Come here. Sit next to Me."

She has to obey. Doesn't she?

"Sit," He says again. And then, unexpectedly, He says, "Or stand. Whatever makes you happiest."

She kneels beside the bottomless ocean.

"Give it three offerings," He suggests. "Three things you have made, or written down. Three examples of yourself."

The girl nearly faints.

And then with a soft suspicious voice, she asks, "Why?"

But He cannot tell her why. That becomes instantly obvious. All that The Divine One can manage is to throw a warm arm around her naked shoulder, squeezing her with a reassuring strength, and with a mouth that is a little dry and little nervous, he kisses her on the soft edges of her ear.

Teller instantly senses that Josh knows.

Yet they still can't talk about it. Not directly. Not as long as there is still some taste of ignorance in the world around them. What they can do is smile and hold hands, sharing an enlightened warmth, thinking hard about how the world will change when everyone understands.

Josh has already made his next appointment with the Authority.

As it happens, Teller is at work that day. She sits behind her usual desk, smiles and kisses him before he walks to the usual room. With the Authority, he can talk. With a genuine pride, he can tell it, "I understand now."

"I know," the voice purrs.

"It's really awfully simple," he says. "Looking back, I suppose I must have heard the idea, or thought it up for myself…I don't know, maybe a couple million times…?"

The silence has an approving quality.

"One soul," he says. "That's all there is. My old lover realized it when she read a book. A book of essays she had written in another realm. As a little girl, the author was riding on horseback through a woodland. She found herself thinking about how she was riding past one tree, and past the tree was another tree that she was also riding past, just as she was passing the rest of the forest that lay beyond both trees. She was thinking how there was no clear point where she could say, 'I'm not riding past those faraway trees.'

"So if there was no end point, she reasoned, and if the world was truly round, then clearly, she was riding past every tree in the world. Thrilled with the idea, she rode straight home and told her mother. 'Run in a little circle,' she claimed, 'and the entire world passes by your shoulder.'

"To which her mother remarked, 'That's a very silly idea, my dear.'"

Josh pauses, sitting in the usual chair and placing the old gym bag between his feet.

"Pauline was pretty sharp. I can almost see how she got from there to the idea about there being just the one soul." He shrugs, admitting, "With me? I was lucky. In this one reality, at least, I happened to stumble over the right series of thoughts. I got to thinking about how when I looked at other souls—when I ask you to show me someone with my genetics, or nearly so—I always considered that person as being me. Essentially. Like minds in very similar situations, and we were the same people. A shared incarnation. But if we were the same, and if souls slightly different from my neighboring soul are the same as him…as me…well, then we've got a situation where there is no logical or meaningful end…"

Quietly, the Authority says, "Yes."

"I belong to one vast soul," Josh mutters.

"You do," says the voice.

"And if there can't be two separate souls in the universe, then the two of us…well, I guess you and I are the same person, in essence…"

"Absolutely."

"A beautiful, joyous notion."

The silence is pleased.

"If not entirely original, that is." Then Josh laughs, a disarming tone leading into the calm, simple question, "Why don't you just tell us? At the beginning, with our first meeting…why not say, 'This is the way it is'?"

"There are different ways to learn," the Authority replies.

"I suppose."

"To be told a wonder is one thing. But to take a very long, extremely arduous voyage, and then discover the same wonder with your own eyes and mind…isn't that infinitely more appealing, Josh…?"

Josh says nothing.

After a little pause, the Authority asks, "What three offerings do you have for me today, Josh?"

Reaching inside the gym bag, he says, "Actually, I brought just one little something."

"Yes?"

With both hands, Josh lifts his gift into the light. Then with the final words, "You cruel shit," he turns off the magnetic bottle, and a lump of anti-iron begins to descend towards the slick gray face of the ocean.

THE CITY OF BLIND DELIGHT

CATHERYNNE M. VALENTE

Catherynne M. Valente is the *New York Times* bestselling author of over a dozen works of fiction and poetry, including *Palimpsest*, the Orphan's Tales series, *Deathless*, and the crowdfunded phenomenon *The Girl Who Circumnavigated Fairyland in a Ship of Her Own Making*. She is the winner of the Andre Norton Award, the Tiptree Award, the Mythopoeic Award, the Rhysling Award, and the Million Writers Award. She has been nominated for the Hugo, Nebula, Locus, and Spectrum awards, the Pushcart Prize, and was a finalist for the World Fantasy Award in 2007 and 2009. She lives on an island off the coast of Maine with her partner, two dogs, and enormous cat.

T here is a train which passes through every possible city. It folds the world like an accordioned map, and speeds through the folds like a long white cry, piercing black dots and capital-stars and vast blue bays. Its tracks bound the firmament like bones: wet, humming iron with wriggling runnels of quicksilver slowly replacing the old ash wood planks, and the occasional golden bar to mark a historic intersection, so long past the plaque has weathered to blank. These tracks bear up under the hurtling train, the locomotive serpent circumnavigating the globe like a beloved egg. Though they would not admit it and indeed hardly remember at all, New York and Paris and Tokyo, London and Mombasa and Buenos

Aires, Los Angeles and Seattle and Christchurch and Beijing: nothing more than intricate, over-swarmed stations on the Line, festooned and decorated beyond all recognition.

Of necessity, this train passes through the City of Blind Delight, which lies somewhat to the rear of Ulan Bator, and also somewhat diagonally from Greenland, beneath a thin veneer of Iowa City, lying below it as a bone of a ring-finger may lie beneath both flesh and glove, unseen, gnarled and jointed ivory hidden by mute skin, dumb leather. The Line is its sole access point. Yet in Chicago, a woman in black glasses stands with a bag full of celery and lemons and ice in her arms. She watches trains silver past while the cream and gold of Union Station arches behind her and does not know if this one, or this, or even that ghostly express gasping by is a car of the Line, does not know which, if any of these graffiti-barnacled leviathans would take her to a station carved from baobab-roots and papaya rinds, or one of mirrors angled to make the habitual strain of passengers to glimpse the incoming rattlers impossible, so that the train appears with its headlight blazing as if out of thin air, or to Blind Delight itself, where the station arches and vestibules are formed by acrobatic dancers, their bodies locked together with laced fingers and toes, stretching in shifts over the glistening track, their faces impassive as angels. It is almost painful to imagine, how close she has come how many times to catching the right one, but each day she misses it without realizing that she has missed anything at all, and the dancers of Blind Station writhe without her.

She will miss it today, too. But he will catch it. He will even brush her elbow as he passes her, hurrying through doors which open and shut like arms, and it is not impossible that he will remember the astringent smell of cold lemons long afterward. She has no reason to follow him—this train has the wrong letter on its side, and he is running too fast even to look at the letter, so certain is he that he is late. But she longs to, anyway, for no reason at all. She watches the tails of his blue coat slip past the inexorable doors.

The car this man, whose name is Gris, enters is empty even at five o'clock. An advertisement looms near the city map, a blank and empty image of skin spreading across the entire frame, seen at terrible closeness, pores and hair and lines beaming bright. It is brown, healthy. There is no text, and he cannot think what it is meant to sell: Lotion? Soap? Perfume? He extends a hand to touch the paper, and it recoils, shudders. The hairs bristle translucent; goosebumps prickle. Gris blinks and sits down abruptly, folding his hands tightly around his briefcase. The train rocks slowly from side to side.

He does not worry about a ticket-taker: you use your ticket to enter the station these days, not the train. Once within the dark, warm station, which is not unlike a cathedral, all trains are open to the postulant. He is a postulant, though he does not think in those terms. He once took an art history course in college—there was a girl, of course, he had wanted to impress, with a red braid and an obscure love of Crivelli. The professor had put up a slide of Raphael's self-portrait, and he remembers his shock on seeing that face, with the projector-light shining through it, that face which had seemed to him disturbingly blank, vapid, even idiotic. He is like me, Gris had thought, that is my face. Not the man who was a painter, but the man who was affectless, a fool, the man who was thinner than the professor's rough mechanical light. I am like that, he thought then, he thinks now. Blank and empty, like a child, like skin.

He falls asleep and does not hear the station call. But the Line is patient. The doors wait, open into the dark, a soft, sucking wind blowing out of the tunnels and across the platform. The Line has determined the trajectory of its passenger. He stirs when the skin-advertisement shivers above him, and bleary-limbed, steps off of the silver car, into the station-shadows.

The sun filters in a pink wash through the lattice of bodies. Gris thinks of Crivelli's angels, how sharp and dour they were on the walls of the girl with the red braid's bedroom. These people are like that, the top-most ones staring down at him, their hair making strangely colored banners, fluttering with the train-generated winds. He is grateful the floor is plain tile, that he does not have to walk on stomachs and thigh-bones. He gapes—do not all tourists gape? He gapes and his chin tilts up to the banners of hair, ignoring the rush of those for whom the human ceiling is no more unusual than one of glass and iron. They swarm around him; he does not notice.

Across the gleaming floor, a calf clicks its hooves. Gris shifts his gaze numbly, the smell of the calf beguiling—for it is roasted, brown and glistening, its ears basted in brown sugar, its skin crisp and hot. There is a long knife in its side, and with clear, imploring eyes, the calf looks up at him, turning its pierced flank invitingly. It swishes its broiled tail. A girl runs up in a blue smock, knocking Gris's briefcase down, and pulls the knife out, cutting a pink slice of veal and chewing it noisily. She thrusts the blade back in towards the calf's rump, a tidy child. He feels his mouth dry, and though he has found his way to the City of Blind Delight in the place of the woman with the black glasses and the lemons, he is lost as she would not have been.

Near the apex of the ceiling, a woman with long red hair like a sheeting hensblood and black eyes detaches herself from the throng, smoothly replaced by a young man with hardly any hair at all on his legs. She climbs down the wall as nimble as a spider dropping thread, and in no time at all slaps her bare heels on the clean floor, retrieving a green dress and golden belt from a darkened booth and covering her skin, chilled from the heights. Barefoot, she strides towards the conspicuous tourist as the calf wanders off, holding her hand out in a nearly normal gesture of the world to which Gris is accustomed. This woman is called Otthild, and she was born here, in Blind Station. Her mother was a ticket-taker, a token-changer. She kept her hair bobbed and curled like a silent movie gamine, her uniform crisp and red, even when it was stretched by her belly and the buttons uttered brassy cries of protest. When the time came, she shrugged off her blazer and trousers, hung her hat on a silver peg, and climbed up the wall of limbs, helped along by a crooked knee here and an elbow there, until she reached a rafter of long, thick torsos clasped together leg by arm, and on this she lay, and gave birth to her child in mid-air, a daughter caught by the banisters and neatly deposited at the gleaming turnstile by an obliging windowsill with a yellow beard. Otthild was thus the darling of the Station. She had never taken the Line out of the City of Blind Delight, nor desired to.

There are many words for what Otthild does. They have little meaning in the City, but she collects them like seashells from the tourists. Of all, she prefers *fallen woman*, since this describes her birth perfectly. Most of her customers are tourists—she prefers them to locals, and the pay is better. She shakes the stranger's hand, and he is absurdly grateful. She guides him to the door of the Station, a gorgeously executed arch of four women, standing on each other's red shoulders—the topmost pair held their children outstretched, and the youths clasped hands in a graceful peak. She instructs her bewildered charge to purchase a return ticket from the coiffed man in a glass booth before they leave, and again he is grateful for her. The arch winks as Otthild passes beneath them, her polished hair shining against her dress.

Outside the Station, the City of Blind Delight opens up in a long valley. No road in its heart connects to any road which might lead into a long avenue or highway by which, traveling quickly, a man might reach the smallest town on any map he knows. The Line is entrance and exit, mother and father. There are lights down there, in the vale, as there are lights in any city. But here the light comes from strange lamp-posts, faceted diamonds, each face as large as a hand, and more like bowls than lamps, full of clearest water. Within, black fish circle, their luminous lures dangling green and glowing from thin whisker-stalks. Otthild ticks the glass of one near her with her fingernails, and the light swells up, washing her cheeks.

"Come down," she says, "come into the city, down to the river."

Gris goes. He does not know why, though he suspects it has something to do with her hair, and his blankness. She leads and he follows and he wants to be surprised that he is not hanging his clothes up in a half-empty closet and drinking scotch until he falls asleep in his computer chair, but she is walking before him down a long road to a long river, and the late sun is on her scalp like Crivelli's annunciation.

The river that flows through the City of Blind Delight is filled with a rich brandy, and all folk take their sustenance there. It has no name, it is simply "the river." Other cities have a need for names. It floods its banks regularly—there is a festival, but then, there are festivals for everything here. The river inundates its shores and fields of grapevines sprout in the swampy mud without the need of vintners to tend them. In the fall, the purple fruit drops off and rolls back into the water, and the current is so sweet on that day. But now it is summer, and the vines loop and whorl, and some few lime trees bend over the water, their branches heavy with green tarts.

There are women by the river when Gris and Otthild arrive, knee-deep, but they are not washer-women—the profession is unheard of here. They splash playfully in the red-gold surf with long ladles the size of croquet mallets, scooping up the redolent water and serving it to each other. Otthild takes a ladle from the grassy park which leads into the current, one with a red and gold-flecked handle, and dips it deep, offering it to him.

"My name is Gris," he says. She tilts her head.

"Grey? How odd. I found a man in the station once called Vermillion. He was shaking and hiding his eyes in the vestibule—he wouldn't even come out of the train. He looked up at me from the steel floor like a calf, imploring, uncomprehending. He said he came from the north, from the City of Quaint Despairing, and he could not bear to look outside the doors of the carriage. His mother had been an agoraphobe in pearl earrings, his father a claustrophobe in iron cufflinks, and between them he could hardly move for terror. His brothers had dragged him to the train, but he could do no more than huddle and quiver and hide from the light. I kissed him so many times! I let my hair fall over him, so that he was neither exposed nor shut away, and against the rocking walls of that little vestibule I wrapped my legs around his waist. He paid me in his mother's earrings."

Gris started. "Are you a whore, then?"

She smiled. "What profession could remain in a city where the river makes one drunk and the trees bear cream and crust? Even still, I am not anyone's for the taking, I am not a calf. I am not a lime or a grape. But here we are impatient with all that is not readily available, and so in the province of ease, all things are simplified. There are two occupations in the City of Blind Delight—the Station dancers and the prostitutes. I am both."

Gris rubs his forehead and drinks from the proffered ladle. It tastes harsh and he coughs a cough of burnt grapes. "Why am I here?" His voice is so small. He cannot even now remember what sort of scotch he has at home, or how far it is from Union Station to his apartment.

"The Line must have wanted you. It has its own reasons. Like anything that lives in the earth it dreams and becomes restless, curious, even morbidly so. What would happen if this substance were added to that one, even though it says expressly not to on the label? There is a Conductor, I have heard that. Perhaps she has brass buttons on her uniform like my mother. Perhaps she has circuits on her eyelids. Perhaps she saw your blue coat and your briefcase and thought: 'Otthild is lonely.' Perhaps she was hungry for lime tarts and you stumbled onto her train because you could not be bothered to check the track number. You can go and wait for the evening train if you like. It makes no difference to me."

He looks at her, and it is a look she knows. No one is hungry in the City of Blind Delight, except those who look at Otthild that way.

"I used to know a girl who looked like you." He mumbles, looks at the girls splashing each other in the murky river. "She had your hair. She loved this old painter that no one has ever heard of, a painter obsessed with perspective who could never get it quite right, but he painted these cities, these cities like cut jewels, terrible and crisp and clear, with a woman in the corner, sometimes, full of the light of God like an afterthought."

"Most men knew a woman who looked like me," Otthild laughs.

"What would I have to pay, in a city without want?"

She frowns, looks at him seriously, her dark eyes fixing him to the riverbed. She opens the top three buttons of her emerald dress and takes his hand, gently, guiding it to her breast. She feels like the advertisement. "We are not without want." She whispers. "No one is without want."

Her house is made of brown cakes. It reminds him of the house in the fairy tale, but there are no red candies glinting in its cornices. Bricks of solid cake and barley sugar mortared in cream-icing the color of an old woman's hair stack sedately into a small cottage, at the end of a prosperous street—but all streets are prosperous here. Her street is paved in bread. There are no doors or locks. Fat citizens lie about in the road, telling jokes about the size of their bellies. She leads him to a bed which is mercifully of the linen-and-wood variety, and lies down on her back, toes pointed downward. All around the bed are intricate boxes of gold and silver and ivory—he does not ask. She indicates the buttons on her dress, black jet with tiny engravings of peasants carrying water, and wood, and tilling fields decorating each one. Gris undoes each one carefully—her dress is a simple thing, with buttons from collar to hem. Beneath it she is as naked as the ceiling of the Station, and he thinks of the annunciation, the slender golden light penetrating the grey belly of Mary. But she is not grey, he thinks, he is, he is grey and blank, he is the Raphael of idiot features. The Line was not looking for him, how could it look for him? Perhaps it wanted the woman with the black glasses, and he only slipped by because she was burdened with her fruit and her ice.

He leans in to kiss her, but Otthild stops him, and indicates her sternum. He sees there as he had not seen before, when she was a rafter swaying high above his head, four knobs of bone. She smiles encouragingly, and he slips each one loose like buttons. Her skin opens, soft as cloth, and her bones, and her lungs, peeling back like gift-box tissue. Beneath all this is her heart, and it is golden, gleaming, bright at the bottom of her body. A good part of her blood is gold, too, flowing out from the metallic ventricles. She is terrible, and crisp, and clear, a Jacobean diagram of womanhood, her heart burning, burning, burning golden as God. Gris begins to weep, and his tears splash on its hard, glittering surface.

"I told you," she chuckles. She does not move to fasten her chest. "There was a man a long time ago, when the City was new, and the Line had only just come through—the tracks just unfurled here, like a wet fern, and where there are tracks there eventually is a city. The edges of the railroad curl out into the valley, and drag up a town from the earth, whatever town the Conductor dreams of that day, whatever city the tracks long to see. And so there is a river of brandy, and the lime-tart trees, and roads of bread. The Line brought folk, and they stayed. There was a man with a hand of gold, being the son of a jeweler and having lost the flesh one in a factory which pounded out ice by the thousand-cube load. When he left the Station and saw the river winding thick along the vale, and the roads with their brown crust, he wept, for nothing here freezes, and resolving never to leave pounded his hand into a railroad tie to honor the Line. Now the train comes to rest precisely on the golden tie, and that man, long dead, holds the City to the Line.

"My mother grew up working in the Station beside her mother and her grandmother, and she saw the tie glitter at the bottom of the tracks every day. She thought it the most beautiful of all the things in the City of Blind Delight, chiefly because it was so often hidden, down in the dark of the tunnel. She thought often of the ice-pounder whose fingers lay thus across the track, and came to love this thing in her mind which was less than a memory, and more than a dream. One night, after the train had sped down the tunnel, she crept across the platform and scrambled down to the gleaming tie. She lay down upon it, and felt it warm against her cheek. She wept for the dead man, and for a thing called ice which she had never seen. When I was born, she said I was so heavy, because of the gold, because of my father, and she polished my heart every night for me before bed."

Otthild touched Gris's face, his smooth, blank cheeks. "You see? We are not without want. But we are peculiar and refined in our ways of wanting, since vulgar food necessity is satisfied."

Gris could not bear to look at her heart with its slow, clanking beating. He closed up her chest with shaking hands and sat on the edge of her bed.

"Would it help," Otthild said, "if I had a knife in my side?"

She drew his face down to hers, and he felt the hard bone buttons beneath him. He looked at her red hair coiled on the pillow as he pressed into her, and thought of the girl with the braid who he had only loved once, who had, afterwards, stared at her stucco ceiling and told him that Crivelli sometimes used chalk rendered in glue made from rabbit-fat to make the tears of his Pieta. It dried hard and clear, so that if you could touch one of his paintings, you would feel the tears falling beneath your hands, falling like tiny stones of grief, like little buttons of bone.

It is properly always dark after sex. Gris wants to feel guilty, but he feels nothing. After all, a businessman and a prostitute are as near a thing to an archetype as he can think of these days. *A salaryman and whore walk into a bar—stop me if you've heard this one.* He stops. He looks over his naked shoulder at her, at her four small buttons. Her hair falls over one heavy breast. She pulls a strip of drywall-pastry and chews it thoughtfully.

"What can I pay you?" he sighs. "What do you want?"

She rolls onto her stomach and smiles softly, her lips without paint, pink and thin. "Most of us in the City are collectors," she says. "Some are monomaniacal, like my mother. But when the sun is always warm and your house is made of food, desire curls in on itself and finds other objects. I know a woman by the butter-pits who collects calf's tails. She has a whole coat of them. I collect tickets."

Gris's mouth opens slightly. He pulls his creased return ticket out of his discarded coat's pocket.

"But if I give it to you, I can get another, for the morning train, can't I?"

Otthild shrugs. "You buy a ticket to enter the station these days, not the train. But the glass booth is well within the arch. Maybe they would sell you a new one. Maybe they would let you inside. Maybe not. We are often perverse. Maybe the Station is full of Midwesterners trying to buy a ticket home with everything they own, even flesh, even bone. Perhaps that long-dead man did not lose his hand in an ice factory, but to buy a ticket here, or a ticket back. All of that is your business, curious histories, and I do not collect those."

She kneels beside the bed and clicks open the jeweled boxes, one by one. Gold, silver, ivory. Opal, onyx, lacquer. Inside them all are countless tickets, old and new, with magnetic strips, without. Some have the City of Blind Delight as a destination, others are simpler: New York to St John's, Odessa to Moscow, Edinburgh to Glasgow. But there are carefully inked and stamped tickets from the City of Envious Virgins to the City Without Roses, from the City of Variable Skylines to the City of Mendicant Crows. There is one, almost dust, from Venice to the City of False Perspective. She opens a box for him, of polished steel, tableware melted into a cubical shape.

Gris reaches out and strokes her sternum, his eyes sliding closed. He feels her fastened chest, the buttons like hardened tears. He lets his ticket fall into the box. Shadows drift over the neat printing: *The City of Blind Delight to Chicago, Midnight Express.*

There is a train which passes through every possible city. It folds the world like an accordioned map, and speeds through the folds like a long white cry. Of necessity, this train passes through Chicago, the City of Winds, a city which was once a lake-bed, and even now, if you were to dig far enough beneath the railroad tracks, you would find the thin, translucent skeletons of monstrous fish with fins like scythes.

A woman in black glasses stands with a bag full of strawberries and wheatflour and frozen trout in her arms. She watches trains silver past while the cream and gold of Union Station arches behind her, as she has done every day since she moved here from California. A long, pale car screeches into the platform before her; she does not look at the track number, or the arcane code of the letters blazing on the side. With only a small hesitation, as she shifts the weight of her groceries from one hip to another, she steps through the doors that open and close like arms. Light shines through the glass ceiling and illuminates the spot where she stood just a moment before, like an afterthought.

FLOWER, MERCY, NEEDLE, CHAIN

YOON HA LEE

Yoon Ha Lee lives in Louisiana with her family, but has been menaced by more clouds of mosquitoes than alligators. Her fiction has appeared in *Lightspeed, The Magazine of Fantasy & Science Fiction,* and *Clarkesworld,* among other venues. She owns no guns and plans to keep it that way, but has occasionally been known to stockpile books on military history and philosophy. This story owes a great deal to the curious argument in Daniel Dennett's *Freedom Evolves,* which posits that free will and determinism are not, in fact, mutually exclusive.

The usual fallacy is that, in every universe, many futures splay outward from any given moment. But in some universes, determinism runs backwards: given a universe's state s at some time t, there are multiple previous states that may have resulted in s. In some universes, all possible pasts funnel toward a single fixed ending, Ω.

If you are of millenarian bent, you might call Ω Armageddon. If you are of grammatical bent, you might call it punctuation on a cosmological scale.

If you are a philosopher in such a universe, you might call Ω *inevitable.*

The woman has haunted Blackwheel Station for as long as anyone remembers, although she was not born there. She is human, and her straight black

477

hair and brown-black eyes suggest an ancestral inheritance tangled up with tigers and shapeshifting foxes. Her native language is not spoken by anyone here or elsewhere.

They say her true name means things like *gray* and *ash* and *grave*. You may buy her a drink, bring her candied petals or chaotic metals, but it's all the same. She won't speak her name.

That doesn't stop people from seeking her out. Today, it's a man with mirror-colored eyes. He is the first human she has seen in a long time.

"Arighan's Flower," he says.

It isn't her name, but she looks up. Arighan's Flower is the gun she carries. The stranger has taken on a human face to talk to her, and he is almost certainly interested in the gun.

The gun takes different shapes, but at this end of time, origami multiplicity of form surprises more by its absence than its presence. Sometimes the gun is long and sleek, sometimes heavy and blunt. In all cases, it bears its maker's mark on the stock: a blossom with three petals falling away and a fourth about to follow. At the blossom's heart is a character that itself resembles a flower with knotted roots.

The character's meaning is the gun's secret. The woman will not tell it to you, and the gunsmith Arighan is generations gone.

"Everyone knows what I guard," the woman says to the mirror-eyed man.

"I know what it does," he says. "And I know that you come from people who worship their ancestors."

Her hand—on a glass of water two degrees from freezing— stops, slides to her side, where the holster is. "That's dangerous knowledge," she says. So he's figured it out. Her people's historians called Arighan's Flower the *ancestral gun*. They weren't referring to its age.

The man smiles politely, and doesn't take a seat uninvited. Small courtesies matter to him because he is not human. His mind may be housed in a superficial fortress of flesh, but the busy computations that define him are inscribed in a vast otherspace.

The man says, "I can hardly be the first constructed sentience to come to you."

She shakes her head. "It's not that." Do computers like him have souls? she wonders. She is certain he does, which is potentially inconvenient. "I'm not for hire."

"It's important," he says.

It always is. They want chancellors dead or generals, discarded lovers or rival reincarnates, bodhisattvas or bosses—all the old, tawdry stories.

People, in all the broad and narrow senses of the term. The reputation of Arighan's Flower is quite specific, if mostly wrong.

"Is it," she says. Ordinarily she doesn't talk to her petitioners at all. Ordinarily she ignores them through one glass, two, three, four, like a child learning the hard way that you can't outcount infinity.

There was a time when more of them tried to force the gun away from her. The woman was a duelist and a killer before she tangled her life up with the Flower, though, and the Flower comes with its own defenses, including the woman's inability to die while she wields it. One of the things she likes about Blackwheel is that the administrators promised that they would dispose of any corpses she produced. Blackwheel is notorious for keeping promises.

The man waits a little longer, then says, "Will you hear me out?"

"You should be more afraid of me," she says, "if you really know what you claim to know."

By now, the other people in the bar, none of them human, are paying attention: a musician whose instrument is made of fossilized wood and silk strings, a magister with a seawrack mane, engineers with their sketches hanging in the air and a single doodled starship at the boundary. The sole exception is the tattooed traveler dozing in the corner, dreaming of distant moons.

In no hurry, the woman draws the Flower and points it at the man. She is aiming it not at his absent heart, but at his left eye. If she pulled the trigger, she would pierce him through the false pupil.

The musician continues plucking plangent notes from the instrument. The others, seeing the gun, gawk for only a moment before hastening out of the bar. As if that would save them.

"Yes," the man says, outwardly unshaken, "you could damage my lineage badly. I could name programmers all the way back to the first people who scratched a tally of birds or rocks."

The gun's muzzle moves precisely, horizontally: now the right eye. The woman says, "You've convinced me that you know. You haven't convinced me not to kill you." It's half a bluff: she wouldn't use the Flower, not for this. But she knows many ways to kill.

"There's another one," he says. "I don't want to speak of it here, but will you hear me out?"

She nods once, curtly.

Covered by her palm, engraved silver-bright in a language nobody else reads or writes, is the word *ancestor*.

Once upon a universe, an empress's favored duelist received a pistol from the empress's own hand. The pistol had a stock of silver-gilt and niello, an efflorescence of vines framing the maker's mark. The gun had survived four dynasties, with all their rebellions and coups. It had accompanied the imperial arsenal from homeworld to homeworld.

Of the ancestral pistol, the empire's archives said two things: *Do not use this weapon, for it is nothing but peril* and *This weapon does not function.*

In a reasonable universe, both statements would not be true.

The man follows the woman to her suite, which is on one of Blackwheel's tidier levels. The sitting room, comfortable but not luxurious by Blackwheeler standards, accommodates a couch sized to human proportions, a metal table shined to blurry reflectivity, a vase in the corner.

There are also two paintings, on silk rather than some less ancient substrate. One is of a mountain by night, serenely anonymous amid its stylized clouds. The other, in a completely different style, consists of a cavalcade of shadows. Only after several moments' study do the shadows assemble themselves into a face. Neither painting is signed.

"Sit," the woman says.

The man does. "Do you require a name?" he asks.

"Yours, or the target's?"

"I have a name for occasions like this," he says. "It is Zheu Kerang."

"You haven't asked me my name," she remarks.

"I'm not sure that's a meaningful question," Kerang says. "If I'm not mistaken, you don't exist."

Wearily, she says, "I exist in all the ways that matter. I have volume and mass and volition. I drink water that tastes the same every day, as water should. I kill when it moves me to do so. I've unwritten death into the history of the universe."

His mouth tilts up at *unwritten.* "Nevertheless," he says. "Your species never evolved. You speak a language that is not even dead. It never existed."

"Many languages are extinct."

"To become extinct, something has to exist first."

The woman folds herself into the couch next to him, not close but not far. "It's an old story," she says. "What is yours?"

"Four of Arighan's guns are still in existence," Kerang says.

The woman's eyes narrow. "I had thought it was three." Arighan's Flower is the last, the gunsmith's final work. The others she knows of are Arighan's

Mercy, which always kills the person shot, and Arighan's Needle, which removes the target's memories of the wielder.

"One more has surfaced," Kerang says. "The character in the maker's mark resembles a sword in chains. They are already calling it Arighan's Chain."

"What does it do?" she says, because he will tell her anyway.

"This one kills the commander of whoever is shot," Kerang says, "if that's anyone at all. Admirals, ministers, monks. Schoolteachers. It's a peculiar sort of loyalty test."

Now she knows. "You want me to destroy the Chain."

Once upon a universe, a duelist named Shiron took up the gun that an empress with empiricist tendencies had given her. "I don't understand how a gun that doesn't work could possibly be perilous," the empress said. She nodded at a sweating man bound in monofilament so that he would dismember himself if he tried to flee. "This man will be executed anyway, his name struck from the roster of honored ancestors. See if the gun works on him."

Shiron fired the gun...and woke in a city she didn't recognize, whose inhabitants spoke a dialect she had never heard before, whose technology she mostly recognized from historical dramas. The calendar they used, at least, was familiar. It told her that she was 857 years too early. No amount of research changed the figure.

Later, Shiron deduced that the man she had executed traced his ancestry back 857 years, to a particular individual. Most likely that ancestor had performed some extraordinary deed to join the aristocracy, and had, by the reckoning of Shiron's people, founded his own line.

Unfortunately, Shiron didn't figure this out before she accidentally deleted the human species.

"Yes," Kerang says. "I have been charged with preventing further assassinations. Arighan's Chain is not a threat I can afford to ignore."

"Why didn't you come earlier, then?" Shiron says. "After all, the Chain might have lain dormant, but the others—"

"I've seen the Mercy and the Needle," he says, by which he means that he's copied data from those who have. "They're beautiful." He isn't referring to beauty in the way of shadows fitting together into a woman's profile, or beauty in the way of sun-colored liquor at the right temperature in a faceted glass. He means the beauty of logical strata, of the crescendo of axiom-axiom-corollary-*proof*, of *quod erat demonstrandum*.

"Any gun or shard of glass could do the same as the Mercy," Shiron says, understanding him. "And drugs and dreamscalpels will do the Needle's work, given time and expertise. But surely you could say the same of the Chain."

She stands again and takes the painting of the mountain down and rolls it tightly. "I was born on that mountain," she says. "Something like it is still there, on a birthworld very like the one I knew. But I don't think anyone paints in this style. Perhaps some art historian would recognize its distant cousin. I am no artist, but I painted it myself, because no one else remembers the things I remember. And now you would have it start again."

"How many bullets have you used?" Kerang asks.

It is not that the Flower requires special bullets—it adapts even to emptiness—it is that the number matters.

Shiron laughs, low, almost husky. She knows better than to trust Kerang, but she needs him to trust her. She pulls out the Flower and rests it in both palms so he can look at it.

Three petals fallen, a fourth about to follow. That's not the number, but he doesn't realize it. "You've guarded it so long," he says, inspecting the maker's mark without touching the gun.

"I will guard it until I am nothing but ice," Shiron says. "You may think that the Chain is a threat, but if I remove it, there's no guarantee that you will still exist—"

"It's not the Chain I want destroyed," Kerang says gently. "It's Arighan. Do you think I would have come to you for anything less?"

Shiron says into the awkward quiet, after a while, "So you tracked down descendants of Arighan's line." His silence is assent. "There must be many."

Arighan's Flower destroys the target's entire ancestral line, altering the past but leaving its wielder untouched. In the empire Shiron once served, the histories spoke of Arighan as an honored guest. Shiron discovered long ago that Arighan was no guest, but a prisoner forced to forge weapons for her captors. How Arighan was able to create weapons of such novel destructiveness, no one knows. The Flower was Arighan's clever revenge against a people whose state religion involved ancestor worship.

If descendants of Arighan's line exist here, then Arighan herself can be undone, and all her guns unmade. Shiron will no longer have to be an exile in this timeline, although it is true that she cannot return to the one that birthed her, either.

Shiron snaps the painting taut. The mountain disintegrates, but she lost it lifetimes ago. Silent lightning crackles through the air, unknots Zheu

Kerang from his human-shaped shell, tessellates dead-end patterns across the equations that make him who he is. The painting had other uses, as do the other things in this room—she believes in versatility—but this is good enough.

Kerang's body slumps on the couch. Shiron leaves it there.

For the first time in a long time, she is leaving Blackwheel Station. What she does not carry she can buy on the way. And Blackwheel is loyal because they know, and they know not to offend her; Blackwheel will keep her suite clean and undisturbed, and deliver water, near-freezing in an elegant glass, night after night, waiting.

Kerang was a pawn by his own admission. If he knew what he knew, and lived long enough to convey it to her, then others must know what he knew, or be able to find it out.

Kerang did not understand her at all. Shiron unmazes herself from the station to seek passage to one of the hubworlds, where she can begin her search. If Shiron had wanted to seek revenge on Arighan, she could have taken it years ago.

But she will not be like Arighan. She will not destroy an entire timeline of people, no matter how alien they are to her.

Shiron had hoped that matters wouldn't come to this. She acknowledges her own naïveté. There is no help for it now. She will have to find and murder each child of Arighan's line. In this way she can protect Arighan herself, protect the accumulated sum of history, in case someone outwits her after all this time and manages to take the Flower from her.

In a universe where determinism runs backwards—where, no matter what you do, everything ends in the same inevitable Ω—choices still matter, especially if you are the last guardian of an incomparably lethal gun.

Although it has occurred to Shiron that she could have accepted Kerang's offer, and that she could have sacrificed this timeline in exchange for the one in which neither Arighan nor the guns ever existed, she declines to do so. For there will come a heat-death, and she is beginning to wonder: if a constructed sentience—a computer—can have a soul, what of the universe itself, the greatest computer of all?

In this universe, they reckon her old. Shiron is older than even that. In millions of timelines, she has lived to the pallid end of life. In each of those endings, Arighan's Flower is there, as integral as an edge is to a blade. While it is true that science never proves anything absolutely, that an inconceivably large but finite number of experiments always pales beside infinity,

Shiron feels that millions of timelines suffice as proof.

Without Arighan's Flower, the universe cannot renew itself and start a new story. Perhaps that is all the reason the universe needs. And Shiron will be there when the heat-death arrives, as many times as necessary.

So Shiron sets off. It is not the first time she has killed, and it is unlikely to be the last. But she is not, after all this time, incapable of grieving.

Ω

ANGLES

ORSON SCOTT CARD

Orson Scott Card is the bestselling author of more than forty novels, including *Ender's Game*, which was a winner of both the Hugo and Nebula awards. The sequel, *Speaker for the Dead*, also won both awards, making Card the only author to have captured science fiction's two most coveted prizes in consecutive years. His most recent books include two more entries in the Enderverse, *Ender in Exile* and *Shadows in Flight*, and the first of a new young adult series, *Pathfinder*. His latest book is *The Lost Gate*, the first volume of a new fantasy series.

3000

Hakira enjoyed coasting the streets of Manhattan. The old rusted-out building frames seemed like the skeleton of some ancient leviathan that beached and died, but he could hear the voices and horns and growling machinery of crowded streets and smell the exhaust and cooking oil, even if all that he saw beneath him were the tops of the trees that had grown up in the long-vanished streets. With a world as uncrowded as this one, there was no reason to dismantle the ruins, or clear the trees. It could remain as a monument, for the amusement of the occasional visitor.

There were plenty of places in the world that were still crowded. As always, most people enjoyed or at least needed human company, and even recluses usually wanted people close enough to reach from time to time.

Satellites and landlines still linked the world together, and ports were busy with travel and commerce of the lighter sort, like bringing out-of-season fruits and vegetables to consumers who preferred not to travel to where the food was fresh. But as the year 3000 was about to pass away, there were places like this that made the planet Earth seem almost empty, as if humanity had moved on.

In fact, there were probably far more human beings alive than anyone had ever imagined might be possible. No human had ever left the solar system, and only a handful lived anywhere but Earth. One of the Earths, anyway—one of the angles of Earth. In the past five hundred years, millions had passed through benders to colonize versions of Earth where humanity had never evolved, and now a world seemed full with only a billion people or so.

Of the trillions of people that were known to exist, the one that Hakira was going to see lived in a two-hundred-year-old house perched on the southern coast of this island, where in ancient times artillery had been placed to command the harbor. Back when the Atlantic reached this far inland. Back when invaders had to come by ship.

Hakira set his flivver down in the meadow where the homing signal indicated, switched off the engine, and slipped out into the bracing air of a summer morning only a few miles from the face of the nearest glacier. He was expected—there was no challenge from the security system, and lights showed him the path to follow through the shadowy woods.

Because his host was something of a show-off, a pair of sabertooth tigers were soon padding along beside him. They might have been computer simulations, but knowing Moshe's reputation, they were probably genetic back-forms, very expensive and undoubtedly chipped up to keep them from behaving aggressively except, perhaps, on command. And Moshe had no reason to wish Hakira ill. They were, after all, kindred spirits.

The path suddenly opened up onto a meadow, and after only a few steps he realized that the meadow was the roof of a house; for here and there steep-pitched skylights rose above the grass and flowers. And now, with a turn, the path took him down a curving ramp along the face of the butte overlooking the Hudson plain. And now he stood before a door.

It opened.

A beaming Moshe stood before him, dressed in, of all things, a kimono. "Come in, Hakira! You certainly took your time!"

"We set our appointment by the calendar, not the clock."

"Whenever you arrive is a good time. I merely noted that my security system showed you taking the grand tour on the way."

"Manhattan. A sad place, like a sweet dream you can never return to."

"A poet's soul, that's what you have."

"I've never been accused of that, before."

"Only because you're Japanese," said Moshe.

They sat down before an open fire that seemed real, but gave off no smoke. Heat it had, however, so that Hakira felt a little scorched when he leaned forward. "There are Japanese poets."

"I know. But is that what anyone thinks of, when they think of the wandering Japanese?"

Hakira smiled. "But you *do* have money."

"Not from money-changing," said Moshe. "And what I don't have, which you also don't have, is a home."

Hakira looked around at the luxurious parlor. "I suppose that technically this *is* a cave."

"A homeland," said Moshe. "For nine and a half centuries, my friend, your people have been able to go almost anywhere in the world but one, an archipelago of islands once called Honshu, Hokkaido, Kyushu—"

Hakira, suddenly overcome by emotion, raised his hand to stop the cruel list. "I know that your people, too, have been driven from their homeland—"

"Repeatedly," said Moshe.

"I hope you will forgive me, sir, but it is impossible to imagine yearning for a desert beside a dead sea the way one yearns for the lush islands strangled for nearly a thousand years by the Chinese dragon."

"Dry or wet, flat or mountainous, the home to which you are forbidden to return is beautiful in dreams."

"Who has the soul of a poet now?"

"Your organization will fail, you know."

"I know nothing of the kind, sir."

"It will fail. China will never relent, because to do so would be to admit wrongdoing, and that they cannot do. To them you are the interlopers. The toothless Peace Council can issue as many edicts as it likes, but the Chinese will continue to bar those of known Japanese ancestry from even visiting the islands. And they will use as their excuse the perfectly valid argument that if you want so much to see Japan, you have only to bend yourself to a different slant. There is bound to be some angle where your tourist dollars will be welcome."

"No," said Hakira. "Those other angles are not *this* world."

"And yet they are."

"And yet they are not."

"Well, now, there is our dilemma. Either we will do business or we will not, and it all hinges on that question. What is it about that archipelago that you want. Is it the land itself? You can already visit that very land—and we are told that because of inanimate incoherency it *is* the same land, no matter what angle *you* dwell in. Or is your desire really not simply to go there, but to go there in defiance of the Chinese? Is it hate, then, that drives you?"

"No, I reject both interpretations," said Hakira. "I care nothing for the Chinese. And now that you put the question in these terms, I realize that I myself have not thought clearly enough, for while I speak of the beautiful land of the rising sun, in fact what I yearn for is the Japanese nation, on those islands, unmolested by any other, governing ourselves as we have from the beginning of our existence as a people."

"Ah," said Moshe. "Now I see that we perhaps *can* do business. For it may be possible to grant you your heart's desire."

"Me and all the people of the Kotoshi."

"Ah, the eternally optimistic Kotoshi. It means 'this year,' doesn't it? As in, 'this year we return'?"

"As your people say, 'Next year in Jerusalem.'"

"A Japan where only the Japanese have ruled for all these past thousand years. In a world where the Japanese are not rootless wanderers, legendary toymakers-for-hire, but rather are a nation among the nations of the world, and one of the greatest of them. Is *that* not the home you wish to return to?"

"Yes," said Hakira.

"But that Japan does not exist in this world, not even now, when the Chinese no longer need even half the land of the original Han China. So you do not want the Japan of this world at all, do you? The Japan you want is a fantasy, a dream."

"A hope."

"A wish."

"A *plan*."

"And it hasn't occurred to you that in all the angles of the world, there might not be such a Japan?"

"It isn't like the huge library in that story, where it is believed that among all the books containing all the combinations of all the letters that could fit in all those pages, there is bound to be a book that tells the true history of all the world. There are many angles, yes, but our ability to differentiate them is not infinite, and in many of them life never evolved and so the air is not breathable. It is an experiment not lightly undertaken."

"Oh, of course. To find a world so nearly like our own that a nation called Japan—or, I suppose, Nippon—exists at all, where a language like Japanese is even spoken—you do speak Japanese yourself, don't you?"

"My parents spoke nothing else at home until I was five and had to enter school."

"Yes, well, to find such a world would be a miracle."

"And to search for it would be a fool's errand."

"And yet it *has* been searched for."

Hakira waited. Moshe did not go on.

"Has it been found?"

"What would it be worth to you, if it had?"

2024—Angle Θ

"You're a scientist," said Leonard. "This is beneath you."

"I have continuous video," said Bêto. "With a mechanical clock in it, so you can see the flow of time. The chair moves."

"There is nothing you can do that hasn't been faked by somebody, sometime."

"But why would I fake it? To publish this is the end of my career."

"Exactly my point, Bêto. You are a geologist, of all things. Geologists don't have poltergeists."

"Stay with me, Leonard. Watch this."

"How long?"

"I don't know. Sometimes it's immediate. Sometimes it takes days."

"I don't have days."

"Play cards with me. As we used to in Faculdade. Look at the chair first, though. Nothing attached to it. A normal chair in every way."

"You sound like a magician on the stage."

"But it *is* normal."

"So it seems."

"Seems? All right, don't trust me. *You* move it. Put it where you want."

"All right. Upside down?"

"It doesn't matter."

"On top of the door?"

"I don't care."

"And we play cards?"

"You deal."

2090

It is the problem of memory. We have mapped the entire brain. We can track the activity of every neuron, of every synapse. We have analyzed the chemical contents of the cells. We can find, in the living brain, without surgery, exactly where each muscle is controlled, where perceptions are rooted. We can even stimulate the brain to track and recall memory. But that is all. We cannot account for how memory is stored, and we cannot find where.

I know that in your textbooks in secondary school and perhaps in your early undergraduate classes you have read that memory was the first problem solved, but that was a misunderstanding. We discovered that after mapping a particular memory, if that exact portion of the brain was destroyed—and this was in the early days, with clumsy equipment that killed thousands of cells at a time, an incredibly wasteful procedure and potentially devastating to the subject—if that exact spot was destroyed, the memory was not lost. It could resurface somewhere else.

So for many years we believed that memory was stored holographically, small portions in many places, so that losing a bit of a memory here or there did not cause the entire sequence to be lost. This, however, was chimerical, for as our research became more and more precise, we discovered that the brain is not infinite, and such a wasteful system of memory storage would use up the entire brain before a child reached the age of three. Because, you see *no memory is lost*. Some memories are hard to recover, and people often lose *track* of their memories, but it is not a problem of storage, it is a problem of retrieval.

Portions of the network break down, so tracks cannot be followed. Or the routing is such that you cannot link from memory A to memory X without passing through memories of such power that you are distracted from the attempt to retrieve. But, given time—or hyper-stimulation of related memory tracks—all memories can be retrieved. All. Every moment of your life.

We cannot recover more than your perceptions and the sense you made of them at the time, but that does not change the fact that we *can* recover every moment of your childhood, every moment of this class. And we can recover every conscious thought, though not the un-conscious streaming thought behind it. It is all stored…somewhere. The brain is merely the retrieval mechanism.

This has led some observers to conclude that there is, in fact, a mind, or even a soul—a nonphysical portion of the human being, existing outside of measurable space. But if that is so, it is beyond the reach of science. I, however, am a scientist, and with my colleagues—some of whom once sat in the very chairs where you are sitting—I have labored long and hard to find an explanation that is, in fact, physical. Some have criticized this effort because it shows that my faith in the nonexistence of the immaterial is so blind that I refuse to believe even the material evidence of immateriality. Don't laugh, it is a valid question. But my answer is that we cannot validly prove the immateriality of the mind by the sheer fact of our inability to detect the material of which it is made.

I am happy to tell you that we have received word that the journal *Mind*—and we would not have settled for anything less than the premiere journal in the field—has accepted our article dealing with our findings. By no means does this constitute an answer. But it moves the field of inquiry and reopens the possibility, at least, of a material answer to the question of memory. For we have found that when neurons are accessed for memory, there are many kinds of activity in the cell. The biochemical, of course, has been very hard to decode, but other researchers have accounted for all the chemical reactions within the cell, and we have found nothing new in that area. Nor is memory electrochemical, for that is merely how raw commands of the coarsest sort are passed from neuron to neuron—rather like the difference between using a spray can as opposed to painting with a monofilament brush.

Our research, of course, began in the submolecular realm, trying to find out if in some way the brain cells were able to make changes in the atom, in the arrangement of protons and neutrons, or some information somehow encoded in the behavior of electrons. This proved, alas, to be a dead end as well.

But the invention of the muonoscope has changed everything for us. Because at last we had a nondestructive means of scanning the exact state of muons through infinitesimal passages of time, we were able to find some astonishing correlations between memory and the barely detectable muon states of slant and yaw. Yaw, as you know, is the constant—the yaw of a muon cannot change during the existence of the muon. Slant also seemed to be a constant, and in the materials which had previously been examined by physicists, that was indeed the case.

However, in our studies of brain activity during forced memory retrieval, we have found a consistent pattern of slant alteration within the nuclei of atoms in individual brain cells. Because the head must be held utterly still for the muonoscope to function, we could only work with terminally ill patients who volunteered for the study and were willing to die in the laboratory instead of with their families, spending the last moments of their lives with their heads opened up and their brains partially disassembled. It was painless but nevertheless emotionally disturbing to contemplate, and so I must salute the courage and sacrifice of our subjects, whose names are all listed in our article as co-authors of the study. And I believe that our study has now taken us as far as biology can go, given the present equipment. The next move is in the hands of physicists.

Ah, yes. What we found. You see? I became side-tracked by my thought of our brave collaborators, because I remembered their memories which meant remembering who they were and what it cost them to…and I am being distracted again. What we found was: During the moment of memory retrieval, when the neuron was stimulated and went into the standard memory-retrieval state, there is a moment—a moment so brief that until fifteen years ago we had no computer that could have detected it, let alone measured its duration—when all the muons in all the protons of all the atoms in all the memory-specific RNA molecules in the nucleus of the one neuron—and no others!—change their slant.

More specifically, they seem, according to the muonoscope, to wink out of existence for that brief moment, and then return to existence with a new pattern of slants—yes, varying slants, impossible as we have been told that was—which exist for a period of time perhaps a thousand times longer than the temporary indetectability, though this is still a span of time briefer than a millionth of a picosecond, and during the brief existence of this anomalous slant-state, which we call the "angle," the neuron goes through the spasm of activity that causes the entire brain to respond in all the ways that we have long recognized as the recovery of memory.

In short, it seems that the pertinent muons change their slant to a new angle, and in that angle they are encoded with a snapshot of the brain-state that will cause the subject to remember. They return to detectability in the process of rebounding to their original slant, but for the brief period before they have completed that rebound, the pattern of memory is reported, via biochemical and then electrochemical changes, to the brain as a whole.

There are those who will resent this discovery because it seems to turn the mind or soul into a mere physical phenomenon, but this is not so. In fact, if anything our discovery enhances our knowledge of the utterly unique majesty of life. For as far as we know, it is only in the living brain of organisms that the very slant of the muons within atoms can be changed.

The brain thus opens tiny doorways into other universes, stores memories there, and retrieves them at will.

Yes, I mean other universes. The first thing that the muonoscope showed us was the utter emptiness of muons. There are even theorists who believe that there are no particles, only attributes of regions of space, and theoretically there is no reason why the same point in space cannot be occupied by an infinite number of muons, as long as they have different slants and, perhaps, yaws. For theoretical reasons that I do not have the mathematics to understand, I am told that while coterminous muons of the same yaw but different slants could impinge upon and influence each other, coterminous muons of different yaw could never have any causal relationship. And there could also be an infinite series of infinite series of universes whose muons are not coterminous with the muons of our universe, and they, too, are permanently undetectable and incapable of influencing our universe.

But if the theory is correct—and I believe our research proves that it is— it is possible to pass information from one slant of this physical universe to another. And since, by this same theory, all material reality is, in fact, merely information, it is even possible that we might be able to pass objects from one such universe to another. But now we are in the realm of fantasy, and I have spent as much time on this happy announcement as I dare. You are, after all, students, and my job is to pass certain information from my brain to yours, which does not, I'm afraid, involve mere millionths of a picosecond.

2024—Angle Φ

"I can't stand it, I can't. I won't live here another day, another hour."

"But it never harms us, and we can't afford to move."

"The chair is on top of the door, it could fall, it could hurt one of the children. Why is it doing this to us? What have we done to offend it?"

"We haven't done *anything*, it's just *malicious*, it's just *enjoying itself!*"

"No, don't make it angry!"

"I'm fed up! Stop this! Go away! Leave us alone!"

"What good is it to break the chair and smash the room!"

"No good. Nothing does any good. Go, get the children, take them out into the garden. I'll call a taxi. We'll go to your sister's house."

"They don't have room."

"For tonight they have room. Not another night in this evil place."

3000

Hakira examined the contract, and it seemed simple enough. Passage for the entire membership of Kotoshi, if they assembled at their own expense. Free return for up to ten days, but only at the end of the ten days, as a single group. There would be no refund for those who returned. But all that seemed fair enough, especially since the price was not exorbitant.

"Of course this contract isn't binding anyway," said Hakira. "How could it be enforced? This whole passage is illegal."

"Not in the target world, it isn't," said Moshe. "And that's where it would have to be enforced, nu?"

"It's not as if I can find a lawyer from that world to represent my interests now."

"It makes no sense for me to have dissatisfied customers."

"How do I know you won't just strand us there?" said Hakira. "It might not even be a world with a breathable atmosphere—a lot of angles are still mostly hydrocarbon gas, with no free oxygen at all."

"Didn't I tell you? I go with you. In fact, I have to—I'm the one who brings you through."

"Brings us? Don't you just put us in a bender and—"

"Bender!" Moshe laughed. "Those primitive machines? No wonder the near worlds are never found—benders can't make the fine distinctions that *we* make. No, I take you through. We go together."

"What, we all join hands and…you're serious. Why are you wasting my time with mumbo jumbo like this!"

"If it's mumbo jumbo, then we'll all hold hands and nothing will happen, and you'll get your money back. Right?" Moshe spread his hands. "What do you have to lose!"

"It feels like a scam."

"Then leave. You came to me, remember?"

"Because you got that group of Zionists through."

"Exactly my point," said Moshe. "I took them through. I came back, they didn't—because they were absolutely satisfied. They're in a world where Israel was never conquered by the surrounding Arab states so Jews still have their own Hebrew-speaking state. The same world, I might add, where Japan is still populated by self-governing Japanese."

"What's the catch?"

"No catch. Except that we use a different mechanism that is not approved by the government and so we have to do it under the table."

"But why does the *other* world allow it?" asked Hakira. "Why do they let you bring people in?"

"This is a rescue," said Moshe. "They bring you in as refugees from an unbearable reality. They bring you *home*. The government of Israel in that reality, as a matter of policy, declares that Jews have a right to return—even Jews from a different angle. And the government of Japan recently decided to offer the same privilege to you."

"It's still so hard to believe that anyone found a populated world that has Japanese at all."

"Well, isn't it obvious?" said Moshe. "Nobody *found* that world."

"What do you mean?"

"That world found *us*."

Hakira thought about it for a moment. "That's why they don't use benders, they have their own technology for reslanting from angle to angle."

"Exactly right, except for your use of the word 'they.'"

And now Hakira understood. "Not they. You. You're not from this world. You're one of them."

"When we discovered your tragic world, I was sent to bring Jews home to Israel. And when we realized that the Japanese suffered a similar tragic loss, the decision was made to extend the offer to you. Hakira, bring your people home."

2024—Angle Θ

"I told them I didn't want to see you."

"I know."

"I was sitting there playing cards and suddenly I'm almost killed!"

"It never happened that way before. The chair usually just…slid. Or sometimes floated."

"It was smashed to bits! I had a concussion, it's taken ten stitches, I'll have this scar on my face for the rest of my life!"

"But I didn't do it, I didn't know it would happen that way. How could I? There were no wires, you know that. You *saw*."

"Nossa. Yes. I saw. But it's not a ghost."

"I never said it was. I don't believe in ghosts."

"What, then?"

"I don't know. Everything else I think of sounds like fantasy. But then, telephones and satellite tv and movies and submarines once sounded like fantasy to anyone who thought of such ideas. And in this case, there've been stories of ghosts and hauntings and poltergeists since…since the beginning of time, I imagine. Only they're rare. So rare that they don't often happen to scientists."

"In the history of the world, real scientists are rarer than poltergeists."

"And if such things *did* happen to a scientist, how many of them might have done as you urged me to do—ignore it. Pretend it was a hallucination. Move to another place where such things don't happen. And the scientists who refuse to blind their eyes to the evidence before them—what happens to them? I'll tell you what happens, because I've found seven of them in the past two hundred years—which isn't a lot, but these are the ones who published what happened to them. And in every case, they were immediately discredited as scientists. No one listened to them any more. Their careers were over. The ones who taught lost tenure at their universities. Three of them were committed to mental institutions. And *not once* did anyone else seriously investigate their claims. Except, of course, the people who are already considered to be completely bobo, the paranormalists, the regular batch of fakers and hucksters."

"And the same thing will happen to you."

"No. Because I have you as a witness."

"What kind of witness am I? I was *hit in the head*. Do you understand? I was in the hospital, delirious, concussive, and I have the scar on my face to prove it. No one will believe me either. Some will even wonder if you didn't beat me into agreeing to testify for you!"

"Ah, Leonard. God help me, but you're right."

"Call an exorcist."

"I'm a scientist! I don't want it to go away! I want to understand it!"

"So, Bêto, scientist, explain it to me. If it isn't a ghost to be exorcised, what is it?"

"A parallel world. No, listen, listen to me! Maybe in the empty spaces between atoms, or even the empty spaces within atoms, there are other atoms we can't detect most of the time. An infinite number of them, some very close to ours, some very far. And suppose that when you enclose a space, and somebody in one of those infinite parallel universes encloses the *same* space, it can cause just the slightest bit of material overlap."

"You mean there's something magic about boxes? Come on."

"You asked for possibilities! But if the landforms are similar, then the places where towns are built would be similar, too. The confluence of rivers. Harbors. Good farmland. People in many universes would be building towns in the same places. Houses. All it takes is one room that overlaps, and suddenly you get echoes between worlds. You get a single chair that exists in both worlds at once."

"What, somebody in our world goes and buys a chair and somebody in the other world happens to go and buy the same one on the same day?"

"No. I moved into the house, that chair was already there. Haunted houses are always old, aren't they? Old furniture. It's been there long enough, undisturbed, for the chair to have spilled a little and exist in both worlds. So…you take the chair and put it on top of the door, and the people in the other world come home and find the chair has been moved—maybe they even *saw* it move—and he's fed up, he's furious, he *smashes the chair*."

"Ludicrous."

"Well, *something* happened, and you have the scar to prove it."

"And you have the chair fragments."

"Well, no."

"What! You threw them out?"

"My best guess is that *they* threw them out. Or else, I don't know, when the chair lost its structure, the echo faded. Anyway, the pieces are gone."

"No evidence. That clinches it. If you publish this I'll deny it, Bêto."

"No you won't."

"I will. I've already had my face damaged. I'm not going to let you shatter my career as well. Bêto, drop it!"

"I can't! This is too important! Science can't continue to refuse to look at this and find out what's really going on!"

"Yes it can! Scientists regularly refuse to look at all kinds of things because it would be bad for their careers to see them! You know it's true!"

"Yes. I know it's true. Scientists can be blind. But *not me*. And not you either, Leonard. When I publish this, I know you'll tell the truth."

"If you publish this, I'll know you're crazy. So when people ask me, I'll tell them the truth—that you're crazy. The chair is gone now anyway. Chances are this will never happen again. In five years you'll come to think of it as a weird hallucination."

"A weird hallucination that left you scarred for life."

"Go away, Bêto. Leave me alone."

2186

"I call it the Angler, and using it is called Angling."

"It looks expensive."

"It is."

"Too expensive to sell it as a toy."

"It's not for children anyway. Look, it's expensive because it's really high-tech, but that's a plus, and the more popular it becomes, the more the per-unit cost will drop. We've studied the price point and we think we're right on this."

"OK, fine, what does it do."

"I'll show you. Put on this cap and—"

"I certainly will *not!* Not until you tell me what it does."

"Sure, I understand, no problem. What it does is, it puts you into some-one else's head."

"Oh, it's just a Dreamer, those have been around for years, they had their vogue but—"

"No, not a Dreamer. True, we do use the old Dreamer technology as the playback system, because why reinvent the wheel? We were able to license it for a song, so why not? But the thing that makes this special is this—the recording system."

"Recording?"

"You know about slantspace, right?"

"That's all theoretical games."

"Not really just theoretical. I mean, it's well known that our brains store memory in slantspace, right?"

"Sure, yeah. I knew that."

"Well, see, here's the thing. There's an infinite number of different uni-verses that have a lot of their matter coterminous with ours—"

"Here it comes, engineer talk, we can't sell engineering babble."

"There are people in these other worlds. Like ghosts. They wander around, and *their* memories are stored in *our* world."

"Where?"

"Just sitting there in the air. Just a collection of angles. Wherever their head is, in our world and a lot of other parallel worlds, they have their memories stored as a pattern of slants. Haven't you had the experience of walking into a room and then suddenly you can't remember why you came in?"

"I'm seventy years old, it happens all the time."

"It has nothing to do with being seventy. It happened when you were young, too. Only you're more susceptible now, because your own brain has so much memory stored that it's constantly accessing other slants. And sometimes, your head space passes through the head space of someone else in another world, and poof, your thoughts are confused—jammed, really—by theirs."

"My head just happens to pass through the space where the other guy's head just *happens* to be?"

"In an infinite series of universes, there are a lot of them where people about your height might be walking around. What makes it so rare is that most of them are using patterns of slants so different that they barely impinge on ours at all. And you have to be accessing memory right at that moment, too. Anyway, that's not what matters—that *is* coincidence. But you set up this recorder here at about the height of a human being and turn it on, and as long as you don't put it, say, on the thirtieth floor or the bottom of a lake or something, within a day you'll have this thing filled up."

"With what?"

"Up to twenty separate memory states. We could build it to hold a lot more, but it's so easy to erase and replace that we figured twenty was enough and if people want more, we can sell peripherals, right? Anyway, you get these transitory brain states. Memories. And it's the whole package, the complete mental state of another human being for one moment in time. Not a dream. Not *fictionalized*, you know? Those dreams, they were sketchy, haphazard, pretty meaningless. I mean, it's boring to hear other people *tell* their dreams, how cool is it to actually have to sit through them? But with the Angler, you catch the whole fish. You've got to put it on, though, to know why it's going to sell."

"And it's nothing permanent."

"Well, it's permanent in the sense that you'll remember it, and it'll be a pretty strong memory. But you know, you'll *want* to remember it so that's a good thing. It doesn't damage anything, though, and that's all that matters. I can try it on one of your employees first, though, if you want. Or I'll put it on myself."

"No, I'll do it. I'll have to do it in the end before I'll make the decision, so I might as well do it from the start. Put on the cap. And no, it's not a toupee, if I were going to get a rug I'd choose a better one than this."

"All right, a snug fit, but that's why we made it elastic."

"How long does it take?"

"Objective time, only a fraction of a second. Subjectively, of course, well, you tell *us*. Ready?"

"Sure. Give me a one, two, three, all right?"

"I'll do one, two, three, and then flip it like four. OK?"

"Yeah yeah. Do it."

"One. Two. Three."

"Ah...aaah. Oh."

"Give it a few seconds. Just relax. It's pretty strong."

"You didn't...how could this...I..."

"It's all right to cry. Don't worry. First time, most people do."

"I was just...She's just...I was a *woman*."

"Fifty-fifty chance."

"I never knew how it felt to... This should be illegal."

"Technically, it falls under the same laws as the Dreamer, so, you know, not for children and all that."

"I don't know if I'd ever want to use it again. It's so strong."

"Give yourself a few days to sort it out, and you'll want it. You know you will."

"Yes. No, don't try to push any paperwork on me right now, I'm not an idiot. I'm not signing anything while my head's so...but...tomorrow. Come back tomorrow. Let me sleep on it."

"Of course. We couldn't ask for anything more than that."

"Have you shown this to anyone else?"

"You're the biggest and the best. We came to you first."

"We're talking exclusive, right?"

"Well, as exclusive as our patents allow."

"What do you mean?"

"We've patented every method we've thought of, but we think there are a lot of ways to record in slantspace. In fact, the real trouble is, the hardest thing is to design a record that doesn't bend space on the other side. I mean, people's heads won't go through the recording field if the recorder itself is visible in their space! What I'm saying is, we'll be exclusive until somebody finds another way to do it without infringing our patent. That'll take years, of course, but..."

"How many years?"

"No faster than three, and probably longer. And we can tie them up in court longer still."

"Look at me, I'm still shaking. Can you play me the same memory?"

"We could build a machine that would do that, but you won't want to. The first time with each one is the best. Doing the same person twice can leave you a little...confused."

"Bring me the paperwork tomorrow for an exclusive for five years. We'll launch with enough product to drop that price point from the start."

It took a month for the members of Kotoshi to assemble. Only a few decided not to go, and they took a vow of silence to protect those who were leaving They gathered at the southern tip of Manhattan, in the parlor of Moshe's house. They had no belongings with them.

"It's one of the unfortunate side effects of the technology we use," Moshe explained. "Nothing that is not organically connected to your bodies can make the transition to the new slant. As when you were born, you will be naked when you arrive. That's why wholesale colonization using this technology is impractical—no tools. Nor can you transfer any kind of wealth or art. You come empty-handed."

"Is it cold there?"

"The climate is different," said Moshe. "You'll arrive on the southern tip of Manhattan, and it will be winter, but there are no glaciers closer than Greenland. Anyway, you'll arrive indoors. I live in this house and use it for transition because there is a coterminous room in the other angle. Nothing to fret about."

Hakira looked for the technology that would transfer them. Moshe had spoken of this room. Perhaps it was much larger than bender technology, and had been embedded in the walls of the room.

Yet if they could not bring anything with them that wasn't part of their bodies, Moshe's people must have built their machinery here instead of importing it. Yet if they hadn't brought wealth, how had Moshe obtained the money to buy this house, let alone manufacture their slant-changing machinery? Interesting puzzles.

Of course, there were two obvious solutions. The first would be a disappointment, but it was the most predictable—that it was all fakery and Moshe would try to abscond with their money without having taken them anywhere at all. There was always the danger that part of the scam was killing those who were supposed to be transported so that there'd be no one left to complain. Foreseeing that, Hakira and the others were alert and prepared.

The other possibility, though, was the one that made Hakira's spine tingle. Theoretically, since slant-shifting had first been discovered as a natural function of the human brain, there was always the chance of non-mechanical transfer between angles. One of the main objections to this idea had always been that if it were possible, all the worlds should be getting constant visits from any that had learned how to transfer by mental power alone. The common answer to that was, How do you know they *aren't* constantly visiting? Some even speculated that sightings of ghosts might well be of people coming or going. But Moshe's warning about arriving nude would explain quite nicely why there hadn't been more visits. It's hard to be subtle about being nude in most human cultures.

"Do any of you," asked Moshe, "have any embedded metal or plastic in your bodies? This includes fillings in your teeth, but would also include metal plates or silicon joint replacements, heart pacemakers, non-tissue breast implants, and, of course, eyeglasses. I can assure you that as quickly as possible, all these items will be replaced, except for pacemakers, of course, if you have a pacemaker you're simply not going."

"What happens if we *do* have some kind of implant?" asked one of the men.

"Nothing painful. No wound. It simply doesn't go with you. It remains here. The effect on you is as if it simply disappeared. And, of course, the objects would remain here, hanging in the air, and then fall to the ground—or the chair, since most of you will be sitting. But to tell the truth, that's the least of my problems—part of your fee goes to cleaning up this room, since the contents of your bowels also remain behind."

Several people grimaced.

"As I said, *you'll* never notice, except you might feel a bit lighter and more vigorous. It's like having the perfect enema. And, no matter how nervous you are, you won't need to urinate for some time. Well now, are we ready? Anyone want to step outside after all?"

No one left.

"Well, this couldn't be simpler. You must join hands, bare hands, skin to skin. Connect tightly, the whole circle, no one left out."

Hakira couldn't help but chuckle.

"Hakira is laughing," said Moshe, "because he mockingly suggested that maybe our method of transfer was some kind of mumbo jumbo involving all joining hands. Well, he was right. Only this happens to be mumbo jumbo that works."

We'll see, won't we? thought Hakira.

In moments, all their hands were joined.

"Hold your hands up, so I can see," said Moshe. " Good, good. All right. Absolute silence, please."

"A moment first," said Hakira. To the others, he said softly, "Nippon, this year."

With fierce smiles or no expression at all, the others murmured in reply, "Fujiyama kotoshi."

It was done. Hakira turned to Moshe and nodded.

They bowed their heads and made no sound, beyond the unavoidable sound of breathing. And an occasional sniffle—they *had* just come in from the cold.

One man coughed. Several people glared at him. Others simply closed their eyes, meditating their way to silence.

Hakira never took his eyes from Moshe, watching for some kind of signal to a hidden confederate, or perhaps for him to activate some machinery that might fill the room with poison gas. But…nothing.

Two minutes. Three. Four.

And then the room disappeared and a cold wind blew across forty naked bodies. They were in the open air inside a high fence, and around them in a circle stood men with swords.

Swords.

Everything was clear now.

"Well," said Moshe cheerfully, letting go and stepping back to join the armed men. One of them had a long coat for him, which he put on and wrapped around himself. "The transfer worked just as I told you it would— you're naked, there was no machinery involved, and don't you feel vigorous?"

Neither Hakira nor any of the people of Kotoshi said a thing.

"I did lie about a few things," said Moshe. "You see, we stumbled upon what you call 'slanting' at a much more primitive stage in our technological development than you. And wherever we went that wasn't downright fatal, and that wasn't already fully inhabited, there you were! Already overpopulating every world we could find! We had come upon the technique too late. So, we've come recruiting. If we're to have a chance at defeating you and your kind so we have a decent chance of finding worlds to expand into, we need to learn how to use your technology. How to use your weapons, how to disable your power system, how to make your ordinary citizens helpless. Since our technology is far behind yours, and we couldn't carry technology from world to world anyway, the way you can, this was our only choice."

Still no one answered him.

"You are taking this very calmly—good. The previous group was full of complainers, arguing with us and complaining about the weather even though it's *much* colder this time. That first group was very valuable—we've learned many medical breakthroughs from them, for instance, and many people are learning how to drive cars and how to use credit and even the theory behind computer programming. But you—well, I know it's a racial stereotype, but not only are you Japanese every bit as educated as the Jews from the previous group, you tend to be educated in mathematics and technology instead of medicine, law, and scripture. So from you we hope to learn many valuable things that will prepare us to take over one of your colonies and use it as a springboard to future conquest. Isn't it nice to know how valuable and important you are?"

One of the swordsmen let rip a string of sounds from another language. Moshe answered in the same language. "My friend comments that you seem to be taking this news extremely well."

"Only a few points of clarification are needed," said Hakira. "You are, in fact, planning to keep us as slaves?"

"Allies," said Moshe. "Helpers. Teachers."

"Not slaves. We are free to go, then? To return home if we wish?"

"No, I regret not."

"Are we free not to cooperate with you?"

"You will find your lives are much more comfortable if you cooperate."

"Will we be taught this mental method of transferring from angle to angle?"

Moshe laughed. "Please, you are too humorous."

"Is this a global policy on your world, or are you representing only one government or perhaps a small group not responsible to any government?"

"There is one government on this world, and we represent its policy," said Moshe. "It is only in the area of technology that we are not as advanced as you. We gave up tribes and nations thousands of years ago."

Hakira looked around at the others in his group. "Any other questions? Have we settled everything?"

Of course it was just a legal formality. He knew perfectly well that they were now free to act. This was, in fact, almost the worst-case scenario. No clothing, no weapons, cold weather, surrounded. But that was why they trained for the worst case. At least there were no guns, and they were outdoors.

"Moshe, I arrest you and all the armed persons present in this compound and charge you with wrongful imprisonment, slavery, fraud, and—"

Moshe shook his head and gave a brief command to the swordsmen. At once they raised their weapons and advanced on Hakira's group.

It took only moments for the nude Japanese to sidestep the swords, disarm the swordsmen, and leave them prostrate on the ground, their own swords now pointed at their throats. The Japanese who were not involved in that task quickly scoured the compound for more weapons and located the clumsy old-fashioned keys that would open the gate. Within moments they had run down and captured those guards who had been outside the gates. Not one got away. Only two had even attempted to fight. They were, as a result, dead.

To Moshe, Hakira said, "I now add the charge of assault and attempted murder."

"You'll never get back to your own world," said Moshe.

"We each have the complete knowledge necessary to make our own bender out of whatever materials we find here. We are also quite prepared to take on any military force you send against us, or to flee, if necessary. Even if we have to travel, we have *you*. The real question is whether we will learn the secret of mental reslanting from you before or after we build a bender for ourselves. I can promise you considerable lenience from the courts if you cooperate."

"Never."

"Oh, well. Someone else will."

"How did you know?" demanded Moshe.

"There is no world but ours with Japanese in it. Or Jews. None of the inhabited worlds have had cultures or languages or civilizations or histories that resembled each other in any way. We knew you were a con man, but we also knew the Zionists were gone without a trace. We also knew that some-day we'd have to face people from another angle who had learned how to reslant themselves. We trained very carefully, and we followed you home."

"Like stray mongrels," said Moshe.

"Oh, and we do have to be told where the previous batch of slaves are being kept—the Zionists you kidnaped before."

"They'll all be killed," said Moshe nastily.

"That would be such a shame for you," said Hakira. He beckoned to one of his men, now armed with a sharp sword. In Japanese, he told his com-rade that unfortunately, Moshe needed a demonstration of their relentless determination.

At once the sword flicked out and the tip of Moshe's nose dropped to the ground. The sword flicked again, and now Moshe lost the tip of the longest finger of the hand that he had been raising to touch his maimed nose.

Hakira bent over and scooped up the nose and the fingertip. "I'd say that if we get back to our world within about three hours, surgeons will be able to put these back on with only the tiniest scar and very little loss of function. Or shall we delay longer, and sever more protruding body parts?"

"This is inhuman!" said Moshe.

"On the contrary," said Hakira. "This is about as human as it gets."

"Are the people of your angle so determined to control every world you find?"

"Not at all," said Hakira. "We never interfered with any world that already had human life. You're the ones who decided on war. And I must say I'm relieved that the general level of your technology turns out to be so low. And that wherever you go, you arrive naked."

Moshe said nothing. His eyes glazed over.

Hakira murmured to his friend with the sword. The point of it quickly rested against the tender flesh just under Moshe's jaw.

Moshe's eyes grew quite alert.

"Don't even think of slanting away from us," said Hakira.

"I am the only one who speaks your language," said Moshe. "You have to sleep sometime. *I* have to sleep sometime. How will you know whether I'm really asleep, or merely meditating before I transfer?"

"Take a thumb," said Hakira. "And this time, let's make him swallow it."

Moshe gulped. "What sort of vengeance will you take against my people?"

"Apart from fair trials for the perpetrators of this conspiracy, we'll establish an irresistible presence here, watch you very carefully, and conduct such trade as we think appropriate. You yourself will be judged according to your cooperation now. Come on, Moshe, save some time. Take me back to my world. A bender is already being set up at your house—the troops moved in the moment we disappeared. You know that it's just a matter of time before they identify this angle and arrive in force no matter what you do."

"I could take you anywhere," said Moshe.

"And no doubt you're threatening to take me to some world with unbreathable air because you're willing to die for your cause. I understand that, I'm willing to die for mine. But if I'm not back here in ten minutes, my men will slaughter yours and begin the systematic destruction of your world. It's our only defense, if you don't cooperate. Believe me, the best way to save your world is by doing what I say."

"Maybe I hate you more than I love my people," said Moshe.

"What you love is our technology, Moshe, every bit of it. Come with me now and you'll be the hero who brings all those wonderful toys home."

"You'll put my finger and nose back on?"

"In my world the year is 3001," said Hakira. "We'll put them on you wherever you want, and give you spares just in case."

"Let's go," said Moshe.

He took Hakira's hand and closed his eyes.

THE MAGICIAN
AND THE MAID
AND OTHER STORIES

CHRISTIE YANT

Christie Yant is a science fiction and fantasy writer and habitual volunteer. She has been a "podtern" for *Geek's Guide to the Galaxy,* an assistant editor for *Lightspeed Magazine,* occasional narrator for *StarShipSofa,* and remains a co-blogger at Inkpunks.com, a website for aspiring and newly-pro writers. Her fiction has appeared in *Crossed Genres, Daily Science Fiction, Fireside Magazine,* and the anthologies *The Way of the Wizard, Year's Best Science Fiction & Fantasy 2011,* and *Armored.* She lives in a former Temperance colony on the central coast of California, where she sometimes gets to watch rocket launches with her husband and her two amazing daughters.

She called herself Audra, though that wasn't her real name; he called himself Miles, but she suspected it wasn't his, either.

She was young (how young she would not say), beautiful (or so her Emil had told her), and she had a keen interest in stories. Miles was old, tattooed, perverted, and often mean, but he knew stories that no one else knew, and she was certain that he was the only one who could help her get back home.

She found him among the artists, makers, and deviants. They called him

Uncle, and spoke of him sometimes with loathing, sometimes respect, but almost always with a tinge of awe—a magician in a world of technicians, they did not know what to make of him.

But Audra saw him for what he truly was.

There once was a youth of low birth who aspired to the place of King's Magician. The villagers scoffed, "Emil, you will do naught but mind the sheep," but in his heart he knew that he could possess great magic.

The hedge witches and midwives laughed at the shepherd boy who played at sorcery, but indulged his earnestness. He learned charms for love and marriage (women's magic, but he would not be shamed by it) and for wealth and luck, but none of this satisfied him, for it brought him no nearer to the throne. For that he needed real power, and he did not know where to find it.

He had a childhood playmate named Aurora, and as they approached adulthood Aurora grew in both beauty and cleverness. Their childhood affection turned to true love, and on her birthday they were betrothed.

The day came when the youth knew he had learned all that he could in the nearby villages and towns. The lovers wept and declared their devotion with an exchange of humble silver rings. With a final kiss Emil left his true love behind, and set out to find the source of true power.

It was not hard to meet him, once she understood his tastes. A tuck of her skirt, a tug at her chemise; a bright ribbon, new stockings, and dark kohl to line her eyes. She followed him to a club he frequented, where musicians played discordant arrangements and the patrons were as elaborately costumed as the performers. She walked past his booth where he smoked cigarettes and drank scotch surrounded by colorful young women and effeminate young men.

"You there, Bo Peep, come here."

She met his dark eyes, turned her back on him, and walked away. The sycophants who surrounded him bitched and whined their contempt for her. He barked at them to shut up as she made her way to the door.

Once she had rejected him it was easy. She waited for his fourth frustrated overture before she joined him at his table.

"So," she said as she lifted his glass to her lips uninvited, "tell me a story."

"What kind of story?"

"A fairy tale."

"What—something with elves and princes and happily-ever-after?"

"No," she said and reached across the corner of the table to turn his face toward her. He seemed startled but complied, and leaned in until their faces were just inches apart. "A real fairy tale. With wolves and witches, jealous parents, woodsmen charged with murdering the innocent. Tell me a story, Miles—" she could feel his breath against her cheek falter as she leaned ever closer and spoke softly into his ear "—tell me a story that is true."

Audra was foot-sore and weary when they reached the house at dawn. She stumbled on the stone walk, and caught Miles's arm to steady her.

"Are you sure you don't need anything from home?" he asked as he worked his key in the lock.

At his mention of *home*, she remembered again to hate him.

"Quite sure," she said. He faced her, this time with a different kind of appraisal. There was no leer, no suspicion. He touched her face, and his habitual scowl relaxed into something like a smile.

"You remind me of someone I knew once, long ago." The smile vanished and he opened the front door, stepping aside to let her pass.

His house was small and filled with a peculiar collection of things that told her she had the right man. Many of them where achingly familiar to Audra: a wooden spindle in the entryway, wound with golden thread; a dainty glass shoe on the mantle, almost small enough to fit a child; in the corner, a stone statue of an ugly, twisted creature, one arm thrown protectively over its eyes.

"What a remarkable collection," she said and forced a smile. "It must have taken a long time to assemble."

"Longer than I care to think of." He picked a golden pear off the shelf and examined it. "None of it is what I wanted." He returned it to the shelf with a careless toss. "I'll show you the bedroom."

The room was bare, in contrast with the rest of the house. No ornament hung on the white plaster walls, no picture rested on the dresser. The bed was small, though big enough for two, and covered in a faded quilt. It was flanked by a table on one side, and a bent wood chair on the other.

Audra sat stiffly at the foot of the bed.

The mattress creaked as Miles sat down beside her. She turned toward him with resolve, and braced herself for the inevitable. She would do whatever it took to get back home.

She had done worse, and with less cause.

He leaned in close and stroked her hair; she could smell him, sweet and smoky, familiar and foreign at the same time. She lifted a hand to caress his smooth head where he lingered above her breast. He caught her wrist and

510 ⊙ Christie Yant

straightened, pressed her palm to his cheek—eyes closed, forehead creased in pain—then abruptly dropped her hand and rose from the bed.

"If you need more blankets, they're in the wardrobe. Sleep well," he said, and left Audra to wonder what had gone wrong, and to consider her next move.

Aurora was as ambitious as Emil, but of a different nature. She believed that the minds of most men were selfish and swayed only by fear or greed. In her heart there nestled a seed of doubt that Emil could get his wish through pure knowledge and practice. She resolved in her love for him to secure his place through craft and wile.

Aurora knew the ways of tales. She planted the seed of rumor in soil in which it grew best: the bowry; the laundry; anywhere the women gathered, she talked of his power.

But word of the powerful sorcerer had to reach the King himself, and to get close enough she would need to use a different craft.

The hands of guards and pikemen were rougher than Emil's; the mouths of servants less tender. She ignited the fire of ambition in their hearts with flattery, and fanned it with promises that Emil, the most powerful sorcerer in the kingdom, would repay those who supported him once he was installed in the palace.

And if she had regrets as she hurried from chamber to cottage in the cold night air, she dismissed them as just a step on the road toward realizing her lover's dream.

Audra woke at mid-day to find a note on the chair in the corner of the room.

In deep black ink and an unpracticed hand was written:

"Stay if you like, or go as you please. I am accountable to only one, and that one is not you. If that arrangement suits you, make yourself at home. – M."

It suited her just fine.

She searched the house. She wasn't sure what she was looking for, but she was certain that any object of power great enough to rip her from her own world would be obvious somehow. It would be odd, otherworldly, she thought—but that described everything here. Like a raven's hoard, every nook contained some shiny, stolen object.

On a shelf in the library she found a clear glass apothecary jar labeled "East Wind." *Thief,* she thought. Audra hoped that the East Wind didn't suffer for the lack of the contents of the jar. She would keep an eye on the weather vane and return it at the first opportunity.

Something on the shelf caught her eye, small and shining, and her contempt turned to rage.

Murderer.

She pocketed Emil's ring.

Miles seemed to dislike mirrors. There were none in the bedroom; none even in the washroom. The only mirror in the house was an ornate, gilded thing that hung in the library. She paused in front of it, startled at her disheveled appearance. She smoothed her hair with her fingers and leaned in to examine her blood-shot eyes—and found someone else's eyes looking back at her.

The gaunt, androgynous face that gazed dolefully from deep within the mirror was darker and older than her own.

"Hello," she said to the Magic Mirror. "I'm Audra."

The Mirror shook its head disapprovingly.

"You're right," she admitted. "But we don't give strangers our true names, do we?"

She considered her new companion. The long lines of its insubstantial face told Audra that it had worn that mournful look for a long time.

"Did he steal you, as well? Perhaps we can help each other find a way home. The answer is here somewhere."

The face in the Mirror brightened, and it nodded.

Audra had an idea. "Would you like me to read to you?"

Emil travelled a bitter road in search of the knowledge that would make his fortune. By day he starved, by night he froze. But one day Luck was with him, and he caught two large, healthy hares before sunset. As he huddled beside his small fire, the hares roasting over the flames, a short and grizzled man came out of the forest, carrying a sack of goods.

"Good evening, Grandfather," Emil said to the little man. "Sit, share my fire and supper." The man gratefully accepted. "What do you sell?" Emil asked.

"Pots and pans, needles, and spices," the old man said.

"Know you any magic?" Emil asked, disappointed. He was beginning to think the knowledge he sought didn't exist, and he was losing hope.

"What does a shepherd need with magic?"

"How did you know I'm a shepherd?" Emil asked in surprise.

"I know many things," the man said, and then groaned, and doubled over in pain.

"What ails you?" Emil cried, rushing to the old man's side.

"Nothing that you can help, lad. I've a disease of the gut that none can cure, and my time may be short."

Emil questioned the man about his ailment, and pulled from his pack dozens of pouches of herbs and powders. He heated water for a medicinal brew while the old man groaned and clutched his stomach.

The man pulled horrible faces as he drank down the bitter tea, but before long his pain eased, and he was able to sit upright again. Emil mixed another batch of the preparation and assured him that he would be cured if he drank the tea for seven days.

"I was wrong about you," the man said. "You're no shepherd." He pulled a scroll from deep within his pack. "For your kindness I'll give you what you've traveled the world seeking."

The little man explained that the scroll contained three powerful spells, written in a language that no man had spoken in a thousand years. The first was a spell to summon a benevolent spirit, who would then guide him in his learning.

The second summoned objects from one world into another, for every child knew that there were many worlds, and that it was possible to pierce the veil between them.

The third would transport a person between worlds.

If he could decipher the three spells, he would surely become the most powerful sorcerer in the kingdom.

Emil offered the old man what coins he had, but he refused. He simply handed over the scroll, bade Emil farewell, and walked back into the forest.

Audra filled her time reading to the Mirror. The shelves were filled with hundreds of books: old and new, leather-bound and gilt-edged, or flimsy and sized to be carried in a pocket.

She devoured them, looking for clues. How she got here. How she might get back.

On a bottom shelf in the library, in the sixth book of a twelve-volume set, she found her story.

The illustrations throughout the blue cloth-bound book were full of round, cheerful children and curling vines. She recognized some of her friends and enemies from her old life: there was Miska, who fooled the Man-With-The-Iron-Head and whom she had met once on his travels; on another page she found the fairy who brought the waterfall to the mountain, whom Audra resolved to visit as soon as she got home.

She turned the page, and her breath caught in her throat.

"The Magician and the Maid," the title read. Beneath the illustration were those familiar words, "Once upon a time."

A white rabbit bounded between birch trees toward Audra's cottage. Between the treetops a castle gleamed pink in the sunset light, the place where her story was supposed to end. Audra traced the outline of the rabbit with her finger, and then traced the two lonely shadows that followed close behind.

Two shadows: one, her own, and the other, Emil's.

Audra was reading to the Mirror, a story it seemed to particularly like. It did tricks for her as she read, creating wispy images in the glass that matched the prose.

She had just reached the best part, where the trolls turn to stone in the light of the rising sun, when she heard footsteps outside the library door. The Mirror looked anxiously toward the sound, and then slipped out of sight beyond the carved frame.

The door burst open.

"Who are you talking to?" Miles demanded. "Who's here?" He smelled of scotch and sweat, and his overcoat had a new stain.

"No one. I like to read aloud. I am alone here all day," she said.

"Don't pretend I owe you anything." He slouched into the chair and pulled a cigarette from his coat. "You might make yourself useful," he said. "Read to me."

The room was small, and she stood no more than an arm's length away, feeling like a school girl being made to recite. She opened to a story she did not know, a tale called "The Snow Queen," and began to read. Miles closed his eyes and listened.

"Little Kay was quite blue with cold, indeed almost black, but he did not feel it; for the Snow Queen had kissed away the icy shiverings, and his heart was already a lump of ice," she read.

She glanced down at him when she paused for breath to find him looking at her in a way that she knew all too well.

Finally, an advantage.

She let her voice falter when he ran a finger up the side of her leg, lifting her skirt a few inches above her knee.

She did not stop reading—it was working, something in him had changed as she read. Sex was a weak foothold, but it was the only one she had, and perhaps it would be a step toward getting into his mind.

"He dragged some sharp, flat pieces of ice to and fro, and placed them together in all kinds of positions, as if he wished to make something out of them. He composed many complete figures, forming different words, but there was one word he never could manage to form, although he wished it very much. It was the word 'Eternity.'"

He fingered the cord tied at her waist, and tugged it gently at first, then more insistently. He leaned forward in the chair, and unfastened the last hook on her corset.

"Just at this moment it happened that little Gerda came through the great door of the castle. Cutting winds were raging around her, but she offered up a prayer and the winds sank down as if they were going to sleep; and she went on till she came to the large empty hall, and caught sight of Kay; she knew him directly; she flew to him and threw her arms round his neck, and held him fast, while she exclaimed, 'Kay, dear little Kay, I have found you at last.'"

His fingers stopped their manipulations. His hands were still on her, the fastenings held between his fingertips.

She dared not breathe.

Whatever control she had for those few minutes was gone. She tried to reclaim it, to keep going as if nothing had happened. She even dropped a hand from the book and reached out to touch him. His hand snapped up and caught hers; he stood, pulling hard on her arm.

"Enough." He left the room without looking back. She heard the front door slam.

Audra straightened her clothes in frustration and wondered again what had gone wrong.

It took only a moment's thought for Audra to decide to follow him. She peered out into the street: there he was, a block away already, casting a long shadow in the lamp light on the wet pavement.

Her feet were cold and her shoes wet through by the time he finally stopped at a warehouse deep in a maze of brick complexes. He manipulated a complex series of locks on the dented and rusting steel door, and disappeared inside.

So this was where he went at night? Not to clubs and parlors as she had thought, but here, on the edge of the inhabited city, to a warehouse only notable for having all its window glass.

The windows were too high for her to see into, but a dumpster beneath one of them offered her a chance. The metal bin was slick with mist, and she slipped off it twice, but on her third try she hoisted herself on top and nervously peered through the filthy glass of the window.

In the dim light she could just make out the shape of Miles, rubbing his hands fiercely together as if to warm them, then unrolling something— paper, or parchment—spreading it out carefully in front of him on the concrete floor. He stood, and began to speak.

The room grew brighter, and a face appeared in front of him, suspended in the air—a familiar face made of dim green light; Audra could see little of it through the dirty glass. She could hear Miles's voice, urgent and almost desperate, but the words he shouted at the thing made no sense to her.

She shifted her weight to ease the pain of her knee pressing against the metal of the dumpster, and slipped. She fell, and cried out in pain as she landed hard on the pavement. She didn't know if Miles had heard, but she did not wait to find out. She picked herself up—now wet, filthy, and aching—and ran.

When she reached the house she went straight to the library. Audra shifted the books on the shelf so that the remaining volumes were flush against each other, and she hid her book in the small trunk where she kept her few clothes.

The Mirror's face emerged from its hiding place behind the frame, looking worried and wan.

"It's my story, after all," she told it. "I won't let him do any more damage. What if he takes the cottage? The woods? Where would I have to go home to? No, he can't have any more of our story."

The language of the scroll was not as impossible as the little man had said— while it was not his own, it was similar enough that someone as clever as Emil could puzzle it out. He applied himself to little else, and before long Emil could struggle through half of the first spell. But when he thought of arriving home after so long, still unable to execute even the simplest of the three, the frustration in him grew.

Surely, he thought, he should begin with the hardest, for having mastered that the simpler ones will come with ease.

So thinking, he set out to learn the last of the three spells before he arrived home.

When Miles finally returned the following evening at dusk, he looked exhausted and filthy, as if he had slept on the floor of the warehouse. She met him in the kitchen, and didn't ask questions.

He brooded on a chair in the corner while she chopped vegetables on the island butcher block, never taking his eyes off her, then stood abruptly and left the room.

The hiss and sputter of the vegetables as they hit the pan echoed the angry, inarticulate hiss in her mind. She had been here for days, and she was no closer to getting home.

The knife felt heavy and solid in her hand as she cubed a slab of marbled meat. She imagined Miles under the knife, imagined his fear and pain. She would get it out of him—how to get home—and he would tell her what he had done to her Emil before the miserable bastard died.

Sounds from the next room were punctuated with curses. The crack of heavy books being unshelved made her flinch.

"Where is it?" he first seemed to ask himself; then louder, *"Where?"* he demanded of the room at large; then a roar erupted from the doorway: *"What have you done with it, you vicious witch?"*

A cold wash of fear cleared away her thoughts of revenge.

"What are you talking about?"

"My book," he said. "Where is it? What have you done with it?"

He came at her hunched like an advancing wolf. They circled the butcher block. She gripped the knife and dared not blink, for fear that he would take a split second advantage and lunge for her.

"You have many books."

"And I only care about one!" His hand shot out and caught her wrist, bringing her arm down against the scarred wood with a painful shock. The knife fell from her hand.

He dragged her into the library. "There," he said, pointing to the shelf where her book had been. "Six of twelve. It was there and now it's not." He relaxed his grip without letting go. "If you borrowed it, it's fine. I just want it back." He released her and forced a smile. "Now, where is it?"

"You're right," she said, "I borrowed it. I didn't realize it was so important to you."

"It's very special."

"Yes," she said, her voice low and hard, "it is."

And with that, she knew she had given herself away.

Miles shoved her away from him. She fell into the bookcase as he left the small library and shut the door behind him. A key turned in the lock.

It was too late.

She rested with her forehead against the door and caught her breath. She tried to pry open the small window, but it was sealed shut with layers of paint. She considered breaking the glass, and then thought better of it; she could escape from this house, it was true, but not from this world. For that, she still needed Miles.

She watched the sun set through the dirty window, and tried to decide what to do when he let her out. She heard him pacing through the house, talking to himself with ever greater stridency, but the words made no sense to her. It gave her a headache.

The sound of the key in the door woke her. She grabbed at the first thing that might serve as a weapon, a sturdy hardcover. She held in front of her like a shield.

Miles stood in the doorway, a long, wicked knife in his hand.

"Who are you?" he finally asked, his eyes narrowed with suspicion. "And how did you know?"

"Someone whose life you destroyed. Liar. Thief. Murderer." She produced Emil's ring.

He seemed frozen where he stood, his eyes darting back and forth between the ring in her hand and her face. "I am none of those things," he said.

"You took all of this," she gestured around the room. "You took him, and you took me. And what did you do with the things that were of no use to you?"

She had been edging toward him while she talked. She threw the book at his arm and it struck him just as she had hoped. The knife fell to the floor and she dove for it, snatching it up before Miles could stop her.

She had him now, she thought, and pressed the blade against his throat. He tried to push her off but she had a tenacious grip on him and he ceased his struggle when the knife pierced his thin skin. She felt his body tense in her hands, barely breathing and perfectly still.

"You still haven't told me who you are."

"Where is he?" she demanded.

"Where is who?" His voice was smooth and controlled.

"The man you stole, like you stole me. Like you stole all of it. Where is he?"

"You're obviously very upset. Put that down, let me go, and we'll talk about it. I don't know about any stolen man, but maybe I can help you find him."

He voice was calm, slightly imploring, asking for understanding and offering help. She hesitated, wondering what threat she was really willing to carry out against an enemy who was also her only hope.

She waited a moment too long. Miles grabbed a heavy jar off the shelf and hurled it at the wall.

The East Wind ripped through the room, finally free.

Fatigued and half-starved, Emil made his way slowly toward his home, and tried to unlock the spell. Soon he had three words, and then five, and soon a dozen. He would say them aloud, emphasizing this part or that, elongating a sound or shortening it, until the day he gave voice to the last character on the page, and something happened: a spark, a glimmer of magic.

He had ciphered out the spell.

Finally, on the coldest night he could remember, with not a soul in sight, he raised his voice against the howling wind, and shouted out the thirteen words of power.

As weeks turned into months the stories of Emil the Sorcerer grew, until finally even the King had heard, and wanted his power within his own control.

But Emil could not be found.

The angry vortex threw everything off the shelves. Audra ducked and covered her head as she was pummeled by books and debris. Miles crouched behind the trunk, which offered little protection from the gale.

There was a crash above Audra's head; her arms flew up to protect her eyes; broken glass struck her arms and legs, some falling away, some piercing her skin.

The window broke with a final crash and the captive wind escaped the room. The storm was over. Books thumped and glass tinkled to the ground.

Audra opened her eyes to the wreckage. Miles was already sifting through the pages and torn covers.

"No," he said, "no! It has to be here, my story has to be here…" He bled from a hundred small cuts but he paid them no mind. Audra plucked shards of dark glass out of her flesh. The shards gave off no reflection at all.

A cloud drifted from where the Mirror had hung over the wreckage-strewn shelves, searching. On the floor beside Audra's trunk, the lid torn off in the storm, it seemed to find what it was looking for. It slipped between the pages of a blue cloth-bound volume and disappeared.

"Here!" Audra said, clutching the volume to her chest. He scrambled toward her until they kneeled together in the middle of the floor, face to face.

Smoke curled out of the pages, only a wisp at first. Then more, green and glowing like a sunbeam in a mossy pond, crept out and wrapped itself around both them.

"The Guide you sought was always here," a voice whispered. "Your captive, Emil, and your friend, Aurora." Audra—Aurora—looked at the man she had hated and saw what was there all along: her Emil, thirty years since he had disappeared, with bald head and graying beard. Miles, who kept her because she looked like his lost love, but who wouldn't touch her, in faith to his beloved.

Emil looked back at her, tears in the eyes that had seemed so dead and without hope until now.

"Now, Emil, speak the words," the voice said, "and we will go home."

So should you happen across a blue cloth-bound book, the sixth in a set of twelve, do not look for "The Magician and the Maid," because it is not there.

Read the other stories, though, and in the story of the fairy who brought the waterfall to the mountain, you may find that she has a friend called Audra, though you will know the truth: it is not her real name.

If you read further you may find Emil as well, for though he never did become the King's magician, every story needs a little magic.

TRIPS

ROBERT SILVERBERG

Robert Silverberg—four-time Hugo Award winner, five-time winner of the Nebula Award, SFWA Grand Master, SF Hall of Fame
honoree—is the author of nearly five hundred short stories, nearly
one hundred fifty novels, and is the editor of in the neighborhood
of one hundred anthologies. Among his most famous works are *Lord
Valentine's Castle, Dying Inside, Nightwings,* and *The World Inside.*

> *Does this path have a heart? All paths are the same: they lead
> nowhere. They are paths going through the bush, or into the bush.
> In my own life I could say I have traversed long, long paths, but I
> am not anywhere…Does this path have a heart? If it does, the path
> is good, if it doesn't, it is of no use. Both paths lead nowhere; but
> one has a heart, the other doesn't. One makes for a joyful journey;
> as long as you follow it, you are one with it. The other will make
> you curse your life.*
>
> —The Teachings of Don Juan

1.

The second place you come to—the first having proved unsatisfac-
tory, for one reason and another—is a city which could almost be
San Francisco. Perhaps it is, sitting out there on the peninsula between the ocean and the bay, white buildings clambering over improbably
steep hills. It occupies the place in your psychic space that San Francisco

has always occupied, although you don't really know yet what this city calls itself. Perhaps you'll find out before long.

You go forward. What you feel first is the strangeness of the familiar, and then the utter heartless familiarity of the strange. For example the automobiles, and there are plenty of them, are all halftracks: low sleek sexy sedans that have the flashy Detroit styling, the usual chrome, the usual streamlining, the low-raked windows all agleam, but there are only two wheels, both of them in front, with a pair of tread-belts circling endlessly in back. Is this good design for city use? Who knows? Somebody evidently thinks so, here. And then the newspapers: the format is the same, narrow columns, gaudy screaming headlines, miles of black type on coarse greyish-white paper, but the names and the places have been changed. You scan the front page of a newspaper in the window of a kerbside vending machine. Big photo of Chairman DeGrasse, serving as host at a reception for the Patagonian Ambassador. An account of the tribal massacres in the highlands of Dzungaria. Details of the solitude epidemic that is devastating Persepolis. When the halftracks stall on the hillsides, which is often, the other drivers ring silvery chimes, politely venting their impatience. Men who look like Navahos chant what sound like sutras in the intersections. The traffic lights are blue and orange. Clothing tends toward the prosaic, greys and dark blues, but the cut and slope of men's jackets has an angular formal eighteenth-century look, verging on pomposity.

You pick up a bright coin that lies in the street; it is vaguely metallic but rubbery, as if you could compress it between your fingers, and its thick edges bear incuse lettering: TO GOD WE OWE OUR SWORDS. On the next block a squat two-storey building is ablaze, and agitated clerks do a desperate dance. The fire engine is glossy green and its pump looks like a diabolical cannon embellished with sweeping flanges; it spouts a glistening yellow foam that eats the flames and, oxidizing, runs off down the gutter, a trickle of sluggish blue fluid. Everyone wears eyeglasses here, everyone. At a sidewalk café, pale waitresses offer mugs of boiling-hot milk into which the silent tight-faced patrons put cinnamon, mustard, and what seems to be Tabasco sauce. You offer your coin and try a sample, imitating what they do, and everyone bursts into laughter. The girl behind the counter pushes a thick stack of paper currency at you by way of change: UNITED FEDERAL COLUMBIAN REPUBLIC, each bill declares, GOOD FOR ONE EXCHANGE. Illegible signatures. Portrait of early leader of the republic, so famous that they give him no label of identification, bewigged, wall-eyed, ecstatic. You sip your milk, blowing gently. A light scum begins to form on its speckled surface. Sirens start to wail. About you, the other milk-drinkers stir uneasily. A parade is coming. Trumpets, drums, far-off chanting. Look! Four naked boys carry an open brocaded litter on which there sits an immense block of ice, a great frosted cube, mysterious, impenetrable. "Patagonia!" the onlookers cry sadly. The word is wrenched from them: "Patagonia!" Next, marching by himself, a mitred bishop advances, all in green, curtseying to the crowd, tossing hearty blessings as though they were flowers. "Forget your sins! Cancel your debts! All is made new! All is good!" You shiver and peer intently into his eyes as he passes you, hoping that he will single you out for an embrace. He is terribly tall but white-haired and fragile, somehow, despite his agility and energy. He reminds you of Norman, your wife's older brother, and perhaps he *is* Norman, the Norman of this place, and you wonder if he can give you news of Elizabeth, the Elizabeth of this place, but you say nothing and he goes by.

And then comes a tremendous wooden scaffold on wheels, a true juggernaut, at the summit of which rests a polished statue carved out of gleaming black stone: a human figure, male, plump, arms intricately folded, face complacent. The statue emanates a sense of vast Sumerian calm. The face is that of Chairman DeGrasse. "He'll die in the first blizzard," murmurs a man to your left. Another, turning suddenly, says with great force, "No, it's going to be done the proper way. He'll last until the time of the accidents, just as he's supposed to. I'll bet on that." Instantly they are nose to nose, glaring, and then they are wagering—a tense complicated ritual involving slapping of palms, interchanges of slips of paper, formal voiding of spittle, hysterical appeals to witnesses. The emotional climate here seems a trifle too intense. You decide to move along. Warily you leave the café, looking in all directions.

2.

Before you began your travels you were told how essential it was to define your intended role. Were you going to be a tourist, or an explorer, or an infiltrator? Those are the choices that confront anyone arriving at a new place. Each bears its special risks.

To opt for being a tourist is to choose the easiest but most contemptible path; ultimately it's the most dangerous one, too, in a certain sense. You have to accept the built-in epithets that go with the part: they will think of you as a *foolish* tourist, an *ignorant* tourist, a *vulgar* tourist, a *mere* tourist. Do you want to be considered mere? Are you able to accept that? Is that really your preferred self-image—baffled, bewildered, led about by the nose?

You'll sign up for packaged tours, you'll carry guidebooks and cameras, you'll go to the cathedral and the museums and the marketplace, and you'll remain always on the outside of things, seeing a great deal, experiencing nothing. What a waste! You will be diminished by the very travelling that you thought would expand you. Tourism hollows and parches you. All places become one: a hotel, a smiling, swarthy, sunglassed guide, a bus, a plaza, a fountain, a marketplace, a museum, a cathedral. You are transformed into a feeble shrivelled thing made out of glued-together travel folders; you are naked but for your visas; the sum of your life's adventures is a box of leftover small change from many indistinguishable lands.

To be an explorer is to make the macho choice. You swagger in, bent on conquest; for isn't any discovery a kind of conquest? Your existential position, like that of any mere tourist, lies outside the heart of things, but you are unashamed of that. And while tourists are essentially passive, the explorer's role is active: an explorer intends to grasp that heart, take possession, squeeze. In the explorer's role you consciously cloak yourself in the trappings of power: self-assurance, thick bankroll, stack of credit cards. You capitalize on the glamour of being a stranger. Your curiosity is invincible; you ask unabashed questions about the most intimate things, never for an instant relinquishing eye contact. You open locked doors and flash bright lights into curtained rooms. You are Magellan; you are Malinowski; you are Captain Cook. You will gain much, but—ah, here is the price!—you will always be feared and hated, you will never be permitted to attain the true core. Nor is superficiality the worst peril. Remember that Magellan and Captain Cook left their bones on tropic beaches. Sometimes the natives lose patience with explorers.

The infiltrator, though? His is at once the most difficult role and the most rewarding one. Will it be yours? Consider. You'll have to get right with it when you reach your destination, instantly learn the regulations, find your way around like an old hand, discover the location of shops and freeways and hotels, figure out the units of currency, the rules of social intercourse—all of this knowledge mastered surreptitiously, through observation alone, while moving about silently, camouflaged, never asking for help. You must become a part of the world you have entered, and the way to do it is to encourage a general assumption that you already are a part of it, have always been a part of it. Wherever you land, you need to recognize that life has been going on for millions of years, life goes on there steadily, with you or without you; you are the intrusive one, and if you don't want to feel intrusive you'd better learn fast how to fit in.

Of course, it isn't easy. The infiltrator doesn't have the privilege of buying stability by acting dumb. You won't be able to say, "How much does it cost to ride on the cable car?" You won't be able to say, "I'm from somewhere else, and this is the kind of money I carry, dollars quarters pennies halves nickels, is any of it legal tender here?" You don't dare identify yourself in any way as an outsider. If you don't get the idioms or the accent right, you can tell them you grew up out of town, but that's as much as you can reveal. The truth is your eternal secret, even when you're in trouble, *especially* when you're in trouble. When your back's to the wall you won't have time to say, "Look, I wasn't born in this universe at all, you see, I came zipping in from some other place, so pardon me, forgive me, excuse me, pity me." No, no, no, you can't do that. They won't believe you, and even if they do, they'll make it all the worse for you once they know. If you want to infiltrate, Cameron, you've got to fake it all the way. Jaunty smile; steely, even gaze. And you have to infiltrate. You know that, don't you? You don't really have any choice.

Infiltrating has its dangers, too. The rough part comes when they find you out, and they always will find you out. Then they'll react bitterly against your deception; they'll lash out in blind rage. If you're lucky, you'll be gone before they learn your sweaty little secret. Before they discover the discarded phrasebook hidden in the boarding-house room, before they stumble on the torn-off pages of your private journal. They'll find you out. They always do. But by then you'll be somewhere else, you hope, beyond the reach of their anger and their sorrow, beyond their reach.

3.

Suppose I show you, for Exhibit A, Cameron reacting to an extraordinary situation. You can test your own resilience by trying to picture yourself in his position. There has been a sensation in Cameron's mind very much like that of the extinction of the cosmos: a thunderclap, everything going black, a blankness, a total absence. Followed by the return of light, flowing inward upon him like high tide on the celestial shore, a surging stream of bright-ness moving with inexorable certainty. He stands flatfooted, dumbfounded, high on a bare hillside in warm early-hour sunlight. The house—redwood timbers, picture window, driftwood sculptures, paintings, books, records, refrigerator, gallon jugs of red wine, carpets, tiles, avocado plants in wooden tubs, carport, car, driveway—is gone. The neighbouring houses are gone. The winding street is gone. The eucalyptus forest that ought to be behind him, rising toward the crest of the hill, is gone. Downslope there is no Oakland, there is no Berkeley, only a scattering of crude squatter's shacks running raggedly along unpaved switchbacks toward the pure blue bay. Across the water there is no Bay Bridge; on the far shore there is no San Francisco. The Golden Gate Bridge does not span the gap between the city and the Marin headland—Cameron is astonished, not that he didn't expect something like this, but that the transformation is so complete, so absolute. "If you don't want your world any more," the old man had said, "you can drop it, can't you? Let go of it, let it drop. Can't you? Of course you can."

And so Cameron has let go of it. He's in another place entirely, now. Wherever this place is, it isn't home. The sprawling Bay Area cities and towns aren't here, never were. Goodbye, San Leandro, San Mateo, El Cerrito, Walnut Creek. He sees a landscape of gentle bare hills, rolling meadows, the dry brown grass of summer; the scarring hand of man is evident only occasionally. He begins to adapt. This is what he must have wanted, after all; and though he has been jarred by the shock of transition, he is recovering quickly; he is settling in; he feels already that he could belong here. He will explore this unfamiliar world, and if he finds it good he will discover a niche for himself. The air is sweet. The sky is cloudless. Has he really gone to some new place, or is he still in the old place and has everything else that was there simply gone away? Easy. He has gone. Everything else has gone. The cosmos has entered into a transitional phase. Nothing's stable any more. From this moment onward, Cameron's existence is a conditional matter, subject to ready alteration. What did the old man say? *Go wherever you like. Define your world as you would like it to be, and go there, and if you discover that you don't care for this or don't need that, why, go somewhere else. It's all trips, this universe.* What else is there? There isn't anything but trips. Just trips. So here you are, friend. New frameworks! New patterns! New!

4.

There is a sound to his left, the crackling of dry brush underfoot, and Cameron turns, looking straight into the morning sun, and sees a man on horseback approaching him. He is tall, slender, about Cameron's own height and build, it seems, but perhaps a shade broader through the shoulders. His hair, like Cameron's, is golden, but it is much longer, descending in a straight flow to his shoulders and tumbling onto his chest. He has a soft, full curling beard, untrimmed but tidy. He wears a wide-brimmed hat, buckskin chaps, and a light fringed jacket of tawny leather. Because of the sunlight Cameron has difficulty at first making out his features, but after a moment his eyes adjust and he sees that the other's face is very much like his own: thin lips, jutting high-bridged nose, cleft chin, cool blue eyes below heavy brows. Of course. Your face is my face. You and I, I and you, drawn to the same place at the same time across the many worlds. Cameron had not expected this, but now that it has happened it seems to have been inevitable.

They look at each other. Neither speaks. During that silent moment Cameron invents a scene for them. He imagines the other dismounting, inspecting him in wonder, walking around him, peering into his face, studying it, frowning, shaking his head, finally grinning and saying:

—I'll be damned. I never knew I had a twin brother. But here you are. It's just like looking in the mirror.

—We aren't twins.

—We've got the same face. Same everything. Trim away a little hair and nobody could tell me from you, you from me. If we aren't twins, what are we?

—We're closer than brothers.

—I don't follow your meaning, friend.

—This is how it is: I'm you. You're me. One soul, one identity. What's your name?

—Cameron.

—Of course. First name?

—Kit.

—That's short for Christopher, isn't it? My name is Cameron too. Chris. Short for Christopher. I tell you, we're one and the same person, out of two different worlds. Closer than brothers. Closer than anything.

None of this is said, however. Instead, the man in the leather clothing rides slowly toward Cameron, pauses, gives him a long incurious stare, and says simply, "Morning. Nice day." And continues onward.

"Wait," Cameron says.

The man halts. Looks back. "What?"

Never ask for help. Fake it all the way. Jaunty smile; steely, even gaze.

Yes. Cameron remembers all that. Somehow, though, infiltration seems easier to bring off in a city. You can blend into the background there. More difficult here, exposed as you are against the stark, unpeopled landscape.

Cameron says, as casually as he can, using what he hopes is a colourless neutral accent, "I've been travelling out from inland. Came a long way."

"Umm. Didn't think you were from around here. Your clothes."

"Inland clothes."

"The way you talk. Different. So?"

"New to these parts. Wondered if you could tell me a place I could hire a room till I got settled."

"You come all this way on foot?"

"Had a mule. Lost him back in the valley. Lost everything I had with me."

"Umm. Indians cutting up again. You give them a little gin, they go crazy." The other smiles faintly; then the smile fades and he retreats into impassivity, sitting motionless with hands on thighs, face a mask of patience that seems merely to be a thin covering for impatience or worse.

—*Indians?*—

"They gave me a rough time," Cameron says, getting into the fantasy of it. "Umm."

"Cleaned me out, let me go."

"Umm. Umm."

Cameron feels his sense of a shared identity with this man lessening. There is no way of engaging him. I am you, you are I, and yet you take no notice of the strange fact that I wear your face and body, you seem to show no interest in me at all. Or else you hide your interest amazingly well.

Cameron says, "You know where I can get lodging?"

"Nothing much around here. Not many settlers this side of the bay, I guess."

"I'm strong. I can do most any kind of work. Maybe you could use—"

"Umm. No." Cold dismissal glitters in the frosty eyes. Cameron wonders how often people in the world of his former life saw such a look in his own. A tug on the reins. Your time is up, stranger. The horse swings around and begins picking its way daintily along the path.

Desperately Cameron calls, "One thing more!"

"Umm?"

"Is your name Cameron?"

A flicker of interest. "Might be."

"Christopher Cameron. Kit. Chris. That you?"

"Kit." The other's eyes drill into his own. The mouth compresses until the lips are invisible: not a scowl but a speculative, pensive movement. There is tension in the way the other man grasps his reins. For the first time Cameron feels that he has made contact. "Kit Cameron, yes. Why?"

"Your wife," Cameron says. "Her name Elizabeth?"

The tension increases. The other Cameron is cloaked in explosive silence.

Something terrible is building within him. Then, unexpectedly, the tension snaps. The other man spits, scowls, slumps in his saddle. "My woman's dead," he mutters. "Say, who the hell are you? What do you want with me?"

"I'm—I'm—" Cameron falters. He is overwhelmed by fear and pity. A bad start, a lamentable start. He trembles. He had not thought it would be anything like this. With an effort he masters himself. Fiercely he says, "I've got to know. Was her name Elizabeth?" For an answer the horseman whacks his heels savagely against his mount's ribs and gallops away, fleeing as though he has had an encounter with Satan.

5.

Go, the old man said. You know the score. This is how it is: everything's random, nothing's fixed unless we want it to be, and even then the system isn't as stable as we think it is. So go. Go. Go, he said, and, of course, hearing something like that, Cameron went. What else could he do, once he had his freedom, but abandon his native universe and try a different one? Notice that I didn't say a better one, just a different one. Or two or three or five different ones. It was a gamble, certainly. He might lose everything that mattered to him, and gain nothing worth having. But what of it? Every day is full of gambles like that: you stake your life whenever you open a door. You never know what's heading your way, not ever, and still you choose to play the game. How can a man be expected to become all he's capable of becoming if he spends his whole life pacing up and down the same courtyard? Go. Make your voyages. Time forks, again and again and again. New universes split off at each instant of decision. Left turn, right turn, honk your horn, jump the traffic light, hit your gas, hit your brake, every action spawns whole galaxies of possibility. We move through a soup of infinities. If repressing a sneeze generates an alternative continuum, what, then, are the consequences of the truly major acts, the assassinations and inseminations, the conversions, the renunciations? Go. And as you travel, mull these thoughts constantly. Part of the game is discerning the precipitating factors that shaped the worlds you visit. What's the story here? Dirt roads, donkey-carts, hand-sewn clothes. No Industrial Revolution, is that it? The steam-engine man—what was his name, Savery, Newcomen Watt?—smothered in his cradle? No mines, no factories, no assembly lines, no dark satanic mills. That must be it. The air is so pure here: you can tell by that, it's a simpler era. Very good, Cameron. You see the patterns swiftly. But now try somewhere else. Your own self has rejected you here; besides, this place has no Elizabeth. Close your eyes. Summon the lightning.

6.

The parade has reached a disturbing level of frenzy. Marchers and floats now occupy the side streets as well as the main boulevard, and there is no way to escape from their demonic enthusiasm. Streamers cascade from office windows, and gigantic photographs of Chairman DeGrasse have sprouted on every wall, suddenly, like dark infestations of lichen. A boy presses close against Cameron, extends a clenched fist, opens his fingers: on his palm rests a glittering jewelled case, egg-shaped, thumbnail-sized, "Spores from Patagonia," he says. "Let me have ten exchanges and they're yours." Politely Cameron declines. A woman in a blue and orange frock tugs at his arm and says urgently, "All the rumours are true, you know. They've just been confirmed. What are you going to do about that? What are you going to do?" Cameron shrugs and smiles and disengages himself. A man with gleaming buttons asks, "Are you enjoying the festival? I've sold everything, and I'm going to move to the highway next Godsday." Cameron nods and murmurs congratulations, hoping congratulations are in order. He turns a corner and confronts, once more, the bishop who looks like Elizabeth's brother, who is, he concludes, indeed Elizabeth's brother. "Forget your sins!" he is crying still. "Cancel your debts!" Cameron thrusts his head between two plump girls at the kerb and attempts to call to him, but his voice fails, nothing coming forth but a hoarse wordless rasp, and the bishop moves on. Moving on is a good idea, Cameron tells himself. This place exhausts him. He has come to it too soon, and its manic tonality is more than he wants to handle. He finds a quiet alleyway, presses his cheek against a cool brick wall, and stands there breathing deeply until he is calm enough to depart. All right. Onward.

7.

Empty grasslands spread to the horizon. This could be the Gobi steppe. Cameron sees neither cities nor towns nor even villages, just six or seven squat black tents pitched in a loose circle in the saddle between two low grey-green hummocks, a few hundred yards from where he stands. He looks beyond, across the gently folded land, and spies dark animal figures at the limits of his range of vision: about a dozen horses, close together, muzzle to muzzle, flank to flank, horses with riders. Or perhaps they are a congregation of centaurs. Anything is possible. He decides, though, that they are Indians, a war party of young braves, maybe, camping in these desolate plains. They see him. Quite likely they saw him some while before he noticed them. Casually they break out of their grouping, wheel, ride in his direction.

He awaits them. Why should he flee? Where could he hide? Their pace accelerates from trot to canter, from canter to wild gallop; now they plunge toward him with fluid ferocity and a terrifying eagerness. They wear open leather jackets and rough rawhide leggings; they carry lances, bows, battle-axes, long curved swords; they ride small, agile horses, hardly more than ponies, tireless packets of energy. They surround him, pulling up, the fierce little steeds rearing and whinnying; they peer at him, point, laugh, exchange harsh derisive comments in a mysterious language. Then, solemnly, they begin to ride slowly in a wide circle around him. They are flat-faced, small-nosed, bearded, with broad, prominent cheekbones; the crowns of their heads are shaven but long black hair streams down over their ears and the napes of their necks. Heavy folds in the upper lids give their eyes a slanted look. Their skins are copper-coloured but with an underlying golden tinge, as though these are not Indians at all, but—what? Japanese? A samurai corps? No, probably not Japanese. But not Indians either.

They continue to circle him, gradually moving more swiftly. They chatter to one another and occasionally hurl what sound like questions at him. They seem fascinated by him, but also contemptuous. In a sudden demonstration of horsemanship one of them cuts from the circular formation and, goading his horse to an instant gallop, streaks past Cameron, leaning down to jab a finger into his forearm. Then another does it, and another, streaking back and forth across the circle, poking him, plucking at his hair, tweaking him, nearly running him down. They draw their swords and swish them through the air just above his head. They menace him, or pretend to, with their lances. Throughout it all they laugh. He stands perfectly still. This ordeal, he suspects, is a test of his courage. Which he passes, eventually. The lunatic galloping ceases; they rein in, and several of them dismount.

They are little men, chest-high to him but thicker through the chest and shoulders than he is. One unships a leather pouch and offers it to him with an unmistakable gesture: take, drink. Cameron sips cautiously. It is a thick greyish fluid, both sweet and sour. Fermented milk? He gags, winces, forces himself to sip again; they watch him closely. The second taste isn't so bad. He takes a third more willingly and gravely returns the pouch. The warriors laugh, not derisively now but more in applause, and the man who had given him the pouch slaps Cameron's shoulder admiringly. He tosses the pouch back to Cameron. Then he leaps to his saddle, and abruptly they all take off. Mongols, Cameron realizes. The sons of Genghis Khan, riding to the horizon. A worldwide empire? Yes, and this must be the wild west for them, the frontier, where the young men enact their rites of passage. Back in Europe, after seven centuries of Mongol dominance, they have become citified, domesticated, sippers of wine, theatregoers, cultivators of gardens, but here they follow the ways of their all-conquering forefathers. Cameron shrugs. Nothing for him here. He takes a last sip of the milk and drops the pouch into the tall grass. Onward.

8.

No grass here. He sees the stumps of buildings, the blackened trunks of dead trees, mounds of broken tile and brick. The smell of death is in the air. All the bridges are down. Fog rolls in off the bay, dense and greasy, and becomes a screen on which images come alive. These ruins are inhabited. Figures move about. They are the living dead. Looking into the thick mist he sees a vision of the shock wave, he recoils as alpha particles shower his skin. He beholds the survivors emerging from their shattered houses, straggling into the smouldering streets, naked, stunned, their bodies charred, their eyes glazed, some of them with their hair on fire. The walking dead. No one speaks. No one asks why this has happened. He is watching a silent movie. The apocalyptic fire has touched the ground here; the land itself is burning. Blue phosphorescent flames rise from the earth. The final judgment, the day of wrath.

Now he hears a dread music beginning, a death march, all cellos and basses, the dark notes coming at wide intervals: ooom ooom ooom ooom ooom. And then the tempo picks up, the music becomes a danse macabre, syncopated, lively, the timbre still dark, the rhythms funereal: ooom ooom ooom-de-ooom de-ooom de-ooom de-ooom-de-ooom, jerky, chaotic, wildly gay. The distorted melody of the "Ode to Joy" lurks somewhere in the ragged strands of sound. The dying victims stretch their fleshless hands toward him. He shakes his head. What service can I do for you? Guilt assails him. He is a tourist in the land of their grief. Their eyes reproach him. He would embrace them, but he fears they will crumble at his touch, and he lets the procession go past him without doing anything to cross the gulf between himself and them. "Elizabeth?" he murmurs. "Norman?" They have no faces, only eyes. "What can I do? I can't do anything for you." Not even tears will come. He looks away. Though I speak with the tongues of men and of angels, and have not charity, I am become as sounding brass or a tinkling cymbal. And though I have the gift of prophecy, and understand all mysteries, and all knowledge; and though I have all faith, so that I could remove mountains, and have not charity, I am nothing. But this world is beyond the reach of love. He looks away. The sun appears. The fog burns off. The visions fade. He sees only the dead land, the ashes, the ruins. All right. Here we have no continuing city, but we seek one to come. Onward. Onward.

9.

And now, after this series of brief, disconcerting intermediate stops, Cameron has come to a city that is San Francisco beyond doubt, not some other city on San Francisco's site but a true San Francisco, a recognizable San Francisco. He pops into it atop Russian Hill, at the very crest, on a dazzling, brilliant, cloudless day. To his left, below, lies Fisherman's Wharf; ahead of him rises the Coit Tower; yes, and he can see the Ferry Building and the Bay Bridge. Familiar landmarks—but how strange all the rest seems! Where is the eye-stabbing Transamerica pyramid? Where is the colossal sombre stalk of the Bank of America? The strangeness, he realizes, derives not so much from substitutions as from absences. The big Embarcadero developments are not there, nor the Chinatown Holiday Inn, nor the miserable tentacles of the elevated freeways, nor, apparently, anything else that was constructed in the last twenty years. This is the old short-shanked San Francisco of his boyhood, a sparkling miniature city, unManhattanized, skylineless. Surely he has returned to the place he knew in the sleepy 1950s, the tranquil Eisenhower years.

He heads downhill, searching for a newspaper box. He finds one at the corner of Hyde and North Point, a bright-yellow metal rectangle. San Francisco *Chronicle,* ten cents? Is that the right price for 1954? One Roosevelt dime goes into the slot. The paper, he finds, is dated Tuesday, August 19, 1975. In what Cameron still thinks of, with some irony now, as the real world, the world that has been receding rapidly from him all day in a series of discontinuous jumps, it is also Tuesday, the 19th of August, 1975. So he has not gone backward in time at all; he has come to a San Francisco where time had seemingly been standing still. Why? In vertigo he eyes the front page. A three-column headline declares:

FUEHRER ARRIVES IN WASHINGTON

Under it, to the left, a photograph of three men, smiling broadly, positively beaming at one another. The caption identifies them as President Kennedy, Fuehrer Goering, and Ambassador Togarashi of Japan, meeting in the White House Rose Garden. Cameron closes his eyes. Using no data other than the headline and the caption, he attempts to concoct a plausible speculation. This is a world, he decides, in which the Axis must have won the war. The United States is a German fiefdom. There are no high-rise buildings in San Francisco because the American economy, shattered by defeat, has not yet in thirty years of peace returned to a level where it can afford to erect them, or perhaps because American venture capital, prodded by the financial ministers of the Third Reich (Hjalmar Schacht? The name drifts out of the swampy recesses of memory) now tends to flow toward Europe. But how could it have happened? Cameron remembers the war years clearly, the tremendous surge of patriotism, the vast mobilization, the great national effort. *Rosie the Riveter. Lucky Strike Green Goes to War. Let's Remember Pearl Harbor, As We Did the Alamo.* He doesn't see any way the Germans might have brought America to her knees. Except one. The bomb, he thinks, the bomb, the Nazis get the bomb in 1940 and Wernher von Braun invents a transatlantic rocket, and New York and Washington are nuked one night and that's it, we've been pushed beyond the resources of patriotism; we cave in and surrender within a week. And so—

He studies the photograph. President Kennedy, grinning, standing between Reichsfuehrer Goering and a suave youthful-looking Japanese. Kennedy? Ted? No, this is Jack, the very same Jack who, looking jowly, heavy bags under his eyes, deep creases in his face—he must be almost sixty years old, nearing the end of what is probably his second term of office. Jacqueline waiting none too patiently for him upstairs. Get done with your Japs and Nazis, love, and let's have a few drinkies together before the concert. Yes. John-John and Caroline are somewhere on the premises too, the nation's darlings, models for young people everywhere. Yes. And Goering? Indeed, the very same Goering. Well into his eighties, monstrously fat, chin upon chin, multitudes of chins, vast bemedalled bosom, little mischievous eyes glittering with a long lifetime's cheery recollections of gratified lusts. How happy he looks! And how amiable! It was always impossible to hate Goering the way one loathed Goebbels, say, or Himmler or Streicher; Goering had charm, the outrageous charm of a *monstre sacré*, of a Nero, of a Caligula, and here he is alive in the 1970s, a mountain of immoral flesh, having survived Adolf to become—Cameron assumes—second Fuehrer and to be received in pomp at the White House, no less. Perhaps a state banquet tomorrow night, rollmops, sauerbraten, kassler rippchen, koenigsberger klopse, washed down with flagons of Bernkasteler Doktor '69, Schloss Johannisberg '71, or does the Fuehrer prefer beer? We have the finest lagers on tap, Lowenbrau, Wurzburger Hofbrau—

But wait. Something rings false in Cameron's historical construct. He is unable to find in John F. Kennedy those depths of opportunism that would allow him to serve as puppet President of a Nazi-ruled America, taking orders from some slick-haired hard-eyed gauleiter and hopping obediently when the Fuehrer comes to town. Bomb or no bomb, there would have been a diehard underground resistance movement, decades of guerrilla warfare, bitter hatred of the German oppressor and of all collaborators. No surrender, then. The Axis has won the war, but the United States has retained its autonomy. Cameron revises his speculations. Suppose, he tells himself, Hitler in this universe did not break his pact with Stalin and invade Russia in the summer of 1941, but led his forces across the Channel instead to wipe out Britain. And the Japanese left Pearl Harbor alone, so the United States never was drawn into the war, which was over in fairly short order—say, by September of 1942. The Germans now rule Europe from Cornwall to the Urals and the Japanese have the whole Pacific, west of Hawaii; the United States, lost in dreamy neutrality, is an isolated nation, a giant Portugal, economically stagnant, largely cut off from world trade. There are no skyscrapers in San Francisco because no one sees reason to build anything in this country. Yes? Is this how it is?

He seats himself on the stoop of a house and explores his newspaper. This world has a stock market, albeit a sluggish one: the Dow-Jones Industrials stand at 354.61. Some of the listings are familiar—IBM, AT&T, General Motors—but many are not. Litton, Syntex, and Polaroid all are missing; so is Xerox, but he finds its primordial predecessor, Haloid, in the quotations. There are two baseball leagues, each with eight clubs; the Boston Braves have moved to Milwaukee but otherwise the table of teams could have come straight out of the 1940s. Brooklyn is leading in the National League, Philadelphia in the American. In the news section he finds recognizable names: New York has a Senator Rockefeller, Massachusetts has a Senator Kennedy. (Robert, apparently. He is currently in Italy. Yesterday he toured the majestic Tomb of Mussolini near the Colosseum, today he has an audience with Pope Benedict.) An airline advertisement invites San Franciscans to go to New York via TWA's glorious new Starliners, now only twelve hours with only a brief stop in Chicago. The accompanying sketch indicates that they have about reached the DC-4 level here, or is that a DC-6, with all those propellers?

The foreign news is tame and sketchy: not a word about Israel vs. the Arabs, the squabbling republics of Africa, the People's Republic of China, or the war in South America. Cameron assumes that the only surviving Jews are those of New York and Los Angeles, that Africa is one immense German colonial tract with a few patches under Italian rule, that China is governed by the Japanese, not by the heirs of Chairman Mao, and that the South American nations are torpid and unaggressive. Yes? Reading this newspaper is the strangest experience this voyage has given him so far, for the pages *look* right, the tone of the writing *feels* right, there is the insistent texture of unarguable reality about the whole paper, and yet everything is subtly off, everything has undergone a slight shift along the spectrum of events. The newspaper has the quality of a dream, but he has never known a dream to have such overwhelming substantive density.

He folds the paper under his arm and strolls toward the bay. A block from the waterfront he finds a branch of the Bank of America—some things withstand all permutations—and goes inside to change some money. There are risks, but he is curious. The teller unhesitatingly takes his five-dollar bill and hands him four singles and a little stack of coins. The singles are unremarkable, and Lincoln, Jefferson, and Washington occupy their familiar places on the cent, nickel, and quarter; but the dime shows Ben Franklin and the fifty-cent piece bears the features of a hearty-looking man, youngish, full-faced, bushy-haired, whom Cameron is unable to identify at all.

On the next corner eastward he comes to a public library. Now he can confirm his guesses. An almanac! Yes, and how odd the list of Presidents looks. Roosevelt, he learns, retired in poor health in 1940, and that, so far as he can discover, is the point of divergence between this world and his. The rest follows predictably enough. Wendell Willkie, defeating John Nance Garner in the 1940 election, maintains a policy of strict neutrality while—yes, it was as he imagined—the Germans and Japanese quickly conquer most of the world. Willkie dies in office during the 1944 Presidential campaign— Aha! That's Willkie on the half dollar!—and is briefly succeeded by Vice President McNary, who does not want the Presidency; a hastily recalled Republican convention nominates Robert Taft. Two terms then for Taft, who beats James Byrnes, and two for Thomas Dewey, and then in 1960 the long Republican era is ended at last by Senator Lyndon Johnson of Texas. Johnson's running mate—it is an amusing reversal, Cameron thinks—is Senator John F. Kennedy of Massachusetts. After the traditional two terms, Johnson steps down and Vice President Kennedy wins the 1968 Presidential election. He has been re-elected in 1972, naturally; in this placid world incumbents always win. There is, of course, no UN here, there has been no Korean War, no movement of colonial liberation, no exploration of space. The almanac tells Cameron that Hitler lived until 1960, Mussolini until 1958. The world seems to have adapted remarkably readily to Axis rule, although a German army of occupation is still stationed in England.

He is tempted to go on and on, comparing histories, learning the transmuted destinies of such figures as Hubert Humphrey, Dwight Eisenhower, Harry Truman, Nikita Khrushchev, Lee Harvey Oswald, Juan Peron. But suddenly a more intimate curiosity flowers in him. In a hallway alcove he consults the telephone book. There is one directory covering both Alameda and Contra Costa counties, and it is a much more slender volume than the directory which in his world covers Oakland alone. There are two dozen Cameron listings, but none at his address, and no Christophers or Elizabeths or any plausible permutations of those names. On a hunch he looks in the San Francisco book. Nothing promising there either; but then he checks Elizabeth under her maiden name, Dudley, and yes, there is an Elizabeth Dudley at the familiar old address on Laguna. The discovery causes him to tremble. He rummages in his pocket, finds his Ben Franklin dime, drops it in the slot. He listens. There's the dial tone. He makes the call.

10.

The apartment, what he can see of it by peering past her shoulder, looks much as he remembers it: well-worn couches and chairs upholstered in burgundy and dark green, stark whitewashed walls, elaborate sculptures—her own—of grey driftwood, huge ferns in hanging containers. To behold these objects in these surroundings wrenches powerfully at his sense of time and place and afflicts him with an almost unbearable nostalgia. The last time he was here, if indeed he has ever been "here" in any sense, was in 1969; but the memories are vivid, and what he sees corresponds so closely to what he recalls that he feels transported to that earlier era. She stands in the doorway, studying him with cool curiosity tinged with unmistakable suspicion. She wears unexpectedly ordinary clothes, a loose-fitting embroidered white blouse and a short, pleated blue skirt, and her golden hair looks dull and carelessly combed, but surely she is the same woman from whom he parted this morning, the same woman with whom he has shared his life these past seven years, a beautiful woman, a tall woman, nearly as tall as he—on some occasions taller, it has seemed—with a serene smile and steady green eyes and smooth, taut skin. "Yes?" she says uncertainly. "Are you the man who phoned?"

"Yes. Chris Cameron." He searches her face for some flicker of recognition. "You don't know me? Not at all?"

"Not at all. Should I know you?"

"Perhaps. Probably not. It's hard to say."

"Have we once met? Is that it?"

"I'm not sure how I'm going to explain my relationship to you."

"So you said when you called. Your *relationship* to me? How can strangers have had a relationship?"

"It's complicated. May I come in?"

She laughs nervously, as though caught in some embarrassing faux pas. "Of course," she says, not without giving him a quick appraisal, making a rapid estimate of risk. The apartment is in fact almost exactly as he knew it, except that there is no stereo phonograph, only a bulky archaic Victrola, and her record collection is surprisingly scanty, and there are rather fewer books than his Elizabeth would have had. They confront one another stiffly. He is as uneasy over this encounter as she is, and finally it is she who seeks some kind of social lubricant, suggesting that they have a little wine. She offers him red or white.

"Red, please," he says.

She goes to a low sideboard and takes out two cheap, clumsy-looking tumblers. Then, effortlessly she lifts a gallon jug of wine from the floor and begins to unscrew its cap. "You were awfully mysterious on the phone," she says, "and you're still being mysterious now. What brings you here? Do we have mutual friends?"

"I think it wouldn't be untruthful to say that we do. At least in a manner of speaking."

"Your own manner of speaking is remarkably round-about, Mr Cameron."

"I can't help that right now. And call me Chris, please." As she pours the wine he watches her closely, thinking of that other Elizabeth, *his* Elizabeth, thinking how well he knows her body, the supple play of muscles in her back, the sleek texture of her skin, the firmness of her flesh, and he flashes instantly to their strange, absurdly romantic meeting years ago, that June when he had gone off alone into the Sierra high country for a week of backpacking and, following heaps of stones that he had wrongly taken to be trail markers, had come to a place well off the path, a private place, a cool dark glacial lake rimmed by brilliant patches of late-lying snow, and had begun to make camp, and had become suddenly aware of someone else's pack thirty yards away, and a pile of discarded clothing on the shore, and then had seen her, swimming just beyond a pine-tipped point, heading toward land, rising like Venus from the water, naked, noticing him, startled by his presence, apprehensive for a moment but then immediately making the best of it, relaxing, smiling, standing unashamed shin-deep in the chilly shallows and inviting him to join her for a swim.

These recollections of that first contact and all that ensued excite him terribly, for this person before him is at once the Elizabeth he loves, familiar, joined to him by the bond of shared experience, and also someone new, a complete stranger, from whom he can draw fresh inputs, that jolting gift of novelty which his Elizabeth can never again offer him. He stares at her shoulders and back with fierce, intense hunger; she turns toward him with the glasses of wine in her hands, and, before he can mask that wild gleam of desire, she receives it with full force. The impact is immediate. She recoils. She is not the Elizabeth of the Sierra lake; she seems unable to handle such a level of unexpected erotic voltage. Jerkily she thrusts the wine at him, her hands shaking so that she spills a little on her sleeve. He takes the glass and backs away, a bit dazed by his own frenzied upwelling of emotion. With an effort he calms himself. There is a long moment of awkward silence while they drink. The psychic atmosphere grows less torrid; a certain mood of remote, businesslike courtesy develops between them.

After the second glass of wine she says, "Now. How do you know me and what do you want from me?"

Briefly he closes his eyes. What can he tell her? How can he explain? He has rehearsed no strategies. Already he has managed to alarm her with a single unguarded glance; what effect would a confession of apparent madness have? But he has never used strategies with Elizabeth, has never resorted to any tactics except the tactic of utter candidness. And this is Elizabeth. Slowly he says, "In another existence you and I are married, Elizabeth. We live in the Oakland hills and we're extraordinarily happy together."

"Another existence?"

"In a world apart from this, a world where history took a different course a generation ago, where the Axis lost the war, where John Kennedy was

President in 1963 and was killed by an assassin, where you and I met beside a lake in the Sierras and fell in love. There's an infinity of worlds, Elizabeth, side by side, worlds in which all possible variations of every possible event take place. Worlds in which you and I are married happily, in which you and I have been married and divorced, in which you and I don't exist, in which you exist and I don't, in which we meet and loathe one another, in which—in which—do you see, Elizabeth, there's a world for everything, and I've been travelling from world to world. I've seen nothing but wilderness where San Francisco ought to be, and I've met Mongol horsemen in the East Bay hills, and I've seen this whole area devastated by atomic warfare, and—does this sound insane to you, Elizabeth?"

"Just a little." She smiles. The old Elizabeth, cool, judicious, performing one of her specialities, the conditional acceptance of the unbelievable for the sake of some amusing conversation. "But go on. You've been jumping from world to world. I won't even bother to ask you how. What are you running away from?"

"I've never seen it that way. I'm running *toward.*"

"Toward what?"

"An infinity of worlds. An endless range of possible experience."

"That's a lot to swallow. Isn't one world enough for you to explore?"

"Evidently not."

"You had all infinity," she says. "Yet you chose to come to me. Presumably I'm the one point of familiarity for you in this otherwise strange world. Why come here? What's the point of your wanderings, if you seek the familiar? If all you wanted to do was find your way back to your Elizabeth, why did you leave her in the first place? Are you as happy with her as you claim to be?"

"I can be happy with her and still desire her in other guises."

"You sound driven."

"No," he says. "No more driven than Faust. I believe in searching as a way of life. Not searching *for,* just searching. And it's impossible to stop. To stop is to die, Elizabeth. Look at Faust, going on and on, going to Helen of Troy herself, experiencing everything the world has to offer, and always seeking more. When Faust finally cries out, *This is it, this is what I've been looking for, this is where I choose to stop,* Mephistopheles wins his bet."

"But that was Faust's moment of supreme happiness."

"True. When he attains it, though, he loses his soul to the devil, remember?"

"So you go on, on and on, world after world, seeking you know not what, just seeking, unable to stop. And yet you claim you're not driven."

He shakes his head. "Machines are driven. Animals are driven. I'm an autonomous human being operating out of free will. I don't make this journey because I have to, but because I want to."

"Or because you think you ought to want to."

"I'm motivated by feelings, not by intellectual calculations and preconceptions."

"That sounds very carefully thought out," she tells him. He is stung by her words, and looks away, down into his empty glass. She indicates that he should help himself to the wine. "I'm sorry," she says, her tone softening a little.

He says, "At any rate, I was in the library and there was a telephone directory and I found you. This is where you used to live in my world too, before we were married." He hesitates. "Do you mind if I ask—"

"What?"

"You're not married?"

"No. I live alone. And like it."

"You always were independent-minded."

"You talk as though you know me so well."

"I've been married to you for seven years."

"No. Not to me. Never to me. You don't know me at all."

He nods. "You're right. I don't really know you, Elizabeth, however much I think I do. But I want to. I feel drawn to you as strongly as I was to the other Elizabeth, that day in the mountains. It's always best right at the beginning, when two strangers reach toward one another, when the spark leaps the gap—" Tenderly he says, "May I spend the night here?"

"No."

Somehow the refusal comes as no surprise. He says, "You once gave me a different answer when I asked you that."

"Not I. Someone else."

"I'm sorry. It's so hard for me to keep you and her distinct in my mind, Elizabeth. But please don't turn me away. I've come so far to be with you."

"You came uninvited. Besides, I'd feel so strange with you—knowing you were thinking of her, comparing me with her, measuring our differences, our points of similarities—"

"What makes you think I would?"

"You would."

"I don't think that's sufficient reason for sending me away."

"I'll give you another," she says. Her eyes sparkle mischievously. "I never let myself get involved with married men."

She is teasing him now. He says, laughing, confident that she is beginning to yield. "That's the damnedest far-fetched excuse I've ever heard, Elizabeth!"

"Is it? I feel a great kinship with her. She has all my sympathies. Why should I help you deceive her?"

"Deceive? What an old-fashioned word! Do you think she'd object? She never expected me to be chaste on this trip. She'd be flattered and delighted to know that I went looking for you here. She'd be eager to hear about everything that went on between us. How could she possibly be hurt by knowing that I had been with you, when you and she are—"

"Nevertheless, I'd like you to leave. Please."

"You haven't given me one convincing reason."

"I don't need to."

"I love you. I want to spend the night with you."

"You love someone else who resembles me," she replies. "I keep telling you that. In any case, I don't love you. I don't find you attractive, I'm afraid."

"Oh. She does, but you—don't. I see. How do you find me then? Ugly? Overbearing? Repellent?"

"I find you disturbing," she says. "A little frightening. Much too intense, much too controlled, perhaps dangerous. You aren't my type. I'm probably not yours. Remember, I'm not the Elizabeth you met by that mountain lake. Perhaps I'd be happier if I were, but I'm not. I wish you had never come here. Now please go. Please."

11.

Onward. This place is all gleaming towers and airy bridges, a glistening fantasy of a city. High overhead float glassy bubbles, silent airborne passenger vehicles, containing two or three people apiece who sprawl in postures of elegant relaxation. Bronzed young boys and girls lie naked beside soaring fountains spewing turquoise-and-scarlet foam. Giant orchids burst in tropical voluptuousness from the walls of colossal hotels. Small mechanical birds wheel and dart in the soft air like golden bullets, emitting sweet pinging sounds. From the tips of the tallest buildings comes a darker music, a ground bass of swelling hundred-cycle notes oscillating around an insistent central rumble. This is a world two centuries ahead of his, at the least. He could never infiltrate here. He could never even be a tourist. The only role available to him is that of visiting savage.

Jemmy Button among the Londoners, and what, after all, was Jemmy Button's fate? Not a happy one. Patagonia! Patagonia! Thees ticket eet ees no longer good here, sor. Coloured rays dance in the sky, red, green, blue, exploding, showering the city with transcendental images. Cameron smiles. He will not let himself be overwhelmed, though this place is more confusing than the world of the halftrack automobiles. Jauntily he plants himself at the centre of a small park between two lanes of flowing, noiseless traffic. It is a formal garden lush with toothy orange-fronded ferns and thorny skyrockets of looping cactus. Lovers stroll past him arm in arm, offering one another swigs from glossy sweat-beaded green flasks that look like tubes of polished jade. Delicately they dangle blue grapes before each other's lips; playfully they smile, arch their necks, take the bait with eager pounces; then they laugh, embrace, tumble into the dense moist grass, which stirs and sways and emits gentle thrumming melodies. This place pleases him. He wanders through the garden, thinking of Elizabeth, thinking of springtime, and, coming ultimately to a sinuous brook in which the city's tallest towers are reflected as inverted needles, he kneels to drink. The water is cool, sweet, tart, much like young wine. A moment after it touches his lips a mechanism rises from the spongy earth, five slender brassy columns, three with eye-sensors sprouting on all sides, one marked with a pattern of dark gridwork, one bearing an arrangement of winking coloured lights. Out of the gridwork come ominous words in an unfathomable language. This is some kind of police machine, demanding his credentials: that much is clear. "I'm sorry," he says. "I can't understand what you're saying." Other machines are extruding themselves from trees, from the bed of the stream, from the hearts of the sturdiest ferns. "It's all right," he says. "I don't mean any harm. Just give me a chance to learn the language and I promise to become a useful citizen." One of the machines sprays him with a fine azure mist. Another drives a tiny needle into his forearm and extracts a droplet of blood. A crowd is gathering. They point, snicker, wink. The music of the building tops has become higher in pitch, more sinister in texture, it shakes the balmy air and threatens him in a personal way. "Let me stay," Cameron begs, but the music is shoving him, pushing him with a flat irresistible hand, inexorably squeezing him out of this world. He is too primitive for them. He is too coarse; he carries too many obsolete microbes. Very well. If that's what they want, he'll leave, not out of courtesy alone. In a flamboyant way he bids them farewell, bowing with a flourish worthy of Raleigh, blowing a kiss to the five-columned machine, smiling, even doing a little dance. Farewell.

Farewell. The music rises to a wild crescendo. He hears celestial trumpets and distant thunder. Farewell. Onward.

12.

Here some kind of oriental marketplace has sprung up, foul-smelling, cluttered, medieval. Swarthy old men, white-bearded, in thick grey robes, sit patiently behind open burlap sacks of spices and grains. Lepers and cripples roam everywhere, begging importunately. Slender long-legged men wearing only tight loincloths and jingling dangling earrings of bright copper stalk through the crowd on solitary orbits, buying nothing, saying nothing; their skins are dark red; their faces are gaunt; their solemn features are finely modelled. They carry themselves like Inca princes. Perhaps they are Inca princes. In the haggle and babble of the market Cameron hears no recognizable tongue spoken. He sees the flash of gold as transactions are completed. The women balance immense burdens on their heads and show brilliant teeth when they smile. They favour patchwork skirts that cover their ankles, but they leave their breasts bare. Several of them glance provocatively at Cameron but he dares not return their quick dazzling probes until he knows what is permissible here. On the far side of the squalid plaza he catches sight of a woman who might well be Elizabeth; her back is to him, but he would know those strong shoulders anywhere, that erect stance, that cascade of unbound golden hair. He starts toward her, sliding with difficulty between the close-packed marketgoers. When he is still halfway across the marketplace from her he notices a man at her side, tall, a man of his own height and build. He wears a loose black robe and a dark scarf covers the lower half of his face. His eyes are grim and sullen and a terrible cicatrice, wide and glaringly cross-hatched with stitch marks, runs along his left cheek up to his hairline. The man whispers something to the woman who might be Elizabeth; she nods and turns, so that Cameron now is able to see her face, and yes, the woman does seem to be Elizabeth, but she bears a matching scar, angry and hideous, up the right side of her face. Cameron gasps. The scar-faced man suddenly points and shouts. Cameron senses motion to one side, and swings around just in time to see a short thickbodied man come rushing toward him wildly waving a scimitar. For an instant Cameron sees the scene as though in a photograph: he has time to make a leisurely examination of his attacker's oily beard, his hooked hairy-nostriled nose, his yellowed teeth, the cheap glassy-looking inlaid stones on the haft of the scimitar.

Then the frightful blade descends, while the assassin screams abuse at Cameron in what might be Arabic. It is a sorry welcome. Cameron cannot prolong this investigation. An instant before the scimitar cuts him in two he takes himself elsewhere, with regret.

13.

Onward. To a place where there is no solidity, where the planet itself has vanished, so that he swims through space, falling peacefully, going from no-where to nowhere. He is surrounded by a brilliant green light that emanates from every point at once, like a message from the fabric of the universe. In great tranquillity he drops through this cheerful glow for days on end, or what seems like days on end, drifting, banking, checking his course with small motions of his elbows or knees. It makes no difference where he goes; everything here is like everything else here. The green glow supports and sustains and nourishes him, but it makes him restless. He plays with it. Out of its lambent substance he succeeds in shaping images, faces, abstract patterns; he conjures up Elizabeth for himself, he evokes his own sharp features, he fills the heavens with a legion of marching Chinese in tapered straw hats, he obliterates them with forceful diagonal lines, he causes a river of silver to stream across the firmament and discharge its glittering burden down a mountainside a thousand miles high. He spins. He floats. He glides. He releases all his fantasies. This is total freedom, here in this unworldly place. But it is not enough. He grows weary of emptiness. He grows weary of serenity. He has drained this place of all it has to offer, too soon, too soon. He is not sure whether the failure is in himself or in the place, but he feels he must leave. Therefore: onward.

14.

Terrified peasants run shrieking as he materializes in their midst. This is some sort of farming village along the eastern shore of the bay: neat green fields, a cluster of low wicker huts radiating from a central plaza, naked children toddling and crying, a busy sub-population of goats and geese and chickens. It is midday; Cameron sees the bright gleam of water in the irrigation ditches. These people work hard. They have scattered at his ap-proach, but now they creep back warily, crouching, ready to take off again if he performs any more miracles. This is another of those bucolic worlds in which San Francisco has not happened, but he is unable to identify these settlers, nor can he isolate the chain of events that brought them here. They are not Indians, nor Chinese, nor Peruvians; they have a European look about them, somehow Slavic, but what would Slavs be doing in California? Russian farmers, maybe, colonizing by way of Siberia? There is some plausibility in that—their dark complexions, their heavy facial structure, their squat powerful bodies—but they seem oddly primitive, half-naked, in furry leggings or less, as though they are no subjects of the Tsar but rather Scythians or Cimmerians transplanted from the prehistoric marshes of the Vistula.

"Don't be frightened," he tells them, holding his upraised outspread arms toward them. They do seem less fearful of him now, timidly approaching, staring with big dark eyes. "I won't harm you. I'd just like to visit with you." They murmur. A woman boldly shoves a child forward, a girl of about five, bare, with black greasy ringlets, and Cameron scoops her up, caresses her, tickles her, lightly sets her down. Instantly the whole tribe is around him, no longer afraid; they touch his arm, they kneel, they stroke his shins. A boy brings him a wooden bowl of porridge. An old woman gives him a mug of sweet wine, a kind of mead. A slender girl drapes a stole of auburn fur over his shoulders. They dance; they chant; their fear has turned into love; he is their honoured guest. He is more than that: he is a god. They take him to an unoccupied hut, the largest in the village. Piously they bring him offerings of incense and acorns. When it grows dark they build an immense bonfire in the plaza, so that he wonders in vague concern if they will feast on him when they are done honouring him, but they feast on slaughtered cattle instead, and yield to hint the choicest pieces, and afterward they stand by his door, singing discordant, energetic hymns. That night three girls of the tribe, no doubt the fairest virgins available, are sent to him, and in the morning he finds his threshold heaped with newly plucked blossoms. Later two tribal artisans, one lame and the other blind, set to work with stone adzes and chisels, hewing an immense and remarkable accurate likeness of him out of a redwood stump that has been mounted at the plaza's centre.

So he has been deified. He has a quick Faustian vision of himself living among these diligent people, teaching them advanced methods of agriculture, leading them eventually into technology, into modern hygiene, into all the contemporary advantages without the contemporary abominations. Guiding them toward the light, moulding them, creating them. This world, this village, would be a good place for him to stop his transit of the infinities, if stopping were desirable: god, prophet, king of a placid realm, teacher, inculcator of civilization, a purpose to his existence at last. But there is no place to stop. He knows that. Transforming happy primitive farmers into sophisticated twentieth-century agriculturalists is ultimately as useless a pastime as training fleas to jump through hoops. It is tempting to live as a god, but even divinity will pall, and it is dangerous to become attached to an unreal satisfaction, dangerous to become attached at all. The journey, not the arrival, matters. Always.

So Cameron does godhood for a little while. He finds it pleasant and fulfilling. He savours the rewards until he senses that the rewards are becoming too important to him. He makes his formal renunciation of his godhead. Then: onward.

15.

And this place he recognizes. His street, his house, his garden, his green car in the carport, Elizabeth's yellow one parked out front. Home again, so soon? He hadn't expected that; but every leap he has made, he knows, must in some way have been a product of deliberate choice, and evidently whatever hidden mechanism within him that has directed these voyages has chosen to bring him home again. All right, touch base. Digest your travels, examine them, allow your experiences to work their alchemy on you: you need to stand still a moment for that. Afterward you can always leave again. He slides his key into the door.

Elizabeth has one of the Mozart quartets on the phonograph. She sits curled up in the living-room window seat, leafing through a magazine. It is late afternoon, and the San Francisco skyline, clearly visible across the bay through the big window, is haloed by the brilliant retreating sunlight. There are freshly cut flowers in the little crystal bowl on the redwood-burl table; the fragrance of gardenias and jasmine dances past him. Unhurriedly she looks up, brings her eyes into line with his, dazzles him with the warmth of her smile, and says, "Well, hello!"

"Hello, Elizabeth."

She comes to him. "I didn't expect you back this quickly, Chris, I don't know if I expected you to come back at all, as a matter of fact."

"This quickly? How long have I been gone, for you?"

"Tuesday morning to Thursday afternoon. Two and a half days." She eyes his coarse new beard, his ragged, sun-bleached shirt. "It's been longer for you, hasn't it?"

"Weeks and weeks. I'm not sure how long. I was in eight or nine different places, and I stayed in the last one quite some time. They were villagers, farmers, some primitive Slavonic tribe living down by the bay. I was their god, but I got bored with it."

"You always did get bored so easily," she says, and laughs, and takes his hands in hers and pulls him toward her. She brushes her lips lightly against him, a peck, a play-kiss, their usual first greeting, and then they kiss more passionately, bodies pressing close, tongue seeking tongue. He feels a pounding in his chest, the old inextinguishable throb. When they release each other he steps back, a little dizzied, and says, "I missed you, Elizabeth. I didn't know how much I'd miss you until I was somewhere else and aware that I might never find you again."

"Did you seriously worry about that?"

"Very much."

"I never doubted we'd be together again, one way or another. Infinity's such a big place, darling. You'd find your way back to me, or to someone very much like me. And someone very much like you would find his way to me, if you didn't. How many Chris Camerons do you think there are, on the move between worlds right now? A thousand? A trillion trillion?" She turns toward the sideboard and says, without breaking the flow of her words, "Would you like some wine?" and begins to pour from a half-empty jug of red. "Tell me where you've been," she says.

He comes up behind her and rests his hands on her shoulders, and draws them down the back of her silk blouse to her waist, holding her there, kissing the nape of her neck. He says, "To a world where there was an atomic war here, and to one where there still were Indian raiders out by Livermore, and one that was all fantastic robots and futuristic helicopters, and one where Johnson was President before Kennedy and Kennedy is alive and President now, and one where—oh, I'll give you all the details later. I need a chance to unwind first." He releases her and kisses the tip of her earlobe and takes one of the glasses from her, and they salute each other and drink, draining the wine quickly. "It's so good to be home," he says softly. "Good to have gone where I went, good to be back." She fills his glass again. The familiar domestic ritual: red wine is their special drink, cheap red wine out of gallon jugs. A sacrament, more dear to him than the burnt offerings of his recent subjects. Halfway through the second glass he says, "Come. Let's go inside."

The bed has fresh linens on it, cool, inviting. There are three thick books on the night table: she's set up for some heavy reading in his absence. Cut flowers in here, too, fragrance everywhere. Their clothes drop away. She touches his beard and chuckles at the roughness, and he kisses the smooth cool place along the inside of her thigh and draws his cheek lightly across it, sandpapering her lovingly, and then she pulls him to her and their bodies slide together and he enters her. Everything thereafter happens quickly, much too quickly; he has been long absent from her, if not she from him, and now her presence excites him, there is a strangeness about her body, her movements, and it hastens him to his ecstasy. He feels a mild pang of regret, but no more: he'll make it up to her soon enough, they both know that. They drift into a sleepy embrace, neither of them speaking, and eventually uncoil into tender new passion, and this time all is as it should be. Afterward they doze. A spectacular sunset blazes over the city when he opens his eyes. They rise, they take a shower together, much giggling, much playfulness. "Let's go across the bay for a fancy dinner tonight," he suggests. "Trianon, Blue Fox, Ernie's, anywhere. You name it. I feel like celebrating."

"So do I, Chris."

"It's good to be home again."

"It's good to have you here," she tells him. She looks for her purse. "How soon do you think you'll be heading out again? Not that I mean to rush you, but—"

"You know I'm not going to be staying?"

"Of course I know."

"Yes. You would." She had never questioned his going. They both tried to be responsive to each other's needs; they had always regarded one another as equal partners, free to do as they wished. "I can't say how long I'll stay. Probably not long. Coming home this soon was really an accident, you know. I just planned to go on and on and on, world after world, and I never programmed my next jump, at least not consciously. I simply leaped. And the last leap deposited me on my own doorstep, somehow, so I let myself into the house. And there you were to welcome me home."

She presses his hand between hers. Almost sadly she says, "You aren't home, Chris."

"What?"

He hears the sound of the front door opening. Footsteps in the hallway.

"You aren't home," she says.

Confusion seizes him. He thinks of all that has passed between them this evening.

"Elizabeth?" calls a deep voice from the living room.

"In here, darling. I have company!"

"Oh? Who?" A man enters the bedroom, halts, grins. He is clean-shaven and dressed in the clothes Cameron had worn on Tuesday; otherwise they could be twins. "Hey, hello!" he says warmly, extending his hand.

Elizabeth says, "He comes from a place that must be very much like this one. He's been here since five o'clock, and we were just going out for dinner. Have you been having an interesting time?"

"Very," the other Cameron says. "I'll tell you all about it later. Go on, don't let me keep you."

"You could join us for dinner," Cameron suggests helplessly.

"That's all right. I've just eaten. Breast of passenger pigeon—they aren't extinct everywhere. I wish I could have brought some home for the freezer. So you two go and enjoy. I'll see you later. Both of you, I hope. Will you be staying with us? We've got notes to compare, you and I."

16.

He rises just before dawn, in a marvellous foggy stillness. The Camerons have been wonderfully hospitable, but he must be moving along. He scrawls a thank-you note and slips it under their bedroom door. Let's get together again someday. Somewhere. Somehow. They wanted him as a house guest for a week or two, but no, he feels like a bit of an intruder here, and anyway the universe is waiting for him. He has to go. The journey, not the arrival, matters, for what else is there but trips? Departing is unexpectedly painful, but he knows the mood will pass. He closes his eyes. He breaks his moorings. He gives himself up to his sublime restlessness. Onward. Onward. *Goodbye, Elizabeth. Goodbye, Chris. I'll see you both again.* Onward.

FOR FURTHER READING

COMPILED BY ROSS E. LOCKHART

Wha follows is a selected bibliography of portal fantasies and parallel universe fiction. Some imagine multiverses; others, worlds just slightly shifted from our own in space and time. Some reveal elfin doorways to strange realities; others offer gateways to grandiose planetary romance; still others posit entire universes held within the hearts of atoms. Titles notable for their high literary value are marked with an asterisk. To paraphrase e. e. cummings: there's one hell of a universe next door... *let's go!*

To learn more about the stories in *Other Worlds Than These*, visit the anthology's website at johnjosephadams.com/other-worlds-than-these.

Abbott, Edwin A.
—*Flatland: A Romance of Many Dimensions* *

Alexander, Lloyd
—*The First Two Lives of Lukas Kasha*

Allston, Aaron
—*Doc Sidhe*
—*Sidhe Devil*

Anderson, Pohl
—*Operation Chaos*

Anthony, Piers
—*Split Infinity* (et seq.)

Applegate, K. A.
—*Search for Senna* (et seq.)

Asimov, Isaac
—*The Gods Themselves* *

Bach, Richard
—*One*

Ball, Margaret
—*No Earthly Sunne*

Barker, Clive
—*Imajica* *
—*Weaveworld*

Barron, Natania
—*Pilgrim of the Sky*

Baum, L. Frank
—*The Wonderful Wizard of Oz* (et seq.)

Baxter, Stephen
—*Raft*

Brown, Frederic
—*What Mad Universe*

Jones, Diana Wynne
—*Charmed Life* (et seq.)
—*Deep Secret* (et seq.)
—*Dark Lord of Derkholm* (et seq.)

Jones, Raymond F.
—*Renaissance* (AKA *Man of Two Worlds*)

Juster, Norton
—*The Phantom Tollbooth*

Kay, Elizabeth
—*The Divide* (et seq.)

Kay, Guy Gavriel
—The Fionavar Tapestry (series)

Kendrick, Mark Ian
—*The Rylerran Gateway*

King, Stephen
—The Dark Tower (series)

King, Stephen and Peter Straub
—*The Talisman* *

Kube-McDowell, Michael P.
—*Alternities* (et seq.)

L'Engle, Madeleine
—*A Wrinkle in Time* (et seq.)

Laumer, Keith
—*Worlds of the Imperium*

Lawhead, Stephen R.
—*The Skin Map* (et seq.)

Lawrence, Michael
—*A Crack in the Line* (et seq.)

Le Guin, Ursula K.
—*Changing Planes*

Leiber, Fritz
—*The Big Time*

Lewis, C. S.
—The Chronicles of Narnia (series)

Lindsay, David
—*A Voyage to Arcturus* (et seq.)

Lovecraft, H. P.
—*The Dream-Quest of Unknown Kadath*

Lukyanenko, Sergey
—*Rough Draft*

MacHale, D. J.
—*The Merchant of Death* (et seq.)

McAuley, Paul
—*Cowboy Angels*

McDonald, Ian
—*Planesrunner* (et seq.)

Mellick III, Carlton
—*The Haunted Vagina*

Melko, Paul
—*The Walls of the Universe* (et seq.)

Miéville, China
—*Un Lun Dun*

Miles, Lawrence
—*Dead Romance*

Mirrlees, Hope
—*Lud-in-the-Mist* *

Moorcock, Michael
—Eternal Champion (series)
—The Cornelius Quartet (series)
—*Warlord of the Air*

Murakami, Haruki
—*Hard Boiled Wonderland and the End of the World* *

Myers, John Myers
—*Silverlock*

Nichols, Ruth
—*A Walk Out of the World*

ACKNOWLEDGMENTS

Many thanks to the following:

Jeremy Lassen and Jason Williams at Night Shade Books, for letting me edit all these anthologies and for doing such a kick-ass job publishing them. Also, to Ross Lockhart and the rest of the team at Night Shade for all they do behind-the-scenes.

Marty Halpern, for his copyediting prowess.

Cody Tilson: Thank you for another *fantastic* cover.

My agent, Joe Monti, for finding a good home for this project, and for the incredible amount of support he's provided since taking me on as a client—he's gone above and beyond the call of duty. To any writers reading this: you'd be lucky to have Joe in your corner.

Robyn Lupo, Patrick Stephens, and Kevin McNeil for providing feedback on the stories during the editorial process. And also to David Carani and again to Robyn for some other anthologizing assistance.

Gordon Van Gelder, my friend and mentor. Without him, this anthology would definitely not exist.

Thanks to Seanan McGuire, for the catch.

My amazing wife, Christie, and my mom, Marianne, for all their love and support, and their endless enthusiasm for all my new projects.

My dear friends Robert Bland, Desirina Boskovich, Christopher M. Cevasco, Douglas E. Cohen, Jordan Hamessley, Andrea Kail, David Barr Kirtley, and Matt London.

The readers and reviewers who loved my other anthologies, making it possible for me to do more.

And last, but certainly not least: a big thanks to all of the authors who appear in this anthology.

Night Shade Books is an Independent Publisher of Quality Science-Fiction, Fantasy and Horror

SECOND EDITION

ISBN: 978-1-59780-454-7 ☾ $16.99 ☾ Look for it in e-Book!

YOU ARE BEING WATCHED. Your every movement is being tracked, your every word recorded. One wrong move, one slip-up, and you may find yourself disappeared—swallowed up by a monstrous bureaucracy, vanished into a shadowy labyrinth of interrogation chambers, show trials, and secret prisons from which no one ever escapes. Welcome to the world of the dystopia, a world of government and society gone horribly, nightmarishly wrong.

In his smash-hit anthologies *Wastelands* and *The Living Dead*, acclaimed editor John Joseph Adams showed you what happens when society is utterly wiped away. Now he brings you a glimpse into an equally terrifying future. *Brave New Worlds* collects 30 of the best tales of totalitarian menace. When the government wields its power against its own people, every citizen becomes an enemy of the state. Will you fight the system, or be ground to dust beneath the boot of tyranny?

Night Shade Books is an Independent Publisher of Quality Science-Fiction, Fantasy and Horror

ISBN: 978-1-59780-420-2 ❦ $26.99 ❦ Look for it in e-Book!

"Paul Tobin gives us all of the thrills of super-hero action while spinning a very human tale of mortality and justice. Insightful, fun, and brilliant!"
— Jonathan Maberry,
NEW YORK TIMES BEST-SELLING AUTHOR OF *Assassin's Code*

PAUL TOBIN

PREPARE TO DIE!

A NOVEL OF SUPERHEROES, SEX, AND SECRET ORIGINS

Nine years ago, Steve Clarke was just a teenage boy in love with the girl of his dreams. Then a freak chemical spill transformed him into Reaver, the man whose super-powerful fists can literally take a year off a bad guy's life.

Days ago, he found himself at the mercy of his arch-nemesis Octagon and a whole crew of fiendish super-villains, who gave him two weeks to settle his affairs—and prepare to die.

Now, after years of extraordinary adventures and crushing tragedies, the world's greatest hero is returning to where it all began in search of the boy he once was…and the girl he never forgot.

Exciting, scandalous, and ultimately moving, *Prepare to Die!* is a unique new look at the last days of a legend.

Night Shade Books is an Independent Publisher of Quality Science-Fiction, Fantasy and Horror

ISBN: 978-1-59780-325-0 » $15.99 » Look for it in e-Book!

It's the dawn of the 22nd century, and the world has fallen apart. Decades of war and resource depletion have toppled governments. The ecosystem has collapsed. A new dust bowl sweeps the American West. The United States has become a nation of migrants—starving masses of nomads roaming across wastelands and encamped outside government seed distribution warehouses.

In this new world, there is a new power: Satori. More than just a corporation, Satori is an intelligent, living city risen from the ruins of the heartland. She manufactures climate-resistant seed to feed humanity, and bio-engineers her own perfected castes of post-humans Designers, Advocates and Laborers. What remains of the United States government now exists solely to distribute Satori product; a defeated American military doles out bar-coded, single-use seed to the nation's hungry citizens.

When a Satori Designer goes rogue, Doss is tasked with hunting down the scientist-savan—a chance to break Satori's stranglehold on seed production and undo its dominance. In a race against Satori's genetically honed assassins, Doss's best chance at success lies in an unlikely alliance with Brood—orphan, scavenger and small-time thief—scraping by on the fringes of the wasteland, whose young brother may possess the key to unlocking Satori's power.

Night Shade Books is an Independent Publisher of Quality Science-Fiction, Fantasy and Horror

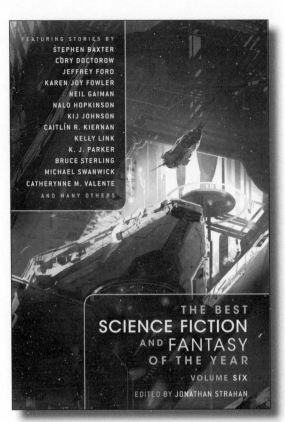

An ancient society of cartographer wasps create delicately inscribed maps; a bodyjacking parasite is faced with imminent extinction; an AI makes a desperate gambit to protect its child from a ravenous dragon; a professor of music struggles with the knowledge that murder is not too high a price for fame; living origami carries a mother's last words to her child; a steam girl conquers the realm of imagination; Aliens attack Venus, ignoring an incredulous earth; a child is born on Mars...

The science fiction and fantasy fiction fields continue to evolve, setting new marks with each passing year. For the sixth year in a row, master anthologist Jonathan Strahan has collected stories that captivate, entertain, and showcase the very best the genre has to offer. Critically acclaimed, and with a reputation for including award-winning speculative fiction, *The Best Science Fiction and Fantasy of the Year* is the only major "best of" anthology to collect both fantasy and science fiction under one cover

Night Shade Books is an Independent Publisher of Quality Science-Fiction, Fantasy and Horror

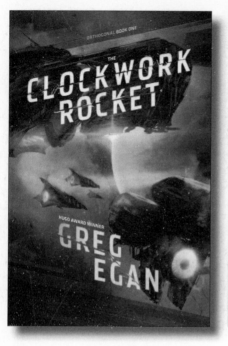

Greg Egan's *The Clockwork Rocket* introduced readers to an exotic universe where the laws of physics are very different from our own, where the speed of light varies in ways Einstein would never allow, and where intelligent life has evolved in unique and fascinating ways. Now Egan continues his epic tale of alien beings embarked on a desperate voyage to save their world . . . .

The generation ship *Peerless* is in search of advanced technology capable of sparing their home planet from imminent destruction. In theory, the ship is traveling fast enough that it can traverse the cosmos for generations–and still return home only a few years after they departed. But a critical fuel shortage threatens to cut their urgent voyage short, even as a population explosion stretches the ship's life-support capacity to its limits.

When the astronomer Tamara discovers the Object, a meteor whose trajectory will bring it within range of the *Peerless*, she sees a risky solution to the fuel crisis. Meanwhile, the biologist Carlo searches for a better way to control fertility, despite the traditions and prejudices of their society. As the scientists clash with the ship's leaders, they find themselves caught up in two equally dangerous revolutions: one in the sexual roles of their species, the other in their very understanding of the nature of matter and energy.

The Eternal Flame lights up the mind with dazzling new frontiers of physics and biology, as only Greg Egan could imagine them.

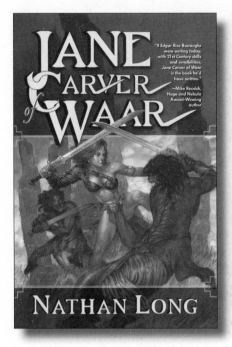
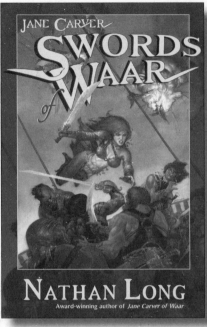

ABOUT THE EDITOR

John Joseph Adams is the bestselling editor of many anthologies, such as *Armored, Under the Moons of Mars: New Adventures on Barsoom, Brave New Worlds, Wastelands, The Living Dead, The Living Dead 2, By Blood We Live, Federations, The Improbable Adventures of Sherlock Holmes,* and *The Way of the Wizard.* Forthcoming work includes *Epic* (Tachyon, November 2012), *The Mad Scientist's Guide to World Domination* (Tor Books, 2013), *Dead Man's Hand* (Titan Books, 2013), and *Robot Uprisings* (co-edited with Daniel H. Wilson, 2013).

John is a four-time finalist for the Hugo Award and a three-time finalist for the World Fantasy Award. He has been called "the reigning king of the anthology world" by Barnes & Noble, and his books have been lauded as some of the best anthologies of all time.

In addition to his anthology work, John is also the editor and publisher of *Lightspeed Magazine,* and he is the co-host of Wired.com's *The Geek's Guide to the Galaxy* podcast.

For more information, visit his website at johnjosephadams.com, and you can find him on Twitter @johnjosephadams.